ARKHAM HORROR™

In the HANDS of MADMEN

An Arkham Horror Omnibus

The LAST RITUAL
BY S.A. SIDOR

LITANY of DREAMS
BY ARI MARMELL

In the COILS of the LABYRINTH
BY DAVID ANNANDALE

ACONYTE

First published by Aconyte Books in 2024
ISBN 978 1 83908 346 4
Ebook ISBN 978 1 83908 347 1

The Last Ritual first published by Aconyte Books in 2020
Litany of Dreams first published by Aconyte Books in 2021
In the Coils of the Labyrinth first published by Aconyte Books in 2022

Printed in the United States of America and elsewhere.
9 8 7 6 5 4 3 2 1

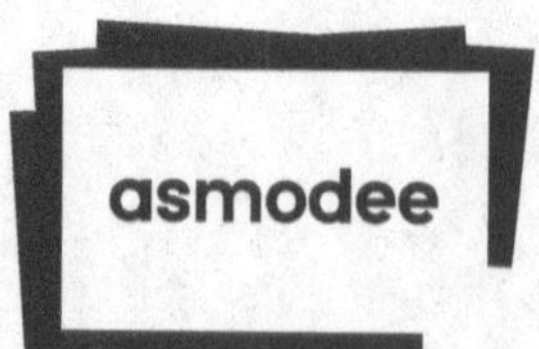

ACONYTE BOOKS
An imprint of Asmodee North America
Mercury House, Shipstones Business Centre
North Gate, Nottingham NG7 7FN, UK
aconytebooks.com

ARKHAM HORROR

It is the height of the Roaring Twenties – a fresh enthusiasm for the arts, science, and exploration of the past have opened doors to a wider world, and beyond...

And yet, a dark shadow grows over the town of Arkham. Alien entities known as Ancient Ones lurk in the emptiness beyond space and time, writhing at the thresholds between worlds.

Occult rituals must be stopped and alien creatures destroyed before the Ancient Ones make our world their ruined dominion.

Only a handful of brave souls with inquisitive minds and the will to act stand against the horrors threatening to tear this world apart.

Will they prevail?

Also available in Arkham Horror

The Adventures of Alessandra Zorzi

Wrath of N'kai by Josh Reynolds
Shadows of Pnath by Josh Reynolds
Song of Carcosa by Josh Reynolds

The Fiztmaurice Legacy

Mask of Silver by Rosemary Jones
The Deadly Grimoire by Rosemary Jones
The Bootlegger's Dance by Rosemary Jones

The Drowned City

The Forbidden Visions of Lucius Galloway by Carrie Harris

More Arkham Horror Fiction

The Ravening Deep by Tim Pratt
Herald of Ruin by Tim Pratt

Cult of the Spider Queen by S A Sidor
Lair of the Crystal Fang by S A Sidor

The Devourer Below edited by Charlotte Llewelyn-Wells
Secrets in Scarlet edited by Charlotte Llewelyn-Wells

Dark Origins: The Collected Novellas Vol 1
Grim Investigations: The Collected Novellas Vol 2

Arkham Horror Investigators Gamebooks

The Darkness Over Arkham by Jonathan Green

Welcome to Arkham: An Illustrated Guide for Visitors
Arkham Horror: The Poster Book

ARKHAM HORROR

IN THE HANDS OF MADMEN

AN ARKHAM HORROR OMNIBUS

THE LAST RITUAL

S.A. SIDOR

"The smoke banked like fog, and the opening of the door filled the room with blown swirls of ectoplasm."

F Scott Fitzgerald, "The Rich Boy"

Chapter One

"The last time…?"

Alden Oakes turned away from the window, staring coolly at the cub reporter who had paused with his pencil raised above the pad. Oakes had avoided his questions deftly so far, employing a defensive combination of small talk and awkward silences.

"I thought we might start there," the reporter said, prodding. He had a deadline.

Alden nodded and resumed pacing inside the hotel suite. "Strange weather we're having. First a dense fog, then blowing mists like gigantic gauzy veils. Now here comes the rain. I didn't need to open this contraption all the way here from the train station this morning." He tapped the window with the umbrella he was using like a cane. The reporter had noticed the famous painter suffered from a slight limp. "The air is strangely mild for midsummer. Don't you agree?"

"It beats the heat," the reporter said. He wasn't interested in talking about the weather, but whatever got his subject to relax and open up to him was worth a try.

Alden gazed out at the gloom as if he were trying to decipher shapes in the clouds.

"How does it feel being back at the hotel again?" the younger man asked, poking again softly, wondering if this afternoon was going to end up being a big waste of time. Usually, there were two ways to handle it. Either you pushed the subject harder and risked losing them, or you went all quiet and let the pressure of no one talking do the trick. He hadn't made up his mind which way to go yet.

"The doorman tipped his cap like we were old acquaintances," Alden said.

Rain hissed and slithered down the glass.

The reporter decided. He had spent hours trying to pry stories out of tight-lipped people in places far less pleasant than the luxurious Silver Gate Hotel. He could afford to kill a little time here in the comfort of a pricey room. So he dropped his pencil on his notepad and pushed back from the hotel room desk, letting out a gentle sigh. Though compact, the desk setup was more comfortable than his cluttered cubby at the *Arkham Advertiser*, where he was forced to share space with a sports reporter, a habitual snacker who left coffee rings and dough-nut crumbs on everything. If the artist wanted to play coy, he'd wait him out, saying nothing. He gazed past the painter at the dim, graying view of downtown Arkham.

Alden pushed off from the window and smiled. He sat stiff-backed on the loveseat, his hands resting on the crook of the umbrella gripped between his knees. Leaning over, he switched on a lamp, casting light into the room which was growing noticeably darker despite the noon hour. "Ready?"

"Yes, Mr Oakes, whenever you want to get started." *Victory!* He snatched his pencil.

Resigned, Alden sank into the pale green velvet sofa cushions, closing his eyes. "The last time I saw the Silver Gate Hotel it was burning. I was burning too, or my jacket was, before an Arkham fireman tackled me to the ground, rolling me in the grass to smother the little fires climbing my back. I escaped with my life, as they say."

"You're a lucky man," the reporter said. Now that the ball was rolling, he just had to keep it going. He might get a decent story out of this yet. After all, the tragic and suspicious fire at the Silver Gate had been the biggest news story in Arkham last year. But Alden Oakes was considered only a minor part of it, a local celebrity footnote. A celebrity *painter*, no less.

"I'm sure some people might consider me lucky," Alden looked at him slyly.

The young man frowned, confused. Would he have rather had his bacon fried?

Alden went on.

"This suite we're sitting in, the one I've booked for this homecoming of mine, survived the catastrophe intact. It suffered serious smoke damage. The whole place did. But you'd never guess that judging from the building's current appear-ance. The bricks scrubbed clean, fresh from the rain, the lobby's glossy marble floor shining like a giant chessboard, and those vases full of maroon heirloom roses and white calla lilies. Such a transformation! Yes, they worked a real mira-cle bringing this hotel back into operation in a little over a year."

The reporter began scribbling notes. "The grand reopening gala is scheduled for tomorrow. Are you surprised the hotel owners invited you?"

"Why? Because of the rumors? My confinement?" Alden's voice rose. "Noth-ing was ever substantiated. Innuendos and idle speculation. The press planted theories to sell more papers. People like you." He checked his anger, pushing it back under the surface. "Others influenced them, of course. The doctors said I needed rest. I suffered from physical and mental exhaustion. No, I don't feel guilty about what happened to the hotel. But I'll admit it was a surprise to receive the invitation. Who are the owners, by the way? Do you know?"

The reporter shook his head. "It's a damned secret. The management company runs day-to-day business. But the legal paperwork is vague, a pyramid of companies, mostly European. Taxes are paid by an anonymous land trust. That's all I could dig up—"

"Don't bother digging. You won't find anything." Alden waved. "It's not important."

"But they wanted you here."

"My presence was demanded." Alden sat forward. "I just finished a gallery showing in New York. I have no real home any more, not in America. I was debating returning to France, or spending a few months in South America painting frogs and orchids along the Amazon. I'd gone as far as hiring a paddleboat with a small crew to ferry me into the jungle."

"Yet here you are," the young man said, shaking his head, incredulous. A trip into the Amazon jungle! Now there was a place where stories were ripe for the picking. They must be hanging from the trees like banana bunches. A journalist could write a big, fat book about it. "Why would you skip a trip like that, if you don't mind me asking? I'd jump at the chance."

"Adventure doesn't require an exotic locale. Only the proper spirit is needed…"

What the heck did that mean? Well, the young reporter wasn't here to argue about foreign travel plans. "Keep talking, Mr Oakes, I didn't mean to interrupt you," he said.

"Not to worry. What's your name again?"

"Andy. Andy Van Nortwick."

"Well, Andy, let me ask *you* a question. How old do you think I am?"

Glad that the artist's mood had improved, Andy screwed one eye shut and appraised his subject. Oakes was slender, his pale coloring bordering on consumptive, except for a penny-sized, raised scar dotting his left cheek. He wore a pencil mustache. His hair receded in a sandy blond wave curling back from a high aristocratic forehead. And he dressed strictly top drawer, a tailored London suit. But his eyes gave it away. They looked watery and old, crowded by lines of worry, sleepless nights, and regret. "I've never worked at the carnival or anything, but I'll guess you're right about fifty. That's a nice round number. Fifty it is."

"I'm twenty-nine. My birthday was two weeks ago."

The reporter's face reddened. "I'm sorry, Mr Oakes. I didn't mean any insult to you."

Alden brought out a gold cigarette case and a banjo pocket lighter. He offered a smoke to the reporter. Then he lit both their cigarettes.

"That's what adventures do to a person, Andy."

Alden winked and settled back on the sofa. He exhaled a plume of smoke into the suite. Andy felt embarrassed. The *Arkham Advertiser* reporter kept his eyes glued to his notepad. He'd been writing for the newspaper for less than a year. Before that he had been delivering them on his bicycle. He was eager to be writing any story more momentous than Mrs O'Reilly's dog gone missing after chasing the milkman off her porch. He silently cursed himself for being so raw. A real dope. He wasn't like the cynical veteran ink slingers, with their grimy fingers stuck in every political pie. They wrote stories as favors or payback. He had no secret agenda. No one was pulling his strings. Not yet anyway. He only wanted to tell the truth. When he looked up again, Alden's expression had softened toward him.

"It wasn't easy walking in this place after what happened to me here the last time," the painter said. "My heart was thumping when I checked in at the front desk and got my key. They've got the elevator operator dressed up like a phony palace guard. So strange. I almost pitied the poor old guy sitting there on his stool."

"I saw him too," Andy said, smiling. "I'll bet it gets boring sitting in that box all day, riding up and down."

"Agreed," Alden said. "Is it me or do the hotel staff seem terribly cheerful to you? I wonder how many of them worked here before the fire. I arrived early to avoid the rush. Most of the invitation-only gala guests aren't getting in until this evening or tonight. As the elevator car rose, I fiddled with my room key, caressing the brass fob. It's shaped like the Silver Gate façade but in miniature. Here, take a look." Alden slipped his room key from his pocket, tossing it to Andy.

"It's heavy," Andy said, before giving it back.

"The fire stopped on twelve. The firehoses never reached this far." Alden tapped the number on the key. "1481. My room for tonight. I entered and hooked the chain behind me. Only smoke invaded 1481 the night of the inferno. Plenty of it. Sniff about I did, once I locked myself inside. Like a basset hound following a scent trail I got down on all fours, but detected nothing more than laundered bed linens and a whiff of lemon oil wood polish. The new carpet feels different, spongier than I recall. They've repainted. The replacement color is horribly bland, less rich and creamy than the original. Your average person wouldn't notice the difference. But I do. Demolition might have been a better option. Start over from scratch. I suppose it all came down to cost. They've chosen to try and cover things up, but the residue is still here, lingering beneath the surface. Hints and echoes. Before you knocked on my door, I smelled smoke in the bathroom. I was *sure* I smelled it. Fleeting, but distinct, not the scent of cigarettes but acrid, choking fumes… I investigated but failed to discover any lasting trace of it, only a bleachy residue rising from the bathtub. Funny."

The reporter couldn't help but take a deep breath.

"You don't smell anything now, do you, Andy?"

"Not a thing, Mr Oakes."

"Maybe it's playing tricks on me," Alden said. "The hotel, I mean. Or, maybe, something else…." The painter seemed lost for a moment, unfocused; his head tilted as if listening for a muffled, distant sound. But then he returned. "The furniture appears solid, elegant yet standard: a bed, dresser, and nightstand. The cozy sofa and chairs, that neat little desk where you're sitting writing out my story. My version of the events as they transpired… what happened to me…"

"What *did* happen to you? It was more than a bad fire, wasn't it?" Andy's eyes sparked.

"You'll make a good reporter someday, Andy. You have the nose for it, as they say. I wonder if you'll believe me if I tell you everything I saw, everything I know is true."

"Give me a try." Andy tapped the ash off his cigarette and licked his dry lips.

"I've got a bottle of gin in my bag," Alden said. He stood up quickly and moved to the closet. Taking down a red crocodile suitcase and setting it on the luggage rack, he pulled a small key from a necklace he wore under his shirt and unlocked the catches. From the case he unpacked a bottle of bootleg gin, a shaker, and a pair of glasses. He left the case open. "Hand me that ice bucket, would you? Thirsty?"

Andy found a full ice bucket sweating on the nightstand. He brought it to the painter.

"I don't drink on the job," he said. "My boss wouldn't like me breaking the law."

"Admirable," Alden said. "But the martini is for me. Ginger ales for you are in the desk drawer." Alden tossed him a bottle opener. When both men had their cold drinks, they settled back in their seats. Alden raised his martini for a toast. "What shall we drink to?"

"Truth?"

Alden shook his head. "Too much responsibility. How about, *my side of things*?"

"To your side of things," Andy said. He sipped his ginger ale.

Alden took a long swallow of gin. "That's all I can tell you, really. All any of us ever can tell, in the end. Nina would agree. She'd like you."

"Who's Nina?" Andy asked.

"She's my best friend," Alden said. "I'll get to her eventually. She's a big part of what this puzzling business is all about. A writer, too, my Nina, 'Alden, if you and I don't tell people what's going on, who will?' she'd say."

"She sounds like somebody I'd like to meet."

Alden smiled wistfully. "Nina isn't here to help us right now. Words are her strength, mine being colors… pencils and brushes, paints, canvas. She would've been much better suited to be your source. But you've got me instead. Let me know if you get hungry. We'll order up room service. Oysters Rockefeller and shrimp cocktails. Put it on the hotel tab."

"Swell. I've never eaten like a rich man before."

Alden set his martini down to light another cigarette. He clicked the lighter dramatically and said, "My curious reporter friend, I'll do everything in my power to set things out right. The dreadful truth of the events as they really occurred, even the unbelievably scandalous details and most gruesome, loathsome facts. But you must know that it all started for me well before that frightful night at the Silver Gate Hotel."

Andy's pencil moved mechanically across the blank page, filling in the lines.

So, Alden began his tale.

Chapter Two

The summer before… well, around two years ago now, I was watching a hot sun set into a cold glittery sea when I heard someone calling my name across the beach at Cannes.

"Oakesy!"

Now, my proper name is Wilfred Alden Oakes. But my father will always be the only Wilfred Oakes, renowned industrialist and philanthropist, et cetera. Everyone else calls me Alden. Except for one person. So I knew, before I saw him stepping through the long shadows stretched out on the sand, that it was Preston Fairmont walking toward me with a martini glass gripped in one hand and the other waving as if he were trying to hail a cab.

"Oakesy! Over here! I can't believe it's you. What are you doing in France?"

I was sitting in a wicker chair beside a small slatted wood table at a beach café, resting my legs after a day of climbing the winding cobbled lanes of the old quarter, Le Suquet, in search of untapped inspiration. Preston grasped the chair across from me and pulled it free from the beach. A bag containing my brushes and paints popped out of the seat but did not spill. Preston removed it from sight. Jubilant and tan, he sat down, beaming.

"What are you drinking?"

"A rose cocktail," I said.

"Splendid."

Preston caught the eye of the waitress. He had a manner about him that service people always noticed. He exuded money. The waitress slid another coaster onto my table.

"*Voulez-vous quelque chose à boire?*"

"I'll have one of these," Preston said, pointing to my drink.

The waitress nodded, smiling, but Preston was already looking away from her at the deep blue waves, the people lounging on the sand, and lastly, as she departed our company, at me. Despite my surprise at seeing him, I was instantly reacquainted with his aloof charm.

"How are you, Preston?" I said.

"Glorious, I've spent the day… I don't know… walking? I never tire of this place."

"Staying long?" I tried to sound neutral. It had been a while since we last talked, and the gap was not entirely by accident. Preston and I shared a lot of mutual background and friends. I preferred the illusion that I was unique in the world. He made that more difficult.

He shook his head. "I leave tomorrow. Sailing in the morning. That's why it's so perfect that I've seen you just now. I've been trying to reach you. You are desperately elusive, Oakesy."

"I've been here all summer," I said, squinting, shading my eyes.

"At the beach? It's no wonder you haven't had an exhibition in ages."

His comment casually found a way to bruise my pride.

Preston's cocktail arrived.

I ordered another and requested the check, hoping to measure our encounter to the most enjoyable length. "Painting isn't all getting and spending. Learning the craft takes time. I've grown this year, but finding my own style has been more difficult than I first anti–"

"Artists throw the best parties," Preston interrupted. "I'll bet you've been to a few."

Preston Fairmont was no amateur about throwing parties. At college he became a Miskatonic University legend. He'd started out at the University of Chicago, but his lack of seriousness as a student caused his parents to want him closer to home. So, reluctantly, he transferred to MU after a year. When we roomed together as classmates, he was still in his hosting infancy and busy establishing himself, keenly assessing maneuvers in the social terrain. During the Great War we talked about dropping out to join the navy because we liked their uniforms. The girls did too, or so we had surmised. There was something romantic yet viscerally tangible about the sea. It's the same reason I've always enjoyed painting in seaside locations. Well, neither of us volunteered to fight, and the war ended the autumn following our graduation. By then Preston was a connoisseur of the party scene and a host of epic renown. I dabbled on the periphery of such events, more comfortable spending my time slapping paint on canvasses in a studio or lugging an easel around outdoors.

"Why were you trying to contact me?" I asked.

"I'm embarrassed to say."

"Impossible," I said. Preston had an innate confidence bred into him. "I've never known you to feel that emotion."

"You'll see when I tell you why."

"Go on."

"I'm getting married." Preston smiled sheepishly.

"Congratulations! That's nothing to be flustered about. Cheers!"

I genuinely felt happy for the old boy, but the joyous surge was quickly throttled.

"To Minnie Devane," Preston added.

The empty glass squirted out of my fingers, tumbling off the table into the sand. Luckily its replacement was due any second. So here was the sticking point. Minnie Devane had been my on-again, off-again college girlfriend, my fiancée and ex-fiancée, my inspiration, the first woman I ever thought I loved. Now, I could write a book about Minnie, but if I did, I'd have to burn it before I was arrested for violating the Comstock Laws. Not that Minnie herself was obscene. See, she was like a piece of broken mirror. Small and shiny, and if you weren't careful she'd leave you bleeding. She reflected back places in yourself that were better left unexamined. I fell for Minnie because she had a smart, sassy way of talking and a wild, fast, shimmery way of whipping herself around a room so that everybody felt charged up. She was all heat and energy.

Sometimes that energy exploded. And people got hurt.

"You and Minnie?" It seemed so impossible, and then, even worse, so obvious.

I picked up the glass and dusted it off.

"Ain't it grand?" Preston said. His forehead beaded with sweat. Dark patches stained his shirtfront. He kept folding and unfolding his arms. His hands were like a pair of birds he was trying to keep from flying away. I noticed his color draining off, like a man about to faint. Was he *that* nervous about telling me? I hadn't thought my opinion mattered to Preston.

"When's the big day?"

"Oh, not until next summer. I've got… We have a year to plan," he said.

The shock of the news still reverberated, of course. I nearly felt concussed. But I was having a hard time coming up with a good reason to object or even to feel bad. I liked Preston. And I liked Minnie. Why shouldn't I be happy for them?

"I don't know if you're looking for it, Preston, but you have my blessing," I said.

The more I thought about them as a couple, the more I saw how they fit better than Minnie and I ever did. I was too solitary to match their robustly sociable personalities.

Preston and Minnie. Linking them up like that would take time to get used to.

"Oakesy, that's real swell of you. I'm relieved." He didn't look relieved. He was scratching his shoes back and forth under the table, peeking occasionally to witness the progress of his dig. He looked worse than when he dropped the big wedding bomb on me. Was there something else? "You're a champ. We hoped you wouldn't be too sore."

"I'm glad you found each other. Honestly, I think I really frustrated Minnie. The lonely artist, I guess, living inside his own head. In an imaginary world. 'But it's always raining in your world,' she'd say. 'That's the trouble.' Maybe I was just too peculiar for her."

"That's what she told me."

Did she now?

Frankly, Preston and Minnie were the kind of people who typically did as they pleased. If they were inconvenienced, they might try to patch things up to see that things would go smoother for *them*. But they were hardly the type to lie awake at night wondering about the impact their actions had on bystanders. I felt sort of honored in a weird way.

"Minnie and I are hoping dearly that you'll come to the wedding. It's in Arkham."

The unexpected invite dizzied me. Certainly, I might get used to the idea of my old flame marrying a college buddy of mine, but did I want to be there to see it happening?

Preston glanced past me over my shoulder. The corner of his mouth twitched in an anxious half-smile. I turned to see what he was looking at. It was a woman in a floppy sun hat with a pink ribbon. Either because Preston had been staring, or because I turned abruptly, she concealed herself, lowering the hat's wide brim to avoid our further attention.

He reached over the table and grabbed my wrist. His look was pleading. I felt sorry for him. "Please say you'll be there," he said. Why was he acting so desperate?

"I'll come to the wedding." I had time to adjust, and he wanted me there so badly.

His face stretched in an elastic, white grin. "That's terrific! They will be so happy!"

"They? Who are *they*?" I asked, confused.

Preston paused, then shrugged. "It's just Minnie and me. No one else."

"Now what about that woman sitting behind me? With the sun hat?" I thumped his shoulder. "I saw you smiling at her." Here I wagged my finger. "Minnie will expect your complete attention and strictest devotion, if you haven't discovered that already."

Preston swallowed dryly. "Well, she's the only one for me."

"Good man! Come next summer, you shall worship the goddess Minnie!" I joked.

"Ha!" His loud exclamation startled the beachgoers around us.

The waitress finally came with our drinks. After I signed the check, I pretended to drop my pen accidently so I could get a second, better look at the woman in the floppy hat. But she was gone.

While I was bending over, I happened to glance under the table. During our conversation, Preston had slipped off one of his white bucks and drawn something in the sand with his toe. A cup-like shape balanced on a triangle. Inside it were two ovals. Next to the cup, and less distinguishable, he'd scratched a three-pronged fork.

How truly bizarre, I thought.

As I tried to make sense of the upside-down symbols, Preston dragged his foot through the sand, obliterating them. Initially he'd come on so very Preston, but now I was noticing his unease. Perhaps this impending marriage really did shake his pillars. Minnie had that effect on some people.

"When are you planning to head back to Arkham?" Preston asked me as I sat up.

"I have no formal plans. I'll be in France for a short while. I was hoping to make a trip along the Spanish coast. My mother wants me home for Christmas. Why do you ask?"

"Minnie and I are throwing an engagement party. No date yet. Probably at my parents' house in French Hill, or maybe at the Lodge. We'd like you there. We have a lot of new friends who'll be attending the wedding. You need to meet them first. Fascinating crowd. Bohemian types, right up your alley. Arkham has a vibrant art scene these days, or so Minnie tells me."

"That sounds intriguing," I said. Since when did bohemians flock to Arkham? "What kind of arts do they practice?"

Preston's skin turned a clammy gray. No longer the tanned picture of good health, he gulped his drink and began sucking on the ice. I worried he was suddenly feeling unwell.

"Are you all right, chum?"

"One too many escargots last night, I'm afraid," he said, wiping his damp forehead.

"And a few too many bottles of bubbly to chase them?"

Preston smiled. "You know me, old friend."

I thought I did.

He asked me to consider a return to Arkham in the fall. He and Minnie needed to start planning for their wedding bash. And weren't the fall trees beautifully colorful around our New England town? Couldn't I find something worth painting closer to my birthplace?

"In any case, get yourself home before all the leaves are gone," he said.

"I'll try my best."

My answer seemed less than satisfactory to him, but we shook hands (his felt like a cold thing washed up on the beach) and said au revoir.

Our waitress swung by, and I ordered an absinthe.

My nerves felt jangly, my inner wiring frayed. For no real reason, my senses felt as if they were set on high alert. It was as if I were living on only coffee and cigarettes.

The water flashed with intricate, metallic-seeming patterns. I noticed one sailing yacht anchored out in the bay, closer to the beach than any of the others. She wasn't the biggest. Her slim white lines lay just above the water like a bobbing shard of ice.

Quickly, on an impulse, I grabbed a pencil and pad and began to sketch her.

Out onto her foredeck stepped a figure visible only in silhouette. Sexless, ageless, viewed at this distance and in the failing light, it might have been any person on the planet. I knew not what drew my eye to it. But I could not look away. The figure glided along the yacht's length. It must have been a sailor carrying ropes, I told myself. Long tendrils looped from the central body and were cast off into the sea. The figure appeared to vibrate. Trick of perspective. The water's reflection was at play with the abundant shadows. My mouth felt dry, tasted of salt. A ripple of nausea passed through me like a sound wave traveling from the middle of the bay. My hand trembled as I traced long, unbroken lines onto the paper, attempting to capture the oddity I saw.

The horizon divided into layers: dark blue, indigo, purple, violet, and smoked gray.

The Bay of Cannes became a sheet of glass.

Those ropes, if they were ropes, retracted. The figure elongated, growing taller by half. This sailor, or fisherman, this distortion of a human form also wore something on its head.

Huge spikes, in the fashion of a crown, a dark cluster of bayonet-like appendages.

That's what they looked like, anyway.

Then the light changed, and soft black fuzz seemed to sprout from the air itself. The yacht became a normal sailing vessel at anchor among dozens of others.

I saw no one onboard.

Night had arrived. I looked around me as if I had been sleeping and wakened in my chair. The corrugated sea came alive once more with twinkling lights mirrored from the cafés and hotels ringing the shoreline. People were talking, sipping aperitifs or cups of coffee.

Normal.

Whatever peculiarity had passed briefly over the bay vanished.

I contemplated the spot where Preston had been talking to me less than an hour ago. He might have been a mirage, a conjuration, a product of my imagination animated in a dream. I picked up my bag from the sand, then stood to put away my sketchpad. I swayed, feeling lightheaded. Was it the liquor? The onset of a fever?

Too long in the sun, I concluded.

I walked back to my hotel in a daze. Falling on my bed, I didn't even bother to undress but slept straight though until morning. I woke instantly at daybreak. The room smelled stuffy, but I felt revived, energized. I might've looked like hell, but, boy oh boy, was I humming. After my breakfast I told the hotel manager I wished to settle the bill. The idea came to me that I must leave Cannes at once. I had no obligations but to myself, so I followed this unexplained urge, curiously compelled to see where it might lead me. I bought a map of Spain and arranged to rent a car. I gave myself through the month of August to prepare for my return to Arkham. If someone had suggested to me, when I went down to the beachfront for a drink by the sea, that I was going be altering my plans and heading circuitously back to the USA early, well, I just might have believed them. But if they had told me that the reason would be a wedding invitation from Preston and Minnie, I would have laughed in their face.

Clearly, I might have said no and stayed in France. Sometimes I've wondered what my life would have been like if I had. Would I be where I am today? And the rumors that inevitably follow me, what would it be like to live without hearing them? The horrible deaths, everything we saw at the Silver Gate event that night, everything that emerged in the unwholesome chaos…

But such thinking is beyond pointless.

I said, "Yes."

And nothing that followed will ever be changed.

Chapter Three

I drove along the coast, saying goodbye to France mile by mile. I had little in the way of luggage, and art supplies took up most of the space in my sleek yellow Renault. I drove dangerously. I never was a particularly good driver and have no sense of direction.

Somewhere between Toulon and Marseilles my map flew out the window and the mountain winds kited it into a ravine. How could I get lost? I kept the ocean to my left and drove on, snaking my way through the stony massifs until it got dark. I looked for a place to get a hot meal and a soft bed for the night. There were no villages to be seen. My eyes burned with fatigue. I considered pulling over to catch forty winks, but the back roads were far too narrow. I didn't want to wake up pasted to the grille of a speeding delivery truck.

To occupy myself I entertained thoughts of Arkham.

Why had I left? What had I missed? How would the city look when I got back?

I was born in Arkham. My family was rich and socially prominent, although my parents were getting older and Wilfred, my father, had turned over much of his company's management to his younger associates. He made most of his money in metallurgy and chemicals. I never understood the specifics of what his Northside factories produced, nor did I care to learn more. Father's life appeared unbearably dull to me. He ranked the arts somewhere below sports and marginally above children's games. I knew the war had been good for the company, good for my family, as horrible as that sounds. My mother, Pearl, had her charity work. She wasn't overly concerned with helping actual people. Her causes leaned more toward public places like parks and museums. I don't fault her too much. I am certain my passion for painting was born out of wandering bored one evening into an exhibition hall during a fundraising dinner. The paintings leapt out at me! Such colors! I really *saw* them for the first time, and I trembled. It was like a religious epiphany without any religion. Or, I suppose, my god was art. In that instant I decided the direction of my life. *I must do this*, I thought with a zealot's clarity. I will make beautiful things. I wanted *my* work to hang in museums. I wanted people, like my mother and her friends, to organize fundraisers to hang pictures I would someday paint and, in return, I'd help people escape their dreary, tedious lives. Conveniently, I'd discovered a way out of the suffocating future that lay ahead of me.

Visions of Arkham flooded my brain for the remainder of my drive, and before I knew it, the world turned blue, then golden, and finally, an almost blindingly sunny white.

I was not seeking out any singular or heightened experiences in Spain. I wanted simply to relax. I settled in a rooming house at the center of a fishing village like many others that exist along the coast. I visited churches and strolled the steep, winding streets, lost in a maze of picturesque dwellings. Like much of the Mediterranean, the buildings I passed were whitewashed with red tiled roofs and tall windows shuttered against the sun's rays during the hottest hours of the day. Cats of every stripe and color napped in the shadows and eyed me with lazy indifference. I moved more slowly and felt myself adjusting to my old roommate's unexpected announcement of what was certain to be Arkham's social event of the year. I warmed to the idea of seeing Minnie and Preston together, and attending their fabulous parties. It would be good to go home again.

Although I was obviously a foreigner the villagers did not stare at me, but neither did they ignore my presence. When engaged they were uncommonly polite. I ate my meals in restaurants, devouring bread, olives, and plates of various small, oily fish, guzzling bowls of gazpacho, often imbibing a glass of Andalusian sherry before slouching off to a soft bed. My condition became one of blissful isolation. Language was like a cage I carried with me everywhere I went. I spoke no Spanish. No one I met spoke English. But I discovered that a mix of French and pantomime was all I needed to get my meaning across.

I completed more paintings there than I had in three months at Cannes.

While they were good, they lacked something almost palpable, as if the real subject had wandered away just before I started to paint. Haunted by absences. I put them away.

Preston was accurate when he alluded to my lack of artistic progress. It was true. I hadn't had an exhibition in ages. I had reached a point of stagnancy, a sluggish creative limbo where my talent and I sat together like a stale married couple who lacked the energy to argue. The truth about my artistic gift is that if I had been born a little better or a little worse, then my life might have been easier. I was never going to be one of those artists who sit in tattered overcoats selling their paintings at weekends on the street in the South Shore of Kingsport. I had no hustle, no salesmanship. I was born rich, so there was always money. Slumming seemed false. My skills revealed a mastery of technique. What I lacked, and what I desired, was originality. I was a copier, an imitator of the painters who came before me with superior vision. I felt like a fraud. I had concluded that the malady I suffered from was an absence of inspiring subjects to paint.

Determined, I left Arkham bound for Europe. Once there, I was drowning in history, museums, and galleries, cloyingly surrounded by other artists doing the same thing I was. What new contribution might Alden Oakes possibly make? Where was my vision? It was a self-pitying view, I know, and like all self-pity it quickly grew tiresome.

Even to me.

So I brooded.

I painted realistic representations of fields, forests, and seashores. Though technically excellent, my work was hollow. I hated each of them, piling the canvases in the corner of a shed I rented from a peasant farmer, only to find later that it had a leaky roof and the paintings I stored there were ruined. There seemed no rush to produce more. I avoided the company of other artists and found myself forsaking the smoky coffeehouses and noisy, cheap cafés. Preston was right about the parties, but I didn't go any more. Still, I held out one last hope of discovering an ideal subject that would unlock my inner potential. The world would have to pay attention. Finally, they would see that I had something unique and powerfully beautiful to contribute to the world.

Such were my daydreams.

One day I decided to leave the village and venture south to Barcelona.

Did I ever get to Barcelona?

I don't *think* so. I know that sounds peculiar, but I've mentioned my horrible sense of direction. I might have reached the lesser known outskirts of the city, or gotten myself sidetracked into an oddly secluded neighborhood. I saw no La Rambla, no Gothic Quarter, or Basilica de La Sagrada Familia, in fact no famous landmarks at all. It occurred to me that I might have mistakenly paid a visit to a completely different town. The architecture had an overcrowded ramshackle quality, not at all what I anticipated seeing. I had gone to the place where I expected Barcelona to be. But no signpost told me definitively whether I ever arrived there. The streets through which I drove had the industrial character of a metropolis. One bizarre thing was this: whichever road I took, I always sensed I was driving downhill. Even when I attempted to backtrack, the Renault pitched downward as if I were trapped in a funnel.

I saw lots of soldiers.

They marched past me in groups, or they lingered in pairs. I never spotted one out walking alone. Their uniforms were tannish yellow, and they wore soft peaked patrol caps with maroon armbands. I couldn't tell how the civilians felt about them, but they made me nervous with their blank expressions and casually thuggish attitude. I looked for a friendly, clean-looking hotel. Everywhere I stopped I was told, "No vacancies." When I asked for recommendations, the clerks indicated there were no rooms to be had in the city.

I parked in front of a bank, thinking I might go inside to exchange some francs and ask the teller to recommend a hotel. I'd enquire offhandedly if this branch was indeed in Barcelona proper. I never had a chance; when I tried the doors, I found them locked.

I cupped my hands to the window.

Deserted, lights out. Nobody home.

It was a weekday. I was sure about that when I left the fishing village.

I lit a smoke and took a stroll. Noting the particularities of the street, I made sure I'd be able to find my car when I returned. Three roads met, forming six corners. A star-shaped island with a dry fountain occupied the center of the intersection.

I went up for a closer look.

Under a layer of foul green water, coins filled the fountain. Curious, I rolled up my sleeve, dipped my arm into the basin, and scooped up a handful of coins. A film of yellow slime covered the coins, which were unpleasantly warm, like little fingertips grazing my palm. I scraped away a bit of scum with my thumbnail. I'd never seen such strange currency. If these were *pesetas*, they must have been very old indeed. The coins lacked any numbers whatsoever. The symbols found there were worn smooth and difficult to recognize, but they depicted mythological beasts unfamiliar to me. I dropped them back into the filthy water. Perhaps it was a local custom to make wishes and toss these peculiar old coins. This fountain had a statue in it at some point; now it was missing. Only the empty pedestal remained. Gazing outward from the font, I surveyed my directional choices.

"Eeny, meeny, miny, moe…"

I picked one of the six streets and started walking.

No shops were open for business. I saw few people. When I passed them, they looked away. With regularity along the avenue there appeared large, dangerous, open holes in the pavement; the air wafting out of these pits smelled of sewage. Puzzled and alarmed, I wondered why they were not covered, reminding myself to use caution on my return journey.

Multiple stairways leading underground offered another clue that I had reached a city center of some size. I assumed they connected to an electrified subway. I knew of no catacombs in this region. But the station entrances bore no names that I could find. The only things differentiating one stairway from another were primitive-looking symbols carved into wooden panels above their subterranean thresholds. Upon closer inspection these hackings seemed to be graffiti, the handiwork of an artistic hooligan with a pocketknife. They reminded me of an exhibit of ancient druidic runes I'd seen once at the Miskatonic Museum.

Locked iron gates were drawn across the stairways.

If they were used for transport they, like the banks, were closed.

The deeper into the neighborhood I explored, the more I noticed the buildings around me falling into obvious stages of disrepair, their architecture looking less structurally sound. Fissures creeping along the buildings' foundations and cracks in their facades had me speculating that the city had experienced a recent earthquake.

The entire scene spoke of disintegration. This could not be Barcelona!

I had arrived during the early evening, and now, a couple of hours later, the sun plunged in the west. Light cut through the alleyways like gold bayonets. I turned at an intersection, always checking behind me to remember a key detail or two. For example, up there was a headless manikin dressed in a red cardigan, leaning forward against a dusty second floor window. Here, glass blocks frame the etched word *Farmacia* over a doorway. Farther on, rows of brown boots are standing to attention on a rack inside a cobbler's dimly humble shop. I planned to follow this trail of breadcrumbs back through the urban forest.

Crimson streaked the bruised sky whose unraveling bandages were merely clouds.

I heard voices, many voices, talking excitedly.

So I followed their sound.

Crack!

A gunshot?

I froze.

Then a volley of loud explosions. A scream. People laughing.

A woman in a black and white ruffled dress ran diagonally across the street ahead of me. She glanced over her shoulder, smiling, I thought at me, but then a young man with curly black hair and a guitar on his back emerged, chasing after her.

I tailed them to a plaza.

Here were the dwellers of the neighborhood. Long tables and kitchen chairs ringed the plaza and branched down the intersecting streets. In the center of the plaza towered a pyramid of old furniture, wood scraps, and even an old, peeling door. Families sat around the tables drinking wine and eating. Children ran everywhere. A man touched a fat cigar to a fuse in his fist and tossed the firework high in the air near the pyramid.

Crack!

The children screamed, laughing, and ran away.

It was a summer festival. I had heard about them from associates in France. It was common to see midsummer bonfires around the solstice throughout Europe, dating back to medieval times or, perhaps, earlier. Many had their roots in ancient pagan rituals. Harmless, good-natured fun said to be effective in repelling evil spirits. Who but the bitterest killjoy could argue against burning pyres and drinking through the night with friends until dawn?

I must've stumbled upon a local custom, I thought. Before I could question it further, the young woman in the black and white ruffled dress offered me a glass of sangria, which I accepted, as her beau whisked her away to listen to him play his guitar in the shadow of the pyramid. I noticed the soldiers mingling with the civilians. It seemed they came from these families. The resemblances between them were undeniable. So any worries I had about civil unrest died there, as I sipped my sangria and smoked, wishing I'd brought a sketchpad and my pencils. Someone offered me a chair. As I sat down, I discovered my glass being refilled. Such hospitality! Waiting for night to fall and the festivities to begin… that is when I first heard mention of the name Juan Hugo Balthazarr. Oh, I didn't hear it strung together like that, but in whispers, an insectile buzz that infected the crowd. "Balthazarr, Balthazarr, Balthazzzaaarrr…."

Could they be speaking of the most shocking living painter in the world?

No, I told myself. It must be a common name in these parts.

Yet I wondered…

Juan Hugo Balthazarr was a Spaniard, born in Barcelona. He was rumored to live there still, inside the walled, crumbling ruins of a Gothic monastery. As I looked around, I convinced myself some of these people at the tables might be his relatives. But no, it couldn't be.

Could it?

Balthazarr was acknowledged, most notably and boisterously by himself, as a genius destined to save the twentieth century from irrelevant art. Renowned as a relentless experimenter, he drew, painted, and sculpted with incredible energy and stamina, often said to spend days, or even weeks, without sleep in order to complete one of his outrageously fantastical visions. Critics either hailed his works as revolutionary or vehemently despised them, but all agreed his creations were as breathtaking as they were indescribable. Yes, there was something of Goya in them, and of those medieval painters who conjured torturous scenes in Hell. But Balthazarr's influences remained hard to pin down. Gustave Doré's woodcuts and engravings. The Dadaists and Cubism, of course. Currently, he was a major force in the Surrealist movement. But he was always his own artist. Incomparable, prolific, and a young man, barely older than I was. How I envied him! If only I could harness the talent I felt I had within me, if only I might push it into the world with such confidence, style, and gusto.

People were turning their chairs to stare down one of the streets.

I looked too.

I had seen only one photo of Balthazarr who, despite his growing worldwide fame, disliked having his picture taken. He was tall and well-known for his athletic physique and long forked beard. I glanced over the heads of the festivalgoers but saw no one resembling Balthazarr. What a shame! If there was one artist in the world whom I admired, it was him.

They said he painted portraits of his darkest dreams. He possessed a perfect memory of everything that ever happened to him, both awake and asleep. Some claimed he was a seer.

Others derided him as the Devil incarnate.

I met a man in Paris, an English muralist, who swore Balthazarr kept him hypnotized for three whole days. Eventually he woke from his trance standing naked on the ledge outside a Moroccan hotel room window with a scorpion in one hand and a bag of semiprecious gemstones in the other. He dropped the scorpion and traded the gems for money to buy a ticket back to London. When I asked him if he held a grudge against the painter he laughed, saying it was the best weekend he couldn't remember in his life. Then he told me that Balthazarr still followed him.

"How do mean 'follow'?" I said.

"Oh, I see him, usually in reflections. Mirrors or windows, the surface of a pond. Never straight on, mind you. Always behind me, he lingers. That beard, and those eyes! When I turn, he's gone. I don't think he's menacing me. He's keeping me company. I only wish he'd stay."

I thought of no reply at the time.

The muralist seemed a bit mad. He had taut, unhealthy yellowed skin, and I noticed he wore two different shoes. One brown, the other black. His fingernails were overgrown and stained from nibbling red pistachios which he kept in every pocket of his jacket and trousers. I heard later that he'd been found drowned in the Seine. But I don't know if that was true. He might've gone home to England. He was quite a character. The kind you might believe anything about if someone told you. Anyway, he insisted that Balthazarr was a mesmerist and he could, if he chose to do so, bring a roomful of people under his power without them knowing it. Part of me loved every wild detail, and didn't care if they really happened or not.

The sound of drums echoed from one of the narrower streets, growing louder. People rose from their chairs and formed a circle in the plaza around the pyramid of items to be burned in the bonfire. I went with them. The noise was deafening as the drummers entered the plaza. They wore rustic costumes. Though simple, they were effectively frightening, a combination of hooded robes and masks made from human hair, dyed red yarn, and grotesquely painted smears of silver, copper, and gold on rough, blackened wood. It was surprisingly easy to believe that instead of people, the drummers were subterranean goblins. The sort of creatures that might've lived down wherever those iron-gated stairways led! They must've worn stuffed gloves to make their fingers appear so crookedly misshapen.

The crowd cheered and clapped.

Round and round the drummers circled the pyramid.

Finally, a tall figure in a silvery robe emerged holding a torch.

"Balthazarr! Balthazarr! Balthazarr!" the crowd chanted.

Caught up in the spirit of things, I joined them. A group rushed in from the rear, blocking my view. Feeling annoyed, I shouldered my way through the throng. "Excuse me. I'd like to see," I said, in English and to no effect. They refused to step aside. I pushed harder, not caring.

"I want to see Balthazarr! Let me see!"

Finally, I broke through to the front.

There was no way of telling who the tall figure really was, because over its head it wore the most startling full-head mask, fashioned like a black sunburst. Each of the daggerlike rays sparkled silver, as if dipped in stardust. The face was round-cheeked and grim, its mouth and eyes thin slits through which the wearer could observe without their identity being revealed. My pulse quickened. Deep interest and anxiety mixed in my blood.

The mask must have weighed an absolute ton. Yet the wearer bore it naturally without a sign of physical strain or restriction.

The robe, I realized, was composed of small mirrors, each no bigger than a playing card, and shards of broken glass secured with wire twists sewn onto a background of dark material. They flashed as the tall figure turned, bending at the waist and touching its torch to the base of the pyramid. The wood pile had to have been soaked in gasoline. That was the only logical explanation for the roar and explosion of flames that climbed higher than any of the buildings in the little street plaza. The tall figure tossed its torch into the conflagration.

The heat caused me to back up and shield my face.

But the other revelers drew nearer.

I don't know how they stood so close.

I felt my skin tighten as it does after a bad sunburn. The drummers marched and banged their instruments louder than before. The crowd swayed and began a chant in a tongue I did not recognize, but it certainly wasn't Spanish.

"*Ebuma chtenff! Gnaiih goka gotha gof'nn! Fm'latgh grah'n ftaghu grah'n!*"

Over and over they repeated… I dare not call them words, but these gross utterances.

"Balthazarr! *Hafh'drn!*" someone cried out.

The tall mirrored figure lifted its arms.

I do not know if I am particularly sensitive to heat. Never had I noticed any delicacy in my skin or nerves. Yet, in this plaza, at this moment, I became terrified that I might begin to burn. That my flesh might melt, sliding off my bones. It sounds ridiculous, but the pain transfixed me. My spine felt as though it were hardening, the fluid inside converting to steam. My marrow bubbled. My panicked brain kicked like a lobster dropped into a pot of boiling water.

Did I hear my bones snapping? Or was it the sound of firecrackers?

Firecrackers, it must be. I watched a belt of them writhe on the plaza floor. A second team of performers entered the circle around the flaming pyramid. This group was nimbler than the drummers. They frolicked and skipped, running up to the crowd and touching them. Why did it make my stomach lurch to see this? The nimble goblins brandished spinning sparklers held aloft on long pikes. As they approached me, I saw the ends of the pikes were three-pronged forks like the one Preston scratched with his toe in the sand under the table.

White-sparking wheels spun on the tips of the prongs. I could not move or look away.

A goblin pushed a wheeled cart to the tall figure who stooped, picking something up.

Two puppets?

They had to be puppets, or large floppy dolls. The first was dressed as an adult man and the other as a woman. What unwholesome effigies!

The curly-haired guitar player strummed his guitar. The young woman with the ruffled black and white dress danced, not in any traditional way, but as if she were possessed.

The tall figure raised the puppets. A man's deep voice spoke through the mask.

"*Ebuma chtenff! Gnaiih goka gotha gof'nn! Fm'latgh grah'n ftaghu grah'n!*"

The crowd squeezed closer to the flames. Someone shoved me ahead. I tried to protest, but my throat was paralyzed. The guitar player thrashed the strings. The dancer flung herself to the ground, and then it was like an invisible hand jerked her body up again.

On the edge of the flaming pyre, I saw a painting propped in the flames.

The crowd pushed me in farther. The temperature was unbearable.

It was a painting of a city…

I strained to see the painting better. But flames licked over it. The canvas burned.

The tall figure, whose mirrors repeated images of the inferno, lifted the man puppet and the woman puppet… was one of them wailing? He muttered in that awful tongue-defying language. The intense heat must have made those puppets wiggle and worm.

"*Lw'nafh. Lw'nafh. Yuyu-Va'bdaa!*"

He spit the final words from his mouth and cast the puppets onto the pyre. His heavy mask slipped. Under it, I thought I saw the end of a long, forked beard.

He put the mask back in place.

"*Yuyu-Va'bdaa! Yuyu-Va'bdaa!*" the crowd shouted.

Facing them now, his resonant voice boomed out like an almighty drum.

"*YUYU-VA'BDAA!*"

They pushed me closer. I breathed in the harsh smoke from the pyre.

Then all was blackness.

Chapter Four

The child's poking woke me at noon. I opened one eye and immediately shut it. The sun, aiming like a sniper through the steeple belfry of a church, blinded me. I shaded my eyes and tried again. The boy smiled, approaching cautiously with a half-burnt stick he had used to prod me from my slumber in a kitchen chair. He was dressed as the male puppet had been during the festival.

I sat up and felt the contents of my skull sloshing like a pail of curdled milk. I was hot, my sweaty shirt peeling from my skin. In my lap rested a sweet-smelling pitcher of macerated fruit, which proved to be the remains of the night's sangria. I set it on the ground and used my shoe to push it away. A fly escaped the pitcher, buzzing past my cheek. My wicked head ached. I had drunk too much, and what lay in my stomach threatened to reappear.

The boy jabbed me in the knee with his stick.

Behind him came the sound of giggling. From under the tablecloth, a little girl of approximately the same age rushed out and stood beside the boy. Her dress matched the female puppet.

"*Buenos días*," I said.

"*Buenas tardes*," the girl corrected me.

I nodded. My tongue twitched like a dying lizard. I had exhausted my Spanish vocabulary for the day. Remaining as motionless as possible, trying to move only my eyes, I surveyed the wreckage of the plaza. Like me, there were other sleepers lying across chairs and under the tables. The cigar man who had lit the fireworks snored like an old tomcat in the doorway of a butcher's.

The pyre had burned to ash. Smoke flavored the air. I attempted to stand and saw the error of my judgment. Daggers cored my eyes. I fell back into the chair, nearly tipping over. The children found this entertaining. Elbows resting on my knees, I held my broken head and tried to piece together the tattered scraps of my memories concerning the festival. The families eating and drinking. Drummers. Goblins twirling sparklers. Pyre burning. The puppets. The tall masked figure with the forked beard. The portrait of a city in flames—

Poke, poke.

The boy was holding a glass of water out to me. His chin quivered. His eyes were a beautifully clear, sugary brown.

"*Agua*, señor?"

Parched, I took the glass with both hands and drank. After swallowing greedily, the smell of sulfur hit my nose, and then came the revolting taste of mold and an oily residue. I spat the water in my mouth back out onto the plaza. Coughing, gagging, I stared into the glass. Green and tan globules floated in the warm liquid. It looked like the water from the coin fountain.

The boy and the little girl laughed and ran across the plaza, screaming happily.

I wiped my mouth with my shirt cuff.

Slowly, I approached the ashes.

No amount of sangria would've triggered a hallucination of the grand appalling ceremony I had witnessed. Or so I presumed. I kicked through smoldering embers. Under the scrim of dust, I perceived the outermost markings of a diagram drawn in chalk. I knelt beside the cinders. Whatever this design was, the bonfire pyramid had been built upon it.

Two large charred footprints were scorched into the plaza stones.

The tall figure with the full-head mask and the forked beard had left them.

I rubbed my grizzled jaw.

What exactly had I seen last night? Under oath, what could I testify to in a court of law? Had there been a crime committed? A double sacrifice?

No.

The events might've been a festival after all. I might've drunk too much sangria. Evidence supporting a more sinister theory was scant. You can't jail people for having an odd dialect. Sure, they acted bizarrely, even scared you. Ever been to an Arkham gala party?

The cigar man groaned as he rolled onto his other side. A hot wind blew. I was a stranger here. Who was I to question their traditions, however disturbing they might appear to my alien eyes? How much of it was my own fantasy? I can't honestly say. Suddenly, I was overcome with a strong urge to return home. I wanted to feel that old familiar strangeness I knew so well. I needed to see Arkham.

It was surprisingly easy to find the Renault. The streets were deserted, and someone had covered the sewers. I dreaded navigating a route out of this city. But this morning I got lucky. I discovered a backstreet that connected to an avenue I hadn't passed on my way into town.

Soon I came upon a highway.

At the first crossroads I spotted a sign with an arrow pointing in a direction away from where I'd come that read: BARCELONA. So I suppose I never visited *that* city.

I started back to the fishing village.

Travel is a liminal state. In such states the mind is often vulnerable, even fragile. Suddenly I was panicked with a sense of being adrift. What was I doing here? In Spain, and in the universe? These questions attacked my head as I drove.

But it might've only been the worst hangover of my life.

I assured myself that I would feel better once I got back to Arkham. Seeing the faces of people whom I recognized; friends, acquaintances from my past, my family, even my old dog, Thorn, would offer me comfort and stability. A solid New England rock under my feet.

Get thee home, Alden, a soothing voice said to me.

I packed my bags, changed my ticket, and did as I was told.

CHAPTER FIVE

"Sir, Mr Alden … sir … ?"

A bony hand grasped my arm. The coolness of the fingers penetrated through my silk pajamas. I recognized their icicle touch. It was Roland, our family's ancient butler.

The hand shook me.

"Uhh … hm … grrr …"

"Sir, are you awake?"

"No." I pulled the blankets to my chin.

"You have visitors, downstairs."

"Send them away. I am entertaining no one this morning."

"It's Mr Preston Fairmont. Miss Minnie is with him. They say you are to lunch together."

Alarmed, I flipped up the edge of my sleeping mask.

"What time is it?"

Roland consulted his pocket watch. "Very nearly noon."

I threw off my blankets and jumped up. The room was dim. Thunder rumbled the house. Wind and rain slashed at the red maples in the courtyard of Oakwood. Our family's Italianate mansion perched near the top of Arkham's historic French Hill, where its architecture stood out among the Huguenot and Colonial-inspired residences like a tiramisu in the window of a Paris patisserie. Oakeses were never shy about being noticed in a crowd.

"What day, man? What damned day is it?"

I tore free from my pajamas. My bare foot landed in a puddle on the floor. My bedroom's doors swept inward from the balcony, the draperies darkened from the rain.

Roland's white eyebrows wrinkled. "It's Monday, the 20th of September … in the year of our Lord 1925 … You've been home for a couple of weeks. You should be adjusted."

"Why are those blasted doors wide open? There's a flood in here."

"You insisted they be kept that way last night, sir."

"I did? And you listened to me?"

"You made me swear to it. You said the rain helped you to sleep."

"Well, obviously I was correct."

Roland handed me a wool suit and a pair of two-tone Oxfords from my closet.

"Thank you, Roland. You know how confused and cranky I am before breakfast."

"And lunch."

I nodded, buttoning a fresh, purple-striped shirt. Roland had dealt with my habitual lateness since I slept in a crib. I was an only child. Roland was the closest thing to a much, much, *much* older brother that I had. While traveling in Europe, I had missed him more than I had my own parents. That isn't saying much. We had been through a lot together, Roland and I. We shared a fondness for each other's sense of humor and amusement at our, often uncomfortable, social predicaments, although Roland had to be careful to keep his opinions secret in order to maintain his position in our household. I ran no such risks. Roland's clear blue eyes twinkled merrily at me.

"Stall them, will you?" I sighed. "I'll be downstairs in a minute. Make coffee."

"I brewed the Ethiopian Harar you prefer. A cup is ready when you are."

"You're a godsend, Ro."

Without so much as a smile, he shut the door.

"Minnie! How long has it been? You look scrumptious as usual." I took her hand and kissed the knuckles. "What enormous jewelry you're wearing. I nearly chipped a tooth."

"Oh, Alden! Preston outdid himself. He must've brought this gigantic diamond over the mountains on the back of an elephant." Minnie's jasmine perfume filled the foyer as fully as her mellifluous voice.

"Without a doubt, your beau has spent many nights astride prodigious beasts," I said.

Preston shared a look of horror with me over the top of Minnie's head.

But Minnie was ignoring both of us as she admired her betrothal ring.

Roland entered silently as a wraith and announced the coffee's readiness.

Minnie jumped at his presence behind her.

"Join me for a coffee before we venture into the elements?" I said, holding out my arm. She linked up with me. Her free hand clasped onto Preston.

Conjoined, we followed Roland.

Minnie pulled me down, whispering, "Your manservant gives me the creeps. There's something sepulchral about him."

"Oh, Ro's a good egg. Recall that he never once reported your late-night presence in my bedroom to my parents."

Minnie nodded in acknowledgment of Ro's discretion and gave me a squeeze in memory of former times spent in each other's company. In the drawing room,

I pulled out a chair for her. Roland brought in a silver cart with a coffee urn and sweet treats. The gray rain beat tiny fists at the windows. Wind, catching in the throat of the fireplace, groaned. Preston acted distracted. He sipped his coffee and paid no attention to the nuptial details as Minnie ran through them. I guessed he'd heard the plans dozens of times. Perhaps he was feeling trepidatious, anticipating the big day. He appeared dashing as usual, but distant, a tad cool. Minnie, on the other hand, glowed. I'd never seen her so animated. Movement enhanced her the same way stillness improved others. No painting I attempted of Minnie did the woman justice. It always felt somehow *less*. One needed to meet her in person to experience her enchantment. Aside from the fact of our broken engagement, I had always liked Minnie. I found I still did.

"Preston, tell him about the tickets," Minnie said, slapping him on the knee.

Preston woke from his trance. "Oh, of course, the tickets … it's a surprise. We want you to come with us. As a gift for returning from France ahead of schedule."

"Tickets to what?" I said.

"Tell him, tell him," Minnie squeaked with joy.

"Houdini," Preston said. He reached into his jacket's inner pocket.

"The magician?"

"What other Houdini is there, silly," Minnie said.

"He's having a show here in Arkham. We're going. And you're going with us." Preston handed me my ticket.

"Why, it's for tonight. At the Ward Theatre," I said, taken aback.

"Afterward we'll go backstage and meet Houdini himself," Preston said.

"Well then …" The idea of spending the rest of the day with Preston and Minnie raised personal alarms. I didn't want to be a third wheel. On the other hand, I'd always hoped to catch a Houdini show. Denying Minnie was also inadvisable. "… I'd love to join you."

Minnie clapped her tiny hands together. "I shall be the envy of every woman in attendance," she said.

"You always are, darling," Preston said.

They kissed.

I studied my ticket. "It says it's a three-part show. I wonder what the parts are."

Caught up in Preston's tweedy arms, Minnie ruffled her fingers through his hair.

"Illusions, Escapes, and Exposing Frauds," she said, breathless.

"Illusions, Escapes, and Exposing Frauds," I repeated, tenting my fingertips and touching them to my lips, as one does while contemplating deep, philosophical conundrums.

"The show is a bit of fun and games. Nothing too serious," Preston said.

"I was only thinking you two might want to pay especially close attention. The lessons you learn may prove helpful after you are wed."

They both laughed.

"Oh, Alden, how I've missed you! You are the perfect antidote to the Arkham gloomies," Minnie said. Parting her lips revealed the intriguing little gap between her front teeth.

"I hope you didn't miss him too much," Preston said, frowning.

I was about to interject something clever when Thorn, my blue greyhound, bounded into the room. He was irresistibly drawn to Minnie and tried to climb into her lap.

She fed him a butter cookie. "Oh! May we take him out with us for lunch?"

"There's a bistro right around the corner where Thorn is a welcome guest," I said.

"I'd love to walk him," she volunteered.

"Be my guest." I fetched the dog's leash from the wall peg.

"While we walk, you tell me all about your time in the Mediterranean. How was it?"

"Hot, interesting, boring… strange."

Minnie smiled. "We're going to have so much fun together this year! Did Preston tell you? Our engagement party will be on Halloween. Doesn't that sound positively bloodcurdling? There are so many fascinating new people for you to meet, Alden. Arkham is changing. Don't laugh, it is. And things are heating up. Remember how hard it was to find a good party years ago? Everyone was still down because of the war and all that dreadfulness. But now it's gotten to be really fun again."

"Who doesn't love fun?" I said, as the three of us crossed the threshold into the chill.

Houdini did not disappoint. He executed the famous East Indian Needle Trick and his own diabolical invention of the Water Cell Torture, which had us gasping for breath in the balcony gallery of the Ward Theatre. Every escape and trick went off without a hitch. The illusionist also took time to debunk the methods of the Spiritualists and other hoaxers. His message was that one may talk to the dead, but the dead never talk back. During this portion of the show, I happened to scan the crowd below us, and to my great astonishment I swore I spotted Juan Hugo Balthazarr sitting in the front row, near the middle of the stage. I did not have the best angle to confirm if it was indeed him, but when the man leaned forward intently, the resemblance to the photo I had seen of the Spaniard was striking. He had a forked beard and was a head taller than his seatmates. And there was no mistaking the animosity apparent in his brutal visage. It was as if he harbored a personal hatred for the debunking Houdini.

Minnie had fallen asleep against Preston's shoulder during this part of the act. But by the end she was awake again. Preston had remained riveted throughout.

"You enjoyed the show?" he asked me.

"Very much so."

He couldn't have known my excitement also stemmed from a possible sighting of Balthazarr in the theatre. This might be my chance to meet the famous Surrealist! I searched for him in the post-performance hubbub. But nowhere in the departing crowd did the tall man with a forked beard appear. Perhaps I was wrong and Balthazarr had never been there at all.

"Ready to head backstage?" Preston asked us.

Minnie nodded enthusiastically. "They call him the Handcuff King, you know."

"Careful. He might lock you up," I said.

"Then saw you in half, darling." Preston pointed. "Through those heavy curtains, there's the door to the backstairs. Lead the way, Oakesy. If we run into security, I'll just tell them I'm a Fairmont. We saved this place from closing. They had a dreadful run, some play about a Yellow King, and people literally died. Which is sad because I heard the play was quite excellent. Who can ever understand the dramatic arts?"

I found the stairway and headed down, with Minnie and Preston pressing in close behind me. The farther I descended, the darker it grew. In the blackness at the bottom, I tripped on the final stair, falling forward against a steel door. It burst open. A narrow hallway. Closed doors on both sides. One weak light bulb dangled from the ceiling by its wire. On the floor, a birdcage filled with white doves. I had crashed through the door so hard that it hit the brick wall behind it, sending a boom echoing down the passage. The doves beat their wings.

I was about to ask Preston if we were in the right place when one of the doors opened.

A head stuck out.

Houdini himself peered at me from around the corner. His intense eyes shone in the semidarkness. Minnie and Preston poured out from behind me, laughing.

Minnie gasped. "Is that him? The real McCoy?"

"Not the McCoy. But if you prefer, I am the real Houdini."

He stepped forward and bowed.

Houdini was not a big man, but compact and solidly muscular. Even in his shirtsleeves, he utterly commanded whatever space he entered. We bowed back to him in reply. He wore a towel around his neck, but on him it appeared a mysterious accessory rather than a cloth to wipe away his sweat after a physically punishing exhibition of his skills.

I remained speechless, paralyzed. But Preston was less awestruck.

"May we visit with you? We have backstage passes," he said.

"Of course, please join me in my dressing room," Houdini said.

We were surprised to find him alone.

He shut the door and squeezed past us.

"My wife, Bess, has gone out to see about our dinner. Please sit, won't you?"

The small room was dingy. A threadbare carpet covered only part of the scuffed floorboards. There was a musty smell and poor ventilation. With the three of us gathered around the magician, I felt cramped, bordering on claustrophobic. Houdini didn't seem to mind. He reclined on a chaise longue, drinking from a glass of ice water.

Now that we had special access, we didn't know exactly what to do.

An awkward silence settled.

Preston coughed.

"I hope you're enjoying your trip to Arkham," Minnie said.

"I love performing here. I have many fans. They are thirsty for magic," Houdini said.

Again, the silence. An unseen clock ticking. Footsteps in the hall.

My tongue loosened. "You have a true zeal for exposing charlatans," I said.

"Vultures," he said. "They prey upon the weak, the grieving. It is an insult to my intellect and yours. I'll fight them. I have offered a $10,000 reward to anyone who professes to have so-called supernatural powers and can prove to my satisfaction they are not conmen. No one will ever claim it. Yet I keep an open mind. I like surprises. 'Show me,' I say."

There came a firm knocking at the dressing room door.

"Excuse me," Houdini said.

He moved around us to greet his new visitor.

Preston leaned into Minnie and me. "Perhaps he might do a few card tricks for us."

I shook my head. "He's already given us a show we'll never forget. We should go."

"At least he can sign our programs," Minnie said.

Preston agreed. "We should have something to remember this night."

"I, for one, will never forget it, whether or not he gives us anything more."

Houdini was talking in hushed tones with his visitor. Suddenly he cried out in pain and staggered backward, bumping into Preston who grabbed the magician around the shoulders to prevent him from collapsing to the floor.

"What happened?" Preston said.

"Why, he's paler than a ghost," Minnie said.

I rushed to the doorway and looked out into the hallway, in time to see the quickly retreating figure of a tall man in a silk top hat and cape disappearing into the shadows.

"You! Stop right there!"

The tall man half-turned. I saw the forked beard. The same person I had been studying in the audience. The one I swore was Juan Hugo Balthazarr! I started after him.

"Balthazarr? Is that you? What is going on here?"

But the tall man kept walking, never breaking his stride.

"Alden, help us!" Minnie shouted.

"I don't think Houdini is breathing," Preston said. "Get a doctor!"

Despite my desire to pursue the phantom, I returned to the stricken illusionist.

"Where am I supposed to find a doctor, Preston?"

He shrugged. Houdini's head lay in his lap.

The magician's eyes were locked on some far-off distance. His mouth fell agape. It was as if he beheld an unnamable terror stalking him, one from whose clutches he could devise no escape.

"Houdini! Houdini!" I shook him.

Then he drew in a deep breath like a man who had been saved from drowning. "I am stabbed. Low, on my right side. The fiend has put his knife into me."

Preston and I searched but found no wound… no sign of any bleeding…

"You are whole," I said. "I cannot see any injury."

Houdini prodded himself, at first gingerly, and then with greater force. He checked his fingers for the red evidence of a wound. "Amazing! I *felt* the blade slicing through me. Like a jolt of electricity! That devil placed his hand on me and spoke in a language I've never heard before. I understood not a syllable. Yet I swear he was killing me. Wait. He did say one thing I understood. As he cut into me, he said, 'Tell me, sir, if this feels real enough.'"

"Did you recognize him?" I asked.

Houdini shook his head. "He was a stranger."

I hesitated to use the name of Balthazarr. I had no proof at all. None.

Sitting up, the magician slowly regained his strength.

"Shouldn't we call the police?" Minnie asked.

"What crime has been committed?" Preston said.

"This man's been assaulted," I said.

"He looks fine now to me. Maybe it was simply a prank," Preston said. "A trick."

With our help Houdini stood. He brushed himself off, checking his lower right abdomen again. "Your friend is right." He squeezed my arm. "I received no damage. And my attacker is long gone by now. I only need to rest."

It was then that Houdini's wife, Bess, arrived. We told her of the incident. While she was alarmed to hear of the baffling encounter, her husband assured her he was feeling normal again. We parted. I felt no small degree of embarrassment when Preston and Minnie presented their programs to the illusionist for signatures. Houdini was friendly and obliging. Holding up his pen, he asked me where my program was. I had it in my pocket but told him I left it in my seat.

"You can sign it the next time you're in Arkham," I said.

"Yes, I will. Thank you for your assistance," he said.

We were about to exit when he exclaimed, "Hold on!" We turned in unison to see the escapologist digging into a lumpy sack behind the chaise. He found what he was looking for.

"Please let me offer you a token of my thanks."

Houdini held out a pair of handcuffs.

As I reached out to take the shackles from him, he snapped them on my wrists.

I struggled to pull them open, with no success. The thick iron bit into my flesh.

"What's the trick?" Minnie asked.

Houdini showed us his empty hands. "No trick. Put out your palm, my dear." Minnie obeyed his instruction. He covered her hand with his closed fist. Then he opened his fingers.

"The best way to open a lock is to have the key."

He deposited it into Minnie's hand, and she squealed with delight. After some teasing, she put the key in the locks and liberated me.

I rubbed my wrists.

Houdini clapped me on my shoulder.

"I will treasure them always," I said, pocketing the cuffs.

My friends and I left the Ward Theatre. The rain had stopped, but the night air was thick. A fog blanketed the city. Downtown, the gaslights flickered like torches afloat in space.

I imagined the tall, bearded man out there in that fog.

Watching us.

Tell me, sir, if this feels real enough.

I shivered. The evening had unnerved me. That man couldn't have been Balthazarr.

Could he?

It was a year later, on Halloween in fact, that the Great Harry Houdini died after a show in Detroit. Doctors determined the cause of death to be peritonitis secondary to a ruptured appendix. Subsequent rumors blamed a Canadian college student who allegedly punched Houdini in the gut days earlier. Houdini's last reported words were, "I'm tired of fighting."

I'll bet he was. He'd had that curse growing inside him for months. I'll leave you to form your own opinion on the matter. I know that I have mine.

Chapter Six

By mid-October the Oakes family mansion was proving to be too confining for my parents and me, despite our habit of keeping to divergent schedules and occupying separate rooms. One morning, Roland brought me an envelope on a silver tray – inside, a note from Mother.

> *Most Beloved Alden,*
>
> *You know that your father and I adore you and are deeply pleased to have you back at Oakwood with us! Yet we can't help but wonder if you mightn't be still happier with companions your own age who are cheered when they hear you knocking about the house regardless of the hour. Of course, you may remain if you so choose, and we would be nothing but delighted if you did. But mightn't it be better for all concerned parties if you were to seek other viable options?*
>
> *With much Support and Encouragement,*
> *M and F*

"Well, isn't that just great? She's giving me notice, Ro. I am to vacate the premises." I always was conscious of being in the way of my parents. Such was the warmth of Oakwood.

I suppose I should've expected this.

Snowy-haired Roland, ever my silent comforter, stood beside my desk staring out into the red maples of the courtyard. The scent of smoldering leaves lifted like sacrificial incense into the sky as the gardeners winterized the grounds. Out back stood a cast iron and glass building shaped like a small Gothic chapel – my mother's greenhouse – where she rotated pots of African violets, regulating their sunlight, checking for aphids, thrips, spider mites, and mealybugs, dipping her pinkie into the soil, monitoring whether it was too dry or too wet.

I scribbled a note on the back of Mother's stationery.

Dearest Mother,

I will begin my search immediately. If nothing surfaces, I've heard there's a "deluxe" vacancy at Ma's Boarding House. Close enough for you and Father to walk over and join us boarders for a plate of Ma's famous homemade stew!

– A

"There," I said. "That'll just about stop her heart." I folded the note in half and tossed it on the tray. Mother loathed teasing, all humor, really. "I will be going out, Ro."

Roland pivoted away from me. He paused before leaving.

"Shall I call you a cab?"

"No, thank you. I'll walk. Do you have today's paper? I need to get a new place."

"I will fetch it from the study. Would you like the Boston papers as well?"

"Start with the *Advertiser*. Tell me, Ro, how does one find lodgings in this town?"

"Carefully I should think, sir," he said. "I've lived at Oakwood for eons. I hardly recall what it's like to stay anywhere else. But I'm glad for it. A person hears stories…"

"What kind of stories?"

"Oh, horrible ones… peculiar happenings, disappearances, strange murders that even the most seasoned police detectives can't explain. Mutilated bodies floating in the Miskatonic River and down along the train tracks. There was a pair of lovely young dancers who went missing. Later their bodies were found burned… It's quite appalling if you think about it." He smiled, toeing the threshold with his pointy black boot. Roland did relish a good gruesome tale.

"I'll keep only happy thoughts in my head as I go about my apartment hunting."

"An excellent idea," he replied. "It pays to stay positive."

He grinned and was gone.

After a few minutes, I was running my razor over my soapy jaw as Roland slid the paper under my door. I toweled off and picked up the news. I heard a curious scratching outside in the hallway and opened for a look. Thorn wandered in.

"What's the latest in Arkham, Thorn?" I threw myself across the bed and began leafing through the *Advertiser*. Thorn slumped at my feet with a deep sigh.

My father had read the *Arkham Advertiser* back when it was still called the *Arkham Gazette*. At first, his goal was to see his name in the paper as his fame grew as a businessman. Once he was rich, he spent more time keeping his name, and his companies, out of the paper. He was no fan of the current paper's editor-in-chief, or the "nosy fiction writers," as he called their team of muckraking investigative reporters. But he paid for a subscription so he could read about his rivals, chuckling at their misfortunes and damning their triumphs with a spoonful of his daily morning grapefruit. Between bites of buttered rye toast, he'd punctuate his perusal of the news with exclamations of "Lies! Nitwits! Horsefeathers!" and an occasional rhetorical question, "Who gives these fools jobs?" and "Why waste the ink?" Also, I think he just liked to complain.

I'd skimmed through most of this morning's edition and was about to chuck everything but the classifieds on the floor when a story on the back page caught my eye.

Sculptor Killed by Crumbling Gargoyle

Arkham, MA, October 13th – Artist Courtland Elias Dunphy was killed yesterday morning at the All Saints Roman Catholic Church of South Arkham while taking measurements for the replacement of a gargoyle statue on the northwest corner of South Church's roof. Witnesses say part of the statue broke loose from the building, causing the artist to lose his balance and plunge to the sidewalk below. Dunphy moved to Arkham from Wisconsin last month after winning a nationwide competition sponsored by an anonymous donor to furnish South Church with new statues. "Court was a sensitive soul and a fine sculptor. I only wish he had more climbing experience before undertaking this job," said Father Michael Cryans, South Church's pastor. Dunphy leaves behind no known relatives.

"How perfectly dreadful." Maybe this was the kind of strange and horrible story Roland mentioned. For no good reason, I flashed to the bizarre festival I had attended in Spain. The figure with the full-headed mask like a black sunburst. And the fire. The painting of a city in flames. As quickly as the vision came, it disappeared. I couldn't figure out why I'd thought it just then. I leaned down to scratch Thorn's head. "You were an unlucky fellow, Mr Dunphy." Thorn shivered and with a whimper curled himself up around my ankles.

"You're right, Thorn. I promised Roland only happy thoughts."

I paged through the classifieds and found nothing.

I decided on a whim to take a stroll around the city and see if anyone had a sign in the window declaring a room for let. I dismissed the idea of buying a house. I'd been roaming Europe for months, and I wasn't ready to sink my roots down. Staying in European hotels while traveling gave me a sense of freedom I'd come to like. I could pick up and go whenever the mood struck. Thinking about doing that in Arkham was different. Everyone I knew here either still lived at home with their families, or were married and starting a new family of their own. I was aware of a few dedicated bachelors left from my college days who now roomed together, but they were as close as married couples, and I didn't want to intrude upon their domestic arrangements. No, it wasn't the idea of moving out that bothered me as much as the fear of not moving on, of getting stuck again in the stagnancy that haunted my time in Cannes. I had taken out the paintings I did in Spain after I resettled in my studio at Oakwood. They were good. Better than the half-starts and failed projects that came before. But they still lacked something. It was like they were waiting for another piece to arrive.

So I put them away.

I hadn't painted anything since getting back to Arkham.

Such was the rambling direction of my thoughts when I looked up to see that I was standing in front of South Church, the scene of the terrible accident where Courtland Dunphy died only a day ago. My feet had carried me to the spot, almost automatically. The brain is an odd organ indeed. It operates at depths science has yet to plumb. Some portion of my consciousness had driven me here. Could it be a coincidence? I dismissed that outright. I'd read about this case. Now here I was. Did I burn with curiosity on an instinctual level of which I wasn't fully aware? Or had something else guided me? A mysterious impulse?

I gazed up at the steeple and realized I was on the wrong side of the church. Here were the front doors securing the narthex, but Dunphy had tumbled off the back end, behind the sanctuary. No gargoyles perched on this section of the roof. The angle of the sun made the stained glass redder, as if it were seeping blood. My morbid imagination! I tramped onward, crunching dead leaves along the side lot of the church. As I turned past the sharp corner of gray, vertical stone, I was surprised to see another person, a young woman, loitering over the scene of Dunphy's demise. She was casting her eyes downward.

I had time to watch her before she noticed me. She cut a smart figure in an olive wool dress and black cloche hat snugged over her bobbed soft curls. She'd been crouching at the edge of the walkway with her fingers stirring a leaf pile. As she rose, she noticed me and cried out, startled, her slender ankle bending awkwardly and tipping sideways at the lip of the cobbled walk.

"Oh, shh–!" she said.

I rushed forward and grabbed her wrist to steady her.

"Sorry," I said.

She pulled herself free from my grip.

"You shouldn't sneak up on people. It's rude," she said.

"I wasn't sneaking."

"Well, creeping then," she said.

Her eyes were nut brown, so too was her hair, and both looked dark under her hat. She lifted her chin to see all of me, and she couldn't help but appear haughty and annoyed as she peered down her nose. At her full height, she stood a good two inches taller than I did.

"I beg your pardon," I said. "It wasn't my intention to surprise you."

"Why are you poking around at the back end of this church?"

"Why are *you*?"

With narrow eyes, we stared at each other.

She went first. "I came to inspect the scene of a man's death."

"I did as well," I said.

Our exchange led to another round of staring.

This time I broke the silence. "I read about it in the *Advertiser*. I was curious."

She nodded.

"Well, I knew him," she said, with the faintest hint of superiority.

"You knew him! I'm so sorry. I feel terrible for you."

She shook her head. "I didn't know him well. We were acquaintances. We said hello when we passed each other in the mornings. He was dedicated to his work at the church." She gestured toward the building.

I looked up, and here I did see gargoyles hunched like stone raptors on the corners of the structure. My mind made quick calculations, and yes, a plunge from that height would most likely be fatal. My stomach flipped in a sympathetic sensation of falling.

"Was he a religious man?" I asked.

"I should think not," she said. A smile curled one side of her mouth. "Art was his religion, I think. We never talked about philosophies. As I said, we were acquaintances."

"I am much the same."

"An acquaintance?" She frowned and cocked her head to one side.

"An artist… a painter." I made an embarrassing flourish with an invisible brush.

"Oh," she said. Her lips were dark red. I wanted her to talk to me more.

"How about you? Are you an artist?" I asked.

She looked away. "No, I write here and there. Bits of things. Small pieces…"

"Writing is an art."

"Not the way I do it. At least that's what I'm told. Mostly by men," she said.

"You can't always listen to what others tell you. Especially men. They are weak creatures. Believe me, I know. I'm one myself. There's little we understand. Only we can't let on how lacking we are, or others of our kind will attack us. Listen to your muse, I say."

"That sounds ancient and fantastical."

"Like gargoyles?" I pointed to the rooftop.

"Like the Greeks."

"Oh, them," I said. "Do you have something in your hand?"

"I might," she said.

"I know you do. I saw it when I snatched your wrist. A stone, maybe? Is it a clue?"

"A clue to what exactly?"

I shrugged.

She opened her palm and showed me a limestone cone, pitted and rough-looking.

"Gargoyle horn," she said. "See how it's sharp and whiter on this side…" She touched the thick end with her fingernail.

"It's broken off from the one up there, do you think?" I squinted, trying to focus on the rooftop gargoyle. He looked older and dirtier than the church he sat upon.

"Courtland must have grabbed hold of it before he fell," she said.

"You found it where?"

"In these leaves." She gave the pile a soft kick. "I guessed this was where he landed. Bang! He hits the walk. His hand relaxes. Opens. The horn rolls away. Or he lets go as he's falling. Anyway, the horn doesn't get very far. The detectives missed it, I didn't."

"What makes you say he landed right here?"

She walked in a semicircle. "Look, there's dried blood between the cobble-stones."

She crouched while I kneeled. She's a cool one, I thought, poring over the details. Maybe she wants to be a crime reporter. It takes a certain detachment if that's your beat.

"I think this was his head. Feet off that way. Arms out like this." She showed me how. It looked like she was praying, supplicating to an ancient demigod. We were close. I felt her breath brush past me. It was chilly outside, but I felt warm. "That has to be his blood. They scrubbed the stones but not in between. You can see dried soap bubbles where it drained off in the mud."

It hurt me to look at her, but I didn't know why. Maybe there was too much to take in all at once, an urgency to soak everything up so I'd never forget.

"Don't you think that's blood?" she said.

There was rusty purplish black residue gummed into the cracks. It made me queasy to think how much liquid probably leaked out of the man. Had he died instantly? I wondered. Or did he lay here watching it all go running out of him like beer from a shattered bottle, the foam of his life escaping as he hissed? I shivered. "I don't know what dried blood looks like."

"It looks like that." She got up.

I followed her lead, dusting off the knees of my trousers.

"Why are you here collecting horns and thinking about death on this autumn day?"

"Boys aren't the only ones who get to be curious. Girls want to know too. I could ask you the same thing. In fact, I will. Why are you here? Do you like sneaking up on people?"

"I told you, I wasn't sneaking. I was out walking. I don't know what drew me here, to be honest. What are you going to do with that horn?"

She studied it. Rolling it contemplatively between her hands. "I think I'll keep it."

"Shouldn't the police have it?"

"Why? They're the ones who left it here. There isn't even a crime according to them."

"Are you interested in crimes?"

She stepped back and studied me. "What if I were?"

I shrugged. "Everyone has a passion. It's spooky… that horn. You're keeping it?"

"Yes," she said, defiantly.

"A sort of lucky charm?"

"Some luck it brought to Courtland. I think it will be a reminder to me, a warning."

"Warning about what?"

She thought for a moment. "Be careful of what you grab." She put the horn in her pocket and started to turn away. I was afraid she was leaving.

"Listen, I like talking to you. I passed a diner back there about a block. If you've got the time, maybe we could get a coffee and talk some more?"

She shook her head. "No, I'm late for an appointment. I only meant to stop here for a moment." She was backing away from me, a little suspicious but smiling. Not afraid.

"How do I know we'll meet again?"

"Arkham is a small place. I'm surprised how often people and things… overlap." She opened her eyes big, as if she'd said something mildly shocking and was trying not to laugh. I wanted to hear what her laugh sounded like. "Goodbye," she said.

She waved to me.

"Goodbye."

She walked briskly around the corner. I hadn't asked her name or told her mine.

I ran after her but I was too late.

The South Church's side lot was empty except for blowing leaves and crooked trees.

CHAPTER SEVEN

"Roland, there's a goblin in the bushes." Mother twitched the drapery. "Roland!"

Turning from the window, she surveyed my costume as I reached the bottom of the staircase. "What are you supposed to be?"

"I'm Pagliacci." I modeled my baggy shirt with its giant, ruffled black collar and pompon buttons, and the sad, droopy spectacle of my pants. My long hat might've doubled for a chef's pastry bag.

Mother's face remained blank. "The clown? From the opera? But you can't sing."

"That's not the point. It's a costume party, not a singing competition."

Roland materialized from wherever he went when we didn't need him.

"Ma'am, you summoned me?"

"Dispose of those trick-or-treaters." Mother ordered.

"Yes, ma'am." Roland picked up a wicker handbasket full of Abba-Zaba bars from the end table and went to the door to pass out the Halloween candy.

"It's only one day a year," I reminded my mother.

"One day too many. What a nuisance! Youths trudging onto the property like vandals. We feed them for free! It's not civilized. But people will talk if we don't answer our door."

Mother adjusted my pompons, checking on me like one of her African violets.

"Found a new home yet?" she asked.

"No." I sighed.

"Have you looked in Uptown? It's where all the Miskatonic U students live."

"I know where they live. And I'm not a student any more."

"Of course not, dear. Don't snap, I'm only trying to help," she said.

I caught sight of myself in the vestibule mirror. I'd painted my face with greasepaint, only using white except for the twin blackened pits of my eyes. A sad clown, indeed.

"Where is this party you're going to?"

"At the observatory. Preston and Minnie's engagement party? I told you about it."

"See! You *should* find a place to live near Miskatonic, Aldie. Ask around. Preston might know of the perfect property for a bachelor. His family has more connections than the New York subway." She stepped back to assess me. "There! You look quite operatic."

Another flurry of low-level knocks jarred Oakwood's stately door.

"Roland!"

Mother's expression softened. She squeezed my fingers briefly, and then let go.

"I wish only the best for you, my little Pagliacci."

"I know you do." In her own distant and cultivating way, she cared about me. "Enjoy the party!"

Preston and Minnie's engagement soiree would, of course, have to be a costume party. They'd rented out the Gerald Warren Astronomical Observatory on the Miskatonic University campus. I'm sure everybody thought it was strange when they got their invitations. The observatory wasn't open to rentals as far as I knew, but like my mother said, the Fairmonts had connections. Fairmont dollars flowed into the Miskatonic coffers, and they could party wherever they wanted. Tradition said that rules didn't apply to the Fairmonts, or people like them in Arkham. I knew that it was true because I was one of those people.

I had the cab driver drop me off on the edge of campus. I didn't want to wait in a long line of cars and partygoers making a big show of their entrance. Not really my style. I'd rather come in on foot, at my own pace, and get a look around before I went in. This used to be my crowd. Now I hesitated, wondering if we'd outgrown each other while I was away.

I was late, of course. The party had already exceeded the confines of the observatory. The untrimmed, but mostly dead, grassy yard behind the small building was filled with ghouls and witches in pointy hats sipping bourbon-spiked punch. A live jazz band played "You'd Be Surprised!" and the singer did a good imitation of Eddie Cantor's jokey, nasal delivery. Orange glowing tips of cigars and cigarettes bobbed in the shadows under the arching warlock limbs of the black cherry trees which spread wide, as if to welcome them. A cherry sweetness tinged the air. It mingled with smoke from a bonfire burning in a rough stone circle near the back of the property, where demons paired off with ghosts or a menagerie of animals, real and fantastical, for more private assignations. I would not be the only clown in attendance at tonight's festivities. My costume choice proved to be popular with both sexes. But I was the only Pagliacci. I smoked a cigarette and came in through the back door. My throat was parched, and I needed something to keep my hands from hanging idly at my sides. The punch bowl was out of glasses, but I found an abandoned one on top of a bookcase, wiped it with my sleeve, and filled it.

I couldn't spot Preston or Minnie. Arkham hadn't been my stomping ground for a couple of years, but I was shocked at how few people I recognized. I chalked some of it up to their clever disguises, but I knew it was more than that. I'd been out of circulation for too long. The social turnover in Arkham wasn't what it was in Boston or New York, but my current state of dislocation had me feeling suddenly old and, like Pagliacci I suppose, more than a bit confused.

The band announced they were taking a break for a few minutes. They reminded everyone about the banquet laid out in the hallway. I wasn't particularly hungry, but I had nothing better to do, so I checked out the hors d'oeuvres.

The revelers weren't interested in eating. I found myself alone in the hallway, poring over deviled eggs, tomato aspics, skewered meatballs, crudités, oysters swimming in a pond of melting ice, fruit salad, stuffed mushroom caps, and shrimp cocktails with most of the big crustaceans picked out. I grabbed a handful of roasted mixed nuts and was crunching them when an old man with a long Whitmanesque beard emerged from the stairway.

He eyed the table with curiosity.

My mouth was full, so I greeted him with a nod.

"My wife, Bernadine, used to say that if you put out a spread of food and scientists are anywhere around, they will soon discover it. I don't like parties. But it seems this gathering has moved on. All these leftovers will go to waste, won't they? That is a terrible shame," he said.

I'd finished chewing. "Go ahead. Fill up a plate. My friends paid for this fête, and they won't mind. There's plenty. Most of them are too busy drinking."

The old gent was surprised by my offer. "Thank you. My wife said I never eat enough when I'm here. 'Head in the stars,' she told me. I get caught up in my work and forget."

I reached for more nuts. Although the hallway was empty, the observatory felt horribly warm from all the bodies bustling through. I saw why people had drifted outside.

"Doesn't your wife want you home for dinner?"

The bearded fellow smiled sadly. "Not any more."

"Given up, has she?" I asked, jokingly.

"No, she died."

Now I felt stupid and awkward, wishing I'd skipped the nuts and followed the others into the backyard. "Please forgive me," I said. "I'm sorry about your wife."

"Not to worry." The scientist went on filling his plate. "I'd rather talk about her than forget how lucky I was. Norman Withers." He held out his hand. "I work upstairs."

"On the big telescope?" I asked, feeling less embarrassed, as we shook.

Norman nodded. "In the lab, too. That's where the real discoveries are made. Reviewing the data. Deducing what the numbers mean. Even so, sometimes I see things I wish I had not."

"Like what?"

I was intrigued. I drained my glass of punch, wishing I had more.

"Oh, lately there have been gaps… perturbations… unexpected deviations."

"Sounds almost spooky when you put it like that."

"The universe is mysterious," he said. "Yet, based on years of research, we know where certain objects are. We can predict their locations. Map them out. They appear and reappear like clockwork. But when I look up and they're not all there…"

I had a feeling that maybe the professor might not be "all there" either. But he seemed nice enough, if more than a little lonely. I'd never had much interest in the sciences, but I liked unexplained mysteries.

He leaned against the wall and devoured a deviled egg.

"Couldn't it just be a mistake?"

"A hiccup in the data?" he asked.

I nodded.

"Yes, it's theoretically possible. I've gone over the measurements, recalibrated my equipment… There's nothing wrong with the telescope. But one too many hiccups…"

"Perhaps you should try holding your breath?" I kidded.

"I wish it were that simple." Norman finished eating his food. He took a second pass at the banquet table and reloaded his plate.

A server came by with a pitcher of the "holiday" punch and poured me another glass. I happened to glance out the back door and spotted Preston waving for me to join him. I was ready to say goodnight to the astronomer when he spoke up again.

"This fellow, Hubble, has argued an earthshattering theory, pardon the pun. Those swirling clouds of dust and gases we call nebulae are, in fact, distant galaxies. The Milky Way is but an eddy in a constant whirlwind. We're spinning like a hurricane on a vast, dark ocean among a staggering number of other hurricanes. Churning, round and round. Our sun, worshipped for millennia and over which gallons of sacrificial blood have been spilled, is but a dingy, minor star. You see, the cosmos is a frightfully bigger place than we ever thought."

"And we humans are…"

"Living on a speck of grit," he said.

Feeling small, slightly dizzy, and apparently insignificant – I gulped my punch.

Norman was obviously a learned man, but in that moment he had the wild, glassy eyes of an asylum patient. Exhausted, haunted. And I'd be lying if I said he hadn't scared me.

The piano player started playing "Fascinating Rhythm."

I tried to find a silver lining. "Life may be Earth's only claim at uniqueness," I said.

The musicians played louder. People were rushing back inside to see the band.

"What if it's not?" Norman said, "What if life is not unique? Who knows the immense sizes and irrational shapes our 'neighbors' might take? They may be our competitors or even our enemies. How will they deal with us when they arrive? We could be at their mercy."

A bowlegged man dressed as a faun, complete with panpipes, leapt up onto the band platform. He planted a pair of fake deer antlers on the piano player. The faun slyly pranced away. It was all in the intoxicating mood of chaotic good fun. The crowd loved it. Not missing a beat, the piano player sang:

"Got a little rhythm, a rhythm, a rhythm
That pit-a-pats through my brain;
So darn persistent
The day isn't distant
When it'll drive me insane…"

Dancers kicked their legs, threw their arms in the air, and shook themselves. A tray of glasses hit the floor, shattering. A woman screamed in mock terror. The pianist hit the keys in a frenzy. It grew hotter in the room. The windows fogged up. Everywhere, people howled with laughter, enjoying what surely was the swankiest party of the year.

I shouted my last question to Norman.

"Tell me, professor. Do you really suppose we aren't top dogs in the new cosmos?"

Norman's eyes narrowed. His gray eyebrows bristled. Gently, but with a degree of urgency, he nudged me into the corner under a candlelit sconce. I soon realized he wasn't concerned with me but instead was staring at the floor along the wall next to the table's edge.

A brown beetle scuttled from under the baseboard.

He crushed it flat.

The old man chuckled. "We might just be the cockroaches."

Holding up his leg, the astronomer regarded the gooey insect remnants sticking to his boot sole, before wiping them off with a napkin and tossing the paper into the trash.

Chapter Eight

After Norman returned upstairs to his lab, I walked to the back entrance to get a breath of fresh air. I was leaning against the doorjamb, lighting a cigarette, when Preston approached me from behind to shout in my ear.

"Was that Methuselah you were talking to?" Preston asked.

I jumped as if I'd been hit with a jolt of electricity, dropping my cigarette in the grass.

"Don't do that!" I said.

"Sorry to panic you, Oakesy. You seemed lost in deep thoughts. I wanted to make sure you were having a good time."

"I'm having a fine time when my friends aren't shocking the hell out of me."

Preston bent over. "Here's your Lucky back."

I picked a bit of turf off my cigarette and stuck the tobacco between my lips. "It wasn't Methuselah by the way. His name is Norman. Norman Withers."

Preston joined me on the threshold. People had to walk between us as if we were standing guard. They nodded cordially at Preston and gave me odd glances as if they were trying to figure out who I was, or maybe if I belonged.

"Never heard of him. Must be from Minnie's side."

"Norman's not from either side." I blew out a plume of smoke. "He's a scientist. Works here at the observatory, studying the heavens. He's an intriguing fella. I don't think he talks to outsiders much. By outsiders, I mean non-academics. He had a lot to say."

"Oh, about what?"

"The cosmos. Deviations floating around up there. He painted an alarming picture."

"Funny old bird." Preston slipped a flask from inside his jacket and took a slug before he passed it to me. "Well, I hope he was having a good time too."

"That's some fine whiskey." I said, wiping my lips. I felt a comforting warmth, like a cozy campfire aglow inside me. "Canadian?"

Preston winked. "You have a good palate. But you should. You're a painter!"

He looked drunker than I first thought. Eyes red, collar askew. A spot the color of dried blood stained his cuff. His clothes smelled like patchouli smoke. "What do you think of this crowd? I know people, Oakesy. Wonderful new people. Soon enough you'll get to know them too."

To me they didn't look very different from the old people we knew.

A cluster of merrymakers – arms linked or hugging tightly as if they'd been cast off the *RMS Titanic* and were clasping together while they waited for the rescue boats, slippery hands grasping slipperier hands – attempted to pass between us.

"We probably should move," I said. The slow crush had me backed up on my tiptoes.

"My party, Oakesy. I'll stand where I want. But you're right, as usual."

They knocked me against the door frame while blasting a mixed chorus of "Let us through!" and "Gangway!" as they passed us. A happy, absolutely sozzled stampede that posed no real threat to anyone but themselves. The next morning their hangovers would arrive overly bright and shiny, clanging pots and pans, marching into their bedrooms as the morning sunbeams cut into their skulls: so many weekend actors in smeary makeup and gaudy rented wardrobes. Preston enjoyed a high status with this crowd – his guests, his *new people* – so I bore the brunt of the bodily pressure. I'm making it sound more unpleasant than it was. What I felt mostly was a thrilling, though fleeting, symbiosis with the others, as if, however briefly, we became a composite creature. Palpable energy surged through the whole group with a crackling power. Preston's Canadian hooch was good, but not good enough that my head was humming louder than the jazz band. It had to be something else at work here.

Preston followed the crowd back inside.

I felt like I needed more air. As soon as I took two steps away from the building, my clown pants began to hang low on my left side, and a heavy weight brushed against my thigh. I reached into my pocket and withdrew a broken piece of limestone carved in the shape of a curved horn. It came from the gargoyle at South Church. Doomed Dunphy's last handhold.

When I'd figured out what it was, I looked up to see the woman I'd met in the churchyard. Now she was standing in the smoky, yellow flickering of the party's bonfire.

I couldn't make out the details of her face, but I knew it was her. She had one leg raised up, her bare foot resting lazily on a tree stump, and there were ribbons hanging off her. She was watching me, the corner of her mouth hooked in a smile. Chin out, head back. I saw that much. So, I walked over. You would have too. Hell, any man would have, possibly a few women as well. Not ribbons, I decided. *Bandages* – that's what they were supposed to be. They wrapped around each of her legs and her torso. She wore a short, nude-colored dress under them. Unraveled bindings trailed from her wrists. Assorted metallic bangles were stacked nearly halfway to her elbows, catching the firelight. Around her throat she'd taken a piece of shroud and tied it in an ascot knot, as if it were the chicest couture. Her head, free of encasement, was topped simply by a small gold crown with an aqua stone set dead in its center. She'd straightened out her bob. The color was a shade darker than I recalled, but maybe the night was doing these things to her, or to me. She looked knowing, yet expectant. Kohl rimmed dramatically around her big, luminous eyes. Bordeaux lips, wet teeth. A person waiting for something, perhaps something owed? Not harmless, not by a mile. Those piercing eyes were capable of shocking and showing outrage in the same instant. *I never want this woman angry at me*, I thought. She's the kind of lady who might stab you with a pair of scissors if she figured you deserved it. Or she might die for you. It all depended.

On what exactly, I wasn't sure.

I tried my best not to look too eager. I'm sure I failed miserably.

"Who are you?" I asked.

She acted insulted. "You mean you can't tell?" She took the cigarette holder from her right hand and clenched it between her teeth. Then, very tall, arms stretching high overhead, she twirled. "I'm an Egyptian mummy."

"But your face isn't wrapped."

"Would you wrap this face if it was yours?" She blew smoke at me.

"I can't say I would."

Her gaze fell to my hand. "What have you got there?"

"I think you know," I said.

"I don't." She was playing a game now.

What was she doing at Preston and Minnie's party? Was she one of the new people?

"You put this in my pocket." I showed her the gargoyle horn.

"I did? My, my, that was awfully presumptuous of me. What business do I have going in your pocket?"

"Let me decide that."

"I'm not making any promises," she replied. Her hands were dusted with a golden powder that sparkled whenever she moved. There were traces of it on her cheeks and chin, from when she had touched her face. Her feet were bare, also gold. I saw a pair of black heels she must have kicked off in the grass behind the stump. She had no drink, but I smelled gin.

"Why give this to me?" I asked, pointing the end of the horn at her. My hand glittered now too.

"To remind you of the unfortunate reason we met," she said.

"Courtland Dunphy?"

She stuck out her lower lip. "He lived across the hall from me. Not for very long, though. He'd recently arrived in town. Did I tell you that before?"

"No, you only said you saw him in passing."

"Court was the serious type, all business. He had a kind face. You know he wasn't the first. There have been quite a few. He was only the latest."

"Latest what…?" I wasn't following her. I thought I was for a second. But I wasn't.

"The latest death… suicides, murders, missing people… It's practically an epidemic."

"Oh," I said. "I heard about them. But I've been out of town so I'm still catching up."

"I'll cross you off my list then." She turned away to light another cigarette.

"What list?"

"Of suspects," she said, offering me a smoke.

Before I could accept her offer, a hooded monk lunged out from the shadows carrying what I took to be a beer keg over his head. Finally, I recognized someone I knew from the old days. It was Clark Abernathy, another of my college classmates, costumed as Friar Tuck. He wasn't carrying a beer keg but a gnarly log, which he tossed on the bonfire. *Craaack!* Sparks exploded into the sky. The black cherry tree branches were lit up. Their fleshless, ghoulish arms hovering above us, making witchy signs over a boiling cauldron.

Clark hadn't seen me. I thought about calling to him.

But I was in a conversation, you see.

"Arkham's always borne its fair share of tragedies," I said. "I've chalked most of them up as legends and rumors. This town likes to tell stories."

"Not all legends and rumors," she said. "These things really happened. People died."

"What are the police doing about it?"

She scoffed. "Nothing. What did they do about Court?"

"I thought what happened to Court was an accident."

"Was it? Court had a premonition a bad thing might happen to him."

I blinked in surprise. "Did he tell you that? I thought you didn't really know him."

She took the horn from me. "I don't really know you. But if you were feeling under threat? I'd pick up on it," she said. "For instance, I could tell if you were scared."

"And am I scared?" I looked right into her eyes.

"Definitely." She smiled. "Anyway, I think something in that church killed Court."

"The gargoyle?" I was puzzled, but intrigued now.

"The gargoyle literally did kill him." She arched her eyebrow, challenging me to argue. When I didn't, she continued. "I don't mean it came to life. That's goofy. I'm talking about a more subtle force. What made Court go up there? Why was he standing so close to the edge? You know it rained that morning? The roof was slick. The gargoyle was scheduled to come down in a week. Its removal had been meticulously planned. They were bringing in scaffolding, ladders, ropes and pulleys; a safe, logical system. Court never told anybody he was going up there.

Father Michael didn't even know. Court had his own key to the church. Why did he grab that horn? Was it for balance in a moment of panic? He knew the gargoyle's condition. He'd inspected it many times. Was his fall simply chance?"

"One might call it fate." But I was beginning to understand what she was poking at.

"Or, maybe, just maybe… it might be something else."

"Like a curse?"

She shrugged. "I prefer to call it an *intelligent influence*."

"You mean someone, or something, made him do it?"

"Oh, damn, here she comes."

I looked through the bonfire flames and spotted Minnie approaching.

"There's my favorite clown," Minnie kissed my painted cheek. She wore a sequined gray leotard. "If you're wondering, I'm a peacock." She turned around so we could appreciate her colorful iridescent plumage. "Have you seen Preston? He was supposed to join me for a duet with the band, but I can't find him anywhere."

"Last I saw him, he was heading inside with the crowd."

"Uggghhh. When was that?"

I shrugged. "Five minutes ago."

Minnie frowned. "I do hope he can remember the words to our song." She paced around the fire, her eyes searching the murky yard for her misplaced beau. "Preston has gotten to be such a worry wart lately. The smallest bump in the road and he startles. I'd think he was cheating on me, too, the way he slinks off without telling me where he's going. Keeping odd hours. A regular Count Dracula. He barely sleeps a wink, even when he's not with me. It's the wedding, I'm sure. We're both terribly excited. But I swear he'd frighten me off if I didn't know the real him. Preston is not one to be bothered. Alden, you lived with the man. He usually takes life as it comes, right? And to Hell with tomorrow."

I nodded. "A cool cucumber is what he is. He looks fine to me."

"Well, he isn't," Minnie said.

What I didn't say was that Preston didn't worry about tomorrows because somebody had always taken care of his, ensuring he'd be given his choice of the best money could buy in all the things life had to serve up. It was impossible to imagine any true harm coming to him. From birth, he'd led a privileged, boyish life. Maybe he thought that was ending.

"Well, I'd better go find him." Minnie marched off. After she rounded the fire pit, she paused – her head swung back – to ask a parting question of me. "Who's your shy friend?" But she wasn't really asking, only being polite. She didn't wait for my answer.

"Who *is* my shy friend?" I said. "You never told me your name. I'm Alden Oakes."

"Nina Tarrington," the mummy queen said.

We exchanged bows.

"Nina Tarrington. Where have I heard that name before?"

"Preston was going to marry me once, too."

If I'd had a drink, I'd have spit it out into the flames. God, I thought, she's telling me the truth. Now I remembered that Preston was engaged to a Nina Tarrington. A Boston woman. Her father was a publisher who owned a newspaper chain. They'd butted heads, Preston and Nina, and fought constantly. Ultimately, the wedding was called off only days before the ceremony. A wild tale accompanied the news. Something about a sword and a wrecked sailboat. Champagne bottles smashed; a man lost tragically overboard.

"You're *that* Nina Tarrington?" I said.

"See, I told you people overlap in Arkham."

"We certainly do."

"Alden, now that we know each other better, do you think you could find me a drink?"

"I'll do my best."

"What more could a woman ask?"

I held out my arm, and Nina took it.

"You know, I was engaged to Minnie. That makes you and I related, I think."

Chapter Nine

"You and Minnie? Knock me over with a feather. We must learn from our pasts," Nina said.

"I plan to do just that." We were returning from a trip to the punch bowl. I raised my cup in a toast. "Here's to learning!" Nina clinked her cup with mine.

We entered the observatory library, which appeared cozy at first, but upon further exploration revealed a warren of nooks and tome-packed aisles that curved around one whole side of the building. People wandered in and out, but no one stayed for too long. For a library it was awfully dim. The room's electrical lighting wasn't working for some reason. I thought it strange, but wiring in Arkham was sometimes a spotty business. Turning the library switches did nothing, leaving us with the moonlight to guide our way. Nina and I found a secluded corner. She curled up catlike on a cracked leather brandy-brown wingback. I perched on a lowboy bookcase filled with scientific pamphlets. Everything was looking very nineteenth century, very Victorian. The music from the band thumped like a heartbeat in the walls.

"What were we talking about?" I asked.

"Outside, before Minnie came over? I was telling you about the unexplained deaths."

"That's right. Arkham's had a run of bad luck lately."

Nina's gaze narrowed. "It's more than bad luck. I think the incidents are connected."

"To what?"

"To each other, for a start," she said.

"Heavens! Do you have any proof of this theory?"

I scooted my bottom back onto the bookcase and bumped into something behind me. It was an orrery depicting our solar system: the sun, planets, and all their moons. I picked it up. The cool brass apparatus resembled a faceless automaton juggling semi-precious orbs in its spindly arms. Gears moved inside the glass dome which formed its base; quite a mesmerizing clockwork model. It reminded me of Norman the astronomer's cosmic lesson.

But I set it aside to listen to Nina.

"I've dug up a few things," she said. "The big picture's still fuzzy."

"A series of murders? That's gruesome." The mood in town seemed dark these days.

"They weren't all murders. Some were suicides."

"That hardly makes it better."

"I agree," she said. "There's been an uptick in missing persons cases too. We can presume a few of those will turn out to be suspicious deaths. And I've come across a couple of other oddities. What the coroner calls 'deaths by misadventure.' But they're far from ordinary accidents."

"Like Court Dunphy's plunge from the South Church rooftop," I said.

"Precisely. My research is leading me to hypothesize an underlying pattern to these deaths. If not in method, then in flavor. They share the same... unique design."

"That 'intelligent influence' you mentioned outside." Now normally, I wasn't drawn to the macabre the way Roland and, apparently, Nina were. But I liked puzzles. However, this puzzle appeared too weird and obscure to feel real. Then I flashed to the bizarre street festival I'd witnessed in Spain. Perhaps the world *was* weirder than I knew. Yet I worried Nina might be more deeply eccentric than I first thought. Would Houdini's debunking have made her angry? I hoped not. I was a fan of logical earthly solutions. "If the design is the same, that might suggest a designer, a unifying personality behind it all. Like an artist compiling a body of work. Do you suspect a hidden force is behind these fatal events?"

Nina considered my question. "Not always hidden. Some of the deaths were violent homicides; people committed them. However, their motives may be... highly unusual."

I breathed a sigh of relief. At least she wasn't talking about vengeful ghosts.

"I'm so glad to hear you say that," I said.

"What do you mean?" She frowned at me.

"These mysterious deaths are like puzzles. They present us with a challenge, and I do like challenges. Maybe I could help you solve them?"

She straightened out her legs. "I never asked you for any help."

Don't blow this, Alden, I thought. "Perhaps, you'd like, what's a good word, a kind of *collaborator*? Someone to talk over the crimes with. Another mind in the mix. A teammate?"

"How would you assist me?" She raised her eyebrows, quizzical.

She had raised a salient point to which I had no ready reply.

"I don't know exactly." I had no investigative experience. I was an artist.

"Well, then." Nina slid to the front of the wingback seat as if she were getting up.

"I have a good imagination," I said, quickly. "I'm a visual thinker. What if you describe the murders, and I'll picture them in my head. Maybe I'll see something useful?"

After a skeptical tilt of her head Nina settled back in her chair again.

"I guess it's worth a try," she said.

"Oh, I think so." Maybe it hadn't started out entirely that way, but now I really did want to hear about these unexplained cases. I wanted to see if I might contribute something.

Nina drew in a deep breath. "Dr Juliana Silva was found hanged from a lamppost in front of St Mary's Hospital in Uptown. She was visiting Arkham from her home in Rio de Janeiro, Brazil. An expert in contagious diseases of the Americas. She traveled here for a year of teaching. A nurse arriving to work her morning shift discovered Dr Silva's body."

"Hanged overnight at the hospital. It wasn't a suicide?"

"Dr Silva's hands were tied behind her back. She was swaying six feet above the sidewalk. No one saw or heard anything. No signs she fought off an attacker. She was still wearing her stethoscope and eyeglasses. She had purple witchweed flowers stuffed in the pocket of her exam coat. Those flowers are not easy to come by, but they grow nearby at Hangman's Hill. Dr Silva was known to take walks there in the daytime, but never at night."

I closed my eyes, concentrating.

Like a sketch, the scene began to develop, stroke by stroke, in my mind's eye.

"Flowers pilfered from a potter's field… Her killer knew where she went for walks. Maybe they picked the flowers knowing she liked them. And used them to lure her." My mental sketch showed a bouquet, an outstretched hand, a length of rope concealed behind the strangler's back.

"Hmm… so she didn't run or fight because she didn't see the killer as dangerous." Nina's voice betrayed her surprise. "I hadn't thought of that. She was killed quickly?"

"I haven't any idea. Go on. Tell me another one…"

"Udo Ganz, union organizer. His body was discovered floating in the Miskatonic River near the docks." This time there was a tinge of anticipatory excitement in her recap.

I opened my eyes. "Hardly much of a mystery there. My father is a local business owner and he hated Ganz, as did most of the industrialists in Arkham. There's a crime there to be sure. Sadly, I don't think it's unusual if a businessman's hired goon drowned Ganz."

"Except he wasn't drowned."

My dull reaction switched to bewilderment. "Beaten to death?"

Nina shook her head. "Mr Ganz had his skin peeled off in one piece. The folded-up flesh suit was mailed to the *Advertiser* on ice. With a note explaining that Ganz had to die. Several elaborate tattoos covering his chest and back made the identification easy. A confidential source told me Ganz had scaled back his union agitating because he was receiving bribes from the same business owners he'd battled for years. In other words, he'd sold out. But union members didn't know. His funeral devolved into a pro-Labor riot. Factories were set on fire. Equipment destroyed. The police arrested over fifty protesters."

I decided not to draw a mental picture of the skin suit. Nina's facts made Ganz's hellish demise plain enough. How could a person commit that crime unless they were insane?

"You have more cases, right?"

Nina nodded. I closed my eyes again.

"The Galinka sisters, Mary Lou and June, perished on the Unvisited Isle. A Boy Scout troop out on a Saturday canoeing excursion discovered their charred bones."

"Oh, my butler told me about this one! They were dancers?"

"That's right. Say, you knew about Ganz and the Galinkas. Maybe you're the missing connection between these deaths?" she teased.

I hoped she was only teasing.

"Ha ha … Just because I know names doesn't make me guilty. Continue, please."

"The twin sisters owned a dance studio where they taught ballet and the latest modern steps. They had vanished after a Friday night recital. The twins were renowned for their cheery, vibrant personalities. Witnesses reported seeing 'a wall of flames' on the island early Saturday. The reports were ignored by the police who figured it was a hobo campfire."

Behind my eyelids, I saw a ring of trees around a blaze. Twisted orange flames licking the sky. Dancers in the dark. "These murders all happened last year?" I was shocked.

She stared at me. "No. That's in the last six months. Go back a year, you can add another half a dozen unsolved bizarre deaths. Each one stranger than the last. My favorite? At the train station, a drifter's body turned up in a boxcar. Throat opened ear to ear by a switchblade knife. The knife clutched in his hand. Not a drop of blood left in him. Or on him. Or anywhere else in the boxcar."

"How did the police explain that?"

"They didn't." Nina threw her arms up and the scent of Chanel No. 5 enchanted me. She ran her fingers through her short, slick hair and gazed out the window at the pale moon.

"Look there," she said, whispery.

I looked.

"No. Not at the moon, silly." Nina blew a gentle breath toward the dusty windowpane.

A spiderweb trembled in a corner of the window.

Where a delicate spider balanced on the swinging threads.

Waiting. Watching.

A shiver crawled over my skin. "All this bloody-minded talk has me tragically sobered up. I plan to address this issue without haste," I said, offering Nina my hand.

We navigated a trail through the stygian, labyrinthine library. The air smelled of mildew, old books, and dust. Nina stopped abruptly. "What's that noise?"

I listened. "I don't hear anything. We're almost to the door."

"The door is the other way." She stopped again and tugged me back.

We were in a very dark aisle, and I began to think she was correct. "Maybe I'm not looking for a door. Ever consider that? Maybe I'm exploring." I turned, hesitating among the oppressive shelves. Which way was the damned door? I squinted without it doing any good.

"Some explorers get lost and are never heard from again," she said. From behind me, she grazed my neck lightly with her fingernail. Then I felt her warm fingertip press down.

"Maybe I want to get lost. That's been my plan all along."

Now we stopped talking. I turned to her.

But I could hardly see anything. Silhouettes.

Nina came closer, so our faces were inches apart. Were we going to kiss? The music from the band had gone quiet, though I swore I heard the blood pumping in both our hearts.

Soft murmurs.

Her face swiveled away from me. "What *is* that noise? I'm not kidding, Alden. I hear people. Two voices, I think." She tipped her head to listen better. "Talking. You hear it?"

"It's just us," I said. "Isn't it?"

But it wasn't just us because I could hear the low voices now too. They sounded … funny. Guttural, deep, and thick. But hissing too, filled with fricatives. I felt an unpleasant creeping chill, like a cold, damp knuckle gliding down my backbone.

"It's coming from this way," Nina said.

I flicked my banjo cigarette lighter so we could see better.

Just under our chins, Nina approached a shelf housing leather-bound, astro-nomical textbooks and star charts, an English translation of Copernicus's *De Revolutionibus Orbium Coelestium*, and a battered tome entitled Morryster's *Marvells of Science*. Quickly but quietly, she unloaded the musty, thick books, piling them in my waiting arms. Once she'd cleared the space, Nina stuck her head inside the vacant cubby.

"They're behind this bookcase," she said. "On the other side of the wall."

"You still hear them?"

"Shuush!" She pointed into the cubby, then nodded.

I snugged myself beside her for a listen.

I held my lighter's wobbly flame up, although there was nothing to see.

There were only sounds.

We leaned forward together.

Voices! Yes, I heard them more clearly inside here; the space made a kind of acoustic amplifier. Voices talking in rhythm, a cadence, as if reciting prayers. Alarmingly close.

Nina held up two fingers.

I nodded in agreement. Two people talking.

She whispered, "A man and a woman."

"Yes. I hear the same."

Almost musical, yet discordant, a harsh pattern. If these were words, they made no sense to me. I could hear them well enough now, but their meaning remained cryptic. I might've even called it gibberish, but despite my lack of comprehension, the utterances were affecting me. I felt uneasy, nauseated. My muscles ached as if I had come down with the flu. We were hearing a sort of chaotic language, nonsense sounds, disorganized but repetitious.

"Yoohoo? LA. Pada," I tried to recreate what I heard.

"Something like that. Not quite," Nina said. "They're saying it over and over. You? You? *Fapada. Vadada? Rabada?*"

The source was frustratingly close. What did the words mean? Who were the talkers?

My brain stirred. A thought in my grasp slipped away. I'd heard something like this language before. But where? Gregorian chants? No. A Dadaist poetry reading?

I smelled a sudden acrid burning. My thoughts derailed.

"What's that horrible smell?" Nina asked as a flame reared up next to her like a darting snake head. "Fire!"

Nina pulled out of the bookcase. The amber serpent of flame followed her. It had coiled itself around her left arm.

Nothing so exotic as a flaming serpent.

In my distraction I had accidently ignited one of the mummy bandages dangling from Nina's wrist. Jerkily, she waved her blazing arm. I grabbed the clown hat off my head and smothered her combusting bindings with my floppy chapeau. The flames quickly snuffed out.

The burnt bandages were a crumbly black mess.

Reluctantly, I struck the wheel of my lighter. Nina's skin appeared slightly pinkish.

"Are you hurt?" I felt terrible, responsible, foolish.

"My skin feels hot but not burned. Don't worry. I'm fine."

When we bent our heads toward the bookcase again, the voices had fallen silent.

"Damn! They've gone," Nina said, disappointed.

"The energy has changed. It's as if I can feel their absence. Do you feel it too?"

She did.

Nina insisted that we had to search for the room beyond the bookcase. I agreed. We began by inspecting the hallway, but found no doors on that side. All the second-floor accesses were locked. We went outside. The area of the building in question had no windows. I wondered if it was storage space. The dome of the observatory loomed above the yard.

"We have to find a way in there," Nina said. "What if someone's stuck in a closet?"

"That doesn't seem likely."

"I need to know where those voices came from."

I fetched us more punch. The alcohol made our quest more feasible.

"Well, we do know one possible way in. Don't we?" I said.

Nina wrinkled her forehead. As we sipped, I watched her eyes grow wide. When she grinned at me, I knew she'd do it. "We're going to need tools."

"And more punch," I said.

The party was enjoying a second wind. The band returned to the stage after a refreshment break. Using the distraction to our advantage, Nina and I returned to the library. We were alone this time. Hurriedly, we blocked the doors from inside to avoid the need to explain our peculiar destructive activities. Having discovered an unlocked janitor's closet, Nina procured a hammer and a sturdy mop handle. She weighed these in her hands.

"Hammer first, then the stick. Are you sure you want to do this?" I asked.

"Fairly sure." She handed me the mop handle and gave the hammer a practice swing.

"Fairly sure or *sure* sure?"

"I'm sure. Let's do it. Preston can pay for the damages later. He owes me."

Experimentally, I rapped my fist inside the empty bookcase, noting the hollow sound.

"Ladies first?"

"I would stand for nothing less."

Nina bashed the hammer through the back of the bookcase. The wood was old and dry. It made a splintery crunch. I jabbed with the mop handle, clearing a wider hole. Even with the band bashing in the other room, I couldn't believe no one heard our demolition.

We discovered a void where there should have been a solid wall.

Like Howard Carter inserting a candle into Tutankhamun's tomb, I slid my hand into the gap, tasting strong musky incense, and something more metallic and far less pleasing.

"Alden, there's something terrible in there. I feel it." She touched her stomach.

"I fear you're right." I had the awful sensation of turning in a forest and feeling lost.

"We've gone this far," she said. "No backing down now."

I didn't argue.

I was preparing to yank out the bookcase, when my grasping fingers entered a notch behind the bookcase's crown molding. It felt like a latch. I popped it.

The bookcase swung free – a hidden doorway: that old gothic trope.

Side by side, Nina and I followed the tiny flame of my lighter into the vault.

"Look at that. It isn't a room after all," I said.

"A secret staircase. Where do you think it goes?"

"One way to find out."

"These stairs are quite narrow," she said. "I'll follow you."

"Oh, thanks!"

I went up one step. Nina was right behind me, her hot hand pressed firmly to my back.

"This might be the closest I've ever come to being frightened," she said in my ear.

"I'm well past that point. We don't know what's at the top of these steps."

The stairway was utilitarian; its wood painted all black. Above us, a soft gray rectangle of space awaited our arrival. I kept seeing bulky imaginary forms oozing into view.

Silence. Except for our quickening breath. The quiet made it worse – the anticipation of noises, unspeakable in the offing. I wanted to fill the quiet with my voice, but I dared not.

"That iron smell is blood. Isn't it?" she said.

"I believe so." Why did the blackness ahead seem to shift to red?

No. It was black.

Nina made a tiny choking sound at the back of her throat. "Keep going."

Five stairs higher and we took them without hesitation. I paused halfway to the top. "We could turn around." There was a pressure now ahead of us and behind. It felt as solid and real as the stair treads under our feet. The pressure pushed. "There's no shame in that."

Nina said, "It feels like I'm underwater. I can't breathe."

We heard something then – a gnawing sound, like tissue being bitten and sawed apart.

"Do you think some poor animal got trapped?" she asked.

"And it's chewing its leg off?"

"Go! However bad, I need to see it," she said. "I can't take it. This wondering."

We rushed to the top of the stairs.

A large room. Faint, lead-colored light over our heads. The air felt cool and drafty, the floor wet. My shoes slipped as if I'd walked out onto an icy pond. But this was no pond, and what lay obscenely before us was no injured animal in need of kindhearted rescuers.

It was far more hideous.

Chapter Ten

The unclothed corpse of a man: awash in blood, shockingly headless.

He lay on his back in a glistening red pool. Arms and legs stretched wide like a stranded starfish, with one key difference: his missing body part would never regenerate. The crimson stain spreading underneath him crept to the edge of the stairs. It was a hard struggle whether to stare at him or to look away. I was transfixed and repulsed in equal measure.

Could this be a particularly well-staged Halloween prank? A bit of artful drama?

The raggedy flesh, the glistening ring of exposed cervical spine told me, "*No*."

This was not a clever prank.

My stomach lurched a little then, and the whiskey inside wasn't helping. Looking away, I found myself observing Nina's face as she comprehended the extent of the horror we had stumbled upon. Her unblinking eyes. Mouth falling open, then the sharp intake of breath.

"What the *hell*…?"

I was about to suggest we go back the way we came, when it occurred to me that the executioner of the unfortunately deceased individual on the floor might still be in the room with us. I did not want to offer the killer my unguarded back.

I swiveled around, my nerves on highest alert.

But I saw no one.

As I stated, the room was large. But it was also open and uncluttered by much furniture. An attacker would have had trouble finding a hiding place, unless they were a contortionist or very, very small. Nevertheless, when I located a switch on the wall, I quickly turned it.

Nothing happened.

Then I remembered the electricity was out in the library. Were these rooms on the same circuit? And had that circuit been cut here, intentionally, in preparation for the act of murder? Despite the impediment of unavoidable darkness, I knew exactly where we were.

Above the body loomed the observatory's most famous attraction, its huge refractor telescope; like a giant metal finger, the narrow end pointed at the headless body. Next to the body stood a wheeled set of steps which the Miskatonic astronomers ascended in order to peer into the telescope's eyepiece. Each wide step served double duty, providing a bench seat for any extended study of the galaxy. "Someone pushed these steps here," I said. "They're far from where they belong."

"The murderer must have done it," Nina said.

"They had plenty of room for killing. Why move things?"

Nina crouched beside the mutilated remains. "See here? Beneath the blood there are markings drawn on the floor. Do you think they're scientific?"

Most of the design was obscured by blood and the corpse. Judging from what remained visible, the dead man lay atop a diagram made of interlocking angles and circles. I bent and dabbed my finger, smudging one of the lines but avoiding any blood. I rubbed my fingers together and sniffed. "It's chalk. I doubt an astronomer drew it. To what purpose?"

"What if the astronomer is also the murderer?" Nina asked. She stood and walked over to a lab table slashed by the shadows. Gazing skyward, she pointed. "That's where the draft is coming from." The observatory's shutters were open. The moon entered through the slit in the dome roof. Nina found the nub of a candle stuck to a table. "Toss me your lighter."

I did.

Candlelight mixed with moonlight, but neither made the sights less dreadful.

"The blood is so red," I said. "And so… everywhere." I gulped sourly.

While I was feeling close to being sick, Nina appeared unnaturally calm.

"I wonder who he is?" she said, returning to the body.

"Doesn't any of this bother you?" I said. "It's all rather graphic and, well… authentic."

Nina shrugged. "I've seen dead bodies before."

"Where?"

"When I was a girl my father had a preoccupation with criminality. He was a newsman and an amateur sleuth of sorts. He took me to crime scenes. Fresh ones. I know it sounds abnormal, but I liked going with him. Seeing Boston's underbelly. It was exciting. I inherited my sordid interests from him. Daddy bought a newspaper, then a few others. We stopped roaming the streets together. Where do you suppose this man's head has gone?"

"The killer took it?"

"Yes. We heard the killer, didn't we? Separating the neck joints moments before we arrived. How did they get up through the shutters with it? It's too high to jump. We were blocking the secret stairwell, which must be a shortcut the astronomers use to get to the library. Going out the main door leads downstairs to the banquet table. It would be too risky."

We could hear the muffled noise of the partiers below us.

Nina's mention of the banquet put me in mind of Norman Withers. "Good heavens! Nina, let me have that candle."

I studied the body closely.

"What is it, Alden?"

I passed the candle flame along the length of the body, careful not to drip any wax. "I met a Miskatonic astronomer at the party tonight. Talkative fellow. Long beard, lively eyes – details which won't help us here. He was working upstairs in this lab. I feared this might be him. But, no." I leaned away from the corpse. "This guy is too young and portly to be the same man. Even lacking a head, he can't be Norman Withers."

"Good news for Norman," she said. "I wonder who…"

A small scuffling noise called my attention to the far corner of the room. A rat?

I do not like rats, though I suppose they were the least of our potential problems.

Still, a rat makes a person feel crawly. Maybe vermin smelled the blood?

An astronomy lab is not the ideal place to find a decent weapon. We had left our hammer and mop handle downstairs. I picked up a slide rule from the table. "Come with me."

"What are you going to do with that?"

"I want to make sure we're alone under the dome."

"And if we're not, you'll take measurements?"

I ignored her jibe. Candle in hand, we made a thorough inspection of the room. I know this may sound callous, but once the initial shock of the gruesome murder had settled in, it was easier to appreciate the inspiring size of the grand telescope we were circumnavigating.

"It looks like Big Bertha. Doesn't it?"

Nina shrugged. "I can't really say. I've never seen a howitzer in person."

"In photos it is impressive." I pointed to an iron track circling the room. "The dome rotates around on rails. Ropes and pulleys move it. That one hanging by the opening controls the shutter. Hey, look! Is that blood on it? The killer must've been covered with the stuff."

"You seem to know a lot about this place." Nina examined the stained cable.

"I visited here on school field trips when I was a kid." Now that we had checked the room thoroughly, I was feeling less threatened by an impending attack. "I think we can say, with some confidence, that the killer has fled. It's time to call the police."

Nina pursed her lips, tapping one knuckle against her chin.

"Do you really think that's wise?" she said.

"A man's been murdered. What other choice is there?"

"How will we explain ourselves? Our discovery of the body, for instance?"

"The police will understand." I was not eager to involve the authorities. People of my class generally prefer to handle life's unpleasant and socially embarrassing events less formally. But here was a decapitated man! "They'll know the right way to handle this."

"That has not always been my experience." She paced nervously. "We should think this all the way through. The body will be found tomorrow at the latest. There's bound to be cleaners coming in after the party. Either way, it won't help him." She tipped her head at the corpse. Then she sighed deeply. "I'll just say it. I don't want to become a suspect, Alden."

"A suspect?" I didn't understand. "Why on earth would *you* be a suspect?"

"I've had trouble with the police… in my past." She looked frightened.

I was curious to know more, but I could see that she was reluctant to tell me. If I pried, she'd clam up. So I lit two cigarettes and passed one to her. We smoked silently in the semi-dark. The two of us. Just thinking. I was waiting for her to make up her own mind. Did she trust me enough to say anything more?

Nina stared at the opening in the dome and watched the smoke escaping. Her big eyes came around to meet mine squarely. "Do you remember when I told you about Udo Ganz's funeral? How there was a riot afterward and protestors were arrested? I was one of them."

"You were picked up at a political protest?" That didn't seem so bad.

"It was more than a protest. But I didn't go for the politics. I went to have a look at the crowd. Maybe I thought the person who killed Ganz might show up. I don't know what I was thinking. That I'd just look at them and somehow know? Maybe it was a fantasy I had of solving the murder. Pretty soon the march turned serious. Out of control. Bottles thrown. Threats and insults traded back and forth between the protestors and the cops. I got caught up in the crowd. I couldn't slip away. Carried along in the river of bodies. The police rushed us. It was terrible. Fists and clubs flying. It felt more like a boxing match than a mass arrest…"

"Nina, I'll make the call to the cops. When they get here, we'll both have to talk to them. There's no avoiding that. But we can stay together. If there's any problem, anything at all, I'll phone my father's lawyer and have him out here tonight. Nobody gets hurt."

Nina hugged me.

I turned my head as we embraced, trying not to see the body in that lake of blood.

"Alden? There's more…"

"More?" I pulled back but held onto her shoulders.

"Just a little."

"Go on."

She turned sideways and started pacing again as she relayed her story. "When the Galinka sisters were discovered on Unvisited Isle? After the story came out in the papers and everywhere people knew what happened? That day, I borrowed a boat. A leaky old rowboat I found tied up on the shore. I rowed out to the island to see things. For myself, you know? Well, the boat belonged to this grubby fisherman. I thought it was abandoned! But he went to the police station and told them I stole it. They raced out with half a dozen big police boats because they thought maybe the person who took this fisherman's boat might be the one who started the fire and burned up the bones of those poor Galinka girls. The cops ran up on the island waving their guns and clubs like wild men. They looked crazy! And when they saw me, I ran too. I tried to get away from them because I was scared. How far could I go? They chased me, high and low, blowing their whistles. I only went out there looking for clues…"

"They arrested you again?"

She nodded. "Handcuffed me. Took me to headquarters. Made me sit in a cell for hours. I explained the whole situation to them. But they acted like I was lying. They dug up my arrest sheet from the Ganz riot. They made me promise to stop investigating things on my own. Leave the police work to us, they said. I promised I would so they'd let me go home."

"And they said if they ever caught you out at a crime scene again…"

"They'd lock me up for a long time. Long enough that people would forget me."

"The joke's on them. I can't imagine ever forgetting you." I wanted us to kiss then, if only a dead man weren't lying there on the floor. Nina looked at me quizzically. Had she misheard me? The trace of a smile said she hadn't. Surprised. That's all. Honestly, I was too.

We agreed that I would say I broke into the telescope room on my own. I'd been taking a whiskey punch-induced nap in the library and heard weird noises beyond the wall behind the bookcase. I'd gone into the hallway and, when I couldn't figure out a way into the room, I grabbed whatever tools I could find in the janitor's closet. I was half-drunk. I thought somebody got themselves trapped inside the wall. I could sell it. The police wouldn't care about that part when they saw the body. Nina would not be any part of my story.

I watched her disappear down the secret staircase.

She vanished into the dark.

I was about to go downstairs and place my call to the cops when I noticed a row of coat pegs on the wall. Hanging from one of the pegs was a brown hooded robe. A monk's robe. I lifted the robe off the peg. Where had I seen this same rustic getup? The spiked punch must have dulled my brain. My mind was drawing a blank until I spotted the thick wooden staff propped in the corner. Friar Tuck!

This was the garb of Robin Hood's tonsured companion.

Clark Abernathy! My old college classmate. He'd chucked that fat log on the bonfire in the backyard while Nina was filling me in on Arkham's string of unexplained deaths. If this was his Halloween costume, then Clark….

We had been acquaintances, never friends. But Clark was a member of my college group of companions. The Abernathys were new money; rough around the edges, eager to please. Ruddy, freckled, and prematurely bald, Clark could be depended on to hoist a bottle of ale, or a dozen. He liked to toss around the ole pigskin and wrestle his comrades into submission on gym mats. Clark was a legend of the dining hall, regaled for his bottomless appetite. By himself, Clark once consumed a stuffed saddle of lamb, three creamed onions, a tray of cinnamon buns, and a Nesselrode chestnut custard pie in a single sitting. The post-collegiate years lured him away from the gymnasium but not the dinner table. His father was grooming him to take over the family's sporting goods empire. Likable Clark was a born salesman. Clark's rise to sporting goods fame had followed right on schedule. Until tonight.

I returned to the body.

During our junior year Clark took a drunken spill off a bicycle onto the railroad tracks. He gashed his knee badly, requiring several stitches and the temporary use of a crutch. I remembered because I was the one who drove him to the hospital that night. I saw the doctor stitch him up.

My lighter flame located the pink scar on the corpse's knee.

Clark's knee.

Poor old Clark. He never did harm to anyone. Yet he ended up like this.

I resisted the urge to cover him with his frock. I didn't want to spoil any evidence.

Instead, I went downstairs to call the police. I'd find Preston first. Clark was his friend and a groomsman at his upcoming wedding. I wanted to tell him before the cops did.

Poor old Clark.

"Oakesy, I can't talk to you privately right now. I'm in the middle of a party! Minnie, darling, come here!" I first thought Preston had come to his party without a costume, but now he was wearing a purple felt top hat with a piece of paper pinned to it that read, "In this Style 10/6." He held a cigar in one hand, an inch of ash about to plummet off its tip, in the other hand he clutched a gin martini poured into a huge china teacup. Partygoers danced around him.

"Preston, Clark Abernathy is dead," I said.

"That's not possible, Alden. I just saw him not an hour ago. He's here at my party." Preston sipped from his martini.

Minnie materialized out of the crowd and rushed to her fiancé's side.

"What is it, my Mad Hatter?"

"Alden thinks Clark is dead. Tell him he's wrong. The boy has had too much punch." Preston fell deeply into a high-backed chair, offering Minnie his knee for a seat. She borrowed his cigar, filling her mouth with smoke, blowing a series of rings at the ceiling. Preston watched her, his eyes hooded with prideful possession, before returning his attention to me. "Now, Oakesy, where have you been?"

"Upstairs, under the observatory dome. That's where I found Clark. We need to call the police," I said, exasperated.

"You're joking! Oh, Alden!" Minnie howled.

People began to drift to our corner to see what they might be missing.

"Please come. I'll show you," I said.

In the background, the trombone player blew a sad vaudevillian solo. Preston rose and put his arm around me, dropping copious ash on my shirt. "Now, now. Oakesy, you're obviously upset. I hate to see that. We'll go with you and clear up this misunderstanding." He turned to the gathering crowd. "Everyone, wait here. We have a private matter to resolve. Minnie, I might need your support." They stood up. Wobbly in each other's arms.

"We should call the police," I said.

Preston looked at me with genuine affection. "You're too damned serious, chum. It's probably a prank. Clarkie loves to pull a good one. These are all my friends here tonight. I'm not about to summon the police and have them hauled away to jail for drinking. Now, how about we three go under the dome and chew out Clark for his poor taste in humor?"

Preston snatched a candelabra from the table. Minnie grabbed onto Preston.

And I led them toward the stairs.

"There's a lot of blood. Prepare yourself."

Preston's expression grew serious for the first time. "Blood?"

"Someone cut off Clark's head. They've taken it." My words sounded insane to me.

Preston looked uneasy. "You'd better go first. I've got a weak stomach when it comes to body fluids. It must be a joke. Don't you see? It can't be real. Fake blood. I'll take Clarkie to task for it. He shouldn't scare my friends. It isn't fun at all when a person takes things too far." In the hall, Preston strode to the door, grabbing the doorknob, twisting. "It's locked."

"There's another way," I said. "A secret passage through the library."

"Secret passage, did you say?" Preston arched an eyebrow.

"Oooh, I like the sound of that," Minnie said. "A touch of Poe!"

I led them to the library, but the doors wouldn't budge.

"We blocked the doors from inside. I forgot."

"Who's we?" Preston asked.

I wasn't going to mention Nina. "It's not important. Maybe if we pushed together?"

We pushed. The doors moved enough for us to squeeze through. Inside the library, I showed them the bookcase and the hidden entrance it concealed.

"What's happened here?" Preston asked.

"Sorry, I'll pay for it. What I must show you is inside and up," I said.

"You're lucky we didn't call the police. You'd be arrested for vandalism," he said.

Minnie forced her way to the front. She peered into the ragged hole I'd made with Nina, then she spied behind the door into the gap. "It *is* a secret passage. Preston, please don't scold him. This is going to be the most memorable party

I've ever had." Before I could stop her, she raced into the opening, her tiny feet thumping up the stairs, feathers brushing the walls as she went. Preston ducked through, chasing after his bride-to-be.

"Wait! Wait!" I tried to caution them. But it was of no use. I had lost control of the situation. *Where was Nina now?* I wondered. I hoped she was on her way home, safe and sound. Reaching the top of the passage's black steps, I followed after Preston and Minnie.

Preston's candelabra glowed, torch-like.

It stopped near the telescope.

I caught up, out of breath. "I'm sorry, Minnie. Preston, I should've warned you what to expect. How bad it really is. No one should ever have to see a thing like this."

"See what?" Preston shone his light on the floor. He pushed aside the wheeled set of steps. He lit up the astronomers' ladder. Walking around the room, he proceeded to illuminate the ropes and pulleys, the work tables, and the rails that circled the dome.

"There's nothing here, Oakesy. Nothing."

Preston was right.

Clark's body was gone.

I thought I must be losing my mind. But there could be no mistake. Here was the very spot I stood with Nina. I crouched and touched the floorboards.

Minnie went over to her beau, and he gathered her in his arms.

They're standing where Nina and I stood, where we nearly kissed not a half hour ago.

Where was the body? Where was poor old Clark?

"Wait. Clark was dressed as Friar Tuck. He had a robe. A staff." I ran over to the coat pegs. But his costume was gone. I wasn't making things up. I wasn't that drunk. Was I? No. And I wasn't alone when I found Clark either. "Nina saw him too."

"Who?" Preston said.

"Nina Tarrington."

Preston looked gobsmacked. "By Zeus! I haven't heard that name in ages. What's gotten into you, Alden Oakes?" Preston wasn't angry with me, confused was more like it. Puzzled at my erratic behavior. "Maybe you've had one too many. That Canadian hooch has your head in a spin, my old friend. Sit down. We'll find you some water or hot coffee. Are you feeling ill? Does he look ill to you, Minnie?" Preston drew Minnie tight against him.

He put the candelabra up near my face.

I winced at the brightness.

"He's very pale," she said.

I did feel sick. My head banging loudly. The light bothered me. I pushed it away.

"He said he saw Nina. Did you hear that, Minnie? Is she even back in town?"

"She was here tonight. At your party," I answered.

"Here? I don't think so." He stared at Minnie. "Can you imagine her showing up?"

"You saw her with me at the bonfire," I said.

Minnie looked surprised. She shook her head emphatically.

"My *shy friend*, you called her."

Minnie thought about it. "The mummy girl?"

"Yes. Mummy queen. Nina *was* here. She and I discovered Clark together."

"I don't think that mummy was Nina, Alden," Minnie said. "Clark's not here either. I haven't seen him. His father called to say he'd hurt his back playing polo and he wouldn't be able to make it tonight. Isn't that right, Preston darling?"

Preston nodded. He looked like he felt embarrassed for me. Pity welling in his eyes.

"Nina was here. She absolutely was," I repeated. "Clark was here too."

Talking mostly to myself. I couldn't have dreamed the whole thing up. *That* was crazy. Crazier than what I thought I'd witnessed in Spain. Rituals and sacrifices. This was Arkham, and I know Arkham. That's what I tried to tell myself.

"Go home, Alden." Minnie pulled a sad face. "Preston, have your driver give him a lift. He looks so very tired."

"I'm not tired. I'll walk home." Is this what cracking up feels like? But I wasn't cracking up, was I? No, I'd had too much to drink perhaps. Got a taste of some bad bootleg that scrambled the inside of my head. It would clear up soon. In the morning I'd be myself again.

"The air might do you some good," Preston said. "Do be careful. Arkham can be dangerous at night."

I searched outside for Nina. Maybe she was hiding somewhere nearby, watching for the police cars to pull up, sticking around just to see if I'd made it out unscathed.

I checked for her by the fire pit. The fire was dying. I tried to pick out any trace of that hefty log Clark tossed in the flames, but everything was embers. Ashes.

No sign of Nina anywhere.

So I left.

Chapter Eleven

Ever walked home late at night and thought someone might be following you? I don't mean muggers. I had a few of those on my tail in Europe, looking to roll a drunk and steal his pocket money. As a man, I've never had the same worries women deal with whenever they hit the streets alone, particularly at night. I'm talking about something different. What I mean is someone is following you, and only you. They haven't picked you as a random target or a victim of bad circumstances. They wanted only you from the start, because you are you. This was a specific brand of stalking I felt that night. Somebody wanted me, Alden Oakes, badly.

But I'm getting ahead of myself.

I left the observatory in a bad mood. Minnie was right about my feeling tired, but I was experiencing more than that. I'd had my head messed with. I was furious. If I had been pranked, I wasn't getting the joke; nothing about it felt humorous. I saw that oozing neck stump and it was not fake. Clark was dead. But how had they erased the crime so quickly? It was like magic. Something Houdini might've pulled on his audience. But with Houdini's act, the audience was in on the game. They knew they were being tricked. That was half the fun of it. My experience finding the headless man left me confused, worried I might be losing my mind. Not really, though. I wasn't insane. Mostly, I was angry at myself for having been manipulated. Who had played me? Who killed Clark?

Why?

After checking my cigarette case and finding it empty, I walked down Crane Hill feeling fidgety. Restless. A carload of Miskatonic U fraternity boys swept past, hurling out insults and impinging my clown heritage and the marital status of my parents at the time of my birth. I gestured at them, immediately regretting it when their car pulled to the curb at the next corner. Several dark shapes exited. They were waiting. I am no stranger to fistfights, having spent enough of my youth at boarding schools and, later, in gritty, illicit barrooms where the masculine pecking order is maintained. I avoided violence when possible. Artists by nature tend to be a hot-tempered, impetuous lot. I was guilty on both counts, though I hoped maturity had improved my judgment. The car moved on. I felt a surge of relief. The boys had simply relieved themselves, leaving a puddle on the sidewalk and a trio of empty beer bottles littering the grass.

The night air had grown wet. Cold fog snuck between the buildings, snagging like cobwebs on the hedges and trees. Without thinking, I found myself veering west. Going downhill to the river. The sludgy black Miskatonic flowed on, mistakable for tar, its odor hardly less noxious, though fishier.

At the apex of the bridge crossing the river at West Street, I paused. I didn't need to travel this way. My house was on the same side of the Miskatonic as the university. But I wanted time to cool off. The river had always been a good place to think, at least during daylight. I never came here at night. Huge warehouses hunkered behind me. Warped piers wandered into the water like suicides. Only a few boats were docked tonight. Scores of gulls slept on the birdlimed warehouse roofs. A tangled pile of fishing nets lay heaped against a brick wall like a formless blob, oddly sparkling under the lights, as if it were covered with a thousand tiny, winking, jeweled eyes. I couldn't imagine eating anything that lived in this polluted sludge. Waves hung dirty lace collars on the pilings. A thick layer of muck the color of leeches sprouted everywhere the water lapped. I caught a darting movement on the dockside: a rat. *Ugh.* I couldn't help but think "*Plague!*" whenever I saw one skittering by. This plump specimen went about its business, paying no attention to me.

Out over the water, squatting in the middle of the river, was the reason I had come here. The Unvisited Isle. The place where the Boy Scouts tramped their boots upon the charred bones of the Galinka twins, and where the police nabbed Nina after her excursion in the pilfered rowboat, if she was to be believed. Why shouldn't I believe her? Because Preston and Minnie told me she wasn't in attendance at their party? I knew she was. I talked with her, and stumbled onto a dead man with her standing at my side. Drunken Preston and Minnie were unreliable witnesses. Though I'd been drinking too, of course. I knew what I had seen. It was absurd to think otherwise, to question myself would be to question my very sanity. I wasn't ready to do that. Honestly, in retrospect, I was only a little drunk.

Squeaking off to my right…

Two more rats were having a polite conversation about the quality of leavings on the shore this clammy Halloween night. Woolly fog collected over the water. I turned up the collar of my clown shirt. To my left, on the other side of this moat, ran the Boston and Maine Railroad tracks, the same site where a collegiate Clark had dumped off his bicycle and split open his knee.

I thought about what Preston had said.

Obviously, I wished Clark were still alive.

Only, I knew he wasn't. True, I hadn't spoken to him at all during the evening prior to his demise. I didn't verify the identity of Friar Tuck. But the man in the monk suit looked just like Clark. Maybe a little more jowly than how I remembered him. Surely it had to be him.

Chattering…

A line of rats now – a night patrol I guessed – advanced along a warehouse loading ramp. The pageant of them sent a chill into me. The docks are notorious for rats, but seeing them in action was repulsive. Their hungry eyes bulged with intelligence; those pale, hairless tails like dirty pulled roots bobbing above the alley, suggesting pestilence. No creature of this Earth should instill a reaction of pure disgust. But I was no philosopher or saint. Rats gave me the willies. I sidestepped farther along the bridge until I was a decent distance away from the rodent activities.

I needed to find Nina.

But where to look for her?

I knew she lived wherever Courtland Dunphy was staying when he perished.

It shouldn't take much research to locate her. We needed to talk. Had she barged her way into Preston and Minnie's party uninvited? That was brazen but forgivable. Perhaps her curiosity had gotten the best of her. She seemed to have that problem on a regular basis. Driven by a need to know. I respected that. More importantly, I wanted to tell her about Clark's missing corpse. In all the excitement it hadn't occurred to me before, but I felt certain that he belonged on Nina's list of recent eerie deaths in our city–

What were those rats doing?

I peered into the hazy light surrounding the warehouses.

That heap of fishing nets. The rats were jumping into it. One after another. And they seemed to be disappearing. It had to be an optical illusion. The number of rats going in was startling. Where were they vanishing to? There must be quite a tasty treat nestled down in that jumble of knotted twine to make them dig themselves in so deep. Something rotten and delicious, and no doubt delectable. I shivered again. I swore I heard the rats chewing.

The sound reminded me of the gnawing noises we'd heard in the observatory.

When Clark's head was removed.

Rats?

No, it couldn't be…

Had they absconded with his body *and* cleaned up afterward?

I laughed. The boom of my voice on the otherwise silent bridge was alarming. I had always entertained notions about individuals who laughed loudly at their own thoughts.

Yet, here I was.

The pile of netting shook. I figured that was possibly natural, given how full it was with inner rats, but what struck me was how unnatural it seemed, a quivering, vibrating, jittery pile of woven–

Those tiny jeweled spots on the nets, at first I thought they looked like eyes, well, now they seemed to act as eyes, because the blob of nets lifted itself off the ground and stood on two sloppy… legs… and the net creature… walked away from its resting place against the wall… Its amorphous head, which sported more eye organs than the rest, swiveled to face me. I swear it looked out over the slick water and picked me out where I leaned on the bridge rail in the fog.

And it beckoned.

I know, I know. How could that be? Impossible, you say. But I tell you, a snarled roll of netting separated from the bulk of the shifting, permeable mass. It was an arm! The arm waved to me. I startled, and then my startlement stretched out into a sense of queasy panic.

Come here, Alden.

I gasped. Words! It used words! With my sleeve I wiped at my face, thinking somehow the fog was altering my vision. Clearly, my eyes were strained. I must've had something in them. Residue. A salty drop of sweat. Contamination from an unknown source. Perhaps a wisp of toxic fog drifted off the rippled surface of the Miskatonic. A smear of distortion from… what exactly? I had no answer. Despite my rubbing, the sight before me did not alter for the better. No. It beckoned again.

Come closer, Alden. Don't be afraid. I've something to show you. Now, listen to me.

I heard it speak. It had no mouth. But I heard it talking to me. Uttering words in a warm, syrupy baritone that was so soothing, so utterly charming. You'd put your trust in this voice. Although, I wasn't sure where it was coming from. The net blob was responsible, but the sounds were emanating from everywhere at once. They assailed me from all directions.

That's good. You keep walking. I'll wait right here for you.

Keep walking? What did it mean by that?

With a sudden, snapping realization, I perceived that I was nearer to the blob. I looked down. My feet shuffled slowly, but doggedly, toward that… knotty thing. Good heavens! I was obeying it without knowing what I was doing. I forced myself to halt. My hand shot out, grabbing the iron bridge rail for support.

"No," I said.

Why do you forestall the inevitable? Who are you to challenge me?

"Who are you?" I shouted.

You know who I am.

"I… I don't…"

You do know. I am no one. I am you, Alden. I am no one and I am everyone.

"That makes no sense. Leave me alone."

You called me. I always come when I'm summoned. You wanted to see. See me, Alden.

"I never called you. Even if I did, it was by mistake. I'm telling you now to go away." My voice sounded weak, as if I were losing the ability to resist. Or worse, the desire.

That is one thing that will never happen. No one turns us back after calling. No one.

It pulled at me then like a magnet that attracts flesh and bone. I felt my body being sucked toward that mound of eyeball-covered, rat-filled, fish-rot-stinking, fibrous threads.

With two hands I grasped the bridge. My fingers slipped on the wet rails. I tightened my hold, my knuckles turning whiter.

The net blob sighed. Its breath of putrid water and vile, greasy mud enveloped me.

If you will not come to me, I will come to you, Alden. I will come for you. We will. All of us. You see us now as you wished, and you will join soon. All makes one. You. Us. In the stars…

It dragged itself along the dockside; the mass of old nets trailed cork floats, broken clamshells, sprigs of decomposing weeds and algae yanked from the Miskatonic's riverbed.

I screamed. Cold sweat ran over me like chilly water scooped from below the bridge.

Was there no one else on the docks at this hour? Nobody guarded the warehouses? Not a single bug-eyed, beleaguered bookkeeper who labored at this late hour with his coffee and cigarettes under a desk lamp? I guess not. Because I screamed my throat raw, yet no one came to my aid.

We are no one. We are coming for you.

The net blob hitched itself along, hauling forth its girth with maximum effort. It shambled onto the bridge. How sluggish it was, but how impressively persistent. The smell overpowered me. Every breath was a taste of slow-cooked garbage, featuring entrails, ripe and green. A halo of flies buzzed around it, ignoring the cold to feast on morsels hidden in its collapsing chambers – its honeycomb of well-aged slimes – slurping at the lumpy, fecund jelly of its malodorous taint.

The lights on the bridge shone through the blob. Inside, the rats tumbled round as if they were spinning on a wheel. Somehow, I knew the swirling energy of their lifeforces fed and propelled this monster. The motion of their rat bodies animated its horror.

If the blob were to consume me, then I would power it like the rats did.

I was not about to let that happen.

I let go of the bridge.

The blob opened its arms and ballooned hugely to catch me.

Be with us. One of us. Be one with us.

I let it pull me close, but in that final instant before its hug would snag me inside its ropy folds, I sprang across the bridge. My muscles strained. Teeth gritted. Rebounding off the rails, I lost my breath in a rush but landed on my feet behind the monster, where its mysterious attraction exerted no pull on me. Go! Run! I told myself. My panic charged me with energy.

Up the hill on West Street I ran.

I did not look back until I reached the Miskatonic University campus grounds.

There I paused, bent forward, resting my hands on my thighs and gulping fresh air. The fog thickened. My view toward the river lay in obscurity. In fact, it appeared as if the fog were advancing out of the river channel and into the city above. The swirls moved too quickly for my comfort and gave me new apprehension. If a pile of old fishing nets could become enlivened through the ingestion of rats, might the fog be vitalized and inspirited? Was this no ordinary weather event but some previously unknown manifestation of a sentient, uncanny phenomenon?

"It's only fog," I said. Only fog…

I made a point to turn my back on it, resuming my journey homeward, this time walking, not running. I tried to talk down my fear. I had to regain some control. Steadfastly, I refused to turn around and acknowledge the heavy dampness in the air. To occupy my mind, I attempted to explain my weird encounter with the net blob. How could I explain it?

It's Halloween! I tried telling myself. You saw a ghost! Wasn't it quaint to think that?

There are no limits to what the mind will do to cast doubt on its own experience of the bizarre, but only after the physical threat is removed. How quickly we reverse our opinions in order to count ourselves among those who are labeled as sane. The inner conversation hammers away at firsthand observations in favor of mundane solutions. Alden, you merely saw someone in a very clever disguise. More University students playing pranks on a lonely drunk stumbling by the river. Students can be awfully clever. What did you *really* see, Alden? What did you hear? You aren't ready for the asylum yet, are you?

I saw a net blob monster, and it knew my name.

Oh, ho ho… who's going to believe you? It was foggy, you admitted that. You'd been drinking quite a lot. You thought you saw a dead man tonight. I think maybe you'd better get yourself home in bed and under the blankets. Take another look at things in the clean light of morning. See if they don't look quite so ominous and dreadful. You got yourself spooked. Good and spooked. Well, one thing led to another and, in the end, this is a classic case of the carried-aways. You panicked, plain and simple. You're a creative type, right? Now see, your excellent and fruitful brain started feeding you the most outlandish ideas. You know what you should do? You should go home and paint. You haven't painted in a while, have you? Anything since you got to Arkham? No? This is your brain giving you inspiration. It's breaking through that wall you put up without knowing you were doing it. Isn't this exactly what you asked for, Alden, old chum? A bolt right out of the blue of good, old-fashioned inspiration. Sure, it was fantastical and well, frankly, weird. But who's to say that's not what the doctor ordered. The Surrealists you admire so much are weird. Maybe you're like them. They have crazy dreams and visions. That's what you had tonight. You weren't asleep. But maybe you were just a little, and you had yourself a waking dream. Don't question it. Or fear it. Paint it, my boy. Go on! Paint it!

Chapter Twelve

I awoke in my bed the next morning and took a hot bath to wash off the grease-paint and any remnants of the night. Steam filled the bathroom. I sank to the bottom of the claw-footed tub, my eyes and nose above the waterline. I soaked for a long time, thinking about all that had transpired at last night's party, and after. When I climbed out, I dried off with a soft, gold towel, digging my toes into a gold velvet rug. All things considered, I felt remarkably well-rested. I was hungry for breakfast. I wiped off the mirror. Shaved. Then I dressed in my painting clothes – a pair of frayed, color-spattered canvas pants and a tan chamois shirt. I put on a pair of moccasins and went downstairs to my art studio. The studio was brick-walled and drafty. I built a fire in the fireplace, tossing in a few birch logs. Roland must have seen me, because he soon visited, delivering a pot of coffee, my favorite chipped mug, and a plate of scrambled eggs and buttered rye toast. I thanked him. Now I was ready to work.

I started the way I usually do: a rough sketch. I broke out my charcoals and a pad of newsprint, whipping through a dozen quick compositions, getting a feel for the best perspective – how much, or how little, to show of my encounter on the bridge. Choosing angles, I settled on a view across the Miskatonic toward the docks. I avoided oils and grabbed my watercolor box. I fixed a board, stretching a sheet of handmade paper, wetting the paper with a sea sponge, securing it to the board using butcher's tape. I leaned the finished board against a wall near the fireplace so it would dry faster. Meanwhile, I planned out my palette, the tubes of cool, earthy colors I'd be using, and a couple of my favorite sable brushes. I kept it simple. When the paper was dry and ready for painting, I picked up a sharp pencil and sketched in the river, the low arc of the bridge, the crooked fingers of the docks. I omitted myself from the picture. I also left a pyramidal blank space halfway up the bridge's span.

I closed my eyes.

Transporting myself backward in time to the night before.

When I saw it again, I took the whole thing in at once, the way you swallow medicine.

I opened my eyes and drew what I had seen there lurking in the fog-draped dark.

Then I put down my pencil, picked up my brushes and paints, and got to work.

By late afternoon I had something that almost satisfied me. I stepped back, walking away for a break. I munched the cold eggs and toast. But I wasn't hungry any more. I'd drunk all the coffee. Loyal Roland had brought me a second pot. I poured a cup, trying to keep my mind quiet and empty from outside thoughts. I only wanted one thing in my head: my ill-formed counterpart on the bridge. I opened the French doors that led out to a pea gravel turnaround and our garages. I smoked three, four, cigarettes. Feeling rejuvenated, I went back inside and looked at the painting I had made.

It wasn't perfect. No painting is.

But I didn't hate it.

It was... close... very close to what I had witnessed last night.

The nighttime docks, pools of curdled light, the river like a sheet of corrugated tin.

Shambling up the bridge: a hideous creature fashioned of nets and fish parts and multiple eyes; the lights shone through it, rats wheeling around inside.

A tangled arm lifted, beckoning to me.

Yes, this would do for now.

I cleaned my brushes, shut the French doors, and left.

Once I'd made the first foray into processing my strange experience on the span over the Miskatonic, I felt I had to find Nina again. I needed to see her. To talk. I wanted to tell her everything that happened after we parted, and to ask her a few questions. Had she crashed the party? Where did she go after she left? Did anything peculiar happen on her walk home? It took me under two hours to locate Courtland Dunphy's building. I'd started down at the South Church rectory, where I went searching for Dunphy's address. The pastor was friendly and no dummy. I spotted him outside the church, smoking his pipe and admiring a pair of crows bathing in the rectory's stone birdbath. I still had my painting clothes on, but I wore a black wool overcoat on top of them, so they weren't obvious. I had exchanged my moccasins for boots. A flat cap kept my head warm. I walked up to the priest.

"They say crows are bad omens. Don't they, Father?"

"God made crows. Just like he made you and me." He removed his pipe, smiled, and asked if I might help him carry a trio of flower baskets inside the sanctuary.

"Sure thing, Father Cryans. You keep up this place by yourself?"

He handed me the heaviest basket. After opening the side door, he wedged it with his foot and took up the other arrangements. "Call me Father Mike. I manage what I can and pay for what I can't. The Lord sends me helpers. Forgive me, but have we met before, Mr…?"

"Rose," I said, caught off guard. I didn't want to use my real name. "Sonny Rose."

"Welcome to All Saints, Mr Rose."

I cringed at my improvised alias.

After the door closed, the hush of the building settled over us. We walked along the communion rail. The priest genuflected. I did the same, not wanting to give offense or rouse any suspicions about my visit. The thickly sweet perfume of roses surrounded us.

I never liked the fragrance of roses. It made me feel vaguely sick.

"Please set those in front of the altar. Now, what can I do for you, Mr Rose?"

"I'm a friend of Courtland Dunphy's, a fellow artist. I wonder if you have Court's address on file. A problem's come up. Having his address would help me solve it."

"You don't know where your friend lived?" The priest poked at the roses, drawing out a bruised bud before stepping back to recheck their appearance. The nave of the church was dim and shadowy behind us. To our right, votive candles burned in a cast iron stand holding tiers of red glasses below a radiant gold crucifix. Scents of damp stone, lemon-oil wood polish, and frankincense lingered. I stepped aside to give the priest a little more room, and my heel stuck in a puddle of wax drippings that had dried on the marble floor. I lifted my shoe while I deposited a few coins into the votive stand offering box. I took a taper and touched it to one of the votives and then moved my flame to one of the unlit candles.

Bowing my head, I offered a silent prayer. *Let this man give me what I want.*

The good father waited for me to finish.

"We'd meet up for coffee and pie," I said. "At a diner. I never visited his apartment."

"But you knew he lived in an apartment?"

"He talked about it. Complained it was small, you know? Artistic commiseration." I was about to blow out the taper, when I noticed the wax drippings on the floor had been spilled in a definite pattern.

A three-pronged fork.

Beside it was another drawing. This one showed a spiked crown, formed by a cluster of wavy-bladed bayonets. A star symbol hung over them both. The star was flying through space, trailing a row of diminishing dots behind the tip of its long, daggered tail.

The pictographs were not the accidental result of spillage, but an intricately fashioned tableau. In the devotional area, the church marble tiles were rusty reddish-hued. So the drawings seemed to boil out of them like hallucinogenic mirages spawned in a scorched desert wasteland. It required an extraordinary amount of self-control for me not to gasp aloud.

My head was spinning. My vision zeroed down to a small, claustrophobic aperture.

"Courtland never struck me as much of a complainer. He told me his place was rather roomy for one person, as I recall."

His unexpected recollection jolted me. I tried to remain outwardly impassive.

The priest blinked at me like a storybook owl over his reading glasses. Plenty of patience this priest had. I suppose it came with the job.

"Ahh… well… you caught me, Father. Maybe I was the one complaining to him."

"Are you feeling unwell, Mr Rose?" he asked.

I shook my head to clear it. But that only made the sudden dizziness worse. The church seemed to be resting on a giant gimbal, where it commenced rotating and tilting like a stomach-flipping carnival ride. I wiped nervous sweat from my forehead and hoped the priest wouldn't notice my unease. Lowering the taper once more, I confirmed the shape of the wax design. "A bit dizzy maybe. The smell of flowers gets to me sometimes. I'll be fine."

"Are you sure?" Father Mike asked.

I gave a small affirmative nod.

He walked away and found a watering can in a closet behind the altar. He started watering the plants, in no hurry.

"You were the one who found him. Is that right, Father?"

I dropped my head and chipped my heel at the wax, hoping I was being subtle enough not to draw the priest's attention to what I was doing. My leg tingled, all pins and needles.

"I was. Unfortunately, his soul was gone. By the time I got to him he was ice cold." He picked a few brown leaves off the altar cloth and put them in his pocket. "Feeling better?"

"What do you think happened? Up there." I pointed to the rafters above us.

My head was clearing; the room steadied. I'm fine if I don't look down, I thought.

The priest stared at me.

It was my turn to be patient.

He rubbed his chin. "Rainy that day. But the roof is flat where Court was. The rain had stopped, too. He shouldn't have fallen. I was in the church when it happened. All those windows were open. Yet I never heard him scream. Can you believe it? You'd think a falling man seeing the ground coming up at him would cry out. His scream would be involuntary. Court broke his neck when he hit. Died instantly, they told me. I can't explain it."

"Me neither." But what if seeing a strange sign made Dunphy as dizzy as I was a moment ago? What if an invisible force drove him out onto the ledge? Red light streamed through the stained-glass windows. The ruddy beams flooded down into the church pews. "The landlord is selling off Court's things to pay the missed rent. He didn't have any family."

"An orphan," the priest said. "Court shared the tale of his lonely childhood with me."

Orphan? That was news I hadn't read. The inside of my mouth tasted sour. It was difficult to swallow. Poor Dunphy. Even more tragic than I thought. What exactly had he gotten when he won that contest and came to Arkham? His luck changed from bad to worse.

"As a fellow artist, I want to make sure he isn't forgotten. Maybe we can exhibit his works. Give him one last show." I had told white lies. I'm sure lying to a priest carries extra penalties if anyone upstairs is keeping score. But what I said was partially true. I *didn't* want Dunphy forgotten. Maybe he'd never get a final gallery show. But if his death was a crime, he deserved justice. My body started quaking. What was going on with me? My throat jerked like I was about to cry. But these spasms weren't from emotion. I checked my boots. My heel was caked with that damned white wax. I couldn't wait to get it off me.

"Nobody deserves what Court got," I said. My lips were twitching.

Smiling kindly, the priest stepped toward me, grasping my shoulder. The man felt sorry for me. Maybe he thought I needed saving. Maybe he was right.

"Sonny, I'm glad to hear that. Let's go to my office. I'll look up the address."

At Schoffner's General Store, I bought a bottle of ginger beer to quench my thirst. I was on the correct street, but it was hard to find any numbers marking the shabby houses and empty storefronts. The evening sky dimmed to plums and oranges, and as the sun set, the wind promised to turn knifing cold.

Rivertown.

Dirty red bricks and the cold, oily shimmer of the water flowing below.

I blew on my hands to warm them.

There was a man on the sidewalk tending a small charcoal grill, roasting chestnuts. I bought a bag. Too hot to eat. I peeled their skins and watch the steam. The man wore fingerless gloves, and three of his fingers were missing. He had an eyepatch and a pucker of scar tissue high on his cheek. He bent to retrieve more chestnuts from a bag he stored inside a child's red wagon. His movements were stiff, as if his joints needed lubricant. He wasn't old. Maybe he'd have been a class or two ahead of me had we gone to the same school.

"Sell many chestnuts?"

"I do better at the holidays. Around Merchant is always hoppin'. It pays to start early." He scored the chestnuts with a paring knife, testing the heat of the coals against his knuckles before adding the nuts to the fire. Using a long spoon, he stirred them on the grill.

I didn't see anybody else on the street. Where did his customers come from?

"How's business by the river?"

"This place is as decent as any, except for where the nicer shops are. But the cops chase away street peddlers like me. I can get into the Merchant District closer to Christmas. Some of them blue boys are all right. Couple of those fellas know me. We fought the Huns at the Marne."

That explained his old injuries. He'd been to the war and lost years and blood there. I was lucky I hadn't joined the navy with Preston. Our bodies were still young and whole.

"I'm Alden," I said, holding out my hand.

"Christophe," he said.

And we shook.

"You move to the neighborhood recently?" Christophe asked.

"What makes you think that?"

"On account of you're a painter by the looks of those splotches on your pant-legs. But you got money for a nice wool coat and polished boots, so you're not a housepainter. You're an artist. Other artists live around here. Never seen you before, so you must be new. How am I doing?"

"Right on target."

He nodded. "I thought so. Just 'cause I got one eye don't make me blind."

I guessed my coverup wasn't enough to fool the observant chestnut man. That had me wondering what else the vendor might be noticing while no one paid attention to him.

"Anything strange ever happen here?"

He eyed me cautiously, as if he thought I might be attempting a joke and failing miserably. "Depends what you mean by *strange*. Arkham's no stranger to strangeness, is it?"

"Can't argue with you there. I grew up on French Hill."

"Ah, French Hill hides her oddities better than the rest," Christophe said. "The Colony wears her peculiars like a badge of honor. She's proud home to an assortment of human curiosities. All shapes and sizes. They grow wild on the riverbanks. Boy, they sure do."

I frowned. "What's the Colony?"

"You're standing in front of it. The big building behind you, that old Georgian mansion. It was abandoned for a decade. A real rathole. About a year ago, they converted it to apartments. Must be fifty people living there. Those fixed-up houses next door? They're part of it too. The whole block got a fresh coat of paint. It's an art commune they call New Colony. Or just 'the Colony' for short. They're inspiring each another, I hear. Hell, some nights they sound like they're inspiring themselves pretty good. They live together, eat together. Do every-thing together, if you catch my drift." He shook his head wistfully.

I did catch it. The chestnuts were popping open, turning black from the fire.

"You ever see a tall woman with dark hair and eyes? High class and knows it?"

"Can't say I have. Must be a remarkable lady."

"Her name is Nina."

"I don't know their names. I only sell chestnuts to them."

"It was a longshot. Thanks anyway. Somebody's bound to know her if I knock on enough doors. She lived across the hall from this sculptor, Dunphy–"

"Maybe Calvin knows her. Hey, Calvin!"

The chestnut seller was motioning to a light-skinned black man walking on the other side of the street. He had short hair and no hat. His canvas jacket was too light for the weather, and his hands were stuffed deeply into the pockets of his faded dungarees. He hesitated to cross the street at first. It was obvious that the reason for his hesitation wasn't Christophe. It was me.

But he came across.

"I thought you don't know names," I said to the street vendor as the man approached.

"I know Calvin. You don't need to worry about him."

"Who said I was worrying?"

Christophe cackled.

"Boy, you been worrying ever since you walked into Rivertown."

Calvin ambled up, and Christophe passed him a bag of chestnuts, free of charge. I watched as Calvin scanned up and down the street. The rumble of a large engine and the grinding of gears resonated behind us. He tensed as if he was preparing to bolt. Around the corner, out of the dark between streetlights, a boxy, dirty white seafood truck emerged. He watched until it passed. His feet were never still, and his eyes moved constantly, but the rest of him stayed poised like a middleweight boxer, ready to duck or throw a punch. I wondered what had him so jumpy.

"Calvin, right?"

I held out for a handshake. But the man just looked at me, terrified.

"How do you know my name?" He flexed his shoulders.

"Easy, Calvin. He heard me calling you. That's all," Christophe said.

"You never said my last name," Calvin said. "How do you know me, stranger?"

His free hand went into his pocket. He had a knife or gun hiding in there, and I had no interest in finding out which, or in seeing if he knew how to use them.

"Last name? I never said anything about a last name." Then I put it together. "Oh, your last name is Wright. Like the flying brothers? That was a coincidence. But if it makes you feel better, I'll tell you my name. I'm Alden Oakes. I live up on French Hill. I'm looking for somebody. A woman who lives around here, I think. Now, her name's Nina Tarrington."

I opened my coat and found my cigarette case. Calvin's hand stayed hidden. I put a smoke between my lips and lit it, no real hurry, hoping my fingers didn't twitch too much. Then I offered the case to Christophe and Calvin. They decided to join me. We stood there smoking. The tension ran off like juice out of a steak when you cut it. I didn't want to think about cutting meat and oozing blood, so I kept on talking. Calvin didn't trust me, and I wasn't sure if I could trust him. But I asked anyway. "You ever heard of this Nina?"

"No."

"How about Courtland Dunphy? He was a sculptor who was working on the new gargoyle at South Church. Is this the address for that building over there?" I showed him the scrap of notebook paper where Father Mike had written Dunphy's street number.

I didn't have to wait for an answer, because I could tell by the way Calvin tucked his chin and shifted that he did know Dunphy. He knew he was dead, too. Because Calvin's face turned as gray as the ash on the end of the coffin nail drooping over his lower lip.

"Yes, I knew Court." His gaze broke away quickly, not wanting to lock eyes.

"That's swell. The lady I'm looking for lives across the hall from him."

He pointed at the Georgian mansion. "Third floor."

"The Colony, see?" Christophe said. "Your lady must be an artist too."

"She's a writer," I said. "So, maybe."

"Calvin here is an artist's model. Aren't you, Cal? That handsome mug of yours." The vendor laughed and struck a pose. "He's always finding one job or another to keep the wolf from the door."

"Is that right? And you live in the Colony?" I asked.

Calvin shook his head. "I stay there sometimes. But I work down on the docks. I load the Burdon's Fishery trucks with the daily catch. Started there this summer."

"That's why you smell like a mermaid!" Christophe pinched his nose. "Whee-ew!"

"There are mermen swimming in the sea too," Calvin retorted, cracking a smile and tossing a hot chestnut at the street vendor. "What do you smell like, Chris? A hobo's campfire?"

I said a quick goodbye and left them standing there, two men joking with each other.

But as I opened the front door to New Colony, I glanced back. Calvin Wright was staring at me, hard. His sunken, dead eyes holding their connection with mine longer than they had during our conversation, and I felt the full weight of his fear. I wasn't sure what had him scared. But whatever it was must've been awfully close.

Because I felt the fear crawl inside me until it became my own.

Chapter Thirteen

My first impression of the Colony was that it needed better lighting. The hall-ways were gloomy. The carpeting suggested a dusty aubergine. Ornate wallpaper intimated a floral trellis. But a second glimpse told me no, there were no flowers here, only the serpentine motif of a writhing, tubular organism that threatened to squirm off the wall if I glanced away for an eye-blink. Outside, one saw three symmetrical stories of red brick and a slate roof. Each floor had seven windows, except the first which traded its middle window for a door crowned by a tri-angular pediment. Two chimneys topped the roof at either end like rooks on a chessboard. Inside, I expected to see a well-lit space, but partitioning of the apartments had created a maze of cramped passages instead, chopping up the common areas into smaller morsels. It was twilight. But indoors, night had already fallen. The windows appeared thicker than normal. Light seemed to have difficulty passing through. Luminous pendant globes dangled from the ceiling, emitting auras the color of cod liver oil. Come to think of it, an unctuous fishy essence permeated the old mansion. Stationed on the banks of the Miskatonic, perhaps it had an earlier life as a fish house. I went up to the third floor, looking for Nina's door.

She lived at the end of the hallway. Before knocking, I turned to inspect Courtland Dunphy's door. Paneled golden oak. In every way it mirrored Nina's. I tried the doorknob.

Unsurprisingly, it was locked.

From behind me came a loud click and a whoosh of fresh air.

"Oooh!" a voice cried, startled.

I spun on my heels.

"Alden!" Nina said. "What are you doing here?"

"Finding you. How's that for amateur sleuthing?"

She leaned out in the hall checking to see if we were alone.

"Come inside." She ushered me into her apartment. Shut the door, locked it. Beneath a Mackinaw coat, she was dressed in men's tweed knickers, thick argyle socks, and a pair of dark oxfords. She'd tucked her hair under a newsboy cap, a cashmere scarf draped around her neck. From a distance, I'd have taken her for a college man. Up close, she was Nina.

"Heading out for a stroll?"

She ignored my question. "How do you know where I live?"

"I told you, I was sleuthing. I needed to see you. A lot has happened since we parted."

"Did the police make an arrest for the murder?"

"No. There were no police, because there was no body. And I know whose body it was. An old college friend of mine named Clark. Clark's body disappeared."

Nina looked astonished. "Disappeared? That's impossible."

I wandered deeper into her apartment. In one corner she'd arranged a comfy reading nook: Chesterfield club chair, torchiere lamp, and a carved mahogany belly dancer balancing a pebbled amber glass ashtray on her head. I sat in the armchair. "I thought so too. But when Preston, Minnie, and I returned to the scene, we observed no signs of a homicide."

"This is a most strange development, Alden." She began to pace about the room.

She unbuttoned her Mackinaw coat. I thumped the chair for her to sit next to me.

"What's also strange is that Preston told me you weren't even at the party."

She squeezed in snugly beside me.

"Oh, did he?"

"He swore to it. Hadn't seen you in ages, or so he claimed."

A bitter smile crossed her face. "Preston would say that. Let me guess. Minnie was there when you said this to him?"

"She was," I confirmed.

"Preston's no fool. He wasn't about to start an argument with his fiancée over me."

"Minnie said she didn't recognize you, even though we talked to her at the bonfire."

Nina pursed her lips. "Minnie and I have never met. I only know what she looks like because I observed her once, leaving Preston's house at a late hour. *She* was the one leaving."

"You were doing what…? Loitering outside?"

She ground her hip against mine. "I happened to be in the neighborhood. Walking."

"Hmm. You did say Arkham's a small town. Are you going for a walk now?"

"Yes."

"Where?"

"Out." She left it at that.

"Acting cagey, are we?" I tried to make it sound light, yet I was terribly curious. When I'd taken my last walk, it hadn't exactly turned out well. I was worried about Nina.

Her spine grew rigid as she sat up. "I don't have to tell you anything."

"Now you sound like you're talking to a policeman." Did she not trust me?

"Well, you're being nosy like one. If you must know, I was heading over to the observatory to investigate. I left in a hurry last night. Remember? Daylight feels safer."

So that's why she was dressed up like a Miskatonic U student. I had a fresher location in mind. "It happens that real monsters were out roaming after hours. I found one lumbering down at the docks. Not too far from here, in fact." I waited for her reaction.

She twisted, staring at me. Intrigued. "You are being too mysterious. Spill the beans."

"I was followed last night. Stalked. The thing that stalked me has invaded my brain. I can think of little else. I'm not sure if it was an elaborate collegiate prank or if I dreamed it up in a drunken haze. But I've spent all day painting the impossible thing I saw."

"What do you mean 'impossible thing'?"

I told her about what had stumbled toward me on that overpass in the dark. The rats and the net blob. Sentient fog rolling off the river. I left out none of the weird aspects. To my relief, she didn't laugh at me or question my grip on sanity.

She simply listened.

Her face provided no hint at what she was thinking. Nina is a modern woman, I told myself. A Bostonian. Educated and independent. That means she believes in reason. But I wasn't sounding very reasonable right now, was I? At the party, I'd been worried for a moment that she was too eccentric for me. Now I was concerned that I might be the overly imaginative one. A painter who sees visions of fishing gear dancing in the moonlight! When I finished relating my fantastic tale, would she ask me to leave and never return? With some trepidation, I reached into the pocket of my overcoat, removing a folded sheet of newsprint. "This is a sketch of the thing I confronted last night. I have a painting of it at home I'd love to show you, but this is the … the substance of it … its hideousness … Words fail me, but here's what I saw."

She took the paper carefully by the edges as if it were an ancient scroll she needed to decipher. Her mouth falling open in astonishment as she studied the portrait. Quietly, she handed the drawing back to me, walked to the door and opened it wide.

I stood. "Look, I know how crazy this sounds. But you were with me at the observatory. You told me about the bizarre events occurring in Arkham. Those unexplained disappearances and deaths … then we found evidence of a ritualistic murder! I hoped if anyone would believe me about the bridge, it would be you. I guess I was wrong."

Her head tilted as she watched me, a look of puzzlement, but she said nothing.

I stepped toward the open doorway. "I'll be going now."

"You mean *we* will be going." She sounded rather firm on the topic.

"We?" It was frustrating enough to feel scoffed at. I didn't need to be flummoxed too.

Now Nina did laugh. She touched my arm. "Oh Alden, I'm not asking you to go. I believe you. Don't you see? There might be a connection between the chimera you met on the bridge, Clark's missing body, and the crimes I'm researching. At least, I'm eager to find out if there is. I trust you feel the same way?" She raised her eyebrows, awaiting my answer.

"I do," I said.

I don't know which was greater, my relief or my determination to forge ahead.

"To the river!" she cried.

"The river!" I rejoined. How could any two people be so invigorated by strange and dark occurrences? Yet here we were, and out the door we went.

But we didn't get very far.

Before we'd reached the stairs at the end of the hall, Nina stopped, glancing over her shoulder. Something was tugging at her curiosity. "What's the matter?" I asked.

"I was thinking about Court's apartment," she said.

"What about it?"

"Do you want to look inside?" She raised her eyebrows and plucked at a loose thread on her Mackinaw's belt. "Maybe there's a clue that will help us."

"You haven't explored the premises already?"

"Until now I lacked the nerve."

"I find that hard to believe."

"We aren't always as bold as we intend to be," she said.

"Fair enough. But the door's locked. I tried it when I came up."

"Locked doesn't mean impossible." Nina reached into her right argyle sock and pulled out what looked like a handle made of animal horn. She touched a brass button and a very long slender blade shot forth. "It's a Frosolone stiletto I purchased in Rome. Useful for a lady who walks alone and goes places others say she shouldn't. I can open doors with it." Nina dashed back down the hall to the Court's door. "Keep watch. I'll be inside in a jiffy."

I blocked the line of vision for anyone coming up the stairs.

"Are you sure you're not a criminal?" I asked.

Nina inserted the point of the stiletto between the door and the frame. She slid it down until she found the bolt. The tip of her tongue poked out of her mouth while she deftly worked the blade around. "Think I've got it."

I heard the bolt spring back into the doorjamb. "You're secretly a cat burglar, aren't you? Stealing precious diamonds around the globe while the good citizens sleep."

Nina smiled as she twisted the doorknob. "Beginner's luck." She retracted her switchblade and slipped it back into her sock without looking. "Shall we?"

I made one last check of the hall for witnesses. Nothing. All was quiet. "This part I *know* is against the law."

"We are working for a higher purpose," she insisted. "Do you think the Arkham police really care about Court's death? Will they do anything to solve it?"

"I suppose not."

"There, you see! We're better suited for the job. And we care."

I followed her into Dunphy's vacant rooms. Instinctively, I reached for the lights.

"Leave them off." She covered the switch. Her hand was hot and as soft as a velvet glove. "What if someone sees the glow under the door? Or a cop walking by notices the window and remembers this unit isn't occupied any more. Pull the curtains, let the moon in."

I did as she said. I tugged the curtains aside. It was a clear night. The moon was a jack o' lantern starting to rot. Stars, like seeds, sprayed in the sky. New Colony's backyard had a nice view of the Miskatonic. Across the water, I saw the railroad tracks. The headlamp of an oncoming train swelling, irradiating the ditch weeds and mud, the sluggish river. The train whistle shrieked.

Even though I saw no one, I backed away, trying to stay out of sight.

"Alden, take a look at this."

I followed Nina's hushed voice behind a lacquered Chinese screen covered with dragons. I jumped. Nerves jolted and tingling. We weren't alone. Hairs raised on my arms. My temples were pounding like a headache.

Nina kneeled on the floor of what was clearly Courtland Dunphy's studio space.

I smelled clay and saw newspapers covering the hardwood boards. Two crates filled with rags and sculpting tools set against the wall.

What had me frightened was a short naked man crouched on a pedestal behind Nina.

He had wings.

Moonlight sliced the studio in half. Nina and the man occupied the center, in and out of the shadows. Neither of them moved. Two cone-shaped horns curved up out of the man's forehead. His skin was pale gray-green.

"I know him," I said.

Nina swiveled toward me. The edge of her cap masked her eyes.

The naked man stared blankly ahead.

"I met him outside of Schoffner's. His name is Calvin Wright. He told me where Court lived." I walked over to the clay statue to inspect it closely.

Dunphy was a talented sculptor.

"It is a smaller version of Cal! He modeled for Court," Nina said. "They worked on the South Church gargoyle. But this can't be the church's replacement, they need stone."

I touched the surface of the clay, admiring the smooth curves and muscular lines. "This is a full-scale model. The final limestone block would've been too heavy to keep in the apartment. Court must've rented another place for his carving." I noticed a second, much larger – but empty – pedestal beside the Calvin gargoyle. "I wonder what was standing here. It's been removed, obviously." There was a stained canvas tarp bunched on the floor. I picked it up and spread my arms. "Big, whatever it was. Dunphy kept it covered. Guess he didn't like what he saw of his other work-in-progress. Did he ever mention working on a side job?"

"No." Nina was opening and closing drawers. She went exploring in Court's spartan bedroom. A neatly made bed and a night table. Against the wall, a bookcase filled with weeksold *Arkham Advertisers* and a Gideons' bible. There was a closet. She struck a match and poked her head inside. She blew out the match before it burned her fingers. She rummaged through the hanging clothes. I heard a jingle. "I found Court's keys," she called out.

Nina backed out into the bedroom.

I pointed to the night table. "What's that?"

She struck another match. Finding a stout black candle, she lit it. Its warm bloom revealed a carving on the tabletop. Only the outermost edges of the design remained visible, a few tantalizingly suggestive dashes and sinewy curlicues bordering on the arabesque; the rest had been gouged completely away. Deep furrows clawed into the table. Blond woodchips littered the floor next to the bed.

"Look! It says something on the wall," Nina said. She picked up the candle and moved it over the pillow on the bed, revealing a square block of letters chiseled into the plaster above the spot where Court would've laid his head each night.

MONSTER

DREAMER

NO MORE

Around the letters was the outline of a house with two chimneys, like rooks on a chessboard. "It's New Colony," I said, feeling myself getting excited. "One letter to represent each of the windows. The blank space is the front door." I lifted the pillow. Underneath I found a chisel. I hefted the tool. "Makes a nice weapon. I wonder why Dunphy thought he needed it."

"Who was he afraid of?" Nina said.

"Or maybe we should ask *what*." I flashed to the rats inside the net, lurching toward me. "Maybe monsters haunted his dreams. Those words might be a kind of protection. Warding off the creatures that chased him when he slept. '*No more…*'"

"Do you hear that scratching?"

I listened.

Faintly, I *did* hear something. Scrape-scraping without rhythm. It continued on. Not a dog or cat caught behind a door. Nothing frantic about it. Measured, deliberate strokes. "It isn't in this room. Is it coming from outside?"

We cocked our heads to listen.

A loud crash exploded in the other room. The sound of glass breaking…

I already had the chisel in my hand. Nina pulled out her stiletto.

We ran into the studio.

"Where's the statue?" I asked.

"It's gone."

"How can that be? The thing was made of clay. It was heavy."

Sure enough, we had heard glass breaking. The window was smashed… outward. No pieces on the floor. Something had gone outside. Whatever it was had been in here with us. My hand was sweaty on the chisel. Heart hammering. I looked down into the back lot. Shards of glass sparkled on the grass.

Nina gripped my elbow. "There! Across the river. On the tracks!"

The gargoyle crouched, looking right at us. Its eyes glowed red-hot in the washed-out moonlight. It raised its hand slowly, waving steely claws in our direction.

"It can't be! It… just… can't be real. Impossible." I felt a rumble in the floor.

A Maine freight loaded with lumber was barreling down the tracks.

"The train's headed right for him," she said. "It'll hit Calvin!"

"Whatever that winged fiend is, it's not Calvin… not even human."

How could we look away?

We couldn't.

A second before the engine made mincemeat of that gray-green monster, the gargoyle pumped its powerful wings and flew up to the smokestack. Grabbing hold, it flattened its body – a streamlined demon – and crawled on its belly over the hot-as-Hell boiler, the sandbox, and the steam dome. When it got to the cab roof, it spun around, sitting up. The gargoyle threw its head back. Although we couldn't hear it, I knew it was laughing at us, whooping madly as it rode the southbound like a bronco-busting cowboy out of Arkham.

Chapter Fourteen

After we watched the gargoyle disappear, we stayed there by the shattered window, not thinking any more about who might be seeing us. Not thinking, period. I knew we were in shock; numbness filling up our bodies like sand, weighing us down, making us move slowly, think slowly. I couldn't believe what I'd witnessed. Yes, I'd seen the net blob come to life and harass me on the bridge, maybe it even planned to swallow me up like it did to those greasy river rats.

But this encounter felt different.

It was much worse.

Maybe because I couldn't doubt it. I didn't have the luxury, if that doesn't sound too funny. Because we were both there together, Nina and me.

And the two of us couldn't be crazy.

"That really happened. Didn't it?" she asked, not in a whisper, forcing her voice to sound firm. Nina was taller than I am by a good two inches. She had an athlete's confident posture. Her physical strength was never in question, but this was not a purely physical threat we had confronted. Our reality was under attack.

"Yes, it did. I don't understand how, or why. But it happened as surely as I'm still standing here with you. We're in a rehabilitated Georgian mansion on the banks of the smelly old Miskatonic River in Arkham, Massachusetts. My family's lived around this moldy old town since before the Revolutionary War. I was born here. Tonight, the moon is putrid but it's still shining. Not a cloud in the sky… and we're both real. We are here."

"I'm shaking. Can you feel me?"

I hugged her tightly. Our hearts thundered. "I feel you as surely as I've felt anything."

"You're shaking too, Alden. So this is no dream."

Not a nightmare. Reality. Our solid flesh was proof of that fact. Knowing this didn't make things better. Dreams are something that end; you wake up and they're finished.

Yet, even abject terror in the face of monsters reaches a lull over time. You manage somehow to get past it. The panic fades to background terror, a jumpiness. But it's no less a threat once it gets behind you than it was when you faced it head-on. The lingering sense of the monstrous becomes worse than its actual presence. It surrounds you, and fills you with an inescapable pressure that builds and wrecks you inside and out. It's personal, an invisible invader who might manifest at any moment. Expectation of evil is your new sickness. The worrying eats at you like acid. You and the monster become one thing, and that feels like the dirtiest trick of them all.

We were only beginning to learn this lesson in fear. We weren't experts.

Not yet.

Her arms, my arms, loosened our holds on one another. We spoke in gentle looks until we found the power of language again. We breathed. The shaking subsided. From outside the broken window came the soft hoot of a screech owl. The grumbling motor of a fishing boat headed out for a night's catch. Cars passing. The chuckle of the river flowing over rock bars. In the distance, a dog howled.

"Why didn't it attack us? Why are we alive?" she asked me.

"I don't know," I said. "We should get out of here."

Nina fixed her cap on her head. "One more look around before we go. This might be the only room in Arkham we know of that has monsters."

We scoured Dunphy's apartment. This time with the lights on. It was when we were leaving that we found the message. It couldn't have been more obvious.

The gargoyle had scratched it on the inside of the door so we wouldn't miss it.

CALvin RiTe

NinA TArrinGTon ALL Den Oaks

WiLL Die by the HAnd of the ONe who CALLs the FALLing sTAr

Thru The GATe

TwsTer of The CoiL

The Un-Sun

yoOYUVABDAA

"He isn't much of a speller, is he?" I said, joking to hold my fear at bay.

"Except for that gibberish at the end, he gets his point across."

Below the words was a series of symbols which were becoming familiar to me. Part of me was happy to see them. They helped to pull the pieces together. Figures I remembered from the Mediterranean coast. Wax drippings on a church floor. Now this.

"What are you doing?" Nina sounded as edgy as I felt.

"Looking for paper," I said.

Inside a drawer I found a sketch pad and a charcoal stick. I tore off a couple of sheets and held them up on top of the etched symbols. "Help me. Here."

"What should I do?"

"Press the corners down. I'm making a rubbing. I've seen these signs before."

I passed the stick over the newsprint. Symbols began showing up on the page like a secret message. "This one's a fork with three prongs. I've seen it the most. Then there's a spiked crown. Not always the same when it shows up but close enough. Here's a shooting star. That's new. But I saw it earlier today. This last one looks like the letter U balanced on a triangle. Maybe it's a cup? With two ovals inside. That's the one I saw when all this started."

"Where did you see these signs?"

"At South Church. In wax spread on the church tiles. I think they might spell out a kind of curse or something. When I looked at them, I felt funny in my head, like I might faint." I was almost finished with my copying. "Tear me off another sheet, would you, please?"

"Do you think someone used them on Court? To make him fall?"

"They might've. I wouldn't have wanted to feel disoriented on the roof. It reminds me of a festival I visited in Spain. Oddest thing I ever attended. The principal player wore a spiked crown. These forks were present too, carried around a bonfire circle by little goblins. People *dressed* as goblins, I assumed. Strange fiesta. Pagan. Very ritualistic. They burned effigies in a mock sacrifice. Massively unsettling. Boundaries were crossed. It left me feeling strange for days." I saw him again, the tall man in the full head mask. The crowd chanting. Then I saw Balthazarr in another crowd, sitting in the front row at the Houdini show. Was that really him, there and backstage? Why was I thinking about Juan Hugo Balthazarr now?

"Ritual sacrifices!" Nina drew me back into the moment. "That *is* creepy."

"Careful. I want proof that we can show to an expert when the time comes."

"Who's an expert on this?"

I shrugged. "I don't know. Perhaps we can find out."

I completed the last of the rubbings.

"Alden, I'm frightened. Human killers are one thing. Supernatural monsters take things to another level entirely. That gargoyle isn't supposed to exist. Should we stop?"

I checked the copies I'd made to see if they were legible. "Look, I'm scared too. It would be insane not to be. I thought you wanted to look for the net blob. To discover any connections to those unexplained deaths. But if you say you want to quit–"

"I'm not saying 'quit.' Only let's think things through. After the gargoyle… reading this message… I don't know if I want to know more. What are we getting ourselves into?"

"I haven't the foggiest. But we have to keep going, Nina."

"Why?"

"Because the first time I saw these symbols was on the beach at Cannes.

Preston drew two of them in the sand with his foot." Saying that out loud felt peculiar. A kind of betrayal.

But who, or what, had I betrayed? Balthazarr leaped into my mind again. I saw images floating in the air of Dunphy's room. Mirages of infamous Balthazarr paintings. Fantastical creatures. Physics-defying acts. The world tearing itself apart, melting and shredding. Provocative. Unnerving. To live in that man's mind had to be a cosmic adventure. The images faded. I hadn't really seen them. They'd come from my memories of his paintings. My stressed brain projected them in the air like shadow figures on a wall.

Nina shook her head. "You sound utterly mad. What's Preston got to do with this?"

Preston. I shook off my fuzzy thoughts. "I don't know how he fits. But he must. Maybe it's like automatic writing. Turn the mind off and let the body draw. He didn't realize what he was doing. It originated in his unconscious. Maybe he'd seen them somewhere. They obviously made an impression. I plan to ask him. Tell me something. What is the Colony?"

Nina frowned, puzzled. "It's an artistic collective. This is the Colony's home."

"A commune? Like Barbizon, or Byrdcliffe in New York?" Why was a gargoyle statue coming to life here? Dunphy was an artist. Isn't bringing art to life what artists do? It felt like I'd taken hold of a string. But I couldn't see what was on the other end of it yet.

"I suppose it's the same idea. A special place for creativity. What are you getting at?"

I wasn't quite sure myself. But I kept pulling on that string. "Why do you live here, Nina? Where do you fit into the picture? Who invited you to the bohemian village?"

I saw the anger flare in her. The muscles of her jaw pulled taut. Her eyes narrowed.

"I applied. I'm as much of an artist as anyone here. As much as you, too."

"You're not a novelist, playwright, or a poet. You don't write for a newspaper. Who's familiar with your work? Who sent you the invitation?"

Nina reined in her anger and thought back. "I received a letter from the Colony Board of Judges. They said I'd been recommended." The weirdness of it struck her for the first time.

"Who recommended you?"

She walked to the shattered window. Looking out at the night. Seeing her reflection. "They never told me. Recommendations are kept confidential from the applicants, they said. I'm writing a study of crime in Arkham. Chronicling Arkham's social decay. I've had a few excerpts published as articles in journals. I figured someone influential read one of them and liked it. I want to write a book. That's what I've been doing here since I arrived. It's my project."

"What better way to keep an eye on you and your project than to bring you close, where they could watch you. I'm not threatened by you, Nina. But who is?"

She brushed her fingers along the broken glass hanging in the window. "What you said about Preston a minute ago, did you mean it? Do you think he's involved in this madness, these events?"

"I can't say. But he knows more than he's admitted. He's acting bizarrely. At first, I thought he was spooked by the upcoming wedding. But I think it's more than that. Something is eating at him. He wants to tell me, but he doesn't know how."

"Preston was the one who got me in here," she said, defeated. "I'm sure of it."

"What do you mean?"

"When I applied to join New Colony, he greased the skids. He made certain my application was approved." She jerked away from the glass. She'd cut herself. A drop of blood welled up. She popped her injured finger between her lips.

The light in the apartment felt too harsh. The shadows, too dark.

I was lost. I felt as if I'd been rolled down a hill in a barrel. What was she saying? Which way was up? Preston and New Colony? I didn't follow her implications.

"What does Preston have to do with whether you're Colony-approved?"

"It's his money that paid for it. Or his father's, to be more precise. Fairmont Senior. Along with someone named Carl Sanford. They bought this block and transformed it. They're behind the New Colony Foundation. They decide who gets in and who doesn't. It's a confidential process, very hush-hush. Cloak and dagger stuff. The Colony Board of Judges allegedly decides, but it might be one or two people. Who really knows?"

I laughed, but the noise I made was hollow. I couldn't believe what I was hearing.

"I figured Preston never gave a damn about the arts."

Nina came closer. "If it was his idea that I move to New Colony, if he invited me, then what does that mean? I only wanted to write my book. I never questioned being here. I like it here, Alden. The people I've met don't feel weird to me. But…"

"But what?" I asked.

She gave me a look of grave recognition. The broken window gaped behind her. "Who invited you to return to Arkham, Alden?"

I folded the rubbings and slid them into my coat pocket.

"We have to talk to Preston," I said.

Nina nodded. "First, we need to warn Calvin. According to that door, he's in as much danger as we are. The gargoyle wasn't an assassin. He was a winged messenger."

Chapter Fifteen

On the street, Calvin and Christophe were long gone. I looked back across the road at the Colony mansion. Lights glowed in the apartments. On an unseen phonograph, King Oliver and his Creole Jazz Band were playing the Dippermouth Blues. It looked so normal from the outside. Just a nice building where people lived. Except I knew it was different. These people were all artists, hand-picked by a mystery cabal. Monsters appeared in their midst. Perhaps I was being overdramatic.

I regarded Nina. "Why would Preston's father sponsor an art commune?"

"Don't know," she said. "He never discussed art while we were together."

"I feel like we have some of the pieces, but we aren't putting them together in the right order. There's no money to be made at the Colony?"

She shrugged. "If an artist sells anything, they keep the cash. It's basically a charity."

Our steps carried us along River Street toward the docks. Soon we'd pass the Unvisited Isle, winding up on the West Street bridge, where I'd had my supernatural encounter. Ramshackle private residences yielded to warehouses and vacant lots. Fences and padlocks. Garbage dumped where no one cared to look: bags of rotten onions, paper waste, a collapsing pyramid of concrete chunks. In a mud patch, a French Provincial dining set waited for guests who would never arrive, unless they were ghosts. It reminded me of ancient ruins.

"The Fairmonts might be profiting in other ways," I suggested.

"How do you mean?"

"Well, maybe it's a place to hide cash, or launder it through the foundation's finances." I wasn't sure how closely Preston monitored the family business and its lawyers.

"Now you sound like a muckraker," Nina said.

"What I'm talking about is buying influence. Making connections they couldn't forge through legitimate channels. People like the Fairmonts pursue money the way roots seek water. My mother says they're connected to everything happening in Arkham. Preston's father is a big wig at the Silver Twilight Lodge. And Carl Sanford is the biggest wig of all. My father's a member, but he never goes, as he is the crankiest curmudgeon in New England. Preston told me *his* father practically lives at the Lodge. He hounds Preston to get more involved, for the sake of their family business. Well, the Colony might be another tentacle of the Lodge reaching into the community. If they control the art scene, no one else does. They decide what's popular. They pick the hot artists in town who get all the attention. Then again, it might be the infamous vanity of Arkham's upper crust. Legacies and all that jazz. Or it might be a scheme we can't even imagine." I threw up my arms in frustration.

"A scheme for what? Taking over the world with art?"

We laughed at that idea.

"Maybe old man Fairmont doesn't want people making anything ugly associated with his fair city. Dragging down its reputation. That's something my mother always says to me. 'Alden, why don't you try painting pictures that people want to look at. Beautiful things. Things that make everyone feel happy.'"

"You don't do that now, do you?" Nina linked her arm through mine.

I thought about the paintings I had attempted in Spain. How an unnamable quality haunted their periphery, hovering just beyond the canvas, affecting every shadow and brushstroke.

"Wait until you see my net blob." Now the unnamable had moved into full view.

"Not pretty?"

I considered her question.

"Depends on your taste, I guess. If you like vampires, ghosts, and ghoulies, then you might love it. Have you seen what the Surrealists are doing? Automatism is a technique they use. You create without thinking. André Breton called it the '*Dictation of thought in the absence of all control exercised by reason and outside moral or aesthetic concerns.*' Pick up the pencil, or brush, or whatever's at hand and draw… paint… just go. No plans. No authorial censor. The Dadaists did it too. You give up control. Chance takes over. The psyche shows itself, unfiltered. They're trying to release the subconscious mind from its prison. Order brought us the war. Chaos might bring peace. I find it exciting. Much of their new work is astounding. There's this fellow from Spain, Balthazarr, who's transcendent. A truly modern explorer. Tapping the inner cosmos of human existence. Uncaging dreams, letting them run loose in the world."

She squeezed my arm. "Nightmares are dreams, aren't they? I'd rather not meet mine when I'm awake. You know mediums and Spiritualists do the same thing. Open themselves up to the spirit world. They let entities pass through. I find it eerie." She shuddered. "I don't want to know what might be lurking inside of me."

"Well, I do."

From the twist of her lip, Nina was about to say something sarcastic, when she froze.

"Is that your blob?"

She pointed with her chin to a pile of fishing nets heaped on the docks. The streetlamp shone on them like a spotlight. It was as if a danger had crawled up out of the waters by its own power and lay asleep on the warped boards. A venomous snarl of sea snakes, perhaps.

"I can't be sure if that's the blob I saw. Nets look alike. But it could be…"

"We ought to make a closer inspection." She took a few baby steps. "I can't believe how nervous I am about a stinky ball of twine." She edged up closer. But not very much.

I found a boat hook, forgotten against the warehouse wall. "I'll give it a poke."

Hesitation makes unpleasant tasks worse, so I strode up to the net and skewered it. Nothing happened. I stabbed harder, swirling the hook around for maximum damage.

"Hey, you there! What d'you think you're doing?"

It was a night watchman. He must've spotted us from his post inside the warehouse.

"What should we do?" Nina asked.

The watchman was a hulking type. He was marching right for us. His boots boomed on the boards. He aimed a flashlight in our faces. It was a blinding slap across the eyes.

In his other hand was a baseball bat. He was snapping it around. Quick wrist snaps that would crack a bone, knock loose a few teeth. My hand went involuntarily to my jaw. I liked my bones and teeth the way they were.

"The hell you think you're doin'? This here's private property." He snapped the bat.

"Get ready," I said to Nina. I hefted the boat hook like it was a javelin.

"Ready for what?"

I threw the javelin right at the flashlight.

"Run!"

There was a clatter, a meaty thump. The flashlight rolled away, casting its beam wildly on the stained waves. Colored orbs floated in my vision, the aftereffects of the light blinding me. Out there in the dark, the angry watchman was picking himself off the boards.

"Why, you sonofa…" he began.

I didn't stick around to hear the rest. I ran for the warehouse. Nina was ahead of me. Inside the warehouse doorway, I could see the hut where the watchman spent his shift. A cup of coffee and an *Adventure* pulp magazine, his pushed-back three-legged stool. I waited to see which way Nina would dart.

Left.

She went around the corner of the facility, vanishing into the dimness between the buildings. If she was going left, I chose right for my escape plan. I hoped it would be an escape, because the watchman was going to exact his revenge on me, *if* he ever caught me. My legs pumped. Thighs burning. My overcoat flying out behind me like a cape. The watchman was puffing, chugging away at my back. Suddenly, he lunged for me – a wide hairy-knuckled mitt swiping at my flappy coattails. Luckily, he didn't grab any material.

My move knocked him off his rhythm.

I veered close to the warehouse wall zipping by my left side. He followed.

"Gaaahhh…!" He grazed his shoulder inside the siding.

A shaft of brightness ahead: Main Street. Then I saw what I needed to get away from my pursuer. I slowed down a tick. Enough for him to think I might be hesitating, deciding which way I wanted to cut when I reached the roadway. He grunted, digging down for one last charge. And as he did, I rolled off smoothly to my right.

He had no time to see the trash barrel.

He ran full force into it. Can and man becoming one thing launched into space, then smashing down on the pavement. All the air blew out of the watchman in a low groan.

Out of the corner of my left eye, I saw Nina emerging from the other side of the warehouse. I switched direction and followed her up the middle of Main Street. She geared down so I could catch her, and we turned up Garrison, not stopping until we hit the campus of Miskatonic U. We collapsed on a bench outside the library. Trying to catch our breath.

Laughing. Tears rolling down our cheeks.

She climbed right up to me and filled her hands with my overcoat lapels. We were in the middle of campus, but the campus was deserted. Library closed. No one out but us.

"He was going to kill you!" she shouted.

"But he didn't."

She kissed me.

"You're crazy," she said. "Reckless man."

"I'm not the one who carries a stiletto in my sock."

We kissed again, longer this time. I reclined on the bench and she lay beside me.

Nina propped her head on my chest.

The air steaming from our mouths.

"I don't sleep," she said.

"What?"

"I'm an insomniac. Have been since I was a girl living in Boston. That's why I always liked going out to crime scenes with my dad. Bad things always seemed to happen to unlucky people at night. He couldn't sleep much either. The house would be quiet, and I'd be awake, just hoping he'd get wind of some news. We could go and look. Find the story. Well, I can't lay around nowadays. Knowing no one's coming to get me so we can go see something sensational and exciting. So I take walks on my own. I look at the world asleep. Nighttime can be beautiful. The best time, really. Quiet, mysterious. It's when I think about solving those terrible crimes in Arkham. I've visited all the crime scenes at night. By myself."

"Maybe you can show them to me, if you like. We can visit places together."

The skin on my neck suddenly touched a cold metal part of the bench.

"You're shivering," she said.

She opened her coat and closed it around us like a pair of wings.

We stayed like that for a long time.

Chapter Sixteen

It was a few weeks later, while enjoying a scrumptious white-tablecloth breakfast, that I confronted Preston with my knowledge of his involvement with New Colony. We were dining at the Harvest, the Silver Gate Hotel's finest restaurant. This was the first time I'd ever visited the hotel. In terms of Arkham's historic grand hotels, there are Silver Gate people and Excelsior people. The Oakes family had always been in the Excelsior camp. I'd seen the Silver Gate many times from the outside. The institution was, and is, a fixture in the city. How amazing that we'd never crossed paths before. I'd walked past the imposing façade always destined for another location. Passing by, often admiring the fine lines and impeccable profile from the street, I felt everyone I knew had been there before me. They all possessed a charming story of some unforgettable private party or a memorable night tucked away in one of the fashionable suites. But I had never partaken, not until this breakfast meeting with Preston. He must've chosen the restaurant and made the reservation, although I'm sure Preston never had to reserve anything in this town. He simply called up and asked for what he wanted, or, more likely had someone else call and use his name like a magic key to open any door, gaining access denied to the lower strata of the acknowledged social order – Those Who Must Wait. I was happy to approve of his choice.

"You've been to New Colony?" He smiled and took a sip of his freshly squeezed grapefruit juice. "What were you doing there?"

"Visiting Nina Tarrington," I said.

He showed no extreme reaction. A twitch in his right eyebrow, perhaps, as he swallowed. Nothing more. "How is Nina? Still a night owl?"

"She is. You might've confirmed that yourself at your engagement party."

Preston nodded. He didn't remark upon his previous denial of her presence at the fête.

"What did you think of the place?" he asked.

"The Colony? It's fine, I suppose. The hallways are narrow, the rooms a bit gloomy."

"Artists do better when they suffer. Or so I've heard. My father poured a bundle into saving that relic. He wouldn't shut up about the cost of the investment he was making. It was rat-infested, the foundation cracked and so on. That whole block of land wants to slide into the Miskatonic and float out to sea. Carl Sanford was the one who found it. They fixed it and turned it over to the bohemian set for fun. So Nina told you we're involved, did she? Well, that's true. For the good of Arkham. The Fairmonts have long held up their end of the bargain as far as local charitable causes go. My father always says we've made so many sacrifices." He sliced into his steak; a little blood ran out onto the plate.

"I've never known you to care about the arts." I lifted my rye toast, pausing midair.

Preston shrugged, chewed. A server approached with refills. He waved him off.

"I don't care for the arts, truthfully. I find my entertainment elsewhere. Thirsty?"

His question surprised me. I had coffee, apple juice, and ice water on the table.

"I'm satisfied."

Preston shook his head with mock sadness. "Oh, Alden. One must never be satisfied. It will kill you faster than anything." He motioned the server over and whispered in the man's ear. The waiter nodded and exited through the swinging door that led to the kitchen. "May I ask why you were seeing Nina? You have a growing interest in her?"

"We're fond of one another. Getting back to New Colony. What goes on there?"

"Art? Who knows?" Preston dismissed the query. "I never interfere. Here we go."

The waiter reappeared with a bottle wrapped discreetly in a towel. With a practiced twist he released the cork. A curl of smoke left the bottle like a djinn. He filled two champagne flutes and placed them on the table. Then he deposited the bottle in an ice bucket, draping the towel over it. No one in the restaurant noticed we were breaking the law. Or maybe they were used to it. The right last name and a pile of cash bought certain privileges.

Preston picked up his glass.

"To never being satisfied."

I clinked and we drank.

"How's Minnie?"

Preston rolled his eyes. "She's on the warpath about the number of fondues, or maybe it's the size of the wedding cake. Possibly both." He rotated his glass, focusing his attention on the bubbles. "I can't keep track. But she isn't happy. We're thinking of moving up the date and having the reception here at the Silver Gate. Don't ask. Nothing's in stone yet. The Silver Gate always puts out a good spread. I'll credit them that." Preston tore away the towel and refilled our glasses. He seemed tipsy. I smelled whiskey on his breath when I arrived. Perhaps Minnie was right to be worrying about his mental state. He looked drawn, his eyes ringed and sunken. Was he still awake from a marathon night of cardplaying? "Let me give you a little advice regarding Nina."

I opened my mouth to protest.

He raised his palm. "If you're happy, then I'm happy for you." Here, he made a puzzled face. "But does Nina ever worry you?"

"How so?" I wondered where this conversation was heading. It didn't matter to me what he thought of my spending time with his ex-fiancée. I was curious about his warning.

"Nina has a vivid imagination. You've learned that by now. She likes to pretend. Gets you to play along. It's intriguing at first, a fun game. But she takes things too far. She loses her perspective and can't judge where the actual world begins. If you aren't willing to follow her then she gets..." He waggled his fingers.

"She gets what?" My voice was loud. I was perturbed by his butting into our relationship with his unwanted commentary. I scraped my chair back. Several heads turned.

Preston leaned forward and whispered. "She gets *serious*. Do you know, she nearly ran me through with a sword? That girl knows her way around a blade. She's a fencer. She can throw knives, and make them stick, too. I've seen her do it."

"What's your point?" If Nina knew how to defend herself, what did he care?

"My point is that you don't want *her* point between your ribs."

He smiled. I flashed to our college days, a pair of thieves watching each other's back. My anger receded like the tide pulling back from a beach. Here I'd come to confront Preston, and instead I felt like he was challenging me, but not out of malice.

"Thanks for the information," I said. Preston was too tipsy to note my sarcasm.

He refilled his flute. "If it all works out for you, I'd be thrilled. More for you?"

"I'm good." I covered my flute. Preston was drinking enough of the bubbly for both of us. I didn't want to talk about Nina any more. I didn't want Preston talking about her. But I wasn't ready to let the topic of the Colony drop, especially because I had a favor to ask of Preston. I didn't want his guard raised too high. I had to keep things friendly to succeed.

"Nina told me you might be able to influence acceptances to New Colony."

Preston ran a finger around the rim of his glass. "I would hope so."

"I want in. Can you do that?"

He acted surprised. "I'll talk to my father. He'll see things get done. It will be a step down from Oakwood. The Colony is little more than a glorified dormitory. Ahh... wait, let me guess. It gets you closer to Nina. See, you *are* playing her games." He shook his head, baffled. "The two of you are very rich. You know that, right? You could live anywhere. Paris? New York? But if you want to play artists starving in the garret, who am I to interfere? Was this her idea?"

"It was a mutual thought we had together." But it wasn't. Nina had presented the idea to me the night before my breakfast with Preston. I agreed because it solved multiple problems. I needed a new place to live, I wanted to be closer to her, and it aided our investigations. Yet I hated that Preston seemed to know my every move before I made it. Before I could stop him, he tried to refill my glass again. Champagne overflowed, fizzing down the outside of the crystal; a spreading stain darkened the linen.

"Oops… I'll have to see what's available for rooms." He sounded like a desk clerk. "The Colony might be full up at the moment. I wouldn't know."

"It isn't. There's an apartment right across the hall from Nina. Rooms previously occupied by a sculptor named Dunphy. He died recently."

Preston didn't blink at the mention of Dunphy's name, though he upended his glass, draining it. "We all die eventually, Oakesy. Oh, that reminds me. Guess who's missing. Clark Abernathy. Isn't that a funny coincidence? You thought he was murdered. Now nobody can find him. His father told me Clark probably ran off with a dancer he'd made acquaintances with at the Clover Club, named Diamond something. But I don't think he really knows. He seemed distraught. It's not like Clark to up and vanish. I hope he isn't in serious trouble."

Clark was well past his troubles. "Where's the Clover Club?"

"Oakesy, we need to reacquaint you with Arkham's nightlife." Preston drained the last drops of champagne into his flute. "It's the only thing stimulating about this place." How quickly had he killed off the bottle? He looked greener about the gills than the glass did.

"I appreciate your efforts on my behalf." I raised an eyebrow. "Are you feeling well?"

"Me? I'm fine, just dandy. It's the least I can do for a friend." He hiccupped.

Preston shifted his gaze to the restaurant windows. A wave of sadness and regret passed over him. Where it originated, I could not say, but a hallucinatory alteration took place. I watched Preston age rapidly in front of my eyes. His brow wrinkled, cheeks sucked in; the patch of hair on his head thinned and grayed, before settling on cottony white wisps. He looked like the spitting image of his father. Was this a psychic vision of my friend's future? Appalled and astonished, I held my breath. The immense pressures of eventually taking up the mantle of the Fairmont clan weighed heavily on Preston. His father constantly measured him up, trying to groom him. One day soon he'd have to live up to the task or be ground to paste by it. Or so his old man said. Preston bent forward as if he were about to be sick. His eyes clouded. The rapid transformation continued until all that sat across from me was a jumble of bones inside a withered, yellow skin sack. Before I could fully comprehend his evolution, the process reversed itself;

Preston quickly returned to the youthful – if exhausted – man I recognized. I rubbed my own eyes, wondering if something was wrong with *me*, or with the champagne. Had we been drugged? Was the alcohol contaminated with a toxin? The illusion passed like a slow-waking dream.

Preston coughed.

"Are you sure you're in decent shape, Preston?" I was checking myself too.

"Right as rain," he answered with a tired half-smile.

I offered him a cigarette from my gold case. We smoked in silence, then he snapped his fingers at me and said, "There's someone you should meet. I fetched him at the train station this morning. He arrived after a long, arduous journey."

"Do you pick up strangers at the train station often?" I said in jest.

"Colony business, to be precise. My father suggested I play the part of welcoming committee."

"Who's the visitor in town?"

Preston pushed back his chair. "He's coming toward us right now." Preston stood and smiled, beamingly. A golden boy displaying all his breeding and charm despite his inebriation. He was motioning emphatically to someone. *Join us, come join us…*

The visitor entered the room behind me.

I turned in my chair.

Preston stepped around our table to receive his guest. Etiquette required me to stand and greet the man. He must have passed behind one of the restaurant's pillars, because I saw no one. Preston appeared dazzled; I might've been a mustachioed hussar on horseback, still he wouldn't have noticed me.

"Pres-TONE! My new friend!" An accented, unmistakably masculine voice impacted us. I felt it as much as heard it. His chic figure arrived. A gust of brisk air accompanied him.

First, I saw his outstretched hand. Long fingers, lean, a network of thick veins visible under the skin. A craftsman's hands, strong and knowledgeable. Preston's pale digits vanished inside the other's grip. He pulled Preston in close and embraced him, thumping him on the back. He was taller than us. Dressed like a raven. Hatless, brunet. He used a chrome ornamental cane. When they parted, the visitor pivoted to face me. It was like opening a high window, the danger.

"Juan Hugo, this is my old friend, Alden Oakes. Alden, meet Juan Hugo Balthazarr."

"Good to meet you, Alden." The artist bowed. His forked beard was luxuriant.

"I am honored." I could hardly breathe. Here was the living artist I most admired in the world. Standing right before me and offering his hand!

Like a blacksmith's vise, he crushed my fingers. It was all I could do not to wince.

"Alden's a painter too. Just back from Europe. He couldn't keep away from home."

"Ah, you are an Arkhamite. I am finding your city most enticing. A dark confection."

Only then did he release me from his dominating clutch.

"I hope you enjoy your visit," I said, rather pathetically. My hand was hurting. The vision of Balthazarr hurt too. He overtaxed the senses. Too vivid, too loud, too aromatic. None of these were unpleasant, but in combination the effect was an intensity unleashed upon the hapless experiencer. I'd never been awestruck until that meeting at the Harvest. If Balthazarr was excessive, he induced the countereffect of making you feel lacking. My flaws suddenly became my very essence. I wanted to run and hide. But his power of attraction prevented me from that.

"Already, my trip has proved fruitful," he said.

Everyone in the Harvest watched him. They tried and failed to look away. He demanded attention; and when you were around him, you surrendered to him gladly, paying your respects. You knew you were going to tell your grandchildren about the time you saw Balthazarr, what he did and said. The encounter scorched itself into your memory with a psychic branding iron.

"Juan Hugo is our first ever artist-in-residence at New Colony. Some Lodge members thought bringing in a master would inspire others to reach for the stars. Does it inspire you?"

"I'm speechless."

"Oh, we must loosen that tongue. I don't want silence. I want exchange." Balthazarr draped his arm across my shoulders. He smelled of saddlery and cigar boxes. Opium incense.

Now that I was seeing him up close and in person, I was sure it wasn't for the first time. "You know, I think we've met before. In October. The Houdini performance at the Ward Theatre? You were backstage visiting Harry Houdini's room. Preston, you remember."

Balthazarr showed confusion. "Impossible. I arrived in town a few hours ago. Before that I was in New York, but only for a short stay. I crossed the Atlantic on the *RMS Aquitania* last week. You see, we could not have met. A Houdini trick would be the only way," he quipped.

"You're thinking of someone else." Preston was irked by my apparent error.

I wasn't convinced I was wrong. Balthazarr's resemblance to the man in Houdini's audience, the one who accosted the escapist at his dressing room door, was uncanny. I tried to recover from my faux pas. "But I did see you in Spain, near Barcelona. At a festival."

"Yes, yesss… now you are talking about my homeland. I was born in Catalonia and have a house by the sea. The festivals are as old as they are exquisite. When were you there?"

I told him, and his expression changed to a frown.

"No, I am afraid you are amiss again. I have been living in London for most of the last year. I haven't visited home, this breaks my heart, in two years. You remind me to return as soon as I have the opportunity. Tell me, how did you like the festival? Was it exciting for you?"

"Very," I replied. "Unlike anything I ever witnessed before."

"You see." He swiveled to Preston. "I told you. No one can resist Spain."

Preston grinned and nodded. "I will have to take Minnie there."

"Maybe for your honeymoon," Balthazarr suggested.

"Maybe," Preston said, noncommittally. "We've finished eating. But would you join us for coffee?" He looked at the dreary weather. "It's nasty out there."

The Spaniard politely declined the offer. "I have an appointment. And I am not afraid of the elements. I brought a cape. Back home I climb the mountains in rain or sun. My mother says I am like a wild beast who always wants to be outside. Sleeping under the stars."

We parted company.

After Balthazarr left the room, several guests concluded their meals. The atmosphere of the dining room deflated. Nothing tasted as delicious as it had previously. Preston and I asked for our coffees, but it was like sipping bitter brown water. I felt run down, vaguely feverish, as if I were catching a cold. We smoked and watched the room depopulate.

Sleet ticked at the windows.

"What do you make of him?" Preston asked. "Our friend with the forked beard."

"Balthazarr's a genius. He knows it. The world knows it."

"He doesn't intimidate you?"

"He intimidates the hell out of me. I don't feel competitive with him because it's no contest. I'll never be a Juan Hugo Balthazarr. But, coincidentally, my work has taken a Surrealist direction as of late. It started with a watercolor I did a few weeks ago, right after your observatory party. I've switched back to oils. Feels like I'm stumbling in the dark. But it's worthy exploration. I'm going places I never dreamed of. Or all I did was dream of them. Now they're happening on canvas. The work's good. I'm going somewhere… I don't know where yet…"

"Perfect timing, then. You take advantage of this opportunity with Balthazarr, and it can only boost your career." Preston ground out his cigarette in a saucer. "I'll be inviting him to my bachelor party. You're coming too. It's after the New Year. Minnie's got us booked through the holidays. We're visiting every damned mansion in Arkham for one social function or other. I've always loathed Christmas."

"Old humbug." Smoke leaked past my teeth. I reached into my jacket for my pocket journal. I leafed through the pages. "Do I have the date of your bachelor party? I can't remember." I unscrewed my pen. "Did you say you're moving the wedding date?"

"Minnie and I are impatient. Why wait until summer? Decisions will be finalized soon. As far as a bachelor party goes, I'll pin it down. My life is so planned out right now. Allow me a little spontaneity, will you?" He slumped back in his chair and shut his eyes.

"You can improvise like a jazzman. Kid Fairmont hammering at the ivory keys."

He stared at me from two sunken pits. "We'll have an old-fashioned boys' night on the town. A real bash. You and me… and all the rest…"

By the time the events of that ill-conceived boys' night ended, neither Preston nor I wished we had been there to see it. But by then it was too late. The die was cast, the play made. The cigarette girl wearing that sparkly red and gold skirt, catching everyone's eye….

What occurred on that ghastly night, lurking the back alleys and secret rooms of Arkham's underbelly? What did Balthazarr really do? A parlor trick, an illusion, or something much worse? Once we realized the level of horror, we couldn't stop it from happening. The blood… everything came bursting through the wall… guns barking, bullets flying… the screams of men and women running for the exits… fleeing an earsplitting roar from beyond.

But I'm getting ahead of myself.

Chapter Seventeen

By the time I arrived at Oakwood after breakfast, the sleet had turned to snow. Whiteness sugared the evergreens, the walk, the hip roof. Barren trees framed the house. I'd pick up a few things, then be out again. A quick turnaround. I hadn't been spending much time at the family hearth lately. Mother was tense because I hadn't moved out yet. That would be changing now. When I entered, Thorn greeted me. Mother was less sanguine. She passed specter-like, silently gliding at the back of the hall, her head turned to note my arrival. I didn't call to her with the good news. I'd tell my parents once I had official word from the Colony that Dunphy's apartment was mine. A few days at the most, I figured, after Preston made his calls. Father wasn't home; he'd absconded to New York to meet with his brokers.

I wiped my shoes and went upstairs. Thorn weaved in front of me. He loved to romp in the snow, the sight of snowflakes made him giddy. Inside my rooms, he dashed to the window and stood up with his paws on the sill, checking if the snow was still swirling. It was. He looked over his shoulder at me, his sad gray eyes pleading.

"All right, I'll take you for a walk. Let me change my clothes."

Thorn's tail wagged.

Roland had my walking clothes ready, hanging on the closet door. The man scared me sometimes with his prescience. He'd looped Thorn's leash on the door handle. I grabbed a satchel stuffed with toiletries, clothes for the weekend, and my sketchbook.

"Come on, boy. I'll show you our new digs."

We descended French Hill, taking a circuitous route. Thorn and I needed our exercise. We cut through the Miskatonic campus. Thorn loved it when the college girls would stop to rub his ears and praise his handsomeness. The quad was empty, and I couldn't guess why until I remembered it was the week before final exams. Everyone was inside, studying. I always loved taking tests. I performed at my best under pressure. Lack of urgency is what plagued me. Sloth and procrastination were my nemeses. If the net blob and the gargoyle did anything positive, they spurred me to get to work. I had painted a life-size canvas of the winged creature riding the train, and, frankly, the sight of it disgusted me, not because the demon was hideous but because it made me realize how I'd wasted years of my life painting anything else. I was born to midwife monsters! As much as they lit my creative fires, I was happy not to have met up with them again. Except in my dreams.

Nina and I were both suffering from frequent nightmares. I was perpetually back in Spain, having the tall, masked man toss me on the pyre or goblins fork out my guts. Nina dreamt she was Dr Silva swinging under a streetlamp. Another night she'd be roasted at the stake side-by-side with the Galinka sisters. Following our run-in with the watchman, I steered clear of the docks. Brave Nina ventured down there on her own in the daytime, inquiring as to the whereabouts of Calvin Wright. Calvin seemed a key to things. He knew Dunphy and had a familiarity with the Colonists. And there was the matter of a living gargoyle flying around town with his body and face. Maybe he could help us. But he'd disappeared. People at the Burdon's Fishery icehouse claimed he quit working there. No one at New Colony had seen him for days.

I spotted Christophe selling chestnuts outside the shops in the Merchant District, but he claimed he hadn't talked to Calvin since introducing us. In the meantime, he added a string of sparkly silver garland to his red wagon, and a fake white beard and elf's cap to his head.

"You're looking festive," I said, handing over coins.

"God bless us, everyone!" He winked at me.

"What's the scuttlebutt?"

"It's cold on the corners and hot behind locked doors."

"What's that mean?" I picked at my bag of chestnuts, trying not to burn my fingers.

"Means I'm freezing my caboose." He dropped his voice to a whisper. "There's trouble brewing in whiskey town. I hear a war's about to break out between rival crews."

"Gangs?"

Christophe's face screwed up. "Ya think I'm talking about knitting circles?"

"I don't often mingle with the criminal element."

"Who you kiddin', pal? Arkham's built on dirty money. Dig under French Hill if you don't believe me."

I thought of all my father's friends and how they'd "made" their fortunes. His point was well-founded. "Do the bootleg wars have to do with Calvin lying low?"

"I never said Calvin was lying low. Only I haven't seen his strong jaw lately. A man could make a pile of dough with those rum-running river boys. Dangerous dough, though."

The Merchant District looked safe and golden on a crystalline wintry night.

Customers expressing holiday cheer. Children frolicked around a faux manger. A string quartet played "Silent Night" outside Lunt's music store. Rosy cheeks and red noses were a symptom of the temperature, not illicit drink. It was hard to imagine a gang war in the offing.

"What's the reason for the war?" I asked.

"You don't listen. I said, 'I hear a war's about to break out' and that's not the same thing as predicting that one will. Here's what I can testify to. Everybody's nervous. It's like they caught some bug and they're passing it around so the whole city's infected. The atmosphere is heavy. Could be a real thing. Or it might be something floating around like smoke. All I know is I smell it. Rotten things are coming. Maybe Calvin tasted it on the wind and left. Who can say?"

Who, indeed?

That conversation had taken place a few nights ago. If the Colony was connected to gangsters, I didn't see how. Art and violence are two different things. One's fantasy and the other is real. Artists like Balthazarr depict scenes of horror. But they were colorful fantasies.

Violence in a painting isn't real.

No one ever died at the wrong end of a paintbrush.

Thorn menaced a couple of Miskatonic squirrels, and I tugged him away. We left tracks in the fresh snow leading to the Colony. He didn't growl at the old mansion. Maybe I expected he would sense evil in the air. I was superstitious that way. Instead, he made friends with Portia and Delilah who lived together in a corner unit on the first floor. They were sculptors like Dunphy, but they'd arrived after his fatal fall. Portia replaced him on the South Church gargoyle project. Delilah was her apprentice. Nina knew them better than I did.

The three drank tea together.

"Alden, who's this?" Portia asked from inside her fur-trimmed hood. The women were headed out. I'd interrupted a chat they were having as they stepped out the door.

"Thorn, my trusted sidekick."

"Your puppy is awfully cute. But we were hoping you'd bring Juan Hugo around," Delilah replied. "Him we're just dying to meet."

Portia gave her a stern look which she ignored.

"You've heard about Balthazarr already?" I asked, surprised. How did they know?

"It's all over the Colony. The notorious Spaniard has arrived," Delilah said.

I petted Thorn's side. "What makes you think I am acquainted with Balthazarr?"

The women looked at each other, passing silent messages.

"We heard you visited him at the Silver Gate," Portia said. "This morning…?"

"Is it true?" Delilah asked, eagerly.

I was taken aback. News spread fast in the commune. I needed to be wary of that, as a rule. Privacy would be a luxury forfeited. "In fact, it is true. But I don't really know him."

"Surely, you do," Delilah said, as if I were playfully deceiving them.

"Will you introduce us?" Portia was trying unsuccessfully to contain her excitement.

I decided not to fight their assumptions. "Well, if the opportunity arises..." Though I was hardly in any position to be escorting Juan Hugo Balthazarr around New Colony. "We have a mutual friend, Balthazarr and I. Simple as that."

"We'll all be friends before too long, I expect." Portia measured her words.

"All makes one in the end," Delilah said.

Portia shot her a look. It *was* an odd way to put things. Yet somehow familiar...

In any case, I didn't want to disappoint them. "Next time I see Balthazarr I'll invite him to come for a visit."

Delilah said, "You don't need to invite him. He's been with us from the very star–"

Portia elbowed her roommate in the side. "We know him by his work, she means."

Straightening, Delilah acted as if she hadn't felt the blow. But she clammed up. When she spoke, her voice sounded tight, breathless. "Can't wait to meet face to face."

The women had me bewildered. But I liked them and wanted to appear amicable, especially since they were Nina's friends. "I don't know about Juan Hugo, but you'll be seeing a lot more of me in the future. I hope to be moving in soon." They were underwhelmed. Apparently, I was small potatoes compared to a world-famous Surrealist.

"Uh huh." Delilah said. She and Portia moved off, waving.

"Be seeing you!" Portia called out, sounding like an enthusiastic, but poor, actress.

The two women crossed the street. Heads tipped together in hushed conversation.

Maybe someday I would be famous enough to excite people, to make their eyes brighten as I passed. To want to meet me. I needed to get used to living among groups again. I'd forgotten how it was since leaving college. In Europe, I chose to live off on my own.

I went up to Nina's apartment. She opened the door before I knocked.

"My, my, what're you dressed up for?" I said. "It's too early for a night out."

"Hello, you two." She kissed me and scratched my dog behind the ears. She wore a shiny black dress that had silver teardrops sewn on; her Mary Janes had rhinestones glued to the straps and heels. Silk stockings. I'd never seen her so done up. She ushered us in.

"I have news," Nina said.

"Me too. But you go first. Is your news good or bad?"

"Good, definitely."

"Mine too."

She poured two whiskies to celebrate. Thorn curled up on the rug by the fireplace. We drifted to the living room. It was all terribly domestic.

"I found Calvin Wright." Nina's eyes glittered, proud of her success.

"Great! Where is he?"

"Staying with friends in Easttown. He's got a new job. Been busy, working."

"In Arkham all along." That made things easier. If he'd left town, we were doomed.

She gulped half her whiskey. "His employer is a bootlegger. Calvin unloads trucks. They're taking the shipments off fishing boats on the river."

"Is that where you got this? It goes down smooth." I flopped onto her sofa.

"Somebody bought me that bottle. I've been out all night at a speakeasy." She waved me off when I furrowed my eyebrows, showing concern. "It was perfectly safe. Listen, Calvin wants to talk. I told him Court's death might not be an accident and that the gargoyle isn't in his apartment any more. He knows something. More than we do. I warned him that he might be in danger." She kicked off her shoes and sat down beside me, massaging her feet.

"What did he say when you told him the gargoyle came to life?"

"I left out that part."

"That's a big part, Nina." I sipped my drink. "You met him at a speakeasy?"

"I had a lead on the Galinka sisters. Apparently they were dancing at the Clover Club to make extra money. I ran into Calvin making a delivery at the club. Our conversation was less than private. So I had to be careful. We can speak freely when we meet again to share what we know." A log popped in the fire. Thorn startled, then heeded the grate suspiciously.

"What exactly do we know?" I swirled my whiskey. Drank it. Added to the glass.

"Something you said earlier got me thinking. I have a theory," she eyed me, tentative.

"The more I think, the more confused I feel lately. Please, I need enlightenment."

"Remember when you were doing the rubbings?" She put her feet back on the floor. "You mentioned 'ritual sacrifices'."

"I saw one in Spain. A reenactment of sorts." I thought about my dreams: the tall man in the mask, the two puppets, a crowd chanting around a pyre. Was it only a reenactment?

"What if the deaths in Arkham are part of a ritual?" Nina watched me, waiting for a challenge. She held her chin out. She'd been examining the crimes on her own for so long that sharing her private theory felt like taking a risk. I was more intrigued than judgmental.

"A ritual for what?"

She shrugged. "Rituals serve many purposes. To worship, to remember… what else?"

I sat forward, trying to think. "Well, maybe… to call something?"

"Yes! Sending a signal for someone, or something, faraway to receive."

"So the crimes are repeating this call?" As the whiskey warmed me, the idea was starting to make sense. But it felt like holding a live fish. I feared it might wriggle away.

"Not repeating, so much as amplifying. Think of it like a radio transmitting more and more powerful waves. Each murder sends the call out stronger than the one before…"

"Until at last something picks up." I felt a victory, short-lived. "And does what?"

"I don't know." She sighed. "Perhaps they find a way to answer?"

"Or they show up." I had a sick feeling in my gut. The net blob. The gargoyle. Were they harbingers? If they were, then whose arrival did they herald? What was hurtling relentlessly toward us? "Tell me the name of the place again. Where you met Calvin last night."

"It's called the Clover Club. Why?"

"You're the second person to mention that place to me today."

"Who was the first?"

"Preston."

"Preston?" Nina acted surprised. But Preston always knew where the best parties were. He'd be intimate with Arkham's speakeasies. For the first time I wondered how well Nina got to know Preston during their time together. I'd had the opportunity to see the part of him that was attracted to the underside of things, the part interested in forbidden pleasures.

"We had breakfast. He told me Clark Abernathy is missing. Clark's father said he might've run off with a dancer from the Clover Club. A woman named 'Diamond,' he said."

"Alden! The Galinkas used fake names at the club. Ruby and Sapphire. Not Diamond, but close. Do you think Clark's dancer was one of them? Did they know him?"

"It's a possibility. Although the sisters have been missing for some time… but if Clark only recently tried to see her, he might not have heard. We *know* he didn't run off."

"News stories of the murders didn't list any aliases. There really might be a connection." She stood up. "We have to talk to Calvin. He's going to be at the docks today."

"The docks? I'd rather not go there. That watchman might remember me."

"We'll be careful. We must see Calvin. He told me something else about a famous artist coming in to lead things at New Colony. He seemed disturbed. I don't know why."

"The artist is Juan Hugo Balthazarr," I surprised Nina again. "I met Balthazarr this morning at the Silver Gate. He makes an impression. Bigger than life. Preston introduced us."

I filled her in on the details of my morning with Preston.

"Let's go," she said, finally. She ran into her bedroom to change her clothes.

"Where're we going?" I called from outside the doorway.

"Calvin said he'd be able to meet us a half hour from now. There's a boat due." She opened the bedroom door. "Say, I never asked you. What's your good news?"

"I'm moving in across the hall." But there was no time for us to celebrate. Instead, we were going to talk to a man about monsters.

Chapter Eighteen

I was worried about showing our faces at the docks. The snow offered obscurity. The docks remained busy regardless of the inclement weather. Longshoremen hauled crates back and forth from the ships to the cavernous warehouses. We were just a couple out walking their dog. Thorn provided a cover story, but we weren't having any luck spotting Calvin. The snow hurt as much as it helped.

We were ready to turn uphill and leave the dirty river behind when a voice called out.

"Hey!"

I froze, recalling the watchman and his wood bat. We wouldn't be so fast running down a slippery alleyway. The shape I saw was a man. Too narrow to be the bulky guard.

"Alden," he said, approaching.

Calvin manifested out of a gust of snow. I couldn't help but check if he had wings. Fortunately, he didn't. He smiled at us.

"Miss Nina." He tipped his head. He wore a knitted cap, a heavy sailor's coat.

"Calvin. I'm glad you were able to come," she said.

Calvin offered his hand for Thorn to sniff.

"You're a fine-looking dog," he said, as he petted my hound.

"Where can we talk?" I asked.

"Follow me." Calvin led us between two warehouses. At the back corner of one building was an unmarked door; he opened it, and we went inside. Calvin pulled a string. A weak bulb. Plank walls. A table and two benches covered with idle pocketknife carvings and cigarette burn marks. The air was stale with men's sweat. Butts and refuse littered the floor; it hadn't been swept out in weeks. A frightened mouse skittered past with a breadcrust.

"Lunchroom," Calvin explained.

"You eat in here?" Nina asked, repulsed.

"Not me," Calvin said. He picked up a broom from the corner. "I don't work here any more, remember?" he said. "I'm along for a ride today. We can talk. Anybody comes in, that changes. We'll have to go someplace else."

"How's your new boss?" I asked.

Calvin shrugged. "A boss is a boss. What'd you want to talk about?"

"How do they sneak the booze out?" I asked, curious.

"Under the fish. Not every truck. I saw them doing it when I was shoveling ice for Burdon's. Then I discovered this other opportunity. Some of the fish trucks take a detour."

I dug out a cigarette, holding out the open case to Nina and Calvin.

"As long as I get paid." Calvin leaned on the broom and put a cigarette between his lips. He raised his eyebrows. "Are we here to chat about running whiskey, or is there something else?"

"Something else," Nina said.

I lit their smokes. "But if it's tied up with bootlegging…"

Calvin picked tobacco off his tongue. "Everything's tied to bootlegging in this town. That's where the money's at. And the police, too. I don't need trouble with them. Nina said this was about Court." He watched me, remaining wary.

"It is," she assured him. "I think… well, *we* think it all might be connected, somehow. The speakeasies, a recent string of strange deaths, and the odd clues we've uncovered so far."

"Probably is connected." Calvin exhaled, tired. "Court didn't even drink. He was too damned serious. At the end, he was acting truly bizarre. Having crazy dreams every night."

"Nightmares?" I asked. "We're having them too. Nina and I. We're getting scared."

"The dreams scared him too. He'd wake up covered in sweat. Couldn't focus. I was worried about him. He'd mumble nonsense to himself while we worked. He thought he was being followed."

"Was that all you did together?" I asked.

"How's that your business?" Calvin's suspicion of me was turning hostile.

"None of it's my business. I'm trying to figure out where everyone fits in the puzzle."

He cooled. "We were friends. Court was too caught up in his art to enjoy more."

I left it at that.

"The gargoyle, the stone one. Do you know where Court kept it?" Nina asked.

Calvin was surprised by the question. "He rented out a garage, not too far from here. The gargoyle was in there. I assume it still is."

"Was Court working on something else? Another sculpture? When we found the clay model of the gargoyle in his apartment, we saw a bigger pedestal. It was empty," I said.

"Nothing I know about." Calvin shook his head. "What's going to happen to that clay gargoyle? It has sentimental value to me. I'd like to buy it if it's for sale."

Nina and I exchanged glances. We had to tell him. No way around it.

"You won't believe this," she started, hesitant, but needing to plunge on. "Dunphy's clay gargoyle came to life." When Calvin made no reply, she continued. "It crashed through the window and flew across the river. We *saw* it ride out of Arkham on top of a train."

Calvin laughed. Waiting for us tell him the rest of the joke.

But we didn't have a punchline.

Understanding our seriousness, he staggered backward as if he'd been physically struck. He sat on a bench, sucking his cigarette and rubbing his chin. His eyes moved back and forth like a man putting together his own puzzle, sorting the pieces out, in the same way we'd done. "It really came to life?"

"It did," I said.

I reached into my pocket and took out the folded rubbings I made from Court's door. I passed them to him.

"What's this?" He seemed afraid to look at the papers.

"We found a message carved on the inside of Court's door. The gargoyle wrote it."

"It wrote something?"

"I made a copy. Words and symbols. Our names are written there. Yours too."

Calvin's hands were shaking as he opened the papers. He spread them out flat on his knees. Ash tumbled onto the newsprint. He didn't bother to brush it away. Concentrating.

"You *are* in danger," Nina said. "We all are, as you can see. That's why we need your help. Together, we might have a chance against whatever evil force is at work here in Arkham." She sat next to him and touched his hand. "Can you help us? Will you?"

Calvin was stunned, and silent.

"What do you know about the Colony?" I sat on his other side. The stark room was cold to begin with, but a new chill creeped in. Bone deep, awful. A palpable presence.

Calvin crushed out his smoke. "I know these signs. I've seen them before."

I jumped up. "Where did you see them? Do they mean something?" I took the paper. Shook it. I turned it around so he could see. "See, here. This one looks like a star. Is it a star?"

Calvin's shoulders dropped. He slouched forward like a prizefighter in his corner between rounds. His breath quickened and grew shallow. "It's called the Falling Star. I've heard others call it the 'Un-Sun.'" He wiped his dry mouth. "They are calling to him."

"We thought they might be trying to make contact. What is the Un-Sun?" Nina asked.

Calvin was twisting his neck, trying to clear his head. Suddenly, he looked exhausted.

"The Gate will open soon," he said. "They'll try to bring him through…"

"Who'll try?" Nina asked.

Calvin bit his lip. "I shouldn't tell you more. Get away. Stay far away. Leave town if you must… you're sure the gargoyle wrote this? He wrote… my name?"

"Yes, all of our names. We need to know what you know. Over the last months several people have died in Arkham under unusual circumstances. Nina and I think it might be a ritual. Dunphy was one of those people. Now we're seeing monsters pop up in town."

"Monsters? Others like the gargoyle?" Calvin looked to Nina to confirm my words.

"We think so," she said. "We've witnessed two for ourselves."

Calvin closed his eyes. He rubbed at his chest. Then his eyes opened and he steeled himself. He pointed to the three-prong fork. "This is their sign. A pitchfork. They've been searching for a leader, a sorcerer to open the Gate without getting them all killed in the process. This mark is the sorcerer." He tapped the spiked crown pictogram. "He might be the Twister of the Coil. I don't know that title. But the sorcerer wears the crown. And they unlock the Gate. The cup with the two eggs in it… I've never seen that figure. A sacrifice, maybe?" Calvin got up. His skin looked slack and gray, as if he'd lost a lot of blood.

"How do you know about this?" I blocked the door. I couldn't have him leaving, and he looked like a man ready to bolt. "Are you one of them?"

Calvin shook his fist in the air. "I'll never be one of them! They killed all that was important to me!" Anguish contorted his face. Hot tears came. But he was not ashamed.

"Who are they?" Nina draped her arm around him as he lamented.

He shuddered. "I don't know. Not exactly. I've been chasing shadows on two… no, three continents. There's more than one group. *That I know about.* They are aware of each other, but not always. It is… very complex. Cults are active in Arkham. They have members inside New Colony. I can't prove my suspicions… not yet. I came to stop them. And I will!"

"I don't understand," I said, frustrated. "Are these secret cultists worshippers of this Un-Sun? Is it a star in the galaxy? Are they sacrificing to the Sun like the Aztecs?"

"They are not like the Aztecs. They do not build. They have no society, no religion but destruction. Their goal is annihilation. You said you saw the gargoyle alive. Well, it was never alive. Animated, yes. But not alive. Did it still look like me? The face?"

"Yes," Nina said.

He gasped. "Sorcerers can copy life. Take a being or an object and control it, like a puppet jerking on a string. But who holds the strings? I've heard they change themselves. Walk around like your twin, a perfect double. It comes before they possess you. Each step is a higher display of power. Masks, all of them. Lies. If it's gone this far… they're close to something big." Calvin surveyed the squalid room, talking to himself as much as to us.

"Slow it down." I grabbed him by the shoulders. I needed to make sense of what he was saying. "You said they have members in the Colony. So which ones are doing it? Not Nina. Or Dunphy. Where did you see these signs?"

"The Black Cave. The signs are there. Painted on the walls deep in the cave. Old paintings. But paint was added to them … *fresh* paint. Wet, bloody smears on the rocks. We heard voices chanting when we moved the hooch… They always come at night… in their cloaks. We can't go back there. Who'd want to? The other boys in the gang ignore it. Keep silent. *Get away from there, son,* they tell me. *Come up to the cave mouth.* But I need to see for myself… under those robes and hoods… they're not human. We have to do something before it gets too–"

Thorn began to whimper.

I knew of a place in Arkham called the Black Cave. Calvin couldn't mean that. It was a minor geological site. Unworthy of a city plaque. Hardly the stuff of sinister machinations.

The lunchroom door burst open.

The doorframe filled. I'd have known him even if he didn't have that ball bat gripped in his right hand. His face was a granite block. But the granite had flaws; a row of stitches crawled along his forehead. Purple wedges under both eyes, and his nose was swollen, bending to the left. When he spoke, it sounded like he had a bad cold.

"What the hell is this, now? A church meeting?"

Calvin snatched up the broom. "I'm just cleaning up. These folks are leaving."

The brute stared at me. "Don't I know you?"

"No, sir. I don't believe we've ever been introduced. My name is Johannes Vermeer." I held out my hand, but he didn't take it.

Thorn growled. I wrapped his leash tighter in my fist.

The night watchman pointed his bat at my dog. "I'll bash his brains out."

Nina slid between us and the guard. "We were hoping to buy a fish for our dinner. I have such a taste for winter flounder in a lemon butter sauce. Johannes was trying to procure one."

The watchman's gears turned. "You can't buy no fish here."

"Off the books," Nina said, smiling. "You can do just about anything off the books."

He wouldn't budge from the doorway. His smell was beer breath and Tres Flores hair tonic. "If it was a fish you wanted, why are you back here jawing with these bums?"

"She opened the wrong door," Calvin said. "The lady's lost–"

"I ain't talking to you." He poked the barrel end of his bat into Calvin's breastbone. "Say, I thought you quit here. Went to work for O'Bannion."

"No, I've been sick is all." Calvin coughed. "Flu, likely."

"Flu?" The watchman backed off a step.

Calvin kept his hand on his chest, ready to snatch the bat. "I'm feeling much better now, though."

"Huh. Tell your story to somebody that cares." He snapped his attention back to me. "I do know that cocky mug of yours. You ever take a tipple down at Donohue's?"

"Me? No, no. I'm a teetotaler. Nothing stronger than a root beer for me."

"Shuddup." Softly, the watchman appraised us, rocking on his heels. He slapped the bat into his palm. It made a meaty thump. "What am I going to do with you?"

"You're going to let us go." Nina threw back her shoulders, moving ahead and taking Thorn's leash from me, ready to slide around the guard. "I've had quite enough of your games." Her free hand disappeared into her pocket. I wondered if the stiletto was hidden there. Was she about to shiv him?

To everyone's shock, the watchman turned to let her pass.

"Good day. Hope you find your fish." He touched the bill of his guard cap.

I went next. Not looking at him. Keeping my gazed fixed on Nina's back as she retreated into the swirling snow with Thorn. After I turned out of the doorway, I let out a sigh of relief and breathed in the crisp, metallic flavor of snow. The waters of the oily Miskatonic rolled in the distance. A fishing boat coasted into my view as sailors moved about the pier, securing its moorings.

Calvin will be behind me.

He'll duck past this overgrown galoot, and we're home free.

Just keep walking. Not too fast or too slow.

You made it.

That was the last thought I remember having before the sky fell on my head, and I watched as a star exploded – a spray of gold sparks – fluttering as they fell in the snow, and the Miskatonic overran her banks, flooding around me, cold, inky black, pulling me down, down, down into its blank heart, a void, and me caught spinning like a snowflake, melting to nothing.

Chapter Nineteen

I woke up under a pile of mackerel. I tasted blood. Not theirs, mine. I tried moving and found I couldn't. Not without a sledgehammer pain squarely smacking my forehead. I puked.

"Easy there, fella." An invisible hand pushed me down. Unfriendly? I couldn't tell.

Another voice. "He's awake. Hoo-wee! Stinks worse than today's catch."

"At least he's not dead. Naomi wouldn't want us bringing in a dead guy."

"No, she wouldn't."

"Nina," I sputtered. My mouth and throat burned, like acid. "Where's Nina?"

"I don't know who that is, boyo. But she ain't here. Keep still, or I'll tie you up."

"You don't need to tie him. He's half dead, poor sap. What a walloping he got."

I let that assessment sink in. Where was I? How did I get here? Ah, yes. The watchman and his bat. I kept my eyes shut because when I tried opening them, scissors stabbed in between them. I wiggled my fingers and toes. At least I wasn't paralyzed.

Cold, I was so cold. I felt like another fish on ice. Limp as a rag, twice as wrung out.

Was this death? When your body gave up and your soul slipped over the brink, is this how it was? The truck hit a bump and jolted me out of my stupor. Someone was moaning.

Me. That was me making a pathetic, gurgling, clubbed-seal lamentation.

I clenched my fists. My fingers dug into scoops of ice. I opened just one eye a slit. Not too bad. There was a man beside me sitting on a Burdon's Fishery crate. They'd tossed me in the back of a Burdon's truck. We were probably taking one of the detour routes Calvin talked about. Delivering contraband whiskey smuggled into Arkham in the bellies of those ships moored at the docks. Riding uphill, the engine growled. Tires spun. Downhill it eased off, but the brakes made a racket, grinding. Axles squealing. Mackerel were sliding around me as the truck negotiated uneven ground. My guess: a dirt road, the ruts clogged with snow and ice. The wind screamed outside the truck, pushing it with each strong gust. The driver was being careful not to end up nose-down in a ditch, because he wasn't headed to any fishery, and losing his shipment might cost him a few years in the slammer, or his life. Through half-lidded eyes, I assessed the man to my right. He was eating an apple, cutting wedges with a short knife, sliding them off the blade into his mouth. Freckles, short red hair. A white man. So it wasn't Calvin.

The driver – the one who called me half dead – didn't sound like Calvin either. It was the voice of a teenager, a farm boy.

Of course, that didn't rule out him being a killer. These two might both be killers, I thought. The night watchman wasn't around. That counted for something.

I went to sleep again. No dreams. Nothing. I was on, then I was off, like a switch.

I don't know for how long.

But when I woke the second time, the truck was parked up, its engine off.

I was alone. My back was wet. I picked up a handful of red ice. I rolled onto my side, thinking I might be sick again. But the nausea subsided. I propped myself up on my elbow. I touched the back of my head. My hair was gummy, my fingertips red. The side of my neck sticky with blood. *My* blood, I realized with a sickening thud. Wide-open, dead moony fisheyes stared at me from the bed of glistening ice – my unlucky travel companions, sleeping the sleep you never wake up from. Hours ago, this school of blue mackerel was swimming in the ocean, making their way in the salty world. Gutted, they were bound for somebody's Friday fish dinner. At least I was still swimming. I had a fighting chance.

The big cargo door was open a crack.

I sat up. My head pounded. I waited to see if it would quiet down.

I looked out.

Men talking, smoking. At work. If I was a ghost, then this was going to be a terrible group to haunt. They looked too tough to scare. Scars and muscles. Just like the dock workers, they hauled merchandise. Illegal merchandise. Loose bottles clinking until they packed them away in crates lined with straw. They were getting the liquor ready to ship out again. I smelled coffee brewing, and spotted a pot chained to an iron tripod over a campfire. There was a kettle over the fire too. Clam chowder by the smell of it. But I wasn't feeling hungry, not that anybody was asking.

My head was a little quieter. Why had they brought me here? Blood trickling from my broken noggin was more pink than red when I dabbed it again with my fingers. The bleeding had slowed down. I didn't go searching too high on the top of my head. I was afraid if I reached up there, I'd feel a crack in my skull, bone chips, and wads of gooey brain.

This way I could almost pretend it was a bad hangover.

Give it a few hours and my normal self would return. Shamed but intact. No permanent damage. Nothing that couldn't be fixed with a meal and sleep. I scooted half out of the truck. Legs dangling. I felt like a broken clock. My springs sprung. The minutes I heard ticking by were my pulse, and it wasn't keeping regular time.

I put ice on my tongue to rinse out the foul taste. Gritty, but better than before.

I sucked. Spit. I mopped my brow with my wet sleeve.

When I checked the interior of the truck, I found the booze was already unloaded.

Just me and the fish left behind.

So long, I thought. Here's my stop, boys. Fare thee well.

I hopped out. Nearly ended up flat on my back again. My legs were rubbery, like the bones were going soft and bendy inside. *Shit.* I was dizzy to beat the band. I held onto the truck.

We were in the backwoods somewhere. A curious cardinal was watching me from a pine. I looked around toward the other end of the truck and saw a hole in the side of a hill.

What had Calvin called that place where he saw the symbols painted?

The Black Cave.

Like I said, I'd heard about it growing up in Arkham. But I'd never been there. Was this it?

Hand over hand, I made my way to the front bumper, out of sight of the men.

Sure enough, the truck was pulled up to a cave. Inside the cave mouth, torches burned. Off to one side stood several copper pot stills, and stacks of firewood for heating up the pots. Above them, a natural chimney formation in the rock let the smoke out. Distillers worked at night to avoid attracting attention. But nobody had been distilling whiskey here lately. The equipment appeared to be stored away. Instead, the cave acted as a kind of warehouse for shipping and receiving barrels and crates of illegal alcohol smuggled in via the docks. The men were working outside the cave today, emptying the Burdon's trucks of their hidden cargo and repacking bottles to fulfill orders waiting on pallets in the snow. Here was a band of pirates divvying out liquid treasure. But the truck I arrived in was parked away from the action. Nobody was bothering with me for right now.

Where were Calvin and Nina? What did the night watchman do to them? I didn't want to think about it. They were smart. Maybe they got away…

I tried standing on my own. Wobbly. But I didn't fall right over like a bowling pin. I stumbled into the cave. I had to stare at my feet to make sure they did their job properly. I bumped into a wall. Or two.

It was darker here. Better for my battered brain. I shuffled in the sandy soil.

Then it was hard rock under the soles of my shoes.

Rock on every side. I ran my hands over the surface of the walls like a blind man.

"Where the hell is he?" a voice said, from not too far away.

"I left him right there. Out cold. I swear to God. I put my hand under his nose to make sure he was breathing. He couldn't just up and go, I'm telling you. Down for the count he was." I recognized the second voice. He was the guy who rode in back with me.

"Well, he isn't here now. Go find Freddie. Maybe he took him somewhere. Go!"

"You got it, boss," said the voice I knew.

"Get back before Naomi hears about this. She'll put both our asses in slings."

I listened to one man walking away. The other climbed into the truck and then jumped out again. I put one foot in front of the other and kept going farther into the cave.

Darker and darker.

It smelled like the sea when the tide goes out and things are left to die on the beach. But I didn't care. It felt good being back there in the blackness. I was protected. The cave floor ramped downward. I kicked something solid that rattled and fell over. Rolling.

"Freddie! Hey, Freddie, that you back there?"

I had to keep low in the dark. If they found me, who knew what they'd do. I wasn't about to go and find out. I knelt on the floor and felt the shape of the thing I'd kicked. Smooth, cool glass. Scratchy metal. When I shook it, liquid sloshed around inside.

I smelled fuel.

A lantern!

I tucked it under my arm and felt my way until I turned around a corner.

It took me a little while to dig my lighter out of my pocket and get the wick lit in near total darkness. When it blazed, I put the cover on and covered it quickly with the flap of my coat. The man standing by the truck, the one who asked if I was Freddie, couldn't see me unless he came deeper inside. My only choice was to explore the cave.

The passage turned to the left. So I did too.

Lifting my light, I continued down the ramp and came to steps chiseled in the rock.

Down I went.

The swinging lantern and the shadows on the bumpy walls didn't help my dizziness.

But I tried to look straight ahead, and I still was climbing down.

A helluva lot of steps this cave had. I had to sit for a while and rest my head on my knees. The effort of walking had my head pounding again. I don't know how long I sat there, quietly. But then I thought I heard footsteps and voices murmuring. Not behind me, where the bootleggers were likely searching for me by the cave mouth, but in the opposite direction, ahead of me.

Deeper inside the subterranean cavity.

I held up the lantern.

Movement… maybe… a piece of the darkness darker than the rest… separated.

I stood up and bent forward, trying to see more. But it was no use. I had to keep going down to make sure.

Eventually I got to a sort of landing. It was as wide as a dance hall. At the far end were more stairs, and I didn't want to walk any more. I was feeling tired. Sleepy. And the blood was pumping from my head wound again. I had to wipe my neck a few times with my wet sleeve. I thought about curling up on the landing and taking a little nap. *When I wake up again, I can go back, or I can take those steps going down.* That's what I was telling myself when I saw them.

I don't know how they got behind me.

But there they were, huddled by the wall with a fire, not yellow-orange like my lantern but encased in a greenish glow all their own.

Three figures in cloaks, like monks.

I remembered Clark Abernathy in his Friar Tuck costume. I recalled how later, when we discovered him, he had no head. Sprawled out on the observatory floor, his neck stump chewed, his cloak hung up on a peg.

The three figures were bent over a little. Close to each other, their backs to me. One was finger-painting on the wall, one chanting, and one stayed silent but attentive.

"You, you," the chanter said. "You, you… you, you…" He said it over and over.

I walked up, more curious than alarmed, and raised my lantern. "Me? Are you addressing me, by chance?"

None of the three bothered to turn.

You, you… you you…you, you youyouyou…

It was as if he were a needle stuck on a record. He bowed slightly with each utterance.

I edged forward, feeling a sour gush of fear kick up inside me but not knowing why.

I tried the finger-painter. "What are you drawing?" No luck. I stepped back, irked. "What is this? A church meeting?" I asked in a raised voice. My head really hurt. I'd heard that question somewhere before. Maybe I was making a joke, but my lines didn't even make sense to me. *You, you…* That sounded somehow familiar too but completely out of context.

The chanting petered off into gibberish.

"*Yuyu! Va-BaDAAAHHH!*" the chanter shouted in a finale that startled me.

The odd phrase echoed in my mind, bringing back thoughts of other voices, the ones Nina and I overheard through the wall in the observatory library. Somewhere else as well. Spain? Was that where I heard these alien sounds the first time?

Never mind, because they finished what they were doing. The finger-painting, chanting, and staying silent were over and done with. They stepped away from their work. The chanter, who was in the middle, was much taller than the other two. The finger-painter was quite short, like an older child, but you could tell by the way they moved they were no child. A petite woman? Their hoods were pulled low, hiding faces. The green light and my light joined on the landing. There were markings on the floor I hadn't noticed before.

Lines. Angles. It reminded me of a geometry problem. Find the missing angle. I recalled the design chalked on the floor under Clark's body.

"You ready to talk now? It's rude not to answer when someone speaks to you," I said.

The one whose job it had been to stay silent responded.

"It isn't time for you yet. Go back." A man. He spoke with a slight German accent.

"Back where?"

The one who had stayed silent pointed up the steps toward the cave opening. I was shocked! His hand and arm had no skin, just wet muscle and sinews, a network of throbbing blood vessels pumping. I should have been terrified, but I didn't feel that way. I was numbed.

"I'm too tired for that now. After I sleep," I said. "It's a long way to daylight. Trust me." I gestured with a sweep of my fortunately skin-covered arm.

"You're injured," the finger-painter said. No child's voice. Feminine, speaking in a hoarse whisper, as if her voice box had been injured. "You have blood on you," she rasped.

"You do too. See?" I shifted my lantern to show the finger-painter her bloodied hands.

The tall chanter in the middle came forward. The green light around the three came out of him. I say "*him*" because the shape had big shoulders, and it stood like a man with its legs spread far apart. The light spiked out of his head like a crown, and green spikes ran down his spine, reminding me of reptiles I'd seen poised on zoo rocks, with their flicking, forked tongues.

"Alden, you are important. Most important. We need you. Please, listen to us." I can't say it was a man's voice. More like a god voice that went through me so that I vibrated. All their voices sounded odd and dreamy. The chanter touched my shoulders.

The pain in my head vanished. I was tingling.

"Are you helping me?"

"Yes," the three said together in a single combined voice.

"You're my friends?"

"Go back, Alden," they said. "We will call you when it is time."

Then I saw the landing was crowded with cloaked figures. There was hardly any room for me to move. Two of them were dancing and leaving sooty footprints on the stone. They lifted me up on their shoulders and carried me up the carved steps. I wasn't frightened, though I should've been. But they felt strong and sure, marching me back to the cave entrance. My lantern was gone. I don't remember where it went, but I didn't need it. We had the eerie swampy green light, and they all knew the cave better than they knew their own homes. Why did I think that? I don't know. But it felt true. I was so light in their hands. It was like I floated above them. Their humming – did I tell you they were humming or chanting or doing something that I could feel, buzzing around me like a swarm of bees, not to sting me, but to save me? – their noise, it relaxed me. Like machines more than bees. A kind of staticky noise that made me sleepy. I wasn't asleep, and I wasn't awake either. When the humming static, or whatever that sound was, when it stopped, it did it all at once. The silence afterward was total. I was lying on the cave floor, near the light from the sun outside, on the rim of the shadows that lived in the cave forever. Not on the hard rock but on the sandy soil, on my back.

My hands were folded across my chest.

"There you are," they told me inside my head, comforting me.

There you are.

Chapter Twenty

"There you are!"

Boots stomped toward me where I lay, dazed. A leather toe prodded me in the side.

"You awake? Or faking it?"

"Man, he ain't faking it. Look at all the blood. His skin's as white as a fried egg."

"I don't know, Freddie. He tricked us before. Boss was mad he wasn't in the truck."

Freddie, who sounded like he was the farm kid that drove the truck, defended me from his partner's accusations. "He probably fell out and crawled in here like a sick tomcat. He's tricking exactly nobody."

"Let's get him up."

Somebody took hold of my legs.

Freddie said in my ear, "C'mon, buddy, you need help for that busted head of yours." Hands under my arms, he lifted me. The men carried me out of the cave, past the parked truck, and over to a table constructed of planks laid across a pair of sawhorses. A tarp corded between two pines tented the table.

I was groggy, nauseated. Freddie looked every bit the rangy teenager, sporting a tousled thatch of hair, the faint hint of a moustache, and a jacket two sizes too large. He ladled out a cup of hot chowder, setting it on a stump beside the table. Then he propped up my head, pressing a canteen to my cracked lips. "This here's water. Drink some if you can. I got tasty soup waiting when you're ready. Doc Unger is coming to inspect that knot on your pumpkin. Boy, that guard feller got you good. I wonder what you did to make him so angry. Doc will fix you up. He's a real steady operator for a dope fiend."

"Stop mothering him," his partner said.

Freddie looked at my eyes, which were getting slowly better at focusing. "Winston's ornery by nature, but he's all bark, no bite. Pay him no mind."

"I'll chomp on both of you," Winston said, snapping his raggedy, tea-colored teeth.

"No, he won't," Freddie assured me.

Winston stood under a corner of the tarp, smoking the shortest, fattest cigar I ever saw. I sipped from the canteen. The water's cold made my teeth ache.

"You want to try sitting?" Freddie asked.

I nodded. He pushed me up. The snowy bootleggers' camp tilted and rocked as if it were built on a platform at sea. But then the motion settled down to a tolerable balance.

"Where're the monks?" I said, slurring my words. But I made myself understood.

"Why, he's been to the pearly gates and back." Winston laughed, slapping his thigh.

Freddie watched my face closely, looking for signs of ongoing impairment.

I didn't feel chipper, but I knew I wasn't brain damaged. I gave Winston a hard look.

"I think you might've had yourself a vision," Freddie said.

I shook my head, which was a mistake.

"In there." I pointed to the cave. "Way at the back. People in robes."

Winston stopped his smiling and gaped at Freddie, then back at me. "You best stay out of there. And don't tell nobody you saw people in robes inside the cave. That's off limits." He chewed on his cigar. It had gone out. He took it from his lips, contemplated it, and put it back. Freddie went to the stump and held up the cup of steaming soup.

"No thanks," I said. "You eat it. My stomach's feeling queasy."

"Suit yourself." He drank half the cup, wiping his mouth with the back of his hand.

"Why am I here?"

"He's a philosopher," Winston quipped.

"The watchman from the docks? Remember him? He clocked you when you wasn't looking," Freddie said. "That's what Calvin told us. Well, Cal, he didn't like that. He fed that head-knocker some bare knuckles. Cal couldn't hang around after that. He stuffed the guard in a trashcan and asked us to bring you here for Doc to patch up. Said he'd hitch a ride here as soon as he could." I'd have preferred a trip to St Mary's Hospital over this gutter medic they kept mentioning. But I understood Calvin's instinct to keep things off the books.

"What about the woman with the dog?"

"We didn't see no woman," Freddie said.

Winston nodded in agreement. "No sir, no dolls or dogs on the docks today."

Where had Nina gone? My anxiety was interrupted by a new source of unease.

"Here comes Doc now." Freddie looked past me. "Make no mention of his wig."

"What wig?" I asked.

"Shush," Winston said, putting a finger to his lips and waving at me to pipe down.

"What have we here, gentlemen?" Doc Unger said, in lieu of a proper introduction.

I was glad they warned me not to mention the man's hairpiece. Because if they hadn't, it surely would've been the first item on my conversational list. As best as I could determine, Doc Unger wore a seventeenth-century French wig in the style of the Sun King, Louis XIV. It was a glossy mass of curls that fell to his shoulders and perched upon him like a slightly snarled, snoozing pet.

"Our boy here suffered a blow to the head from a wooden club," Freddie said.

"Did he now?" The faux courtier set his leather bag on the ground. With firm but gentle pressure he turned my face away from him. His fingers delicately probed my injury.

"Is it fatal, Doc?" Winston asked, snickering. "Should we call a priest?"

"I think not." The real exam began then. I yelped in pain. Doc rustled in his bag. He numbed me, cleaned my wound, stitched me. Then he bandaged my skull, wrapping my battered crown in a gauze turban. He handed me a small brown bottle of pills for pain, two of which I swallowed immediately. And he added that I should drink fluids, but not liquor, and to rest for a few days. "The human skull is a natural helmet, and yours, luckily, has not been breached. Not for lack of trying, you dear hooligan."

After my treatment, I tried to pay him, using damp bills dredged up from my pockets.

He refused. "My work here is charity. For the good of society, I endeavor."

With that he exited, dissolving into the snow like an extravagant ghost.

"I've never met a doctor like him before," I said, astounded.

"Oh, Doc's not a real doctor. He was a patient at the asylum before he escaped. He does quality work. Long as he gets his dope, he's pleasant as can be. Keeps us fit as fiddles."

I thought about my sewed-up head under the turban, the fat numbness sitting on me like a giant snoozing spider. This formerly institutionalized man had put his fingers inside a rip in my head. I surprised myself by feeling less worried than impressed. Though that might have been the pills already at work.

Freddie refilled his cup from the kettle. Steam rose, a scent of the sea too.

"Want a little soup now?" he asked.

"Sure, why not? What have I got to lose?" Lunatic surgery relaxes one's standards.

"That's the spirit."

Even grumpy Winston appeared buoyed by the shift in attitude. "You really see monks in the cave?" he asked, earnestly.

"I did. They carried me back up the steps from down on the landing."

The bootleggers exchanged quizzical stares.

"What?" I asked. "What did I say?"

"There ain't no steps in the cave," Freddie said. "It's twisty back there, and it pitches down to the caverns that fill up when the tide's in, but no steps. No landing neither."

"But… but I was there," I said, thinking about my memory; how unlikely it really was.

"Oh, you got conked and went to dreamland. It's no big thing," Winston said. He fished a flask out of his coat pocket and, after taking a swig, offered it to me.

"Doc said, 'No liquor.'" Freddie reminded him. He kicked snow at his criminal cohort. "But give me a taste, Win."

The two bootleggers drank, staring into the pines and falling snow.

"Strange life," Freddie said, finally.

I didn't disagree.

Darkness crept into the woods around the Black Cave. Winston and Freddie pointed out a gap in the pines and told me the Miskatonic River was less than a hundred yards right that way. Through the trees, I thought I could make out distant church steeples. So, we weren't all that far from the docks and the city. But I couldn't walk it in my current shape.

"The hooch goes out to a boat after nightfall. We load it on the beach," Freddie said.

"Does the booze always come in and go back out again?" My pain had reduced to a pounding, but tolerable, headache.

"That's called distribution," Winston chimed in.

"Rum-running boats ferry shipments down the river. A part stays here and goes to the O'Bannion joints. The rest leaves by truck, headed inland," Freddie said.

"The Clover Club? That's an O'Bannion place, right?" I felt recovered enough to join them for a smoke. "Naomi O'Bannion. She owns the place?"

The men nodded.

"That's one thing her family runs," Freddie said. "Quite a lady–"

"Don't say no more. He's a stranger," Winston cautioned. "No offense, mister."

"None taken." My new bootlegger friends lit torches and staked them in the ground so their fellow brethren in the whiskey trade could see their work. The other members of the bootlegging crew were off nearer the road. We were on our own. "I know a lady like that."

"The one you lost at the docks?" Winston asked.

"That's her."

"You called her *Nina*," Winston remembered my ramblings from the ice truck.

"Did somebody say my name?"

Nina glided out of the trees.

Freddie and Winston jumped like a couple of spooked squirrels.

I nearly fell off the table. Nina approached, red-cheeked from her hike in the woods.

"What the hell? She's a damned witch!" Winston pulled a pistol.

"Easy, fellas," Nina said. "I'm no threat." She raised her hands in the air.

"Where'd you come from?" Freddie said. Winston still had the pistol trained on her.

"Back there. Down by the river. After the watchman attacked Alden, I ran and hid in a toolshed. It was so abominably frigid, I thought I might emerge an icicle. When I worked up my courage enough to climb out, I saw Calvin in the alleyway looking for me."

"Calvin? Where is he?" Winston's finger hooked tight on the trigger.

"Point the gun down at the ground, please," I said.

He seemed unsure. He switched the barrel back and forth between us. "I don't know you. You sure as hell don't know me. Don't go telling me what to do."

"Easy, Win. Don't do nothing you can't take back." Freddie said.

I turned to Nina. "It's awfully good to see you. Where's Calvin?"

"We found a boat. Calvin rowed up to a spot on the banks and dragged the boat ashore. I raced up here to see if I could find you. You looked so lifeless at the docks."

I touched my turban of bandages. "Now I look like Rudy Valentino in *The Young Rajah*. It's nice to hear you haven't lost your skills as a boat thief. I do hope Calvin shows up soon." Boots stepping in snow. *Crunch, crunch.* "Ah, here he comes now."

Calvin pushed past a snow-heavy branch. A shower of ice crystals danced in the torchlight. A sweaty-faced Calvin smiled before his expression turned to surprise at the sight of Winston's pistol. "What's this? Winston, are you going to shoot me?"

Winston lowered the gun.

Freddie said, "Cal, you about gave us a heart attack."

Sensing the danger had abated, Nina rushed into my arms.

We kissed.

"You two should leave," Calvin said. "The current will carry the skiff into town."

"I can steer," Nina said. "My father had me sailing my own dinghy when I was ten."

"Can you walk?" Calvin asked, helping me down from the table.

"If I go slowly." I grabbed Calvin's thick forearm. "Thank you for everything. They told me you took care of that bat-wielding maniac. I owe you."

"After I took his club away, he wasn't so tough."

"We need to talk. Soon. I saw things in the Black Cave. Monks… well, they weren't really monks. It's difficult to explain."

Calvin looked at Freddie and Winston. They shrugged.

"We'd better go," Nina said.

I followed her through the pines to the black river, where Thorn, with his tail wagging, waited for us in the boat. Home to New Colony we went.

Chapter Twenty-One

Two weeks later I finished moving into Court's old apartment. The property manager had cleaned the place out. He sanded the inside of the door and slapped on a new coat of varnish. If I peered from the side in the right light, I could still read the message and see the symbols the gargoyle had carved there. The three butchered names of Calvin, Nina, and me followed by the threatening ominous prediction.

CALvin RiTe

NinA TArrinGTon ALL Den OAks

WiLL Die by the HAnd of the ONe who CALLs the FALLing sTAr

Thru The GATe

TwsTer of The CoiL

The Un-Sun

yoOYUVABDAA

I read our names again. It dawned on me that, apart from the random capitalizations, the creature had gotten the spelling of Nina's first and last names correct. That's interesting, I thought. *Tarrington* was the longest word, and the animated clay thing had even managed the double "r" bit, which might've meant nothing, of course. He'd succeeded with a series of double "l" spellings in the next line. Perhaps it was random chance; I was looking for clues where none existed. Or maybe he was more familiar with her Boston clan, or a namesake in another city. Or did Nina mean more to him? And to the Twister of the Coil? And the Un-Sun?

I set aside my ruminations about our names.

It was the last word that interested me the most. This *was* the word I heard from the tall monk in the Black Cave. *You, you… Va-BaDAAAHHH!* Something like it came to Nina and me through the library wall as well. I was convinced I'd heard it at the ritual in Spain.

But what did it mean? It might have been a kind of prayer or interjection.

Yet I suspected it was a name. So many of the words in the gargoyle's message were names: Calvin, Nina, my name....

The others were less clear: Falling Star, Twister of the Coil, and...

Yooyu Vabadaa.

It had to have meaning. Two parts. It felt like a name when I spoke it aloud.

I wanted to ask Calvin. He was vital to our solution. But where had Calvin gone?

Since that night we left the bootleggers' camp, we hadn't seen him. He never came to New Colony. We certainly weren't going to return to the docks. Nina tried to persuade me to pay a visit to the Black Cave. I wasn't ready for that. How could we go there without the risk of being shot by gangsters? I was sure we could find its location. We knew the side of the river it was on and how far from town. It was only a matter of picking the correct dirt road.

But no, it wasn't safe.

Calvin knew where to find us. We simply had to wait for him to make contact, as hard as that might be. I'd shared my idea about *Yooyu Vabadaa* with Nina. She agreed it sounded like a name. Beyond that we were stuck. Oh, we had plenty to keep us busy. But none of it related to Arkham's mysterious deaths or monsters. My head was feeling better. I was grateful for that. I had used up the pills Doc Unger gave me.

Nina and I mostly did what lovers do. Mother called it "playing house." All I knew was that I was in love for the first time in my life. Every scrap of evidence told me that Nina loved me too. We did make a cute couple, as Preston said. I hadn't seen Preston either lately, not since our breakfast at the Silver Gate Hotel. Preston never came down to New Colony. He was a silent partner.

Balthazarr had arrived at New Colony.

I wasn't the one who brought him around. He didn't need a handler. The man made his own way. The whole Colony buzzed with new energy. Our artist-in-residence, Juan Hugo Balthazarr, the Shocking Spaniard, was no wallflower. More like a carnival barker, combined with a one-man band and a living fireworks display. He had the instincts of a master thespian and the charm of a motivated salesman pushing the snazziest, gaudiest product in the world: himself. He knew how to attract attention. His artwork was brilliant, ground-breaking, and relevant to modernity like no other's, yet he still managed to outshine what he did with who he was, a true celebrity. He gave a few lectures, even taught a class or two. Mostly he talked. During one class I attended, he had us paint a communal painting. Each student added a brushstroke, a color, or a line scraped with a palette knife.

In the end, the painting itself was abstract. A chaos of styles.

"Do not think. Create," he said. "Forget logic... order. Tap into your elemental self."

I had difficulties. If I abandoned logic and order, then how could I pick up a brush?

When it was finished, Balthazarr had us gather around the canvas.

Around him.

We sat on the floor – like his worshipful disciples.

He lit a match and burned the painting.

I excused myself, suddenly feeling ill. I was back in Spain watching the pyre.

Christmas came and went. Nina and I bought a small tree. We tied red velvet ribbons on the branches. Put our wrapped gifts under its pagan branches. We drank eggnog and built fires.

I met the other Colonists. For the most part they were examples of types, and if you've spent any time around artistic communities, you'll likely know exactly what I mean. There were the brooding loners. You met them once, then saw them only from afar, or in passing. The society-seekers were the opposite, always around, even when you wished they'd stay in for a night. They spoke outrageous things into a crowd and watched to gauge the reactions. Drank too much, ate off other people's plates, smoked constantly, and you'd better keep a hand on your partner, or you'd find theirs in its place. They broke things, including themselves, and, bright as they were, the shine would not last for too long. This you discovered soon.

I know I must sound critical, but you misunderstand me if you think I didn't like the Colonists. They were my people. I was among my own kind. They were the crazy makers of art. Creators whose acts of creation typically involved an equal, or greater, measure of selfdestruction as a price paid. A self-fulfilling myth. They glowed from inside, like hot embers, and whatever color existed in Arkham only existed because of them. For the most part, as cohabitators, they were never easy.

Take Portia and Delilah, the sculptresses I mentioned before, who were our downstairs neighbors. They fought with each other. Screaming matches we could hear through the walls. At other times, they were so sweet and perfectly fitted to each other, you'd swear they were twins. But twins fight too, I guess. I liked them. Portia's new gargoyles were better than Court's.

"Do you really think so?" Portia asked me one frozen afternoon, while the ladies drank Oolong tea, after I'd returned from the bakery with warm doughnuts and a sour cream pound cake. Delilah and Nina were in the other room slicing up the cake, putting it on plates.

"That gargoyle could sit atop Notre Dame," I said. "*Très magnifique.*"

Portia nodded and nibbled at her doughnut, unsure whether to believe me.

That's one of the big problems with artists. We're inner people, despite the outer drama and colorful displays. Selfish by nature, consumed with our own visions and dreams. We alternate between delusions of grandeur and crippling self-doubt. It lures people, then drives them away. *I love you – I hate you. I love me – I hate me.* No wonder the world thinks us mad.

"I guess it could be turning out worse," she said. "How's your painting coming along? Do you have anything to hang in the gallery this weekend for New Colony's winter show?"

Balthazarr had insisted that we present our art. Permit ourselves to be judged publicly, so he organized a show. Everyone was thrilled … and equally terrified.

"I'm working on a couple pieces." That was all I wanted to share. *See? I'm like them.*

I had three completed paintings in Court's old studio. There was the watercolor I painted at Oakwood of the net blob shambling across the bridge toward me. Since my arrival at the Colony, I'd done two new oils. The gargoyle hopping the train, cackling with its head thrown back and wearing Calvin Wright's face like a mask. And my latest creation, an interior of the Black Cave: the processing monks in hooded robes carrying me aloft, the chiseled steps and knobby walls cast in a sickly greenish hue. I painted my damaged, bloody head, but my eyes were wide open, staring at the viewer, entranced. In the background, on one of the cave walls, small details: finger-painted symbols – smears of scarlet defacing the rocks – and angular geometric lines crisscrossed the landing, half-concealed in shadows. I made some of them look like the gargoyle's symbols I kept finding. I wasn't even sure what I'd seen on the walls of the cave. My memory was too foggy, the details already fading.

I hadn't shown this painting to Nina. Not yet. I told her it wasn't ready, but that was a lie. The painting was finished. I wasn't ready for her to see it, or anyone else. It was still too enigmatic to me. Had I traveled that far into the depths of the cave? Or was this canvas the cryptic hallucination of a shaken brain after it suffered a pummeling with a bat? Who knew?

I had a fourth painting, an oil I'd begun after the net blob's portrait, but I had abandoned this work. It showed the inside of the Warren Observatory, the telescope dome. Clark Abernathy's headless body ceremonially arranged on the floor. Preston and Minnie were there but facing away. I was pointing at the corpse, covering my mouth, horrified.

I'd pushed Preston's bachelor party from my mind, when one evening I checked my mailbox at the Colony mansion and discovered an invitation, unstamped, hand-delivered, waiting for me. I tore into the envelope as I climbed the stairs.

You are cordially invited to a night of debauchery and excess in celebration of the eminent departure of Preston Fairmont from the domain of the unmarried into the bosom of his bride.
We shall convene in Independence Square at 11 o'clock on the night of January 28th, 1926.

> *Bring nothing but your imagination. Expect nothing but pleasure and*
> *future legendary stories.*

The invitation card was engraved on fine handmade paper. In the lower left corner of the card was a woodcut print that I recognized immediately as a never-before-seen design by Juan Hugo Balthazarr. Another abstract – stark black against the creamy paper – it hinted at the contours of a twisted limb, possibly botanical, but more suggestive of animalistic inspiration. The fleshy tip reached up like a decomposing finger from a cursed and diabolical grave; it sprouted from an ink splat. Looping tributaries leaked off the page. I felt my heartbeat catch. First from seeing an exclusive, obviously very recent, Balthazarr creation, but secondly, something unnamable in the pattern drew my fixation and stimulated a sense of compounding dread in me.

"You're not dressed yet?" Nina's voice startled me from the top stair.

I nearly toppled backward. Regaining my balance, I quickly covered the invitation with its envelope. I *was* dressed. I just wasn't dressed for tonight's affair. We were headed to the opening of the New Colony's inaugural Winter Show.

"I have time," I answered, composing myself as I mounted to the third floor.

Nina wore a sleek red dress that clung to her – a second skin, smooth and shimmery as a salamander – radiating the spirit of a creature born in, and impervious to, fire. She tilted her head while affixing a pearl earring. "You'd better hurry. What have you got there?"

"It's nothing." I attempted to pass her in the hall. But the lady was faster.

While I reached for my doorknob, she darted in a slender hand and snatched the invitation from my grip. A laugh on her face, celebrating her quickness and victory, soon dissolved. She handed the invitation back to me.

"Do be careful about Preston," she said.

"How do you mean?" Was she worried on his behalf, or that he was a threat?

"Steer away from trouble. That's all." She went back into her apartment.

I went inside mine to get dressed.

When I came outside again, Nina was there, waiting in her furs.

She assessed me up and down and smiled.

"You look smashing," she said.

"Likewise. Care to take my arm?"

She did care to.

Ours was a short walk in the chilling New England air. The gallery showing was being held in one of the New Colony buildings, down the block from the mansion. This ancient house once belonged to an Atlantic sea captain who was lost, along with his ship and crew, in a freakish storm. Fully restored, the domicile provided a viewing gallery and hosting site for parties like the one we were attending tonight. Someone had lit the path to the front entrance with rows of long black candles set in wrought iron stands. Their flames twinkled brightly in the crisp stillness.

"How pretty," Nina said.

I nodded, gazing at the Indian teak double doors as they parted to receive us. This was my first visit to the "Sea Captain's House," as it was called within the Colony. While I had passed it many times, I had never been close enough to notice the detailed carvings on the doors. Now I read symbols there which resembled the spiked crown, the falling star, and the trident fork. Was I seeing these signs everywhere I looked because they inhabited my brain? Or did they encroach upon us?

I tried inspecting them more thoroughly after we crossed the threshold. But there was a rush to shut the doors against the wintry blasts. Our greeters blocked the carvings in question with their bodies. They asked for our coats. Still, I hoped for another chance to review what I thought I saw. A waiter carrying a tray of champagne swept past. Laws that ordered the outside world seemed suspended in the Colony. Or maybe Preston paid the police to look the other way. Nina captured two flutes, passing one to me. A cluster of artists, mostly other painters I'd met since joining the Colony, pressed in, offering a chorus of warm, boozy hellos and taking us politely, though firmly, by the elbows, ushering us into the confusing warren of rooms that served as the gallery.

Francine, a miniaturist, led the group. "They've done a fabulous job," she said, showing us a path to the hors d'oeuvres. "I don't know who ordered the food but it's the tops, I tell you."

She handed me a crab pastry.

Nina picked out a skewered meatball dripping with gravy, popping it into her mouth.

"The bar's through there." Francine gestured to the next room, its wallpaper crowded with tropical fruit and exotic birds. "There's a harpist plucking away upstairs, and a man playing pan flute. It's so luxurious I might die. Oh, get me a mint julep will you, dear?" She waved to Oscar who threw enormous pots on his potter's wheel, decorating them with ferocious jungle cats and popeyed monkeys swinging by their tails. Oscar waved back. "There are people with money here tonight." Francine jerked her head toward a couple in the corner, conversing with Dexter, an experimental sculptor. He liked to glue string to objects, layering the strings, varying colors and thicknesses. I doubted they would buy anything from him. I'd gone to prep school with the male of the pair, and he was strictly a fan of realism and female nudity. However, his wife I didn't know. The room was crowded. Overcrowded. I fought off a surge of claustrophobia.

"Quite a group," I said over the noise of multiple conversations going on at once.

"Lots of money," Francine said. "Hear it? *Chang, chang…* pockets of gold."

I turned to ask Nina if she could hear the money, but she was gone from my side. When Francine paused to accept her mint julep from Oscar, I slipped out into the foyer and spotted Nina's red curves halfway up a winding staircase, leading to the house's second story. She was smoking a cigarette and talking to someone. A man. She laughed at something he said, nodding dramatically and resting her hand on his arm, which in turn leaned casually on the banister. As Nina inclined to take a sip of her cocktail, I wondered briefly how she'd gotten a drink so quickly when the bar was packed, but then I saw the man had the same drink in his hand. I realized both that he'd offered the sip to her and that he was Juan Hugo. When he saw me looking up, he motioned for me to join them.

"The man I wanted to talk to," he said. His beard looked longer than the last time I saw him. It split at the end into two dark wedges. It was hard to keep from staring.

"Why are you looking for me, Juan Hugo?"

"Because you have the most beautiful date, and I must tell you I intend to steal her."

I said nothing.

He turned to Nina, white teeth smiling. "I think he believes me."

Nina held her chin up like she was balancing a china cup on her head. Amused or embarrassed? I couldn't tell what she was feeling. She took the glass from Juan Hugo and drank.

"I never believe anything. It's the key to my happiness," I said, taken by surprise.

Nina frowned.

Juan Hugo broke into laughter. "I am joking. Not about this woman's beauty but my intentions. I want to talk to you about your paintings, Alden. I've seen them. They are hanging in a room upstairs. Can we go there now?"

"We are free," Nina said. She didn't look at me, but she held out her hand. I took it.

"Let's go," I said.

"Excellent!"

Usually the crowd followed Juan Hugo wherever he went. They hung on his words for sustenance. Engaging him in conversation elevated anyone's status in the community. To have his full attention the way we did was the envy of every artist in the Sea Captain's House. It seemed peculiar how empty the upstairs hallway was; almost as if the others had been told beforehand to stay away, to keep their distance while Juan Hugo talked with us. It was crazy to think you were the center of everyone's awareness, that you as a couple were objects of their total absorption. Why did it feel slightly sinister? Even conspiratorial?

Yet that's precisely how it felt.

Balthazarr guided us to the room.

"This must have been a bedroom, no?" He considered the chamber. The walls and floorboards were strangely blacked. Shutters sealed off our view from the only window.

But it was the paintings we had come for.

My three paintings were the only artworks on display in the room. They were large, but still they seemed to float on the otherwise barren walls. Each painting positioned alone.

Every other room was a shared exhibition space. I didn't know if I was lucky or not.

Balthazarr approached my watercolor portrait of the net blob. He folded his hands across his chest and stroked at his beard with the fingers of one hand. "Here." He pointed to the blob. "Yes, yes…" He stepped back and took me by the shoulders, positioning me directly in front of my work. "What you did here, Alden, is extraordinary. I have never seen anything like it before."

"It marked a new direction for me."

"A new direction for New Colony!" Balthazarr clapped his hands. The explosive sound hurt my ears. "What to make of this one? A train to Hades? Don't tell me a word. The painting speaks for you. Never explain your paintings, Alden. That is not your job." On the adjacent wall, hanging separately and alone, was the vision of my experience in the Black Cave. Balthazarr framed his hands around the edges of the canvas as if he were trying to squeeze the ritual images together. "I feel like I was there with you. In this Black Cave. You are painting nightmares, whether you know it or not. Dreams. The landscape beneath the conscious mind."

"How do you know about the Black Cave?" I said, trying not to sound suspicious.

His arm struck out toward the wall. His finger indicated the white card with the name of the painting typed on it. "It is titled *The Black Cave.*"

"Oh, right. So it is."

"But my favorite of your paintings is this one."

Balthazarr stepped over to the wall behind us. There was a canvas on the floor, facing away from the room, tilted against the wall. He turned it around. Then he hung it on a nail.

"What do you call this one? *Witness to A Ceremonial Beheading*?"

It was my unfinished depiction of the observatory's dome room. Clark's body lying on the floor. Preston and Minnie. My self-portrait refusing to deny the mutilated corpse.

"How did this get here? It's not supposed to be in the exhibition. It's unfinished."

"The incomplete condition is unimportant. It is finished, Alden."

"No, I abandoned it."

"It is a work of genius. If I were you, I would not change a thing."

Nina hadn't said a word.

"What do you think?" I asked her.

"We should listen to Balthazarr." Her voice had a flatness, as if she were hypnotized.

"There! You see!" He grabbed the back of my neck with his pincer hand. "I want to say it is my privilege to be in the Colony with you. To belong to this commune with *you*." He kissed my cheek with effusive affection. "What an exciting time to be alive and in Arkham!"

Chapter Twenty-Two

After Balthazarr left us alone to rejoin the party, Nina and I stayed there in the room. Outside, we heard the gathering regain its former volume, as if they'd hushed up to eavesdrop on our meeting with the Spaniard.

"He called you a genius, Alden." She held tight to both my hands.

"I know." I squeezed her and looked again at my paintings, one by one. "What do you think it means?"

"I think it means you're a genius, silly boy." She kicked the door closed and switched off the light. Did she feel, as I did, that my paintings were somehow watching us?

Nina and I kissed for a long time in that dark room. We couldn't see each other, but we could feel. Weirdly, I started imagining these amoeboid lifeforms crawling in the black air around us. Some trick of the eyes caused by the absence of light, no doubt. Like gigantic pseudopodal protozoans trapped under a microscope, the magnified apparitions constantly reshaped themselves. Slither and flow. Had I had not been otherwise preoccupied, I might've watched in fascination. As it was, my observations came from the periphery of my vision. The mirages shone iridescently as drops of oil in water do. There was a chance that at any moment someone might walk in and catch us. Short of breath, we paused for a laugh at the absurdity, the headiness and unreality of it all.

"Things are changing for you," Nina whispered.

"You're the cause of it. Surely you can tell that."

She nuzzled my neck, her warm breath tickling me, sending shivers.

"I don't mean that. I'm talking about your career. Things *there* are changing."

"Yes, that too." I stroked her back. "They really are. Aren't they?"

She laced her fingers in my hair and pulled me in for a last kiss.

"We'd better join the party before they find us," she whispered.

"Reluctantly… I must agree." I switched the light back on.

We repaired our states of dishevelment. At first, I detected what seemed to be a chorus of chanting emanating from down below us. Chanting! But it was only the end of some sea shanty type of song the attendees were finishing. An alien and unfamiliar tune, which the harpist and pan flutist both seemed to know, for they played in support of the voices. We'd worried about a romantic interruption for no good reason, apparently. The hallway stood vacant, eerily so. We felt a bit like a pair of children sneaking down to see what their parents are up to at the grownups' party. In any case, that was how I felt. How was it we hadn't been missed?

I followed Nina downstairs into the only room large enough to hold all of the visitors. It must have been a dining room in bygone days; long and rectangular, with accesses from both ends, and a chandelier hung in the center where a table might've been. Despite the size, the crowd had packed themselves in. It was a ridiculous sight, like a game almost. See how many we can fit in here. The light fixture above looked like a dead spider flipped on its back, trapped in a chain web of its own fashioning. Beneath the spider stood Balthazarr beside a circular stand, atop which rested an odd golden bowl. He had a little space cleared out around him, but he was the only one. I almost turned back.

"You are here right on time, my friends." Balthazarr beckoned us closer to the action.

We proceeded to the front of the crowd.

In the center of the odd bowl, a thin spike protruded; it looked alarmingly sharp.

"What is this old relic?" I was amused by the ornately embossed basin, its outer shell decorated with rows of concentric circles aligned and alternating bands of hammered nubs.

"Alden, you jest. But do you know you are correct. It is a relic."

"Where's it from?" Nina said. She traced her finger along the rim of the bowl.

"I brought it with me from Spain. But it is much older than Spain herself. Are you aware that people have lived on the Iberian Peninsula for thirty-five thousand years? Before the Romans, Phoenicians and Celts lived there. Is this Celtic?" He shook his head. "I don't think so. More likely Phoenician. Its origin is mysterious. Suffice it to say, it is ancient."

"What's it used for?" I said.

One of the attendees chuckled behind us.

"It's a tub for taking bloodbaths," the man said, sounding intoxicated.

A woman shushed him. Balthazarr's stare grew hostile at the interruption. Two men slid quietly across the room and removed the drunken man.

"Hey, whaadid I do? I wanna watch. Aw, c'mon guys. Don't be sore. I'll be good from now on and keep my trap shut. Lemme go back. *Pleeease...*" But he did not gain reentry.

Balthazarr pointed to the hole in the crowd where the man had been. "In a way he was right. Though the gin has given him a flair for the overdramatic."

The crowd laughed.

"It does involve blood," Balthazarr said.

"Whose blood?" I asked.

"All of ours! We are going to swear an oath of artistic dedication. Of brotherhood and sisterhood. We are proclaiming ourselves New Colonists. To mark our bond with one another, we are going to give a symbolic offering of our physical selves. A drop of blood. No more. I don't want anyone fainting."

I felt unsure and glanced at Nina, but she was transfixed by the bowl.

The crowd laughed again. A nervous tension was building in the atmosphere, like a coming lightning strike. The crackling of electrically charged fields.

"You want us to cut ourselves, so we bleed?" Nina said. She didn't sound afraid.

"No, no, no. Not a cut. A simple quick tap on the end of this nail. Use your pinkie finger if you like. You won't even feel it, I assure you. The nail is so sharp. Then a drop in the bowl. A token act to represent our vital connection, our collective lifeblood, if you will. You'll be surprised how good you will feel once we have all taken our turns."

"Shall I go first?" Nina said.

"Please, yes. Unless you prefer that Alden takes his turn before you."

I said, "Maybe one of the people who came down earlier should do it." I was no fan of bloodletting. The bowl seemed unclean, though I couldn't pinpoint why.

Balthazarr stiffened his back. "I am offering it to you out of respect, Alden. Artist to artist. It is my bowl, and I want you to be the first. Think of it as a game we are playing. We will all have our chances. Please, don't insult me."

"I'll go first," Nina said. "I'm not afraid of a little blood." She pushed up her sleeve.

Balthazarr spread out his arms. He looked like a statue standing there.

"Your hand… I will guide you."

Nina stretched out her arm. I wanted to stop her. But I didn't. She'd be mad at me. It was only a little prick on the finger. Hell, I was pushing up my cuff and thinking about what it would be like when I went next. That might sound cowardly. But I felt very brave.

Balthazarr seized Nina's wrist and pulled her over the bowl. In a swift motion, he pressed her hand down and the end of her middle finger touched the ancient golden needle.

"Ow." She winced. "You promised it wouldn't hurt." Nina stuck her finger in her mouth and sucked the tip.

"See? I'll bet it's already stopped bleeding, hasn't it?"

Nina inspected her fingertip. "No. It's still bleeding."

Balthazarr was reaching for me. "Alden, it's your turn."

I hesitated. But I couldn't back out after my girlfriend went, could I?

Balthazarr took hold of my wrist. His fingers were like a shackle pinching too tight. I knew that I couldn't pull away from him if I wanted.

"I'd prefer to do it myself. If that's permitted."

He smiled. "By all means."

I tried not to stare too hard at the pointy thing. It looked worse the longer you stared. But you had to keep it in your sight, or you might end up impaling your hand! So, what I did is, I went sort of soft-focus. In the blurry haze, I reached for the spike. I tapped my finger down like I was checking for wet paint. The blood bubbled out, a swollen red berry. And I squeezed my finger with my other hand. The drop made a soft ping when it hit the bowl. I must've squeezed too hard because I heard a couple more pings. I put my finger in my mouth and tasted salt and copper.

After that, the line went faster. There was champagne making its way around the room on new trays. The waiters must've been hanging around until the made-up ritual ended. That's what it was really, a ritual. And like I had in Spain, I felt I'd witnessed something forbidden.

More than witnessed this time. I'd acted a part in it.

The blood offering wasn't the end, though.

Balthazarr had something more to give than blood. He offered his drops last. Last man standing, I thought. Because I felt kind of drunk even though I'd only had that one flute of champagne and now here was my second that I hadn't even sipped yet. But word went out that we were supposed to wait to drink this glass. Balthazarr was going to make a toast. Everyone who was a member of the Colony, and a few rich people who'd come to buy art (they gave their blood offerings too) paused. Balthazarr was like a conductor. We were the orchestra. The members of the orchestra looked a bit glassy-eyed, like I felt. I saw a spirit of sleazy debauchery traveling around the dining room like a secret. Mixed in with the alcoholic lushness was a glaze of lechery and a languid slothfulness, an overripe sense of gluttony and satiation. We were like a den of fat vipers, our bellies full of a fresh kill and our mouths dripping venom, slits for our eyes.

"Attention!" Balthazarr called out.

He tapped a spoon against the side of his crystal flute.

To my ears it sounded like a gong. So loud and piercing.

The vipers met his gaze.

Nina was at my side. The two of us slumped against the wall. Her hot fingers were playing with mine. I felt a desire to look at her, to do more than that. First, I had to hear Juan Hugo make his toast or whatever it was happening in the center of the crowded house party.

"Each of you has made a blood sacrifice to New Colony. This cannot be changed. We are linked, brother to brother, sister to sister, brother to sister, sister to brother. A commune with a single cause. To change the world."

"Hear! Hear!" voices agreed.

I mumbled along. But my lips felt fat. I touched my face. Hot and numb.

Balthazarr lifted his champagne. "New Colony!"

"New Colony! New Colony!" people began to chant.

"Success to our ventures! Merciless vengeance to our enemies! Power is ours alone!"

The crowd cheered.

I thought I hadn't heard the outlandish Surrealist correctly. Had he said, *"Merciless vengeance to our enemies!"* and *"Power is ours alone!"*?

The moment passed. My legs were weak. I braced my back against the wall.

Balthazarr said, "Drink, Colonists. Drink!"

We all did. Maybe it was the heat, the room being too close. My head was swimming. I thought drinking something might help. The champagne must have come from different bottles than the first round. It tasted metallic, a tad briny. The bubbles were slack, and the temperature grew so it was like standing in front of a furnace. I made a sick face.

Balthazarr smashed his glass flute on the floor.

We copied him.

My movements were automatic. As if my body mimicked what it saw.

Shards flying. Broken glass crackling under our best shoes. The harpist and the pan flute player began a peculiar melody. Dissonant and sour; their instruments had fallen grossly out of tune. But no one seemed to care. I felt both exhausted and frantically awake.

Balthazarr, after throwing down his empty glass, had not moved. Now he picked up the golden bowl from the stand and he raised it over his head. His deep voice rang out.

"Ebuma chtenff! Gnaiih goka gotha gof'nn! Fm'latgh grah'n ftaghu grah'n!"

He lowered the bowl, tipping it into his open mouth, and swallowed our blood.

The music grew louder and louder. Flutes and harps and unseen gongs.

I gasped for more air.

As the house and all its occupants fell into a dizzying and impenetrable darkness.

Chapter Twenty-Three

I awoke to the sunshine blazing through a window. The curtains were open. Nina lay by my side, curled away from me, the blankets pulled up to her ears. My head ached dully. I sat on the edge of the bed. This was Nina's apartment. At some point during last night's delirium I had shed my tuxedo; like flotsam from a shipwreck, items snagged on the rocky coast of Nina boudoir. Nina's red dress was also there, hanging over the back of a chair, a shed skin. Also, I had apparently collected Thorn from my place. He perked up his ears, but left his narrow face resting on his paws; his lithe form stretched on a Persian rug at the foot of the bed, tail wagging to greet me.

I stumbled like a sailor to the bathroom and drank for a long time from the sink tap. Thorn appeared in the doorway, looking concerned. The room shifted at sea under my feet.

"I'll live," I told him.

He answered with a small whimper. He wanted to go outside. What time was it?

Nina had no clocks. How could anyone function with no clocks?

I washed my face but tried not to view my reflection. I feared I looked as bad as I felt.

When I came back out, Nina hadn't moved. I gathered my clothes and dug for my pocket watch. A quarter to twelve. Poor Thorn had been holding it a while. The thought of putting my tuxedo back on repelled me. It smelled of sweat, wine, smoke, and musky incense. Had we burned incense at the gallery house? I couldn't remember doing that. But I couldn't remember much of anything after Balthazarr's bloody rite. Certainly not coming home. Or the end of the party, for all that it mattered. I felt as though I'd been drugged, or the way I did as a child emerging from a case of the measles. Drained, depleted. Luckily, I kept some clothes in Nina's closet. I found pants, a flannel shirt. I retrieved my cigarette case and shut the curtains before slipping out. Nina snored, a soft burring sound. The gray room put me in mind of a zoo.

Thorn's leash was on the counter. Nothing appeared disordered in the apartment. It was in strange contrast to my state of mind, which felt uncannily dislodged, and vaguely guilty of something, though of what I couldn't say. Here were our shoes and an empty bottle on the floor.

I took the dog out to do his business. I dropped the bottle in the trash.

Fortunately, the weather had warmed. A sulfurous fog loomed over the water. Dampness clung to me like pond slime. I lit a smoke and squinted at the sun, glaring diamond-sharp in the sky. Thorn snuffled at the ground. I unhooked his leash, and he appreciated the freedom, trotting around the apartment house's backyard toward the riverbank but never straying out of my sight. God, my head hurt.

"Alden, hey Alden," a voice said to me from the fence at the far end of the yard.

I turned, seeing no one.

"Alden, over here." The fence on that side of the property was made of tall pickets. The slot between two of the pickets was darker than the others. It was a person standing on the other side, blocking out the light. I saw them pressing their face tight against the boards.

An eye blinked.

"Calvin, is that you?" I started to walk over to the fence.

"Stay there."

"Why? Where have you been? We've waited for you. You've taken your damned time showing up."

"What did you do last night?"

"What?"

"You heard me. What did you do last night, Alden? At the Sea Captain's?"

I took another step.

"Don't come any closer, or I'll go." The eye blinked again. It was bloodshot, red.

"We went to a gallery party. Things might've gotten a bit out of hand. I can't remember." The gong ringing. Pan flutes, vibrating harps. Balthazarr's arms outstretched.

The flash of teeth. A smile filled the gap. The husky rasp of a man laughing.

"A bloodletting. Yes? You gave them your blood to taste?"

"Calvin, come around and let me see you. Nina and I, we want to talk to you."

"Talk, talk. No! No more talk. You must kill her, Alden. Before she kills you."

Why did he sound so stilted and strange?

I threw my cigarette away. I glanced around for Thorn but couldn't spy him anywhere. "I don't know what you're going on about. Is this a joke? Now, you've helped us, so I'm giving you the benefit of the doubt here. But if you say anything like you just did again, I don't know what I'll do to you." I marched up to the fence.

The eye stared. It backed away. A metallic flash glittered in the air above our heads. He threw something over the fence to me. It twirled, landed at my feet. A knife. Nothing fancy, the kind of blade they used to gut fish at the docks.

"You go on and kill her, Alden. She's not real."

"Why are you saying this?" I picked up the knife. The handle felt dirty. My head hurt. I saw the figure behind the fence shift. A shrug? He'd be lucky if I didn't cut him first.

"No reason," he said. The dry husky laugh again. "I'm telling her the same thing."

There was a sound like flags flapping in the wind, like big yellow flames in a bonfire.

The gargoyle exploded into the air. He flew straight up to the roof and perched there.

He swiveled his head, looking at me, and then, hanging upside-down from the roof's edge, he tried to see in the window of Nina's bedroom. "Bastard, you closed the curtains." I was too stunned to speak. My feet rooted to the grass.

Letting go of the roof, he spun and pumped his skin wings, swooping down. I ducked.

The gargoyle laughed, slicing into the fog over the river.

The fog boiled behind him.

Thorn barked from the river's edge. The thing that was not Calvin had disappeared. I looked up at Nina's window. Was he there too, like he'd said? Impossible. *"I'm telling her the same thing."*

I called my dog and raced back inside the mansion.

Skipping stairs and shouting, "Nina! Nina!"

I threw open the door and ran to the bedroom. The sheets were a tangled mess. She wasn't there. My God, I thought. They've taken her! Thorn dashed past me and into the bathroom. He bumped the door open with his nose and slipped in. A single sharp bark.

"Thorn! Privacy please, you sly old dog."

It was Nina's voice, muffled but unmistakable. My heart leaped in my chest.

I crossed the room in two strides and pushed past the door.

"It's a party now," she said. "Shut the door. I feel a draft." Nina lay up to her chin in steaming hot water. She'd filled the clawfoot tub as high as it would go without overflowing. She'd slicked back her wet hair, and her cigarette holder was clamped between her teeth. There was an ashtray on the floor beside the tub and a snifter of what looked like cognac.

Thorn rested his head on the rim of the tub.

"Don't even think of joining me, Thorn." Nina petted his snout with her drippy hand. "Darling, do tell me that's not a knife you're brandishing." She looked at me with mild concern.

I stared at the weapon the gargoyle had tossed over the fence. I was gripping it so tightly my fingers were changing colors. I put it on the sink. The rust-speckled steel, its edge shining like wet silver paint. I ushered Thorn from the room and closed the door.

"Did anyone visit you?" I asked.

"Besides Thorny?"

"I'm not joking. Has someone been up here talking to you?"

"Quiet down. You're killing my head. Of course no one's been up here. What's gotten into you?" She closed her eyes, reclining against the back of the tub. A damp hand removed the cigarette holder; she tapped ashes toward the ashtray on the floor. "Hand me my brandy, would you? Don't judge. Hair of the dog, as they say."

I stepped nearer to the bathtub, starting to bend over for the glass, when I paused.

"Do you have a knife?"

"Alden, you just put one on the sink. What do you need a knife for?" She yawned. One of her hands dangled over the tub, a foot above her glass, but the other remained hidden under the murky, milky jade water. I smelled sweet pine bath salts. The bathroom tropical with steam. Wisps floated in the air, mixing with her cigarette smoke. I was sweating.

The gargoyle's words echoed in my brain. *"I'm telling her the same thing."*

Had the demon given her a knife? Did he suggest she murder *me* because I wasn't real? How did he know about last night? And about Balthazarr's blood ritual?

I inched forward, attempting to see through the bathwater. It was impossible.

Nina's eyes remained closed. She clenched the cigarette holder between her lips.

"Quite a party," she said, smirking. "You certainly enjoyed yourself."

"Yes ... I'm having trouble recalling how things ended."

"What a pity. You were having the time of your life." She let out a low growl from the back of her throat. "My finger still hurts. Will you kiss it for me?" She extended her middle finger, the one she'd pricked on the nail over the blood bowl. "Pretty please?"

I moved closer, never taking my eyes off the surface of the jade-colored water. "My memories grow fuzzy after Balthazarr's rite."

"Really? You seemed fine. You were talking to everyone. Balthazarr's enthusiasm over your paintings boosted your confidence to new heights. He's quite the character, isn't he?"

"What was your impression of the great Surrealist?"

I leaned against the tub at an angle slightly behind her. If she were going to stab me with a knife secreted in the water, she'd have to twist around to do it. I thought I might be able to back away and defend myself with the ashtray, if need be. Not hurt her but deflect the attack. Would she obey the gargoyle? I hadn't. I wasn't sure of anything. Not even Nina.

"Ummm. He's handsome and *very* charismatic. It's all part of his act, I should imagine. I've noticed him buzzing around the Colony but never met him properly." She shifted in the tub. Her pink skin squeaked against the porcelain-coated cast iron. I startled, but she didn't notice. Her eyes were heavily lidded. "Though come to think of it, I actually might have seen him before. Much earlier…"

"You saw Balthazarr before last night's party? Really? Where?"

"He was with Court, I think. Maybe coming out of his apartment? Or when I visited South Church. All I remember is a tall man with a black beard split at the bottom. *He's striking,* I thought. It might've been the day when you and I first met. Isn't *that* funny to think about?"

How could that be? Unless Balthazarr somehow projected himself across the ocean. Or he was lying about his arrival in the country. Or both. I crouched behind the tub, watching.

"What are you doing back there?" She lifted her head and sat up, craning to look at me over her naked shoulder. "Have you gone batty? Did the champagne do it?"

"That second round did taste strange," I said. "A chemical aftertaste, chalkiness."

"I'm kidding. *God.* Hand me the cognac, will you?"

"Let me see your hands first. Both hands." I stood, my back to the tile wall.

My request amused her, despite her current post-celebratory suffering. She took her hands out of the water. They were steaming, as if she'd crawled fresh from a hell mouth. She flipped her cigarette into the ashtray on the floor. She maneuvered around, so now she was half-kneeling, half curling on her haunches in the bathtub. It was a good position to spring at me. A wave sloshed over the side and doused her cigarette. She smelled like the pine woods. A forest creature I'd encountered in a fable. A wood nymph to enchant me. Her body was gleaming. I could count the nubs of her spine down to the waterline.

"Here are my hands," she said. "Now what should I do?"

"Is anything hidden under the water?"

"Practically everything." Her long arm reached for the cognac. She gulped it down.

"I'm not playing games here."

"You *are,* you silly boy. But I like this game. Keep going."

"There was something in my champagne. That's why I can't remember anything."

"You think I slipped you a mickey?" She pantomimed dropping something in her glass. Acting on the assumption that I was being playful. None of this was to be taken seriously.

Lovers' games.

That's what we were doing. Or she was pretending to think so.

I wouldn't have objected, except I'd met a monster outside at this very hour, in broad daylight, and he'd told me to kill my lover. I was dizzy. My head hurt where the night watchman had bashed me. The fog on the river that swallowed the gargoyle – I felt like I had some of it trapped inside my skull, like smoke blown inside a bottle and corked. Hazy, I was hazy.

"What happened after the lights went out? You remember, don't you?" I said.

She nodded. "Balthazarr must've had someone switch the power off to the house. It was a performance. Surely you realize that." I could see her playfulness ebbing. She wondered if I was serious. "He tried out a bit of hocus pocus. For mood. To bring the Colony closer together. No different than fraternity initiations. Secret handshakes. Clubby foolishness."

Nina pulsed her fingers at me like the fronds of a sea anemone. Trying to recapture the mischievous mood she'd felt before. She refused to acknowledge anything real had happened last night. I wished I could believe that too. But I couldn't. Everything can't be imaginary.

"My tuxedo stinks from incense. Tell me it doesn't. When did they burn incense?"

"I will not sniff your tuxedo. C'mon, my Oak Tree. Let's take a bath and get clean." She shifted and another wave slopped noisily over the tub.

I jumped back, snatching the knife from the sink.

"Stay away!" I shouted.

Her jaw fell open. Her anger arrived in a rush. "Don't you pull a knife on me! Are you crazy? Look at yourself!" She pointed to the mirror.

I turned to witness my frightened face. Eyes bulging. Me, in the fogged-over lookingglass, clutching a brutal blade. In horror, I threw the knife away.

"What am I doing?" My lungs were heaving, my throat constricted as I struggled for a breath. "Why can't I remember anything after Balthazarr drank the blood? It's a void in my mind."

Nina rose from the bathtub. No weapon. She reached for a towel and wrapped it around her torso.

She put her arms around my chest. "Poor baby, you *are* scared. Of me?" She laughed, astonished at that. "Easy now, easy..."

"I love you, Nina."

"I love you too." She hugged me.

I shivered in the overheated bathroom.

"Maybe you've come down with something." She put her lips to my forehead. "You're burning."

We walked into the bedroom.

I lay on the bed, my head in Nina's lap. "Tell me what you remember of last night. After Balthazarr drank the bowl of blood."

"Someone turned the lights out. It was only for effect. Like a magic show. We all knew it wasn't real. A minute or two later, the lights switched on again. People clapped. Balthazarr took a bow. He'd done some trick with the floor, too.

I don't know, it was like charcoal outlines of his shoes. They'd been burned into the wood. If he was hoping people would be shocked at that, it didn't work. They hardly paid any attention. You noticed them. The burn marks, or whatever he'd done to fake them. You said you saw him do the same thing in Spain."

I had seen them in Spain. But last night was still lost. "Did he say anything to me?"

"He called you a clever man." Nina combed her fingers through my hair.

"I think I was drugged. I didn't drink enough booze to knock me out."

Nina considered what I had said. "You were drinking quite a lot after the second round of champagne. But I suppose you might've been given something against your will. There are cacti that grow in Mexico, and vines from the Amazon in Peru, that cause hallucinations. Or opium might do it. It's possible…"

"When I went to take Thorn out this morning, I saw the gargoyle. He was behind a fence in the yard. And he gave me that knife. He told me to kill you." I made a fist. I was trembling with rage. "That you weren't real. He said he told you the same thing. To kill me…"

"You saw the gargoyle again?" She was shocked. "I'd almost convinced myself that never happened. That we dreamed it. No one told me to do anything, Alden."

We stayed in bed, silent. I wasn't asleep. When I turned my face to look at Nina, she was awake too, smiling down at me like the statue of a goddess. Serene, yet powerful.

"Did you see Balthazarr before last night? Are you sure of it?"

She shook her head. "No, not sure. But you saying you felt like you were drugged has me thinking. I wonder if they all were. The Galinka sisters. Udo Ganz. Dr Silva. That drifter in the boxcar with his throat cut, and even Clark Abernathy. If the killer, or killers, drugged them first, then it might've been easier to manipulate them like they did. I wonder if someone was trying some drug out on you. To see what would happen."

"A test?"

"Yes. A test. Or a preparation. I didn't tell you before. But I found out new facts about the murder victims. They all came from wealthy, aristocratic families. Oh, they didn't necessarily have mountains of cash now. For some it was in their lineage. The Galinka sisters were the granddaughters of a Russian princess. Dr Silva's family is one of the wealthiest in Rio de Janeiro. Udo Ganz's father owns an emerald mine in South Africa. The drifter was the one who didn't fit the pattern. That's because the police didn't know who he was. Well, his relatives showed up at the county morgue last week to claim his body. They're royal blood from Luxembourg, of all places. Clark's family is new American money. Rich people like us, Alden. We're the ones getting murdered."

Chapter Twenty-Four

The next day Nina decided we needed a car. My father owned three Rolls-Royce automobiles. His favorite was a Silver Ghost, the only car he ever drove himself. Asking him for it was laughably out of the question. He also had a Phantom, reserved for special trips, and a smaller Twenty that Roland used to chauffer Mother around to appointments.

I paid my father an early morning visit. It was best to catch him at the end of his breakfast. His mood slid downhill as the day progressed, from irritation to aggravation.

"May I borrow the Twenty?" I asked.

My father's eyebrows lifted. A dramatic display for him. "What for?"

"I have a new girlfriend. I'd like to show her around town."

The corner of his mouth twitched. This was a smile.

"Mother said she won't be needing Roland to take her anywhere."

Father sat at his enormous desk, tapping his fingers on the mahogany. Deciding.

"It had better come back the way it leaves," he said, finally.

"Thank you."

Father put on his spectacles and rustled his newspaper.

I was dismissed.

Nina practically ran to the curb. A handful of curious bystanders gathered outside the Colony to gawk when I pulled up. I got out to meet her on the sidewalk. Nina bypassed me, walked around to the driver's side, climbing behind the wheel. She patted the other seat. "Get in."

"I cannot allow you to drive Wilfred's car."

"He'll never know. Will he?" She dared me to deny her.

"Fine." I got in. "Let's not have a wreck. If we do, make sure I die."

Nina drove fast. The roads were slick from a recent dusting of snow. I felt the Twenty lose traction a few times, but Nina always corrected the car. She had no patience, I was learning. Rush into everything. Catch up on the details as you go.

Don't talk yourself out of risk. Find the limits, race up to the line, see if you might be able to push things out a little farther, or in deeper.

I won't lie and tell you she didn't excite me.

Life since Nina had more color. Bigger ups and downs. It was a thrill ride, to be sure.

Speaking of thrills, I reached into my pocket and removed an item wrapped in a rag.

I opened the cloth.

A gun.

Nina glanced down at it. Then looked back at the road. The car accelerated.

After the gargoyle's second appearance, Nina managed to wear me down about visiting the Black Cave to search for more clues. Not hearing from Calvin sealed the deal. I insisted we didn't have enough protection to go near the bootleggers' camp by ourselves. Nina disagreed but didn't argue. One night, she went out for a walk while I was asleep and came home with a pistol. She'd bought it at the Clover Club. "It's a Colt 1903 Pocket Hammerless. Compact. Holds seven rounds." She was quite proud of herself for having procured it.

"Are you serious?" I asked, sitting up in bed. I'd awakened at the sound of the door.

"You said we needed protection. Here it is."

"Who sold it to you?"

"What difference does it make?" She aimed the semiautomatic around the apartment.

The next day we took turns drawing the weapon, blowing bottles off stumps, in a vacant lot along the river. We were no marksmen, but in a jam, we might get off a few shots.

Now, riding beside Nina, I rechecked the magazine. Tucked the gun into my waistband. In case we ran into trouble. Which we certainly would.

Now that we were mobile, we didn't have to worry about walking everywhere in the freezing January cold. After a bit of poking around on lanes that dead-ended at the river, we found the one that led to the bootleggers' camp. Better to let them see us coming from a ways off with the sun in the sky, I thought. We didn't need them feeling any jumpier than they were going to be already. Pine branches hid the entrance to the camp road. We passed it a few times before I noticed the long gap running back into the trees. Nina pulled over, and I dragged the branches out of the way. Once she drove in, I arranged them back the way they were. Farther up the old dirt road, we encountered a heavy log crossing our path. No way to drive over it. But together we managed to roll the log off the lane. Momentum carried it out of our hands and into the ditch. We drove on. The Miskatonic flashed through the bare trees to our left. I hadn't spotted any lookouts watching the road for trespassers. I almost wished I had. Then they might've turned us back around and sent us home.

"We're getting close," I said.

The Twenty rocked and skittered up and down the hills.

"I'll talk first," Nina said. "They'll be less suspicious of a woman."

"Don't bet on it. How do you explain us driving on their road?"

"We're from out of town. Honeymooners. We got lost."

"After we removed their camouflage and barriers?"

"They'll believe me. I can be terribly convincing." Her cheeks turned rosy in the cold.

"Remember, when we get there, we can ask about Calvin. If we don't see him, we try to find Freddie or Winston. But don't get out of the car. Any sign of danger, we leave," I said.

"Life is danger, Alden."

"I prefer mine moderated."

We reached the camp.

She hit the brakes.

Squirrels. Cardinals in the pine branches, flashing like torn red flags. Junk on the ground. Cigarette butts. Broken bottles. Empty cans of beans. Footprints chewed up the snow. Truck tire marks slashed the ground, as if a giant had been digging with his fingers, but none of the tracks were recent. They had ice in them. Quiet as a saint's confessional box, it was. Nobody home.

"Where did they go?" I said.

Nina opened her door.

I grabbed her arm. "We're not getting out. Remember?"

"That was if they were here. The bootleggers have cleared out, obviously." She pulled away from me. Her shoes made glassy, crackling noises on the crusty snow. I hadn't opened my door.

"Then why get out at all? Calvin's not here." The sight of the camp made my head start to ache. Perhaps it was psychosomatic, a physical recollection of my head injury and treatment. My temples throbbed.

She turned. The wind was picking up, snatching at her words. Her hand held her hat down, keeping it from blowing away. "I want to look for clues. If nobody's here, we can explore the cave." She walked on before I could object.

I bit my lip. "This is a mistake," I whispered. My fingers rested on the gun grip.

I climbed out and followed her.

Honestly, I was curious. Visions of the scene I witnessed in the Black Cave still showed up in my dreams most nights along with the night watchman's swinging bat. My ride in the Burdon's ice truck with the mackerel. It was all there in my head. Nothing burned as brightly as my memory of the green lights in the cave. Hooded figures finger-painting on bumpy cave walls, their buzzy voices chanting as they carried me up the steps.

"Wait for me," I shouted.

Nina paused inside the cave mouth, as if she were about to be swallowed.

"You have your lighter? Fire up my torch. I found one leaning against the wall. I want to go investigate back there." She pointed to the depths of the cave, past the places where I'd seen the barrels and crates stacked for deliveries. They were gone. You could see their impressions in the sandy soil. I lit her torch, and she held it over our heads. The copper pot stills were pushed farther inside than they had been. Maybe they were too heavy to bother moving.

"They left in a hurry. Didn't take all their equipment," I said.

The torch reflected in the copper.

"Nobody with a half a brain is going to sneak in here and mess with their stuff."

"What does that say about us?"

"We're only taking a look around," she said.

I tried to take the torch from her.

"Let me have the torch. You've got the gun," she said.

"We must stay together," I insisted. "I don't want either of us getting lost."

"Of course, darling. We're a team." She kissed my cheek.

Side by side we searched the underground hollow. Just as I recalled, the cave turned to the left and the floor angled downward, like a ramp. It was clear that previous explorers had removed several small and medium-sized rocks from the pathway, stacking them on either side of the passage. At the bottom of the ramp-like descent we reached a level surface, and soon discovered a large fragment which had broken from the ceiling in a collapse. It blocked our progress. This chunk of geologic debris resembled a toy top, or cone; its point smashed into the floor, eons ago. Nina's torchlight revealed a blank circle on the ceiling where the fragment had once hung. We had no choice but to climb over the obstacle. With a little extra effort, we overcame the impediment. What bothered me was that I had no memory of encountering this obstruction on my first trip down.

"You said there were steps." Nina probed the darkness ahead. "How far ahead?"

"Just a bit," I said. But I could've sworn we should have reached them already.

We continued to hunt for the stairway. The cave walls narrowed, not to the degree they inspired any claustrophobia or fear of entombment. However, like the top-shaped obstacle, I didn't recall this constriction of the passageway. No wider than a doorway, the walls had pressed in around us. The flow of air lessened, or perhaps I was breathing heavier.

"Why didn't you tell me it got this tight? Does it open again by the steps?"

"The steps are wide across." Had we somehow turned the wrong way? All of this appeared unfamiliar to me. Perhaps my damaged brain had ignored or erased this interval.

I didn't know.

"I see something," Nina said.

"The steps?" I felt a momentary rush of relief. I'd simply forgotten this tunnel portion.

"No. Not steps."

Thankfully, the stone corridor did open wider. The walls disappeared completely, and we entered an enormous cathedral-like space, with high, ribbed ceilings of wavy colored rock; dark blues and purples streaked upward in serpentine ribbons, like the bottoms of many velvet drapes. Others took on more fleshy colors, reminding me of clam gills or the undersides of mushrooms.

"This isn't the way I came before."

"But there was no place to turn. We walked the only way we could go." Nina stuck the torch out in front of her. Fiery flashes answered her movement in the dark ahead.

"What's that?" I whispered. "There's somebody out there." I drew the Colt. If anyone rushed at us, I planned to shoot them. I heard a moist glugging.

Nina raised her torch again.

The flashes multiplied in reply.

"How many are there?" she said, astonished.

"It might be that group I met. The hooded ones who carried me back to the cave mouth."

Nina raised and lowered her flame, quickly. She repeated the action. Then did it once more, but slowly. "I think I know what's happening." She took several long strides forward.

"Where are you going?" I bolted after her.

She stopped abruptly and threw her arm out to block me from going any farther.

"Careful," she said, lowering her torch. "We don't know how deep it is."

A huge glassy pool of obsidian water stretched before us as far as we could see. The lights were reflections of Nina's torch, mirrored on the rippling surface. Water? I had no memory of this! "What's making those wrinkles… those undulations in the pool? Is it fish?"

"What else could it be?" Nina crouched, splashing her fingertips in the shallows.

"Don't do that." I didn't want us attracting anything closer. I felt suddenly like prey.

"Why not? I thought you wanted to see if they're fish." She splashed some more.

"Don't." I touched her shoulder. The ripples moved rhythmically, making bigger wavelets. Muscular waves churned farther out; the source skulked beyond the limits of our light.

"Is it a big fish? Or an animal that lives down here?" she asked.

"I can't see anything. Stop it. We have to turn back."

Nina withdrew her fingers from the black water and stood up. She put one finger to the tip of her tongue. "Saltwater. It must be connected to the river and the ocean beyond."

Something thick and weighty wallowed below the surface. A pale bulge of belly, or was it dorsal? The bloated body rotated under the water, twirling a few feet from us. We backed up.

From the unseeable borders of the pool came a loud slapping and the dull thud of – well, of I don't know what… some creature cavorting in the underground reservoir. The merriment of it nauseated me. How can I explain other than to relate that I experienced an instant and powerful physical revulsion when I perceived the sound and its vile echo inhabiting the ancient chamber?

"We have to go," I said, urgently. I had the horrible sense of time running out.

She felt it too, because she did not hesitate to retreat from the lake's perimeter. When we had gone twenty yards, or it might've been more, we turned our backs to the pool and made a quick evacuation from the Black Cave. The narrow portion of the passage seemed narrower. Behind us, at a distance not terribly close, but not as far as would have made us comfortable, a wet smacking of meatiness on rock – I won't say stalked, but trailed us.

Nina scrambled over the cone-shaped fragment that resembled a toy top.

I stared into the dark. If the cause of the wet smacking suddenly appeared, I would kill it.

But nothing emerged.

I pocketed the gun and went over the top too.

At the base of the cave ramp, we allowed ourselves to experience a sense of reprieve from the strange perception of threat emanating from that dismal, sea-connected, jet-black lake. I clutched Nina's cool, sweaty hand. The air seemed less thick, breathing easier.

Too soon we felt safe.

For we had not taken more than three steps up the ramp when we discovered the corpse. How we didn't smell it beforehand defies easy explanation, since the body showed clear signs of advanced decomposition. A leaky, leathery, human bag wrapped in a shawl of struggling maggots. It exuded a green, black, and brown rainbow of liquids – a slow, rancid waterfall of putrefaction oozing down the slope. Whatever we had been spared of the odor now advanced upon us ferociously.

I retched.

Nina buried her mouth in her sleeve, gagging.

I have left for last the most shocking fact: the corpse had no head.

I bent over the remains, feeling fascinated and disgusted. But, ultimately, my curiosity won the day. I searched the cave in vain for a stick to prod the body. Instead, I was forced to use the tip of my shoe to nudge the cadaver's lower leg. "Hand me the torch, please."

"What for?" Nina asked, her voice dampened by the crook of her elbow.

"Please give it to me. I want to see something."

She passed me the flame. And for the second time in recent months, I employed firelight to identify Clark Abernathy's scarred knee. It was a positive match.

"This is Clark Abernathy's body," I said, confirming what I suspected.

I returned Nina's flame.

"How do you know?"

"He has a long scar on his leg. See the mark? I spotted the same cicatrix on the body in the observatory. Before it was hustled away. I knew it! I am not crazy! Clark was, and is, dead. Murdered. Beheaded. His life offered as a sacrifice. Something… stole his corpse from the observatory. The gargoyle! Of course! It flew him out the window before I could show the remains to Preston and Minnie. He's been hidden away somewhere. Somewhere cold. Because he'd have been more decayed than this if the body were left to rot naturally. No. They've iced him. Now they've dumped him down here like a sack of garbage." I felt a modicum of vindication.

"Who?"

"Who what?"

Nina lowered her arm from shielding her nose. "Who dumped Clark?"

"His murderers. The ones who've been killing Arkham's unfortunate elites. Clark may have learned something from the Galinka girl he met at the Clover Club. Maybe he saw something he shouldn't have. But I'm sure it's no coincidence."

"He wasn't here when we came down the ramp an hour ago."

We turned simultaneously to gaze up the ramp, toward the cave mouth. Though I heard nothing, I knew we were not alone. Threats ahead of us and behind.

The Colt Hammerless was in my hand once more.

Gingerly, we stepped around Clark. He'd been dragged. A trail of putrid fluids illustrated the way. We came to the turn that led to the cave entrance. It was a blind curve. Light from the outside brightened the passage, after the turn. Nina's torch shone on the cave walls where we paused to gather our nerves.

"If they're waiting for us, it'll be right around the corner," I whispered.

Nina nodded.

"You stick the torch out to distract them. I'll take a look," I said.

"Don't get killed." She squeezed my hand.

Nina stretched out her arm and waved the torch in front of us. We waited. The appearance of our flame triggered no response. But if they were being patient… I put my back to the cave wall. I started forward.

"Wait," Nina seized my shoulder.

"Wait for what?" My heart hammered in my chest.

"I don't know…"

"Neither do I." It was no use prolonging things.

I ducked my head, and the gun, around the junction.

No one. Nothing.

Together we proceeded to the cave mouth. No discernible footprints stood out from those already left in the sandy soil near the opening. The stains from transporting Clark's mushy carcass began at the ramp. His carrier had fled the scene.

"Alden, look at this."

Nina pushed her torchlight at the wall. It was where the barrels had been stacked the last time I visited.

"A new drawing!" I said, startled. Then disgust took over. "These marks have been made with Clark's… fluids."

"Oh, God." Nina covered her mouth. But she didn't look away.

The blackish greenish lines flowed over the stone, as if a powerful grip had forced them out of Clark, using him like a tube of paint.

"Two ovals inside a cup. This was the first pictogram I saw, when Preston drew it in the sand with his foot back at Cannes."

"Over here," Nina said. "There's more. Words." She slid her light along the rocks.

I read the message out loud.

WELCOME ALDEN

NINA

YOU OPEN THE GATE!

"*We* open the Gate?" Nina said. "Why would we do that?"

"They know we're looking for them. We must go. Now!"

Moving quickly, we retraced our steps back to Father's Rolls-Royce. I got behind the wheel and tried to start the engine. But it kept stalling out. Damn! I pounded the wheel. Nina took the Colt from me. "Be ready!" I said. Finally, the motor turned. I turned the Twenty around and sped away. Every tree trunk hid a monk to my mind, each cluster of evergreen branches provided a roost to a clay-faced gargoyle. It wouldn't have shocked me to see the net blob lumbering along the road.

I wasn't even sure if I planned to report Clark's body to the police. I didn't want to be involved. What if his body disappeared again before the cops got here to retrieve it? Would I be a suspect in his disappearance? No. I was going to keep my mouth shut. Nothing would help Clark anyway. I pressed the gas pedal. Did my best to steer clear of the potholes and deeper ruts.

"Look!" Nina shouted. She pointed the barrel of the Colt at the windshield. "Someone rolled the log back across the road."

I slowed the car. Was this a trap? Would snipers have us in their sights? A pair of sitting ducks parked in a Rolls-Royce on a lonesome back road. How long would it take anyone to discover our bullet-riddled bodies? Until springtime? I had no choice. Only forward.

I stopped the Twenty. My tires crushed the icy mud in front of the log.

"That's no log," I said.

I climbed out. Nina's door opened. She joined me at the bumper of the running car.

Exhaust swirled at our backs.

On the frozen ground. Two more bodies. Lying head to foot in a neat row.

Freddie and Winston.

Lying face-up in a mockery of silent repose. Arms folded across their chests. The only thing that betrayed their peace was the matching look of horror petrified on their faces.

Mouths locked wide in eternal screams.

Throats cut, ear to ear.

They might've been caught staring, gaping at the blank white sky, except…

They had no eyes.

Chapter Twenty-Five

I felt guilty for not burying them.

Nina and I carried Freddie and Winston over to the ditch where we'd rolled the log. We lowered the men into a trough of soft snow and covered them with pine boughs. Our conclusion was that whoever disposed of Clark in the cave had also killed Freddie and Winston. They were freshly deceased, their blood still warm when it ran from their terrible wounds through our fingers.

"Were they guarding the camp?" Nina asked.

"If they were, then whoever murdered them did it prior to our arrival. Freddie and Winston would've recognized us on the road. If we drove past their guard posts, they certainly would've caught up with us at the camp." I wiped Freddie's blood off my hands on the rag I'd brought for the Colt. Nina did the same. We threw the rag into the ditch.

Back home at the Colony apartments, I reconsidered calling the police. I'd leave an anonymous tip about the bodies in the woods and the cadaver inside the Black Cave. I picked up the phone.

Nina grabbed my hand. She convinced me not to call.

"Half the force is on the O'Bannion family's payroll. News will reach them eventually. When the boys don't report back, the bootlegging crew will check the camp. They'll find the bodies."

"I don't know. We hid them pretty well."

"They'll notice the log missing and look in the ditch. Trust me, Alden. The O'Bannion gang takes care of their own. No one's calling the cops. Not us, anyway."

She was worried about the police again. My call wouldn't help the dead.

Nina poured two whiskies and handed me one. "It's for the best. You don't want Freddie and Winston buried in some Potter's Field owned by the city of Arkham, do you?"

"I guess not." I polished off my drink, feeling it burn all the way down.

Nina played with her glass, rolling it between her palms. "Listen. I've been thinking. Clark's murder fits with the others. It matches the pattern. He's from the elite class, and that's who's being targeted. If the murders are rituals, maybe they're leading up to something bigger. First, they send out a call. To what? We don't know yet. Then the rites offer a kind of protection to the ones doing the killing. It can't be just one person doing it, either. It's too complicated. All those murders… physically it must be a group behind them. For whatever reason, this group attracts a spirit or entity, sends out a signal. If the entity is pleased, it bestows power on the offeror."

"I like what you're saying, except Freddie and Winston weren't elites. Freddie was a farm boy. They were… ordinary."

Nina exhaled and shook her head. "Their deaths weren't sacrificial. They were killed because they got in the way. The method wasn't ceremonial. They were simply dispatched. The only signal being sent was to you and me. Like that message on the cave wall."

"You think these men were killed because they helped us?"

"I'm afraid so." She looked sad but not defeated.

"It makes me sick to think it's my fault." It tore me up thinking those two guys had their throats cut over me. Dead in a cold ditch. If I hadn't snooped around, they'd be alive.

"You can't blame yourself."

"But I do." I finished my drink. "What about Calvin? Think he's alive?"

"I hope so. We have no reason to believe he's dead. In danger? Certainly."

So, in the end we didn't call the police. I saw no story of the killings in the city papers. As far as we knew, the dead men were still out there on the dirt road, under the pines.

I was in my apartment a few days later when someone knocked on my door. Nina and I had made a habit of locking our apartments. But we had keys to each other's places. Nina never knocked. I knew it couldn't be her. Besides, she was out tracking down a lead on the dancing Galinka sisters act and who hired them to work at the Clover Club. Nina thought maybe that's how they were selected to be sacrificed. She took the Rolls, which I hadn't bothered to return.

I lifted the Colt off my dresser, holding it behind my back as I answered the door. I opened it a crack and was surprised to see Minnie's cat eyes blinking at me.

"Hiya there, Alden. May I come in?"

I stepped back, tucking the gun into the small of my back. Pulling out my shirt, I hoped she wouldn't notice the pistol.

"Funny seeing you here. Shouldn't you be out planning a wedding?"

Minnie walked in, in a rush. She threw off her hat and dropped her purse on my sofa, and then plopped herself there too. With a smooth scissor move, she slipped off both her shoes, pointing her silk-stockinged toes at the rug and flexing her tight calves while letting out a deep, exhausted-sounding moan. "Oh,

Aldie, I'm so worried I don't know what to do. I didn't know who else to come to. Because if you can't help, I don't know where I'll go. Insane, probably. It's all too much. I can't take it. I absolutely can't, not like this."

She started crying. Not big heaving sobs, but shiny, bubbly tears like glass beads rolling down her cheeks. Her dimpled chin quivered.

"Minnie, dear, what's got you so upset? It can't be all that terrible, can it?"

Minnie looked at me, and her eyes flooded.

I sat beside her. She draped her arms around me. Her breath smelled of peppermints.

"I think Preston's in real trouble," she said. "We both are."

I was alarmed but didn't want her to see that. "I've known Preston a long time. Longer than I've known you. He's gotten into plenty of pickles. But I haven't seen one yet that he can't wriggle out of. Usually smelling like a prize rose."

I rubbed her back.

She scooted closer. Her forehead brushed my cheek. I felt her laughing. Not happy but laughing. That's a start, I figured. "Tell me what he's done."

Minnie sat back. But her face stayed near to mine. The last time we were this close we were lovers, I thought. My heart tripped faster. I tried easing back and ran into the stiff arm of the couch. My gun did, anyway. So I moved up again.

"Ever got in your head that somebody you love has changed?" she said.

"That's why we broke up. Isn't it?"

"I don't mean that. I mean that the person you knew checked out, and somebody, a stranger, checked in. Preston is not himself. He looks like Preston. It sounds like his voice. But he's different. I can't explain it exactly how I want. He's Preston, but he's not Preston, too."

"I'm lost here, Minnie." I didn't want to dismiss her concerns. I'd noticed Preston changing too. A man under pressure, I thought. Slowly cracking. I'd chalked it up to wedding jitters. It sounded worse than that. "He hasn't called the wedding off, has he?"

"Called it off? No. He's actually moved it up! To March! Oh, I know he's hiding something from me. That's nothing new. We lie to each other. Small things, the way all couples do. I'm not talking about that." She wore poinsettia red lipstick, dark and artificial, but it looked good on her, a dramatic contrast to her complexion.

"He mentioned pushing up the date to me. But I thought that was a mutual decision?"

"It was. It *is*." Minnie seemed a woman bombarded by thoughts and emotions. "I'm not against getting married earlier than we planned. I love him. I think he loves me. It's just such a total turnaround. If anything, I would've guessed Preston wanted to delay the wedding. He was anxious. He told me so. Now it's just the opposite. He'll only say he wants us together sooner. But where did that idea come from? It's not like him. Preston puts things off. His father is the restless one. Lately, it's as if a stranger were wearing Preston's body as a disguise. The way he moves. The expressions on his face. They're off kilter." Minnie squeezed her tiny hands into tinier fists. "Oh, it's so frustrating. You think I'm crazy. A crazy woman who complains about her new man to her old man…"

"I'm your old man?"

She punched me lightly in the chest, right over my heart. "You know what I mean."

Minnie left her hand there. Her fingers spread and pressed against my shirt. She felt my heart pounding. How could she miss it? I held her wrist, gently moving her hand away.

"Men often don't know how to express their feelings. Might it be simple as that?"

"Don't you think women get nervous too? Is he the right man? Is this it?"

An idea dawned on me. "Are you having second thoughts, Minnie?"

She waited a few beats, thinking it over. "No," she said, with finality. "Preston and I are perfectly matched. Only, I want him back the way he was. Do you know what I think it is?"

"What?"

"It's not a what but a *who*." Minnie dipped her chin and aimed a lacquered nail at me.

"Who then?"

"Juan Hugo! He's the one that's changed him. The man's practically taken over our lives. He would've if I didn't stop him. Preston is under the man's spell. Worse than another woman."

"But Balthazarr spends all his time at the Colony. I've never seen Preston there." I was surprised to hear her mention the Surrealist's name. If Preston existed at one remove from New Colony, then Minnie was at least two away. How was a visiting painter having any impact whatsoever on her relationship?

"That's just it!" Minnie jumped from the sofa. "Is it always so dreadfully chilly in your rooms?"

"I hadn't noticed."

"Don't you have a bottle we can open?"

I frowned, confused. "Of alcohol?"

Minnie put her hands on her shapely hips. "Alden. I want a drink."

"Why didn't you just ask?"

"I just did. Give me a cigarette, sweetie. I'm going through difficulties."

I handed her my case and lighter and went to fetch a bottle of whiskey.

"*God!*" I heard her calling out. "Men are so literal. And they can be frightfully dull."

I returned with the bottle, handed it off to her, and went in search of glasses.

"Where is Preston off to constantly? I'll tell you. It's Balthazarr. Balthazarr at the Lodge with Carl Sanford and his pops for brandies. 'I'm out for a drive with

Juan Hugo, love'. We're the two getting married. He needs to think about us. *Our* event. Especially if everything is happening sooner than we planned."

I guided Minnie back to the sofa. She snuggled against me.

"You're saying Balthazarr is influencing Preston in a negative way…"

"Yes, he is." I noticed Minnie's perfume. Loud and citrusy when it first touched the nose, then settling back into a warm blue vanilla scent. Elegant, sad. Silk sheets and hours alone. I wondered how life would turn out for her.

"Care to elaborate?" Without thinking, I saw my hand stroking her bare forearm, the light fuzz rising from my attention, an appearance of goosebumps. I noticed I had them too.

Minnie relaxed; her shoulders drooped like a hypnotist's volunteer.

"Preston moved the wedding because of him. He won't admit it. But I know that's the cause. He's got me to shift the party over to the Silver Gate Hotel."

"Balthazarr suggested that? Preston told me you were thinking about it the morning Juan Hugo arrived. Oh now, see there, he couldn't have put the idea into Preston's head."

"Well, I don't know how he did it. But he did. Like a Houdini trick or something…"

I was the one having doubts now. About Preston and Balthazarr. Was Preston under the man's influence to a degree I had not perceived? I felt a fool for missing it if it was true.

"Having the wedding at the Silver Gate *will* be so terrific," Minnie continued, unaware of my mental reevaluations. "I'm not complaining about the quality of things. Preston keeps telling me how bright our future is becoming with each new day."

The winter sun broke from the clouds and shone white on the floor of my apartment.

We watched it like our ancestors watched their fires. Mesmerized. Seeking meaning.

"He said that? Here I always thought you two had a bright future together."

"Me too…" Minnie topped off her glass. "It's like he's suddenly gotten a vision, or something, about not only the wedding. But about everything. As if he's made an investment and the payoff is coming in bigger than he expected. He sounds like one of those creepy old schemers. It's not that bad, really. Only… there's something else attached to it. A secret. A double event that he's not letting me in on. Saying it out loud sounds crazier than when it's murmuring on in my head."

Dread, when it arrives, is like a falling inward. I was falling now. My two friends…

Minnie curled against me. I felt a kind of exposure then; involuntary fear crept over me like sickness. I was afraid to touch her. Yet I did and said nothing about it.

"Is Preston in some sort of secret society?" I asked, shifting my inquiry.

Minnie lifted her head to look at me. "The Silver Lodge? That's more his father's thing."

"What about here at New Colony? Has he said anything curious related to that?"

Minnie blinked. I could tell she was reviewing conversations past. "I don't think so."

"I only ask because Juan Hugo is the big cheese at the Colony. People worship him. Hell, I do too. It's almost cult-like, the following he has." I gazed at the bright sun scouring the wooden boards. "He does these mock rituals. Stagecraft, I thought. A bit of showmanship. But in front of the right crowd the effects are entrancing. Preston might find he's charmed. Afterward he acts as though he's still under the influence of Balthazarr, his Master, so to speak." I did my best not to introduce to Minnie any of the panic that was growing inside me.

Minnie had enough worries.

She sat heavily against me; her eyes fluttered. I took her glass. When she spoke, the edges of her words were rounded off and softly slurred. "When we're alone together, Preston is not Preston. He smiles at me like he's pulled some awful trick. Like inside, he hates me."

"That sounds awful." I cared for Minnie. But in that moment, I wanted to flee.

"Tomorrow is Preston's bachelor party," Minnie said.

"I know. I'm going."

"Balthazarr is his new best man. Did Preston tell you? It was supposed to be Clark, but Clark has vanished. His family hired a private detective. They think he might be dead." Her head tipped back. Eyes closed.

My throat rippled. I could not speak.

"Be careful when you're out with them, Alden. I have the most awful premonition that something ghastly is going to happen and ruin all our lives."

Minnie started to snore.

The clouds hid the sun. The floor, the apartment and everything in it grayed out.

Chapter Twenty-Six

Hours later, I woke up alone in the dark on the sofa. Minnie was gone. I heard noises in the hall, a kind of scuffling, and two voices, tensed and rising in volume. I couldn't make out the words. After a moment of disorientation, I shook myself awake and lurched for the door, hoping Nina hadn't caught Minnie slipping out, still a little drunk and looking guilty as hell of something.

Nina was there.

But she wasn't arguing with Minnie.

The other person was a man I didn't recognize, dressed in pinstripes and a snapped down fedora. "Mind your own business, pal," he said to me. I smelled his whiskey breath, and his eyes were pink from drinking and smoking in illicit establishments. The bulge under his arm was hard to miss. But when he grabbed Nina's elbow, jerking her away from her door, I had no choice.

"She is my business," I said.

I decked him.

He was slow from over-indulging, or I got lucky, because I caught him right on the knockout button. The tough guy collapsed in a heap. I took away his weapon, and as I did, his eyelids fluttered. I hammered him with the pistol grip, sending him back to hoodlum dreamland.

"Did he hurt you?"

"Just what you saw," Nina said. "I told him I appreciated being escorted home, but our night was over. He didn't like that. I could've handled him. But thanks."

"Don't mention it."

I couldn't help but notice Nina was dressed for an evening of entertainment. She'd done herself up flapper style. Sequins and beaded fringe; her silks rustled when she moved. Her feet looked like she stepped in black tar and then dipped them in a sack of gold dust. She wore a feathery bandeau and enough pearls around her neck that any pearl diver finding her might retire. This wasn't Nina's usual look. She'd made a point of getting herself noticed tonight, and I guess it worked. "I tried to lose him at the door. He pushed his way in."

"What should we do with him?"

I decided to roll him downstairs. Out the front door. Then I dragged him by the heels across the lawn to the street where I dumped him in the gutter. "That poor suit!" I said to myself as I lit a smoke.

"Amigo! What are you doing outside with no jacket?"

Balthazarr crossed the street diagonally toward me. He wore a long black overcoat, and if he hadn't said anything, I never would've noticed him blending into the shadows.

"Taking out the trash."

Nina watched us from the doorway to the mansion. When she saw Balthazarr, she hurried down the steps to join us. "A guest overstayed his welcome."

"Rudeness is a crime I cannot forgive." Balthazarr asked us for a detailed account of what transpired. Nina told him. He acted impressed by my decisive action.

"It's all over," I said.

"I think not." Balthazarr picked up the goon and threw him over his shoulder.

"What are you doing?" I asked.

"Teaching a lesson in manly behavior."

Balthazarr marched through the Colony mansion's snowy side yard and out to the back. I was freezing in my shirtsleeves, but I went with him. Nina had never taken off her coat and she trailed after us, negotiating the icy grass in her gold-heeled pumps.

"I'm not defending this guy," I said. "He was drunk and stupid. But I took him out. I don't think he's going to be happy when he finds out I kept his gun. We can let him go."

Balthazarr remained silent. He carried the unconscious man lightly, as if the body weighed nothing. He wasn't even breathing hard. His powerful legs crashed through the frozen weeds that grew at the back border of the property. He stomped them down, heading to the river, only halting when he reached the bank. Steam curled from his mouth, as thick as white smoke. What was he going to do? He couldn't take the guy past the water.

The Miskatonic hadn't frozen over completely. Along its edges, cloudy lips of ice made long, smooth curves out into the black water. The man on Balthazarr's shoulder groaned. The artist stared across the river, unblinking. He murmured something, a prayer, in an alien tongue. I couldn't make out all the words. Only it wasn't Spanish.

"Wait!" Nina shouted.

But it was too late.

In a remarkable display of strength, the Spaniard lifted the unconscious hooligan's body straight over his head and threw him far out into the water, beyond the snow-covered shoreline. There was an explosion of water. The body sank. Balthazarr walked away from the river without looking back. I stared dumbfounded, waiting to see if the man might break the surface and begin thrashing about for a saving hand. I studied the bank for a stick, something I might use to hook him back to shore.

But the man never popped up.

"He killed him," Nina said. She couldn't believe what she'd witnessed.

I couldn't either. I refused to.

"The current has taken him downstream. He must have come up. Only we didn't see."

"That water is deadly. Throwing him in is as good as tossing him in a fire," she said.

Like a pyre, I thought. Like a ritual sacrifice.

We turned to the mansion. Balthazarr was already at the apartment house. He was singing to himself. A song of joy and exuberance, perhaps a drinking song, but not in Spanish. The language had a cloggy sound. Guttural, throaty. He belted it with gusto. Did he sing out, "*Yuyu-Vabadaa*?" I don't know. He may have. He really may have.

When we caught up with him, he was smiling. He ensnared us in his great woolly arms, pulling us tight. "You are my friends! New friends! I love Arkham in winter!"

"Juan Hugo, what did you do?" Nina asked, incredulous.

The painter looked back over his shoulder at the Miskatonic.

"I gave a gift."

"A gift?" Nina was having none of it. His flippant attitude caused her agitation to grow. "How can you care so little about human life? You murdered that man!"

Balthazarr drew his head back and howled with laughter.

"I think we'd better go back inside," I said to Nina. I didn't want to anger Balthazarr.

"Murder? Did I murder a gangster who tried to force his way into your home? This brute who could not control himself. You have sympathy for him? No, no." Balthazarr shook his head.

"You've gone too far, Juan Hugo. We don't condone murder here in Arkham," I said.

"Murder again. What is this talk of murder? Look around you, Alden. Nina. Your town is rife with crime. Its industries have at their very foundations the exploitation and violence of one class of people carried out upon another. Bones. This is a city built on bones. But I am only a visitor here. Yet, I am accused of doing what? Drowning a mongrel who attacked my friends?"

Nina pointed her finger at Balthazarr. "You won't get away with this. It's barbaric."

"I think you do not understand barbarism," he said. "You only think you do."

We started to walk away.

Balthazarr called out. "My friends! Do you see? There! Under the lamppost?"

Nina and I stopped, looking to the end of the block, where the river veered close to the road. The bank was terraced and lined with stone steps for fishermen to sit and cast their lines.

The shape of a man plodded into the circle of light. He was composed of shadows, really, little more than an animated mass, drizzling water onto the pavement, exuding tendrils of fog, and shivering so profoundly that his vibrations smudged his outer silhouette to an indistinct blur.

"He is alive! Your worries are for nothing!" Balthazarr laughed again, and he took up his gruff, rasping song; its hoarse refrain like croaking from a swamp, a phlegmy cough repeated and repeated. "Good night, amigos. You are softhearted. Dream, my dreamers. Dream!"

"Is that the man who walked you home?" I asked Nina. "Is he up from the river?"

"Too far to tell… but who else… ?"

The shape at the end of the block shuffled off.

"Balthazarr is right. He taught the man a lesson. No one died. We can go to bed."

"He didn't know what would happen." Nina opened the front door.

"Nothing happened."

Nina mounted the stairway to our floor. At the top of the stairs, she paused.

"Something did happen," she said.

Without inviting me in, she passed over her threshold, shutting the door behind her.

I went into my room and fell into bed, asleep with my clothes on, right until morning.

CHAPTER TWENTY-SEVEN

"I have to go. You said so yourself. Preston needs a friend to steer him from trouble." I stood at the mirror in my bedroom, tying my bowtie. The darkness had come on quickly. Black velvet night pressed its face to my window; a thin beard of ice spilled frostily over the sill.

Nina was adamant. "I've changed my mind. You're more important to me than Preston ever was. And remember, I know him as well as you do, or better. He's quite resourceful and responsible for his own actions. The situation's too dangerous. We saw what Balthazarr was capable of yesterday. The man's unpredictable. You can't say what will happen tonight. You can't, because you don't know."

I went over to the bed where she was reclining and kissed her. "That is precisely why I must be there. To protect Preston from unforeseeable events." I hadn't told Nina about Minnie's visit or her disturbing report on the recent changes in her fiancé. I was more worried about my old friend than I was letting on. Sharing that with Nina would only cement her determination to keep me at home. Preston needed my support. "I predict that several foolish men will drink too much alcohol, speak boldly, and smoke too many cigars. They will grow weary of each other's company because they are not so young as they once were. The end."

Nina rose from the bed, brushing me back.

"I don't like it. But it's your decision." Her coldness conveyed utter disapproval.

I combed my hair, watching Nina in the mirror, in the doorway, slowly receding.

I finished grooming. Yet I stayed where I was, my eyes locked on Nina's reflection. She opened her mouth about to speak. "Please save your arguments," I said. "I'm going."

A flash of red-hot anger. "Go on, then! It's you who'll regret not listening." She stormed out. Her heels clicked as she crossed my bedroom, not slowing down as she entered my studio. Soon she would be gone. Out the door. I turned and ran after her.

"Wait! Nina!"

Her hand rested on the doorknob. She was staring at the wood panels, the ghostly message the gargoyle had left for us, though it was barely visible in the lamplight. She saw it.

"I'll find you when I get home," I said. "If that's what you want me to do."

Without another word she left me standing there.

I went into the closet and fetched my overcoat, leather gloves, and black bowler.

A long chilly night awaited me.

I took a cab to Independence Square.

I wasted no time entering the park. The brutal temperatures inspired me to keep moving. The park shelters occasional unsavory characters after dark. I quickly recognized the loiterers hanging around Founder's Rock at near midnight, polluting the air with expensive tobacco smoke. My fellow partiers *pour la nuit*.

"There you are, Oakesy!" Preston said around his imported Havana.

"Let me have a look at you," I said, sounding more worried than I had intended.

Preston made a strange face and held out a silver flask. A tad gaunt, dark around the eyes, but his skin was flushed with drink. Overall, he did not appear as a man bedeviled.

"You need to catch up," he said. By the proof of his breath and wobble in his steps, he was speaking the truth. He slugged me boyishly in the upper arm. He and Minnie were very fond of administering a light pummeling during conversation. I pictured them aged in the Fairmont mansion, having abandoned language entirely, relying on biffs and thwacks.

"Who's on board with us tonight? Connors and Read? Bug-eye Westy? Did you wrangle Thurlow, Shattuck, and Nettleton? I fear a reunion with that gang might kill me off for good."

But, as it turned out, I had no worries. None of the old gang made it to Preston's bachelor party. Had they drifted away only to have their shoes filled by New Colonists? Not including myself, I counted six Colonists in tonight's group. I'd never seen Preston with any of them before now. From the far side of Founder's Rock emerged the caped, top-hatted Juan Hugo. He was walking with a cane, not because he needed it, but for the effect; his stick was blackthorn, its knob might have been a natural bulbous peculiarity, but it seemed carved and cycloptic.

"A few days ago, I read in the newspaper that my countryman Ramón Franco crossed the Atlantic in an airplane. From Spain to South America in less than two and a half days. Imagine what the Conquistadors would have done if they had airplanes. Our world is shrinking fast, *mis amigos*. Getting smaller each day.

Soon it will implode violently, like a massive star. Where do you go when there is nowhere to run? When it collapses, where will you be?" he said.

"I'll be good and drunk." Preston tipped back his flask. It was empty. He tapped the last drops of whiskey into his mouth then capped the flask before chucking it into the bushes.

"Hey, that was silver! Wasn't it?"

The Colonist who had spoken was named Devereaux. He wrote Dadaist-inspired poetry, cutting up epic poems – *Beowulf* and Dante's *Divine Comedy* were favorites – mixing in local newspaper advertisements, and reassembling the random fragments into blocks of text, out of which he removed every other vowel. He performed these aloud. His aim, he said, was to destroy language. He complained his task was impossible. Although, I thought he did a pretty decent job.

"Damn my silver! I've twenty-nine more at home!" Preston shouted.

Balthazarr rubbed his bare hand on the Founder's Rock, looking at the sky.

"Isn't it cold?" a painter named Fowler asked, crouching at his feet.

The Surrealist studied the oblong stone dedicated to Arkham's *original* colonists.

"Not to me, it isn't. The menhir boils with energy surging from the earth's core."

"That's frostbite you're feeling," I said.

As Balthazarr watched me, his rubbery mouth pulled into a clownish grin. Shadows filled the hollows of his face. He was a handsome man, but a grotesque animation enlivened his sneer, or perhaps it was the spotty electric lighting in the park. Glass shards from multiple damaged lamps littered the pavement. Vandals, I guessed. Ruffians. Nothing more sinister than that. Was I trying to convince myself? Or did every detail hint at a hidden threat?

"I am going to die tonight." Preston's tone startled me, forcing me to regard him with genuine unease. He pointed at the ground. "I will literally freeze right where I am standing."

"Where to next, Mr Balthazarr?" It was the other painter who tagged along with Fowler. Jeremy Whipple. He died not too long after that night. After sailing to Australia to paint scenes of farming life, he fell under a Sundigger cultivator.

"La Bella Luna," Balthazarr chewed on the words, biting into succulent fruit.

"La Bella Luna!" Preston yelled.

Nine well-dressed men of the city intoned his mantra.

I was too sober to enjoy our parade up Garrison Street. It was a relief to reach our destination. The warmth inside La Bella Luna seemed overmuch, a tropical contrast to the tundra of the park. Preferable, but soon I was sweating, my forehead beaded. The Italian bistro was unpopulated at this late hour. I hadn't realized we were planning to dine. My companions, apart from Preston and Balthazarr, appeared equally puzzled. Balthazarr tapped his stick on the podium, summoning a slouching concierge who counted out nine menus.

"Allow me," Preston said.

Balthazarr acquiesced, letting one of Arkham's native sons take the lead.

"Marco! It is Marco, isn't it?" Preston asked.

The concierge inclined his head a fraction of an inch in acknowledgment.

"Marco, can you serve a private party of our size? Downstairs?" Preston flashed a playful gaze back at us.

"We are crowded at the moment, sir," Marco said. "Maybe if you come back later."

I gawked at the empty tables.

Then I smirked as the reality of the exchange dawned on me.

"I always have a table waiting for me *downstairs*." Preston added a theatrical wink.

"Right this way, sir. Please follow me." Marco put the menus back.

We trailed him through the bistro, its walls papered with gold velvet *fleurs-de-lis*. Past the kitchen entrance was a second door, hidden behind the corner. Marco opened it, revealing a wooden stairway and strains of live jazz piano rising from below.

Preston tipped Marco. We descended into the passage.

"Tell them Marco said to let you in," the concierge called down after us.

At the bottom of the steps: a steel barrier. A spy hatch slid open in the center of it.

Preston repeated the concierge's words.

Bolts were thrown. A roar of music escaped as we were admitted.

"Welcome to the Clover Club, boys." A towering redhead in headdress greeted us. She had arachnid eyelashes, large hands, and a six-shooter on her hip. "No weapons permitted. Check your pieces here. Lie to me, you'll regret it. Ooh, I like your beard, hon."

The hostess stood nose to nose with Balthazarr and tweaked his chin whiskers.

"You are a very tall woman," Balthazarr said, blushing.

"I'm from Texas. Everything's big in Texas. What about your stick? Got a sword inside?"

"No, madam. It is natural solid wood."

The hostess held out her palm. Balthazarr laid the cane across it. She checked the stick for concealed blades, then returned it. "You coldcock anybody, we'll use that thing to break your legs. Understand? This here's a peaceable joint. We don't like shenanigans."

Balthazarr's eyes grew large in mock terror. He pretended to quake.

The lower level of La Bella Luna housed a speakeasy in full swing at midnight. Brick walls, part of the building's original foundation, contained most of the noise; the opulent dark green draperies, hanging ceiling to floor around the club, smothered the rest. Adorned with silver palms, the stage glowed in the center of the main room. A jazz band was playing. The same band that played at Preston and Minnie's party at the observatory. The piano player began to sing of lost love and memories best left undisturbed.

"Get a load of this place!" Whipple's head swiveled left and right.

Fowler nudged him with an elbow. "Act like you've been here before."

"But I haven't. Have you?"

Fowler shook his head and pointed to a row of archways at the back, their openings partially concealed with clacking strings of multicolored glass beads. Men and women parted the curtains, heading in and out, offering glimpses of felt-covered tables, card players, and spinning roulette wheels. "The high-rollers must hang out in there. I'd like a peek."

"Go on, fellas. Make yourselves comfortable. Oakesy and I will find a table. Come back when you're good and ready. Here's some seed money." Preston peeled off bills from a stack of crisp green lettuce. "Let's see who's lucky tonight."

Fowler, Whipple, and Devereaux headed for the card room. The other three New Colonists, whose names are not important, grabbed their allowances and advanced like a line of windup automatons to the club's poker tables, where they leave our story, never to return.

Balthazarr, Preston, and I ambled over to the bar in the corner.

Preston bought three whiskies. Balthazarr made a beeline for an empty table. A bull wearing a tuxedo stopped him, informing him that table was reserved, and he needed to look elsewhere. Balthazarr apologized but never broke eye contact with the bouncer.

"There's a table," I said. "Those people are leaving." I grabbed a chair, sat down.

"That's Naomi O'Bannion's table you tried to steal, Juan Hugo. Strictly off limits," Preston said, sliding into a seat nestled between Balthazarr and me.

I recognized Naomi's name from the bootleggers' camp. Winston had mentioned her talking to Freddie in the ice truck, while I was rolling around with mackerel. My mind flashed to the ditch, on their eyeless faces gaping at the stars through the pine needles.

"Who is O'Bannion?" Balthazarr asked, sipping his bootleg drink.

"Her family sells vice in this city. Naomi's fiancé is Peter Clover. This is his place."

"Ah, so that goon is her goon." Balthazarr was still watching the club muscleman.

"Somebody's making a killing tonight. The place is packed," I said.

"Alden's never been here," Preston said. "But Minnie and I love it. The club really swings. You wouldn't believe what we've seen happen down here. Crazy things."

"I'd believe it." I looked at Balthazarr. He turned to meet my gaze. Raised his glass. Did Preston know about his friend's temper?

Preston waved to a cigarette girl.

She saw him and smiled, sashaying our way. Everyone in the room noticed her.

Short brassy curls and dancer's legs, her sparkly red and gold skirt bounced with each step. That didn't completely explain the attention. There was an energy in her, bright and infectious, you knew she'd have a husky laugh and brains to match her sassy looks. She might be a cigarette girl tonight. She wouldn't be for long. The world had big plans for her. She did too. When she arrived at our table, a sea of faces directed themselves to our table. There might as well have been a spotlight on her. She waved her hand in a practiced motion over her tray of goods. "What'll you have, gentlemen? Cigarettes, chewing gum, candy. A flower for a lady."

"Do you have cigars?" Balthazarr said.

"I sure do. How many?" Her gold pillbox hat tilted on her head so it made you worry it might slip off. You wanted to catch it before it fell. But she knew what she was doing. It stayed put. Her eyes were dark like buckwheat honey; her skin held a misty golden shimmer.

"One will do." Balthazarr pressed coins into her palm.

"I'll take a pack of cigarettes. Those right there with the dromedary." Preston pointed. "Say, do you know if they have any champagne tonight?"

"Is it your birthday?"

"No, I'm getting married."

"What a lucky lady."

Preston took the cigarette pack from her, letting his fingers graze her wrist.

She pushed out her lower lip. "You might ask Glenda about the champagne. She's the girl in the Egyptian getup."

"Thanks," Preston said. "Keep the change."

She looked at the bill he gave her. "Thank you!"

Heads turned as she passed by.

The lights came down so the room was almost black. After that, the jazz played even louder. People crowded the dancefloor. Others shimmied wherever they were, at the tables – or on top of them – pressed against the bar rail, even the most hardcore gamblers couldn't help but tap their toes to the drums and bass.

Preston got his bottle of champagne. It tasted like ice-cold liquid money.

As the night wore on, we hardly left our seats. I felt my face growing numb. Devereaux stopped by for a drink, reporting that Whipple and Fowler were winning at baccarat. He'd lost his last few bets and was taking a break to change his luck. He went off into the dark confusion of bodies to talk to a girl at the bar. He appeared ashen and either he'd had a drink poured over him or he'd broken out in a drenching sweat. In the men's room I met him again. He was hunched over a sink, coughing or sobbing. When I asked what was wrong, he waved me away. Somebody's night had taken a bad turn. Whipple and Fowler did win some money. But Fowler drew the ire of a Russian aristocrat at the baccarat table, and the Slav challenged him to a duel. Fowler laughed in reply, setting the man off, and the Slav exploded, clawing at Fowler's face, getting both men tossed from the club. Whipple agreed to take Fowler to the hospital for sutures.

Despite the lateness, or earliness, of the hour, the crowd only swelled to greater numbers. Lights brightened and went low again. At some point, without my noticing, the musical act changed, a woman was singing, but I had trouble making sense of her words. It was like one of Devereaux's poems, a jumble, with vowels missing or added in, ululations that didn't seem like jazz at all but a spiritless cry from centuries and continents away. Nothing energetic, only pain. I even thought I heard her sing something like, "Yuyu, Yuyu."

But I was drunk by then and doubting my own ears.

The singer announced they were taking a break. I was surprised to see Balthazarr standing in the shadows on the stage. The house manager came up to the microphone.

"We've got a real treat in store for you tonight. Who likes magic?"

The intoxicated crowd cheered.

The manager hushed them. "Easy now, my celebrants. I give you Balthazarr the Magnificent!"

I poked Preston. He shrugged and blinked, glassy eyed at the circle of light on stage.

Balthazarr approached the microphone. He had his black cane and a gleam in his smile. "I will need two assistants from the audience." He shaded his eyes as he pretended to seek in the crowd for volunteers. For all our carousing, he seemed as sober as a hatchetwielding teetotaler. I could barely keep from toppling out of my chair. What was he doing?

"I hope he doesn't pick us. I don't think I can walk," I said.

Preston put his head down on the table.

"You... and you, sir. Yes, you. Please, everyone. Encourage the fine gentleman." Balthazarr began clapping. The audience joined him with vigorous applause.

Preston looked up in a panic. But Balthazarr hadn't chosen us.

The cigarette girl and the bullish goon in a tuxedo stepped into Balthazarr's light.

"Thank you. Now, I need everyone to concentrate on the top of my walking stick. Look at it. Empty your minds of thoughts, logic, and reason. Think only of a depthless void."

"That shouldn't be too hard for–" a heckler tried to interrupt.

"Silence!" Balthazarr's command quieted the man, and the rest of room as well. The gambling rooms had emptied. No dealers dealt cards, no dice rolled, every wheel ceased its spin. People were transfixed on the stage. Every eye focused on the Surrealist.

"Stand next to each other. Very good." He guided the girl and the goon together.

From behind the two, Balthazarr lifted his stick overhead. The cycloptic handle was too far away from the table for me to pick out any detail, or really to see it at all.

Yet I did.

I saw the wood-carved eye, the lidless orb no bigger than an ordinary glass marble – it glowed, and I looked at it as if it were right before my face, a few inches away, burning and wide open. How was this possible? I blinked, but nothing changed. The eye burned into me.

"This is an illusion called *The Two Keys*. I am the Locksmith, if you will. They are the keys." The crowd chuckled nervously. "I use them to unlock…! What? What do you see?"

The silence continued. I heard not a breath being drawn, not a crinkle of clothing.

Nothing.

I was somehow seeing everything on stage in perfect clarity. I was at the same time staring into that wood pit, that unpeeled lidless orb, the cyclops Balthazarr raised into the air.

"Do you see it? Answer me!"

"We see it!" My lips moved. I felt the involuntary spasm of my vocal cords, the vibration of words formed in my throat and mouth, my teeth and tongue and lips, but without my control.

Everyone in the room had spoken simultaneously. Our voices speaking as one.

"Do you see a doorway opening, perhaps?" Balthazarr said.

"We see it!"

The orb expanded. It was like looking into a telescope. Stars, galaxies, dusts and gases. Nebulae. The cosmos. An immense shape swam across the vastness. Both dead and alive, for whom life had no meaning, death no consequence, it turned its intelligence toward the watchers.

Toward *us*.

On the stage, a long, looping tendril dropped from the murky ceiling. Then another and another. Dozens of them. They danced and interwove their lengths. One bundled cluster of thick, vine-like appendages braided themselves together and coiled around the cigarette girl with her tilted pillbox hat and her brassy curls, her sparkly red and gold skirt and her stockinged legs. The other tendrils entwined and tightened around the stocky neck of the tough bruiser beside her.

"Beholder from Beyond, God of Dimensions Unimagined, Lord and Servant of None and Nothing, I call to Yuyu! Take this Man and Woman. Falling Star! Un-Sun, be born!"

"Falling Star! Un-Sun, be born!" every person in the Clover Club repeated.

The conjured cords snapped tight around the two volunteers and lifted them off their feet, carrying them high out over the crowd. Transfixed, we watched as they began to choke.

The man's legs kicked. He grabbed at the coils cinching taut, closing his airways.

The cigarette girl twitched, her whole body encased in a bone-crushing vise. I wanted to react but could not. I felt at a distance from myself. An observer. A disembodied eye.

Behind Balthazarr, as if projected on the wall, a vision of the cosmos swirled. Inside that deeply dizzying vision, the immensity that pulsed and swam, came closer.

Closer.

Balthazarr's body became a blur, vibrating with the Thing invading dimensions.

Colors beyond our visible spectrum of light radiated. But I could see them! Patterns overlapped. Ribbons and wavy bars of shifting fluorescence. Scribblings, blooms, and radiances like ink drops falling into dark water. I rubbed my burning eyes. Panic erupted from within me. The deeper I gazed into the wall, the deeper I was able to see. I peered out over vast distances, across the universe, agape, awestruck at its endlessness. While, at the same time, the objects floating before me were being x-rayed by unseen, increasingly powerful machines, exposing their underlying structures and the essential building blocks of all creation. Dizzyingly, my perception zoomed in and out. My brain felt pulped. My senses stretched past reasonable limits.

Others were experiencing it too, a stomach-churning cosmogonic seasickness.

The immense void loomed.

Then it roared. I have never listened to a dragon's roar, but this one also breathed fire.

The crowd suddenly awakened from their communal trance.

Men and women screamed. A gun went off. The club guards drew their weapons and began shooting haphazardly, without targets, at the stage. Bystanders were struck down in the barrage of gunfire. A stampede for the door started without warning. Clubgoers trampled one another. They tore at anyone they perceived in their way, blocking their escape. From what?

They couldn't name it. From fear. The spiking blood-rush of pure, insanity-inducing fear. It didn't matter who they were outside the club. Outlaws, judges, and regular joes. Jazz lovers, flappers, or busboys. Rich or poor, society page veterans or everyday citizens out for a night in the city of Arkham. Everyone was included.

They all picked the wrong night, the wrong place to be.

Chapter Twenty-Eight

I don't remember going outside. Preston and I somehow fought our way through the river of Clover Club customers flooding out of La Bella Luna's doors. When the rush to exit through the restaurant momentarily screeched to a standstill – after a clumsy, sozzled couple tripped and went sprawling over the threshold – a frustrated group of men picked up La Bella Luna's choicest table and tossed it through the plate glass window. Shards sprayed onto the sidewalk. Marco the concierge looked on, mystified.

I couldn't tell if I was leading Preston or he was leading me. We seemed to switch back and forth, one of us supporting the other who lagged behind, physically and mentally exhausted, our minds hindered by too much hooch and champagne and lingering visions of impossible geometries, the abysmal field of swirling objects conjured on the Clover Club's brick back wall.

I must've blacked out briefly. I remember grabbing hold of Preston's hand and hauling him down the block, dodging away from the police cars and paddy wagons racing to the club. We cut through an alley and hopped a fence, delirious with dread and a case of uncontrollable nervous laughter. Shadows darted past us. Ghostly human-sized smudges hastened down gloomy avenues, their features appeared partly erased; pencil sketches of people, quick facsimiles, running amok. Were these the other Cloverites fleeing a scene that got too hot?

It must've been so.

I was covered in cold sweat.

Preston gasped. His ribs rattled with spasms.

I was about to ask him what he saw at the club when a sliver of the void must have caught up with me, because the next thing I knew I was sitting with my back against the hard, weathered contours of Founder's Rock, noticing my sock and my wriggling toes. "Hey, would you look at that?" We were still holding hands. I shook our conjoined fist. "I lost a shoe somewhere in the melee."

"You lost a shoe, but you gained a glimpse into something beyond."

It wasn't Preston's hand I was holding.

"How did you get out? You started the whole damned thing!" I let go.

Balthazarr held up his empty palms, defensive of my accusation. "What did I do?"

"Are you kidding me? People died back there!" I glanced around the side of the rock. Then I got up. Not a black Oxford wingtip in sight. My shoeless foot was freezing on the cobbled path.

Balthazarr waved for me to sit next to him. "I did a magic trick. An illusion."

"You call that a trick? No way, Juan Hugo. Pardon me, but that was not hocus pocus."

"Hypnotism. I put the audience in a trance. And you saw what you wanted to see. Somebody panicked and started shooting. That club was filled with drunken gangsters. Don't blame me." Balthazarr was taking slugs from a bottle of champagne.

"Where'd Preston go?"

"Home. His driver picked him up. You don't remember?"

"It's almost as if I were drugged. This has happened to me several times in the last few months. Maybe I have a problem with my brain. My toes are turning to ice. End to end I'm falling to pieces." I sat, crossing my ankle over my knee and massaging my numb foot. Spain and the Colony's Winter Show. It had happened to me again. A brain fog. Confusion.

"Let me see," Balthazarr said, passing me the champagne bottle.

"What? My foot?"

He nodded. Before I could object, he pinched the toe of my sock and pulled it off. Then his rough sculptor's hands began to knead at my chilled flesh. I expected to feel something like shock or embarrassment, at the least an awkwardness from the physical contact. But it felt marvelous. Instant warmth, an almost ecstatic relaxation. Tension was leaving my body through the sole of my foot. Balthazarr removed my other shoe and sock, without my stopping him. Two men in the park after hours, one undressing the other. There was an aura of social impropriety, but despite the incredible strangeness of this unexpected act, it didn't strike me as weird. I was like a patient seeing his physician. I wouldn't have wanted to explain that to the police. But they were otherwise occupied this night.

I tipped the bottle, closing my eyes. Balthazarr's soothing voice surrounded me.

"My friend, Luis Buñuel, is a film director. He is also a hypnotist. He claims that motion pictures are a form of hypnotism. He writes that he is working on a picture in France. His boss tells him, 'Luis, you seem rather surrealist. Beware of surrealists, they are crazy people'. Do you think that's true, Alden? Are we like the unfortunates who live across the street?" Balthazarr gestured to Arkham Asylum, the hospital lit up like a haunted ruin. Were the massive gray cobwebs in the windows spirits or patients? The moon attracted them like bugs.

"I don't know what you are," I said.

"I am you. We are the same thing."

"Who is Yuyu-Va'badaa?" I blurted out. "I'm not sure I'm saying that right."

Balthazarr smiled. "It sounds like your own invention. I like it. Baby talk. A word the Dadaists might've come up with."

"It isn't. I heard it in Spain. And around Arkham, at the Colony. Now again at the Clover Club. All places you've been, coincidentally." I watched him for signs of recognition.

The Spaniard shrugged. "Maybe it comes from your imagination. I cannot say."

"I'm not making it up." Was he calling me crazy? A person who hears voices.

"If you were … is there anything wrong with that?" He stood, stretched. Letting out a gaping, cavernous yawn. "We must get you home before you doubt your sanity, eh? I will telephone for a cab." Balthazarr marched off across the street to the asylum. Taking the steps two at a time, rap-rapping loudly on the doors. I was certain they would turn him away. But they didn't. They let him inside. Minutes later he reemerged. "Your cab is on its way. I'm walking back to the Silver Gate. The air does me good. Ah, look, your ride is already here."

A black cab slid to the curb. Shining, insectile. The driver: gloomy and lumpen.

I got in. Balthazarr murmured something to the cabbie. His voice buzzing in my ears.

As the car was about to pull away, I touched the cabbie's shoulder. "Wait."

I leaned out of the window. Balthazarr watched me, amused.

"Why don't you live at the Colony with us, Juan Hugo?"

He considered my question. His eyes gleamed like smoky brown gemstones. "Because, Alden, *mi amigo*, gods dwell apart from their followers."

I sat there, unable to tell if he was being serious.

His caped figure turned, melting away into shadows and river fog.

I told the driver to take me home.

Upstairs, I hesitated outside my apartment. I looked at Nina's door. I wondered if she was still awake. Would she be angry with me still? If I woke her up, would I make things worse?

I decided to take the risk. I needed to tell her what happened at the Clover Club, everything I'd seen and heard. My conversation with Balthazarr. I needed her to tell me I wasn't losing my mind.

As I knocked on her door, it swung open.

Nina would never go to sleep and leave her door unlocked. I felt panic rising in me.

"Nina!" I called out, rushing inside. I raced room to room. Empty, empty, empty.

Her bed was made. She hadn't gone to sleep there. But her purse was in the kitchen. Cash in her wallet. Her apartment hadn't been broken into by thieves. Nothing was missing.

Except Nina.

I did a slower, more thorough search. My head was full of bootleg alcohol and fear.

On the floor, by the edge of her bed: a broken pearl necklace. The pearls scattered. Were those scuff marks scratched into the floor? Had she been physically dragged away?

Kidnapped?

Too fast now, images flickered through my mind. The gargoyle. All the cases of those missing and murdered Arkhamites: Dr Silva, the Galinkas, Ganz and the boxcar drifter…

Headless Clark…

Would Nina be another name among the missing? Or worse?

The next phase of the ritual: another sacrificial elite. Was Nina's theory correct?

I tried to think… Think, Alden… I could almost hear her coaching me along. *Look for clues.*

But where? What was I even looking for?

I went through Nina's closets, her dresser and nightstand. In the drawer of her writing desk I found what I needed. A reporter's notebook. I'd never seen her with it, but she must've taken it along when she went out alone. Jotting more notes after she got home.

I flipped the cover.

Blank. Not a single scribbled word. Why keep it in her desk if she didn't use it?

Damn it!

Wait. Caught in the spirals at the top were fringes of pages that had been torn out. Why would she tear pages out of her private notebook? She wouldn't. But someone else might. I held the notebook under her desk lamp. I saw impressions of handwriting pressed into the paper. I rummaged in the desk and found a pencil. I rubbed the pencil back and forth over the impressions, until the words of the last page she wrote became, mostly, readable. It was the same thing I'd done to copy the gargoyle's message off the door. Here I knew the author. I recognized Nina's handwriting. These were *her* words.

> *out last night to dig up info (Galinka sisters) Found who hired them*
> *to dance at the CC. The girls were popular!!! Had avid fan turned up*
> *some nights. After shows, they sat with man. Alone, private. He took*
> *them out. Where? Unknown. Not far away. In town. Maybe Clark???*
> *Not Clark. Descript all wrong. Tall, handsome, beard. Accent?*
> *Man bought gifts. Dresses, jewelry, etc. Paintings!!!*

JHB???!!! Who else? But was months ago. How did he?

Balthazarr in Arkham, months before he said he arrived. Was it possible? It was only Preston and Juan Hugo himself who told me when he'd gotten into town. The bottom half of the page was spottier. Not all the words transferred through from the ripped-out page.

Black Cave. Underground lake. Unvisited Isle. Docks. Hospitals and
Hotels!!!?
Arkham police too dangerous – infiltrate every aspect
Must tell A Smarten up. Watch out especially for
be playing games with us. Don't trust N. Colonists. Spying – listen
through walls – the mail
They do rituals. Not everyone but… Will ask more ???s
P&M in deep. P suspected but – unknowingly controlled them puppets
JHB again 2PLACES AT ONCE?
Tell A it has to be

I reread the page a dozen times, then I read it some more. What did I see?

Nina listed locations of strange activity in Arkham. The cave, the pool we found there. The island where the sisters were burned. The docks where the bootleggers operated and where the net blob pursued me. Dr Silva was hanged outside a hospital. What about hotels? Balthazarr's current address was at the Silver Gate and it might be the new location of Preston and Minnie's wedding. Then came Nina's constant worries about the police. Here's where the gaps started to take a toll. "*Infiltrate every aspect*" could mean the police or it could mean someone else. But who? The murderers? I didn't know. "*Must tell A. Smarten up.*" I assumed I was "A." Who did I need to "*watch out*" for? Perhaps the answer lay in the next line. The New Colonists. Playing games, spying, eavesdropping…

"*They do rituals. Not everyone but…*" But mostly everyone. The Colonists couldn't be trusted. We lived among them. Nina was going to ask more questions. Of whom exactly?

I didn't have any suspects in the Colony itself. But *P* and *M* had to be Preston and Minnie. Our friends. Well, my friends at least. Nina didn't know Minnie. Preston was her ex.

Preston "*suspected*" something. Who were the "*puppets*" she mentioned? The Colonists? Nina and me? Or none of the above. It was too damned vague.

Too many pieces were still missing.

Juan Hugo Balthazarr in two places at once. What could that possibly mean? Did he control the "*puppets*"? The gargoyle leapt into my mind, wings flapping, laughing in my face.

Nina was gone. Who took her away? There was no obvious solution.

"Tell A it has to be..."

It didn't have to be! Not if I could help it.

I ran back downstairs and outside, seeing if I could find more evidence of Nina's kidnapping. A piece of clothing. A footprint. Blood in the grass. No, not that. Because I was certain she'd been taken against her will. I knew it in my gut. In my heart too. While I was out partying at the Clover Club with Preston and Balthazarr, witnessing God knows what taking place on that stage, someone or something crept into the Colony mansion and stole Nina.

The sky was still dead black. The only color came from factory smokestacks and the flash of early-rising gulls searching for breakfast scraps.

I was trembling.

What *had* I witnessed at the Clover Club? Was it a feat of hypnotism like Balthazarr said? It felt more real than a magician's parlor trick gone awry.

Or was it a preview of a cosmic catastrophe? Dimensional collapse? The cigarette girl in her pillbox hat. Did she die? Had Balthazarr murdered two people in a room full of witnesses and walked away?

What was my role in all this?

Nina. I had to find her.

Nina...

Chapter Twenty-Nine

Following the events that transpired at the Clover Club, I went to the newsstand daily and bought the *Advertiser*, hoping to read a report of the incident. I wanted to know what the police uncovered, the number of victims, names of those who were arrested, and what explanation the authorities provided for the calamity. But there was nothing. Only a local business article relating that La Bella Luna bistro was closed temporarily for remodeling.

It was baffling.

How could such damage and human turmoil be ignored? It had to be a cover-up. Nina's suspicions concerning the police explained how these odd deaths might be kept hidden from the public. Now I believed she'd been correct all along. Here was the proof.

I couldn't go to the police about her disappearance. No. I was convinced they wouldn't help me. Talking to them might lead to false charges against me. Who knew who pulled the strings in Arkham? I'd thought I did, but I was wrong. I didn't want to end up in jail.

At least two people died in the Clover Club. I saw it happen.

With my own eyes.

Balthazarr said he hypnotized the crowd, including me. But Nina didn't trust him. And now I didn't. He'd made me doubt myself. I couldn't easily shake off that feeling either.

Self-doubt hounded me. I was paralyzed by the idea that anything I attempted would be destined to fail. How *could* I find Nina? I stayed close to home at first, hoping she'd turn up. That I'd been mistaken about her leaving against her will. She'd taken a trip. That's all.

She did not miraculously reappear.

I walked the streets of Arkham looking for her. What else could I do? I didn't trust my New Colony neighbors any more. Preston and Minnie were nowhere to be found. When I stopped by the Fairmont house, the family butler told me Preston was not at home. He was out of the country, in fact. Beyond contact at the moment.

"Out of the country? Doing what?"

"Traveling."

"Traveling?" I sneered, obviously unsatisfied with that answer. Unwilling to leave.

"Perhaps he is working out details for his wedding. The date is officially changed."

"Changed to when?" I asked, confused and insulted that I hadn't been informed. I was still in the wedding party, wasn't I? An old friend, a confidante. Or so I had been led to think.

"March, sir. Saturday the 27th," he said, one hand on the door, already closing it.

I stuck my foot in. "Are you sure?"

"Quite sure. The event is scheduled at the Silver Gate Hotel."

"I'd like to talk to Mr Fairmont. Please tell him to call me as soon as possible."

"Very well, sir. Good day." He shut the door in my face.

To pass the time and distract myself, I painted, my work diving deeper into surrealist territories. I painted with oils exclusively during this period. A large vertical canvas depicted the gargoyle soaring skyward from behind the rickety wooden fence. His proffered knife twirling in the air, as the viewer's feet (my feet) stayed planted in the yard, the foggy Miskatonic to our left. Another canvas, horizontal, showed a panorama of the Black Cave's subterranean lake, a pale sea monster disturbing its sable depths. But my greatest project during this burst of creative energy was a triptych of the Clover Club. The three panels captured phases of the ritual I witnessed. Balthazarr himself at the microphone. The floating bodies of the cigarette girl and the goon. And, lastly, the transfigured brick wall leading to an imaginary world of threat and terrors.

Without knowing it at the time, I had just painted myself into the history of Surrealist visionaries. I was one of them now. But, in the moment, I was emptying my mind as it continually refilled with hallucinatory images, a relentless parade of dreams that invaded me daily, nightly.

January became February; February leaked into March.

One afternoon that felt more like a memory of winter than the promise of springtime, I ventured out from my studio, returning to the docks. It was reckless. I felt desperate, foolhardy. My latest work endowed me with a sense of immortality, and at the same time I yearned for something to break my world, even if the broken thing knocking inside it was me.

At the corner of the last dock, I was surprised to find Christophe and his little red wagon, roasting chestnuts, stirring them with a long spoon on his charcoal grill.

"One bag," I said.

The one-eyed former soldier recognized me immediately.

"Haven't seen you in a while." He scooped up the hot chestnuts into a paper bag.

"I've been around. Isn't it late for chestnuts?"

Christophe shrugged. "It's never too late if I have customers."

We stood there watching longshoremen unloading cargo from a ship. The air was cold, but you could sense the pressure of a coming change, a new season in the offing, the passing of time like smoke from Christophe's grill floating, disappearing.

"I've been looking for my friend, Nina."

Nina, Nina. She was never far from my thoughts.

"Isn't that what you were doing the first time we met? Looking for the same girl?"

I smiled. "You're right. I was."

"And I introduced you to Calvin."

"You did."

"He was just here," Christophe said.

My heart jumped. "When?"

"Oh, maybe a minute ago. I sold him a bag. He went walking down that way. Where are you running to? Are you crazy? You dropped your bag." Christophe pointed with his spoon to the chestnuts I spilled on the gravel.

I was running after Calvin. I went in the direction Christophe pointed.

But I saw no one.

I kept going.

I came to an intersection and scanned the cross street both ways. There!

The easy-flowing walk of a man of slender build. He wore a heavy overcoat and a dark wool stocking hat. He was smoking a cigarette, and in his fist was a rolled-down paper bag. I chased after him.

"Calvin!"

The man turned as I descended on him. It was Calvin Wright. He looked shocked to see me. I grabbed him by both shoulders. The cigarette fell from his mouth.

"I found you," I said. At last, a chance! Did he know the whereabouts of Nina?

"Alden! I'm working for the same people. We have a ship coming in tonight."

"Where is she? Where is Nina?"

Calvin acted as if he didn't understand my question. He rested his hands on my wrists until I released him. He looked at me with pity. "I don't know where Nina is. I haven't seen her since that day we were at the camp when you were hit so badly in the head. Are you feeling… better?"

I laughed bitterly.

Calvin shook his head, worriedly. "The O'Bannions broke up the camp on the Miskatonic. The cops were onto us. The gang moved me up to Canada for a while. The other end of the operation. I helped bringing shipments down to the states. I got back a week ago."

I hung my head in disbelief. "Freddie and Winston are dead."

"I know. A rival crew caught them out at the camp."

"No, no. That's wrong. We think the Colonists killed them."

Calvin stepped back. "The Colonists?" His hand went into his coat pocket. I wondered if he had a knife. Was he with them? I didn't know what to believe any more.

"Nina and I went down into the Black Cave. They were dumping Clark's body…"

"Who's Clark?" He took another step away from me. Wary, perhaps even frightened.

"He was my friend. It isn't important. You're telling me you haven't seen Nina since the day that watchman cracked me over the head with his bat?" My temples were pounding.

"That's right."

"My God. Where is she? Where could she be?" I said to myself, walking away.

Calvin tried to get me to go to a diner with him. He wanted to calm me down, to find out what I knew about Balthazarr, the Colony, and the Clover Club. I refused to go.

"I have to find Nina," I said. "No one is helping me."

"That's what we'll do, you and I together. First, you need to get control of yourself."

"Where's that warehouse?" My mind raced. "You told us it was around here. The place where Dunphy did his stone-carving." My hands balled up; all my muscles clenched. I had to do something, anything. It felt like my skeleton wanted to free itself from my flesh.

"It's up the street. But that was months ago. I don't expect they've kept anything."

We went up the street and, no, they hadn't kept anything. Because where the warehouse once stood was now a vacant lot filled with the charred rubble of a building.

"I hadn't heard about a fire," Calvin said, at a loss.

"No. How could you? Thank you for your time." I tried to leave.

"Wait. Let me walk with you. I'll get us smokes. We can talk." Calvin ducked into a shop to buy cigarettes, and I left. Turning quickly around corners. But I didn't go home. I wandered the streets of the city, thinking, trying not to despair, failing miserably.

The other Colonists shunned me now. I didn't want to talk to them. Or even see them. Life in New Colony had become terribly, awfully ordinary. Nina's disappearance was accepted, a tasty piece of communal gossip that faded and was replaced by more recent news. It drove me mad. I only stayed in case she came home. If only she were still here…

I had to find answers. So I decided to go where the answers were most likely to be.

To do what I'd dreaded doing for so long.

I had to see Balthazarr.

Balthazarr had taken up residence in the penthouse suite at the Silver Gate. He lived and worked on the top floor, with a view of the entire city available to him. I showed up at the hotel one afternoon, while cold March rain slashed the hotel façade. I asked at the hotel desk for them to ring Balthazarr's suite. I knew the artist had a reputation for sleeping late, but he'd be awake by now. In effect, I imagined he knew I was coming down to the hour, maybe even the minute I called on him.

"Mr Balthazarr says you should come right up. Elevators are across the lobby."

"Thank you."

The old guy operating the elevator greeted me cheerily.

"Good morning, sir!"

"Good morning."

"Oh, sir, don't I know it. I know it in my heart. Every morning is a good one."

What a peculiar man, I thought. Happy in his work. Ignorant of the dangers lurking.

He transported me up to the penthouse.

"To your left. Enjoy your visit. Once you stay here, you'll never go anywhere else."

I thanked the old man and watched the doors close on his grinning face. I walked the long hallway. The carpet was plush. The wallpaper geometric and modern. I felt as though I were inside a work of art. An artificial facsimile. Fake. Unreal. What is real? How can one know? At the end of the hallway, the door stood ajar. I was peeking in when I heard him.

"Welcome, Alden. It has been too long. Please, don't be shy."

I pushed the door open. I didn't see anyone. The main room of the suite was a tremendous mess. No maid had cleaned in here for weeks. Balthazarr transformed the rooms into a version of his home studio from Spain. Paints, canvases, brushes soaking in muddycolored jars. Beautiful wreckage wherever the eye landed. Someone had attempted to spread several drop cloths on the furniture and carpeting. They'd been moved and shifted around so that whatever protection they had offered was now nil. I found the bathroom. Empty. The sink was running. I turned the faucet off. Balthazarr's untidy, vacant bedroom. Cushions arranged on the floor. The bed stripped. The nightstand covered with drippy, melted candles and bottles of varying design. It reminded me of the floor tiles of South Church. But I tried not to look too hard. I didn't need distraction or to feel more uneasy. Wet roof. Dunphy falling.

Where did Balthazarr sleep?

I had concluded he must be hiding from me, when I felt his hand touch my shoulder.

"Ahh!"

"Sorry, did I frighten you? I am enjoying a cup of herbal tea. Would you like some?"

He offered his teacup for me to smell.

It was pungent, musky. I couldn't imagine drinking it.

"No, thank you."

"As you wish." He was dressed in a flowing silk kaftan of pale yellow. A medley of other colors had been splashed and dried across its surface over the years, so that it was like a modern Balthazarr canvas he wore. "Let's sit and talk. Not for too long. I have work to do."

I joined him on a pair of oversized ottomans in the middle of the room. All the curtains had been taken down. I had a dizzying sense of pitching over the end of the building as I looked out. Rain slithering on the glass. Shapes in the clouds. Billowing, gray, opaque.

"I'll get right to it," I said. "Where's Nina?" *JHB? Who else? Two places at once.*

"Ha! You're asking me? I thought she was your girlfriend."

"Do you know?" An edginess slid into my voice. I sound crazy, I thought.

"I'm sure she'll come back to you when she is ready. But I see you are serious and in pain. I am sorry I cannot help you. How is your painting going? Doing anything interesting?"

"I've had a productive few months." My surge of pride bothered me.

"Excellent. The Colony has been good to you, no?"

"They don't talk to me any more."

"Talk is not the only way to communicate. You are making art. That's what's important."

He sipped his horrible tea. I could smell it on his breath, like rotten flowers.

"What is going on in Arkham?" I asked. "Why are you really here? Don't lie to me."

"There are no lies. Only stories … pictures … our fantasies."

I shifted on my cushion. I could not find a comfortable position. My muscles ached. I had a new headache sprouting. "I know what happened at the Clover Club wasn't simply a case of hypnotism. You did something … something real …"

"We manufacture reality. Make it new every day on the assembly line of a shared consciousness. But truth is what *I* dream it is. There is no such thing as a fiction. My dreams are as real as their bricks. I am going to use my dreams to smash the windows of this world. Look around you. It is a dead universe we struggle to survive in, Alden. A graveyard only capable of breeding more graves. They will fill the earth with death. But not I. Balthazarr wants no part of their scheming. I am a destroyer and a creator. I annihilate death and replace it with my art."

He looked totally serene as he told me this. My spine was twisted, stiffening. "You are trying to break reality." I mopped my forehead. The suite was humid as a greenhouse.

"That's one way of putting it. Ask yourself, whose reality? Not mine, I guarantee you that. Politicians, generals, and businessmen conceived this reality. I reject it. I demand a revolution. Artists, dreamers, and the so-called mad people will have their chance. Reality must be broken." He finished his tea, placing the cup on the floor. He fluffed out his tunic.

"Is that what your paintings do?"

"Paintings? Yes, but they are so much more. Your thinking is too small. We must be big to triumph in these days of modern wonders. Live boldly." He spread his arms out.

"I'm a painter. I might even be a surrealist like you. 'Live boldly'. What does that even mean?" I loosened my tie. My head throbbed. I felt the veins under my skin, netting my skull.

"It is about time. Paintings, novels, sculpture, poetry, films… any work wrought by the mind and human hands. Once we conquer time, everything becomes meaningless. My life's work is digging an escape tunnel out from this dimension, my reality prison cell. My knuckles are bloody from tunneling out of their sterile world. When I go out, I'm leaving the Gate open for whatever haunts the other dimension to come in. It is of no concern to me! Come with me, Alden. Let's break out together. Everything is death except for dreams. We are artists. You work for my dreams. I work for yours. Together, we become the future. Our work will live for eternity. There isn't much time left."

I took off my jacket and folded it across my knees. Outside the windows, the distant grayed buildings appeared to be warping. "The night of Preston's party, when we were alone in Independence Park, you asked me if I thought you were crazy. I still don't know how to answer that question."

"Fair enough. That is how you choose to interpret me. I am too busy to be a critic."

"What comes next? What is your best reasonable alternative?"

The question bored Balthazarr. "If reason gave us this, what good is reason? Don't you want to see something new? Even if it's nothing? I have no plan. Perhaps we shall try chaos. If there is no order, then everyone has the power of a god. Do you want that too?"

"I've heard enough." I got up, nearly losing my balance. I caught myself teetering.

"You have everything you need to decide. I hope you make a wise choice."

Without answering him, or saying goodbye, I turned and left the suite. The elevator operator was waiting for me at the end of the hallway. His empty smile stretched wide like a mask. His blank eyes never blinking. I left the hotel, but the feeling of vertigo and the aroma of Balthazarr's tea lingered.

Chapter Thirty

Preston called me the next day. He had decided to join his parents down at their winter home in West Palm Beach. They built a place there during the war, when the Mediterranean became inhospitably treacherous. The Florida land boom was over; real estate prices were dropping, but the Fairmonts had enough cash and diversity in their investments to ride things out. Preston had planned to travel south for some sun and leisure after his bachelor party, but I was stunned when I heard him say he'd left town by train the very next day. Doubly surprising was the news that Minnie left with him. Why hadn't they sent any word to me?

"Oakesy, we need to tell you something. It's terribly embarrassing. Shameful, really."

"What is it?"

"We've called off the wedding," he said. His voice was jarring. A hoarse croak.

"Called it off. I've only just learned the date was changed. Why on earth…?" It was beyond belief. I'd come home from Europe. For this! If not for them, Nina might still be…

"I'd rather not go into particulars. Father advised me to cool things off. Let's say it's postponed. Less grim, don't you think?" Preston sounded so far away. Not the other end of the country, the end of the galaxy.

I gazed out my window, combing my fingers though my hair. The Miskatonic ran fast with runoff. There were things floating in the water. Bloated, mottled. Rolling like fat barrels.

"Is anyone sick?" I asked. My mouth felt dry. I licked my lips, papery and cracked.

"No." Preston echoed as if he'd fallen down a deep well. "I can't talk much longer."

"Did you know Nina's gone missing? Since the night of your bachelor party…"

"Not Nina too." He gasped. His words bounced off the walls of that murky well. I heard a deep, gravelly voice in the background. His father? Or someone else? A cacophony of other voices suddenly interrupted us, talking all at once.

"Preston? Preston are you there?" I pressed the handset hard to my ear.

"Get away." That's what I thought I heard him say. I can't be certain. Not of what I heard or who said it. Too much static on the line, then the connection was cut off. Dead. I hung up.

The following morning two letters arrived in my mailbox. One was from Preston and Minnie, their apologies and a notice of the cancellation of their ceremony.

The other was an invitation.

> *The honor of your presence is requested at*
> *Juan Hugo Balthazarr's Masquerade*
> *In the Main Room*
> *At the Silver Gate Hotel*
> *Masks are required*
> *Midnight, March 27th, 1926*

The date and location were identical to Preston and Minnie's aborted wedding.

The time was later, of course.

The days leading up to Balthazarr's masquerade ball passed in a blur. From Oakwood, I received a delivery: my tuxedo and a note from Ro wishing me good times. New Colony was a hive of activity. Colonists who had shunned me in the months since Nina's departure now showed a renewed camaraderie and friendliness in the hallways and walking on the grounds. I wrapped up my finished paintings for storage, and Roland was kind enough to pick them up and take them to the house for me, in case anything unexpected happened. I told him I was worried about a leaking roof. He knew better but didn't ask questions. I wasn't sure what was going to happen. I wanted my work salvaged in any case. I worked too hard to lose it all.

I busied myself with a final piece that I planned to unveil at the ball. It was something I'd never attempted before, an arts and crafts project. Glue, paper, an elastic string.

The day before the party I happened to see Balthazarr mixing with Colonists on the front lawn of the mansion. His piercing gaze locked on me as soon as I exited the building.

I walked right up to him.

He extricated himself from his conversation. The crowd moved off to give us privacy.

"I got your reply. I am immensely pleased you are attending my event," he said.

"I had a chance to think about what you said to me that day at your penthouse. Well, I've made up my mind. I'm following you."

"Excellent, excellent. See you at the Silver Gate."

I don't think he believed me. But that didn't matter.

The night of the ball, I put on my tux and took out my arts and crafts project to study it one last time. It was a full-face mask. I'd made it myself from papier mâché, glue, and paint. I put the mask on and checked my reflection in the mirror. It wasn't perfect, but it suited my purpose. I thought about writing a letter to Mother and Father. You know, if things didn't work out. But what would I possibly say? Would they believe me? In the end I decided against it. What would last, would last. All else was destined to be forgotten, lost in time.

One final thing.

I opened the drawer of my dresser. I moved aside my undershirts. I still had the gun I'd lifted off the tough guy in the hallway, the man Balthazarr tossed in the river. I wasn't sure if he was dead or alive, that bully who went for a swim into the icy, onyx Miskatonic. What we saw dripping on the banks that night might've been him, or it might've easily been a monster made of nets and rats. Either way, I had his gun. I checked the bullets. Then I tucked it into the small of my back and covered it with my jacket.

I was ready.

I drove the Rolls-Royce to the hotel, parked it out front where everyone could see me.

The Silver Gate was a real beauty. That night she looked white and shiny like an ocean liner, or a huge stone cliff covered with snow and ice. Maybe, from a certain angle, she looked like a wedding cake covered in diamonds. She sparkled to beat the band.

Outside, the night air was fresh and clean. It would be a good night for sleeping.

Inside, they'd filled the lobby with roses. Explosions of red everywhere you turned.

I saw Colonists loitering in the lobby, smoking. They already had their masks on.

"Hiya, Alden! Where's your mask?"

I held up a paper bag. "Got it right here. See you inside."

Balthazarr's ball was in the Silver Gate's main room. I hadn't felt anything unusual the other times I entered the hotel. But I felt something now. A low, steady vibration humming from the structure itself, as if it were a tuning fork. I wondered how long ago the wheels of this scheme started turning, because Balthazarr and his Colonists weren't acting alone in this. They were in the final phase of a long-range plan. This was the last ritual in a string of others. Was it global? Who knew how far the tendrils reached? But whatever entity they had been calling to across dimensions, sending out their blood-soaked signals… Whatever they called it… Yuyu-Va'badaa or the Un-Sun… the Falling Star… that shapeless void careening through space and time had been drawing nearer to Earth, and tonight, finally, they hoped it would arrive in glory. The Gate would open. They didn't even try to hide it. The Silver Gate. I bet they had a good laugh at that. Hiding in plain sight, biding their time. As patient as they were deadly.

The doors to the main room were shut. Masked sentinels guarded them.

"You need to put on your mask," one said to me. It was Portia's voice, our downstairs neighbor, the sculptress who replaced Courtland Dunphy. Did she know how they killed him?

I removed my mask from the paper bag and put it on.

Portia drew in a sharp breath.

"Can you dispose of this for me?" I asked.

She took the bag but said nothing.

I opened the doors and went inside.

I could see why they wanted to keep outsiders from seeing the ballroom. They had removed all the tables and chairs. There was no bar, no banquet. Only the gleaming marble floor. From the ceiling hung lit chandeliers; tall black candles in wrought iron stands stood around the perimeter of the room, their wicks unburnt. The floor itself was the real stunner. Elaborate glyphs covered every available inch of tile. It must've taken them hours to create it, I thought. A small army of artists at work, following a mathematically precise occult diagram that was magnificently intricate. What was the purpose of this design?

It wasn't a map of any known universe.

I don't know what it was, to be honest. A symbol, or series of interlocking symbols, drawn on the floor is my best guess. In some places, the lines were poured in powders – rusty auburns, gray-speckled blacks, and bone whites. Brushstrokes of gold, silver, and red traced angles and spirals. At the center was a perfect circle. Within it, a falling star, the same symbol I'd seen before, dripped in wax at South Church and carved into Dunphy's apartment door.

Here, it appeared to be burned on the marble.

If a visitor wandered into this room by mistake and didn't look down, or notice the lack of furniture and refreshments, they might've thought it was just a bizarrely themed party. The attendees gathered in small conversational groups, smoking cigarettes, gossiping, killing time until things got swinging. *I* was the most shocking part of the night so far.

It was my mask.

Many of the masked chose to hide their eyes only, but I wore a full-face disguise.

I'd done my best to get the features right, but the dead giveaway was my long, forked beard. I used hair clippings from a barbershop. Oh, I was too short and slim to be mistaken for the actual Balthazarr. But at a distance, especially in profile, a quick glance might lead someone to think I was the sorcerer, the Twister of the Coil. It was disrespectful, my mocking their leader. At worst, the mask was blasphemous.

Balthazarr hadn't made an appearance yet. That was who they were all waiting for.

Well, one of the things they were waiting for, anyway.

The chandeliers dimmed. The candles were lit. Music – a thin, eerie wailing of strings from an instrument I could not identify, and whose player remained concealed – began. *Ah, the show is starting.* I made a path to the middle, on the rim of the circle. The crowd parted before me. The sentinels entered, securing the doors behind them with chains and padlocks. A group of busy Colonists passed out robes. The masqueraders cloaked up.

Someone handed me a robe. The garment was celestial blue.

"I expected black," I said.

No one responded to my remark. I slipped the robe on.

Juan Hugo Balthazarr knew how to make an entrance. Not from the background or some curtained wing off stage. No. He simply arrived inside the circle. Perhaps we were all hypnotized already. He glided among us, a moving blind spot. I don't know how he did it.

He was not the focus of my attention.

Because Balthazarr did not arrive alone.

Nina stood at his side.

I could not breathe. My torso experienced a temporary paralysis. Worrying I might lose consciousness and sabotage my mission, I struck my fist against my chest. Slowly, I inhaled. Had she succumbed to the allure of this cult? She was too good, too strong. But there was no denying her standing there assisting Balthazarr. His companion in this sorcerous rite.

Wisps of fragrant smoke floated in the room, scribbling up from bronze censers.

Balthazarr raised his hands overhead.

"New Colonists, allies, and benefactors… Welcome to the end of the world!"

The crowd cheered.

"This is a new day, the last day. We call to the Un-Sun, the Falling Star. We open the Gate for Yuyu-Va'bdaa. The old ways of reason, order, and logic are no more. We hunger for chaos and thirst for insanity, so that we may lose the burden of our servitude and be free from the dungeon of laws, rules, and commandments. Lies are true. We are our own gods."

The masked congregants fell to their knees.

All except for me.

I stood there, wearing Balthazarr's face.

My plan was to shoot him, to empty my pistol into his chest. An artistic statement as well as an assassination. What was more surreal than Balthazarr killing Balthazarr? But I hadn't expected Nina to be there. I was willing to take a chance with my personal escape from the scene. Her survival was another matter. Through the eyeholes of my mask I tried to make sense of her. She didn't seem to recognize me. How would she? All the people wore robes, and no part of my true face showed. Nina wasn't looking at anyone, just staring straight out. Her pupils were dilated. Entranced, that much I judged for certain, perhaps they'd drugged her. When did they catch her that night? How? It didn't matter, not now.

I made a gambit to play along with the ritual for now.

"Unmask yourself, Alden," Balthazarr said.

I obeyed.

Pain licked my fingertips. The mask was on fire. I dropped it to the floor and watched the paper curl and whiten to ash.

Nina's wrists were crossed under the sleeves of her robe. When she drew them apart, I saw she held the cycloptic cane Balthazarr had used to orchestrate the ritual at the Clover Club. She raised the diabolic stick into the air.

"Balthazarr! Yuyu-Va'bdaa!" she cried.

"Nina! Yuyu-Va'bdaa!" Balthazarr replied.

"Balthazarr! Nina! Yuyu-Va'bdaa!" the kneeling supplicants repeated.

"*Ebuma chtenff! Gnaiih goka gotha gof'nn!*" Nina said, slamming the tip of the wooden ritualistic instrument into the floor. The outer boundaries of the ballroom drifted away. The candles became pinpricks of starlight. A darkness enshrouded us. Slowly, a pale greenish hue tainted the surrounding air.

No, Nina, no…

How was this woman my Nina?

She always ran ahead, I thought. Sometimes ahead, there is a trap.

Balthazarr pointed at me. I was pulled into the circle as if a rope were cinched around my body, and I could not resist its urgent tugging. Balthazarr wore his robe from Spain; the mirrors and shards of broken glass glittered, a galaxy in motion, breaking down, tumbling into oblivion.

"Where do I stand?" I asked him. My will was slipping. The puppet master pulled my strings. I was determined to fight him. But it was so much easier not to fight…

Balthazarr pointed to a glyph drawn on the marble, a cup with an oval balanced inside. "You are the final sacrifice," he said to me. "The First Key."

"And what is she?" I asked.

"I am the Bride," Nina answered. "The Second Key."

"Whose bride?" I asked.

Neither of them said a word.

A roar came from not far off. Its volume grew stronger until my eardrums ached.

The same roar I'd heard in the Clover Club. The fire-breather, the voice of a dragon flying through space to consume our human race. To swallow us like a moistened crumb.

Nina raised the cyclops stick. Its lidless eye glowed, an orb containing galaxies.

"This is the ritual. I am the Sorcerer," Balthazarr said. "We are at the dawning of a new sun, never witnessed before by impotent human eyes, a sun that burns without light, that consumes all. I, the Twister of the Coil, open the Gate! Do you see it? Do you see?"

"We see!" the supplicants answered.

Our circle tilted on its axis – a disk floating free in outer space. The masqueraders clung to their own geometric platform as it lifted and fell, crest to trough, again and again, riding on a cosmic sea. Mirages materialized in the zone above us. Each vision a tableau of one of Arkham's recent ritual murders. Dr Silva swinging from a lamppost, her pockets stuffed with witchweed. Udo Ganz unzipped of his tattooed skin. The Galinka sisters kicking their dancers' legs as they burned on a pyre. The tramp bleeding outside a boxcar. Dunphy clutching a gargoyle horn as he plummeted toward the ground. Clark's naked, headless corpse splayed beneath a telescope pointed at the stars...

Somewhere outside of linear time, the murders were still happening, *would always be happening* in a continuous, never-ending loop.

They flashed like lighthouse signals to Yuyu-Va'bdaa as it navigated the cosmos.

I saw the murders for what they were: impersonal, cold as a mechanism, tumblers in a lock, but also lights, like candles, stationed along a dark path.

They led to the Gate and they opened it, too.

Smoke-like tendrils began to form out of Balthazarr's body. An array gathered around his head and as they solidified, they fashioned themselves into a spiked crown. From his hand sprung a long, three-pronged fork with which he stirred the air.

"Beholder from Beyond, God of Dimensions Unimagined, Lord and Servant of None and Nothing, I call to you! Take this Man as a final sacrifice of the last ritual. This Woman is your eternal Bride. Falling Star, Fall Here! Un-Sun, be born! Yuyu-Va'bdaa, come to us!"

"Be born!" the worshippers called out, even as turbulence rocked their platform and tossed numbers of them screaming into the ether. "Come to us! Yuyu-Va'bdaa!"

I drew my pistol and, pointing it squarely at Balthazarr, I pulled the trigger.

The trigger did not move. The weapon scorched my hand. I smelled hot metal and my burning flesh. Balthazarr's piercing eyes transformed into pits of swirling kaleidoscopic colors. The pistol glowed orange. Furnace-hot. My skin sizzled. The gun turning to liquid.

I screamed.

"Fool! I offered you the opportunity of a lifetime. Beyond any lifetime!" Balthazarr flicked his wrist, and the molten metal scattered. A glob landed on my cheek, searing into my cheekbone. A thick tentacle of ectoplasmic fog snapped out of the Surrealist's ribcage and looped around my throat, strangling me. A vile energy passed through him, entangling me.

As I choked, my fingers dug into the viscous substance.

"Chaos is the new order!" he shouted. "Lose your sanity! Abandon old logic. Yuyu-Va'bdaa shatters time. There is no future. No past. Now is All! See it! We are with Yuyu!"

Stars exploded in my eyes.

Not real stars, but the blood vessels in my head. I was dying. My body crushed. I would not follow Balthazarr. No one would. After the Gate opened, it would be death.

Only death.

In the dimming light of my receding consciousness, I reached out to feel the sleeve of Nina's robe. I could not see, but I could feel. Was that her hand touching mine? Yes! But she could not hold onto me. Nor I hold fast to her. Our fingers lost their grip. Soon our sanity would follow. I clutched the material of her robe in my fist. Then it too pulled away from me.

Gone, she's gone.

I am too.

Nina did not make a sound. The silence was worse. I called and called, "Nina!"

No reply came.

Only a whirling of winds greater than any earthly storm. And the roar of Yuyu.

My vision zeroed down to a tight tunnel.

In that tunnel with me was the face of Balthazarr, huge and triumphant, victorious. His grimacing mouth fell open. The noose around my neck slackened. Blood rushed into my starved brain. I struggled to see what was happening in front of me. Balthazarr spun his arms wildly, striking out at nothing. A flash of quick movement. A tall woman, the woman I knew.

Nina backed away from him.

He clutched at his neck. The tendrils looping from his body evaporated.

The handle of Nina's Frosolone stiletto protruded from the hood of his robe. She had stabbed him sideways, slicing through meat and bone. The slender blade transected his spinal cord. Strings cut, the Spaniard crumpled. His face transformed to a mask of total disbelief.

But what of her? Was it too late? My heart flooded with sudden hope of our survival.

"Nina!" My words lost amid a constant roar.

The void – arrested at the threshold!

The Gate split open. It was, and is, impossible to describe. Call it a dilation between dimensions. A tearing of the veil between our reality and an otherness. An evanescent portal.

It started to close. To seal itself like a cosmic wound clotted with stars.

Full of stars.

I strained with every muscle fiber to reach her. She took a step toward me, but a powerful funnel of air was sucking inward – a cosmic inhalation drawing everything to the Gate and the lightless immensity perching on the brink of universes. Balthazarr tumbled, flipping end over end, into the vanishing gap. Nina watched him go. She had saved me. She held out her hand for me to take. "Now, Alden." Fear seized me instead. Controlling me. Thoughts of the Gate and what lay beyond it: an unbounded chasm. Endless nothingness.

So, I am ashamed to admit I hesitated. A fraction of a second. No more.

Then I lunged for her. But it was too late. I was too late.

I watched the Gate take her.

It closed.

Back inside, the ballroom was chaos. The room was dark. I crawled on the floor, over bodies, dead and dying. The candles had fallen over, most of them extinguishing themselves.

But not every candle.

I found the doors. Locked. I smashed at the padlocks with my fists. I was too weak, my hands too soft. My eyes had trouble seeing things. I turned to the chasm of the ballroom, the moans of the injured, the giggling gibberish of those driven utterly insane by what they had witnessed. I groped for an iron candle stand. I ripped a burning candle from its holder and threw it at the wall. Taking the stand, I smashed open the lock. The doors flung wide.

"Alden! Is that you?"

Calvin caught me as I pitched forward. Behind me, the wall where I threw the candle started to burn, a wavering curtain of flame. "We need to get out of here now," he said.

"Nina."

"Where is she?"

He pulled me upright.

I bolted back inside the ballroom, yelling her name, the smoke thick and poisonous.

The Silver Gate feeding itself, and everyone still inside, to the inferno.

Chapter Thirty-One

Van Nortwick put down his pencil and massaged his tired hand. He reached for the last bottle of ginger ale and tilted it against his lips, but found it empty.

"That's quite a story, Mr Oakes." He was going to write it up. It would make the paper. But he wasn't sure how much of it he believed.

"We're out of cigarettes, Andy. I think that means it's time to stop."

The painter leaned against the dresser. He'd left the sofa hours ago, complaining that his bad leg felt stiff. He paced around the hotel room as he talked, settling back on the window ledge or propping himself up on the furniture, like he was doing now.

"You never told me what happened to your leg," Van Nortwick said.

"Ceiling collapse. Not in the ballroom but the lobby. A beam hit me. I thought that might be the end, but I managed to wriggle free. A fracture, they said at the hospital. But I limped outside. That's when the fireman tackled me. My jacket was burning. I mentioned this to you already. Don't want to start repeating myself. Anyway, I'm healed up. My body is."

The reporter picked up his pencil again, tapping it on his notepad.

"Preston Fairmont and Minnie Devane…?" Van Nortwick's pencil stirred.

"They went traveling for a while. Sent me postcards from around the world. Preston felt guilty for leaving town, but he needed to escape. He saved himself. And Minnie too. I don't blame him." Alden pushed off the dresser, walked to the window. "I saw it in the papers that his father died. I can only imagine the pressure Preston's under now." Gray rain fell steadily.

"Well, thank you for your time. You've certainly given me a lot to digest."

Alden turned to him, smiling thinly.

"You think I made it up."

Van Nortwick shrugged. "It's not my place to judge. I gather facts, write them down in neat columns the way my editor likes. It's up to our readers to decide what they think."

Alden nodded. "Care to try an experiment?"

The reporter paused, considering the offer.

"For the benefit of your readers, of course. It'll be easy," Alden said.

"Sure, Mr Oakes. You've been generous with me. I can do that."

The artist looked at the window again. Then, as if he'd come to a decision, he swiveled around and positioned himself in front of the hotel room's only mirror. "Come stand behind me, Andy, over my shoulder here, and look into the glass."

Skeptically, Van Nortwick rose and joined Alden at the mirror.

"How's this?" he said.

"Perfect," Alden said. "Now, concentrate on our reflections."

Van Nortwick did his best, focusing on the room as it was doubled in the glass.

After a long minute, Alden met his gaze. "Well, see anything? Besides the two of us."

Van Nortwick stared hard. Then, shaking his head, he stepped to one side.

"Sorry, Mr Oakes," he said.

"That's fine. I'll give you credit for trying. Good luck with your story." Alden started packing his gin, shaker, and glasses into his red crocodile suitcase. When he finished, he drew out the necklace he wore. Van Nortwick saw there were two keys on the necklace. Alden locked the case. The reporter prepared to go. At the door, they exchanged goodbyes.

"Have fun at the gala," Van Nortwick said, stepping out of the suite into the hall.

They shook hands. The reporter startled for a moment at the rough scar tissue. How had he been burned? In an accident of some sort? Or it might be self-inflicted, he thought.

Probably the hotel blaze. He was lucky to have survived.

Alden was smiling wanly as he shut the door.

Have fun at the gala. How stupid can I possibly be? Van Nortwick chastised himself as he rode down in the elevator with the creepy old operator outfitted like an organ grinder's monkey. Alden Oakes might be as crazy as people said. But after a tragedy like the Silver Gate fire, who wouldn't be traumatized? He didn't need to be told to have fun reliving the experience. Stupid.

Van Nortwick lingered in the lobby. It wasn't that Oakes hadn't given him enough for a good story. Just the opposite. He'd given too much. How was he going to turn all that talk into a clever bit of journalism? Van Nortwick bought a pack of cigarettes from the hotel newsstand. He was watching the rain, hoping it would let up so he wouldn't get completely soaked walking back to the *Arkham Advertiser* offices, when he spotted Alden emerging from the elevator. The artist had a small satchel over his shoulder. He headed straight back toward the event rooms.

Van Nortwick followed him.

He was going into the newly renovated ballroom, the heart of the tragedy, and the location of tonight's party. Van Nortwick waited for as long as it took him to finish his smoke, then he crushed out the butt in a standing ashtray and went inside.

The room was mostly dark. He searched for the painter but found no trace of him.

"Back here," Alden said.

In a far corner of the great room, the painter sat cross-legged on the floor. His satchel was open, and a small array of paint jars and brushes were arranged beside him.

He was painting on the wall. The outline of the image was the size of a person.

"Start at the bottom and work your way up. That's how I'm doing it." Alden smiled.

"Some people would call that vandalism," Van Nortwick said.

"Everyone's a critic. But you're right about one thing. No one will be happy if they catch me doing this. I'll be quick, though. I've been practicing." He'd moved into a crouch, then up on his knees. His brushstrokes were fast and sure. It *was* a person he was painting.

"It's a woman."

"It's Nina," Alden said.

"*Portrait of a Lady?*"

"*Portrait of a Lady in Another Dimension.* Will you hand me the red, please?"

Van Nortwick passed him the paint.

"And that brush there. Don't worry, you're not my accomplice. I take full responsibility."

"I suppose an Alden Oakes original is worth a lot of money these days."

"The hotel couldn't afford me if I charged them." Alden was standing, leaning forward. He'd almost finished the painting of the woman, of Nina. Full of motion, stylized. She wasn't wearing a robe but a red dress. Her head was tipped back slightly, chin up, the hint of knowing smile barely perceptible on her lips. "I see Balthazarr in reflections, but he is not alone. Nina is there, too. I don't know if they are even aware of each other. They never interact. I think their spectral figures are like a double exposure, two overlapping images combined in the same photograph. I've studied the images. Balthazarr's paintings. Others I've found in my research that I'm sure are connected to their rituals. I've painted them over and over. Balthazarr's way isn't the only way to open a gate, you see."

Van Nortwick didn't see now, just as he hadn't when he looked deeply into the mirror over Alden's shoulder, but he wasn't going to interfere.

"Why did she have the blade with her, if she was a believer and follower of Balthazarr? Think about it, Andy." Alden put the final touches on his portrait. "She was still my Nina. I don't know who took her the night I went to Preston's party. It was either the Colonists, or maybe Juan Hugo himself. If Nina was right, he could project himself in two places at once. It doesn't matter now. The past is past, they say. I'm not sure I totally agree."

"You want to bring her back?"

"Not exactly. You'd better stand back over there. I can't predict everything that might happen next."

Andy started to move away to where the painter had directed him.

"Wait! I forgot something." Alden slipped the necklace from around his collar. "The gold one opens my gin case. It's yours. Here's my room key so you can fetch it afterward." He fished the hotel key out of his pocket.

Van Nortwick looked at the pair of keys on the necklace.

"What's this other key for?"

"Get back a bit farther. Farther. There. That should do it." Alden pushed his art supplies away from the portrait. He looked at Van Nortwick. "I failed Nina. As the Gate pulled her through, I hesitated. I lacked courage." A haggard smile, resolved, etched in pain.

He reached into his satchel and pulled out a pair of thick iron shackles.

"Houdini's handcuffs," Van Nortwick said. What did the artist have in mind?

Some magic trick of his own design? He hoped the result wouldn't be too awkward. Or sad. That would be even worse. To watch a fragile mind breaking in front of you. If that happened, Van Nortwick decided, right then and there, he wouldn't put it in his story.

Alden wasn't paying attention to him any more. He was reciting words in a strange guttural language, chanting in a singsong cadence. Van Nortwick was too far away to make out the exact phrases, but they would've made no sense to him.

The wall.

The portrait of Nina pulsed. Then it shone and rippled like the surface of a sunlit pond. Van Nortwick dropped the necklace on the floor. His mouth hung open like a fish thrown on the dock. It was truly supernatural! He felt hugely excited and terrified at the same time. If this were happening, then what other parts of Alden Oakes' tale were true? Could it be accurate in every detail? Van Nortwick's mind was boggled. He staggered. The world was not what he thought it was. It was deeper and darker.

And so much more.

Nina Tarrington reached out to Alden.

This time he clearly wasn't going to let fear get the best of him. Alden snapped one cuff on Nina's wrist, and then he snapped the other on his own. He took a deep breath as they crossed over the threshold, disappearing together, forever, through the Gate.

ACKNOWLEDGMENTS

At Aconyte I'd like to thank Marc Gascoigne, my most excellent publisher, for the opportunity to work on this exciting and rewarding adventure. I owe a special debt of gratitude to my editor, Lottie Llewelyn-Wells, for her keen eye, brilliant insights, and crystal clarity in all matters. And thanks to the whole talented Aconyte team for their dedication, hard work, and support.

Thanks to Asmodee Entertainment, Fantasy Flight Games, and *Arkham Horror* for the world.

Lastly, I wish to thank my wife, Lisa, and my children, Emma and Quinn. Without their love this book would not exist.

About the Author

S A SIDOR is the author of four dark crime thrillers and more recently two splendid supernatural-pulp adventures, *Fury From the Tomb* and *The Beast of Nightfall Lodge*. He lives near Chicago with his family.

sasidor.com // x.com/SA_Sidor

ARKHAM HORROR

LITANY OF DREAMS

ARI MARMELL

PROLOGUE

The aromas of life, rich and cloying and congealing in the back of his throat, danced arm in arm with the stink of putrefaction and death.

Wilmott Polaski, a pale and scrawny figure whose element included musty books and dusty shelves, jabbering students and bickering academics – and most assuredly did *not* include copses of thick boughs, glittering eyes peering from the shadows, swarms of insects and waterlogged socks – found himself uncertain as to which collection of scents was worse.

The boots he had hurriedly purchased for this sojourn fit poorly, and his coat was woefully inadequate. Mosquitoes, for which he would have thought the lingering winter chill would be too cold, hovered in thick clouds over the languid waters. Strange birds, or what he assumed to be birds, called in the distance. Ragged moss sagged from tired branches that always seemed to be reaching his way, perhaps attracted to his warmth in lieu of a spring thaw that refused to come.

Did Hockomock have alligators? He didn't think so, couldn't recall ever hearing of such creatures here. With every glance toward the dark and rippling surface, always lapping uncomfortably close to the roadway, however, he grew less and less confident.

In short, the good professor deeply did not wish to be here. With any luck, he wouldn't have to be for long.

Another twenty minutes' walk produced nothing akin to an alligator, nor anything more hostile than those mosquitoes, but it did – finally! – bring into view the community he'd caught the train down from Arkham to find.

If, he observed with some disdain, one could even dignify it with the term.

It had no name, so far as he knew. No fixed borders, no shops, no municipal center or identity. Just a collection of scattered homes and tiny farms huddled on the edge of the Hockomock Swamp, a "community" only in the sense that the several dozen families who lived in these ramshackle domiciles interacted with one another on a somewhat regular basis, and seldomly with anyone else.

The houses were old, rickety, shingles and walls beginning to rot, the supports that held them above the muddy flats and potential floods bowing like the legs of a tired grandfather. While Wilmott heard sporadic sounds of labor in the distance, the striking of tools on wood or wet soil, he saw no one.

Nervously, he dug into his coat pocket, once more checking a bundle of handwritten notes and a hastily sketched diagram. He'd anticipated an unfriendly reception – from Henry Armitage and other fellow academics, he'd heard many a report of just how mistrustful some of these insular Massachusetts communities could be – but somehow the total absence of reception was more disturbing still.

According to his haphazard little map, however, he was still on course. With a sigh he returned the papers to his pocket and continued.

The water of the swamp puddled before him, occupying a shallow dip in the roadway. Mud squelched under his steps, threatening to yank the ill-fitting boots from his blistering feet. Wilmott swallowed a stream of profanity. Damn the useless Arkham police, damn Chester and damn himself for getting caught up in the young fool's endeavors!

He glanced skyward, hoping to estimate the time of day, how long he had to accomplish his self-assigned mission before he had to turn back if he wanted to beat the sunset. The sun, however, skulking behind layers of white cedar branches and fat, ponderous clouds, told him nothing. With more silent cursing, he turned his gaze once again to the path ahead…

Was that it? That house there, hunkered at the very edges of the deeper waters? Its wood sagging, windows sloping like sleep-heavy eyelids?

It could be. To judge by his last look at the map, it should be. Defying the nervous agitation in his gut and drawing himself up to his full, impressive – if woefully spindly – height, Wilmott marched forward and pounded his knuckles on the door.

It shuddered. Paint flecks snowed down to his feet. Nothing more.

Wilmott waited what he judged a polite interval, then knocked again, harder still.

And again.

What to do if nobody was home? Somehow, in all his deliberations about whether to even come, all the time it took him to pinpoint and then reach his destination, he'd failed to consider so basic a hurdle. Perhaps this sort of thing was more complicated than he'd given–

The door finally swung open, with less a creaking than an angry and fiercely startling *crack*, as he raised his fist to try once more. Wilmott found himself staring at a yellowed shirt under frayed denim overalls.

He craned his head upward. An angry, reddened face, covered in the thick stubble of untended weeks, glared down at him.

"What?" The man's voice was as coarse as his chin and cheeks.

Wilmott removed his hat – as much to give himself a second to recover as out of courtesy. "Afternoon. Are you Woodrow Hennessy?"

"Who's askin'?" He spoke with a near-impenetrable drawl; Wilmott, for all his efforts to be kind, couldn't come up with a better term than *backwoods*.

"My name is Professor Wilmott Polaski, from Miskatonic University. I–"

"Got no use for university folk. If you're lookin' for a guide, go back'n ask over in Taunton." The door began to shut.

"No, you don't understand. I'm searching for a missing student. Chester Hennessy."

The door halted.

Taking that as an invitation to continue, Wilmott bulled on. "Chester's been gone for several weeks now, and I'm afraid the authorities have been stymied. I recalled that he'd mentioned you on occasion, and I thought perhaps–"

"Ain't talked to Chester in years. He an' his don't have truck with our side of the family."

Well, *that* wasn't right, not based on what Chester had said. "Mr Hennessy, perhaps if I might come in, we could discuss–"

"I said I don't know. Leave."

And now Wilmott was growing irate, not merely at the constant interruptions but the man's entire attitude. Did he not recognize the seriousness of the circumstances? Was he not concerned for his kin?

Perhaps the man somehow failed to understand. He was, after all, but an uneducated yokel.

"Mr Hennessy, I think perhaps I've failed to make myself clear. Chester is–"

The door opened all the way once more, and while Wilmott might not have been clear, the message conveyed by the pair of steel barrels that now hovered mere inches from his suddenly pallid face was unmistakable.

"Leave!"

Hands rising in sudden terror, one of them still clutching his hat, Wilmott backed away from the shotgun. Sheer luck prevented him from tripping over his own heels, or the rickety steps, as he retreated from the porch. He'd barely reached the roadway when the door slammed, hiding Hennessy – and his weapon – from view. The professor barely even heard it over his pounding heart.

He released a long, shaking breath.

"Well," he muttered. "That could certainly have gone better."

Instinct and rationality both urged him to turn around and leave, to head back to Taunton, check into a hotel for the night and hop aboard the first train back to Arkham in the morning. He'd already gone above and beyond the call of any duty owed a student by his professor.

But the project…

Nor was it merely his own ambitions that made Wilmott hesitate. He knew, absolutely knew as surely as if he'd read it in one of his own textbooks, that Woodrow Hennessy was lying to him.

It wasn't merely the man's behavior, though that, even for so isolated and unfriendly a community as this one, was certainly suspicious enough. It was Chester himself. On one of the rare occasions his relations had come up in conversation at all, Chester had specifically told him that he got on much better with the low side of the family than his parents did.

While "better" didn't necessarily mean "close," it certainly implied a stronger relationship than Woodrow claimed.

Although he turned and walked away from the Hennessy house, although it ran counter to his better judgment, Wilmott Polaski had already made a decision.

He didn't go far. Perhaps a mile at most, distant enough that Hennessy should think him gone, that no random member of the community – not that he'd seen any – would connect the stranger with that particular house.

And there, sitting upon a log at least marginally free of mildews or fungi or other swamp substances, he waited.

He knew the delay would mean stumbling his way back to civilization in the dark of night, at best; and at worst, genuine bodily harm. He deliberately shunted those thoughts aside. He felt himself on the verge of answers, possibly of saving not only his prize student but the project that would cement his own name in the textbooks he so valued.

Night fell, the avian and insectile songs of the Hockomock changed from one chorus to another and Wilmott Polaski shuffled his way back toward the crooked house.

He approached at an angle, wincing as he deliberately set his path through the cold waters, soaked almost to his knees. Should Hennessy open the front door and gaze out through the curtained, drooping windows, he ought to notice nothing amiss. And thankfully the sodden earth rose again around the house proper, if only just, so Wilmott shouldn't have to remain long within the muck.

The back of the place was, if anything, even more dilapidated than the front, whole sections softened with moisture and inner rot. The good professor had to remind himself more than once that such disrepair didn't necessarily reflect a slovenly nature on the part of the inhabitants, that the environment might well seep into the wood, strip the paint, bestow a patina of filth, regardless of all efforts to hold it at bay.

Not that he was *too* terribly inclined to give Hennessy the benefit of any doubt.

Lamplight leaking out from the ill-fitting shutters, and a bright moon glowing through the clouds that had grown thinner as dusk fell, provided just enough illumination for him to get by. Enough to note details of the house that he'd failed to observe earlier, when his focus has been entirely on the front door and the man within.

The most salient of those details was the lower level, beneath the house proper.

It had, perhaps, been constructed at a time when the surrounding waters were a bit lower than today. Standing mostly above ground, it couldn't rightly be called a basement, yet it was too large and structurally sound to be simply an under-floor hollow someone had bricked up. Whether it had existed since the structure was built, or whether someone had added it later, Wilmott wasn't architect enough to say.

Neither could he say with certainty why that lowest level didn't fully match the width of the rest of the house, creating a peculiar combination of partial cellar, partial crawlspace. It wasn't unique to the Hennessy place, either, as he'd seen similar construction on some other homes he'd passed. Perhaps it was to do with the inconsistent earth here at the swamp's edges, with portions solid enough to support construction standing adjacent to others that were far too soft? He didn't know.

He knew only that, beneath the sagging floor and between the wooden supports, stood walls of uneven stones and thick mortar.

A half-sunken cellar certainly felt like a good place for Hennessy to hide his secrets, and, if nothing else, one of its own narrow windows might provide ingress. Crouching low, shuddering at the slick mud beneath his fingers as he scrabbled for balance, Wilmott slid beneath the house's outer edges.

Picking his way between puddles and discarded, rusted tools, biting his lip to keep from exclaiming his revulsion at the cobwebs and skittering bugs, he neared the first of those windows…

"*Isslaach thkulkris, isslaach cheoshash… Vnoktu vshuru shelosht escruatha…*"

It might have been five voices or fifty; he knew only it was more than one. Resonating off one another, echoing in brick-walled rooms, filtered through cracked wood and the natural songs of the swamp, it seemed somehow more than the foreign tongue – or perhaps simple gibberish – that reached his ears.

"*Svist ch'shultva ulveshtha ikravis… Isslaach ikravis vuloshku dlachvuul loshaa… Ulveshtha schlachtli vrulosht chevkuthaansa…*"

On it went, intertwining until he couldn't tell one phrase from the next, and then repeating once more from the beginning.

Over and over as he sat and listened, trying and failing to make the slightest sense of it, growing somehow *heavier* with each repetition even though it never varied in volume. Something about the litany was… off. Unclean. He felt violated, as though something slick had wiggled on the back of his tongue as he swallowed a bite of what should have been a mundane meal. He found himself lightheaded and nauseated, staggering back a few steps from the window as he struggled to restrain his rising gorge.

The handle of the old shovel on which he stepped was rotten most of the way through, but with enough of a solid center to resound like a gunshot when it snapped beneath his foot. Disoriented and now terrified of being discovered, the professor turned and fled, splashing through the swampy waters and into the night, leaving the Hennessy house behind.

The house, but not the ghastly phrases, which now seemed determined to dog his every step.

"Isslaach thkulkris, isslaach cheoshash… Vnoktu vshuru shelosht escruatha…"

Two nights later, he returned yet again.

As before, he'd initially intended to flee, and found himself unable. Thoughts of Chester Hennessy and their shared endeavors occupied his waking hours, most of which he spent staring at the walls of his rented room or aimlessly wandering about town. When sleep had finally claimed him, he'd tossed in the grip of horrific nightmares, shivering so violently he'd bolted awake from vistas of frigid ice… howling winds… endless shadow… *something* reaching out for him, stretching, grasping…

And always, asleep or awake, nesting at the back of his mind, winding and twisting and coiling around itself over and over, that abhorrent, damnable verse. Had he been honest with himself, Wilmott would have admitted there was something to the mantra itself, far more than his concern for his missing student or even their endeavors, that kept him here.

Even when preparing his return to the house, however, he never allowed himself to consider it.

This time, thanks to a quick trip to Taunton's shops, he came prepared. A set of screwdrivers and miniature blades sat tucked in a bag at his belt, and he clutched a small lantern in one fist, an iron prybar in the other. Flimsy as the wood was, the last was almost overkill. The window frame scooped away like oatmeal; he could practically have made entry with his bare hands.

Wiggling, grunting, he wormed his way through the window and flopped to the mildewed stone floor, flinching from both the impact and the choking scent.

Only as he picked himself up did he realize that the odd recitation continued, that the people down here, whoever they were, were still repeating their mindless refrain. Up to that point he'd thought the words were merely in his head, as they had been for the past days.

That realization brought with it another wave of disorientation, as if the thought itself made him more susceptible. The hallway tilted around him, splintered in a kaleidoscope of fragments, before pulling itself back together and leaving only dizziness in its wake.

Wilmott staggered forward, one hand on the wall while the other clutched the lantern that now seemed a woefully insufficient source of light. The uneven floor made the vertigo harder to deal with, as broken stones reached up to trip him or sudden dips threatened to topple him. More than once the swamp crept in between the stones at the lowest points, resulting in puddles to splash or, on one or two occasions, even wade through.

Surely the passageway couldn't be this long? It must be his own confusion that had him nigh convinced he'd taken scores of steps already, rather than a mere handful.

When he stumbled yet again, glancing down angrily at his traitorous feet, he discovered it hadn't been the floor that tripped him this time.

The blue-gray of a Postal Service uniform, now tattered, hid most, but unfortunately not all, of the half-stripped skeleton beneath. Nor had it been time, the waters, nor even vermin that had torn away the flesh and tissue. Even through his disorientation, his horror, Wilmott clearly saw the jagged indentations on the bone that could only have been left by human jaws.

He found himself continuing, with only the faintest memory of clambering back to his feet. He couldn't remember at precisely what point he'd collapsed, nor did he recall vomiting, though the acrid taste on his tongue suggested he had.

He thought, too, that he might have seen the remains of other savaged corpses beyond that of the unfortunate postman, had flashing, sporadic images of additional limbs, additional skulls, but once more his memory refused to cling to them well enough to be sure it was anything more than overwrought imagination.

His head ached, the skin uncomfortably tight around his skull. By the time the obvious notion of "Turn back! Get out!" penetrated his feverish mind, he'd already reached the end of the hall.

A cage of some sort, or a makeshift cell. He couldn't seem to focus on it clearly, or at least only bits and pieces stuck in his memory. He recalled stone walls and haphazard iron bars.

He recalled the stench of old sweat, of human filth.

Recalled not the one young man he sought but a small collection of faces, caked in mud and spit and blood and worse, some merely soiled but others subtly misshapen. If Chester had been among them, Wilmott never saw him.

It was from them, from chapped lips and ragged throats, that the alien chorus emerged. Over and over, almost but not entirely in unison so that the words seemed to vibrate in the ear.

"*Svist ch'shultva ulveshtha ikravis…*"

And Wilmott stepped toward them, his empty hand outstretched to tug at the chain and padlock that sealed them in, his own mouth beginning to move, no thought or instinct in his head save to *join them.*

The vicious report of a shotgun, and the patter of stone fragments falling from the buckshot-marred ceiling, shook him from his trance.

In the entryway to a perpendicular hallway Wilmott had previously overlooked in his distraction, stood Woodrow Hennessy. He gripped his weapon in corpse-knuckled fists, and twisted fabric of makeshift plugs protruded from his ears.

"I told you to leave, God damn you!"

Had Wilmott been more together, more himself, he might have heard not only the fury but the horror and grief burdening the man's outburst.

But he was not, and did not. Howling in confusion and in fear, the professor spun and raced back the way he'd come.

He sloshed through pools, stumbled over corpses, scraped his hands as he scrabbled back through the open window. Even in the pitch dark, he only barely remembered to keep hold of his lantern. His thoughts – all those not wrapped up in the litany, endless, pounding – were of escape only. In his panic, then, it seemed to make sense that the monstrous rustic with madmen locked in his cellar would be far less keen to pursue him into the wild than back along the road.

By the time his pounding heart had slowed and his head ceased spinning long enough for him to recognize the downsides of such a plan, he was already hopelessly lost.

Hours passed. Wilmott shivered violently, soaked to the waist. Beneath the dark waters, the mud had finally sucked the oversized boot from his left foot, forcing him to limp with fear that he would step on something piercing, slicing… or biting.

Unnamed creatures shrieked in the distant dark. The swamp rippled in the wake of swimming things.

From the muck below and the cedars all around, limbs snagged at his clothes, at his skin, making him start with frightened cries no matter how tightly he tried to keep his lips shut. Surely they were only branches, roots, vines. Yet in the flickering light of his lantern and in his thoughts – which felt ever warped, ever more sluggish, compressed in some mental vise – he could have sworn he saw them moving, flexing as they reached for him.

And that light itself had begun to fade, its dancing growing ever more frantic, as the flame licked thirstily at the last few traces of oil.

They both flared, then, the firelight and the panic together, in a final burst.

Before him, half-sunk in the swamp, vine-wrapped and coated in slime, was a black stone. He peered at writings carved in an alphabet unlike any he had ever seen before and could not possibly read – and yet which seemed, at some level below the conscious, perhaps even beyond the sapient, familiar. It tugged at him, a sensation that felt as physical as it did emotional. A shiver began at the back of his neck but died before it traveled far, as though his body no longer remembered how to move.

His lantern died, to reveal another source of illumination, coming up through the swamp behind him.

"Professor!" Woodrow Hennessy's voice was hoarse. He must have been calling out for some time. "Professor, can you hear me?"

He stepped into view, water sloshing around his calves. Wilmott Polaski tore his gaze from the stone, advanced toward the newcomer, and responded in the only way he could, with the only words he knew.

"Isslaach thkulkris, isslaach cheoshash…"

Hennessy might not have heard him – he still wore the plugs of fabric in his ears, seemed more frightened of what he might hear than of braving the swamp while deafened – but he clearly recognized the recitation all the same.

With a scream of fury, of guilt, of denial, but above all else of fear, he raised the shotgun toward the oncoming professor and fired.

Chapter One

It was a soft song, its notes made up of the shuffling of papers; the thump of leather-bound covers; the rolling of ladders and the scuffing of chairs; the swish of trousers, of skirts; and the dull hum of quiet conversations that were never *as* quiet as the students believed they were.

A soft song, filtering from dozens of rooms and arched halls, from every floor of Miskatonic University's famed Orne Library – and one that, on the average day, Daisy Walker found empowering, energizing for all its subtleties.

Today was not an average day. She had not, in fact, had many average days at all for the past few months.

At first, part of her unease might have been anxiety over her new responsibilities. This new term, spring '23, was only the second since Dr Armitage had put her in charge of the Special Collections, the restricted tomes and writings for which the Orne Library was most well known. The least precious of the books therein was worth more than her yearly salary, the value of the entire lot immeasurable, not just in money but in irreplaceable lore.

Daisy knew herself well enough, though, to realize that while nerves might have overcome her poise at first, she'd more than adapted to her new duties in the intervening months.

And some of that unease might be down to the contents of those tomes, which she'd made a point of studying once the position had opened and Armitage had first hinted he might consider her to fill it. While most of the Special Collection was merely old, some of its contents were… peculiar.

She'd perused a few of them, when she had the opportunity: *De Vermis Mysteriis*, John Dee's partial *Necronomicon*, the del Arrio translation of the *Cabala of Saboth*. They spoke, those books, of ancient things, of sorceries long forgotten and of names that should have been. As windows into ancient cultures and beliefs, they fascinated her, but their actual content? She didn't believe a word of it, of course; it was no more real than the imaginings of Gogol or Stoker. Still, that hadn't prevented her from turning on a few extra lights during the later hours of her shifts, double-checking the locks before turning in for the night, or – now and again – waking in a panicked sweat from nightmares she could never clearly recall.

But again, Daisy knew herself well enough to know that no musty old myths or fairy tales would disturb her so thoroughly, or for so long.

No, it was—

"Miss Walker?"

"Oh!" The young librarian jolted in her chair, hands gripping the edge of her desk. It was, to the best of her memory, the first time anyone had opened the door to her office without her noticing.

That idea still took some getting used to: her office.

"Oh!" The echo came from the even younger woman, wide-eyed and round-faced, standing in the doorway. "I'm so sorry! I didn't mean to startle you."

Daisy brushed back a long curl of blonde hair. "That's quite all right, Abigail. I was just… lost in thought, I suppose." Not that she had any intention of revealing said thoughts, either regarding her books or… other concerns.

"I did knock," Abigail offered shyly. "But you didn't answer, and I *knew* you were in here, and I wanted to make sure you were all right." Then, perhaps noting a lingering vacancy in Daisy's expression, "*Are* you all right?"

"I'm fine. I suppose I was even more lost than I realized. You, ah, you needed something?"

Those wide eyes flickered aside, down, back to meet her own. "I just… That is, I thought I should ask if you needed anything done in the, um, the Special Collections?"

"I see." With an iron will, Daisy kept her lips from quirking in a knowing grin. "No, dear, nothing just now."

"Oh." Again the brief gaze off in the direction of the restricted chambers. "Are you, um, are you sure?"

The grin fought even harder to slip onto her face – but at the same time, she had to fight the urge to shake her head. Abigail Foreman was an industrious student worker, and Daisy would be happy to have her stay on once she'd graduated, should her interest in library economics lead her in that direction.

She was, however, a bit too readily diverted by particularly boy-shaped distractions.

"Your duties, Abigail, include providing assistance to students and patrons when they solicit it – not to go foisting it upon those who have made no such requests."

Abigail flushed until her skin practically glowed.

"Yes, miss. Sorry, miss."

Now Daisy did allow herself to smile, hoping to take some of the sting from the rebuke. "Now, I believe someone told me South American Studies needed re-shelving?"

Abigail took the offered escape, fleeing from the office, and Daisy released the sigh that had been building for the past few moments. She liked the girl, would normally have made far more allowances for her latest infatuation, might even have encouraged it.

Raslo. Why, of all the fine young lads Miskatonic's campus could offer, did the poor girl's attentions have to fall on Elliot Raslo? Even if he hadn't been mired in uncertainty and grief, even if everything in his life, everything at Miskatonic University, been fine and dandy, even then…

But that wasn't her secret to tell. The boy would have been mortified even to know that she knew.

Daisy stood – chair scraping across the floor – carefully smoothed her blouse and skirt, and left her office, turning in the opposite direction from Abigail's flight.

The outermost chamber of the Special Collection was a reading room, consisting only of a table, a handful of comfortably upholstered chairs, and a lamp. Students and visitors were permitted to make use of the collection only individually or in small groups, and only on limited occasions depending on seniority, the nature of their research and in exchange for volunteered labor. Over the past weeks, assuming nobody else had reserved time, it was a coin toss whether or not Elliot would be here. Thus, Daisy wouldn't have been surprised to see him even if she hadn't already known, thanks to Abigail's blatant interest, that he was there.

The young man sat, elbows on the table, head in his hands, so that Daisy wasn't certain he was awake. His brown coat and his black hair were both rumpled. Time was, not so long ago, he'd have been chagrined even to be seen outside in such a state.

"Elliot?"

He was, indeed, awake. He looked up at her, bleary with exhaustion and churning emotion. His face – a bit darker complexioned than her own due to a Mediterranean grandparent – sported several days' worth of stubble.

"Is there news?"

It was his first question almost every time she saw him, no matter that she'd told him over and over that she would let him know the instant she heard anything.

"No." She pulled up a chair and sat across from him. "Nothing."

"Damn!" Then, quieting himself before she had to remind him to do so, "Useless, the lot of them."

She knew he meant the Arkham police. This, too, was part of the ritual, a conversation they'd had so often she had to assume he took some meager comfort in its repetition.

"They've precious little to go on," she told him. Indeed, they had almost nothing. Chester Hennessy, Elliot's best friend and roommate, had vanished without trace – a feat duplicated some weeks later by Professor Polaski, Chester's mentor and advisor in ongoing research.

"They're ignoring what little they have," Elliot insisted, rubbing a knuckle into his eye. "They're still treating them as separate incidents when any idiot can see they're not. Still insisting that Chester ran off because of that bitch–"

"Language, Mr Raslo!"

He recoiled as if she'd slapped him. "I– Of course. I'm so sorry, Miss Walker."

Daisy knew he meant it. Elliot was, if nothing else, a gentle, courteous soul. At least when he wasn't exhausted and frustrated and scared.

She laid her hand atop his, and managed not to wince as he clutched it like a life preserver. Normally she'd have moved the book that sat before him on the table, would have refused to let them rest their hands on its cover this way for fear the oils of their skin might damage the old material, but a brief moment or two wouldn't hurt it.

It wasn't the first time he'd asked for this one, either. He'd been weeks trying to retrace Chester's research, hoping that something in the missing student's recent endeavors – the project that had absorbed him, body and soul, for months – might shed some light, however feeble, on the mystery of his disappearance.

So far, unless he was keeping secrets from her, he'd had precisely the same amount of success as the police he cursed for idiots and fools: none whatsoever.

She didn't mind his presence, and certainly appreciated his help. Like Chester before him, in order to earn himself more time in the Special Collections, Elliot had volunteered to help sort unimportant documents for the Orne Library and the university as a whole: letters and personal papers willed them by alumni; old newspaper clippings; reports of historical artifacts stolen from museums and other universities for which they should be alert; and so forth. He claimed it was solely due to his efforts to find his missing roommate, but Daisy believed it was a way to feel closer to the friend he'd lost. Elliot was, on those days he could focus, even better at such mundane but essential tasks than Chester had been. Still, she'd grown worried at his mounting obsession, to say nothing of the damage to his academic standing. Daisy knew he must be missing classes in order to be here at all hours.

Had her leniency with the Special Collections and his research somehow led Chester Hennessy into harm's way? Unlikely as it seemed, it was that fear more than anything else that kept her awake nights, ate at her composure during the day. It was not a mistake she cared to repeat with his friend, however much he felt the need to follow.

"Elliot," she began finally, "you need to–"

It was only because Daisy hadn't shut the door to the reading room that the commotion reached them at all, that she heard the sudden cacophony intruding on the library's song. Not shouting, not yet, but voices raised in disagreement that could readily *become* shouting.

Or worse?

She rose, her back as stiff as her expression. Even at the best of times, Daisy had no patience for those who would disrupt the peace of her library. Whoever had foolishly elected to do so today, in the midst of all her other concerns, was liable to get an unfriendly piece of her mind. "I'm so sorry. Excuse me."

A swish of woolen skirts, and she was gone.

Elliot watched her go, his weary mind not immediately registering the significance of what they'd heard.

Miss Walker, his instructors, his fellow students. They all attributed his constant distraction to grief and to worry, even if they couldn't possibly understand just how strongly he…

Well, they were partly right. But only partly.

And they attributed his research, his burning compulsion to retrace Chester's research, to an obsessive and almost certainly futile hope of locating him when the police and the man's own family could not.

They were partly right. But only partly.

The other part, he'd mentioned to no one.

That Chester had told him excitedly, on one particular evening, that the clue to finally break his mystery project – the one he claimed would exceed all his ambitions, would cement his name in the annals of archeological studies before he even completed his education – had been found. Though he had then balked at explaining precisely what he had found, or how it could help.

That in the final days before his disappearance, Chester had become distant, listless, constantly preoccupied. He'd slept poorly, barely spoken. Had taken to muttering to himself, sometimes in French, or in languages Elliot couldn't identify, let alone interpret.

Elliot's own studies, focusing as they did on the psychology of the human mind, led him to believe that his friend's efforts had transformed into a dangerous, perhaps even pathological obsession. He had finally committed himself to confronting Chester, though his heart pounded and his stomach coiled in on itself like a dying worm at the thought of what such an intervention might do to their relationship – but Chester had disappeared before he'd gathered the courage to speak up.

And ever since…

Ever since, Elliot himself had awakened from jagged, half-remembered nightmares on more nights than not, shivering from a deep chill unrelated to the temperature of the room in which he slept. Nightmares not only of ice, but of things that moved in shadow, things that dwelt behind endless sheets of hail and sleet.

The dreams alone, he could have managed. It was the constant repetition that threatened to drive him mad.

Just a few words, a partial phrase. Something in that unknown language, something Chester had murmured only the once where Elliot could hear it. It lodged in the back of his mind, a constant itch he couldn't scratch, couldn't stop *trying* to scratch, echoing over and over, winding through every conversation, bubbling beneath every lecture, until he wanted to scream.

To scream those words.

It was that phrase, that fragment, that distracted him more than any search, more than any grief. And he knew, without knowing entirely how he knew, that it would have been far worse, might truly have stripped away all sanity and self-control, if it hadn't been for his *other* discovery in following Chester's research. That *other* mantra.

It *was* just a mantra, was it not? It couldn't really be–

Another burst of raised voices, not quite shouting, from whatever commotion was occurring out in the library, snapped him from rumination. Elliot forced himself from his chair. He doubted Miss Walker or the library staff would require any help to deal with whatever problem had arisen, and on the off-chance they did, he couldn't imagine what help he might be able to offer. So it was with more of a desperate need for diversion than any sense of duty that he proceeded down the hallway in her distant wake.

All normal activity within the library's main hall had come to a halt as students peered over their books and their papers at the confrontation brewing by the massive entryway. Several of the Orne staffers, and two of Miskatonic's uniformed security guards, were gathered in a clump around a stranger who'd apparently attempted to access the library.

The man didn't look remotely like student, staff, or alumni, and while the Orne Library was open to others, they either had to be invited researchers or to have made a formal appointment well in advance. To judge by the raised voices, some of which were clearly tired of repeating themselves, the stranger met neither qualification.

Elliot hadn't the faintest idea what to make of the man. He wasn't particularly tall, but his broad shoulders and proud bearing made him seem so. He wore a long, heavy coat that would have blended in well enough on the streets of Arkham, but the boots visible below his trouser cuffs, made of some supple leather, were of no style or fashion the young man had ever seen. Nor, for that matter, were the fellow's features, which were flatter and darker than Elliot's own. The young student was not especially well traveled, much as he wished otherwise, and unable to place the stranger's land of origin. He put Elliot in mind a bit of a Mongolian researcher he'd met once, and a bit of American Indian, but not precisely either.

"It's only a few questions!" The stranger's voice was deep, resonant; his accent, like everything else about him, far enough beyond Elliot's experience that he couldn't place it. "Surely one of your librarians can spare me five minutes!"

One of the security guards began again to deny him, taking a menacing step nearer. It was, perhaps, the threat of the confrontation turning into a genuine brawl that inspired Daisy Walker, hovering at the edges of the commotion, to finally intervene.

"And what questions are those, Mr…?"

"Miss Walker," the security guard protested, "I don't think you oughta–"

"It's all right, Floyd."

The stranger turned her way, his coat drifting open to reveal an array of charms and amulets that hung from his neck by a veritable thicket of leather thongs and animal gut. From where he stood, Elliot thought, but couldn't be certain, he saw old bone, wood, stone, and thick leather trinkets, all of which were carved or stitched with small designs he couldn't, from this distance, make out.

"Shiwak," the man replied to Daisy's implied question. "Billy Shiwak."

"All right, Mr Shiwak. What's so urgent that you had to raise such a fuss in my library?"

No, not bone, Elliot decided, idly wondering why he was so focused on this man's – Shiwak's – accoutrements. *Ivory.*

After the past few moments of tension, Shiwak seemed almost confused now that he had the opportunity to pose his questions. He cast about for a few seconds, as though seeking his words.

"To begin with," he began, "I'm hoping you can tell me where to find a man by the name of Jebediah Pembroke. I've been told–"

Elliot never found out *what* he'd been told, because Daisy Walker went deathly still at the mention of the name, though it meant nothing to Elliot himself. In his three and a half years at Miskatonic, Elliot had never seen her react that way to anything.

"How dare you?!"

Everyone, including the security guards and the newcomer himself, took a step back in shock.

Daisy continued, her voice nearly vibrating. "I don't know what sort of rumormongers and gossip you've been listening to, but I will not subject myself or these halls to your… your *slander.*"

"Miss Walker, I'm certain I intended no insult. I simply–"

"I'll thank you to leave my library now, Mr Shiwak."

"Please, I–"

"I will thank you. To leave."

The ice enveloping her every word, and a glance at the stern expressions on the two security guards, apparently convinced the man that further argument would do nobody any good. With a stiff nod, he made for the doors, the guards falling into step behind him.

Daisy spun, her heel digging a divot into the thin foyer carpet. "This is still a library," she announced firmly to staff and student alike, "not a theatre."

Faces swiftly turned back to books or notes or regular tasks. Head high, the librarian swept through the main room, making her way back toward her office.

Elliot alone continued to stare at the doors, contemplating the fellow who'd disappeared beyond. For it was only now that the damnable phrase returned to its accustomed volume in the back of his mind, that he realized it had briefly quieted, if only slightly.

Quieted in the presence of the peculiar Billy Shiwak.

Chapter Two

William "Billy" Shiwak stormed from the Orne Library, jaw clenched, swearing violently – though only in his thoughts, not aloud. The journey had turned poor enough already; to risk attracting the attentions of a hostile toornaq with an ill-phrased curse would be the height of foolishness.

And you've already acted the fool enough for one day, haven't you, Billy?

Over a year spent among them, longer than that studying them, most of his life spent speaking their tongue as well as his own – and for all that, Billy still couldn't even pretend to understand Americans. No doubt the woman had good reason to find his mention of Pembroke offensive, but for the life of him he couldn't imagine what. Personal history, perhaps? A familial feud? Something else entirely?

The Ujaraanni. *I should have led with questions about the* Ujaraanni.

After all his efforts, after coming this far, he'd rushed where he should have been patient. Made for the campus straight from the train station, given no careful thought how to best approach the people here. Foolishness!

No help for it now. Miskatonic University had been his best lead, but not the only one. He would have to pursue the others, and hope that either they proved fruitful, or at least took long enough that he might find a more effective way to approach the school.

A school which, apparently, the two guards intended to make certain he left. He realized now, as his anger at Daisy Walker and, even more so, himself, began to fade, that the men were still with him, several steps behind. He remained on the clearly delineated pathways, between massive stone structures – any one of which would dwarf every home in Itilleq combined – and alongside grassy lawns so neatly tended that they'd maintained their greenery even through a winter that the folks of Massachusetts doubtless considered harsh.

What did *they* know of harsh winters?

As they neared the edge of the sprawling campus, Billy halted and turned. "Could either of you gentlemen recommend inexpensive lodgings?"

The thinner and older of the two – had the librarian called him Floyd? –

scoffed and turned away, but the other nodded. "There's a couple flophouses up in the Merchant District. Ain't fancy, most maybe ain't even too clean, but if you're not picky about where you bunk, they'll do you fine."

Billy tried to map in his head what he'd seen of Arkham thus far. "Up near the train station?"

"Yeah, more or less."

"I would prefer somewhere else." If he was picturing the right place, he'd seen several blocks cordoned off by the local police on his walk from the train. "There's some sort of disturbance…?"

"Oh, right. There's a flu spreading out that way." The guard pondered a moment, then, "Ma's."

"I'm sorry?"

"Ma's Boarding House. Southside. She's usually got a few rooms to let, if you ain't dippy enough to break her rules."

"I see. And how would I–?"

But either because Floyd was sighing theatrically and tapping his foot, or because his own patience had run dry, the security guard was done answering questions. "Just head down Garrison," he said, already walking away. "I'm sure you'll find someone who can direct you from there."

Billy didn't bother calling a thank you. He wasn't sure the man would either have heard or cared.

"Father," he muttered, "whatever anersaat or toornat caused your misfortune, I hope your pain sated them. I've got enough difficulty with *human* impediments, thanks very much."

Still grumbling, he hunted for a street sign to confirm that he was indeed on Garrison, then turned southward.

Asking for directions proved more difficult than the Miskatonic security man had implied.

Not due to any dearth of people to ask. Even in the drifting fog and the abnormally chill early spring breeze of the evening, citizens wandered on business of their own. Motor cars and horse-drawn carriages passed him by on the streets, and the walkways bustled with pedestrians.

No, the problem was finding someone willing to speak to *him*.

Other than his seal-skin boots – he'd just never been able to find any comfort in American footwear – and the amulets he tried to keep largely concealed beneath his coat, Billy had dressed to blend in. And if he'd been trying to vanish into a crowd, or to remain anonymous and keep his head down, that would have been enough.

Coming anywhere near enough a stranger to speak to them, however, was another matter. His features were more than enough to mark him as an outsider, and while he'd visited cities where foreigners – or anyone with a skin tone much darker than a corpse – were treated far worse, that didn't mean the average Arkhamite welcomed him with open arms.

It was, in fact, a young black man, the fifth person he'd stopped, who'd finally (and even cheerfully) given him directions, as well as warning him three separate times not to miss out on either Ma Mathison's Sunday night soup or her apple pie.

"Better'n Velma's cherry pie, even! And you *know* nobody'd make *that* claim lightly!"

"I'm… sure they wouldn't."

Then, later, a second set of directions, when the first proved somewhat insufficient for a man who knew nothing about Arkham's byways, this time offered by a kindly old white couple – a fact that made Billy feel a bit better about the town in general – tooling around in a spotlessly clean Ford Model-T.

And finally, tired and hungry, he found himself on the front steps of Ma's Boarding House, a surprisingly large structure whose severe peaks and almost ominously sharp lines were oddly offset by the bright lights, both inside and out, and the sounds of cheer from beyond the door.

His entrance drew any number of stares, but only a handful appeared suspicious or hostile; most expressed mere curiosity, and all swiftly returned to their own business. People sat about a large common room, in a wide variety of chairs that, though mismatched, had been chosen and placed with care toward which colors and patterns complimented one another.

The room's far end opened into a smaller chamber containing what appeared to be a communal dining table. Although currently empty, to judge by the lingering, mouthwatering aromas, it played regular host to expertly prepared meals.

A large, dark-haired woman in pearls and a floral dress bustled over to meet him. In an accent he'd never encountered, and so thick he nearly had to wade through it, she introduced herself as Ma Mathison, welcoming him to her house, to Arkham, etc.

"Jus' two dollars a night, or twelve for the week, and you won't find yourself any better in Arkham for twice that! And that includes dinner, too, long as you're at the table to say grace with us at six. Six sharp, you hear me? Else you're on your own, 'cuz I don't fill no bellies that miss grace!"

"Uh, I hear you. Yes, ma'am."

Ma ran down the rest of her rules as she guided him to a desk across the room where she happily took both his name and his money. They were numerous, those rules.

"No guests downstairs past nine, no guests in the rooms past eight, no guests of the opposite sex ever. I won't be having scandalous doin's in my house!

"Luncheon costs sixty cents and is served from eleven to whenever the food runs out. You can bring a guest, but it's sixty-five cents for anyone not payin' for a room.

"You can come'n go as you like, but I won't be having my other guests disturbed, so if I hear complaints about noise in the wee hours, out you go!"

Then finally, after catching a glimpse of his amulets, "And you practice whatever you want at home, but there'll be no prayers to anyone but Our Lord an' his son Jesus Christ in this house, you hear?"

"I still hear you, yes." Billy stared briefly at the key in his hand, unable to remember when during the torrent of words she'd stuck it there, and felt vaguely dizzy. *I may need a translator.*

Or earplugs.

"You got any questions," she finally concluded, "you just let me know."

She was already stepping away as she spoke, clearly anticipating none. Most of her guests were probably either regulars, or too overwhelmed by the verbal barrage they'd just endured, to come up with any.

"Actually, yes." Billy waited until she'd halted, processed the unexpected reply, and turned back his way. "I'm wondering if you can tell me where I might find…" He paused, dredging the unusual names back to mind. He had them written down, but he'd rather not have to dig.

"Either the Curiositie Shoppe or a place called Ye Olde Magick Shoppe." *Whatever in the world "Ye" means…*

He watched the narrowing of Ma's eyes, the scrunching of the skin around her lips and chin, and only then realized – given some of what she'd said to him already – why she might take the question amiss.

Doing a marvelous job on the diplomacy so far today, Billy.

"I'm not a, uh, practitioner," he told her, and it was at least partly true. He was certainly no angakkoq, though she would doubtless consider the beliefs he held, the gods he venerated and the spirits he feared pagan enough. "I'm only trying to track down some… cultural relics."

Which was also partly true.

Though the suspicion never left her face entirely, she relented enough to offer general directions to both establishments, and Billy wanted to curse again. He'd been within a couple of blocks of the Curiositie Shoppe, had practically passed it on his walk from the train to Miskatonic. And Ye Olde Magick Shoppe, while more out of the way, had been closer to the university than it was to him now.

"But if you're really lookin' for historical pieces," she continued, "you oughtta start at the Historical Society. They can probably set your feet on the right path, an' they got no truck with the sorts of people who frequent dens of witchcraft and iniquity."

"Historical Society?"

"Yep. Keep all sorts of writings an' pictures an' art an' old gewgaws. Biggest collection in Arkham outside of Miskatonic. Maybe bigger, if you're lookin' for local history in particular."

He wasn't, not at all. Still, this sounded like the sort of place that might, at least, have an ear to the trade in stolen historical objects, or be able to point him toward those who did, if he asked carefully enough. A frisson of excitement ran through him – to say nothing of relief that he might yet recover from the earlier mistakes of the day.

"Would they still be open at this hour?" he asked, shoving his room key in a pocket.

Ma Mathison shrugged. "Couldn't say." She did, however, glance somewhat obviously at the clock across the way.

Billy followed her gaze, saw it was little more than an hour until "grace," then shrugged in turn. "I guess I'm on my own for dinner tonight, then. Thank you, Mrs Mathison."

Though his stomach and his feet both rebelled, he turned from the soft chairs and the scents of dinner to come and headed out once more into Arkham's streets.

The Arkham Historical Society was a massive three-story Georgian manor towering over the surrounding houses, doubtless the home of some obscenely wealthy family before it was willed to the organization. The wrought iron fence coiled around it was not a welcoming sign – but the *literal* sign, a bronze plaque on the gate identifying the society for what it was, proved more enticing.

While several lights shone through various curtained windows, however, nothing about the edifice indicated whether it was currently open to visitors. The evening was still young, but the heavy clouds, lingering since winter had technically ended, made it feel later.

Should he treat it as a private residence, knock and wait to see if it were answered? Or as a shop or public facility, assuming that if the door was unlocked it meant he was welcome to enter?

When a twist of the handle proved that it was not, in fact, locked, Billy chose the second option and stepped inside.

He found himself in a long, carpeted hall, lit from above by fancy electrical chandeliers. Along both walls were portraits of men and women, doubtless important folks in Arkham's history, looking over glass display cases of documents, journals and the like. Beyond, the hall led into further rooms, this size or larger, with their own displays. He couldn't see from here what might be in them, but they were far more numerous, and in many cases larger, than those beside him.

Beyond a sense of vague amusement at what these white folks considered "old," Billy found himself largely uninterested in their history, built as it was on the bones of those who had come before. Perhaps he'd have been a little more curious under other circumstances, if he hadn't been so driven by concerns of his own – but *only* a little.

Doorways led to other rooms, off to either side, but as he had no notion of what might lie behind them, he chose instead to wander along the main way.

He'd not yet reached the end of this first room, however, when one of those side doors opened, startling him, if only mildly.

"While I'm always delighted to welcome a newcomer to the Historical Society, young man, I'm afraid that I'll be locking up soon, as we're members only after hours. You've scarcely the time to see anything. Perhaps if you'd like to return tomorrow?"

The speaker was an older fellow, spindly almost to the point of frailty, with vaguely colorless hair sprouting from atop a vaguely colorless head. The only real spots of color anywhere about him were the dull plaid elbow patches on his otherwise gray suit coat.

That and a blueish amulet hanging from his neck. It boasted a peculiar design, an uneven star with a circle – perhaps an eye – in its center.

Different from his own amulets as it was, coming from a culture he could not even guess at, Billy knew a protective talisman when he saw one.

From what, he wondered, could this old man need to protect himself?

"I'm not actually here for a tour," Billy told him, "but on behalf of my people." He wasn't sure why, but he felt that this stranger, obviously a man who valued his history, might be sympathetic to such a claim. "If you could spare just a few minutes before, ah, locking up, you would be doing us a great service."

The old man cocked his head, examining Billy as he might one of his displays, and then his face suddenly split in a grin. "You're Eskimo, aren't you? I haven't met one of your people in decades!"

As often as he'd heard that term in his travels, Billy still felt himself stiffen. "Yes, I am. Though we call ourselves Kalaallit. Or Inuit, if you prefer."

"Right, right. I've heard that about many Eskimos."

Billy forced his teeth not to grind.

"Well," the other said, "my name is Peabody. Reginald Peabody. I'm the curator of this hallowed establishment."

"William Shiwak."

"Very well, William. You've got your few minutes. What can I do for you?"

They'd drifted, as they spoke, to the doorway from which Peabody had appeared. Beyond it lay a small office, cluttered with unfiled papers, unshelved books, and some old broken tools that Billy assumed were being cataloged for storage or display.

Peabody did not, however, return to his desk and sit, nor offer one of the chairs – which would have required some excavation to unearth anyway – to his guest. Clearly, when he offered a "few minutes," he meant it.

Billy almost asked about Jebediah Pembroke, but thought better of it. He still had no idea what about that name had set off the librarian, so he couldn't be certain it wouldn't have the same result here.

Instead, for the first time in weeks, he told an outsider the truth, albeit far from the *whole* truth, about his travels.

"I'm looking, Mr Peabody, for something that was stolen from Itilleq. That is, my nunaqarfik, my… village." Not an exact translation, but it would do. "I have reason to think it might have made its way here to Arkham, and while I do not believe for one moment that you or your Society would have anything to do with stolen goods…" A bit of buttering up, as well as heading off any possible offense, couldn't hurt. "… I have to believe that a man in your position, working to acquire artifacts of your own people's history, must hear things. Or at least know someone who could direct me further."

"I see. I'm afraid I don't recall seeing or hearing of anything lately that struck me as Eskimo. But perhaps if you were to describe it to me?"

"It's a stone." He shivered even as he spoke of it, such was the power it held in his mind, in the traditions and taboos of his family. "Blacker than ink, worked smooth on some sides, broken and rough on others. And on it are carved an array of symbols. They might be letters, but not of any alphabet I or my people have ever–"

"Oh! As a matter of fact, I *have* seen something like that."

"I… You *have*?" Billy almost staggered, so unexpected was the response.

"Indeed, yes. It's in the Miskatonic University antiquities collection. I'm afraid I don't remember what it was called, or what might have been written about it – my own focus has always been on Arkham's history, specifically – but I'm sure it…"

Billy was no longer listening. He'd been there. He'd been *right there!* So close, if only he hadn't led with the absolute wrong question.

Well, no sense fretting over it now. He would just have to–

"I'm sorry, what?" Something Peabody said had finally snagged his attention once more.

"I said, young man, that you might have some difficulty finding anyone who knows much about it, even on campus, as it's been there gathering dust for decades. Perhaps generations."

But that wasn't possible. The Forsythe Expedition had come to Itilleq, had betrayed their hospitality and stolen the *Ujaraanni*, less than ten years ago. He'd been in his adolescence, not yet privy to many of the conversations, but still he remembered the commotion, the exchange of stories, the sharing of meals.

The fury of his people and of nature when it was taken.

The grief of saying farewell to his father.

He found himself outside, having made thanks and polite farewells to Peabody that he couldn't recall. Something bizarre was happening here, was waiting for him at Miskatonic University. Even if it wasn't what he sought, the similarities couldn't be pure coincidence, could they? He must, at least, find some sort of clue as to where to go from here.

So yes, he would return to the school this very night.

Only this time, he wouldn't waste his time asking questions – or permission.

CHAPTER THREE

Sleet, falling in thick curtains, glittering blades that sliced skin and muscle and sinew; gaping red wounds that steamed in the cold. Rock blacker than the night sky; treacherous, slick and precarious on its own even before the layers of ice that froze atop it in invisible sheets.

Screams, distant, muffled by the blizzard yet echoing from the stone. Screams of agony. Screams of terror.

Screams of friends, he somehow knew, though he did not know their names, could not bring their faces to mind.

And shrieks of something else, something far less merciful than the indifferent winter. Something that slipped between the falling shards, skittered across the stone, slid into the mind and sluiced beneath every conscious thought…

It would be inaccurate to say Elliot awoke with a scream, for he was screaming long before the pounding of irritated students in the next room over finally roused him.

Nor was that scream a simple, wordless cry of fear. Better, by far, if it had been.

"Isslaach thkulkris, isslaach cheoshash…"

The same four words – and they were words, he recognized them as words, though he hadn't the faintest idea of what they meant – that Chester had muttered to him, just the once, the day before he'd vanished. The same four words that had resounded in his mind ever since, over and over, murdering focus and devouring thought, every hour, every minute, until he'd been certain they must drive him mad.

Until he'd found…

He staggered from the bed, tripped over his feet, bruised an arm catching himself on a chair. With the wobble of a drunk he crossed the room, hands pressed futilely to his ears – as if he might somehow block out sounds coming from within – until, after what felt like a thousand uphill miles, he reached the squat desk jammed in the corner.

A framed photo of his parents and sister crashed to the floor as he fell against that desk, hauling open a drawer and grabbing for a particular half-crumpled sheet of paper covered in carefully copied French.

Shaking, he read it aloud.

Then a second time. And a third.

With each recitation, the maddening litany faded, though it never fell entirely silent, never faded completely from his consciousness.

In fact, it lingered more today than it had yesterday, nagging at him, making him fret. He'd have to go back to the source soon…

Elliot dropped into his chair, shivering with a chill born of both the icy dream and the sweat coating his brow. He stared, unseeing, at the dormitory room around him: several banners for Miskatonic's football and baseball teams, photos framed and unframed, a poster advertisement for Coca-Cola.

And, across the room, Chester's own bed and desk, neither of which had been used in weeks – unless one counted Elliot's worried snooping through his roommate's papers as "use."

He felt a bit guilty about that violation of his friend's privacy, but Elliot didn't truly regret it. He'd done it in hopes of finding the missing student – and if he hadn't, if he'd not located a few copies of French text, he might not have wound up looking through the same tomes in the Orne Library that Chester had.

Might not have found the mantra.

Although he was having more and more trouble convincing himself that "mantra" was the proper word for it. Elliot looked back at the paper in his hands.

He'd found it in the *Livre d'Ivon*. One of many ancient treatises Chester had said he'd perused in the Special Collection, it was a French translation of what purported to be a far older tome originally scribed in a language predating even Ancient Greek. The Special Collection was home to quite a few such works, though as they focused largely on obscure legend and superstition, or forgotten forms of the occult, he couldn't imagine what Chester might have been looking for.

The passage he himself had found – the mantra – was, based on Elliot's limited fluency in French, some sort of protective incantation. A … spell.

Nonsense, of course. When reading it had first quieted the refrain in his mind that he'd somehow picked up from Chester's troubled mutterings, Elliot had, as a student of psychology, leapt to the more sensible conclusion that it had served him as a distraction, a mental exercise or meditation. Certainly that, and not some ancient sorcery, was why it had helped him focus and temporarily shut those other, more alien words away.

And yet… And yet…

If that were so, why did his handwritten replica only work for several days before its efficacy began to fade? Why did going back to read the original text in the *Livre d'Ivon* seem to "recharge" its ability to help him, as if it contained some genuine power that his poor copy couldn't completely capture?

And why did the period in which his copy was useful, the interval before he had to go back and re-peruse the original, seem to be gradually growing shorter?

Elliot had a potential answer to that last one: he was slowly losing his mind, developing some sort of genuine psychological condition of which his mental repetition of Chester's nonsense phrase was only the first symptom. It wasn't an answer he much cared for, but if he was genuinely considering magic to be the other alternative, surely that was further evidence.

It was only then, as his mind calmed, as the litany faded as much as he could hope it would, that Elliot realized something else. Something new.

There was another word in his head now, one he had never heard before and assumed must have come to him in some noxious dream. Not part of that terrible repetition. It made him queasy to think it, repulsed him on some reptilian level; but it didn't fit with the phrase, didn't threaten to drive him once more into paroxysms of confusion, didn't make him feel almost compelled to repeat it until his jaw was sore from clenching.

But he also couldn't forget it. It refused to fade with the rest of the dream from which it must certainly have come. It was, perhaps, another symptom of the lunacy he was now half-convinced he suffered, just a random collection of sounds coughed up by a diseased brain.

That didn't feel right either, though. Elliot realized he firmly believed, though he had no basis for such a belief, that it meant something, that word. That *sound.*

Tsocathra.

Elliot rose from the chair and began digging through his clothes. He wasn't getting back to sleep any time soon, that much was certain. He hadn't the focus to read, and he had no interest whatsoever in sitting in this room, staring at the walls or at the reminders of his missing friend. A walk in the cool night air carried risk of a reprimand, but the notion was too enticing to pass up. He threw on a pair of slacks, pulled on a shirt and sweater and made for the door.

For over an hour he simply wandered the Miskatonic campus, illuminated by fog-dampened lampposts and cloud-veiled moon. The cold breeze rustled his hair, forced his hands into pockets, but he wasn't nearly so uncomfortable that he would consider turning back. This, at least, felt natural; the occasional shiver a healthy response to the chill, not the feverish or claustrophobic remnant of nightmare.

He tried to keep quiet, his pace slow. The campus had only a handful of security men, so the odds of running into one were low, but not so slim that he could afford carelessness. Nor was the penalty for violating the nighttime curfew particularly severe, but Elliot was well aware his academic standing had suffered of late, due to his inability to concentrate, his frequent absenteeism, and the fact that, with Chester missing, he couldn't bring himself to care much about his studies. No sense adding more weight to what was an already troubled semester.

It gave him something else to worry over as he walked, in those few moments he wasn't preoccupied brooding over Chester.

Only once did he come vaguely close to being caught, but he heard the clunk of footsteps and saw the glow of lantern or flashlight in the fog with more than enough time to change direction. He cut swiftly across one of the lawns, skirted the edge of a fountain, and then realized precisely where he was.

Had he meant to come here, if only unconsciously, or was it pure coincidence? In either case, he knew the Orne Library now stood ahead of him and to the left, which meant off to the right…

The museum.

It hadn't been intended as such, initially. Rather, this was originally a private archive of the various historical and cultural relics acquired by the university over its many years. At some point, one of the deans had decided that it would be educational – as well as good publicity for fundraising efforts – to make those exhibits open to not just the faculty and select students, but to the public.

The building, which was not the first in which the collection had been housed, was large and imposing, with a great stone facade and ornate windows. Inside, Elliot knew, it more closely resembled a standard campus structure, with broad open halls surrounded by smaller side chambers and offices, as well as a massive semi-basement in which artifacts were examined and sometimes stored when they were deemed either too valuable, too fragile, or too uninteresting to warrant public display. As with the library's Special Collection, students normally required staff approval and supervision in order to study the basement's contents.

Of course, none of the museum was open to the public or the student body at this time of night, but that hadn't stopped either Chester or, on occasion, Elliot in the past. Elliot had been horrified, at first, when his roommate told him of his illicit visits, but Chester had only laughed at his concerns. When his project was complete, he'd insisted, nobody would care that he'd sneaked in to study one particular artifact after hours.

The caretaker and chief curator was the only man technically permitted within during off hours, but one particular security guard each night walked a beat that put him within sight of the entrance every few minutes. As was so often the case, tonight that duty fell to a young man named Jeremy Casterline, who had made quite a tidy sum over the past months – first by allowing Chester to conduct some of his research after hours, and then by allowing Elliot to follow up on what Chester had been doing.

Or, on occasion, to simply stand before one exhibit in particular and wonder what about it had so fascinated his friend. What Chester had seen in it that nobody else had.

Whether it was somehow related to whatever had become of him since.

A few dollars changed hands. A key rattled in a lock. Elliot darted through shadowed halls and darkened alcoves, ducking once into a closet when he mistook the creak of settling foundations for the footfalls of Mr Combs, the caretaker.

It was dim, but not dark. Occasional lights left on for Combs' convenience were more than sufficient for Elliot, who'd walked this path more than once. To the far end of the main hall, through one specific storage room with a door in the back, down the stairs to the half-underground lower level.

And from there, through smaller rooms, around tables, between dusty crates, to the enigmatic monument Chester had spoken of, on which most researchers had given up literal generations back, tucked away unseen because nobody much cared about it any longer.

The Lindegaard Stele.

Except tonight, when he'd casually walked most of that route and was but two rooms shy of his objective, a faint breeze where there ought not be one halted him in his tracks.

By now his sight had adjusted well to the gloom, and it took little effort to pinpoint the problem. There, above a stack of crates and a set of metal-frame shelves, one of the semi-basement's ground-level windows had been left ajar.

No, not "left." Forced. It hung loose from its frame, some of the braces snapped, open wider than it had been built to allow.

Wide enough to permit someone to sneak inside, perhaps.

Elliot froze, sweating despite the chill, struggling to think. He ought to go. Fetch help; Jeremy, or even the police. If not, then simply return to bed, let whatever was happening go on without him, as it would have on any other night.

Whatever he did, no matter what choices, he absolutely must *not* proceed on his own. God only knew what a thief or intruder, caught in the act, might do to a witness.

Yet that was precisely what Elliot Raslo did. This had been his way of connecting with the missing Chester, his own private ritual. That someone had the audacity to sully that, however unknowingly, made his blood pump fiercely with a rage he'd rarely felt.

Besides, might this not be related to Chester's disappearance, or that of Professor Polaski? So far as Elliot knew, nobody had broken into Miskatonic's antiquities collection in living memory. For it to happen now, with everything else going on, would certainly be a remarkable coincidence.

Casting about, Elliot spotted a collection of tools on one of the shelves. After wiping his palm dry on his trousers, he selected a small mallet, swung it a few times to get a feel for the heft, then crept onward.

Peeking around a doorframe two rooms further, he spotted the stele: an obelisk of glossy black stone, taller than any man. It had once been taller still, but the top portion – probably only a small bit, though nobody could say precisely how small – had broken away long before the thing came into the university's possession.

A piece that Chester had said was a major part of his ongoing project – and that he'd claimed to have located. He'd sworn his friend to secrecy on that score and, thus far, Elliot had kept his word. He worried about keeping information, any information, from the authorities, but he couldn't imagine how learning of that broken stone, however ancient and mysterious, could aid in their search.

One smooth side of the stele was covered almost entirely in what looked to be writing, but not in any alphabet Elliot – or any of the many scholars who had studied the thing in decades gone by – could identify, let alone pronounce or hope to translate. It was ancient, that much had been determined with certainty, but the carving of those symbols, letters, sigils, whatever they were, had been achieved with a degree of finesse even modern tools had difficulty matching.

A fascinating mystery indeed, when it had first been uncovered, but one that, after countless years of no progress whatsoever, had been pushed aside and forgotten.

Of more immediate concern was the mystery of who had broken into the basement and now stood, back to Elliot, staring up at the obelisk and muttering under his breath.

As stealthy as he could manage, Elliot crept closer, struggling to keep his breath even, steady, when every nerve prodded at him to gasp. Something about the man seemed familiar, and once the young student was near enough to better hear him, he knew why.

While the language wasn't one Elliot spoke, the voice was unmistakably the same he'd heard earlier that day in the library, raised in aggravation.

Except the muttering abruptly stopped and the intruder whirled, hands rising to defend himself. Elliot, despite all his efforts, must have made some sound that gave him away.

For several long breaths they sized each other up.

"What are you doing here, Mr Shiwak?" Elliot finally demanded, his own tension compelling him to break the silence.

Shiwak's attentions flickered briefly to the bludgeon in Elliot's hand, then settled on his face. "This doesn't concern you. You shouldn't be here."

"And you should? Has the university hired a new caretaker? They should have said."

The intruder's scowl deepened.

"This being your first day on the job," Elliot continued, bravado forcing him on lest he lose his nerve entirely, "I suppose we can forgive you forgetting your keys, but that window'll be costly to fix."

Shiwak, however, had sussed him out. "You're no caretaker, either, boy. Seems neither of us are supposed to be here. So why are you … ?" He drew himself up stiff, a thought seeming to occur to him, and he gestured vaguely back at the stele. "This? You study this?"

"I–"

"The *Ujaraanni*! Have *you* got it?"

"The what?"

"The other piece!"

Elliot's gut clenched and drums pounded behind his eyes. The other piece? The man was after what Chester had found.

"You! You did something to him, didn't you? Where is he?!"

Shiwak blinked and took a step back, clearly unprepared for that reaction. "I don't know who–"

"Where is he, you son of a–?"

Elliot didn't even realize he'd charged the stranger, raised the mallet over his head to strike. He knew only that this man *must* be responsible for what had happened, that all his frustration, all his fear, finally had an outlet.

Except Shiwak was no longer there to be struck.

The stranger slipped aside like an eel and lashed out with the edge of his closed fist. The impact caught Elliot in the chest, driving the breath from his lungs, bruising flesh and slamming him painfully to the floor on his back. Shiwak leaned down, startlingly fast, smacking the hammer from Elliot's slackening grip even before he landed and sending it spinning across the darkened room.

"I'm unsure what you think I've done," Shiwak said, backing off rather than pressing his advantage. "But I *am* sure that this… Is not a good idea."

Elliot scrambled to his feet, slightly dazed, still driven by anger. No, it probably wasn't – especially as, from the floor, he'd seen something, a sheath or the like, hanging at the stranger's back, beneath his coat. If it was a weapon, however, the man hadn't gone for it yet, and Elliot wasn't planning to give him the chance, or to let him get away.

He'd been caught by surprise, that was all. While hardly an experienced brawler, Elliot practiced with Arkham's boxing club. He knew how to handle himself. Grimly, he advanced, fists raised.

"Don't do it, boy."

He did it.

With a cry, Elliot lunged, leading with a swift jab.

Shiwak caught his arm, twisted inside his reach, hammered the younger man's throat – not nearly at his full strength, which might well have killed, but enough to make Elliot gasp and gag. Still maintaining his grip, he dropped himself to the floor and rolled, slamming Elliot once again to his back and then winding up atop him, Elliot's arm bent painfully between them. Shiwak scissored his legs, immobilizing Elliot's own between his knees.

Agony coursed through him, but Elliot forced himself not to thrash. He wasn't sure how he'd wound up pinned this way, but he realized that if Shiwak so much as rolled, his trapped arm might well break.

"Are we done?" Shiwak asked him.

"Oh, you're quite done," someone else answered on Elliot's behalf.

Chapter Four

Daisy Walker, the librarian, stood shaded in the doorway, scarcely more than a silhouette. "Get off him, please."

Then, when Shiwak hesitated, "Miskatonic is currently missing both a student and a well-respected professor, and we've no idea what happened to them. In light of that, many of the staff who have reason to be on campus after nightfall have taken to arming ourselves. A derringer may not be the most fearsome weapon, Mr Shiwak, but I daresay you still shouldn't like to be shot by one."

With a faint grunt, he released Elliot from his grip and rose to his feet. Elliot scampered away, wincing, and then pulled himself upright as well.

"Miss Walker–" he began, worry and relief vying for space in his throat.

"Later, Mr Raslo, you will have ample opportunity to explain to me why you're here, and why I shouldn't report Mr Casterline for allowing you entry. In the meantime, kindly go find either him or Mr Combs and have him summon the police."

"Do you think it's safe to leave you alone with him, Miss Walker?" Elliot asked, though in truth, the alternative – for him to stay while she went to fetch help – wasn't any more appealing.

"I'm sure I can manage," she said from her darkened doorway. "Now hurry along. The faster you call the police, the sooner they'll–"

"Wait!" Shiwak took a single step forward, not enough to be threatening but definitely attention-getting. Then, far more softly, "Please."

Even in the dark, Elliot sensed Daisy's scowl. "Mr Shiwak, you've broken into the university's archive, you're assaulted one of our students–"

"It was he who attacked me, actually." Then, before she could continue, "You're correct, though, I broke in. And if that means I must go with your police and face the consequences, so be it. But please, I ask you – I beg of you…" Those last words sounded as if they twisted in his mouth, pridefully fighting to remain behind his lips, yet he forced them out. "Tell me something first. Tell me of this." He turned to gesture at the Lindegaard Stele. "Tell me where it comes from, how it came to be here, all you know of it. Do that, and I give you my word I'll wait for your police, and go peacefully when they arrive."

Daisy and Elliot both stared, bewildered by the bizarre request. The young student wondered if he might not be stalling for time, but it seemed an odd tactic, and he sounded so very sincere. Almost plaintive.

"You first," Daisy decided. She still hadn't come any nearer than the doorway. "Convince me of your intentions. Tell me why this matters to you."

Now it was Shiwak's turn to stare, but he took even less time to make up his mind than she had. "Very well." He sat in place, cross-legged, visibly calming himself. "It's been some time since I told the whole tale to anyone."

One final breath, almost a sigh.

"Itilleq, my home, consists of a very large extended family. My immediate kin, those related to us by marriage, those related to *them* by marriage, and so on. You might call it a 'clan,' though that word has no precise equivalent for us.

"And for so long as we have been a community – longer – it has been the task of one of our angakkut to stand guard over the *Ujaraanni*."

"Um?" Elliot asked in what was, perhaps, not his most eloquent or insightful question.

"The angakkut are wise men and women," Daisy said, her tone suggesting she was casting back to information read long ago. "Shamans. I've no idea whatsoever what the other word means."

Shiwak nodded. "Nor should you. The *Ujaraanni* is a wicked thing. A magnet for malevolent anersaapiluit – ah, 'evil spirits' would be a near enough translation, I suppose."

Elliot scoffed silently. More superstition.

And yet, thinking of the litany he had "caught" from Chester, and the incantation in the *Livre d'Ivon*, he couldn't quite dismiss the notion as readily as he once might.

A thought that, in turn, made him realize that the refrain in his head had grown even quieter in the past few moments than it earlier had been. That, once again, it appeared to be proximity to this peculiar newcomer that helped suppress it.

"It is a stone," Shiwak continued. "A large black stone, smooth on most sides but broken and jagged along the bottom." He nodded again as both members of his audience glanced openly at the stele behind him.

"Yes. The same stone. The same writing, that even the eldest and wisest angakkut could never read. They knew nothing of what it meant, only that it was dangerous.

"For generations, they kept it in a cave some distance from our homes. One angakkoq was chosen to watch over it, and he or she would do so for many years, even decades. Until exposure to the *Ujaraanni* became too much. It slowly drives those near it mad, you see. Perhaps something in the stone itself, perhaps the spirits it draws. Eventually, even the most powerful angakkoq would slip into dotage, unable to function. Then we would care for them, as long as they lived, and the next would take their place."

Elliot found himself drawn into the tale despite himself, his mistrust. "Why not get rid of it?"

"What would we do? Shatter it? Even if our tools proved up to the task, the angakkut worried that doing so might anger the spirits drawn to it, or that its own magics would lash out. Abandon it? Someone else might find it and be threatened. No, it was our sacred duty to ensure the *Ujaraanni* harmed none."

"But something happened," Daisy guessed. Like Elliot, she must have been fascinated, as she'd taken several steps further into the room.

Shiwak gave her a peculiar look, but continued. "Yes. Perhaps nine years ago, a number of travelers came to Itilleq. White men, Americans, and several Kalaallit guides from elsewhere in Greenland. The Forsythe Expedition."

"I've heard of them," Daisy told them. "They were said to have brought back several artifacts of great historical and anthropological... Oh."

"Yes," the Kalaaleq growled. "We didn't learn of their betrayal immediately. They spent several days with us, exchanging stories, trading supplies, learning some of our customs and beliefs. When they departed, we wished them well, told them we hoped the kindly toornat and anersaat would protect them from the hateful. And they repaid us by..."

He paused, choking down the fury and the hurt. "It was only when my cousin made a journey to bring food to the angakkoq guarding the *Ujaraanni*, something we did about twice a week, that we learned how greatly they'd deceived us.

"I don't believe they meant to kill old Palleq. But he was growing older, his health poor due to his isolation, and his mind beginning to go. Even the stress of being restrained might have proved too much. In either case, we found the angakkoq dead in the snow, and the *Ujaraanni* gone."

Daisy visibly flinched, and Elliot could guess why. The Forsythe Expedition had nothing to do with Miskatonic University, but it had likely been funded, at least in part, by a similar institution of academia – and Miskatonic, in its day, had sponsored similar expeditions. The librarian probably felt pangs of guilt, by association if nothing more, and perhaps wondered if any of those efforts had employed equally disturbing methods.

The rest of Shiwak's tale passed swiftly, in that darkened room, with the stele looming behind. His father, one of the community's traders, highly fluent in English and familiar with some of America's ways, had been chosen to go forth and seek out the *Ujaraanni*, to return it if he could, at the very least to learn where it had ended up. Shiwak spoke only briefly of the day his father left, but he remembered it well. The tightness in his voice was proof enough of that.

"For a time," he told them, "we would receive occasional messages detailing my father's progress. Or rather, his lack thereof. Then, about three years after he left, those messages stopped."

"Why?" Elliot asked.

It was Daisy, who had done the math in her head, who answered. "Because that would've been in 1917."

"Indeed," Shiwak said. "When your nation joined the 'Great War.'"

Silence, for a bit.

"I still don't know precisely what my father did for all that time. But it was a couple of years after the war ended that we received a traveler. A Canadian Inuk. He told us that my father had come to them, planning to sail eastward, but was badly injured and could travel no further. I set out immediately, to be by his side and to take up his quest if need be, but by the time I arrived, he had already died."

He spoke it so plainly, without inflection, that Elliot's own heart seized up. Such intense control could only mask an equally intense pain.

His father, Shiwak explained, had given his hosts information to pass along. He had learned, in his travels, that the Forsythe Expedition had been sponsored by the University of Virginia.

"It may not have been the institution itself," Daisy pointed out. "Such things are often financed by alumni, on their own or as part of one of the silly secret societies all these prestigious universities seem to sprout."

Shiwak waved a hand; the difference was irrelevant to him. In either case, the stone was no longer there when he traveled to Charlottesville, but in asking around it didn't take him long to determine what had happened.

"The university suffered a theft from its collection. In May of last year, an object was brought to them for study. The 'Blackstone Meteor.'"

"I read about that," Elliot chimed in.

"Yes, much fuss was made over it. A fuss that also allowed one of their security guards, a Mr Addison, to conspire with several outsiders to steal and sell a number of goods. The *Ujaraanni* was among them."

"How did you find that out," Daisy asked him, "when apparently the university and the police couldn't?"

"Oh, they suspected Addison, even terminated his employment, but the authorities had no proof. To me, he confessed."

"Why would…?"

Carefully, moving slowly to make it clear his movement was by no means a threat, Shiwak pulled back his coat and patted the sheathed blade.

"You didn't!"

"I didn't have to. Merely holding it to his face and making clear how strongly I felt about the matter proved sufficient. I did find it fascinating that he couldn't say precisely *why* he chose the *Ujaraanni* as one of his targets, when other possibilities would have been easier to move and just as valuable, if not more so. He said it 'just spoke to me.'"

"In any event, he gave me the names of several men, who gave me the names of several more. And so, after a great deal of work, I found myself here with a handful of clues – only to discover this Lindegaard Stele, and a host of new questions."

What in God's name had Chester gotten himself caught up in? Elliot's thoughts whirled with questions of his own, but even had he been willing to interrupt, he couldn't decide where to start.

Daisy's brow furrowed – Elliot could see it, even in the gloom, and knew she wondered at many of the same things he did – but Shiwak spoke again before she could speak.

"On that topic, Miss Walker, I would like to apologize."

"Oh?"

"It only occurred to me tonight, as I was thinking over all of this, precisely why it might be so offensive – even, perhaps, damaging to one in your position – for me to have asked you publicly about a man like Pembroke. It was ill-considered and rude, and I'm sorry."

"Oh." She seemed uncertain what to do with such a statement from someone she'd clearly viewed as quite a rough man. "Well… Thank you."

Elliot, with the instincts of a student, actually half-raised a hand before remembering these were rather different than classroom circumstances. "I'm afraid I don't understand."

"Jebediah Pembroke," Daisy told him stiffly, "is one of Arkham's dealers in stolen goods. Antiquities in particular. Miskatonic has nothing to do with him or his kind, obviously, but tongues will wag. And as the new overseer of Special Collections…"

"Ah. Right."

"Now, please, Miss Walker," Shiwak said. "I've answered your question, and in rather great detail. It's your turn."

Chapter Five

It was, indeed, her turn. Daisy didn't ever seriously consider going back on her word. It would serve no purpose – nothing she could reveal was sensitive in any way – and while she wasn't opposed to a bit of falsehood where necessary, lying without need rubbed her, as a lover of knowledge, the wrong way.

"I'll tell you all I can," she said, "though I'm afraid you may find it largely unsatisfying."

Some of it, she remembered. The rest she found in the small bound stack of notes tucked away on a shelf near the Lindegaard Stele.

It had been found on the property of Helfred Lindegaard, a Danish magnate digging for cryolite in Greenland. "It was unearthed from deep within one of the mines," Daisy read, "near Ivigtût." She paused. "Is that anywhere at all near your home?"

"No. Itilleq is many hundreds of miles north of there."

"Hmm. Well, in any event, there are few specifics to speak of. None of the local Inuit made any claim to the stele…" She paused again, then added somewhat apologetically, "Or at least, so it was reported. Your own story makes me wonder, but I'm afraid there's nothing to indicate otherwise.

"Lindegaard had anthropologists study it, but none were able to translate it, nor connect it to any known historical cultures. He then sold it to an American collector of historical oddities, who also had it studied, with the same lack of success. He, in turn, willed it to Miskatonic University, where…" She trailed off with a shrug.

"Where it was studied," Shiwak guessed, "with no success."

"Just so. They finally gave up. Without being able to say much about it, and given how much space it would occupy, they decided it wasn't worth making a display. So they stuck it down here where it's essentially been gathering dust for a few generations. Every now and again, someone takes a stab at translation, or further study. All futile.

"Or," she added with a pointed look at Elliot, "perhaps all futile until now."

He turned his gaze toward his feet and remained silent.

"Elliot," she pushed, not unkindly, "I respect your desire to keep your friend's confidences, but the time for that is past. I made a point to never press him for information on his project, even though I can't remember the last time a student spent so much time studying books in the Special Collections. Most students wouldn't even have been *allowed* to, but he had several professors vouching for his efforts, and of course he volunteered a great deal of time toward helping around the library.

"I didn't press even when it became clear he was deliberately obscuring his tracks, asking for more books than he needed, so even though he was always accompanied by another librarian or myself, we couldn't guess at his goals."

Despite himself, Elliot nodded.

"But I do know, thanks to Mr Combs, that he spent much time here as well – and, given your own presence here tonight, I'm guessing that his studies weren't limited to the museum's proper hours."

"A… Are you going to report him for that?"

Daisy didn't know whether to smile or to sigh. Everything going on, the boy missing for so many weeks, and Elliot was still worried about Chester getting in trouble…

She settled for telling him, "I think we have larger concerns right now."

That, however, seemed to spark another question in Elliot's mind. He gingerly sat on a wooden crate, checking to ensure it would take his weight, and then asked, "How did you know to find *me* here tonight?"

Oh, because Abigail Foreman is obsessed with you, has been watching you, worried sick, since Chester vanished. Because she followed you tonight, saw you bribe the guard, and then – sneaking around the building to try to see what you were doing – spotted the broken window. And because she was also worried about getting someone in trouble when she should have been focused on his safety, and so came to get me from the library instead of running straight to security. God only knows what would have happened if I'd not been working late tonight!

But of course, she wasn't about to tell him a word of that. She *would* have a long and pointed talk with Abigail about proper behavior – for a young lady in general, and an infatuated one in particular – but that wasn't Elliot's business.

"Larger concerns," she said again. "Elliot, it's time to come clean – for Chester's own sake. He *was* studying the Lindegaard Stele, wasn't he?"

The boy's face twisted in a riot of conflicting emotions, but, finally, he nodded. Daisy, for all her talk of "larger concerns," felt a tingle of excitement. Mysterious secrets, hidden studies into ancient lore… This was like something out of her favorite novels!

Of course, many of those hadn't turned out so well for the characters involved, had they? Her excitement faded, replaced by the first stirrings of fear.

"Yes," Elliot admitted. "He swore he'd found a means of translating the stele. He never told me how, only that he'd made some connections nobody ever had before. He was certain this would cement his position in the archeological world, before he'd even graduated. And…" His eyes twitched in Shiwak's direction. "He said he'd located the missing part of it, too. But he never said where," he added quickly.

Shiwak growled something under his breath in what Daisy assumed was Kalaallisut. Switching back to English, he asked, "Who else knew of this?"

"A few of his professors knew part of it," Elliot answered slowly, almost unwillingly. "But I think only his chief advisor on the project had any real detail."

"Professor Polaski," Daisy guessed, irate. She understood why Elliot had kept silent, she truly did, but that knowledge might have helped convince the police that the two disappearances were connected.

"Yes."

She also, Daisy realized, felt more than a touch of annoyance at Chester and Polaski themselves. Damn them and their academic paranoia. Nobody else had access to the missing bit of the stele, nobody else was even *trying* to translate it any more. If they'd been less secretive about their whole endeavor from the start, if they'd let anyone know what they were working on, this might all have been avoided – or at least given the police more to go on.

"Who is this Polaski?" Shiwak asked.

But Elliot's suspicions had clearly resurfaced. "Why should I tell you? Why are we telling you *anything*?"

Daisy understood his reluctance, but she was growing impatient. "Elliot, I don't believe Mr Shiwak is our enemy here. I don't think he did anything to Chester."

"Why not?!"

"Because he probably wouldn't need to ask you about the *Ujaraanni* if he had. More to the point, because he had every opportunity to hurt you, and he chose not to."

Elliot's face flushed. "I didn't do *that* badly."

Shiwak's answering grin was perhaps meant to be kind, but he couldn't quite hide the amused pity beneath it.

"Yes, dear," Daisy said. "I'm afraid you did. And he was holding back." Then, when Elliot's expression turned stubborn, "Mr Shiwak, would you show him, please? Slowly," she added.

Using only three fingers, the Kalaaleq reached under his coat and drew his knife. It seemed to take forever.

The blade itself was well over a foot long, straight-backed, curved and thick along the edge. The handle appeared to be made of old ivory or bone, and was carved with an array of animalistic figures.

"My pana," he said. "Snow knife. Made to carve packed snow and ice for constructing igluvijait. So you can imagine what it does to flesh and bone."

The red in Elliot's face drained away as swiftly as it had gathered, leaving his cheeks pallid, as it finally dawned on him just how their scuffle could have gone if Shiwak had indeed wished to hurt him.

"You should also consider the fact," Shiwak continued, "that I have kept my promise to sit here peacefully, and wait for your police, despite the fact that Miss Walker is not, in fact, in any way armed."

Elliot stared at her, and now it was her turn to blush, if only lightly. *I thought I was doing so well.*

"What gave me away?"

"You gesture a great deal with your hands while you speak. Even in this light, I've had plenty of opportunity to see that you're holding only your purse, not a gun. But also your posture. I've had weapons held on me before by those not accustomed to their use. As best I can put it into words, you are… not relaxed, no, but the wrong sort of tense."

"Well. I appreciate the consideration, then."

Elliot seemed rather more bothered by the revelation – and by Shiwak's awareness of it – than Daisy was. "Do… Do we still run for the police?"

"I don't think fetching the police is in anyone's best interests here," Daisy said thoughtfully. Then, before Elliot could protest, "As I said, Mr Shiwak hasn't hurt anyone. His search is clearly connected to Chester's disappearance."

"Then the police should know about it!" Elliot protested.

Shiwak shook his head. "And they, of course, will listen to, and believe, my story. They will believe I had nothing to do with the missing men. They will ignore the convenient foreign suspect, on whom they can blame the whole thing, and continue to devote manpower to a search that has so far proved fruitless. No, boy, Miskatonic has been more welcoming to me than many American cities, but I'm not foolish enough to believe that would last one minute if I drew police attention."

Daisy wished it wasn't so, but he was right. Furthermore…

"It might not be in Chester's best interests, either," she pointed out. "You said he'd located the *Ujaraanni*. And Mr Shiwak traced it to Arkham through connections to men like Pembroke."

She saw the question in Elliot's countenance. He wasn't following, or perhaps didn't wish to follow.

"How do you suppose," she asked gently, "Chester got hold of such a thing? From what sort of people?"

Again Elliot looked away, fists clenching angrily. He doubtless wanted to protest, to defend his friend – and doubtless knew he could not.

"What will you do now, Mr Shiwak?" she asked.

The Kalaaleq sheathed his blade and rose to his feet, legs seeming simply to unfold beneath him. "Assuming you're not calling the police? Continue my search." He turned to gaze at the Lindegaard Stele. "Although I admit, if you can tell me nothing else about, ah… Chester?"

"Chester Hennessy, yes."

"About Chester's research, I'm not hopeful about my other options. There are others I can ask about Pembroke, but I don't imagine most will be any more willing to speak to me about him than you were, even if they do know something. And while I've no compunction about threatening thieves, I'm less eager to treat honest folk that way."

"To say nothing of less likely to get away with it," Elliot said.

"That, too, yes."

Daisy found herself chewing her lower lip in thought. She could tell him that it might just be possible for her to learn more of Jebediah Pembroke. Her declaration that nobody at Miskatonic would deal with such a man was based as much on hope as on fact, and she'd long suspected that several of the university's less scrupulous faculty members took the occasional legal shortcut with their acquisitions. She could ask. As both a historian and, she hoped, a good person, she felt for Shiwak, and he deserved the best chance of recovering his people's stolen relic.

But her first loyalty had to be to Miskatonic. If she *were* to learn something, and it ever got out why she had access to such information…

No. No, she couldn't risk it. Not just for the university, but also for Elliot. She couldn't expose him to the dangers and temptations of that world. Maybe, maybe if she could be *sure* it would help them find Chester Hennessy and Wilmott Polaski, she would feel differently. But not as things stood now.

"The Hennessys are in town," she said instead.

Shiwak turned. "Pardon?"

Damn. She shouldn't have said that. She'd just been so anxious to find *some* way to help, some lead to offer, other than Pembroke…

Too late now. He'd simply press the issue – either with her, or worse, out on his own – if she clammed up.

"Chester's parents. They live in Boston, but they're staying at the Excelsior Hotel while the Arkham police search for their son. I'm certain," she added swiftly, as Shiwak drew breath to speak, "that the police have already spoken to them, though. And I can't imagine it's a topic they much care to discuss, let alone with a stranger. I was just thinking aloud." Maybe that would deter him from pursuing the matter.

"The police might not have known what to ask," Elliot said. "Whether he'd said anything to them about his research, about Mr Shiwak's stone. The Hennessys might know something important and not realize it."

"I still doubt they would speak to him," Daisy protested. *I really should not have said anything!*

"Probably not. But what if it's not just him?"

Daisy stared, horrified. Shiwak didn't appear much happier, though for very different reasons.

"My hunt is my own," he said. "And if I *were* to work with someone–"

Elliot didn't let him finish. "–It wouldn't be me. I know I made a… less than flattering first impression. But Chester is my best friend. If there's even a chance someone might find him where the police can't, I refuse to sit by and not at least try to help. And I know Arkham. I won't just be able to get you into places you couldn't go on your own, I can take you to ones you'd never even find."

Daisy's hands very nearly flailed in protest. "Elliot, this is a bad idea. It's dangerous. And you've already been ignoring your studies, missing classes…"

Shiwak, however, had grown thoughtful. "You might be of some help, at that. And I certainly cannot fault your loyalty to your friend."

Elliot smiled his way, then turned toward the fuming librarian. "I know all of that, Miss Walker. But I have to do this."

Shouting at him would do very little good, Daisy knew, but she very much wanted to anyway. She understood his need to do something in the search for Chester – understood his feelings better than he would have wanted her to – but this was foolish. Dangerous. Now that she knew Shiwak wouldn't have hurt him, she wished she'd never interfered at all.

"Even if I accept that, what makes you think the Hennessys would speak to you either? So far as they're concerned, you're just another student. Even as their son's friend, you've nothing to offer them and no authority."

"No, I don't. But you would."

"I… what?"

"As a representative of Miskatonic, concerned that the police haven't found Chester yet – or Professor Polaski – you and some of the other faculty have taken it upon yourself to see what you can find, and you'd like to ask them a few–"

"No. Absolutely not."

Elliot's face fell, and it was probably only his pride – bolstered by Shiwak's presence – that kept him from crying. "Miss Walker, please. *Please.* What would this take, maybe a few days? No great loss, if it's a waste of time, but what if it's not? What if we find something?"

He stepped forward, hands out, beseeching. "Daisy…" His choice to use her given name was deliberate, she knew. He was too courteous to do it by accident. "They're out there somewhere. Chester, Professor Polaski. In God knows what sort of trouble."

Oh, don't do this to me…

"I… I'm no investigator, Elliot!"

"You're a researcher. Is that really any different? It's certainly closer than Mr Shiwak or I."

Daisy's shoulders slumped. This was wrong in a dozen different ways – but she could not deny to herself that, despite all her objections and all the logical arguments against it, it *felt* like the right thing to do. They just might be able to find something the police could not, they'd convinced her of that, and if she didn't try…

"All right," she sighed. "Meet me outside the library, tomorrow evening at five, and we'll see if we can do this without causing anyone – including ourselves – *too* much trouble.

"Mr Shiwak, have you found a place to stay? I can make some recommendations."

"Thank you, no, I have a place," Shiwak replied. "And if we'll be working together… call me Billy."

Chapter Six

The faint drizzle soaking Arkham the following day might have dampened the Miskatonic campus, but it had no such effect on the gossip among its students – and, though they were perhaps more discreet about it, the faculty and staff.

The broken window at the museum had, of course, been discovered, leading a horrified Mr Combs to call in everyone who worked with the collection, and every professor who knew it well, for a frantic cataloging of relics and displays. As efforts proceeded throughout the day, everyone wondered if this was some isolated incident, or if indeed it was somehow linked to the missing professor and student.

When the caretaker announced, somewhat disbelievingly, that not one item was missing, nor even out of place, the peculiarity only served to exacerbate the spread of rumor, rather than to mitigate it.

Daisy Walker and Elliot Raslo spent the bulk of the day fiercely biting their tongues and, at least in the librarian's case, having more than a few second thoughts. *What are we doing?* Even if they learned something, and Daisy felt less confident about that possibility today than she had in the heat of the moment last night, she wasn't sure what they might do about it.

It didn't stop them, however, from meeting up with Billy Shiwak at the appointed time, to begin their unofficial, unauthorized and quite possibly unwise investigation.

Walking halfway across town would have been an unpleasant proposition even without the chill of the rain, so – given there were three of them to split the fare – Daisy suggested hailing a taxi, to which the others readily agreed. It didn't take long for one of the black-and-yellow Fords to come thumping and puffing their way; a great many drivers made a habit of lingering around the edges of campus toward the end of classroom hours.

How much of Elliot's and Billy's unspoken agreement to pile into the back seat, leaving the front for Daisy, was due to courtesy, and how much to both of them trying to avoid conversation with a stranger, she couldn't say. She wasn't especially inclined to thank them in either case.

"Where to, doll?" asked the slouch cap and thick mustache that seemed to make up the entirety of the cab driver.

"Excelsior Hotel, please."

An eyebrow rose at that, proving the man was not, in fact, all mustache and cap. "You sure?" His gaze flickered toward the back seat.

It might have been a comment on the fact that, while hardly dressed shabbily, neither of the men – nor Daisy herself, for that matter – wore clothes of quite the quality one might expect for guests of that establishment. It might have been doubt that Billy, in particular, would be entirely welcome there.

Or it just might have been coarse commentary on the notion of a young woman visiting a hotel accompanied by two men.

"Quite sure." She kept her smile, though it felt fragile as cheap peanut brittle. "We're visiting a guest." *Not that it's any of your business.*

"Hey, it's your dime." He arm-wrestled the car into gear, and they were off.

The rattle of the engine was sadly insufficient to keep the driver from beating his gums the entire drive, going on about how he rarely got to head out this way, making unwarranted comments about anyone they passed who looked the slightest bit out of the ordinary and sneaking (poorly and blatantly) constant glances at his blonde passenger. Throughout it all, Daisy maintained her Librarian Voice, answering all questions with a formal courtesy, while inwardly she allowed herself many a vision of throttling the man – possibly followed by Elliot and Billy, each of whom gazed out his respective window and seemed utterly unaware of the cloud of discontent filling the vehicle.

The combination of unwanted conversation and the constant bumping of narrow tires over Arkham's roads – only some of which had been paved with automobiles in mind, the rest consisting of old cobbles – had Daisy's head aching by the time they finally arrived. With rather less poise than was her wont, she gathered coins from the others, practically dropped them in the driver's lap and slammed the car door behind her.

Then, standing on the sidewalk, light rain falling on their faces and pedestrians irritably shuffling around them, the trio looked up at the massive edifice that was the Excelsior.

One of Arkham's tallest structures, it boasted a stone facade intended to make it appear far older and more historic than its relatively recent construction. Ionic pillars, glass-and-brass revolving door, a doorman in formal coat and cap, all shouted lustily to all and sundry that this was a place of class, refinement and, of course, no small expense.

Yet the Excelsior boasted that it made the amenities of wealth available to the middle class as well, making some of its rooms and services more affordable than its appearance might suggest. The result was a place considered unnecessarily hoity-toity by some, while far too welcoming to those of "lower status" by others.

Still it remained popular, as it was one of the best Arkham had to offer.

Daisy politely declined assistance from the doorman, hoped Billy either wouldn't notice or wouldn't react to the man's disdainful sneer and pushed her way through the revolving door.

The lobby of the Excelsior was a veritable cavern, boasting broadly spaced columns, as well as lush pathways of carpet across an expanse of marble floor. People clad in their "Sunday best," or outfits more formal still, wandered this way and that, sat about the various tables in elegant leather chairs or spoke with the staff at the counter. Rich cigar smoke filled the air, and what had once been a bar along one wall now, in these days of Prohibition, served coffees and, oddly enough, deli sandwiches.

And every last patron, or so it felt, stopped to glower at the new arrivals.

A few of the guests were not white, though they were a minority. A few of the guests were underdressed, though they, too, were a minority.

None were both.

Billy's expression hadn't changed, but Daisy, for all that she'd known him less than a day, could sense his hackles rising. Uncomfortable as the unwanted attention made her, she couldn't imagine what he must feel like, regularly drawing that sort of scrutiny.

Worse, their reaction had apparently reminded Elliot of something he previously hadn't thought of. Discomfort splashed across his face, as though it had fallen on him along with the drizzle outside, he said, "It's, uh, it's just occurred to me…"

"Yes?" Daisy prompted.

"Chester's told me a bit about his parents. They're, um, old-fashioned. In their attitudes."

He directed that last remark pointedly at Billy, flushing as he spoke.

"I'm sorry," he added. He looked like he wanted to fold in on himself.

"This is my search," Billy began, voice low but hot. "If you think I'm going to sit any of it out–"

Daisy wanted to agree with him. It was unfair, unjust. Instead, she forced her anger down and laid a hand on his arm. "What good will it do if they won't speak to us? We're in this together. Elliot and I will tell you anything and everything we learn. I give you my word."

"And mine," Elliot added, drawing himself up to his full height.

Billy glared, turned away and paced several steps, then back, fists clenched.

"All right." It clearly took everything he had to keep from erupting, but he was no fool. "I'll trust you. I'll wait."

Daisy squeezed his arm, then she and Elliot moved to the desk to ask after the Hennessys' room number.

Billy watched, first as they spoke to the concierge, and then made for the elevator. The mechanical contraption swallowed them up, and only then did he turn, casting about for a place to sit.

He met a veritable sea of hostile, or at least suspicious, expressions. Without his local companions, loitering here alone, he stood out more than ever. Scowling, he crossed his arms, stubbornly planting himself, silently daring anyone to say anything.

It was a pose he retained until people began literally drifting away from him, to sit at a greater remove. Until two of the staff began whispering to one another behind the welcome desk, one of them allowing his hand to drift ever nearer the phone hanging on the wall behind them.

It might not be related to him. And if it was, it might not be the police the man intended to call. Still, that wasn't a risk Billy was prepared to take, not a hassle he remotely needed.

Muttering under his breath in Kalaallisut, he made for the revolving door to continue his wait outside.

The drizzle hadn't stopped, but thankfully the Excelsior boasted multiple canvas awnings. Even distancing himself from the front door, he could at the very least keep himself relatively dry. And while he drew occasional sidelong glances here as well, they were less frequent – not everyone walking by was nearly so parochial as the bulk of the hotel's clientele – and, as he was no longer "invading" an exclusive space, less openly hostile.

He wanted to go home.

Hands in his coat pockets, he leaned back against the stone wall, watching the sopping city moving around him, snickering occasionally at peoples' shivers or expressions of discomfort – nobody here had the *slightest* notion of what "cold" truly meant – until…

Billy Shiwak had grown up a hunter, first and foremost, and he had learned to keep alert, to heed the world and its creatures and its spirits, to *notice*. This time he wasn't certain, at first, what had drawn that notice, but he knew far better than to ignore it.

A car sat parked down the street, one of many. He knew almost nothing of automobiles, their makes or models. He could only say this one was of a different sort than the taxi that had brought them here; longer where the taxi had been squat, green instead of black and yellow.

Nothing about it should have drawn his attention.

The same held true for the driver. A white man in a tan suit and hat. He seemed to be watching Billy, true, but so were many others. So what…?

Wait. Had he seen them before?

He had spent the ride here from Miskatonic staring out the window. Ignoring the blather from up front with which the driver pestered Daisy Walker; ignoring, too, the rattle of the engine and the shake of the vehicle, sensations which discomfited him more than he'd care to admit. Billy wasn't afraid of technologies unknown to Itilleq, but he didn't entirely trust them, didn't care to be cooped up inside them. Give him a sled and a team of dogs over any clattering contraption.

But in his glancing about, his casual perusal of Arkham as it flowed past, had he seen this precise green car, with this man behind the wheel? Was this stranger following him, or one of his new companions?

He couldn't say for certain – most of these white folks looked alike – but that the thought had even occurred to him made him think he was onto something.

It might have been wiser to ignore the man, pretend he hadn't noticed him. To wait until Elliot and Daisy returned, and see if the green car continued to show up wherever they went next. Billy was irate, however, frustrated, and patience was not currently an enticing option.

Instead, he moved down the street, not straight toward the potential watcher but in that general direction.

At first, the stranger didn't react. He continued watching, but his attention appeared casual, just a local curiously observing an obvious foreigner wandering by. When Billy finally drew near, however, and abruptly turned to make his way directly toward him, the man immediately fired up the ignition and pulled into traffic.

Coughing and growling, the car took long enough getting up to speed that Billy could have caught it in a sudden sprint, but then what? Throw open the door and climb inside? Scare the wits out of someone who, probably as not, had done nothing wrong, had merely panicked at a stranger's sudden approach?

He watched the car merge into traffic and fade away into the rainy twilight.

Probably nothing, anyway, he told himself as he wandered back toward the hotel, and his comfortable waiting spot beneath the awning. *You're letting this unpleasant city get to you.*

Even as he leaned back against the stone facade of the Excelsior, however, he wasn't certain he believed it.

In the years they'd known one another, Elliot had seen Chester truly angry on only a handful of occasions. While he wasn't quite so courteous as Elliot himself strived to be, and was quite a bit more garrulous, his jests a bit rougher and his observations more pointed, Chester remained, for the most part, reasonably polite. Rarely crude, rarely boorish.

In those rare circumstances when he had become truly heated, however, he'd shown a tendency toward not merely disrespectfulness but genuine cruelty. It was a side of him Elliot strenuously disliked, and had hoped, with some effort, to coax him away from.

Tonight, after meeting Chester's parents, Elliot at least had a much better notion of where that side of his friend came from.

In the long walk from the elevator, down hallways adorned with thick car-peting and gold-patterned wallpaper, he and Daisy had decided that she, as the proper representative of the university, would do most of the talking. He, they would explain, had come along as Chester's best friend, just in case a line of discussion sparked additional questions in him that Daisy wouldn't think to ask.

When he answered their knock, however, the look of angry disdain Mr Hennessy had greeted them with had driven most potential questions from Elliot's mind.

The man had Chester's deep brown hair, and a shaggy, old-fashioned mustache to Chester's neat, pencil-thin one, but otherwise they didn't look terribly much alike beyond basic build. It was clearly Mrs Hennessy after whom Chester had taken, with her angular features. She reclined in one of the sitting room's brightly upholstered chairs, a cup of tea upon the table at her side, and the glare she cast him, framed within red hair tied severely back behind her head, was even less friendly than her husband's.

"Good evening," Daisy began. "My name is Miss Walker, from Miskatonic University. This is Mr Raslo, one of our students. We–"

"You told us all this when you called up from the lobby," Mr Hennessy barked, lowering himself into a chair across the room from his wife – and not, Elliot noted sourly, asking his guests to do the same. "What news?"

"Ah…" Elliot swore he could see Daisy pulling her "cloak of librarian" around herself, shifting into formal and proper mode. While neither of them had expected the Hennessys to be in a jolly mood, given the circumstances, this was not the welcome Elliot had anticipated. "We've no new information to speak of, I'm afraid. We–"

"Then what the hell are you here for?!" Mr Hennessy exploded right back out of his chair, finger aimed like a weapon. "Why are you wasting our time?"

Daisy drew breath to answer, but now that he'd begun, Chester's father wasn't about to wind down again so readily. "This *town*." He practically spat. "The Arkham police. Useless fools, every last one of them. 'No news.' It's the same every time we speak to them, when we can speak to them at all, when they aren't more concerned in avoiding our questions than in *finding our son*. He's only been missing for coming up on two months now."

"They don't care," his wife snapped in turn. "Nobody cares. Nobody who *matters*."

Elliot recoiled at the implied insult, very nearly snapped something impolite, but thankfully, Daisy answered faster than he could.

"We agree," she told them. "The Arkham police are overworked and overwhelmed, particularly now." She didn't specify what she meant; it wasn't necessary. The memories of the worldwide Spanish Flu epidemic were less than half a decade old. So far, the fever near the Merchant District hadn't spread, and the Arkham municipal government was spending most of their resources, the police included, on keeping it that way. "They can't focus on finding your son, not to the degree he deserves. That's why we're here. The university is concerned–"

"The university." Mr Hennessy stalked across the room to stand by the window. His furious expression, softened only marginally by fear and sorrow, glared back at them from his reflection in the darkening, rain-spattered glass. "For all the good you've done him. We already *had* someone from Miskatonic asking after him, weeks ago. One of your professors. And what did that accomplish? What answers has *he* come up with?"

Elliot felt a small charge run through him. If nothing else, that was confirmation of what everyone on campus had already figured: Wilmott Polaski's disappearance was, indeed, connected to Chester's own.

"We don't know what Professor Polaski might have found," Daisy told them with a growing frown. "He's disappeared, too. I would have thought the police had told you that."

Their host waved a dismissive hand. "They might have mentioned it." He turned back their way, shaking his head. "I should have sent Chester to Harvard, but no. Miskatonic had the better ancient languages program." He scoffed. "Where's the prestige in that?"

"It's what he loved," Chester's mother protested from her chair. "What made him happy."

"It was stupid. Childish. He should have devoted himself to something that *matters*."

This was threatening to blossom into what was clearly an old argument – but at least the topic had come up. "Did Chester ever talk to you about his work?" Elliot asked. "Particularly his current project? Did he mention his research or… or a… black stone…?"

He wanted to duck back behind Daisy, to get away from the twin murderous expressions now turned his way. Oh, he'd headed off their argument, all right – by giving them both something new on which to focus their frustrations.

"Chester didn't tell us much about his studies," Mrs Hennessy told him, her words nearly leaving a wake of frost between them on the carpet. Her glare darted briefly back toward her husband, blaming him for their son's reticence, but when it settled back on Elliot it was more hostile still. "I expect you enticed him to talk to *you* about such things far more than anyone else, Mr Raslo."

Her obvious hatred nearly sent him reeling, and he didn't for the life of him understand why, where it came from. Daisy took a step nearer to him, and he found himself grateful for even that gesture.

Possibly as much to draw their attention from Elliot as anything else, she took it upon herself to ask the next question. "I'm certain the police must have asked this already, but is there any other family Chester might have gone to? Any relatives you might–?"

"No." If anything, the missing young man's father grew even angrier at the change in topic. "No, there's nobody. We have no other family. It's just the three…" He stumbled on that, as if struck again by the very real possibility that he might have to revise his count. "…just the three of us."

His wife opened her mouth as if to speak, then decided against it, pressing her lips firmly together. To comfort him in his obvious distress, despite the sharp mood and harsh words of a moment before? Elliot wasn't sure. He almost had the sense there had been something else she'd wanted to add…

It was, instead, Mr Hennessy who spoke again, after taking a few heartbeats to recover himself. "I think you had better leave now."

Daisy clearly agreed. "Yes, we've taken up enough of your time. Thank you for seeing us. We'll let you know if we learn anything." She started toward the door.

For his own part, Elliot wasn't certain they'd learned everything they could from Chester's parents – they'd not really learned anything at all! – but hadn't the slightest notion how to ask any further questions in the face of such obvious unexplained hostility. No, Daisy had the right idea. It was time to go.

Still, his own sense of decorum, his deep concern for Chester and his sympathy for what his parents must be going through, wouldn't permit him to simply depart without another word.

Would that he had.

"Mr and Mrs Hennessy, I… I know how worried you must be. I'm worried too. We care about Chester, and I promise you I don't intend to stop until–"

"Don't you dare." Mrs Hennessy spat her words, her hatred, as if they were venom. Even in rising finally from her chair, she seemed almost, snake-like, to uncoil. "He told us all about you, Mr Raslo. You were supposed to be his friend. I know he told you what he was doing. You could have stopped him at any time. Whatever trouble he's in is because of you!"

The blood drained from Elliot's face so swiftly he felt on the verge of passing out. His feet took root in the carpet of the fancy suite. "Wh– What…? It was a *research project*! I didn't know he was in any danger. I–"

"You should have! I know he was sneaking around behind his professors' backs, getting up to all sorts of things, and you let it go on. And if… *when* he returns home, I promise you I intend to make certain he has nothing more to do with Miskatonic University, or any of his so-called *friends*. This is your fault. *Yours!*"

The room blurred. The world tilted. It took an iron grip, absolutely everything Elliot had, not to fall to his knees and empty his stomach. He didn't recall moving, only knew that he was passing through the door when he slammed a shoulder into the frame.

Later, it might bruise. In the moment, it only barely registered.

Mrs Hennessy was angry.

Is she right?

Grieving. Lashing out. It didn't mean anything.

Is she right?

Whatever had happened to Chester, it wasn't his fault. It *wasn't*.

Oh, God, is she right?

Behind him, he heard Daisy bidding the Hennessys good day in a tone icier than any Chester's mother had managed, than he had known she was capable of. And then he heard her in the hall behind him, calling out his name.

He didn't halt. If he did, he wouldn't start again.

Step by step, the hall swaying like a rope bridge beneath him, he staggered on. He should have reached the elevator by now, shouldn't he? He should…

He'd turned the wrong way upon leaving the room, gone right instead of left. He realized it now only because the door to the stairs appeared before him. It took him four tries to read the sign through welling eyes.

He pushed through it, stumbled down two steps, three, and finally stopped, clinging to the bannister.

He couldn't go any further. However embarrassing, however unmanly, the tears began to fall.

Then Daisy was behind him, folding him in her arms. "That witch! Elliot, I'm sorry. I'm so sorry."

He turned, face pressed to her shoulder, and she held him while he sobbed as though his world had ended.

Chapter Seven

Not even two full days ago, it had taken every argument young Elliot Raslo could muster to convince her to take any part whatsoever in the investigation on which he and Billy Shiwak intended to embark.

So how is it, Daisy wondered irritably as she maneuvered through the early bustling traffic that marked the start of Arkham's business day, *that I'm the only one doing any investigating this morning?*

It wasn't a fair question, seeing as how it had been her own suggestion that she make these first excursions alone. Still, even if she'd have admitted it to nobody else, she was feeling out of her depth and not a little bit put upon to be the one running all over town while the others waited. At least Dr Armitage had been happy to approve her sudden request for time off, and the rain had briefly ceased, even if the weather remained unseasonably chilly, the sky streaked with gray as if by a frustrated painter.

Today, she intended to ask questions of any number of strangers, questions that – even if they accepted her implication that she spoke on behalf of the university – many might feel disinclined to answer. It was why she'd recommended, however reluctantly, that Billy allow her to handle these errands, and why he, with equal reluctance, had agreed. These folks were going to be hesitant enough as it was; they might react poorly indeed to an obvious outsider.

As for Elliot, well … He seemed barely there at all this morning. Last night's emotional wound had sent him spiraling back into the exhaustion and preoccupation he'd suffered since Chester's disappearance. Daisy was sure there was more to it than worry, that something was genuinely wrong with the young man, but he hadn't confided any such thing, and she wasn't ready to press.

All of which left her, but just because it was logical for her to lead the investigation didn't mean she had to like it. Holmes or Dupin she was not.

The bulk of the day was spent in near-constant motion. Occasionally by taxi, when crossing much of the city was necessary, but mostly on foot, wandering from this place to that, one interview to another.

She decided to get Saint Mary's out of the way first. Not only did she anticipate learning nothing of use, but she thought this, of all their ideas, was the one where she was most probably retracing steps the police had already taken.

The hospital seemed a drab, depressing place, though how much was the building and how much her own dislike of such places she couldn't say. She spent almost an hour sitting in the lobby, staring at the slightly yellowing walls, watching white-coated doctors and white-uniformed nurses escorting patients, talking to relatives, wheeling gurneys, and so forth. Every now and again an ambulance crew delivered emergency cases, and then the relative quiet was broken by a mad bustle of activity.

Given their own uniforms, she couldn't help but picture those ambulance attendants, disrespectful as it might be, as milkmen delivering particularly large and uncooperative bottles.

It was, finally, Dr Regensteiner, Saint Mary's old and perennially exhausted chief physician, who finally deigned to take a few moments out of his busy schedule to address her queries.

"As I told the police some time ago, Miss Walker," he scolded from behind a white beard held to his face entirely by the folds of his wrinkles, "no, Chester Hennessy is not currently a patient at Saint Mary's. And if you'd checked with them before coming here, you could have avoided wasting both your time and mine."

Daisy kept her professional smile plastered to her face. "Has he, perhaps, been a patient here in the recent past, then? Or has he sought treatment for any particular malady? You must understand, any information at all could lead us to–"

"Any such information at all," Regensteiner interrupted, "would certainly be inappropriate to share without his consent, or at least that of his family. Whatever interest Miskatonic may have in his whereabouts, or whatever your reasons for not leaving this to the authorities, doesn't change that."

"But, Doctor–"

"Now, unless you *have* written consent from the family, or you're suddenly empowered to make a legally binding police request, I will bid you good day. I have a hospital full of patients, to say nothing of influenza raging through the Merchant District slums, thank you very much."

He swept away, coat billowing like a melodramatic stage cape, before he'd even finished speaking, leaving Daisy inwardly seething in his wake.

Daisy's visit to the offices of Joe Diamond, Arkham's most famous private detective, was equally fruitless if, at least, less unpleasant. Frustrated as they were, she'd thought that Chester's parents – and she still almost shook with fury when she thought of them and their treatment of Elliot – might have hired the man to hunt for their son. If so, Daisy hoped she might be able to wheedle a bit of information out of him. But…

"I'm afraid Mr Diamond ain't here." Daisy stood before the desk in a cramped but surprisingly personable outer office, speaking to a brunette in a dress surprisingly fashionable for a receptionist. "I can take down a message, or if you want to share some details, I can pass it along when he gets back, see if it's a job he's interested in."

"I, ah, didn't want to hire him, actually. I wanted to find out if he's already *on* a case."

The secretary's nose did a bit of a twitch, almost retracting into her face. "I don't share the boss's beeswax, lady."

"No, I know." She sighed, perhaps a tad theatrically. "Someone very important to me is missing. I just figured, if he was on the job, maybe he'd found something out he could tell me."

Nothing for a moment, then the other woman's expression loosened ever so slightly. "Look, I can spill this much. Mr Diamond's over in Salem, has been for a few weeks. And yeah, it's a missin' person, but it's a guy from out that way. So unless your friend lives in Salem … ?"

Daisy shook her head. "Arkhamite. A student at Miskatonic."

"Then no. Got no cases like that. Sorry."

Daisy thanked her, left her a card in case Diamond somehow found himself on the case once he returned and cared to share notes, and then once more went on her way.

Those two stops might have been useless, but they were also the easy ones. The next? Daisy was going to have to ask, or at least dance around the edges of, precisely the same sorts of questions that had gotten her hackles up when Billy first approached her. And while these were no proud, centuries-old institutions to be threatened by ill rumor, nobody wanted to be caught up in possible scandal.

Especially not where their livelihoods were involved.

Uptown, not terribly far from Saint Mary's hospital, sat Ye Olde Magick Shoppe, a cramped establishment spilling over with purported eldritch writings, mystical reagents, and the occasional relic or talisman. Clear across Arkham, in the Northside district, was the Curiositie Shoppe, a larger storefront specializing in the unusual, the intriguing and the historical; odds and ends from all corners and all times.

Polar opposites in terms of owners and their attitudes. Miriam Beecher, a venerable and gray-haired woman wearing fashionable blouse and slacks, but enough antique jewelry to supply an entire stage production, was notorious for taking her "magic" seriously indeed. Walk into her store with the intent of purchasing "tricks" or mastering illusions, or offer up the slightest hint that her grimoires were anything but genuine, and one could expect only disdain in return.

Oliver Thomas, however, a British expatriate, saw his curiosities solely as product. So long as they looked interesting enough to sell, the man couldn't appear to care less what one thought of them, and the only "magic" that mattered to him took the form of hard currency.

Both shops, however, marked two of the most likely locations – alongside the Historical Society and Miskatonic's own collections – where the general public might cross over into the world of historical or anthropological oddities, to say nothing of the obscure religious sects that cropped up now and then, that always seemed to ebb and flow beneath the civilized skin of Arkham.

Surrounded by the scents of dried herbs and musty old books that permeated Ye Olde Magick Shoppe, and then the aged dusty atmosphere of the Curiositie Shoppe, Daisy asked her questions. And in both locations, with both proprietors of such wildly differing attitudes and beliefs, the conversation ran much the same way.

"Yes, indeed," Beecher told her, earrings and bracelets jingling like distant church bells. "Mr Hennessy was here, and more than once."

Thomas, too, admitted as much. "Don't normally talk about my customers, you understand. Keeping their business private's part of mine, right? But what with him gone missing and all… Yeah, Mr Hennessy was here, quite regularly."

"I'm afraid I couldn't begin to tell you what he might have been seeking," the old woman continued. "He looked through several of my books, even bought a few. Nothing of any note or significance, mostly general overviews. Initiate material. The bulk of his interest lay in my selection of talismans and objects of power, though. He was looking for something specific, but he never saw fit to tell me what it might be."

"Nah, love, couldn't say what he was after. Every few weeks, he'd come in, spend time looking over the shelves, as if he was waiting for something specific to turn up. Never did, though. Even let him look in the back room once, where I keep the *really* good stuff. Don't usually do that for blokes his age, but he'd been in enough… Still didn't have whatever he wanted, though, and he never told me what that was."

Both shopkeepers agreed that Chester had finally stopped coming in a few weeks before they'd heard about his disappearance, and both suspected that was because he'd finally found whatever he was hunting.

No real surprises, then. Given his efforts, Daisy would have been rather shocked had Chester *not* paid visits to either establishment. Hoping to learn more, she'd then asked both Beecher and Thomas about the *Ujaraanni*, since Billy wasn't here to ask himself. Unfortunately, both denied having ever come across such a thing.

And, as both had grown stiffly reticent when Daisy asked if they knew of anyone who might trade in such materials under the table, insisting that their establishments were entirely proper and above board, she'd chosen not to pursue any further questioning about Jebediah Pembroke or his ilk.

Finally, she asked both proprietors if they knew of any other dealers or private collectors – legitimate, of course – who might trade in such artifacts, and thus might have received a visit from Chester, or have heard of something like the black stone she sought. Both of them had provided her with a list.

"This doesn't represent all my clientele, of course," Beecher clarified. "That wouldn't be proper."

"This is just the ones who've given permission," Thomas told her. "Y'know, said I should feel free to pass their names along to anyone looking to buy or sell the sort of goods they're interested in."

It was, at least, a start, and Daisy thanked each of them, hopeful and heartened to have acquired *something*, no matter how she might have preferred a more comprehensive listing. She found herself an open table at a small café; no Velma's Diner, this little place, but she couldn't face any unnecessary walking after all the travel she'd done today. There she spread out the handwritten notes while waiting on the coffee and pie she'd ordered in lieu of a proper luncheon.

Most of the names on each list were, as best she could determine, just random citizens of Arkham with a bit more money and a bit more historical, or perhaps religious, interest than most. A few were on both lists, and it was those she found most interesting:

Dr Armitage and Mr Combs, as well as several others from the staff and faculty at Miskatonic. No surprise there.

Mr Peabody and a few other members of the Historical Society. Again, no surprise.

A handful of Arkham's wealthy, whom she knew – particularly as some were frequent visitors to the Orne Library or the museum – as either students of history or dabblers in the esoteric and the occult. One name, a Victoria McCutcheon, drew a moue of personal distaste.

Carl Sanford, leader of the local Twilight Lodge, New England's very own Freemasons-esque elite club and fraternal order. She'd have been surprised *not* to see his name on both lists.

And at the bottom of each, where one might anticipate finding the newest clients, one Hyrum Lafayette-Moses.

Daisy frowned over her newly delivered rhubarb pie. It would be the height of arrogance to assume she ought to know of every collector or student in Arkham, but this one not only rang no bells whatsoever, it didn't even strike her as local. "Lafayette-Moses" sounded, to her ear, far more like a Southern family name than one likely to be found in Massachusetts.

Perhaps not much of a lead by itself, but combined with the fact that he appeared to be a new customer to both locations… Well, Daisy was coming to distrust coincidence.

A quick visit to the rear of the café, and the payphones located there, and she had her answer, straight from Dr Armitage himself – who was also good enough not to inquire as to why she was asking such questions, particularly on a day off.

Lafayette-Moses, he'd explained, was an old-money gentleman from Louisiana with a fascination for all materials both historical and purportedly mystical. Armitage knew who the man was because he'd visited the Orne Library on several previous visits to Arkham. Apparently he'd even attempted to buy a few of the university's rarest books. Unsuccessfully, of course.

Armitage didn't know for sure if Lafayette-Moses was back in Arkham now, but Daisy found herself assuming he was, or at least had been not long ago. That his name appeared on the lists meant he'd been in contact with both shops, and, again, its place at the bottom suggested said contact had been recent.

Which meant his visit might well have overlapped with Chester's efforts on his project. Perhaps even his disappearance.

Another "coincidence." Nothing she'd found was remotely sufficient to assume Mr Lafayette-Moses was guilty of any wrongdoing, but she definitely wanted to learn more of him.

Daisy considered the matter as she left the café to rejoin the constant pedestrian traffic, pleased to have made some progress, fretting that it might be insufficient or leading her in the wrong direction. She had no idea how to find or to contact the man, nor did she know for certain that he'd done anything other than patronize the same establishments as the missing student. Nothing she and the others could take to the police, but she would certainly mention it to Billy and Elliot as a name they ought to keep in mind.

And speaking of Billy and Elliot…

Chapter Eight

Afternoon now, moving rapidly toward evening. As the more sensitive of the day's tasks were complete, Daisy had returned to campus to fetch her companions.

Billy, who'd spent his day waiting around Ma's Boarding House, was raring to go. They'd all agreed the town's train station was a potential source of clues, and that was a part of the investigation in which he could actually participate. Though his life as a hunter had taught him patience, Daisy was sure anyone else would be all but vibrating in their shoes.

Elliot was another matter.

His shirt was wrinkled beneath his coat, his hair a tangle, and the bags under his eyes deep and dark as the inside of a pocket. How much of his condition was due to yesterday's unpleasantness and how much his ongoing issues, she couldn't say. When she'd proposed that she and Billy go off on their own, however, and leave him to get more rest, he'd all but barked at the suggestion.

All three of them headed out, then, though more than once she questioned that decision. On occasion, throughout the remainder of the day, she heard Elliot muttering under his breath in what sounded like French, a strange mantra against some nameless evil, the precise details of which she could never fully make out.

It made her worry for him, but, more than that, it made her afraid for reasons she could not begin to name.

As Daisy didn't want the taxi driver to overhear, she'd filled them in on all she'd learned, or failed to learn, before and after the ride across town. When she finally finished, evening had well and truly arrived, and they stood in a small cluster before their destination.

The train station resembled nothing so much as a fortress, looming over the winding currents of the Miskatonic River and the iron pathways that were Arkham's greatest connection to the world beyond. The stone was old, worn, particularly on the two great towers that flanked the rails, almost as if the place had actually weathered a siege or two.

Those gates, however, were always open, and the constant flow of humanity nearly matched the aquatic flow of the Miskatonic. The trio of would-be investigators were hardly the only clump of people standing about and talking. The throng simply parted almost mindlessly around them.

Although he'd been here once before, upon his arrival in Arkham, Billy's expression as he took in the size of the constantly shifting crowd was dismayed. "This is ridiculous. No chance some overworked porter or ticket vendor will remember one particular passenger who might or might not have come through more than a month ago!"

Daisy had to admit she wasn't feeling much more optimistic, especially as this was almost certainly another avenue the police would have followed up themselves. She was running short of ideas, however – or at least of ideas she was willing to pursue. "We won't know until we try," she said. The bright lilt to her voice sounded forced and false even to her own ears.

They split up, then, Billy toward the nearest porter, Elliot the ticket counter. Daisy went looking specifically for Bill Washington.

The chief porter was an Arkham staple, a mainstay of the station for nigh on twenty years, not counting his brief service in the Great War. He was friendly, honest, a man who enjoyed the chance to welcome newcomers and wish his fellow Arkhamites safe travels, and if anyone *would* remember a single face amidst the protean mass of humanity, it'd be him.

Tonight, as business – despite the Kalaaleq's chagrin – was actually relatively slow, Washington had hauled his guitar out from where he kept it behind the counter, and casually strummed to entertain the passersby. Nobody would mistake him for a professional musician, but he was talented enough that his efforts were generally appreciated.

"Good evening, Mr Washington."

"Well, good evening, ma'am!" The porter rose with a touch of awkwardness, thanks to an old war injury.

She identified the expression he wore immediately: he recognized her, but couldn't entirely place who she was. Well, that was fair. They'd only interacted a handful of times. She wasn't a frequent traveler, and Bill Washington wasn't precisely a regular on campus.

"Daisy Walker. I work at Miskatonic."

"Of course, Miss Walker! What can I do for you?"

Unfortunately, the answer turned out to be "nothing." Recognizing Chester Hennessy from an old photograph Elliot had provided, and then recalling if he'd been one of the hundreds to pass through the station at any point in the past few months, proved beyond Washington's abilities.

When Daisy reconvened with the others, just beyond the station's entrance, their looks of frustration mirrored her own feelings perfectly.

"We're wasting our time," Billy insisted. "We should be asking after Pembroke."

Daisy shook her head, blonde curls bouncing. "And how would you go about that, exactly? You're talking about a man who deals in stolen goods. Most people have no idea how to find someone like that, and those who do? Aren't likely to admit to it."

"I know how to make people talk," he grumbled. Then, before she could object, "But you're right. I've no idea where to start."

A surge of guilt made Daisy's stomach clench, and she could only hope the others saw nothing in her expression. *I can't,* she reminded herself. *I can't risk it.*

"What about Hennessy's friends?" Billy asked. "One of them might have an idea where he's off to. Or perhaps a sense of where he might hide something valuable to him."

It was Elliot's turn to shake his head. "I'm Chester's best friend." Was it Daisy's imagination, or was there a touch of bitterness in his voice? "I can't think of anyone he'd tell such things, if not me."

"Besides," Daisy added, "the police would surely have followed that line of investigation as well."

Billy growled something unintelligible, then asked, "What about a lover, a girlfriend?"

This time Daisy knew she hadn't hidden her reaction well enough, felt her jaw twitch before she could stop it, and Elliot looked suddenly sick. Billy's eyes flickered between them, then narrowed.

"What aren't you telling me?"

Elliot answered first, almost spitting. "Nothing!" Even his obvious anger, however, couldn't keep him from slowly wilting beneath Billy's disbelieving glower.

"Miss Walker?"

"I…" *Damn it, why did he have to ask* this? "I really don't feel this is a proper topic of discussion…"

The man standing before her went as cold as his homeland. He wasn't "Billy" any more, but once again the stranger who'd first set foot in her library. "I thought we were working together. That you wanted to find your friend as much as I want to find the *Ujaraanni.* That I could trust you."

Daisy felt herself floundering. She *did* want to find Chester, they *did* need his help. "It doesn't matter. I can't imagine she'd be willing to speak to us, anyway."

"She *who?*"

Then, when Daisy and Elliot both hesitated, Billy shrugged. "Fine. I'll start asking around campus about who Chester Hennessy was seeing. I'm sure someone will prove willing to tell me about whatever it is you won't say. Gossip's always best when it's 'inappropriate' anyway, isn't it?" With that, he started away.

"No!" Elliot called after him, a cry less of defiance than of pain.

Damn, damn, damn. "Mr Shiwak. Billy. Wait." Daisy jogged a few steps to catch up with him, put a hand on his shoulder. "Wait, please. Let's talk."

They shuffled down the block, away from jarring shoulders and curious ears, settling in the mouth of a narrow alley where only the rats might overhear.

"Chester *was* seeing someone," Daisy admitted. "Not many people spoke of it openly, but it was all over Arkham high society – and campus. A woman by the name of Victoria McCutcheon."

Elliot's gaze dropped to his shoes and his fists clenched, but as much as Daisy knew he didn't care to discuss this, didn't even want to hear that woman's name spoken aloud, he held his place.

Billy appeared no happier, though for very different reasons. "And you felt the need to keep this secret… why?"

How to make him understand? If what she'd read of his people was accurate, his own cultural understanding of taboo was primarily religious, not social.

"Chester's family have done very well for themselves," she told him, "becoming quite wealthy. But McCutcheon comes from old money, one of Massachusetts' elder families. Even more to the point, she is only recently widowed, after a marriage one might most courteously describe as 'turbulent,' and more than twice Chester's age."

Then, as Billy continued simply to stare, "Am I not being clear at just how inappropriate this was? The scandal, where both parties are concerned is… not insignificant. Chester might well have found his attendance at Miskatonic called into question if–"

"For this, you jeopardized my search?" Billy exploded. "For *this*?"

Daisy felt the last of her patience evaporate in the heat of his anger. "Because of precisely this reaction." Then, when he appeared sufficiently taken aback by her reply that he might listen despite himself, she continued, "Because I knew you wouldn't understand the significance. That you'd want to run off and find Mrs McCutcheon, demand answers of her. Which would, at best, offend her to the point that she would refuse to help and might spread word of your actions throughout Arkham's elite. And at worst, would be another means of drawing the police down on you."

"You believe she would call the police simply because I approached her with this?"

"Very possibly. But she might not even have to. Do you suppose they're ignorant of the gossip about her and Chester? They would have been careful with her when he disappeared, questioning her lightly, if at all, but they would have watched her for a while, in case she's involved. And as I've no idea how long 'a while' might be, I can't say they aren't still doing so."

Billy slowly nodded, his anger receding. "You've given this a lot of thought."

"Her name was among the list of customers at the shops I visited," Daisy acknowledged. "Not surprising, really. A lot of Arkham's wealthy are dabblers in history. Or," she added, lips quirking in distaste, "the occult. So it's been on my mind."

"All right." Billy took a final, steadying breath. "I would have preferred that you had simply told me and explained all this up front. But I understand why you didn't."

"I'm glad. Thank you."

"Damn it!"

The both of them jumped, turning at Elliot's sudden curse, having all but forgotten his presence. The student had wandered paces from them, punctuating his exclamation with a kick aimed at a loose length of broken wood. It skittered across the alley to rebound from the far wall.

"What's wrong?" Daisy asked, moving to his side.

"Listening to you talk about that… about McCutcheon. We missed something."

"How do you mean?"

"I mean, we've been asking the porters at the station about Chester. One young man in a crowd, with no reason to stand out. But…"

It appeared he couldn't bring himself to utter the words, but he'd said enough. And he was right.

If Chester and Victoria McCutcheon had done any traveling *together*, a wealthy and well known older woman with a younger man might well stick in the mind where a lone traveler would not – particularly if the observer had heard the gossip of her scandalous affair.

"I'll go back," Daisy offered. "You can wait here."

And indeed, salaciousness and scandal proved the key, as it so often did. When she spoke to Bill Washington once more, this time with her new approach, his memory proved far better than it had.

"Not only did he remember seeing them together more than once," she told Elliot and Billy upon her return, "but now that he had context, he remembered seeing Chester come through the station on his own. He bought a ticket – at right around the time he disappeared."

Oh, but she had both their attentions now. "He said Chester looked… rough," Daisy continued, with an apologetic glance to Elliot. "Unkempt, exhausted. Talking to himself. Washington doesn't recall his destination – he helps so very many travelers – but he remembers Chester muttered something about going to see family."

Elliot frowned. "Was he sure?"

"He was." Daisy had asked him the same, and for the same reason she knew Elliot brought it up.

Chester's parents had told them he *had* no other family.

Someone was lying to them – and they'd no reason to suspect it was Bill Washington.

Furious as she was that Mr Hennessy had lied to her face, confusion won out. What was he so determined to hide? Or was he truly so enraged at anyone to do with Miskatonic that deceiving them was an end unto itself, even with so much on the line?

To a mind that clung to order as hers did, that cared for others as hers did, it was truly unfathomable.

"What now?" Billy asked. "Do we go back and demand the truth from his father?"

"I doubt that would accomplish much," Daisy said, pulling herself from her contemplations. "He wasn't precisely cooperative the first time."

Elliot cocked his head, brow furrowed, as though struggling to think. Then, "Christmas lights."

Daisy and Billy both stared. "Pardon?" she asked.

"Chester told me that when he was a boy, he and his parents would go to visit family for a Christmas light display. I guess, when his father said he had no other relatives, I assumed whoever they used to visit was gone, but if they're not… If he lied to us…"

"And where was this display?" Billy asked.

"Taunton." This much, at least, Elliot had no difficulty remembering, and no wonder. That town put on the most famous Christmas display in the state of Massachusetts. "They went to see the lights on Taunton Green."

Chapter Nine

The sleet no longer bit, no longer sliced. Instead it had somehow thickened, until it was no precipitation but a chilling weight, a constant pressure that impeded every movement, rendered the entire world a gelid slurry.

He staggered onward, fighting that pressure; fighting the snow that slurped at his ankles, his calves; fighting the slope of the earth itself, the base of a mountainside whose contours he couldn't see beneath thick banks of devious white. He never so much stepped as staggered, falling with each pace and catching himself with a jolt of effort, praying every time that he'd moved forward more than he'd listed to one side or the other.

Every inch of him burned with the cold. His breath warmed his teeth only just enough that they throbbed anew with every inhalation of the frigid air.

In the distance, blunted by the sleet and snow, the screams of allies, friends, family. He wished, more than anything else, those screams would stop, though that would almost certainly mean they were, to the last of them, dead.

At least they would only be dead.

For those shrieks never ceased, never paused even to draw breath. They were continual, constant as the roar of winter wind. No human lungs could have sustained them, no human throat endured them, yet they continued. They were needles in his ears, fire in his mind.

And they would. Not. Stop.

He couldn't tell from where they might be coming, had long since forgotten if he struggled to reach them or to get away. He knew only that, at some point back before the furthest reaches of his memory, he'd chosen a direction, and he dared not deviate now.

Dared not… until a new sound echoed above the wind, above the screams. A constant, dreadful pounding, paired percussions like the beating of some dreadful heart.

Dared not, until the mountain before him shifted. Visible only as a darkened shape beyond the sleet, something impossibly huge, thicker around by far than any boulder or any tree, winding and writhing in twitching segments unlike any serpent, stretched his way. Seeking, reaching.

Maintaining his course no longer felt quite so vital.

He retreated before it, or tried, but the deep snow that had impeded him before redoubled its efforts. It clung to his legs, tighter with every step, as though a co-conspirator with whatever it was that came now to claim him. For half a dozen paces he fought it, wresting a foot free every time, though each was slower, more difficult than the last.

Until finally he could not free himself at all.

The snow held fast. The thing in the sleet, sliding this side to that like a questing tongue, drew near. The terrible heartbeat grew louder, louder, until he scarcely heard the distant screams, until the mountains shook.

Desperately he twisted, pulled, striving to free himself.

His leg separated just below the knee, leaving his foot and the better part of his calf behind.

There was no blood, no bone. No pain. Only a dull tugging sensation and peculiar fibers, dangling, stretching long and thin before finally splitting, like ropes of drool or tufts of cotton candy.

The formerly clinging snow now felt solid as stone beneath his back as he toppled. With both hands and his one good leg he scrabbled back, desperate to escape, a single nerve-thin strand still linking him with the bit of himself he'd left behind.

Already dimmed nearly to midnight by the clouds and the sleet and the shadow of the mountain, the day grew darker still as the unseen thing loomed high. The far-off screams grew suddenly louder, blending into a single shriek that rose even above the pounding heartbeat, and his own cry of despair rose high to meet it...

Billy nudged him hard by the shoulder, rocking him in his seat. "Elliot. We're here."

Elliot clawed toward consciousness, toward understanding, his gaze bleary and blinking, his pulse pounding until the back of his skull ached. The shrieks lingering in his head transformed into the squeal of wheels braking on iron tracks; the heartbeat into the oh-so-familiar *clack-clack, clack-clack* of the train.

He started to speak, to answer his companion, until he felt the words forming in his throat, lurking on the back of his tongue in wait to spring forth.

Isslaach thkulkris, isslaach cheoshash...

Instead he clasped his teeth shut and began digging in his coat pocket for a familiar piece of folded paper.

"You all right?" Billy asked.

"I... Yes. Just... a bad dream." With an addict's shaky desperation, he opened the paper and read through the French printed there, vocalizing under his breath. He almost sobbed in relief as the *other* words, the beginning of the litany, once more faded to the recesses of his mind.

He'd returned to the library mere hours before departing Arkham, reread the *Livre d'Ivon*'s original copy of the protective spell. It should be some few days before he needed to again; his handwritten version should be sufficient for the duration of their journey.

Should.

What might happen to him if it weren't, or to others if he found himself unable to prevent himself from repeating the phrase that seemed to have spread to him, as a virus, when he heard it from Chester, didn't bear thinking about.

Elliot wished Daisy might have come with them. Yes, he'd grown more comfortable in the company of Billy Shiwak – especially since, for reasons he still couldn't begin to understand, the litany seemed less intrusive, to hold less power in his mind, in the Kalaaleq's presence – but he didn't really *know* the man. He certainly couldn't consider him a confidante, couldn't openly express himself, or his fears, as he could with the librarian, whom he viewed more as a colleague than as a member of the Miskatonic staff.

As much as she wanted to help, however, Daisy couldn't abandon her job duties for multiple days on end to go chasing down an amateur investigation. She'd been fortunate indeed to have had even the time she'd already devoted to it, to have a supervisor as understanding as Dr Armitage. Disappointed as he might be, Elliot could hardly blame her. She might poke around a bit more in the probably vain hope of tracking down Lafayette-Moses or other leads, but otherwise would be returning to her professional duties while he and Billy were away.

As it was, Elliot himself was missing yet more class time for this. Had he room in his thoughts for any more worry, on top of his concern for Chester, his nervous fascination with the mystery Billy had brought them, and his fear of his own deteriorating mental state, he would have been deeply troubled over the possible consequences for his academic future. As it was, however, he could scarcely find it in himself even to care.

Both of them rose, along with most of the other passengers, and began shuffling out onto the platform of Taunton Central. The traffic in the station was enough to shame Arkham's own. In addition to being slightly larger than that more infamous city, Taunton also served as a nexus for train travel across much of the state. A great many passengers wandering the platform, the station and the surrounding block were simply killing time between one train and the next.

That the station itself was larger, more open and certainly more welcoming than the one with which Elliot was familiar helped alleviate some of that sense of crowding. Where Arkham's station resembled a hunched fortress, this was almost more akin to a church, with a more cheerily hued brick facade, broadly arched windows and a single steeple.

The difference in architectural attitude carried over into the city itself. If Arkham seemed determined to stew bitterly in its history, Taunton had elected to age more gracefully. Its structures were less tightly packed, their style not so Old World, not so overwhelming. The streets and sidewalks looked wider, though that might have been an illusion evoked by the larger property lots and the multiple open parks, of which Taunton Green was only the most renowned.

Even the weather seemed to embrace a more open feel. While it was no less abnormally chilly for being this far into spring, the clouds weren't quite so gray, nor did they crouch so low to the earth.

Under other circumstances, Elliot might have enjoyed this brief sojourn. As it was, that he was even aware of these differences was due mostly to a deliberate effort to distract himself from tumultuous thoughts.

A few quick questions of one of the porters, and they were off. The walk was relatively pleasant as they fell in with the rest of the pedestrian traffic. Conversation and the chug of automobiles embraced them, making it difficult for the two of them to speak much to one another. Elliot welcomed that fact, as his lingering nightmare and other preoccupations disinclined him to friendly chat.

It was only after several moments of travel that he noted Billy's stiff expression, and then the occasional glances thrown his companion's way by a few of the more uncouth locals. Perhaps, given how unsociable Billy appeared to be feeling, Elliot hadn't needed any excuse to remain silent.

Their path carried them through Taunton Green, and even in his dour mood Elliot could understand why so many might travel to see it. The green was a massive open space of walkways drifting between verdant lawns, punctuated by a handful of trees here, a rippling fountain or polished statue there. It wasn't the largest urban park he'd ever seen – though it certainly dwarfed any Arkham had to offer – but it was somehow the most dignified, for lack of a better word. Clearly Taunton's citizens took great pride in their parks. When decorated with light displays and other adornments for the holiday season, it must be quite the sight indeed.

Not far beyond was Church Green, a much smaller park, and it was at the edge of that one where they finally reached their destination.

Taunton City Hall.

It seemed, at least for a municipal office, a welcoming place, designed in the Renaissance Revival style, its facade adorned with attractive but unnecessary arches and columns. Perhaps it was that same sour mood, but Elliot couldn't help but feel almost patronized, even deceived, by its demeanor.

Which is why he wasn't surprised when they walked inside, toward a secretary's desk, and the bespectacled woman behind it – who had just been all smiles, waving and nodding a few of the locals past her – turned suddenly stone-faced.

"Is there something you need?" she asked, the blatantly deliberate lack of discourtesy in her tone somehow, in and of itself, discourteous.

She had, Elliot observed, scarcely noticed him at all. The bulk of her attention, and doubtless her ill-concealed hostility, was reserved for the obvious foreigner beside him.

With a smile that might have appeared genuine to this stranger, but which Elliot already recognized as the unhappy baring of teeth, Billy replied, "We're here to consult your public records."

"And your business?" she demanded.

Time to step in. "I'm trying to track down the family of a close friend," Elliot said, casually sliding himself somewhat between the two of them. "I understand they're from here."

Which wasn't necessarily true, of course. He knew only they'd *come* here at some point. As Elliot and his friends had decided even before leaving Arkham, however, it was the only place they had to start.

For a long moment the secretary looked at him, attention darting between Elliot and Billy. If he had to guess, she was trying to come up with a valid reason for denying the request.

"They are," Elliot asked in what was clearly not a question at all, "*public* records, aren't they?"

With a final, put-upon sigh, she pointed down a hallway and rattled off a brief set of directions.

"Thank you," Billy told her, before Elliot could. Her lips twitched.

They turned and entered the hall, footsteps echoing on the stone-tiled floor. "I'm sorry about that," Elliot said finally, ashamed at how his companion had been treated.

Billy shrugged. "Not your fault. You can't choose what people you're born into."

Not entirely sure how to take that, let alone address it, Elliot kept quiet.

The public records, occupying several large rooms, were overseen by a stuffy little man in a slightly threadbare suit and a substantially more threadbare head. He was quite proud of his little fiefdom, however, and more than happy to order one of his minions to assist Elliot and Billy in their search. It took almost no time at all before they had the addresses of all properties owned by a Hennessy within the limits of Taunton.

Of which there were, surprisingly, five.

The two seekers exchanged exasperated sighs, then Billy began scribbling down the addresses while Elliot went in search of a city map.

The first home they visited was a tiny house on a tiny lot, one Elliot might have called a "hovel," if it hadn't been so neatly painted and well kept. The young couple who lived there glowered at the interruption once Elliot knocked on their door, and insisted they'd never met anyone named Chester, before firmly closing said door in his face. Not that he'd really required an answer; it was pretty clear just to look at their facial features that neither could be related to Chester in any way.

The second was a butcher shop, its proprietor living in the apartment above. The establishment had already closed for the evening, however, and either the owner wasn't home or was ignoring the pounding, however fierce, upon his door.

Dark had fully fallen by the time they reached the third, a house larger, but older and more decrepit, than the first, on the edge of one of the town's business districts. Elliot's feet ached at the unaccustomed walking, his jaw hurt from constant clenching in frustration at their failures so far, and while the refrain hadn't returned to the forefront of his mind, it tickled at his thoughts, twisting them just enough that he felt a constant mild dizziness.

"We should have found a room for the night already," he complained to his fellow traveler. "Saved this one for tomorrow."

Billy, who didn't appear remotely tired, merely cast him a look and went to knock.

Nothing. A second knock…

"Just a moment!" The voice floated to them, soft and fragile as cobweb, scarcely audible through the wood. It was well over a minute before they heard the sound of the latch, and the door creaked open to reveal a hunched old woman leaning on a cane. She barely came up to Elliot's shoulders, though she was sufficiently wrinkled that, if fully stretched out, he could imagine her as ten feet tall.

"So sorry," she told them. Even without the intervening door, hearing her was something of an effort. "Not as quick on my feet as I once was. Something I can do for you?"

"Mrs Hennessy?" Elliot hazarded.

"I am."

"I'm terribly sorry to disturb you," he said, "and I'll try not to take much of your time."

She smiled at that, revealing a marked insufficiency of teeth. "I don't get many visitors, my boy. You take as much time as you like. In fact, would you care to come in? I've just made some tea…"

She was already shuffling back from the door, clearly anticipating no refusal. As he didn't want to be rude, Elliot followed, Billy a moment later.

The place could have used a good scrubbing, but it was the simple patina of age rather than a sign of sloppy housekeeping. The walls boasted several photographs, black-and-white images of a woman Elliot took to be their host when she was younger, and a bearded man of the same age.

He squinted at the photos as he passed. The man *could* have been a relative of Chester's – but none of the pictures were clear enough to be sure.

Other than those, the house was decorated with crocheted and needlepoint designs, mostly of the floral or snowflake variety.

She sat them down at a rickety table with a worn tablecloth, and poured them each a cup of tea in yellowing china. Only when they'd both taken a few sips, and she'd asked them a few polite questions about how they were liking Taunton so far, did she cease bustling about and seat herself across from them.

"Now, what was it you wanted to talk to me about?"

"Ah." Elliot swirled his half-empty cup, realized he was fidgeting, and put it down in its matching saucer with a rough *clink*. "The truth is, Mrs Hennessy, I don't even know for certain if you can help us or not. You see, I'm looking for a friend of mine. He's gone missing."

"Oh, dear. How awful." While she sounded genuine, however, there was something else to her tone, a hesitation so tiny Elliot wasn't even positive he'd heard it.

"Thank you. I… don't really have a strong reason to suspect he's here in Taunton, but I know he's visited in the past, and he has – or at least had – family somewhere nearby. And as his family name is Hennessy…"

The old woman was already nodding, to herself it seemed more than to them. "Tell me, is your friend named Chester, by any chance?"

For a heartbeat or two, Elliot couldn't move, could barely even draw breath. He felt as though he'd been struck by lightning.

Perhaps sensing the younger man's reaction, Billy spoke in his stead. "So you *are* related!"

"Oh, my, no. I'm afraid I don't even know the poor young man."

And now Elliot felt only confusion. "I'm sorry, I don't understand. If you don't even know him…"

Their host took a sip from her teacup. "Then how do I come to know his name? He must be quite popular, your friend. Or important. You aren't the first to come looking for him, and to find me instead."

"Professor Polaski," Elliot whispered.

"Yes. Yes, that was his name. I couldn't call it to mind. More tea?"

"Uh… No, no thank you."

Billy shook his head.

"Suit yourself." She shifted in her chair, wincing at some unspecified pain in her tired bones. "Yes, your professor came to my door, with many of the same questions you have, and I'm happy to tell you what I told him."

Elliot leaned forward, fingers clasped tight on the table.

"I've been in Taunton more than half my life. Can't say I know everyone who lives in town, of course, or even swear I've met everyone who shares my family name. Far as I can remember, though, there's never been a Chester Hennessy lived here, nor even made any sort of regular visits I ever heard of."

Now it was a good thing the young student had a solid grip on the table's edge. The world tilted beneath him, and without it, he might have slid from his chair. All his effort, all his *hope*, for nothing. He'd continue going through the motions, visit the last few Hennessys on the list, but he couldn't pretend it would matter. This whole thing had been a waste of–

"But…" the woman across from him continued, arresting his spiral into despair. "That was before Professor Polaski mentioned the swamp."

Elliot stared at her. Blinked in confusion. Stared at Billy, who could only blink in return.

"Swamp?" he finally asked.

"Indeed. He said he remembered something Chester had mentioned in passing, about his kin holding property near a swamp." Again she smiled that broken-window smile. "I guess you didn't know that?"

"I didn't, no." Elliot choked back an irrational surge of jealousy. Chester had worked with Polaski for months. It was to be expected they might have exchanged occasional conversation about their histories or personal matters. And Chester had always been reticent where his own family was concerned. That he'd told Polaski something about them which he'd never mentioned to Elliot was hardly any sign of mistrust or deliberate slight.

He couldn't help feeling, however, as if it were. Just a bit.

"Well, of course he meant Hockomock." She said it as though it were the most obvious conclusion in the world. "Only swamp around here. Goes on for miles and miles, big as you like. And I told him, like I'm telling you, there's a whole lot of folks who live out there, more than you'd ever think. Bunches of little towns, 'cept you can't really even call them towns. Just handfuls of people living as neighbors, here and there."

Elliot felt sick from the constant emotional up and down, the hurdles that seemed to rise up every time hope was nearly within his grasp. He took another sip of his tea, now unpleasantly cool, so that he might have a moment to think.

It was another lead, another possibility. That was good news.

But Hockomock… He didn't know all that much about it, but as an educated citizen of Massachusetts, he possessed a passing familiarity. The old woman hadn't exaggerated the enormity of the freshwater swamp. Surveys and estimates placed it at over *fifteen thousand* acres. He wasn't giving up, would *never* give up, but…

"'How are we supposed to find his family in all of *that*?" Elliot didn't realize he'd uttered the words aloud until he felt the weight of both his companion's and his host's attentions.

The woman *tsked* at them over her cup. "You boys didn't do your research before coming all this way, did you?"

Billy offered a shallow grin. "He's the local. I'm not *supposed* to know these things."

"I…" Elliot flushed. "I've been a bit preoccupied." In truth, he wasn't even certain what he'd missed, what she intimated he ought to have known, but embarrassment washed over him all the same.

"Even folks living out by the swamp," she explained kindly, "have got to buy their land, don't they? All neat and legal, if they want the government men to leave them alone. And nobody lives out there doesn't want to be left alone. Told your Professor Polaski that, too. No reason you can't find those Hennessys same way I assume you found me."

Deeds and property records. Of course. But, "Those wouldn't be in Taunton, would they?" Elliot mused.

"Not in City Hall. But Taunton's also the seat of Bristol County, with its own offices. Hockomock Swamp's not entirely in Bristol," she acknowledged, "but most of it is. And if your Hennessys aren't in that part, well, there's other county seats you can go to."

She was right. They still had a chance. "Is that what Professor Polaski did? Did he find anything?"

"I couldn't rightly say for sure. It was the last thing we talked about, though, and if he had any troubles after that, he certainly never came back to talk to me about them."

Which meant whatever had happened to Polaski might well have happened out there. In the swamp.

Might be waiting to happen to them, as well.

Elliot shivered once, then shrugged it off as best he could. It was all they had, and Chester – and possibly the professor, too – might need them, danger or not.

He saw little point in lingering much after that, though he remained long enough to assist their host with cleaning the cups and the kettle. The night was dark and cold by the time they bid their farewells, but he scarcely noticed, nor did he say much to Billy beyond a brief discussion of where they might find a couple of rooms for the night. Tomorrow, first thing, he intended to be waiting at the Bristol County Hall of Deeds.

And after that? If luck was with them, by midday they'd find themselves within the Hockomock Swamp – and perhaps finally within reach of some answers.

Chapter Ten

Except where Chester's attentions were concerned, Elliot had never been one for envy, or for the resentments it caused. His family had always been comfortable enough that, when he saw the luxuries available to his wealthier compatriots – travel, finer clothes, fashionable trinkets – he'd shrugged them off as unimportant. When a fellow student had a greater facility with a classroom topic, and thus an easier time keeping their grades up, it had only inspired Elliot to work harder. Even as he'd suffered the hideous affliction he battled constantly, the repetition in his mind he'd somehow "caught" from his friend, he'd never once wished it had struck someone else instead of him.

Right now, however, as he struggled – his breathing grown labored and his calves protesting in agony – to keep up with Billy's constant, tireless pace, he felt himself harboring the first glowing embers of a desire to kill his traveling companion.

Finding county property deeds in the Hennessy name had been the work of mere minutes, narrowing those down to a single property at the Hockomock's edge a few minutes more. They'd retreated to the cheap flophouse on the edge of town where they'd spent the night to discuss the matter, and both agreed that, while they had no guarantee this Hennessy property was the right one, it fit their parameters better than any other. They had little choice but to try.

Which had left only the question of how to make the trek. All eleven and a half miles of it.

The business of car rentals hadn't yet come to Taunton. No trains ran out that way. Even if they'd found someone willing to rent them horses, neither man had any experience in the saddle.

Eventually, though it proved pricier than Elliot would have liked, they'd hired a taxi – but the man was willing to take them only a bit more than halfway.

"Roads out that away ain't any good," he'd explained at their protest. "Muddy and uneven, barely fit for horses'n wagons, let alone automobiles. It's more'n my hide's worth to return my taxi to the company damaged, savvy?"

So they had disembarked on one of said muddy roadways, with a hike of over four miles to their destination. Hardly an insurmountable distance, but on the unfamiliar surface, after days of wandering and toil far in excess of his custom, Elliot was ready to have his legs surgically removed.

Or he was until that thought reminded him of the previous day's dream, and he firmly yanked his thoughts off in a different direction.

Cedars began to line the roadsides, sprouting from shallow waters, fresh but murky. Moss dangled, waved in the breeze, shedding moisture gathered from the thick humidity. *Beards*, Elliot mused. *The tangled, unkempt beards of old winos.*

The mud grew thicker, until every step was accompanied by a moist *squelch*. Between the added exertion and the midday sun – even shaded, as it was, behind what had become a ubiquitous layer of cloud – Elliot found himself perspiring despite the cold. He removed his coat, slinging it over his shoulder, and rolled up his shirt sleeves. The newly exposed skin instantly formed goosebumps, but the extra chill was welcome, for a few moments at least.

The mosquitoes were not. One alighted on Elliot's wrist, fat and black and buzzing. He stared at it, more fascinated than disgusted.

"I'm hardly an expert," Billy observed when Elliot lifted his arm for a closer look, "but I'd have thought it too cold for them."

"So would I." Elliot's response was distant, almost hypnotized. Then, sharply awakening to the real world, he grunted and smashed it flat with his other hand. It burst, already ripe with someone else's blood.

As if in response, the buzz of other insects grew louder from far over the placid waters, along with the cries of frogs, the calls of birds, and other voices less readily named.

"Elliot," Billy rumbled, a warning in his tone.

"It's just a mosquito. I don't think–"

"Elliot!"

He looked up from the crimson and black mess on his wrist.

Ahead of them, the trees grew thicker, looming over the roadway – but it was what stood *in* the roadway that had Billy concerned.

Several automobiles – open-bedded pickups, mostly, all covered in layers of dried muck suggesting they belonged to folks who lived and worked out here – had been parked in a cluster, blocking the path. A wooden horse-cart and an array of logs and branches, dragged from the surrounding swamp, lay alongside them. Together, they formed a barricade, one clearly intended to bar passage.

A few other trucks had apparently attempted to skirt around them. They sat, now, halfsunken into the mud and the swamp water. They had failed in their efforts, and were never likely to move again, at least not under their own power.

Not a soul stirred. Whoever had been here, either blocking the road or attempting to traverse it, was long gone. The outermost layer of mud, only partly dry and adorned with fallen leaves, implied perhaps a day or two, no more than four or five at most.

Elliot and Billy took in the tableau, breathing the flowering and rotting aromas of the swamp. Neither of them spoke, but a shared glance indicated they'd both noticed one last, troubling detail.

This was no defensive construction, the effort of a community of country locals who, for whatever reason, had believed some terrible threat bore down on them from outside.

The cars that had gotten themselves mired, half-swallowed by the swamp in a failed effort to go around the barricade, were all pointed *out*, back the way Elliot and Billy had come. The townsfolk who'd arranged the makeshift barricade had meant to keep their own neighbors and kin from departing.

"What does this mean?" Elliot asked when he finally unearthed his voice from the nervous fear that suddenly weighed it down.

"I have no idea." Billy opened his coat and rested a hand on the hilt of his pana. Freed abruptly of their confinement, the collection of talismans, leather and ivory and stone, clattered where they hung about his neck. "But unless there's some truly bizarre local custom you've not told me about, I'm confident in saying it's probably bad."

Carefully they approached the collection of metal and glass, rubber and wood. While no other vehicle could travel this road, as pedestrians they ought to have little difficulty working their way through. Either the townsfolk had had no concerns that anyone might depart on foot, or the barricade had at some point been manned.

That last thought gave Elliot some hope he might find a weapon with which to defend himself in one of the cars, and he paused to check. If anyone had stood sentry here, with gun or blade, they'd taken their arms when they'd departed. He did, however, locate an old axe handle in the bed of a truck, and while a makeshift bludgeon might not have been his first choice, he felt better for the solid weight in his fist.

Billy offered an approving nod, and they continued – more slowly, more warily – on their way.

The calls of the wildlife grew softer; still present, but at what felt a far greater distance. It didn't make sense, and Elliot was about to ask his companion if he'd noticed it too, when he realized another sound had begun to take their place.

A sound not from without, but within.

Isslaach thkulkris, isslaach cheoshash… Isslaach thkulkris, isslaach cheoshash…

Elliot staggered, nearly falling. Several paces ahead of him, Billy failed to notice.

No! Please, God, not now!

He whispered his French mantra, which he knew now by heart. It calmed the other, more alien words, but not so well as it normally did. The incomprehensible phrases seemed not louder, precisely, but more insistent.

As though something new somehow reinforced them. As though they were, nonsensical as the idea might be, fighting back against his efforts to subdue them.

Still, he wasn't so disoriented, not yet at least, that he missed the grim concern – in tone, if not in vocabulary – when Billy murmured something in his native tongue.

"What?"

Billy pointed.

At first Elliot saw only a small farmhouse, old and rickety, listing drunkenly where its soft foundations had shifted. Not an enticing place to live, but otherwise nothing worth remarking on.

"It's not the Hennessy place," he began. "They're supposed to be at the far side of–"

Then, finally, he noticed the door. It hung wide open, idly drifting in the sporadic breeze.

"Maybe they just didn't bother shutting it." His protest sounded weak even to himself. "If they're just coming right back, or… I mean, everybody knows everybody in a community like this. I'm sure they all trust each–"

"Do you see anyone running errands? Do you hear sounds of work? Any at all?"

Elliot hadn't paid much attention to any such things, thanks to the warring phrases in his head, but an instant's deliberate effort proved Billy correct. There was nothing. No nearby movement, no sound of tools on wood or vegetation, no grunts of exertion or time-passing conversation, no motors.

He heard the remote animals and insects, the uneven wind, the slow lapping of the waters on the muddy banks. No more.

Not good. Really, really not good.

"Should… Should we go inside? Take a look?"

"We should find who we came to find and finish our business here. Quickly."

With that, Elliot couldn't begin to argue. They moved on.

More houses, shacks really, and occasional barns, on either side of the roadway. All were more or less as decrepit as the first. Many also had doors or windows gaping wide, and none produced a single human soul.

Elliot's heart pounded until he could feel his pulse in his limbs, his neck. Sweat beaded on newly raised hackles.

Isslaach thkulkris, isslaach cheoshash…

Over and over he forced the French mantra through his throat in a counter-rhythm, punctuated ever more often by a plaintive "Shut up, *shut up!*" that he never once realized he'd spoken aloud.

"Look out!"

He failed to register his companion's shout, finally snapping back to awareness and retreating only when the flapping, thrashing brown mass appeared in his face.

It squawked and screamed, some sort of swamp-dwelling bird he'd never seen before. A bit smaller than a crow, it was all coffee-hued feathers and long yellow legs and beak – a beak that drove at Elliot's flesh, a living piston, over and over as he fell back before it.

He'd encroached on the territory of an avian nest before, been swooped at a time or two by an irritated songbird, but he'd never suffered this sort of aggression. He flailed his coat and his makeshift bludgeon wildly, face turned away from the living dagger stabbing at him. Something in his path, or perhaps the muck of the roadway itself, snagged at his heel and he tumbled, landing on his back with a wet smack.

Still it came. He felt a sharp, ragged agony across his cheek as the tip of the beak ripped at him.

Then Billy stood over him. A single swipe of an arm and the bird hurtled aside, struck by an impossibly swift backhanded blow. It fluttered about, half-stunned, before finally hauling itself, soggy and dripping, from the water and flying on its wobbly way.

"The anersaat of this place are angry," he said, reaching down to offer a hand. Elliot took it almost mindlessly, not even looking at it. "Perhaps they've even been sickened somehow." He hauled the student to his feet. "Unless you want to tell me that sort of behavior is normal here?"

No response. Elliot continued staring straight ahead, jaw clenched but eyes glazed, oblivious to his companion, to the blood running down his cheek, to the mud coating his back, soaking into his trousers, matting his hair.

"Elliot? *Elliot!*"

He finally turned, offered a single slow blink. "Yes." It came out in a rasp, as though he'd gone for days without a drink.

"We need to keep moving."

"Yes."

Billy cast him a long look, then started walking. Elliot followed.

He'd had to strain to hear Billy at all, even to see him behind a haze of… Of what? Nothing stood between them, nothing obscured his view, yet he felt as though the other man was unclear, obfuscated as if by a thick vapor or mirage.

Isslaach thkulkris, isslaach cheoshash… Isslaach thkulkris, isslaach cheoshash…

Ever nearer, in all directions, louder, louder… Not as though any one speaker had raised their volume but as if the chorus itself had grown, as if what had been a single voice, or perhaps a handful, was now a choir, its numbers expanding until it blotted out the world, blotted out the mind, leaving no room in his brain for his own thoughts or notions or dreams…

The sucking patches of mud became open mouths, tongues slurping out for him, wetly wriggling throats contracting in the wake of his footsteps. The puddles in his path transformed into misshapen pupils that tracked his progress. To either side, stretching as far as he could see, the ripples in the swamp became the wake of hidden things, slipping ever closer beneath their aquatic veils, and the great trees loomed ever more inward, stretching over the road as grasping tendrils so they might reach down upon passersby. Massive heaps of wood and stone pretended feebly at being simple structures, but they knew not how to rest at angles recognizable by human senses, and he saw an inkling of the alien truths and unnatural passages beneath their careless facade.

Elliot began to shake, to whimper. He turned as he walked, struggling to look every which way, lest something unspeakable creep up on him. A voice called to him, emerging from a looming shape some paces ahead, but he could make out none of the words, nor the ever-shifting features of the speaker, melting like spent candle wax before reforming to melt once again.

A limb stretched toward him, impossibly long, grasping with countless talons. He screamed his terror, his defiance, hefted his axe handle and swung it hard.

A second limb appeared and yanked the weapon from his grip. He was helpless.

And now it came closer, that waxen figure, and he saw not merely the two great limbs to either side but an array of smaller ones, dangling and thrashing from its chest. He wailed, retreated until he felt it latch onto his shoulder, then beat his fists upon it. All to no avail. It drew him closer, closer, and now he couldn't help but sob in the face of the unclean thing, roaring its nonsensical syllables at him, syllables he barely even heard for the litany.

The litany.

Isslaach thkulkris, isslaach cheoshash…

He fell, and it leaned over him, holding him so he didn't strike the earth. Dangling, one of those smaller tendrils drifted over him, brushed his face…

Elliot gasped, a drowning man finally surfacing for air. The swamp around him, though unpleasant, was merely the Hockomock once again. The road was mud, the trees simple plants, the waters rippling slow and lazy, with nothing of sinister intent below. The houses of the village were, again, just that.

The words in his head, though not silent, once more occupied only a single dark corner of his consciousness.

It was, of course, Billy who had caught him, who stared down at him in deep concern. Billy whom he had instead imagined as some shifting, waxen thing.

And it was one of his many talismans, an ivory amulet carved with sharp angles that resembled, in the proper lighting, some manner of caribou or other antlered beast, that hung loose enough to drift against his bloodied cheek.

That amulet – Inuit protections, Inuit magic – had saved him. Had brought him back. He realized, too, that it must have been the presence of those talismans that had quieted the litany previously, had made him more comfortable in Billy's presence.

Tears welled at the corners of Elliot's eyes. Tears of relief, yes, that the madness had passed – but tears, as well, for a life, for a *world*, he had lost. For he could no longer cling to even a thread of pretense that what afflicted him was mere mental illness, that the spell he recited from the *Livre d'Ivon* served as nothing more than a mantra to focus his thoughts.

Curses. Sorcery. Magic. All real.

"I'm sorry." He allowed Billy to help him stand, then flushed and looked away as he realized he had attacked his companion in his madness. He didn't immediately recognize the terrain or the specific houses nearby; they must have walked farther than he'd realized during his delirium. "I … I don't know what to say."

"The truth would be a good place to start." Billy took a step back once Elliot proved able to stand on his own and made no further violent move. He still hadn't returned the axe handle. "Something's troubled you. Even for as scant a time as I've known you, I could see that much. I ignored it as no business of mine, but if it's going to drive you to fits of madness–"

"Not … madness. Not exactly." Elliot pointed to the talisman that had brought him back to himself. "That saved me."

Billy glanced downward, inhaled deeply. "You're beset?"

"Beset?" Even having acknowledged the truth to himself, it took Elliot a moment to admit it to another. "You mean by… spirits. I suppose I am."

The Kalaaleq fingered his collection of talismans, then removed the one in question and handed it over. "For the moment only," he warned.

Elliot almost burst into tears again – particularly when he placed the cord over his head, and instantly felt the pressure of the refrain lessen further. Not since he'd first heard it, since the words had initially taken root in his soul, had they felt so distant.

"Thank you." It felt woefully insufficient.

"Now, the truth. All of it."

He would have told it, right there, in the middle of the swamp-kissed road. Even as he opened his mouth to speak, however, the alien phrases grew loud once more. Indeed, he could make out nearly a dozen separate voices, coming from multiple directions. He trembled, nearly fell to his knees in the mud, despair washing over him in a suffocating wave.

Until he saw Billy turn, hand reaching for his blade, seeking the source of the sudden chant, and realized what was happening.

The litany wasn't coming from inside his head, not this time. It came instead from all around them.

Chapter Eleven

From behind several houses, from inside one of the barns, emerging from copses of white cedar and tussocks of underbrush to wade through the murky waters, nearly a score of the locals at last revealed themselves.

They might, at a casual glance, be taken for average rustics, the sort of folks who carved out a laborious life here at the outskirts of the Hockomock. Most wore thick trousers or overalls, heavy boots, hats or caps to keep their hair from their faces and the sun from their eyes.

Most, but not all. Several were half dressed, shirtless or barefoot, and a couple dressed only in filthy underclothes. Their skin was mud-slicked, covered in abrasions, and they seemed utterly oblivious to the pain of those minor wounds and the bite of the unseasonable cold.

Many were empty-handed, but others carried rakes, shovels, saws or knives, tools of gardening or farming or butchering far too easily wielded as weapons for Elliot and Billy's comfort.

It was none of that, however, that sent the first frisson of terror dancing spider-like down Elliot's back, set his brow to sweating and his limbs to shaking.

"Isslaach thkulkris, isslaach cheoshash… Vnoktu vshuru shelosht escruatha…"

The litany, more of it than he'd heard from Chester, more than had ever infected his thoughts, drifted over the swamp in an unending chorus. It pounded over him, a heavy rain, a noxious fume.

"Svist ch'shultva ulveshtha ikravis… Isslaach ikravis vuloshku dlachvuul loshaa…"

The chanters drew breath at awkward moments, between words, in the midst of words – but unlike the syllables, all uttered in unison, they sucked the humid air at different intervals. The result was an incantation that never broke, continued even when a voice or two dropped briefly away.

Within Elliot's own mind, the single phrase he knew, that had troubled him for so long, swelled in joyful echo of the recitation without, until it felt like a physical pressure, and he feared his head might burst.

Yet it also remained clear, as if the sounds could not quite gain purchase.

Perhaps it was his recent recitation of the protective spell – and he knew now, beyond any doubt he ought to feel as a modern student of science, that it *was* a spell – from the *Livre d'Ivon*. Perhaps it was the talisman Billy had offered him, or some combination of the two.

Oh, God. Billy.

He turned, seeking any sign of incipient madness on his friend's visage, but that concern, at least, seemed unfounded. Although clearly troubled by the approach of the entranced villagers, and disturbed by the alien sound of their refrain, Billy showed no signs of an ill mind. Elliot remembered how he'd faltered when he'd first heard the words, as though struck a physical blow, and saw no such reaction here. He could only assume that Billy, too, benefited from the warding magics of the remaining amulets he wore.

Which hardly, he realized as the first trio closed to within reach, made them safe.

Billy passed the confiscated club back to Elliot, then took a single step toward the advancing mob. He raised his hands defensively before him, empty left fist further forward than the knife in his right. "I don't want to hurt you ..." he began.

A heavyset man, who looked, between his beard and his build, more lumberjack than farmer, raised a heavy spade like an axe over his head.

He never brought it down. Billy stepped in, staggered his attacker with a fist to the side of the head, then slashed upward. His snow knife drew twin lines of blood across both the local's forearms, lines that swiftly opened into deep smiling maws of red flesh and a glimpse of bone. The spade dropped wetly to the mud.

The agony should have been crippling. The arms should have been useless. Instead, without so much as a gasp of pain to break the cadence of his mantra, the bearded man swung his arm from the side, twisting at the waist. Not the strongest blow, or the swiftest, but its sheer impossibility caught even the hunter by surprise. Billy grunted, staggering several steps.

And cried out in pain as a young woman, barely more than a girl, opened the meat of his own arm with a wild swing of a rake.

Not a severe wound – Billy's coat and his own reflexes absorbed the worst of the blow – but it bled freely through the rent sleeve, and his face twisted briefly before he resumed his mask of stoicism. The woman raised the rake again ...

Elliot's club cracked viciously into her right knee, sending her tumbling to the roadside. Even in the face of the obvious threat, it had taken all his will to strike her that way, and he felt a surge of nausea that had nothing to do with the constant litany or his mounting fear.

When she began to stand back up, though, oblivious to the unnatural sideways angle at which that knee now bent, it absolutely *was* fear that spurred Elliot to retreat to Billy's side. The third of the initial trio of attackers lay bleeding at Billy's feet; Elliot hadn't the slightest idea how he'd gotten there.

"We have to get out of here!" He sounded hysterical, knew it, and couldn't bring himself to care.

"Yes."

Elliot tore his attention from the approaching throng, only steps away. Billy's reply… Had he hesitated, for just a heartbeat? Had Elliot heard just the smallest hint of distraction in his tone?

It might well have been his imagination – but just maybe, perhaps due to their proximity, the litany was beginning to penetrate his ward. Elliot himself felt no different, but already tainted by his earlier exposure, he wasn't sure he'd notice.

"Run, then!" Elliot screamed at him.

Whether the hesitancy had indeed been in his imagination or whether that shout snapped Billy out of it, the hunter obeyed, Elliot following close behind. Billy made his break along the very edge of the road, ankle-deep in the swamp. Tricky footing, but not impossible, and the route took them between two of the larger oncoming groups.

One man moving ahead of both clusters, wearing only long underwear and a single tattered shoe, put himself in Elliot's path. A desperate swing of the axe handle swept him aside, and Elliot forced himself not to look back and see what damage he'd inflicted.

Another, armed with a hatchet, leapt from a grassy tussock toward Billy. Elliot couldn't entirely track what happened next, saw only a blur of hands and blades. Crimson fountained halfway across the roadway. Billy kept running, shaking his knife clean. The other man dropped, twitched twice and lay still.

It happened so fast, Elliot was already past when it finally registered on his beleaguered mind that he'd just watched a man die. Now he did turn, twisting as he ran to stare behind him in horrified fascination at the unmoving corpse. He found himself strangely furious with Billy, not because he'd killed his attacker – he'd had, Elliot knew, little option – but because it didn't appear to bother him much.

A ludicrous objection, particularly when they were fleeing for their lives, but one he couldn't shake.

Not, at least, until his backward gaze rose from the dead body to the living ones still in pursuit.

The locals ran after them, but it was no sort of gait Elliot could fully comprehend, let alone accept as normal. With each pace they nearly toppled forward, rear leg unnaturally stiff, only just catching themselves on the front before straightening up and repeating the process. They didn't appear injured or pained so much as somehow unfamiliar with their own bodies. The result was a peculiar lurch, unnatural yet somehow rapid enough to keep them from falling too far behind. Through it all their arms remained straight – ahead of them, carrying weapons, or rigid by their sides – and their breath barely seemed to quicken or deepen despite their exertions.

And still the chant, never ending, a profane liturgy beyond religion, beyond fanaticism. "*Vnoktu vshuru shelosht escruatha…*"

Gradually, Elliot and Billy indeed increased the gap between them and their pursuers, but the cost was high. Elliot gasped for breath, shook with the sharp pain digging into his left side, and even the seemingly indefatigable Kalaaleq was panting lightly. If they failed to change their circumstances soon…

Billy broke right, the move so sudden Elliot almost failed to follow. He ducked past a pile of old straw, through a small copse of trees and pointed.

Ahead was a small shack, far more decrepit even than the rest of this ill-kept, swamp-battered community. It leaned so precariously to the side that Elliot worried even Billy's gesture, meant to draw his attention to it, might be enough to topple it.

It was, however, the only shelter in sight that, thanks to the trees, they just might reach unseen by those who followed.

Elliot burst in and fell to his knees, started to gulp for air – and then froze, nearly choking, as Billy clasped a gloved hand over his mouth.

"Dust," Billy hissed in his ear, before turning back to quietly latch the door behind them.

Indeed, Elliot realized their entry, to say nothing of his near collapse, had kicked up huge amounts of dust, dirt, mildew, and God knew what else. Gasping that in, as he'd begun to do, would have sent him into a coughing fit that nobody outside could have failed to hear.

Pulling his shirt over his mouth, Elliot battled with his lungs, his instincts, forcing himself to take slow, controlled breaths. Billy did the same, for only a moment. Then he examined the blood and worse still clinging to his pana, and casually wiped it clean on his sleeve.

"What?" he whispered in response to Elliot's clear disgust. He moved his arm, so the rips from his earlier wound flared. "Going to have to either throw it away or get it cleaned and mended anyway."

Elliot looked away. A minute later, having finally gotten himself somewhat under control, he studied their feeble shelter.

No interior walls, no furniture. Only the dusty floorboards and the structure itself, slumped enough to be almost dizzying, the wood sporting a roadmap of cracks and faults. The door was a thin bit of lumber with a simple latch, a pitiful barricade against any determined assault. What had once been an open window was now roughly boarded up, rusty nails jutting awkwardly every which way.

The coughing fit Elliot had barely avoided wouldn't have had time to draw their attackers, he figured, before it brought the whole rickety heap down on their heads.

"This place looked better from the outside," he grumbled, wandering over to the thick boards covering the window.

"Mm. I'd hoped for a little more," Billy admitted.

Elliot placed his hands on the wood, careful not to lean too heavily – and only then realized both his hands were empty. He'd lost both coat and bludgeon somewhere in his mad scramble.

Nervously fingering the talisman now hanging from his neck, he turned to ask Billy what their next step might be. Instead, he caught the briefest glimpse of a shadow, faint in the light of the overcast day, beneath the ill-fitting door.

He hissed, pointing. Billy glanced downward, nodded, pressed his ear to the wood, softly lifted the latch…

Then, in a wild flurry of motion, he swung the door open, lunged out and hauled one of the townsfolk inside. Billy swung a swift blow to the side of the man's head, grabbed his shoulders and hurled him to the ground, then slammed and latched the door once more.

By the time the villager began to rise, garden trowel clutched like a dagger in his fist, Billy had his own knife drawn and buried in the man's throat.

Elliot swallowed his gorge and averted his gaze until the thrashing and gurgling stopped.

"Was that…" He gagged, tried again to maneuver the words around a suddenly dry tongue. "Was that necessary?"

Billy kicked the trowel his way. "What do you think?" Then, without waiting for an answer, "Whatever's come over them, they can still think. Still plan."

"How do you mean?" Elliot reluctantly picked up the makeshift weapon, wishing desperately for his lost axe handle. A club was one thing, but the idea of striking someone with this dull blade, trying to drive it into moving, resisting flesh…

"I mean one of them came close, alone. A scout. And he was quiet. No chanting."

Or maybe he was quiet and alone because you just slaughtered an innocent man who hadn't yet succumbed to the litany! Elliot wanted to shout. It wouldn't do any good, though – and he recognized, even as he struggled not to voice the protest, how improbable it was.

More improbable still when, not seconds later, the mantra began once more from outside the shack.

"*Isslaach ikravis vuloshku dlachvuul loshaa…*"

Billy had been right; the dead man had been a threat. Under other circumstances, Elliot would have been relieved to know that.

"Get away from the window!" Billy growled, before shoving the fresh corpse up against the door and retreating toward the center of the room.

Elliot took a moment to obey, struggling to listen. "I don't think they're on that side," he said, pointing at one of the walls. "Maybe if we can break through…"

"*Isslaach thkulkris, isslaach cheoshash…*"

He started forward, but Billy halted him with an outstretched hand. "Why? Why not surround us?" He paused. "Why aren't they already inside? That door should barely slow them–"

A roar from outside, distant but swiftly growing closer, drowned out the chanting. The dust near the floor began to dance.

And the wall – on the "clear" side, where Elliot had meant to stand – disintegrated as the pair hurled themselves aside, one to each corner.

Rust-splotched red metal and water-stained wood paneling tore through the shack. Driven by a slack-faced, chanting young man probably no older than eighteen or nineteen, the light truck – a Chevrolet model 490, Elliot would later recall, though of course he had no thought for such details at the time – seemed utterly unimpeded by the flimsy walls. Whether he even tried to hit the brakes or not, it ripped apart the flooring beneath its spinning tires and punched through the back as easily as it had the front.

Boards and old lumber screamed as they leaned, twisted, snapped. Scrambling to their feet, Elliot and Billy dashed for the newly made gap, stumbling and scrambling over broken floor. Mere paces behind them, the structure that had threatened to come down from the moment they'd seen it finally made good on its promise in a cacophony of shrieking and shattering.

Wood settled. Dust cleared.

On the other side of the debris and all around the idling truck, as though coalescing out of the waters and the drifting mists of the swamp, the throng appeared once more. Still. Unblinking.

Chanting.

Billy winced, shaking his head as through trying to clear it. This time, even Elliot felt the pull. Their defenses against the litany wore thin.

They turned to run once more, only to discover a second group – far smaller than the first, but plenty large enough to slow their flight until they were overwhelmed – approaching from behind.

Billy's face once more settled into its grim mask, but he couldn't entirely hide a faint quiver in his jaw. He raised his pana, prepared to fight until the option was lost to him. Seeing no other choice, Elliot did the same, trowel trembling in his sweat-slick palm.

A fearsome crack rang out across the scattered community, echoing through the hollows and branches and waterways of the Hockomock.

Elliot yelped despite himself, and even Billy started. He wasn't certain, initially, what the sound had been; wasn't certain until he saw one of the smaller group of locals tumble to the mud, bleeding from a wound in his thigh that hadn't existed an instant before.

A second shot. Then a third, a fourth. With each, another person fell to a bullet placed with expert precision, an injury that was not – or at least, with proper treatment, might not be – lethal.

Nor did Elliot require anything rivaling Billy's keen eye to note that the unseen gunman had selected targets to clear the two of them a path through their attackers.

Again they required no words between them. They just ran.

A short way down the road, they spotted a figure atop what might have been a barn built, in part, to resemble a church, or might have been an actual church, constructed with unusual simplicity. A squat steeple protruded from the roof, the only bit of construction that marked the building as different. From that, in turn, jutted a thin rod of metal, almost invisible against the low clouds, that might once have been the base for either a cross or a weathervane.

The gunman crouched beside that steeple, braced against the brick, rifle aimed downward. The weapon barked, and another of the distant figures fell.

"Keep goin'!" Now, having heard the heavily accented voice, Elliot recognized their mysterious savior as a woman, despise his inability to make out much detail from this distance. "You'll want the house with the red door, white trim. Get upstairs." She slammed a hand against the bolt, fired yet again.

Billy and Elliot resumed their sprint, electing to trust her advice. Whoever the stranger was, she'd rescued them, drawing attention to herself in the process. More significantly, she hadn't succumbed to the litany.

Two more shots, but no more. Elliot glanced back and saw her scrambling down the roof, out of sight. At least for the nonce, nobody pursued the two of them any longer. All those who'd been close had fallen to their guardian angel's rifle, and the rest had now turned her way, converging on the barn or church or whatever it was.

"Should…" He struggled to breathe, to speak, as he ran. "Should we go back… and help her?"

"We should do exactly what she told us to," Billy insisted. "She's been here longer than we have, and she saved us. Trust that she knows what she's doing."

"And if… we're wrong?"

"Then there's not much we could have done anyway, is there?"

Chapter Twelve

By the time they reached the house she'd described, some three or four lots away, Elliot's run had become a stagger. Again his side felt as if he'd been stabbed, and spots danced in his vision with every labored breath. He stumbled up the steps to the porch, through the door and found himself bent double, leaning against the railing of a staircase.

Billy slammed the door, far heavier than that of the shack, behind him and twisted the bolt. It fell into place with a reassuringly weighty *clunk*. He then left Elliot to recover while he made a quick circuit of the first floor.

"House has been abandoned for a few days," he reported upon his return. "Most of the food's gone, and what's left is rotten. Whatever reason they had for leaving, they had time to prepare. Furniture's been moved to block the back door and the windows, so we should be secure for a while. She said to go upstairs."

Elliot nodded, waved off Billy's offered hand and clumsily followed him up the steps. The whole house, now that he had the presence of mind to notice, smelled foully of mold. He suspected it had little to do with being abandoned; it was hard to imagine anyplace built in the swamp *not* harboring such an odor.

On the second floor, too, the windows had been blocked and many of the doorknobs were dusty, but the bed looked as though it had seen recent use. Next to it was an American infantryman's footlocker from the Great War. Elliot opened it while Billy expanded his search to the neighboring rooms. Inside he found a canteen of lukewarm water, some smoked meat and half a chocolate bar, a roll of gauze, a broken bit of soap and a pile of bullets. A quick examination showed him ".30-06" stamped into the rim.

Elliot wasn't certain why it was here, but gift horses, mouths and all that.

When Billy returned, he carried a stack of clothes and towels scavenged from the other rooms. The folks who'd lived here might have packed to leave, but they hadn't taken everything.

When Elliot showed him the stash in the footlocker, Billy only nodded. "Our friend, or someone, left emergency supplies here." He poked at the rumpled bed. "Probably in a few houses around the community, I'd imagine. Wise."

Helping one another where necessary, they peeled off the filthiest bits of their clothes – Billy's coat, Elliot's shirt – to get at the bloody contusions beneath them. "Maybe she's just staying here," the younger man suggested. As he spoke, he moistened a towel with the canteen, scraping it with soap before using it to scrub at a nasty cut.

"I don't think so." Billy stoically poked at the gashes in his arm, nodded in contentment at the scabbing they'd already done. "This bed's been slept in recently, but not *too* recently. Not last night. I guess someone's using it as an emergency shelter. And I guess anyone who'd think to do that probably has more than one."

Elliot considered asking him precisely how he could figure when the bed was last used, then thought better of it.

"That's a good sign," he said instead. Then, at Billy's quizzical look, "It means they've been active for a while, right? If they've had the time to set up emergency shelters since this… this nightmare started? Whatever means they have of avoiding or resisting the litany, it works long-term."

"Hmm."

After slaking their thirst and cleaning the worst of their wounds, the canteen was nigh on empty, and while the property doubtless had a well, neither man felt particularly inclined to step outside to find it. Elliot's skin crawled with the feel of the mud drying across his back, where it had sluiced in under his shirt, and in his hair.

As best they could, then, working with dry towels, they worked at scrubbing away the worst of the filth.

They were still at it when…

"See you two've made yourselves nice and cozy."

Elliot jumped, but more startling even than the woman's sudden appearance in the bedroom doorway was the soft but unmistakable gasp of shock from behind him.

"How…?" Billy gathered himself. "How did you get inside? If you'd unlocked the front door, I'd have heard the latch!"

"Nuh-uh." Rifle aimed their way, she braced herself on the doorframe, then carefully took her left hand from the barrel. With two quick tugs, she removed twisted wads of fabric from both ears, then resumed her grip on the weapon.

Protection against overhearing the litany, Elliot realized. He found himself almost disappointed that the solution was so mundane, even if it proved him correct that she – and probably others – were aware of what was happening and had found ways around it.

"You're the ones owe me for savin' you," she continued. "And you're the two strangers come to my home after the devil himself reached up outta hell to damn us, so *you're* the ones gonna be answerin' *my* questions, unless you wanna get up off that bed and march right the hell back outside!"

She didn't actually shout that last, clearly too smart to risk attracting attention, but from the way she snarled each individual syllable through a cage of clenched teeth, Elliot hadn't a doubt in his head that she meant every bit of it.

Under other circumstances, he wouldn't have found her remotely intimidating. She was quite slight; the top of her head barely reached his chin, and she couldn't be much more than half his weight. Furthermore, the smattering of freckles, and the fact she wore a coat and trousers clearly intended for someone taller and broader, gave her an almost childlike mien, even if she was probably, in truth, a few years older than him.

Today, though, between the fury in her tone and the rock-steady steel barrel gaping at them – a weapon she'd already proved herself quite willing and able to use – Elliot found her more than sufficiently frightening.

He raised his hands, though it felt a foolish gesture given that they were full of nothing more deadly than a filthy towel.

"First off," he began, "we're not your enemies."

"Oh, yeah? I just shot down folks I know – my neighbors, my friends, my *kin* – to save you, so you best be *real* convincing."

"I assume there's no coming back, then?" Billy asked softly. "From whatever's come over them?"

The young woman flinched, though still the rifle never wavered. "Why… Why'd you think that?"

Elliot wasn't certain he'd ever heard the Kalaaleq speak so softly, so gently. "Because I know what family means to people like us. People who live away from the large cities, off what the land chooses to provide. And while I am deeply grateful for your rescue, I don't believe you *would* have shot at kin to saveus, even if only to wound, if you still had hope they'd return to you."

Tears rolled down her face, cutting furrows into the dirt she'd picked up running through the swamp.

"My name is Billy. Billy Shiwak. This is Elliot Raslo. And what he told you is true. We're not the enemy. We didn't do this."

"No. No, I know you didn't." She sighed, wiping her face with the back of her hand – and, in the process, finally lowering her weapon. "Wouldn't have needed savin' if you did, I suppose."

Then, "Ida Glick. And I guess I'm pleased to meet you, considerin.'"

Elliot let his hands fall. "So, uh, Ida. Would you mind terribly…?" He poked at his mud-caked shirt.

He took her wan smile as permission, started to dig through the pile of garments Billy had found, and then stopped. "Uh… Your family's?"

"Naw. This house belongs – belonged – to a friend of my daddy's. Go ahead an' take what you need. They… won't be comin' back for any of it."

Most of the men's clothes were a touch big on Elliot, but not too badly. Billy's broad-shouldered build proved more of a hindrance, but eventually he found a long canvas coat, almost a duster, bulky enough that it wasn't too restrictive.

"We're searching," Elliot explained as they changed what clothes they could while remaining decent in front of Ida. "A friend of mine's gone missing. So has a carved stone – a religious relic, basically – from Billy's people."

Ida looked Billy's way at that. "You Injun?" At least the question sounded merely curious, not hostile.

"Inuit," he replied. Then, at her obvious confusion, he sighed. "Eskimo."

"Wow. Long way from home."

"I am."

Ida leaned the rifle against the wall – still within easy reach – and sat on the floor. "What kinda stone?"

Billy described the *Ujaraanni* as he struggled into the coat, but all Ida could do was shake her head. "Can't say as I seen anythin' like that. Why'd you figure it was here?"

"Mostly because we traced my friend Chester here," Elliot explained. "He was researching the stone – or one much like it – when he disappeared, and we think he's got family in your community."

The young woman frowned, tapping a finger to roughly chapped lips. "Can't say as I know anyone by the name of Chester, either."

Elliot's stomach dropped. They couldn't have found *another* family of the same name but no relation, could they? But no. Whatever was happening here, the litany – the same one he'd "caught" from Chester – was involved. That *proved* a connection.

"Are you sure?" he pressed. "Chester Hennessy. He's about–"

He never finished the description. Ida was back on her feet with a feral growl, the rifle once more in her hands and pointed with terrifying stability at Elliot's skull. "Hennessy? You're with the Hennessys?!"

He retreated to the wall, hands again held high. "Whoa, whoa! We're not *with* anyone! I just want to find my friend. That's all."

Billy tensed beside him, ready to spring if he had to, though the odds of him reaching Ida before she could fire were poor at best.

Thankfully, it proved unnecessary. With a foul curse Elliot had never heard from a woman before, she lowered the weapon once more. "I dunno about your friend, but you'll want to take care who you tell about him. None of us left got any love for the Hennessys, may they rot in hell!" Then, at the puzzled looks from across the room, "Was the Hennessys brought this curse down on us in the first place."

True or not, Elliot couldn't even find it in himself to be surprised she thought so. That sort of luck just seemed par for the course at this point.

He and Billy glanced at one another, peeled themselves off the wall, and settled on the edge of the mattress. "Maybe you'd better tell us exactly what's happened here," Billy said.

Ida turned away, paced as far as the room allowed, then faced them again.

"It was more than a week ago. I... Maybe two?" Her expression shifted, anger draining away to reveal the sorrow and the lightest touch of the fear it had masked. "I've lost track. It's hard to..."

"Anyway, more than a week. We already knew somethin' wasn't right, 'cuz a few folks round here'd already disappeared. Bobbie Marsh went out fishin', never came home. Sarah Loomis, she... Well, a few of us, just gone.

"'Cept we found out they *weren't* gone. That day, somethin' happened at Woodrow Hennessy's place. Dunno what. We heard gunshots inside the house, a lotta yellin'. Then, for a few minutes, nothin'. Bunch of the men got together, went over to see what was goin' on. My daddy and... others..."

Ida held herself together, for the most part. She cried for only a short while, all but silently.

"They got to the house," she resumed, sniffling, "just when the door opened and the missin' folks all come pourin' out. Them, and most of Hennessy's family. And every last one of them was like the people you've seen for yourselves. Violent. *Empty*. And all of them chantin' that horrible chant."

"Your father was killed?" Billy asked, his obvious sympathy doubtless stemming from the loss of his own father. But Elliot knew better, knew the answer to that question was no even before Ida shook her head.

Knew what was coming, knew the fate of her father, of the others who'd dared approach the Hennessy place, was worse than mere murder.

"He ain't dead. None of them are. That *chant*. Those unholy words, whatever they mean... They *infected* everyone! They're *part* of it now!"

Elliot dropped his head into his hands, groaning softly. He'd known this was coming for a while, or part of him had. He'd refused it, buried it, unwilling to face what it could mean for Chester.

For himself.

Billy stood and wandered to the far side of the bedroom, arms crossed, expression unreadable.

"I know how it sounds!" Ida protested. "But it's true. You gotta believe me!"

"I believe you," Elliot reassured her. "Go on, please."

"Not sure there's much more to tell. More of us went to see what was happenin'. By the time we figured it out – by the time any of us believed it – more than half of us were already... gone. Taken or mad or whatever it is.

"Some tried to escape, but the... the mad ones, they got there first. Blocked the roads, waited for anyone to try to run."

"We saw. On our way in."

From the corner, Billy said, "Some of you might still have gotten out on foot."

Again Ida shook her head. "There's some of them still waitin' in the swamp. You never know where they'll come from, or when. Tryin' to get out on foot, it's suicide. And even if we did, where would we go? We don't have much money, don't have much use for it here. Nobody in Taunton's gonna believe us. They'd turn us out or lock us up – or worse, send someone back here to see for themselves."

"How long does it take?" Elliot asked, hoping he didn't sound too panicked. "From the moment someone hears the litany, I mean? Is it instant? Minutes? Hours?"

Ida could only shrug. "Ain't always the same. I've seen people turn in mid-step and start repeatin' those words, and I seen people take *days*. Got no idea what makes them different."

Elliot's head spun. He'd hoped for a pattern, a solid answer. He'd hoped to learn whether he'd simply gotten lucky, how much time he might have if he couldn't get back to the *Livre d'Ivon*, whether he'd done better because he'd heard less of the alien speech. If what Ida said was true, however, if there was no pattern to it, no sense…

He had to learn more. He had to find Chester.

A single footstep and the rustling of clothing snagged his attention. He turned to find Billy facing them again, arms still crossed, looking even more inscrutable than normal.

"I'm sorry. I'm having difficulty believing this."

Him? Of the two of them, *he* was proving the skeptic? "Billy," Elliot protested, "everything we've seen…"

"I don't doubt that some great wickedness has beset this place. But while I am no angakkoq, I grew up with their tales and their warnings. All the children of Itilleq did, more so even than most of our brethren. You know why."

"Uh, I don't," Ida reminded him, but he ignored her.

"And I spoke to the angakkoq for many days before I set out to take up my father's burden, before he gave me these." Billy brushed a hand over the cluster of talismans about his neck. "I know much of the anersaat of beasts and men, how they can grow hateful or corrupt after death if mistreated or sickened in life, and of the toornat, who never wore flesh or bone, or ever lived as we understand life. I know the many ways the evil among them can harm us, punishing us for violating taboo or tormenting us simply because they can. If you wish me to believe this misfortune was drawn down on Ida's people because the stolen *Ujaraanni* was brought here, or because Chester Hennessy had contact with it and then came here, I accept that as an unfortunate possibility."

His knuckles tightened until they turned white, and he couldn't entirely hide a scowl. "But a toornat or anersaapiluk that possesses people, one after the next, through the speech between them? Or passes on a curse through echoed phrases implanted in living minds? Not the wisest of my people have ever heard of such a thing, and you'll find it difficult to convince me that, as long as we've watched over the *Ujaraanni*, we've remained ignorant of–"

"But you never transliterated it."

Elliot hadn't meant to interrupt; it just came out. Now that he'd done it, however, now that he had Billy's attention – not to mention his ire – he knew he couldn't let the man's pride in his people, his steadfast faith in their spiritual awareness, get in the way of his seeing the truth.

Even if it was a truth against which part of Elliot himself still howled in protest.

"You said so yourself. Your people could never read the carvings on the *Ujaraanni*. But we know Chester had made some new discovery – of the *Ujaraanni* or the Lindegaard Stele. And you told us that your shamans, your…"

"Angakkut." Yes, Billy sounded angry, but he was also listening.

"Yes. Your angakkut went mad, if only slightly, after spending years watching over the stone.

"So what if Chester *did* transliterate it somehow? What if the litany is the pronunciation of the carving on the stones? Who's to say they *couldn't* transmit that madness, far stronger than mere exposure? Your people would never have known."

Silence for a moment. Ida gawped at them, and Elliot wondered how much of this she truly followed. Enough, at least, to remain quiet, to listen and learn.

"Even if your friend could have done this," Billy replied, his tone making it quite clear how he felt about that particular possibility, "you're only guessing that it's those words, and not some other unseen force, causing the–"

"They infected me."

Billy's jaw snapped shut like a bear trap. Then, "You said my talisman protected you."

"It did. I don't mean today. I mean weeks ago. Before Chester disappeared."

Ida could no longer remain a bystander. "Not possible! It takes days, at most!"

"I got less of it. Just one phrase. And I've been … taking precautions." Then, at Billy's glare, "I told you I was 'beset.'"

He revealed it all then. Chester's growing peculiarity, his utterance of the single phrase shortly before vanishing. Elliot's own distraction, his nightmares, his efforts to hold the litany at bay with the protective spell from the *Livre d'Ivon*. How he'd nearly succumbed when they arrived, when he drew nearer the other "infected," until the Inuit talisman brought him back.

For the first time, he spoke it all aloud. With it came the trembling, the fearful tears at the thought that he must eventually succumb, and his horror now that he'd seen what he might become once he did. But with that also came relief, the lifting of a weight he'd forgotten he carried. At least the burden was no longer his to shoulder alone.

Billy remained silent through the entire tale, for several long breaths after it was complete. Then he burst into a long diatribe in his own language, spitting words so harshly and savagely that Elliot knew, without translation, they could only be the vilest profanities.

"What is it with you?!" he finally demanded in English, his breath ragged with fury. "Is it an American thing, or are all white people liars?"

"Hey," Ida protested.

Elliot said, "I'm not sure what—"

"You and Daisy Walker. First Victoria McCutcheon, and now this. We are supposed to be partners. Working together. I should be able to trust you!"

Something coiled, worm-like, in Elliot's gut. The man wasn't entirely wrong, he knew that, and some small bit of guilt gnawed at him. At the same time…

"This isn't easy for me to tell, Billy. I spent weeks believing I was going mad. I still may be, only now I know there's some… some curse or black magic or evil spirit behind it. Things I didn't for one instant lend the slightest credence to before all of this began!"

"You still—"

"And besides, you doubted Ida's claim that the litany caused the madness, and that was after you'd seen the results for yourself. Would you have thought me anything but a lunatic if I *had* told you?"

Billy's gaze narrowed. "You owed me the opportunity to decide for myself what I believed." Some of the rage seemed to have faded from him, however, his face and posture relaxing, if only just. "It's obviously far too late for me to decide not to work with you," he said, "even if I wanted to. You are going to tell me *everything*, though. No more secrets."

"There are no more. You know it all now."

Elliot lied without hesitation, without flinching. Because the final secret was one he'd kept for years, one that was nobody's business but his own. It had nothing to do with Billy, nothing to do with the *Ujaraanni* or curses or Chester's disappearance.

One that he'd no intention of sharing with anyone until and unless the day came where he told Chester himself.

After a moment, perhaps deciding whether he believed Elliot or not, Billy nodded. "So. Your spell protects you in part from this… litany. My talismans are effective as well. But neither is inviolate. Exposure to enough of these… corrupted souls, or for too long, and the wards fail. We'll need to be careful."

Elliot nodded. "Ida, I saw that you'd fashioned earplugs of a sort…"

"I did, but they don't work real well. Okay from a distance, but you wouldn't ever wanna count on them."

"No, I'd imagine not, but every little bit helps."

"Won't be enough. I don't know about your, uh, spells and charms." Her mouth twisted around the words. Elliot wasn't sure if she still, despite all she'd seen, had difficulty believing, or if perhaps she felt some religious objection. "But even together, those ain't gonna get you outta here. They'll grab you in the swamp, drag you down and drown you or hold you until you can't help but hear 'em."

The two men again exchanged glances, each confirming with the other what they already knew.

"We're not trying to leave," Billy told her.

"Not without Chester or the *Ujaraanni*, if they're here," Elliot added. "We're going to the Hennessy place."

Chapter Thirteen

That declaration had gone over about as well as Elliot expected it would.

Ida spent some time informing the two of them, in no uncertain terms, that they didn't *need* the effects of the litany as they were clearly quite out of their minds to begin with. She'd grown even more emphatic when Billy asked if there was any way she might assist them. She literally laughed at the suggestion before declaring that, if she'd any intention of either committing suicide or succumbing to the spreading madness, she'd already had far easier opportunities to do so. She'd even gone so far as to retrieve her rifle in preparation for leaving the pair of them to whatever idiocy they were determined to undertake – with the stern warning that she'd not go out of her way to rescue them a second time – when Elliot had stopped her cold.

"You said there only a handful of you left?" he'd asked.

"Yeah," she said, shouldering her weapon. "Me and a few others."

"And how long do you expect you'll survive, or be able to protect them, if nothing around here changes?"

She'd frozen in the hallway, almost twitching.

"You said it wasn't worth the risk of trying to escape," he'd pressed, "because you have nowhere to go. But I can fix that."

His family had never been wealthy, not compared to Chester's parents or their peers, but the Raslos were well-off enough. Elliot could certainly afford train fare for a "handful" back to Arkham, and to put them up in cheap lodgings for a time. Months, even, long enough for Ida or some of the others to find employment. Even a flophouse, he reckoned, would be more comfortable, and certainly far safer, than their constant fearful sheltering here.

"But only if I help with your lunatic plans, right?" she'd demanded, her shoulders slumping.

"No." That had earned him two shocked stares, one Ida's, one from Billy. "Assuming I survive…" He had to rush through those words. He'd never counted himself courageous, and wouldn't have been today, either, if it hadn't been Chester who needed him. "… I'm not going to leave you or the others to suffer or die, whether you help us or not. But I'd also be lying if I said the likelihood that I *will* survive wouldn't be greatly improved by your help. It's up to you."

And so she'd led them from the house, through a hatch beneath a throw rug in the downstairs hall to the muddy crawlspace beneath the floor. After listening for long moments, to be sure none of the "corrupted" were near, she'd pushed aside a cluster of loose brush concealing the entrance to that crawlspace, and they'd found themselves outside.

Billy had expressed a quiet delight at the whole affair, as he finally had his answer as to how she'd gotten inside without him hearing the door.

From there they'd crept through shallow swamp waters and scattered cedar copses, quietly working their way around the edges of the community. Quietly and *slowly*, as Elliot – and even the others, to a lesser extent – flailed and stumbled in the dark of night. Inwardly he cursed the gloom, for all that he understood why a flashlight or a lantern were utterly out of the question. Ida had insisted the darkness would help conceal them, but Elliot still wished they'd waited for dawn.

"The mad ones don't use fire," Ida had whispered at one point while they crouched behind a thick tussock. "Least not that I ever seen. So you gotta keep your ears open, 'cuz you won't see them comin.'"

Nerve-racking as the journey was, they reached their destination without incident. It was another house, little different than the one they'd just left.

"My aunt and uncle's place. Or it was." She led through a similar brush-hidden entry, a similar crawlspace, and up through a similar hatch.

"Wait here while I tell the others I ain't alone. Don't want one of you gettin' shot."

"That would be inconvenient," Billy agreed blandly.

Elliot sat on the floor, back to the staircase, while Ida proceeded upward. This place smelled subtly different than the previous house. It had the same atmosphere of mold; inescapable, as he'd expected, given the environs. It held other scents as well, however, odors he couldn't identify but that might well have told him, even if he hadn't already known, that this place was occupied where the other had not been.

Maybe this is the sort of thing Billy's learned to pick up on, he mused, entertaining himself by trying to focus in on the smells.

A faint odor of cooking, perhaps? Nothing strong, maybe just a simple soup or the like. Sweat? Could be old sweat. And…

His nose wrinkled. He wasn't sure he wanted to know why, but he'd have sworn he'd caught just the faintest hint of feces.

Ida's call, barely more than a whisper, drifted down from above. "All right. Come on up."

Elliot and Billy obeyed, the stairs creaking beneath their feet. Ida stood in a narrow hall, its carpeting so old and cheap and worn it appeared the floor just hadn't shaved lately, outside an open doorway. She fidgeted as they drew near.

"Listen, before you go in…"

But they both had already looked over her shoulder, drawn perhaps by the sound of muttering.

There were several people in the room, some furniture, another door, but they scarcely noticed any of that.

In the room's center, a man wearing a filthy shirt and trousers was tied to a chair with heavy rope. His hair and beard were wild, tangled, partly hiding his face, but not so thoroughly that Elliot failed to spot a family resemblance to Ida.

His head rocked limply side to side, and with every breath, every move, he murmured those dreadfully familiar words.

"Isslaach thkulkris, isslaach cheoshash…"

Elliot cried out, wrapping his fingers instinctively around the amulet Billy had given him. His friend hissed something unintelligible, his own hand dropping to the pana at his waist.

"No!" Ida stepped in front of them, hands raised. "He's harmless!"

"How can you say that?" Elliot demanded, even as Billy reached out to shove her aside.

"*Listen*! What do you feel?"

"I…" Elliot stopped, jaw dropping. Nothing. Even with the protection of the talisman, of the spell, he'd felt the litany's pressure on his mind every time he'd heard it spoken. But now, other than the familiar pull that had been his constant companion for weeks, he felt almost nothing. After the first shock of it, a peculiar sense of initial impact, they were just normal – if disturbing – sounds.

Billy, too, froze, frowning. "I don't understand."

"I told you before," Ida said. "I told you folks don't all respond the same to hearin' the chant. Well, some of the infected don't seem the same *sayin'* it as others, either. A few of them, it's like they can't spread it. You hear them, and it feels like you got punched in the head, but nothin' else happens. You don't go crazy, don't start repeatin' it. It's the only reason I'm still me," she admitted. "One of them caught me by surprise."

Then, possibly anticipating the questions and concerns that might follow, "It was only a day or two after this all started. If I was gonna… gonna change, I would've by now."

Elliot struggled to think. *God, every time I'm starting to get a handle on this…* "There's no commonality? Nothing about them to suggest why they may not be able to pass it on?"

"If there is, I don't know it." She was about to say more, stopped and quailed beneath Billy's glower. "I wasn't keepin' secrets from you!" she insisted, doubtless remembering his angry rant from before. "I just got distracted by everythin' else we was talkin' about and didn't think to mention it. I swear."

His only response, after a long pause, was "Hmm." Without another word, he walked into the room. Ida and Elliot, each hesitant for their own reasons, trailed in behind him.

Now that he had the attention to spare, Elliot took in the somewhat dim surroundings and the other survivors. In addition to the bound man, the room held a rickety table and several mismatched chairs, probably dragged in from elsewhere in the house. An oil lamp glowed from atop that table, a risk they could afford because the only window was both boarded over and heavily curtained. The other door was only slightly ajar, and Elliot couldn't begin to make out what might be in the next room.

Two figures waited beside that table, a young woman and another man, both clad in heavy cottons and denims, and both as pale as most of the community's inhabitants. She was dark-haired, her eyes surrounded by deep hollows of exhaustion so she appeared almost skull-like, making it difficult to guess her age. She stared absently into the burning lamp.

Her companion was lightly bearded, perhaps in his early thirties, his hair the color of summer hay.

"This is Virgil," Ida said, pointing first to the man, then the woman, "and Lucy." Then, indicating with the other hand, "Billy and, uh, Elliot."

Virgil advanced, warily, and extended a stiff hand for the newcomers to shake. "Don't really trust outsiders right now," he told them pointedly. "But Ida says you're okay, so you're okay. Until you're not, hear me?"

"Uh, yes," Elliot agreed. Billy nodded.

Lucy glanced vaguely up from the lamp, then went right back to her staring.

Ida's voice dropped to a near-whisper. "Forgive her. We ain't seen her husband Abraham in almost a week now. She don't say or do much, except when she's helpin' me care for–"

A faint, ragged groan floated in through the second door. Ida sighed.

"And that'd be him." She headed that way, and the two newcomers followed.

In that next room, she struck a match and lit a second, smaller lantern. Here, too, the windows were boarded and curtained. The room held another table, a rocking chair, an open chest full of linens, topped by ratty cards, discolored dominoes and the like…

And a narrow bed, on which a young man tossed and turned beneath rancid, sweat-stained sheets.

"This is Alfred. Alfie. My fiancé." She reached down with a sad smile and brushed a lock of blond hair from a forehead sticky with perspiration.

Alfie was probably about the same age as Ida, though furrowed brow and clenched jaw made him appear somewhat older. He gazed up at her touch, eyes fluttering open, but they were glassy, unfocused.

"Oo's 'at?" he mumbled at her.

"Just some travelers, hon. Go on back to sleep."

"'Llrght." He was out once more almost instantly, and swiftly resumed his tossing and turning. Mechanically, Ida began carefully stripping the filthy sheet and blanket from atop him.

"There're clean ones over in the chest, if you don't mind?"

Elliot stepped over, cleared away the bits of games and other entertainment, and returned to Ida's side with an armful of blankets. This close, he could smell the alcohol on Alfred's breath, even in his sweat.

She must have seen something in the flicker of his expression. "He ain't a drunk, you know." As she changed the blankets, his legs were revealed. The left was swathed in thick bandages, with two wooden planks set to hold the limb immobile. "He broke it real bad, gettin' away from the crowd that came pourin' outta the Hennessy place that night. We set it best we could, but all we can do for the pain is keep him in moonshine."

Not wishing her to feel she had to defend herself, Elliot said, "It looks to me like you're doing everything you can for him."

"Yeah. I… I'm tryin', but it's hard. Lucy watches him when I'm out huntin' supplies or just need a break, but she's got her own loss…"

"And you're still caring for him, in the midst of everything," Billy added. "That speaks well for you, and your feelings for him."

Ida turned away so they couldn't see her face at that. When she spoke, her voice was thick.

"Virgil'll find you some more blankets, show you where to bunk, where we keep our food and water. Get some sleep. Tomorrow we'll start figurin' on how to pull off your suicide mission without the actual suicide."

Elliot welcomed the meal, even if it was only beans and dried meats, washed down with well-water.

Sleep he welcomed even more, as the exhaustion of the day overwhelmed him. He tossed and turned at first, trying to absorb all he'd learned and seen, to say nothing of his fear that they might be attacked in the night. Ida assured him, however, that the corrupted, though occasionally cunning, were not especially smart, had so far failed to realize there were survivors holed up in this house. Further, she and the others took turns standing watch at night, just in case. They were safe here, or at least as safe as might be managed.

None of those precautions protected Elliot from more of the snow-swept, flesh-rending nightmares, but one could hardly expect miracles.

He awoke several times – sometimes from those awful dreams, once because he could have sworn he heard what sounded very much like a slamming door. No other noises followed, however, neither movement from within the house nor chanting from without, and he eventually drifted off again, convinced it had been a remnant of a dream, or perhaps the shaky old structure doing a bit of settling.

The following day had brought countless aches and pains, to say nothing of a fatigue against which a single night's sleep was woefully insufficient. For that, and because Ida was in no rush to engage in what she still considered a fool's errand, Elliot and Billy did little more than catalog their supplies and discuss various possibilities – What if Chester wasn't here? What if the *Ujaraanni* wasn't here? – over which they had little power anyway.

It wasn't until the following day, then, that their planning began in earnest. Lucy and Virgil faded in and out of their conversations, which ranged throughout the house but always returned to the small room upstairs so Ida might spend time with Alfie, or so one of the three could try – usually with little success – to force Richard, the man in the chair, to eat or drink something.

Five final, untainted survivors, so far as any of them knew, of what had been a thriving community.

A rough map of the community – which Ida had sketched in chalk on old paper – and several guns lay on the table. She had insisted that Billy and Elliot help themselves to the small arsenal she'd collected from the many abandoned homes. "If you think I'm goin' anywhere near the Hennessy place with an unarmed man," she'd told them, "you're madder than they are."

The Springfield rifle, which she'd carried the day she met them, and the Colt pistol, however, were off limits. "Daddy brought them back from the war, and ain't nobody usin' 'em now but me."

Billy had selected the next largest rifle, a lever-action Winchester. Elliot had no idea if his people used guns, but the ease with which the man worked the breach and loaded the weapon proved he had some experience with them.

It was experience Elliot himself lacked. Eventually he'd chosen a simple revolver, similar to the sidearms he'd seen the Arkham police carrying, under the assumption – the hope, really – that it would be the easiest to manage. Ida gave him a few pointers, showing him how best to use the sights, correcting his stance, and eventually told him, "Look, just try not to use it till you're close enough you can't miss."

Perhaps not the most inspiring words he might have hoped for.

Evening had fallen once again, and the three of them sat about the table, twisting torn bits of cotton into makeshift earplugs. Alfred snored loudly from the next room, and even Richard seemed to have dozed off, though he mumbled occasional bits of the litany even in his sleep. They'd given him one of his regular cleanings earlier in the day, so the room smelled a bit less foul than it had.

"... ran just fine the day before all this started," Ida was telling them as they worked out the kinks in their plan. "I figure it still ought to. We do this right, it should draw any of them away from outside the house."

"From inside, too, if we're lucky," Billy said.

"Maybe, but we still don't know how many're even in there. I don't like–"

"Ida…"

The trio rose from the table, turning toward the door at the weak, shaking call. Virgil stood in the adjoining room, hunched, hands clutching his head as if to keep it from bursting. He staggered toward them, his steps less steady than any drunkard's, only to collapse halfway. He struck the table on the way down, making no effort to catch himself, and landed with a dreadfully hollow sound. Knocked askew by the impact, the lamp on that table – currently and thankfully unlit – dribbled a stream of oil, glistening as it crossed the wood.

Billy acted first, reaching the man's side almost before he hit the floor. Seeing no obvious injuries, he carefully lifted Virgil in his arms and carried him back toward his companions, rather than leaving him to lie near the spilled fuel. There he and Ida carefully looked the stricken man over while Elliot grabbed the nearest fabric, an old tablecloth, to mop up the all too flammable mess.

"What happened to him?" he asked, upon returning from his task.

"Don't know," Billy said, not glancing away from Virgil's supine form. "We haven't found any wounds."

Ida, however, did look up abruptly from her friend. "Lucy! Where's Lucy?"

"I'll go–" Elliot began, but a groaned word from the floor stopped him.

"No…" Virgil opened his eyes, jaw taut with even that much effort. "She's gone. Left."

"Left?" Ida grasped his shoulders as if to shake him, visibly restrained herself at the last second. "What do you mean left? What *happened*?"

"Left after… after she told me…"

"Told you *what*?"

But Elliot knew what the answer would be even before Virgil confirmed his fears. "Told me *them*. The words."

"No. No!" Now Ida did shake him. "It ain't possible. She couldn't have been exposed!"

"She's been… sneaking out at night. To look for Abraham."

Ida cursed, shoulders slumping and head hanging. "Of course she did. I shoulda known. And *you* shoulda told me!"

"I know." Virgil managed a faint smile. "But she knew you'd try to stop her. She begged me, and I thought… I thought she was OK."

"Virgil," Ida said then, the words cracking, "there's no way…"

"I know," he repeated. "No way back. No way to know how long I got. No way to know if I can spread it. Just… make it quick."

Billy stood and stepped aside, thinking. "No need for that yet. We know my amulets offer some protection. We can wait until you succumb, let me feel it when you begin to chant. I should be able to tell if you're dangerous. If not, we can–"

"Can what? Tie me to a chair for the rest of my days, like Richard? That ain't any kinda life. I told you before, Ida, you ain't doin' your brother any favors – and I'm tellin' you now, I don't want that for myself."

Elliot turned away, brushing past Billy to reach the far side of the room, standing near the sealed window beyond the table and the chest. This wasn't an argument he wanted to hear.

He didn't want to be reminded of the choice he himself might have to make.

They'd actually gotten lucky, he realized, in a twisted sort of way. Lucy could well have exposed more of them than just Virgil, with only the tiniest twist of fortune. Particularly if – like Chester before he'd disappeared – she'd only slipped into the recitation on occasion, had otherwise kept control of herself, she could, without even meaning to, have worked her way through the entire household, and they would never have known until–

"*Iiiiiii…*"

A single, drawn-out sound, high-pitched and trembling, ended the argument across the room, drew Billy's attention, drew Elliot's. He fought a moment to keep himself from turning. Every nerve in his body, every instinct, every thought in his head, shrieked in a single chorus that he did not, oh, God, he *did not want to look.*

He turned. He looked.

They all did.

Alfred stood beside the bed in which he'd lain, swaying with an unsteadiness that didn't look to be caused by either pain or drink. His leg bulged obscenely where it shouldn't, the makeshift splint failing to hold it entirely straight, but he seemed oblivious to the injury. He stared, but now it was not intoxicated bewilderment Elliot read in the man's gaze.

It was nothing. Nothing at all.

"*Iiiiiii….*"

Ida was gasping, her body unsteady. Billy, so unshakable, so ready for anything, seemed paralyzed. Elliot wondered, crazily, if he looked as horrified to them.

The sweat beading up across Alfred's face, his neck, his arms, thickened as if purging all the impurities from his body at once. A pungent mélange of sickness and rot and alcohol made eyes water throughout the room.

Finally, after an eternity of seconds, the syllables began to emerge.

"*Isslaach thkul–*"

Ida screamed, a piercing, banshee's wail, swept her rifle up from the table on which it lay, and pulled the trigger.

Chapter Fourteen

Well into the following evening, frogs, insects and night birds conducted their nightly orchestra, hidden behind curtains of darkness and trees. The slow-moving waters lapped almost silently at the skirts of solid ground. Dozens of near-mindless townsfolk, chanting softly, wandered about the Hennessy property where most of them – save a few scattered stragglers and lurkers in the swamp, waiting to waylay would-be escapees – gathered every night as the sun descended.

Elliot and Billy, huddled behind a fallen log across from the discolored old house, worked hard at making no sound at all.

It hadn't been long enough, not by far, to call the plan a failure. Ida might reasonably need more time, several more minutes at least, to complete the first stage of her task. Intellectually, Elliot fully understood that.

Emotionally he was a disaster, bordering on sheer panic. Bad enough he was already neck deep in circumstances that would petrify or even drive mad braver men than he, with every intent to dive in deeper still. But to be relying so heavily on Ida Glick, after all that had occurred…

She'd sworn, time and again, that no vile chorus resounded in her head, that her fiancé's abortive chant had failed to take hold. Indeed, Elliot had no good cause to doubt it; he saw in her expression and her posture, heard in her voice, none of the vague preoccupation that had fallen over him after he himself had been exposed. She could, of course, just not be showing symptoms *yet*, but it truly seemed – perhaps because she'd heard so little of it, perhaps because her own scream had deafened her to it, perhaps because Alfred had been one of those incapable of spreading the malady – that she'd been spared.

Elliot almost wondered whether she believed that to be a mercy or a curse.

In the twenty-some-odd hours since she'd fired those three shots – the second one to save Virgil from his own oncoming transformation, at his request, and the third to put down her brother Richard – she'd spoken almost not at all. She insisted her mind was whole, insisted the plan would go ahead as discussed, and otherwise retreated to some inner sanctuary where Billy and Elliot could not follow.

If she slept, it was only moments at a stretch. If she ate, the others hadn't seen it. Worst of all, after a single initial outpouring of grief, during which she'd dropped her weapon and fallen to her hands and knees in the blood of those she'd loved, she hadn't shed a tear.

Elliot certainly understood. He couldn't imagine how he'd react if he had to do the same for Chester, and she'd lost a friend and a brother as well as the man she meant to marry. It hardly required Elliot's many courses on the topic of human psychology to suggest that her reactions to what had happened and what she'd felt forced to do, however understandable, were neither healthy nor hopeful. That counting on her playing her part in a plan on which their own minds and lives depended was perhaps ill-advised.

Even as his stomach redoubled its efforts to tie itself in knots, however, and he began to feel that things had fallen apart, a new sound filled the Hockomock night, drowning out all the others. First a series of mechanical sputters, and then a steady chugging roar, announced that Ida remained on task.

As she'd expected and they'd all hoped, the gasoline-powered tractor belonging to the Hennessys' nearest neighbors – one of the most modern pieces of equipment in the entire community, albeit only usable on the highest and driest portions of the property – still ran perfectly well.

Also as they'd hoped, the sound was more than sufficient to attract attention. Almost in perfect unison, the chanters on the Hennessy grounds turned their heads, their stares somehow simultaneously intent yet empty. They raised their voices, until the refrain grew louder than the tractor and Elliot began to flinch from the pressure in his mind. He muttered his own protective spell, time and again, and clutched at his borrowed talisman. Billy, too, clenched his own amulets in his fist. They could remain only a few moments, if the corrupted didn't…

But they did. In some foul midpoint between a marching platoon and an advancing hive, they set off, every one, toward the mechanized siren's song. Their voices faded with distance, if only somewhat, and the young student gasped in genuine relief.

They still had no way to know if any of the locals remained inside the house, but that was what their weapons were for. Elliot prayed it wouldn't come to that.

"Go," Billy breathed at him. Bodies bent low, they dashed from behind their cover and made for the next nearest hiding spot: the Hennessy barn.

It wasn't large, as barns went, but it looked to be in solid shape; more so, in fact, than many of the nearby houses. The main doors were chained shut, but trying to haul those open without attracting attention would have been a fool's errand anyway. Instead they moved to a smaller side door. It, too, was padlocked, but a blow with the butt of Billy's Winchester fixed that.

The single, sharp sound shouldn't prove sufficient to draw the attention of those who currently pursued the rumbling engine.

They hoped.

They meant to slip inside for only a moment, to wait long enough to be certain the corrupted had all gone, that nobody loitered or had returned to spot them, and then continue on to the main house. They hadn't thought to find anything of import here in the barn itself.

Once they were inside, however, and convinced it was safe to do so, Elliot switched on a small flashlight he'd taken from Ida's store of supplies. He'd intended to take only a swift glance around, to get his bearings and ensure nobody else lurked in here with them, though they would surely have heard chanting already if anyone had.

Instead he found himself staring at a deep red Lexington series T, one headlight shattered, its whitewall tires coated in dried, cracking mud.

It was very much not a practical vehicle, nor an inexpensive one, certainly not the sort any of the locals were likely to own. It would have stood out for that reason alone, even if Elliot hadn't recognized this automobile in particular.

But he did.

"That's Chester's car!" It was the weight of a hundred conflicting emotions, more than deliberate caution, that kept his voice low. Billy whispered something in reply, but Elliot didn't hear it. He'd already sprinted to the vehicle, flashlight thrust out before him, peering intently through the open windows.

It was empty. Of course it was empty. He already felt foolish for thinking it would be anything else.

Billy appeared behind him, placed a hand on his shoulder. "Look at the dust. Thing's been here for weeks, at least."

"Yeah. I know, I…" He stopped, considering. "But Chester took the train to get here."

"Hmm." A moment, then, "Obviously he'd come here more than once recently."

"That makes sense, but why leave the car?"

It was puzzling enough for a second, more meticulous inspection. Unsurprisingly, it was Billy, with his keen hunter's gaze, who spotted it.

A few shallow tears in the upholstery of the back seat showed where something had pressed deeply into the leather. Something that had sat there for some time before finally being moved. Something weighty, for its relatively small size. Something generally rectangular, with one side rough enough to snag.

They absolutely were here, then, or at least lately had been. Chester and the *Ujaraanni* both.

Elliot was too worn down by the past few days, too frightened by what might yet lie ahead, for the elation he might otherwise have felt. Still, it was a hopeful enough sign to draw a ragged grin, one that Billy mirrored with his own.

The flashlights clicked off, and the two men crept back to the side door of the barn, listening for any trace of movement. It was time, and past time, to get to the main house and, God willing, the end of both their quests.

Their ignorance of who or how many might remain within the Hennessy place made entering via the doors, or any of the obvious windows, a foolish endeavor. Ida had assured them, however, that – as with many of the community's dwellings – this house contained both a partial cellar and a crawlspace beneath, the latter occupying what space the unevenly shaped former did not. Through that crawlspace, they ought to be able to locate a viable means of access.

And so they found themselves, after a swift but uninterrupted dash across the open yard, amidst the muck and the cobwebs below the house. From unseen sources, the soft drip of water and the occasional skitter of some small creature provided a constant background noise. Listening past those, they could still hear the chug of the tractor's engine, far down the road.

Once or twice, they heard the report of Ida's rifle. When Elliot had turned to Billy, his worry written clear across his face, the older man had shaken his head. "Nothing we can do for her right now but see the plan through. Remember, long as she's still shooting, she's still alive and still herself."

And was still in enough danger that she needed to keep firing. It wasn't the reassurance Elliot imagined Billy thought it was.

They searched about them, covering themselves in mud and worse. They kept their hands hovering over the bulbs of their flashlights. This ensured they wouldn't be spotted by anyone on the property, but in exchange they had only a weak, diffuse illumination to work with.

Still, after long, uncomfortable moments, it proved sufficient. Several windows looked to provide access to the house's cellar. One of them, in fact, appeared very much as if it had been pre-prepared for them: it had been completely removed, the rotten wooden frame all but destroyed, and then haphazardly shoved back into place. A simple nudge should pop it right back out.

"Some sort of lure?" Elliot asked.

"For who? Not us. This happened a while ago."

Cautiously, suspiciously, they worked together to pull the window free without knocking it off to the inside, where it might shatter and alert someone. Once they'd cleared it, Billy slid through first, falling a short way to a broken stone floor, Elliot close on his heels.

Complete silence was not an option, though they did their best. The uneven stone floor occasionally tripped even sure-footed Billy, and puddles of the intruding swamp splashed now and again beneath their feet. Elliot, not generally claustrophobic, felt trapped, suffocated, and the hallway seemed to him the worst combination of sewer and tomb. As though encouraged by his fear, the chant reared up in his head, requiring he split his concentration even further in order to mouth his protective French words against it.

Because of that distraction, it took longer than it should for him to realize that his difficulty breathing wasn't entirely an illusion of his mind. The aroma of mildew sat not only in his lungs but on his tongue, so thick he tasted it – of mildew, and of worse. He gagged suddenly, keeping his most recent meal in his belly only by an act of will.

"God! What *is* that?"

"Rot." Billy's voice was grim as Elliot had ever heard it. "Don't look down."

Elliot, of course, did exactly that – and could no longer stop himself from vomiting.

At least it kept him from an embarrassing, and possibly dangerous, scream.

The swamp water had collected at a low point in the corridor, creating the largest puddle yet. It was larger, in fact, than the hallway was wide, for here a break in the wall created something of a natural niche.

Within that hollow, and spilling out into the corridor, lay a heap of decayed and waterlogged corpses. One wore shreds of a blue uniform, though it was too far gone to identify what it once had been. Police, maybe?

The freshest of them wore a suit coat, perhaps of tweed.

Even had the body been saintly, untouched by a hint of decay, it would have been impossible to name. Whatever had killed the poor soul, probably a small detonation or a shotgun blast, had obliterated his face.

"Get up!" The tone wasn't unsympathetic, but clearly brooked no argument. "We have to keep moving."

Elliot straightened from where he'd hunched against the far wall, having caught himself there when his stomach heaved. "In a hurry?" he asked, wiping his lips.

Either Billy missed the sarcasm or chose to ignore it. "Since some of those bones have been *gnawed on*, yes, I'd prefer to be elsewhere."

Not for half a second did Elliot believe his friend might be joking. He felt his gorge rise again, and he knew his eyes must be wider than the empty sockets of the skulls at his feet, but he nodded and resumed walking.

After a bit of thought, he realized that the walk itself had begun to bother him.

The hallway couldn't be this long, not unless this underground level extended further than the house above. It turned and doubled back a short way ahead; also peculiar, but that, at least, might be due to irregularities in the earth. This was swampland, after all. Perhaps the cellar had to be constructed around patches that were too soft to serve. That didn't explain though, why the cellar would be broader than the stories above.

Once they rounded the "U" in the corridor, they saw a junction coming up. To one side, it led into what appeared to be a storage or utility room, which in turn contained a staircase leading up into the main house. To the other...

They stared, neither entirely sure what they were seeing. Or rather, why they were seeing it *here*.

A long, open chamber, its brick walls covered in stains of mold, mud, and – to judge by the smell – far worse, held a number of cots and several scattered chairs. The bedding on those cots was balled up, torn, tossed aside, stained with urine, sweat and blood. Most of the chairs lay scattered on a floor partly stone, partly mud, and entirely covered in perhaps an inch of sitting water. Other lumps of ripped or discolored fabric appeared to have once been various pieces of clothing.

The entire room was divided from the hall by iron bars, unevenly and inexpertly mortared into place at some point well after the cellar was constructed, possibly quite recently. A gate of those same bars hung open, and a heavy padlock lay on the floor where it had fallen nearby.

What was this place?

When Billy finally spoke, he sounded almost casual. "Were you aware Chester's family had their own dungeon?"

Elliot raised his hands, dropped them again. He found no words with which to answer.

The hall continued beyond the makeshift cell, but a quick look revealed only more storage space, either filled with old detritus that hadn't been touched in years, or entirely empty.

They found themselves left with no other option but the stairs. Billy unslung the Winchester from where it hung at his shoulder, Elliot reluctantly drew his revolver, and they crept nervously up the steps. Elliot flinched with every riser, the creak of old wood, the dull slurp of the wet mud scraping from his shoes.

The trapdoor at the summit stood open, allowing ingress into the darkened house. After a whispered consultation, both men decided reluctantly they'd have to keep their flashlights on, despite the danger of being seen; the other choice was total blindness. Again they kept their palms near the bulbs, hoping at least to minimize their chances of discovery.

They stood in a wide hall that, other than its larger size, would have fit quite well in either of the other houses they'd recently experienced. A throw rug lay in a crumpled wad, up against the wall. Perhaps it normally covered the hatch to the cellar?

Also on the floor were a number of broken frames, torn paintings and photographs lying amidst shards of wood and glass. Between the peculiar passages, the trapdoor and now the signs of rage and ruin, Elliot found himself thinking back on various gothic novels. The association was far from comforting.

At the hall's far end, invisible from where they stood, what sounded like an old grandfather clock hollowly ticked away the passing seconds. Seeing no reason to choose otherwise, they moved toward the sound.

The clock coalesced from the shadows, a genuine antique, but it, too, had suffered from whatever happened within this sulking beast of a house. Though the brass pendulum still swung, the glass casing had been shattered, the intricate hands bent and mangled so they pointed outward instead of at the Roman numerals surrounding them.

The intruders now saw a pair of rooms off the main hall, one to each side. From the right came a constant mumble of those phrases now as familiar and as unwelcome as a recurring nightmare. Elliot felt only a minimal pressure at the base of his skull. Against a single speaker, his protections held. He advanced into the room, Billy at his side.

It was, or had been, a sitting room of some sort, to judge by the various chairs and upturned table, the ash-coated fireplace, the old radio atop a credenza. Another door led back into what Elliot guessed would be a kitchen, and a broad staircase ran up to the second floor, an overhead world currently doused in gloom.

In the center of the chamber, hunched in an upholstered chair, sat the man whose voice they heard. He was older, filthy and unshaven, and he cradled in his lap a double-barreled shotgun.

At the realization that he might actually have to use it, Elliot's own gun suddenly weighed a hundred pounds, his fist growing numb around it.

Even as they entered, he ceased his recitation and looked up. Infected he might be, but he wasn't gone yet, not utterly. His grip shifted on his weapon.

"Who're you? Why're you in my house?"

Elliot advanced a single step, pistol held to the side so the stranger could see it wasn't aimed his way. "We're sorry to intrude."

At this, the old man cackled until he choked. "If you ain't yet, you surely will be," he wheezed.

"Um. Yeah, we've gotten that impression. My name is Elliot Raslo. We're looking for–"

"Chester. You're lookin' for Chester."

"Yes!" God, at last someone here had *heard* of him. Elliot felt a tiny ember of hope. "Do you know him? Is he here?"

"My nephew," the old man said. "Chester's my nephew."

From behind Elliot, Billy cleared his throat, stepped more fully into the room. "Chester's father told us he had no other family."

"Yeah, he would. Bastard. Never had much use for the 'lower' branch of the family, not after he struck it rich." For an instant, the old man – *Woodrow*, Elliot recalled from the property deed; *this would be Woodrow Hennessy* – seemed incensed enough over the old grudge that he forgot to be frightened, forgot his incipient madness. "Wanted nothin' to do with us any more. Chester wasn't that way, though. Chester never forgot where he came from."

Again Woodrow cackled, but this time it ended in a sob and a wet, ugly spit. "Wish he had, now."

He went on, before Elliot could ask. "Raslo, was it? Yeah, he mentioned you, before he… Before. Said he was glad he hadn't dragged you into his 'research.' Guess he shouldn't have been, huh? Huh?"

Elliot knelt beside the chair. Part of him wanted to weep at the revelation that Chester had, at least for a time, remained sane enough – *himself* enough – to care about Elliot's safety. He swallowed the urge, knew this wasn't the time. "Mr Hennessy, what happened here?"

"Chester happened!"

The shout nearly knocked the young student back on his heels.

"Chester and that damned *thing* he found."

Billy's head cocked to the side. "If it's what I believe it to be, that 'thing' is the sacred charge of my people."

If Woodrow heard, he made no acknowledgment. "First he only wanted to hide it here a spell, while he went on researchin'. Said it wasn't safe any more where it'd been, that he'd figured out he couldn't trust somebody. Don't recall if he ever said who. Kept it in his car, in the barn. And that was fine. The animals didn't care for it much, wouldn't settle down around it, but we figured it was just somethin' about the car they misliked.

"But then he came back. He wasn't… wasn't right in the head. Wanted our help to get rid of it. So we took the damn thing, carried it into the swamp. But the swamp…" He grinned, showing browned teeth, but tears flowed down his cheeks. "The swamp refused to take it."

Elliot heard a soft hitch in Billy's breath.

"And then," Woodrow told them, "then Chester started… blithering. I didn't hear it myself, then. Ears ain't what they once was. But my family… It disturbed them, but that was all, at first. Chester tried to leave, but we wasn't sure it was safe, so we locked him in a room. Then my Sally, she started…"

More tears, now. Snot leaked from his nostrils, saliva dribbled from the corner of his lips.

"We needed a place to keep them, see? And we had the cellar my great granddaddy built as a stop on the Underground Railroad. Me and my boys, we mortared in some bars, started keepin' the mad ones there till we could figure out what to do.

"But I never *did* figure out what to do. And the madness kept spreadin', until my whole family… And then some of the neighbors…"

He looked up, and Elliot wondered if the man wasn't seeking some form of absolution. "I couldn't stop it. I couldn't spend much time with 'em; even stoppin' up my bad ears with cotton, I almost heard it. I kept workin', much as I could, but one man can't manage this property alone.

"And we got discovered. A few of the folks from the far end of town. A nosy postman. Some professor from Chester's school."

It was Elliot's turn to choke. Polaski *had* gotten this far! So what had happened to him? Was he one of the corrupted wandering the town? Was it sheer luck Elliot and Billy hadn't run into him?

"I couldn't… I couldn't let them leave, let them bring the authorities. They'da took my family. And I couldn't let them change, spread the madness any further! You see that, right? You see that?"

The temperature of the room seemed to drop by twenty degrees. "Mr Hennessy… What did you do?"

"I couldn't let them. I couldn't." Woodrow began rocking his chair, hunched around the shotgun. "But I didn't let them die for nothin'. The crazy ones, they don't care what they eat, and God knows I couldn't keep them fed on my own…"

Now Elliot *did* fall back, scrabbling away from the old man like a crab until he struck one of the overturned tables. He'd have vomited, then and there, had he not emptied his stomach moments before. For now he realized just who the faceless corpse in the tweed jacket must have been.

"I got careless, finally." Woodrow didn't appear to have noticed Elliot had moved, still gazed down at the spot in which he'd crouched. "Didn't know they was clever enough to play a ruse. Went downstairs, saw my boy Thomas face down in the mud. I ran in to check on him – and he grabbed me, pulled the cotton from my ears. Hissed that damned chant until I couldn't help but hear…" Another sob.

"Been here ever since, just waitin' on my turn to… turn. For a while, the mad ones went out, takin' folks from wherever they could find them and bringin' them back here for Chester to infect. After a while, though, they just started spreadin' out, convertin' more and more on their own. Dunno if there's anybody left, now."

Billy moved to the table, reached down to assist Elliot to his feet. He remained strong and steady as ever, but his face had gone sickly pale. "This is worse than we thought."

He had no idea how true that was. Because, for once, Elliot had caught something his friend had missed, something that turned his stomach to ash, his blood to ice.

"What do you mean," he asked Hennessy, voice quivering, "they brought people 'back here' for Chester to infect?"

"What do you think I mean, boy? Chester ain't never left the house."

Chapter Fifteen

The sound began in that instant, as if summoned by Woodrow Hennessy's declaration. It came from overhead, somewhere on the darkened second floor: an uneven pattern of thumps, like staggering footsteps, but not quite.

Thump… thump-THUMP. Thump… thump-THUMP.

Slowly growing louder as they neared the broad staircase.

Thump… thump-THUMP.

Billy turned his flashlight on the stairs, but the beam was weak, illuminating only a tiny pocket beyond the topmost step. He swept it, first to one side, then the other, hoping to see whoever – whatever – might be moving along the landing, but between the feeble luminescence and the shadows cast by the wood-barred railing, anything up there remained invisible.

In the far reaches of his mind, nearly as distant as the litany he fought constantly to keep locked away, Elliot wondered if that felt right, if the light hadn't seemed more potent mere moments before.

Then they heard the voice.

It was low, quieter than the shouting of the other corrupted they'd encountered, yet somehow stronger, more zealous.

Thump…

"*Isslaach thkulkris, isslaach cheoshash…*"

…thump-THUMP.

"*Vnoktu vshuru shelosht escruatha…*"

Elliot recoiled, crying out, the chant pounding against his skull, against the magics warding him. Billy's flinch and the sudden pallor of his skin made it clear he felt it too.

Thump…

"*Svist ch'shultva ulveshtha ikravis…*"

…thump-THUMP.

"*Isslaach ikravis vuloshku dlachvuul loshaa…*"

Though the flashlight now shuddered in his hands, Billy kept it trained above – and finally the figure stepped into the woeful puddle of light.

Elliot's scream was one of a horror confirmed, not a horror discovered, for he'd already known. He'd recognized more than the words; he knew the voice that uttered them.

Thump…

"*Ulveshtha schlachtli vrulosht chevkuthaansa…*"

Chester Hennessy stood unblinking, hair and skin and tattered clothes stiff with dried mud, blood, and God knew what else. With every second step he seemed to fall forward, barely catching himself with the opposite foot before he completely toppled. The effect was a peculiar, almost alien back-and-forth sway that no thinking man could have maintained for long.

And still the venomous liturgy poured from him, phrase after phrase, verse after verse, at least twice as many as Elliot had heard from any of the corrupted before. They hammered at him, called to the partial echoes already embedded in his soul. He shook, his skin clammy with cold sweat. This was a power he'd never experienced, as far beyond the chanting he'd heard so far as that chant had been beyond ordinary speech, and he knew the protections on which he and Billy were counting could hold for only minutes at best.

"Chester!" His cry was loud, carrying despite the tremor in his throat. "Chester, it's me. It's Elliot."

Chester heard, he must have. Yet he showed no reaction at all, let alone a hint of recognition. He took two steps down the stairs, again catching himself well beyond the point where physics and human anatomy demanded he fall, and the litany continued without interruption. When he finally reached its conclusion, some dozen or more lines beyond those Elliot had heard before, he simply began again from the start.

"*Isslaach thkulkris, isslaach cheoshash…*"

"Damn it, Chester." Elliot felt his voice break, his stomach drop. Had his heart stopped, frozen solid in his chest that instant, he wouldn't have been at all surprised. He felt almost betrayed that it hadn't. Unshed tears turned the room into a cracked kaleidoscope of blurred, partial images. "This is me. Don't do this. Come back to us." And then, far more softly, "Come back to me."

Another two steps. Another near fall. Another line of that cursed refrain.

Billy charged, leaping onto the credenza and from there to the stairs, vaulting the bannister to land on the broad step beside the filth-encrusted Chester. Rifle in his left hand, he struck with his right, and Elliot experienced a split second of gratitude. He knew the hunter's instinct – to say nothing of his fear, the pressure of the alien syllables in his mind – must have driven him to shoot, to end the threat as swiftly and surely as possible. That he made the effort to strike without killing was a gesture Elliot hadn't been sure he could expect.

For all the good it did.

As was his wont, Billy struck with the edge of a closed fist, delivering what should have been a debilitating blow to the madman's temple.

And Chester's head… *bent*.

From the jaw downward, he did not so much as budge. Above, the rest of his skull canted sharply to the right, lips compressed tightly together on one side, stretched far apart on the other, as though the joint itself had dislocated and separated by nearly the thickness of the striking fist.

Arm still half-extended, Billy froze, unable to absorb what he was seeing.

Still chanting, the sounds only marginally garbled by the deformation of his jaw, Chester lashed out casually as though shooing a mosquito. Billy crashed through the bannister, wood shattering and splintering, to land with a painful impact back on the floor.

Elliot couldn't move, wasn't certain he even breathed. Chester once more began his descent down the stairs.

Billy shouted, but Elliot didn't hear the words. Only the litany rang in his ears.

When he realized his companion would not or could not listen, Billy scrabbled for his rifle, lifted it toward Chester…

Now Elliot found the strength and the freedom to scream, trying to stop his companion before he fired.

And Billy *did* stop, but not because of Elliot. Woodrow, his own lips now once again moving in that alien tongue, leapt at Billy from behind, swinging his shotgun as a club. Billy rolled aside at the last second and the pair of them crashed away into the far side of the room, wrestling and striking at one another.

Leaving Elliot to face Chester alone.

He found his revolver in his hand, barrel pointed toward the advancing figure. He couldn't recall drawing it, let alone aiming.

"Oh, God. Chester, *please*! Please stop."

Two steps. Another line. Well more than halfway down the stairs now.

"*Please!*" He couldn't truly see Chester at all through his tears, could only aim at the center of the moving blur. "Please don't make me."

Two more steps. Elliot could barely tell where his mind, his memories, his soul, left off and the litany began.

A new phrase. The beginning of another step.

Elliot opened his mouth. What emerged was so soft, it was scarcely a breath. "I love you."

He tightened his finger. The trigger twitched.

Chester finished his step, another, nearly falling, impossibly catching himself. The revolver didn't fire.

Elliot couldn't do it. The last fraction of an inch that would drop the hammer might as well have been a thousand yards. Elliot couldn't shoot, only sob, as Chester neared the base of the staircase.

But *someone* fired, twice in rapid succession.

The shots were the trumpet of Gabriel signaling the end of days. Everything in the room – even, for a heartbeat, the litany in Elliot's head – went silent.

Chester's skull rocked back. Thick, black blood ran from a hole in his forehead, slightly right of center, and from a second through his befouled shirt, just above his heart. Slowly he straightened, as if even these were but a mild inconvenience – and then pitched forward, toppling face first to slide and bump to a heap at the bottom of the stairs.

Bits of glass tinkled audibly to the floor, and at that signal the world began to move again. The pained grunts and bruising blows of Billy and Woodrow's struggle again sounded from the chamber's far corner, but Elliot paid them no heed, his shocked gaze drawn inexorably leftward.

One of the room's windows bore a pair of shattered holes, from which cracks still spread and chunks still fell. Beyond, barely visible in the darkened yard, stood the pale shape of Ida Glick, the Springfield in her hands, her eyes wide with shock, presumably at however much of the impossible tableau she'd witnessed before acting.

Something inside Elliot broke.

Where his hand had trembled earlier it now stood steady as a rock, cold steel aimed squarely at Ida's chest. Every other part of his body, however, every molecule, shook and twitched and burned. He screamed, shrieking until the pain in his throat grew near to rivaling that in his heart.

He wished, later, that he could blame his behavior solely on the litany, on some unnatural outside force. But it would have been a lie.

He never could remember, afterward, exactly what he said. What foul epithets he called her, what protestations he made, what threats he uttered. Vaguely he recalled branding her a murderer, wishing her to Satan's deepest pits, swearing that he could have – would have – reached Chester, talked him back from his insanity, reclaimed his soul, if only he'd been given that one final chance, those last few miraculous words.

Utter nonsense, of course. Even in the moment he knew it, but he buried that knowledge deep rather than accept it. He stoked his near-murderous rage, made it his furnace, searing away all other thought, because what it held at bay – the unfathomable grief, the clenching, gut-wrenching loss, the knowledge of what had just happened and the overwhelming guilt despite knowing there was nothing, *nothing* he could have done to change it – would have frozen him as surely as any blizzard.

Through it all, beyond the slightest tilt of her head and the twitching of a cheek, Ida did nothing. Said nothing. Whether the night's events had cast her into her own exhausted state of shock or because, after the fate of her last friends and family, she didn't care if Elliot gunned her down – or some other cause known only to herself – she made neither move nor argument to save herself.

Elliot wondered, afterward, if he would ever have truly fired on her, or if his mad fury would have wound down, run itself out, and it shamed him that he did not know. He was never to find out, though, because finally Ida's expression *did* change, becoming a mask of limp horror as she stared past Elliot's shoulder.

At first he didn't notice, as he failed to notice the faint sounds of something shifting, sliding across the floor. Even in his frenzy, however, what came next he could not help but hear.

"*Svist ch'shultva ulveshtha ikravis…*"

He didn't deliberately turn around; it simply happened, his body racing ahead of his mind.

On the far side of the room, the struggle between Billy and Woodrow had paused in mid-grapple. Both men stared at a sight so impossible it had reached even the corrupted elder Hennessy, snapping him briefly back to sanity.

Chester, head still contorted partly to one side and his forehead still gaping wide where Ida's bullet had passed through, had clambered back to his feet.

"*Isslaach ikravis vuloshku dlachvuul loshaa…*"

Elliot emitted a primal bark, a sound of tangled, undifferentiated emotion, neither laugh nor sob. Rational thought was a squirming eel in his grasp, and he felt himself tempted to let it go, to sink into either the litany or some more mundane delirium, rather than try to grapple with what could not be, yet undeniably was, the reality before him.

Chester was dead. Surely he *must* be dead, yet he stood, moved, spoke. His chant continued unbroken, no longer even pausing for breath, and Elliot once again nearly let himself submerge in a wave of lunacy when he observed the faint wriggling of the torn threads around the rent in Chester's shirt. Saw that they danced in measure with the recitation.

Somehow Chester drew air into his lungs, into his voice, *through the bullet hole in his chest.*

Yet, for all the horrors tormenting Elliot, pounding in his mind like a wild stampede, he also found one train of thought grown suddenly and absolutely clear. It parted the confusion, the rage, the madness, all of it, his very own cerebral Moses at the Red Sea.

This thing before him, possible or impossible, living or dead, was not Chester. It had been, once, but his friend, the man he loved, was gone.

Again the room grew smeared behind a new font of tears, but this time when Elliot raised his revolver, he felt no hesitation.

Six rounds, rapid; he continued to pull the trigger, producing nothing but metallic clicks, well after the weapon ran dry. How many struck their target he couldn't say, but the being that had once been Chester Hennessy staggered, catching itself on the end of the bannister.

Still it didn't fall, didn't cease its recitation, but Elliot's action freed the others from their own paralysis. With thunderous reports, Ida and Billy both emptied their rifles into the wavering thing.

Ida dropped her empty rifle, drew her Colt and kept firing, even as Billy began feeding bullets into the open breach of the Winchester. When her magazine ran dry, she retrieved the rifle, ejected the spent clip and snapped in a new one.

But the barrage had finally proved too much. Chester fell yet again, the impact heavy and wet, and even had he somehow remained upright, somehow survived, not enough remained of his throat and jaw to make sounds at all, let alone form coherent words.

Woodrow staggered to his knees, reached to tug at Billy's sleeve, not in any attack, but a feeble call for attention. As Billy knelt to hear whatever the old man had to say, Elliot – and, soon after, Ida – carefully advanced on the mauled and mangled corpse.

It's not Chester. It's not Chester. It's not!

Easier to tell himself that earlier, though, when it stood as a man couldn't, survived what a man couldn't. When it spoke horror into the thoughts of all who could hear.

Now, when it was just raw, dead flesh…

Elliot screamed, an anguished howl, and collapsed. The world faded, his memories faded, his own name began to leave him. He grew hollow, empty.

And from within, those Godforsaken words – not the entire litany, though he'd heard it all several times now, but the fragment planted within him so many weeks ago was more than enough – surged up to fill that emptiness.

Chapter Sixteen

Not, however, for long.

In truth, it was but a scant few minutes – though Elliot didn't know that, having lost all sense of time along with the rest of himself – before his mind, his soul, began to return. It spread from a peculiar warmth in what he slowly recognized as his right hand, a sensation sharp yet somehow comforting. It spread, and carried awareness with it. All he was seeped back through his body as the refrain fled back to the closet in his soul where he locked it away, leaving room for his return, and he was again Elliot Raslo.

He felt unyielding wood beneath him, looked up to see Billy kneeling over him, hands clasped around Elliot's own, muttering in Kalaallisut. The cadence sounded very much like a prayer, or perhaps a protective mantra. The many cords around his neck were gathered into a single thick strand, for the many amulets…

Elliot blinked. The talismans were clutched in his own fist. They had been the source of that strange sensation, were – at least in part – what had driven back the darkness to which he had nearly succumbed.

"Th…" His throat, raw and abused by his earlier screams, produced a sound that couldn't even be called a proper croak. He swallowed, sucked in a deep breath, tried again. "Thank you. I'm… all right."

He wasn't, of course. Might never be again. But he was himself, and in control.

Billy broke off his prayer with a nod and a faint smile. Gently, he released his grip and carefully disentangled his protective amulets from Elliot's fingers. Elliot felt a surge of fear over their absence, but the words did not return. His own protections, and the borrowed talisman around his neck, were once again enough.

Leaning on Billy until his equilibrium returned, he climbed unsteadily to his feet. Ida still stood by the body, from which Elliot swiftly turned his attentions lest grief overpower him again. Woodrow Hennessy remained on the room's far side, watching them all, lips quivering with the battle taking place behind them.

Then, when Billy saw Elliot stand, he nodded once and turned back toward where Woodrow Hennessy had collapsed.

He was gone.

Elliot tried to speak, to wonder…

From the next room came the shotgun's roar. A dull, hollow thud followed. And Elliot didn't wonder any longer.

Neither Billy nor Ida appeared especially surprised, nor inclined to speak, so Elliot didn't either. Not out loud.

Please, God, let that be the last of it. He didn't think he could take any more horrors that night, or for a long time to come.

Instead he shuffled to the young woman's side, approaching at an awkward angle to keep the terrible mess at her feet out of sight.

"Ida, what I said… I'm sorry."

It took a moment for his words even to register. "Hmm?"

"Before? When I was… After you shot… I wasn't myself. I didn't mean those things I said to you."

"OK."

That was it? After his vicious, shrieking tirade? Elliot felt a flash of anger, until he reminded himself of all she'd gone through. That she'd seen the same horrors he had, and lost even more than he had. No wonder she might be distracted, numb, with far more to concern her than the insults of a grieving, selfish boy.

Instead he asked, "Are you all right?" Then, to clarify what would otherwise be a truly foolish question, he managed to gesture down at Chester's ruined body without letting himself think about it. "I mean, his chant…"

"Oh. Yeah, I'm fine. Couldn't hear him, out in the yard."

That made sense. Chester's recitations had been rather quieter than the others. Lucky, damned lucky. They–

A loud scrape scattered his thoughts like a flock of doves. They looked toward the noise to find one of the doors open, and Billy gone. Whatever they'd heard had originated in the next room.

Elliot bent to retrieve his fallen pistol, digging in a pocket with his other hand for the spare rounds. "Billy?"

He was relieved beyond measure when he received an answer. "Yes, be right out."

Indeed, the hunter emerged from the doorway seconds later, carrying a small steamer trunk he'd salvaged. Thick dust covered the old leather and the brass fittings, announcing that it hadn't seen use for quite some time even before everything here had gone to hell.

Billy let it drop to the floor, flipped open both latches, and prodded at the central mechanism. Then, with a shrug, he took his rifle and smashed the lock until it snapped completely off.

As the others watched, he opened the trunk to reveal old bottles, jars and smaller boxes, which he proceeded to dump. Then, finally looking up, "I can carry it by hand if I have to, but if you can help me find some straps, that'd be better."

Understanding finally dawned. "You mean to use that to carry the *Ujaraanni*," Elliot guessed.

"I do."

"But we've no idea where it is. He said they dropped it in the swamp."

Billy rose and began rummaging around the chamber. "No, you see, that's what Woodrow Hennessy told me in his last moments of sanity. He told me how to find it."

They set out not long after morning light, from that house of horrors further into Hockomock Swamp.

Billy wore the trunk strapped to his back with a number of belts he'd found in one of the rooms, an arrangement that couldn't possibly have been comfortable – and that would doubtless be even less so with the weight of the stone added. It failed to slow him down, however, and whatever directions or pointers or landmarks Woodrow had given him were sufficient that he pressed on through the shallow waters and across muddy knolls with little hesitation.

Nobody stood in their way, and no sound of chanting interrupted the natural song of the swamp. They passed several bodies on their way out of the community, bullet wounds serving as mute testament to Ida's struggles of the previous night. Elliot recognized one of them as having been her friend Lucy, the source of the infection that had driven them from her uncle's home.

Whatever hesitation she'd previously shown to kill, whatever spark of hope or affection had driven Ida to attempt disabling injuries rather than lethal ones, had died with Virgil and Alfred. Most of the bodies displayed wounds to head or heart, and more than a few boasted those in addition to other, less severe damage. The inescapable conclusion, Elliot realized with a shudder, was that she'd made a deliberate point of finishing off the wounded.

The majority of the community's citizens hadn't died by gunfire at all, but by fire of a far more literal sort. One of the largest barns was nothing more than a pile of charred wood, still smoldering, tendrils of black smoke winding upward to merge obscenely with the lowering clouds. The metal skeleton of the tractor stood in the center of the ruin, and Elliot couldn't doubt that, were he to go look, he'd find a sizable collection of bones. Perhaps even evidence that the door had been barred from the outside after the corrupted were lured in by the rumble of the engine.

He did *not* go look.

He also remained unsure just how long their sojourn in the depths of the swamp took them. He retained only broken, sporadic memories of the trek, and he never quite figured out why. It wasn't the litany; though it troubled him – and his protective mantra was growing less effective, suggesting that time ran short before he would need to get his hands once more on the *Livre d'Ivon* – it wasn't strong enough to account for his fractured memories. Even if it were, why only this, their travel through the muck, beneath the shadow of the looming cedars, and not the morning before, or the afternoon after?

No, it was as if the swamp itself had absorbed some measure of the ambient madness that had afflicted the community, a madness through which these foolhardy intruders must pass to reach their goal.

He remembered the water, cold and murky and still, usually shallow enough to ignore, but occasionally so deep as to soak them to the knees or even higher. It felt vaguely gelid, as if the fluid itself strove to impede them.

He remembered the cries of the animals turning discordant, hostile. The swoop of birds, as he'd suffered before; the thrashing of small reptiles, of mink, even of a deer or two splashing through the water or struggling across the clinging mud, not fleeing from the three humans but *advancing* on them, teeth bared. He remembered gunshots, his own and the others', and the hot spray as Billy's pana drank freely.

He remembered the trees, clustered like bitter old men around a cigarette or a bottle, casting baleful glares over their shoulders at those whose lives still lay before them. Occasionally they hunched further still, their branches dangling fingers that brushed the wanderers' heads and shoulders. Elliot was certain they must surely clench into a sudden fist, yanking him from his feet by his skull.

And he remembered the stone.

Although they couldn't possibly have crossed so much of the sprawling Hockomock, it waited within a hollow of ridges and tussocks that felt like the very center of the swamp, perhaps of the world entire. The press of the water grew stronger, and he thought they approached through one of the wetland's random currents, or perhaps the remnants of a feeding stream.

Until they drew nearer, and he watched the ripples, the tiny waves, and realized the water flowed away from the stone *regardless of angle or direction.*

The glistening black rock protruded only a few inches from the swamp, but even that was far too much. Assuming it was roughly the size Billy had claimed, small enough to fit within the trunk, and particularly given how much it must weigh, it should have been completely submerged, perhaps even having buried itself within the subaquatic muck.

It wasn't, yet neither did it appear to float. It sat absolutely still, without the slightest bob or drift, as if set in a base of hard soil or even cement. And Elliot recalled what Woodrow Hennessy had said in his half-mad rantings.

The swamp refused to take it.

"I heard tales," Billy whispered, though whether he tried to explain what they were seeing to his companions, or to himself, Elliot wouldn't guess. "That at times, when wicked anersaapiluk grew numerous and plotted against the Kalaallit, when the *Ujaraanni* sang to them more loudly than normal, the angakkoq would approach the stone, and say his ceremonies. Call upon friendlier toornat to guard us from the enemy spirits and lull the *Ujaraanni* to sleep again. And sometimes, he found the *Ujaraanni* buried deep within the ice of the cave – but inside a hollow. A bubble, as if even the ice drew away from it."

Carefully he unstrapped the steamer trunk and lay it on a thick tussock beside him, then stepped carefully toward the stone. "Whatever the *Ujaraanni* really is, even nature rejects it. I don't know if I fully believed... before."

Then, with a quick lunge – perhaps so he had no time to think twice – he bent and plucked the stone from its swampy cradle. His muscles bulged with the weight, but otherwise he seemed to meet no resistance. Although it sat in the water as though held in place, it emerged without struggle, slimy and dripping. Billy twisted, dropped it into the waiting container, and slammed the trunk shut.

Just that simple.

Elliot had caught only a glimpse of the symbols etched into the stone. He still couldn't begin to read it. Nevertheless he knew, with absolute certainty, that he'd been right. The litany in his mind, that had driven Ida's entire community to madness, came from that ancient, unknowable writing.

You did it, Chester. I wish you hadn't, but you did. I hope enough of you remained, at least for a while, to be proud of your achievement.

Billy hefted the trunk, straining with the weight until he found the proper balance. Elliot and Ida assisted him with the straps, and they set off once more, back the way they'd come.

"Why?" Ida made the demand, sounding more alive than Elliot had heard her since the death of her nephew. "Why in the name of Christ would you wanna go back there?"

Billy said nothing, but the narrowed glower he wore conveyed the same question.

They stood once more on the border of the now-dead community. Billy and Ida had just begun discussing whether they ought to shelter until tomorrow, rest up or head out for Taunton and then Arkham immediately – and, if the latter, whether they should travel by foot or attempt to make use of one of the remaining vehicles. The conversation hadn't gotten far, however, when Elliot had announced his own intentions.

"Look, nobody here wants to see the inside of that house again..." *And the tattered body of poor Chester.* "... any less than I do. But I've got to find something, come back with *something*. A token, an heirloom. Something for his parents." *And for me.* He sniffed once, otherwise refusing to break down again, to let the emotion take control.

"I don't think–" Ida began, but Billy interrupted.

"No, he's right. Chester's family deserves something of him to hold onto."

Somehow Elliot felt that the "family" he referred to wasn't Chester's mother or father. He smiled his thanks, though he received only the usual stoic facade in return.

Ida looked from one to the other, then shrugged. "Fine. A few minutes."

They entered by the front door this time, and Elliot went nowhere near the sitting room with the stairs. He might need to yet – it was the only way to the second floor, and he'd no idea if he could find what he required elsewhere – but he fully intended to put it off until absolutely necessary.

Instead he slipped down other halls, leaving his companions to their own devices, and back down the hatch to the peculiar cellar. His flashlight occupied one hand, while he kept the other pressed over his mouth and nose in a futile effort to mitigate the terrible scent of the cell where multiple corrupted souls had dwelt in their own filth for days or weeks.

Slipping through the open gate, he found himself again facing the bunks, the scattered bedding, the odd piles of abandoned clothes. Wondering how he could possibly have thought to find anything worthwhile here, he idly prodded at those heaps, first one, a second…

The third partly fell aside, the top part a single chunk glued together by mud and worse, to reveal a familiar coat.

Away from his friends, Elliot allowed the tears to come again, stood over this remnant of Chester as sobs racked his whole body and his gut felt like a pit that would never again be filled, that he could only wish would swallow him whole.

It didn't, and eventually his eyes ran dry, burning and raw. Only then, finally, did he pick up and examine the coat. He couldn't bring the garment itself back; it meant nothing much to him, would mean little to Chester's parents, and was indelibly soiled in any case. But maybe something within?

The outer pockets were empty, nothing but fabric meeting his questing fingers. In the inside left breast pocket, however, Elliot found a fountain pen – which might have been quite nice, before it spent days not merely coated but filled with the muck's seeping fluids – and a thickly folded array of small papers. This, he carefully removed and laid out atop one of the cots.

Most was unsalvageable, the ink having run into meaningless smears, the paper itself soaked through and discolored. A few bits in the very center, however, had been partly protected by their less fortunate brethren. Elliot looked them over in brief perusal.

Before him were, in fact, two very different sorts of document. Most of the collection, and thus most of the survivors, were small sheets of modern paper torn from a pad. These bore notes in a handwriting Elliot immediately recognized as Chester's. Later he might read through them, see what he might learn, but for now it was enough to identify them as his.

The others, of which there were only a very few remaining scraps, were of a far older, thinner, less hardy material. It might even be some manner of parchment, rather than true paper. The few portions that weren't soaked were, instead, so old they had dried, and threatened to crack if not creased *just so* along preexisting folds. Even after lying in the filth, even in the heart of the room's thick miasma, they gave off the slightest whiff of age.

Elliot couldn't guess where Chester might have acquired them, and was even more at sea regarding what they might say. He was learned enough to recognize the writing as Greek, but he had no education in the language.

This was something, at least. He frowned, though, as he carefully refolded the documents and slid them into his own pocket. It was Chester's, yes, but it held no special memory or emotional association. It wasn't anything his parents would appreciate, and to Elliot himself, they were, as far as their value as a memento, worse than useless. They were a symbol of the obsessive project that had taken Chester from him.

He'd have to keep searching, then, and not down here. Hardly a surprise, but he'd hoped–

"Elliot!" Billy's shout echoed from the hatch atop the stairs. "You'd better come up here."

Oh, God, no more. How can there possibly be anything more?

Oddly stiff, as if his body anticipated whatever latest horror his mind could not conceive, he shuffled back to the staircase, hauled himself up, riser by riser, through sheer habituation and muscle memory.

As he crested the hatch, he saw Billy and Ida waiting in the hall, and while both stood still, they somehow conveyed the impression of nervous fidgeting.

"What's happened?"

Both of them glanced away a moment, reluctant to answer or even meet his gaze. Then…

"Chester's gone," Billy told him.

The words literally had no meaning, not any more than the litany had. "I don't understand."

Ida tried now. "Elliot, Chester's body. It's gone."

He waited for understanding to dawn. When it didn't, he simply walked forward, pushing past them both and toward the sitting room.

"Elliot…"

He ignored the call, turned the corner.

The furniture remained overturned, the room crimson-spattered.

Other than a pool of drying blood and scattered bits of unrecognizable carnage, however, nothing remained of Chester. Not where he'd fallen at the base of the stairs, nor anywhere else in the room.

"Animals," Elliot announced, even as he swept the room for paw prints, claw marks, a blood trail, and found none of them. "Animals took him. We should have covered up the broken window."

"No animals of significant size have been here, Elliot," Billy told him, speaking slowly, as to a child.

"One of the corrupted, then. Surely Ida didn't kill *all* of them. One of them crept in, dragged him off."

"To what end?"

"*I* don't know, do I? They're *mad*!"

Ida shook her head. "Ain't any sign of that, either. Besides, why'd you think we left you alone down there long as we did? We looked around first. All down here and upstairs. No trace, no tracks."

"Then you missed something! You saw him! You saw what we…" The room spun. Elliot put a hand on the bannister to steady himself, then recoiled when he discovered it was still tacky with drying gore.

"You saw what was left," he muttered, staring in terrible fascination at the red on his palm. "He sure as God's in his Heaven didn't get up and walk out of here!"

"Probably not," Billy agreed, though his refusal to rule it out wasn't lost on Elliot, even in his dismayed and distracted state. "But then it means someone else was here, strong enough or numerous enough to carry him out, and stealthy enough to do it without leaving a trail. We don't know who, and we don't know why."

"That means we go. Now. Before he, or they, or *it*, comes back."

"We can't leave." Why couldn't he tear his attention from the filth on his hand?

Why did part of him want to let the mantra rise once more from the corner of his thoughts and wash his concerns and his grief away?

"We can't leave until we know what happened to him. We can't. We just can't!"

He was still protesting, screaming even, but still staring intently at his open palm, as Billy took him by the collar and dragged him from what had long been, but would never again be, the Hennessy house.

Chapter Seventeen

No matter how Daisy wished the lingering chill would break already, spring refused to commit itself, like a reluctant swimmer dipping a toe now and then into a frigid pond.

It was especially peculiar, as Daisy and her compatriots at Miskatonic frequently discussed because, according to the radio – when it wasn't going on about the Influenza outbreak near the Merchant District, and the economic damage it was causing Arkham – the weather was properly seasonal across the rest of the country. Even other portions of New England had long since warmed and thawed, their grasses green and their flowers blooming. Only over this pocket, from Vermont to Rhode Island, from the coast to the Catskills, did winter's shadow refuse to wane.

If only the weather had remained the most significant of her problems.

Daisy wrapped her arms around her and leaned into the breeze, to keep warm in her heavy overcoat and to keep her cloche from flying off her head – but mostly to protect the parcel, wrapped in multiple layers of waxed paper and thicker packaging paper, clutched to her chest. Although she'd left work a bit early, the heavy cloud cover accelerated the fall of night, so she made her way home illuminated primarily by the glowing streetlamps and the headlights of passing cars.

What she was going to *do* when she got home, she'd no idea.

Elliot and Billy Shiwak had returned to Arkham yesterday, accompanied by a young woman they'd introduced only as Ida – and even that she'd had to coax from them, as none had been in any state to hold intelligible conversation. They'd simply showed up at her door, begging shelter so they might recover in privacy. She'd not yet even discovered how they'd learned her address, as she was fairly certain it didn't appear in Arkham's quite limited telephone directory.

She knew her neighbors would talk if they saw she had two single men staying with her, let alone a university student, and even Ida's presence made it only moderately less scandalous. She'd had to sneak them in past the tenants on the lower floors then, and insisted on silence.

Elliot's condition was threatening to make even that requirement impossible to enforce.

Whatever in God's name that condition might be. Concerned as she was, she also wrestled with more than a little irritation – legitimate, she felt, under the circumstances – that they seemed reluctant to share the whole story.

She'd gotten *some* of it out of them, mostly from Billy. He'd explained that they tracked down the Hennessy family, that they'd discovered not just Chester but the whole community gripped in some sort of mania, that things had gotten... ugly. They found many dead, including Professor Polaski. Blood was spilled, Elliot had been forced into acts for which he was emotionally unequipped and they'd barely escaped with their lives, fighting off multiple ambushes in their flight. That they had retrieved the *Ujaraanni*, but were uncertain as to the fate of Chester himself.

When Daisy told him, with some heat, that he obviously wasn't revealing everything, and that she didn't appreciate being kept in the dark, he'd muttered about evil spirits and ancient curses and strange things she would never believe, and was happier not knowing.

Oddly enough, she didn't *feel* any happier.

Oh, the whole bit about spirits was hogwash, of course. Her study of ancient tomes and the cultures that produced them left her more openminded than many in this modern age of science and industry, but she drew the line at this occult nonsense. She didn't even like to *imagine* how horrible a world it would be if such possibilities, worse by far than the ghosts and revenants and vampires that occupied her leisure reading, could be real. Billy's beliefs might include those sorts of things, and Ida might be a poorly educated yokel, but Daisy knew better – and she was surprised Elliot Raslo, a student of psychology and all-around modern fellow, bought into it.

Then again, right now he was delirious at best. Daisy suspected that Chester, having gone mad with his own obsession, had introduced the community to some sort of intoxicant or hallucinogen, and it was Billy's own beliefs that had encouraged the three of them to see a more uniform pattern in the villagers' behavior. Whether she was correct or not, however, whatever truly had happened there, she certainly couldn't deny its impact on the poor boy. Between that and whatever violence he'd committed to defend himself, whatever crazed behavior he'd witnessed on Chester's part, he'd broken.

For the entire night after their arrival, Elliot had tossed and turned as though stricken with terrible fever, muttering in his sleep, waking frequently with a sudden cry that was, often as not, in French rather than English. His sweat soaked the sheets of Daisy's bed – she'd given it to him, letting Billy sleep on the floor beside him, while she and Ida shared the living room – and his somniloquent murmurs had somehow floated through the closed doors to disturb her own dreams.

Like Jonathan Harker at the convent, she mused despite herself. The recurring notion that this whole situation mirrored her beloved novels was no longer remotely enticing.

When she'd asked about the French, Billy explained that Elliot had found a warding spell in one of the books he'd studied, but that, even though he'd kept a copy, it grew less and less effective if he didn't return on occasion to reread the original.

More mystic absurdity, but if he'd convinced himself the mantra protected him, it might serve as a meditative focus. Again, however, while she might dismiss the Kalaaleq's explanations, she couldn't argue with what she saw occurring with her own eyes: Elliot was, indeed, deteriorating, even over the course of the single night.

But how to help? She could hardly go to the police. Billy – and even Ida, who'd remained sullenly quiet most of the night, doubtless out of grief – made it very clear that the entire town had died in the violence. That, without evidence to support their story of a community gone mad, any claims of self-defense would almost surely be waved away.

Indeed, under other circumstances, it was a tale she herself would almost certainly reject. Yet Daisy had already known Elliot Raslo for a trustworthy and upright soul before he became this muttering shell, and she'd come to feel, in the time she'd known him, that Billy was not one for wild flights of fancy. So even if she doubted some of the specifics, she couldn't dismiss the entirety of their account.

No police. Which also meant, unless they could come up with a convincing and unimpeachable lie, no hospital for Elliot – assuming medical science could even do anything for him.

It also meant, though Daisy did not consider this until later, she could never reveal to his friends and colleagues the fate of poor Willmott Polaski. She couldn't possibly justify her knowledge that he was dead, killed in a tiny unnamed village in the Hockomock Swamp. His was a fate that would have to remain an unsolved enigma for all concerned. It was a guilt she would struggle with for many nights to come.

All of which left her only one way to help, and it terrified her.

At first, she'd dismissed it. It couldn't do much *real* good, anyway, just play into Elliot's delusions. Then again, what if that were enough? What if that gave him the fortitude he needed to gather his wits?

It was foolish, an incalculable risk to maybe, *maybe* help someone to whom she didn't really owe anything. Someone for whom she'd already gone out of her way. Someone who, while she liked him well enough, was just one of her many student patrons at the library, not even a proper friend.

She could lose her new position, her employment, her whole career. She might face charges. Worst of all, she might, if anything untoward happened, be responsible for the damage or loss of precious writings and the knowledge, the history, the culture contained within.

A dozen times throughout the day, she'd talked herself out of even considering it. And a dozen times, after a few moments, she recalled Elliot's clenched features, trembling with an inner suffering.

A face that, in the past, she'd seen slowly lose its accustomed cheer as his friend – someone she knew he loved, though he would never tell a soul – had failed to reappear. Seen the determination in it, how unhesitatingly he'd risked himself when he saw the most minuscule chance to help locate the missing Chester.

And for all those efforts? Nothing in return but violence and guilt, loss and, perhaps, lunacy.

So Daisy Walker had sighed as the workday neared its end. She made excuses for her early departure, claiming headache. She'd gone into the Special Collection, after making sure nobody was there and Dr Armitage was nowhere in the building at all. And she'd broken what she considered her near-sacred charge as a librarian.

Her home, only a few blocks from the Miskatonic campus, came into view, and she clutched the parcel ever more tightly.

Thank God and all his angels it wasn't raining that evening.

The next island of mist-diffused illumination revealed a row of brownstone townhouses, one of several nearly identical blocks. Constructed deliberately close to the university, they had served for many decades as homes for large swathes of the faculty, staff and student bodies, though a smattering of inhabitants without connection to the school dwelt here as well. No formal divisions or bylaws prevented one group from living near the others, but through unspoken agreement, the staff and the students had largely segregated themselves. It made things less potentially awkward for all concerned.

Daisy swept up the steps, grabbing her mail from one of the hanging boxes purely out of habit, and let herself in. Lace curtains and an unfortunate paisley carpet, neither of which she'd have chosen if the whole place belonged to her, welcomed her home. She ignored them, as well as the doors to either side, making directly for the stairs.

Miss Albertson and Miss Lindsworth, who shared the second floor, had a Ted Lewis record on the gramophone, audible as fuzzy, muffled sounds even on the staircase. Louder, really, than it ought to be, but Daisy wasn't the sort to complain even on a normal evening. Tonight in particular, she welcomed it, as it should serve to cover any excess noise from her own chambers.

Finally, she reached the door to the third-floor flat she called her own.

It wasn't large, as such places went. Living room, bedroom, a couple of small closets, a tiny washroom, an only slightly less tiny kitchen. The place felt even smaller than it was, for while her decorative tastes were minimal – a few pictures and a historically old Miskatonic banner hung on the walls, and a couple of potted plants sat here and there – she owned rather more bookshelves than the place was designed to accommodate.

Living alone, the lack of space had never disturbed her. Three guests, however, were more than enough to strain the flat's limits.

Ida looked up from the sofa as Daisy latched the door behind her. The younger woman had a bottle of Coca-Cola on the end table beside her – Daisy had told them to feel free to raid whatever they liked from the refrigerator – and an open copy of *The Mysterious Affair at Styles* on her lap. It didn't appear she'd gotten very far into the text, and Agatha Christie certainly wasn't the most challenging writer on Daisy's shelves. Nevertheless, the librarian found herself taken aback. She realized then that she'd assumed the rustic Ida to be so uneducated as to be an indifferent reader, if not downright illiterate, and felt a flash of shame at her presumption.

Perhaps she'd allowed the swiftness of her rise at the Miskatonic library to go more to her head than she'd thought.

She thought about asking Ida how she was enjoying the mystery – her own way of making up for her ill-considered suppositions, even if the other woman couldn't possibly know about them – but Ida spoke before she had the chance.

"They're still in there," she said, inclining her head toward the bedroom. "Have been most of the day. Billy's real worried."

"I see." Casual chat later, then. Dismissing any last-minute doubts about her course of action, Daisy removed her hat and coat, hung them in the closet, and proceeded to the next room, nervous fingers plucking at the wrapped parcel.

Elliot sat in bed, reclined against a few pillows and the headboard. Although ostensibly awake, he stared at nothing, and his mouth moved in silent shapes.

Beside him, Billy had removed most of the amulets from around his neck and held them like a bizarre bouquet against Elliot's chest. He chanted a ritual or prayer in his native Kalaallisut, the sounds formed in his throat more than by tongue or lips or teeth, and waved his other hand in simple patterns in time with the cadence. He ceased, however, mid-word and mid-gesture, at Daisy's appearance.

"Please, don't let me interrupt," she said.

"You're not. I've been through the song a hundred times, but it doesn't do a lot of good. I'm no angakkoq, and even if I were, I lack the drums, the masks and the other tools to make the spirits obey. Elliot's sickness isn't in his body or even his mind, I think, but his anersaaq. His soul."

She wasn't about to argue it with him, and besides, even if it *was* in his mind, as she believed… "Here." She held out the package, began to unwrap it oh so carefully. "This might help."

Billy raised an eyebrow, and even Elliot turned his head, seeming to pay attention for the very first time, as the scent of old paper filled the room and the light fell upon cracked leather binding. A faint gasp emerged from the feverish young man, and he extended both hands as though beseeching a benediction.

"How did you know which one?" Billy asked. "I couldn't remember a name."

"You said it was a protective incantation in French. Not many books it *could* be, and I've a record of every text Elliot requested." She turned her attention to the student, slowly passing him the *Livre d'Ivon*. "Elliot? Elliot, can you hear me?"

It took him a moment, but he nodded.

"*Please* be careful. If anything happens to this… 'I'll be in trouble' doesn't begin to cover it. I would lose everything. *Everything*."

Again, he nodded, and though his head literally twitched with whatever insanity or illness he battled, his lips trembled and the veins in his neck stood out, he took the book from her with surprising care, turned the pages with a gentle touch. Daisy released a breath she hadn't meant to hold.

"Come." Billy rose, taking most of the talismans with him, though he left the one Elliot wore about his neck. "We should give him some space."

Daisy frowned, reluctant despite Elliot's surprising caution to leave the book unsupervised.

Billy came around the bed, stopping beside her. "It's better for him."

With many a fretful glance back, she allowed herself to be guided to the living room, and she insisted on leaving the door ajar.

They sat with Ida – Daisy on the sofa, Billy in a small chair – and tried to focus on the other puzzle before them.

The centerpiece of the room was an oak coffee table, its base carved with intricate patterns of ivy and leaves. It was, by far, the fanciest element of Daisy's furniture: a gift to her from her parents when she'd set off on her own, years before. It still carried a sheen, as though freshly polished, even though she'd have been forced to admit that she'd left it untreated far longer than her mother would have approved.

Scattered atop that table were the scraps Elliot had salvaged from Chester's abandoned coat. In all the chaos of the trio's arrival last night, and then her work today, this was her first opportunity to look them over in any depth.

For several moments, then, she did just that, barely touching them – particularly the older, more fragile fragments – prodding lightly with a fingertip, at most, when she needed one moved. Other than the occasional crinkling, and the sounds of whispered French from the bedroom, she worked in silence.

Elliot's hushed voice dissolved into soft snores, and she finally straightened, nodding more to herself than to the others.

"This," she announced, pointing at the writing on the older pieces that resembled parchment as much as paper, "is Ancient Greek. There's not enough of it left, and I'm afraid I'm not near sufficiently fluent, to tell you what it says or what its source might be.

"But I can tell you that Chester was using it as a step in some sort of transliteration. These," and here she pointed to the student's own notes on more modern paper, "is a list of sounds and syllables."

Billy and Ida continued to watch her, clearly awaiting further explanation.

"All right. You have Language A, Language B and Language C. They all use different alphabets. If you can find a guide for pronouncing Language A, written in Language B, and you know Languages B and C, you can use it to spell out an acoustical translation in Language C. It won't tell you what the words *mean*, but you could pronounce them aloud. You… What's wrong?"

Her two guests stared at one another, expressions grim, before focusing on her once more.

"So Mr Hennessy," Billy said, "somehow found a way of transliterating some language to Ancient Greek, and then wrote himself instructions for transliterating from Ancient Greek to the English alphabet?"

"That's what this suggests to me, yes."

"And the original language?" He seemed particularly driven on that point. Recalling their discussion in the university's museum, Daisy understood why.

"If you're asking me if it's the writing on the Lindegaard Stele, I'm afraid I can't say. If he wrote down the original script at all, it's not among the notes that survived."

"I think it a safe assumption, though."

She nodded. "Probably."

"I'll need to destroy those notes, or take them with me. I don't *think* the infection of the litany can be passed from the notes themselves – I guess it only works if the original source is the *Ujaraanni* or the stele – but I'm not willing to take the chance, or risk someone else using them to translate the stele."

All right, enough. Daisy had tried to respect his beliefs, but she wasn't about to let him take the last remnants of Chester's work, to say nothing of the surviving scraps of what was clearly a far older text, because he was afraid of passing along some curse.

"I'm sure we can discuss that," she said delicately, "when the time comes for you to return home. But–"

"The time *has* come. I intend to leave tomorrow."

Daisy gawped, and Ida seemed fully intent on the conversation for perhaps the first time. "But this ain't done!" the younger woman protested.

"It is for me. My task was to retrieve what was stolen from my people. I've done that. I must deliver it to them."

A cold burning, a protective urge mixed with a dull fury, welled up from Daisy's stomach. "You're going to just leave? With Elliot in his condition?"

Billy at least had the grace to look abashed, casting his gaze first at the steamer trunk he'd left in the corner, then down at the table. "I've done all I can do for Elliot. My amulets seem to help, and I will happily leave several with him, but beyond that–"

Biting back an angry retort, Daisy rose and swept into the kitchen, hoping the time it would take to fetch herself a cup of tea might calm her down.

It did no such thing. When she returned, the warm china in her fingers, she still seethed, her fury at the Kalaaleq's stubbornness unabated. Nor was she the only one; Ida and Billy argued still in rasps and whispers, fighting to keep their voices down lest they wake Elliot in the next room.

"…a sacred responsibility." Billy was insisting as she returned to the sofa. "This was my task, and my father's task before me. My duty is clear."

"Aw, bullshit."

Daisy spluttered into her tea, but Billy… Billy went first pale, then flushed. The tendons stood out in his neck, and his breath quickened. "Because we've fought side by side," he growled, "and because you cannot possibly understand the offense you've just given, I will forgive that. But—"

"Bullshit," Ida insisted again. "Ain't me who's offending your people or your father here."

"Um, Ida…" Daisy carefully set her cup down on the table, well away from the paper. "Perhaps you might consider—"

The other woman obviously had no intention of stopping, however. "We got no idea if Chester Hennessy's even alive, or where he might be, or even *what* he might be!"

If he's alive? "What" he might be? How much of the story haven't they told me? Even if Daisy had meant to ask, however, Ida didn't pause long enough for her to get a word in.

"We don't know how many of those twisted madmen might still be alive out there, or if Chester's got any way to start the whole damned mess all over again. Right?"

Stiff-necked with injured pride and boiling rage, still Billy eventually nodded.

"And all because of that damn stone. So you tell me, William Shiwak, how exactly are you honoring your daddy or doin' right by your people if you ignore the harm caused by you losing track of your 'sacred charge'?"

Silence for a time, broken only by the harsh rumble of Billy's angry breathing. Finally, however, his fists unclenched and his stare lost its edge.

"Perhaps I'm not," he conceded, leaning back in his chair. "Maybe… your words have merit."

Daisy's shoulders relaxed like someone had just taken her off a clothes hanger.

"Tell me, then," he continued, in what could have easily been a challenge, a genuine query, or both. "Say I agree. Say I decide to stay until this matter is concluded. What does that mean? When is it over? What exactly must I do that I haven't already done?"

To that, neither Daisy nor Ida had an answer.

Chapter Eighteen

All about him, the ravaging ice, the barren snow; the jagged peaks and the hollow, hungering skies.

The howl of distant winds and even more distant voices, and none to say which was in greater pain.

His own horrified shrieks, as he once more saw his leg separate from the rest of him, linked only by thread-like strands without blood or flesh, without even pain.

And the massive scrape of something on frost-covered stone, as the tree-broad tendril crept its way toward him around the slopes – followed, this time, by a second, a third.

Not wood, not stone, not scale, not bone, but something entirely… other. A hide that was not hide, a flesh that was not flesh. A substance that was not, in some indescribable way, even substance. Solid, tangible, real, and yet… not.

Nor was "tendril" even the proper term, he realized with the tiny portion of his mind that wasn't lost to thoughtless gibbering at what drew near. This was not the long, stringy appendage of some floating medusoid, nor the thick, grasping tentacle of a cephalopod, nor even a winding serpent.

No, each seemed more an impossibly long digit of uncountable segments, a giant's finger with not two knuckles, or three, but hundreds upon hundreds of separate phalanges until they formed a grasping chain of skin and bone – or rather, of whatever comparable substances made up this inconceivable monstrosity.

He scrabbled backward, pushing himself along with hands, his remaining foot and the awkward stump of his leg which left almost paintbrush-like strokes in the snow. The flailing limbs followed after, no matter how far from the mountainside he scurried, until at last he reached the end of their length. The source of the first shambled into sight, followed by the other two.

Each was a cluster of people grouped together, their mouths stretched into gaping maws with nothing but hollow darkness beyond. Every person had their arms stretched forward, and it was these that had lengthened, twisted, twining and knotting together to form the base of a questing coil. It should have been too heavy, overbalancing and toppling the throng of people who supported it, but they appeared not to struggle with it at all.

"Isslaach thkulkris, isslaach cheoshash…"

From those cavernous mouths emerged the opening phrases of that familiar damned liturgy, repeated over and over – not by these wretched souls, for their lips and tongues and throats did not move, but through them, as if they were naught but megaphones or radio speakers. From a few score faces, in three separate clusters, emerged the voice of a chorus of hundreds, perhaps thousands.

Yet even this was not the worst of it, not the final horror that dragged a last soul-rending scream from the pit of his stomach, the depths of his soul. No, that was elicited by a few specific faces, faces whose deathly slack and hideous stretching could not prevent a flash of recognition.

Professors. Fellow students. The inhabitants of that poor, nameless hamlet on the edge of the Hockomock.

Polaski. Woodrow. Jeremy, the security guard. Lucy. Virgil. Alfred.

Ida. Daisy. Billy.

Chester.

And though he struggled to flee, as fast as his maimed body could go, he found himself sliding toward the nearest tendril, the first of the shambling group, his own limbs betraying him, and he felt in his heart nothing so much as a fearful yearning to join them, to offer up the flesh of his own limbs to become part of that writhing, seeking whole…

Elliot thrashed, flipping himself over on the sweat-soaked mattress, blankets and sheets flailing around him like shed feathers, pillows hurtling across the room to bounce from the walls or tangle in the curtains. He couldn't breathe, gasping, hyperventilating. Resounding in his head, louder even than the partial refrain, was that other word, that strange word he'd awakened to before, laying so heavy on his mind that he couldn't help but whisper it aloud.

"Tsocathra…"

It helped, in a peculiar way. It forced him to break his pattern of gasps, allowing him to draw a slower, more controlled breath. And that, in turn, made him realize something else.

Namely, that he *was* realizing. That he was thinking.

That he *was*.

For the first time since being dragged from the Hennessy household, Elliot – exhausted, terrified, grieving as he might be – was fully himself.

He cast about, taking in the bedroom that was clearly not his own. The quilt he'd sent tumbling was patterned in blue and gold, with a neat frill running along its edges. The sheets and pillows were a light violet, the curtains a darker shade of the same.

Across from him stood a mirrored vanity, with an array of perfumes and toiletries laid neatly atop. Only sheer luck had prevented the cushions he'd hurled from taking any number of them to the floor, or knocking the mirror askew. God knows Daisy wouldn't have been happy with–

Daisy! This was Daisy's bedroom. He must have been in a state indeed, for her to let a young man, even one she trusted, sleep it off in here.

Bits and fragments flooded back to him. He recalled their careful walk to the edge of town, in order to open a gap in the barricade of cars. Ida had trailed behind him and Billy, ready to pick off any lingering corrupted who ambushed them. He couldn't remember if she'd needed to or not.

Once they'd cleared a path, he'd held it together long enough to drive one of the community's abandoned cars to Taunton, but he couldn't possibly manage it any further. He couldn't recall if Ida had driven them back to Arkham – she knew the basics, though she'd never driven more than a few miles combined in her life – or if they'd taken the train.

Then nothing, nothing but the litany and the grief and the dreams, until Daisy had come into the room, and he'd somehow *felt* what she brought with her.

He turned, afraid to look, but the *Livre d'Ivon* sat on a small end table to his left, still pristine. He gasped in relief; if he'd damaged it in his flailing, it would've been the end of him. Even if Daisy hadn't killed him, he was doomed without access to the spell within.

Finally, Elliot looked down at himself. Someone had made a cursory effort to bathe him, freeing him from most of the swamp's mud, from the blood and sour sweat of their ordeal. They'd dressed him, too, and he wondered who he owed for what must be a brand-new suit of men's pajamas, and how much.

He sat up, anticipating that the room would probably spin around him, and clutched a bedpost when his prediction proved accurate. Once the worst of the dizziness passed, he stood, testing his balance. He wouldn't care to attempt the stairs, let alone actually go anywhere, but the next room should be manageable. He needed a glass of water; his throat was parched, painfully so, and he wondered how much screaming he might have done, and whether he'd disturbed Daisy's neighbors.

Staggering steps and one near collapse brought him to the door, which stood open a few inches. He didn't mean to eavesdrop, but the others were deep in conversation, and he found himself pausing to get a sense of it.

"… as though we've covered all this," Daisy was saying.

"I agree." That was Billy. "Which brings me back around, yet again, to the same question. If I stay, it would be to accomplish… what?"

If I stay? What had Elliot missed?

He continued with, "We have no more of a trail to follow now than we did before Taunton. Less, in fact. Chester might have gone anywhere if he's still alive. Or might have been anywhere even *before* he went to his uncle, and infected any number of people! Even if we find a way to prevent what happened to Ida's home from happening elsewhere, we might well be too late."

The room fell into a helpless silence that Elliot knew all too well, not only from their previous efforts but his own studies. This was a group that had gone round and round in conversational circles, and come up with nothing new.

They didn't know Chester, though. Not the way he did.

"He won't have gone just anywhere," Elliot rasped, pushing the door open.

Immediately Billy and Daisy were up and at his side.

"Are you all right? How are you feeling?"

"Do you need anything?"

"What do you remember?"

The questions overlapped until he could barely keep them straight, wasn't certain who had asked what. Without requesting it, and almost against his will, he found himself physically helped to the sofa. The glass of water Daisy pressed into his hand was welcome, however, and he allowed himself a moment to gulp it down, nearly choking in the process.

Finally everyone settled. Billy and Daisy watched him intently, he standing, she seated in a chair across the coffee table. Ida, too, waited for him to speak, though he seemed to have only a portion of her attention. He felt a deep pang of sympathy, and hoped the others hadn't been rushing her to recover from her own losses any faster than she was able.

When he spoke again, the water had restored some of his voice, though it still felt, and sounded, rough as tree bark.

"Chester lost himself to his obsession," Elliot said, forcing himself not to flinch when speaking the name. "And to the object of his obsession. The madness, the litany, it came from the *Ujaraanni*. Everything in his life has revolved around that damn… Around that stone." He cast an apologetic glance at Billy, who merely shrugged.

He noticed, though, that Daisy was looking quizzically at him. He wondered how much of the tale his friends had shared with her, and how much of that she'd believed. Indeed, he thought he sensed a tiny flash of disapproval, even disappointment, directed his way.

Well, he understood. He wouldn't believe either, in her position. But she hadn't been there, and he had.

"I don't know how much of Chester is left. I don't know if he's thinking or remembering or… guided by something else entirely. But I'm quite certain that, if he's not… gone… then he'll be looking to retrieve the *Ujaraanni*. Or at least to be near it, or the Lindegaard Stele, again."

Various shifting and sidelong expressions met that assertion. "It's possible," Billy allowed. "But I would hate to rely on it. There's a great deal of supposition involved. And even if you're right," he bulled on, holding up a hand to forestall Elliot's objection, "knowing that he might 'be near,' *if* he's alive, isn't much to work with."

"What about his notes?" Elliot gestured to the paper spread across the table.

Shaking her head, Daisy explained to him what she'd learned going through them, that they were a transliteration from some language – probably but not definitively that of the stone – through Ancient Greek, to English. Nothing that would help them here.

"Perhaps if we had more of his notes…" She trailed off with a meaningful look.

"Not in our room, certainly," Elliot said. "He always kept any notes of significance on him. He took them with him when he left. Although…" His forehead creased in thought. He wished the remnants of the dream and the constant echoes of the alien tongue would let him think!

"He didn't keep his research materials there," he finished. "We didn't have the room."

"Would those offer anything that would be useful to us now?" Billy asked doubtfully.

Daisy frowned. "I don't see that we have anywhere better to look. Elliot, do you know where he might have kept them?"

"He never said, but I assumed…" Again he paused, letting ideas and memories catch up and slowly realizing the implications of what he was about to say. "He was working with Professor Polaski's help. I assumed the materials stayed with him."

The librarian shrank in her chair. She knew the question that was coming before Billy voiced it.

"Do you know where Polaski would have kept such things?"

"I might," she admitted, "have some idea."

For God's sake, was she *trying* to get herself fired?

Elliot, though greatly improved, was not yet in any position to leave the townhome, and he'd begged her to leave the *Livre d'Ivon* with him a bit longer. To let him spend more time with the original copy of what he truly seemed to believe, much to Daisy's dismay, was a genuine protective incantation.

She'd acquiesced, as he certainly seemed enough in his right mind, now, that the book itself should be in no danger. Still, her gut churned at letting it out of her presence, and at missing what might have been a perfect opportunity to return it unnoticed.

What was she up to instead, then, in the deepest hours of this blustery Arkham night? Why, merely leading a pair of relative strangers across the Miskatonic campus, hoping to evade the patrolling security guards, with the full intent of *breaking into a missing professor's office.*

"Fired." She almost laughed aloud at herself. Was she trying to get herself *arrested*?

She couldn't help herself, though. For all that common sense told her to extract herself from this entire affair, both the fascination of a mystery unsolved and a sense of fidelity to Elliot, and even Billy, given all they'd gone through, demanded she continue to assist.

No matter how foolish.

She worked at convincing herself that Willmott Polaski would approve of what they meant to do. He'd gone off on his own to find the missing Chester, even if he was motivated by his own vested interest in their project. She might not be able to tell anyone what had befallen him, let alone do anything about it, but if the materials in his office could help them learn more about what had happened to Chester, or even locate him again, she thought the old man, from wherever he now watched them, would welcome their prying.

Of course, while that might assuage her conscience, it did nothing to mitigate her worries regarding…

"Hey, you three! Hold it right there!"

… possible discovery.

"Don't say a word!" she hissed at the others, then turned to face the oncoming guard, smoothing her coat with hands suddenly sweaty despite the chill.

"Good evening, Floyd," she said with a forced cheeriness.

The old security guard, his face an unfortunate leathery amalgamation of flat patches and deep wrinkles, drew himself up, blinking in confusion. "Uh… oh. Miss, uh, Miss Walker! What…"

It wouldn't do to laugh at the poor thing, but she'd so thoroughly short-circuited his expectations it was difficult not to. Obviously he'd anticipated corralling a group of youngsters, shooing them back to their dormitories and writing up a disciplinary report.

Unlike the student body, faculty and staff had no curfew, no regulations prohibiting them from wandering the campus at any hour, no matter how ungodly. Technically, Floyd had no authority and Daisy was committing no infraction.

That didn't make seeing her here in the middle of the night any less unusual, though.

"Uh, Miss Walker, if you don't mind me asking…"

"Of course, Floyd. I was up late working, and I'm afraid I only just realized that I needed some particular paperwork to finish up my task."

If one turned it sideways and squinted at it a bit, it wasn't even a lie. A single nervous finger tapped against her palm, a fidget she couldn't quite suppress, but otherwise she forced her posture, her expression, to remain relaxed.

"I see. And, uh…" He glanced at her companions, lingering on Billy as though he recognized the man but couldn't place where from.

She waved dismissively. "Friends from out of town who are staying nearby. It wouldn't do for me to be wandering around this late on my own, of course."

Floyd chewed on that, quite literally. She could see his jaw moving.

Eventually, he conceded, having no other real option. "Well, all right, Miss Walker. Just, uh, you be careful. And I don't know that I'd make a habit of this sort of thing."

"Oh, believe me, Floyd, I've *no* intention of *that*." It felt like the truest thing she'd said in days.

He wandered away, still glancing back, as Daisy and the others resumed their trek.

The pathway wound about several small lawns, a fountain, a gated garden around the base of a statue, through various patches of Arkham's nearly ubiquitous fog, before finally delivering them to the front of a building a short way from the library itself. Like most of its brethren, it wore a stone facade, stood several stories in height, and somehow conveyed a sense of great, looming weight.

Ignoring a sudden attack of nerves, Daisy removed a heavy keyring from her purse. Getting into the building itself was no trouble; most of the educational halls on campus, including the library, made use of the same key. It was far easier than assigning different ones to the cleaning and security staff, to say nothing of swapping them out any time an individual professor's classes might be shuffled about between terms.

If only finding a means of ingress was their biggest hurdle.

Maneuvering through a gloom broken only sporadically by the cloud-diffused moon and fog-scattered lamplight leaking in through the windows, they proceeded down broad, echoing halls. Polaski hadn't been the Orne Library's most frequent patron on the faculty, not by half, but she'd been to his office often enough before she'd obtained her current position – delivering or, more frequently, retrieving old books – that she remembered well enough where it was. Up those stairs there, down that hall there, fourth door on the left.

Just one amidst a row of offices, distinguished only by the name carefully stenciled onto the frosted glass window in the door.

Daisy tried that door. It was, to nobody's surprise, locked fast.

"I live in hope," she said a bit defensively, able to sense the disbelief from her companions that she could only scarcely see in the dark.

"What's your backup plan," Billy asked, "now that hope hasn't proved sufficient?"

She sighed, and then had to confess, "I'm not entirely sure. None of my keys will work here." The buildings might have a more universal lock, but individual faculty offices most certainly did not.

"Perhaps this is something we ought to have discussed before we got here."

"To what end? My answer would have been the same. 'I've no idea how we're to get in. We'll have to figure something out.'"

"Hmm." He moved past her and rapped a knuckle against the wood. "I could probably break it down, given a few minutes. It wouldn't be easy, and it wouldn't be quiet, but unless someone's in the building, or just outside–"

"I'd *really* rather not. Campus is still buzzing over the break-in at the museum last week, and security's still deeply unhappy about it. Another would almost certainly draw more attention from administration and from the police than we–"

"Oh, for heaven's sake!" Ida pushed between them, literally shouldering Billy away from the door. "Stand back and lemme work." She crouched down on one knee, putting herself at eye-level with the latch. "Either of you think to bring a flashlight?"

Billy dug into his coat and tried to hand it to her, but she shook her head. "Just hold it so I can see what I'm about."

Then, bathed in the yellow illumination, she drew a small pouch from one of her pockets, and a few bits of wire and metal from that.

Apparently she, like Daisy, could feel the weight of the others' stares. "What? How'd you figure I gathered all those supplies for our hideout back home? Not *everyone* went nuts with their doors unlocked, and not every house had a crawl-space I could get into."

"Break a window?" Billy suggested, shrugging.

"Sure, and leave a big sign I was in there in case anyone wandered by. They were nuts, not dumb." Metal scraped and mechanisms clicked as she worked. "I ain't hardly an expert, but I known the basics since I was a girl. I don't guess a teacher's office ought to be too tricky."

Perhaps not, but it was a good three minutes, filled with aggravated grunts and a few curses that made Daisy's hair curl, before a loud click announced that the door was finally unlocked.

At least the diversion might have done Ida some good, Daisy hoped. That effort, and the accompanying conversation, had been the liveliest she'd seen the young woman since they'd first met. Unfortunately, if it *had* helped, it was only in the moment. By the time Daisy stepped past her, felt her way to Polaski's desk, and switched on the lamp, Ida's expression had reverted to the same preoccupied, half-defeated mask she'd shown earlier.

Daisy moved back and carefully shut the door behind them. The office had no window to the outside, and while the glow of the lamp was visible through the frosted glass, there shouldn't be anyone walking the building's halls to see it. Barring the truly unexpected, they had some time.

The office wore a light coating of dust, suggesting that nobody had been in here since Polaski locked up and embarked on his ill-fated journey almost a month past. It didn't bother Daisy much – she was used to handling old tomes that had gone untouched for far longer – but Ida sniffled a few times behind her, and Billy sneezed outright with a blast Daisy imagined was not unlike a small explosive.

He could only offer an apologetic grimace.

Other than that dust, the office was precisely as she remembered, and as she would have expected even if she'd never been here. The desk held a typewriter, several pens, an old mug and a stack of folders. Multiple shelves, and an old sofa, displayed books and yet more documents. A large filing cabinet occupied one corner, and, throughout the entire room, an array of boxes sat stuck into whatever niches they would fit, stacked two and three high.

"Lot to go through," Ida said.

"Yes, well… Professor Polaski spent as much time in his own research as he did teaching. And I doubt Chester's was the only student project he was assisting with, even if it was his priority."

Billy carefully moved a stack of books so he could sit on one arm of the sofa without knocking anything askew. "Why *would* he be so involved in Chester's research?"

"At first, probably just as an advisor and a guide. Students who are assigned such projects, or think they've found something worth pursuing on their own, often ask for that sort of assistance.

"I think it went beyond that, though. Even before either of them disappeared, they both spoke about their endeavor in emphatic terms, and I saw them together in the library on multiple occasions. So many students feel they're on the verge of some great breakthrough that will make their careers, cement their reputations – and, not incidentally, show up all the stodgy old codgers who've come before them and grown too tradition-bound and intransigent to accept anything new."

That drew a soft chuckle. "I take it you've heard a lot of these complaints."

Daisy grinned. "More than a few, especially when I was only a junior librarian, not much older than the students." She sobered swiftly. "A lot of them feel that way," she repeated. "But it seems Chester actually *was*. And Polaski saw it. I think he hoped some of Chester's coming glory would rub off on him, give him one last boost among his peers."

That he might have meant to steal the younger man's discovery, to pin his name on Chester's work, crossed her mind. She dismissed it as best she could – Willmott Polaski had never struck her as any such a fraud – but she wished the suspicion hadn't even occurred to her.

"You're right, though, Ida," she said, putting on her best all-business librarian voice. "There's a lot here to go through. We'd best get started."

Chapter Nineteen

For a discomfortingly long while, the trio dug through the late Willmott Polaski's boxes, crates, folders and files. Daisy swiftly adopted the leadership role, not merely because of her organizational expertise but because she, of them all, had by far the strongest grasp of what they were looking for, what sorts of materials might prove informative.

Still, there was much to sift through, and her frustration mounted in almost perfect sync with the minutes, and then hours, as they passed.

Stacks of material developed, sorted into three broad categories in descending order of size: irrelevant to their purposes; potentially related, pending Daisy's closer examination; and materials unquestionably linked to Chester or his project. As that last pile grew to a volume that, while still dwarfed by the others, at least suggested their cause wasn't hopeless, Daisy found her frustration fading, replaced by equal parts anger and admiration at Chester's cleverness.

"He's not even supposed to have these!" she blurted at one point, startling her companions where they sat, backs hunched, on the office floor. She held a small stack of photos and written reports, information on missing or stolen materials disbursed by other universities. These were some of the materials Chester had sorted during his hours of volunteer work. He'd undertaken those labors to earn himself extra time in the restricted collections, but apparently he'd had other, ulterior motives even then. Whatever track Chester had followed, he'd been on it for many months, perhaps more than a year.

Finally, as the hour grew late and they found themselves nearer to dawn than to midnight, Daisy called for her companions' attention. They huddled together, each nursing stiffened fingers and a collection of jagged, painful papercuts. The librarian had an array of files and photos spread before her like the fan of a peacock's tail, and she felt literally dizzy from piecing together the trail she now believed Chester's search had followed.

He really had been a genius, in his way. A shame his obsession had cost the linguistic and archeological fields a brilliant, possibly even world-changing, mind.

"All right," she began, "I think I've got it. I don't know when Chester decided to focus on translating the Lindegaard Stele as his great triumph, or why. I suppose it was just one of those fascinations people develop sometimes."

Billy seemed less inclined to wave it off. "Perhaps. Or perhaps it called to him, even then."

"Yes, well. At any rate, he surely studied all the existing writings, and ran into the same walls everyone else had. He must have been disheartened, realizing there were good reasons nobody had even taken a crack at it in decades.

"Now look here." She pointed at the photos and reports she'd indicated earlier. "The various universities that keep collections of relics like Miskatonic does… we've something of an unspoken arrangement. If we discover a fraud, or an artifact is stolen or goes missing, we alert the others to be on the lookout for it."

"I see where you're going," Billy said, leaning back against the sofa. "Addison's theft of the *Ujaraanni* from the University of Virginia."

"Right. Of course, it doesn't mention Addison here. As I recall, you said he was never formally charged. And the *Ujaraanni* wasn't the only artifact stolen. But the report includes photographs and sketches, and Chester must have immediately recognized the writing."

"And decided he had to get his hands on a relic stolen from my people, without concern for what was right or just."

"Well… Yes, I suppose, though of course there's nothing in here about *that*. It clearly stoked his ambition, though, because it was after this report that he started digging into other university documents." Her head drooped. "I'm afraid, by accepting him as a volunteer, I gave him the position that offered him access to such things."

"You didn't know."

Daisy cleared her throat, wishing she'd thought to somehow bring a beverage with her. Of course she couldn't have known, but she felt culpable all the same. She was supposed to be the responsible one. The authority. "In any event, his next discovery appears to have been these." Again she reached out and shifted a few documents around, indicating a new bundle.

"These are the personal notes and records of one Lemuel Abernathy, a Miskatonic alumnus and something of an adventurer and explorer. Upon his death, he'd willed his notes and related documentation to the university. We receive a great many such bequests from former students," she explained, "and I'm afraid we're quite behind in having them all sorted, and anything useful cataloged."

Ida chimed in, then, nearly making Daisy jump; she'd all but forgotten the young woman was there. "So Chester found somethin' you all hadn't yet?"

"Um, indeed. From an expedition Abernathy had undertaken in Mongolia before the turn of the century."

She pulled an old ferrotype photograph from the pile and passed it around. It showed a slab, possibly granite, at the base of a rocky slope. The stone itself might or might not have been artificially shaped, but there could be no mistaking the symbols carved upon it as anything natural. It held but a few lines of text, roughly chiseled and partly worn away by the elements, but those sigils that remained were familiar enough.

"Mongolia?" Billy breathed in confused wonder.

"Whoever the language once belonged to," Daisy said with just a tinge of humor, "they were certainly well traveled."

"Clearly."

"Obviously, Chester also noticed the connection," she told them, resuming the narrative. "According to Abernathy's notes, the locals told him this was some sort of protective incantation, meant to ward off evil spirits. I imagine that must have made him wonder if the same was true of the *Ujaraanni* and the stele, because his own scribbled notes here…" A finger indicated yet another document. "… suggest that he started specifically looking for defensive and warding rituals in the restricted books he was researching.

"I'm sure he found quite a few. Such things are quite common in the occult writings of older cultures. He appears to have found a reference in the *Livre d'Ivon* – it contains many such wards, so I suppose it's not surprising Elliot found his own, ah, mantra there – to incantations in Ancient Greek, supposedly copied from an even older tongue."

She was nodding to herself as she spoke, putting the pieces together, remembering when Chester had come in, asking for some especially restricted books, how he'd needed Polaski to sign off on the request before she'd grant it.

"And as there aren't many grimoires older than the original *Book of Eibon*, and even fewer that were originally in Greek, process of elimination led him to the *Pnakotic Manuscripts*." She couldn't help it; her voice hushed as she spoke the name of one of the rarest of the Restricted Collection. "But it says here even that frustrated him. He found a few lines of a spell in Ancient Greek, yes, and even a few of the older symbols that matched those on the stele, enough to convince him he was on the proper track. That's all the English translation had for him, though, and we haven't got any of the others. Certainly it wasn't enough for him to transliterate the *Ujaraanni* or the stele."

She paused, tapping a finger to her lip. "His notes don't indicate where he went next, I'm afraid, and I'm not sure I can think of any options. Obviously, if he had access to the *Pnakotic Fragments* in the original Greek, prior to any of the abbreviated manuscript translations like the ones in our library, that might have offered him some answers, but I can't imagine where–"

Daisy must have shot upright, beginning to stand, as the full implications of what she'd already seen finally dawned. Must have, though she didn't recall it, because the next thing she *did* remember was slumping back down, half-sitting and half-sprawled in the midst of the scattered notes, Billy rushing to her side in a belated attempt to catch her.

"What is it?" he demanded. "What's wrong?"

"The *Fragments*…" She felt herself on the verge of tears, heard the same tremor in her words she felt in her gut, in her hands.

Ida was beside her, too, now. "I don't understand."

"In Chester's coat. Ancient Greek, written on parchment. Those were genuine. From the *Pnakotica*!"

Probably not torn from the true Pnakotic scrolls, no, but even if they had been copied from the original – or even copied from copies – that made them, by far, the oldest documents Daisy had ever handled, some of the earliest mystical and occult writings in the *world*. Irreplaceable, both for what they were and for what they might have contained, if they'd happened to include any of the lost segments never before collected or translated.

Destroyed, save a few incomplete scraps. Lost to the mud and filth beneath the Hennessy house, soaked through, smeared and disintegrated. Gone forever. As a librarian and a historian, her life devoted to preserving such cultural treasures, she found this hit her harder than the deaths of strangers, or even Polaski's, and the guilt over that realization only added to her misery.

"Would that have allowed Chester to complete his transliterations?" Billy asked. Whether the query was meant to distract her, snap her out of her shock, or simply because it was the next logical question, Daisy wasn't sure, but either way it gave her something to cling to.

"It, um…" She coughed and tried to regain some of her earlier poise, though embarrassment over the brief breakdown kept her from meeting his gaze at first. "It might, if it contained a sufficient sample of the original writing along with the matching text in Ancient Greek. Chester was a linguist, and now he would have had at least some idea of the… spell's purpose. It would have taken work, I imagine – being able to read Ancient Greek isn't the same as knowing quite how to properly pronounce it – but yes, that may well have been the last piece he required."

"So," Ida said, "that's that, then?"

Billy stood, stretching. "That is most certainly not that."

No doubt he had the same question Daisy did. "Where in God's name could Chester have gotten hold of these? Leaving aside the exorbitant cost, you can't just walk into a library or somewhere like The Curiositie Shoppe and ask for the *Pnakotic Fragments*! People in our field spend years, sometimes lifetimes, hunting handfuls of scraps."

"Perhaps Chester was less concerned with propriety or…" Billy cast about for the proper term. "… or provenance than your fellow archivists. And maybe he had a more personal connection."

Daisy looked up, the gesture and her expression both sharp. She could think of only one person with whom Chester had a "more personal" connection, and Daisy had hoped never to hear the woman's name again in the context of the investigation. Or at all. "Are you suggesting…?"

"You did tell me, did you not, that she was a customer at several of the shops you visited? That she was a 'dabbler' in history and the occult?"

"Who're we talking about?" Ida asked, but Daisy barely heard.

"*Dabbler* is precisely the word. I sincerely doubt that woman has the connections necessary to come up with anything even close to the age or significance of the *Fragments*. And if she did, you'd be asking me to believe that, in addition to his good fortune in stumbling on these clues here, Chester also had the miraculous stroke of luck to be involved with one of the few people who could… could…"

The spark of suspicion Billy had ignited in her thoughts flared abruptly into a crackling bonfire. She raised a hand toward him, with which he kindly helped her to stand. Then, her steps slowed by stiffness from sitting on the floor – but also by a deep reluctance, an intense desire not to risk discovering her unpleasant notion had any foundation in truth – she hobbled her way around Professor Polaski's desk. A quick shuffle through the documents on top, then a series of rough rumbles and thumps as she scoured drawer after drawer…

There, in the bottom right, a small leather-bound parcel. His address book.

Almost unwillingly, tense enough that she earned herself another papercut for her troubles – drawing from her a sharp hiss but no other response – she flipped the pages toward the center.

When she got there, all she could do was sigh.

McCutcheon, Victoria. Address. Phone number.

Polaski knew her. Had known her for some time, based on the page's general wear and other nearby entries.

Given his parents' wealth, it had never before occurred to Daisy to wonder just how Chester had met the attractive and relatively young widow in the first place. Now that she knew, it left a deeply sour taste in her mouth.

"He sought her out," she told the others, unaware it emerged as a partial growl. "Chester Hennessy involved himself with Mrs McCutcheon because they thought she might be useful." She dropped the address book and its damning entry, now stained ever so faintly with a smear of her own blood, back into the drawer and slammed it shut with a resounding *crack*.

"All of this is important to know," Billy said, "but it doesn't tell us anything about where he might be now, or where he might have been prior to his uncle's home. We're going to have to speak with McCutcheon after all." If he had any thoughts about ending that declaration with *As we should have done before*, he was good enough to keep them to himself.

Daisy shook her head, but it wasn't a refusal so much as a commentary on their situation. "Certainly not tonight. It's nearly morning. We'll take a day, try to figure out some way to approach her that won't get us immediately shown the door, or worse."

And for me to sneak the Livre d'Ivon *back into the collection. I'd rather at least cut down the number of incredibly foolish chances I'm taking at any one time.*

Grudgingly but swiftly, they began shoveling documents back into the boxes whence they'd come, though they didn't bother attempting to sort them into their prior order. It only mattered that nobody who might come into Polaski's office down the road – to clean, or to empty it out once Miskatonic acknowledged he'd never be returning – had any reason to suspect they'd been here.

"Billy, Ida." She closed the box on which she'd been working and turned to face them. "Elliot doesn't need to know this. He's suffering enough with his friend's loss. We don't need to poison that memory with this new insight into Chester's behavior."

Two quick nods, and they were at the boxes once again, racing to be out of here and back home before the dawn.

Chapter Twenty

Keeping the less savory elements of their discoveries from Elliot proved easy enough. While bedrest and access to the *Livre d'Ivon* had greatly improved his mental state, he remained exhausted, worn out by his ordeals and the internal battles that followed. If he wasn't fully satisfied with their abbreviated account of the night's activities, then at least he was too tired to press.

He didn't object even when Daisy informed him, somewhat nervously, that she would be returning the ancient text to the library in the morning. He seemed to feel that he'd spent enough time with the original spell that his scribbled copy, or even his memory, should be enough to sustain him for a few days.

Rather more startling was the fact that finding an opportunity to speak with Victoria McCutcheon also turned out to be easier than anticipated.

It was again the same trio that had broken into Polaski's office. Elliot remained behind once more, at Daisy's insistence. She felt further rest would do him good, but she also didn't fully trust his ability to keep his emotions in check when dealing with Chester's former paramour.

Heading out that evening after her shift at the library, she and the others had concocted a fiction they hoped might at least get her into McCutcheon's lavish apartment building. Approaching alone, she informed the doorman in his starched navy-blue coat and cap that she had come on behalf of "the shop" – she deliberately failed to specify which. She must see Mrs McCutcheon on the matter of a rare book in which she'd expressed interest, and might now be available for purchase.

They'd had some hope that the tale, vague but believable, would satisfy the sentinel's sense of protocol. Once inside, she would then slip around to the servants' and delivery entrance and let the others inside.

Instead, the doorman told her, with a sort of apologetic boredom, that Mrs McCutcheon had only recently left the premises, and he could hardly venture to guess how long she might be out. A bit of dissembling about the need for haste, as other parties were interested in the book – combined with a few dollars discreetly slipped into a white-gloved hand – persuaded him to reveal that, while he couldn't say with certainty where McCutcheon might have gone, she'd recently made a habit of dining at Salton and Lindall's, a newly opened restaurant just a few blocks distant.

"Can we risk talking to her in public?" Billy asked as they made their way along winding streets, through crowds perhaps a bit thinner than normal thanks to growing fears of the Merchant District flu. "When I wanted to question her before, you said the police might still be keeping an eye on her."

"They might, yes, but I shouldn't think they've got officers *inside* an establishment such as Salton and Lindall's. They'll see us enter, but we won't mean anything to them. They won't know we're speaking with her unless she's right by a window or willing to make a public fuss. And if they do, well, I'll tell them my worry over Chester inspired me to confront her." It wouldn't make the Miskatonic administration happy, but it ought to earn her nothing worse than a reprimand. It most certainly wasn't as grave a transgression as many she'd already committed in the name of this investigation.

"You weren't prepared to take that chance last week."

"Our options weren't so limited last week."

"Hmm."

Ornate signage, gold script on green, and a pair of Corinthian columns adorned the restaurant's entrance. Through broad windows, Daisy saw rows of tables, their cloths and the upholstery of the chairs a matching verdant hue to the exterior, and great glass chandeliers hanging above. She also saw that she and her compatriots, garbed in reasonably nice but everyday outfits, were a bit underdressed compared to the more formal – or simply wealthier – patrons within.

Well, nothing to be done for it now. Thankfully, other than an involuntary twitch that might have grown into a grimace had he allowed it, the tuxedo-clad *maître d'* made no objection.

"May I help you?"

"Ah..." Daisy scanned the room and swiftly found what she sought. "Thank you, we're just meeting a friend." She brushed past him, shoulders back and stride purposeful, as if daring him to interfere.

Daisy had never met Victoria McCutcheon, but she'd had no difficulty picking her out. The restaurant was not crowded that evening – perhaps explaining why their outfits hadn't elicited more of a protest – and she'd both heard McCutcheon described by those who knew her, and read similar descriptions in the society pages, which she would, if questioned, have strenuously denied ever perusing.

A physical description might have proved insufficient on its own, but the fact that the woman was dining on her own – not only without companions, but with a barren no-man's land of empty tables surrounding her, as though the other patrons feared social ostracism was contagious – was indication enough.

Chester might have been gone for months, but the stigma she suffered for the relationship would linger quite some while longer.

She sat with her head held high, her red hair hanging freer and longer than the current style. She wore a fringe-layered dress in even brighter crimson, one that seemed almost to challenge anyone who would judge it – or her – and she steadily stared back at anyone who glanced her way until they returned to their meal.

Daisy found herself admiring the woman's courage and, though it neither justified nor excused McCutcheon's own inappropriate choices, the discovery that Chester had deliberately taken advantage made it difficult to maintain the simmering anger she'd nursed.

So it was with genuine feeling, not mere etiquette, that she announced, "Apologies for disturbing you, Mrs McCutcheon." She, and then Billy and Ida, seated themselves at the woman's table, ignoring the shocked gawking of the other patrons. The woman hadn't been here long, apparently, as the table held only a near-empty cup of coffee and a plate of cheese, olives, and crackers. If she'd yet ordered an entrée, it hadn't arrived. "But I'm afraid we require a few moments of your time."

This close, neither McCutcheon's regal bearing nor her expertly applied makeup could quite conceal the line of worry, nor the circles of fatigue, marring a visage that otherwise defined statuesque. The look she turned on the newcomers, however, was full only of suspicion and defiance.

"I don't believe I know you," she said. "And I'm quite sure I didn't invite you."

"No, you don't. And you didn't. I promise, we won't take long."

"No, you won't." McCutcheon twisted in her seat, as though to signal the waiters.

"We're friends of Chester Hennessy."

She stopped, turned back. Her expression was, if anything, even stonier than before. "No, I don't believe so. Colleagues, perhaps, but he told me of all his friends."

"Fine, then. Colleagues. The point is, we're looking–"

"I have spoken to several of his friends. I have spoken to one of his professors. I have spoken to the police. I had nothing helpful to tell them, I have nothing helpful to tell you, and I will thank you to leave me to my supper in peace."

My, this is going well. "Mrs McCutcheon, please. We have information the others didn't, we might–"

"I will ask, politely, only one more time. Please leave me alone." This in the unmistakable tone of a woman out of patience, and unaccustomed to being refused.

Daisy struggled to remain calm. McCutcheon's anger and uncooperativeness were entirely understandable, and they were strangers to her. Nevertheless…

"We have reason to believe that Chester got into trouble, in part, thanks to some of the connections you helped him make. Don't you want to try to set that right?"

McCutcheon tensed so violently that Daisy recoiled, frightened for a moment that the older woman might actually come at her over the table. "Chester was his own man," she snarled. "His studies were everything to him, and I was *delighted* to be able to help him!"

And with that, Daisy had one of her answers. The anger was deep, genuine – but so was the faint tremor beneath it, a frisson of worry and guilt that, just maybe, her "help" *had* contributed to her lover's disappearance.

Which proved, so far as the librarian was concerned, that McCutcheon didn't know. She'd never discovered that, whether the relationship had later become at all real to him or not, Chester had sought her out specifically to advance his cause. If she had, the emotions wound and woven through that response would assuredly have been quite different.

Daisy found herself uncertain how to proceed. The part of her that made her living on research, on fact, insisted she tell McCutcheon the truth, rebelled at leaving the lie in place. The other, the part that remembered past times in which she'd given her own heart away unwisely, ached in sympathy with the other woman; disliked the idea of causing her further pain, of shattering the memories that were all she had left of the lover she'd lost.

And though it shamed her, she also had to contemplate which option was more likely to lead to the information they sought, which would advance their own investigation – but then, would acting based on those considerations make her any better than Chester?

Her hesitation cost her. Before Daisy could choose her next words, McCutcheon had raised a hand and waved, attracting the attention of a young waiter across the dining room. He excused himself from the fellow employee with whom he was speaking and began wending his way through the tables. Daisy, who couldn't come up with a single argument as to why McCutcheon shouldn't have them removed from the restaurant, felt disappointment welling like bile within.

Billy leaned over the table and hissed, "Chester Hennessy has been cursed!"

Well, that tears it. No chance, now, that McCutcheon would waste one more breath on them, save to have them expelled. Anger at the impulsive and frankly outlandish assertion burned in her cheeks as she made ready to rise…

"What?" Every dish and utensil on the table jerked toward McCutcheon, and Daisy realized she must have clenched her fists on the tablecloth. "What are you saying?"

"The *Ujaraanni*." He lowered his voice further, barely whispering, so that the approaching server couldn't overhear. "When he unlocked the writing on the stone, he unlocked something else, too. It drove him mad, along with dozens of others, and it hasn't finished corrupting him, twisting him. We can't say for certain if he's even alive or dead, but if he lives, he is beset, and it will only get worse – for him and all who come near him – if we don't–"

"You require something, madam?"

Four pairs of eyes turned to the waiter, and then three of them dipped toward Victoria McCutcheon, wary and waiting.

Seconds passed, until the waiter began to shift where he stood, the situation growing awkward.

"More coffee, young man," McCutcheon said almost too softly to hear. "Please."

"I… Of course, madam," he agreed, though clearly confused. "Will your friends be needing anything?"

"No, I… don't believe they'll be here long."

More time to converse was precisely what Daisy and the others needed, but she almost wanted to protest. For Billy's argument to have carried any weight with an educated, modern woman of high society… Even as a dilettante student of the occult, she couldn't possibly believe such things.

Except, based not only on her response but her sudden pallor, she so very obviously did.

Until the waiter returned with her refill, McCutcheon said nothing. Once the hot liquid was poured, she took a large, indelicate gulp. It must have been near to scalding, but she appeared not to notice. Reaching into the purse by her chair, she removed a silver flask and poured a sizable dollop of something clear and acrid-smelling into the cup to make up the difference. Daisy swallowed nervously, glancing around to see if anyone had spotted the lawbreaking that had just blatantly occurred in the middle of the restaurant, but if it had been noticed, it went unremarked.

McCutcheon proceeded to empty well over half the coffee cup in a series of quick swallows, then dabbed at her lips with a napkin.

"Tell me what happened."

Billy did, with occasional commentary from Ida. Much of the story Daisy had already heard, but the Kalaaleq delved into details here he'd never so much as hinted at previously – doubtless because he knew that the librarian would never have accepted them. He spoke not merely of the spreading madness, the power of the litany, to a degree she hadn't yet heard, but also of *physical* alterations Chester had undergone, and his apparent inability to die.

Still she felt he left out a few gruesome specifics, but the tale was complete enough.

And no matter that she knew it was rubbish, that they could not have seen what they claimed to have seen, Daisy couldn't entirely repress a shudder. Billy and Ida were confident they spoke nothing but unvarnished truth, she could see that in their expressions, hear it in their tone. McCutcheon was equally convinced; her hands shook as she clutched the cup, and though her cheeks were no longer pale, the only color they held was the redness caused by the potent spirits in her drink.

It was enough to start just the faintest crack running through Daisy's own bastion of doubt. Not enough to make her believe, but enough that she could not quite dismiss the tiny, burrowing worms of "What if?"

McCutcheon once again raised her napkin, this time to blot away a wayward tear. "I never thought… There's always danger in unearthing forgotten things, learning of the old powers, and I knew something must have gone wrong when he disappeared, but I didn't…" Another dab of the napkin. "If I'd any idea something like this could happen to Chester, I would never have helped him. Never."

She went on, before any of the others could speak. "I spend very little time in that world, you understand? I make a… poor student, and I never meant to be anything more. It was fascinating to get a peek behind the curtain, that's all. But I know people, people part of the Silv… part of brotherhoods and orders who take these things far more seriously. Even some who claim to be part of witch cults older than Arkham!

"I don't know if I ever believed them, but it didn't matter. I didn't want to know more. I was happy where I was. Even happier when I realized my position meant I could help Chester with his work."

She paused long enough to finish the last of her coffee. She half-raised a hand to signal for yet another cup, then seemed to think better and dropped it to her lap.

"I asked them for help," she confessed. "When Chester had been gone a week or so. I thought, if he'd run into trouble delving into… into matters he shouldn't, perhaps those who studied that same lore could tell me something. Or maybe, if even a bit of it was true, *really* true, they might have… other means of finding him. Methods the police would never know existed.

"They agreed to help, at first. But only a few days later, they reneged. Told me they weren't to get involved, that Chester had nothing to do with them. I… said some things that cost me friends I could ill afford to lose, but none of them would budge. One let slip that the decision was made by someone from out of town, though why anyone in the Arkham occult community should care to listen to an outsider is beyond me."

Something about that rang a very faint bell of familiarity, though Daisy couldn't say why and hadn't the spare attention to devote to it just now. She found herself caught up in the implications of the woman's story. She knew Arkham had more than its share of occultists, of secret societies, but that there were apparently so many who were such fervent believers they would accept a tale like McCutcheon's… It made her wonder how much she truly understood about the town she called home.

"I think…" McCutcheon's eyes, which had gone blurry with unshed tears and the effects of drink, steadied for an instant. "I think they were afraid. I think they were instructed to stay away by someone they didn't dare disobey." She seemed to go fuzzy again. "I realize how paranoid that sounds…"

Did it? Daisy wasn't sure any more.

She *was* sure, however, that the conversation was nearing its end. That the woman had finally shared a guilt, a burden, she'd long carried – her tongue loosened by fear for Chester and by alcohol – but had little more to say.

So she asked the most pressing question, the one for which they'd sought out the twice-bereft widow in the first place.

"How did Chester get his hands on the stone? On the *Pnakotic Fragments*? How did he manage *any* of this?"

"One of my friends knew a man who could help him. She introduced him to Chester – and then later to me, when I was looking for connections to help me *find* Chester."

"Yes? And who was that?"

"His name was Jebediah Pembroke," said McCutcheon.

They'd convinced her to dig into her address book and scribble out the information they needed before retreating from the restaurant and leaving her to her lonely meal. For the journey back across town to her home near the university, other than her instructions to the taxicab driver, Daisy had remained silent. Even after going upstairs, getting settled in, filling Elliot in on the basics of what they'd learned – while still avoiding the less pleasant revelations regarding Chester – she'd allowed Billy to do the talking.

It was only after a good half hour, when everyone had grown weary but remained too energized over the new revelations to take to their beds, that she finally made her decision, and her announcement.

"I'm sorry," Elliot said softly, disbelievingly, sprawled across half the sofa. "You want us to what?"

He'd been half-dozing, while Ida had her face buried in the mystery she'd borrowed off the shelf and Billy played dominoes against himself on the coffee table.

Now he was wide awake, the others paying complete attention as well.

"I said," Daisy repeated, as she stepped to the table, digging in her purse, "I'll need all of you to leave come the morning."

Still Elliot appeared to be the only one willing to speak. "I don't understand. I thought we–"

"You're well enough now, Elliot. It won't hurt you. You have your room, Billy and Ida can easily take lodgings." She gestured toward the steamer trunk they'd taken from the Hennessy household. "You can take that with you, or I can hold it until you're prepared to return home. And, of course, you can still access the library, through Elliot. I'll help you find anything you need there."

"Then why…?"

Daisy carefully lay a scrap of folded paper on the table and slid it across. Billy opened it to reveal the address they'd acquired at Salton and Lindall's.

"I'm through," she told them. "Finished, with all of this. I'm truly sorry, but I have to be. I've already taken risks, not only with my own wellbeing, but others' as well. I *cannot* be seen dealing with a trafficker in black market artifacts. Not in any capacity, not by anyone. If so much as a *rumor* were to spread that we were dealing with Pembroke, the damage to Miskatonic's reputation, its standing in the academic and historical worlds, would be catastrophic.

"It's why I tried to steer us to alternate avenues of investigation, back when we had any. We don't any longer, and I ... have no choices left to me."

It was the truth, but not the *entire* truth. The primary reason to extricate herself, but not the only one.

Their tales of what had happened, what they'd seen, were impossible. Utter madness, without even delving into what they *hadn't* told her. And yet ...

Yet a part of her, a very tiny part, the part that had insisted she keep the lights on after flipping through those ancient tomes, was starting to wonder. She'd begun to cast Billy and Elliot, in her own thoughts, as akin to Henry James' literary governess: a disturbed woman who imagined she saw ghosts—unless, of course, she wasn't. Unless they weren't.

Daisy, who if nothing else had to keep her head as a librarian and caretaker of the Special Collection at Miskatonic, couldn't afford to let herself slip into the flights of fear and fancy that must surely result if she ever seriously allowed herself to follow them down that path.

So she could do nothing but harden her resolve.

Elliot looked as if he wanted to cry, and she felt as though she'd just kicked a puppy out of her home. A worm of guilt writhed in her gut, trying to gnaw its way out. She desperately didn't want to do this, and would still assist them should they require any further library research, but beyond that, her responsibilities permitted no further option.

Even as she watched, Elliot's expression smoothed out as he thought it all through. "I understand," he finally told her.

"You don't, not entirely, because I haven't finished yet. I don't know everything that's happening, and I'm unsure how much I believe of what I do know." An understatement at best, that last! "But Chester is still missing, and we have a genuine lead that I cannot pursue, but I also cannot ignore. I do not want to get any of you – or anyone I work with – in trouble with the authorities, or do any harm to the university. But I also can't sit on this indefinitely if there's still even a chance of saving Chester or preventing harm to others."

"There's *no* chance of–"

She raised a hand, halting Elliot's protest. "I am giving you until the weekend to find him, or at least to find me additional reason – reason I can *believe* – to continue leaving this in your hands. If you cannot do so by then, I will have no choice but to tell the police what I know of Pembroke's connection to Chester, no matter who – or what – might be damaged."

Silence fell. Nobody cared for the ultimatum, or for the repercussions. Again, Daisy didn't like it any better, but faced with an array of nothing but bad options, she had to choose the one that felt the most right or, failing that, the least wrong. Had to obey the dictates of her conscience. She'd skirted the edges too often lately as it was.

Even when the following day had come, however, when her guests – her companions, people who could have been her friends – had gone their way, when she'd returned to her work at the Orne Library and tried to put all thoughts of mystery and investigation behind her, she still found herself wondering, with every free moment, if she was doing the right thing.

CHAPTER TWENTY-ONE

After something of a scramble the following morning – Billy once more taking a room at Ma's Boarding House, and Ida, with a few dollars of Elliot's money, doing the same – the trio were all but exhausted. Neither of the newcomers to Arkham had slept much the past two nights, and while Elliot had done little *but* rest, he found himself craving a little longer to put himself together. He might understand intellectually why Daisy decided as she had, but that didn't make him any happier about it, and while the abrupt change in accommodations wasn't difficult, it was a hassle he didn't need right now.

Thus, though they begrudged the wasted time, particularly with Daisy's deadline weighing on them, they reluctantly granted themselves the remainder of that day, and the following night, to recuperate.

Shortly before noon on the second day after leaving Daisy's flat, they assembled in Ma Mathison's dining room for an early luncheon. All three looked to be in a healthier state than they had been, though only some of that was due to the extra rest; the remainder from the opportunity to thoroughly clean up and change into freshly laundered clothes.

It was a somber and subdued meal. Planning had neither taken long nor accomplished much. As none of them knew a lot about Pembroke, his organization, or his activities, they seemed to have little choice but to play whatever came by ear. And as none felt any desire to rehash recent events or previous speculation, they found themselves with little to talk about.

A couple of hours later, with luncheon and an equally taciturn cab ride behind them, they found themselves braving the cold drizzle and damp breeze of the Merchant District streets.

It would have been a gross exaggeration to say the neighborhood felt abandoned, and it was entirely possible that neither Ida nor Billy even noticed anything amiss. To Elliot, however, those streets were definitely underpopulated. For a weekday afternoon, foot traffic on the sidewalks was mild, the automobiles in the roadway a sporadic trickle.

Every now and again, a glance down one of the longer cross streets, during a pause in the mild but steady downpour, provided a hint as to why. In the distance, barricades and police vehicles marked the line of demarcation between the district proper and the poor warehouse and residential blocks beyond, where Arkham's authorities still worked to keep the localized outbreak of influenza from becoming an epidemic. According to the radio and the papers, they'd so far been successful, and patronizing the Merchant District posed no risk at all. Elliot could certainly sympathize, however, with any who elected not to take the chance, to put off their shopping or conduct their business elsewhere.

Here, however, was where the address McCutcheon had provided them was located, so here they must be.

Elliot and his companions found themselves before a plain brownstone, a structure that, while of more recent vintage than much of Arkham's Colonial or faux-Old World construction, was hardly new. The paint had begun to peel off the window shutters and doorframes.

He couldn't help frowning at it. "This doesn't look very like the lair of a fence and smuggler, does it?"

Ida snorted, and Billy raised an eyebrow.

Elliot flushed. "Okay, yeah. Dumb thing to say. What room?"

"2C," said Billy, who had memorized the address rather than bring the note along.

The front door led to a dim hallway with numerous smaller doors. None were open, or showed any sign of activity or even illumination through their frosted glass windows. Most didn't even name whatever enterprise they belonged to, displaying only a suite number. Those few that did provide more information had unhelpful names such as "Bellington and Windsor" or "Neidermeyer Inc."

"Business ain't boomin'," Ida observed.

A broad staircase groaned beneath them as they ascended to find a nearly identical hall above.

Billy pointed. "There. 2C."

It was one of the few doors with a business name as well as a number, though that name – West Side Rental and Storage Management, Ltd – was scratched and worn enough that one had to be right next to it to read it.

Elliot shrugged, knocked and opened the door.

There had been a time, he couldn't help but note, when this sort of thing would have had him racked with nervousness. After the past week, it barely made an emotional impact at all.

Within stood a few chairs against one wall, a rust-stained drinking fountain and a desk. Behind that desk was a door leading into another room, and the room's only occupant.

Her complexion was dark, making her bright red lipstick stand out all the more dramatically. She wore a stylish scarlet beret and a navy pantsuit, and –

other than being just a few years older – would not have looked remotely out of place among a group of Miskatonic seniors on a Friday night.

And if she was excited to see potential customers, she did a masterful job of hiding it.

"Something I can help you with?" she asked, polite but a touch cold.

"Well, yes," Elliot replied. "We'd like to see Jebediah Pembroke."

Naive he might be, but the young student wasn't a fool. He knew, before he spoke, that one probably didn't just walk in and ask to see a black marketeer by name. On the other hand, he had neither the slightest notion what the proper criminal etiquette might be, nor the patience to try to figure it out.

A sharp blink was the woman's only indication that he'd startled her. "I'm afraid there's nobody in today who can help you. If you'd like to leave a name and an address or phone number–"

Billy, it turned out, had even less patience than Elliot. "We haven't the time for games. Is he back there?" He took two steps toward the door behind her.

Something metallic clattered, the source of the sound hidden by the desk, and the woman finally stood...

An M1921 Thompson submachine gun in her hands, muzzle gaping wide, the heavy ammunition drum dangling like some monstrous growth beneath the barrel.

"He's not, and you're not going there, either."

Ida drew her Colt, dropping into a crouch. The other woman twisted to aim her way; every muscle in Elliot's body clenched as the barrel passed across him on its way toward Ida...

And Billy, too, drew a pistol. The part of Elliot that wasn't screaming recognized it as the revolver he'd carried during the horrific confrontation with Chester. He hadn't even known Billy had picked it up, let alone brought it back with him.

"Whoa, *whoa!* Everyone just... wait a minute!" Elliot kept his hands raised. "Calm down!"

Then, "Look, Miss... Uh, Miss," he continued when she didn't fill in the blank for him, "we're not here to rob you, or to hurt Mr Pembroke. Or you."

"Damn right you're not."

"Um. But I do think you should talk to us."

"And why's that?"

"Because there are lives at stake. Because something terrible may be happening – maybe even here in Arkham. And because the very best you can hope for, if everyone starts shooting, is a real ugly cleaning job."

The woman finally cracked a faint smile. "You don't scare easy, do you?"

"Are you kidding? I'm terrified. But after what we've seen in the last few days..." He shuddered, despite his best efforts. "You wouldn't believe it."

"You might be surprised what I believe, Mr Raslo."

And here he'd thought he was done being surprised for a while. "How... ?"

"Big hulking Eskimo like your friend here comes to Arkham, and suddenly people start asking around the shops about an item we... moved? Of course I've had people shadowing you. Or at least I did until you left town."

"Inuit," Billy corrected. Then, abruptly, "The man outside the hotel *was* watching me, then!"

Elliot tried to ask what in God's name he was talking about, but the woman didn't offer the opportunity.

"Yeah, and he wasn't real happy you spotted him. Neither was I." She paused, mulling something over. "All right, here's the deal. That you're here looking for Mr Pembroke already answers some questions I had, but it opens a whole lot more. So yeah, I'll talk to you – soon as you hand over your bean-shooters."

Ida and Billy both protested, but Elliot shushed them. "We need answers. Miss..."

This time she proved more forthcoming. "Bentley. Alice Bentley."

"Miss Bentley might have those answers for us. And besides, Daisy knows where we are, and she's waiting to hear from us." That last was as much for Bentley's sake as for his friends', and another quick smile suggested she well knew it.

She didn't know, of course, that Daisy didn't expect to hear from them for several days – and Elliot saw no reason to clarify.

Ida grumbling, Billy deathly silent, they handed over their pistols. Bentley put them in a drawer and slung the Tommy back under the desk. "Don't think that means I'm unarmed," she warned.

Elliot and Ida nodded. Billy – who, Elliot knew, still wore his pana beneath his coat – merely smiled in his turn.

Bentley opened the door behind her and led them into the next room. Based on its size, and the additional doors, the bulk of the floor must have actually been devoted to Pembroke's business. The other offices were facades.

Bookshelves covered most of the open walls, containing both rare tomes and modern ledgers. Here and there were a variety of old statues, bits of jewelry, bronze weapons – tiny relics of a dozen cultures that had presumably caught Pembroke's fancy.

Again, Elliot yearned for simpler times when he'd have had the energy to be fascinated. Though he couldn't help but think, with a touch of amusement, at the collective apoplexy the staff at Miskatonic's museum would have over it all.

Their host directed them to a table in front of one of the bookcases, and the chairs surrounding it. Elliot and Ida sat, but Billy crossed his arms and glared.

"Does it bother you even a little that you're dealing in treasures and sacred objects stolen from any number of–"

"No. I've never stolen anything, and if anyone wants to come to me with the proper provenances to prove ownership, I'll be happy to make them a good deal." With that, she joined the others around the table.

Growling softly, Billy finally did the same.

Elliot decided to go first. "Your boss won't mind you talking to us?"

"I don't know. I'll be sure to ask if I ever find him."

His companions were taken aback. Elliot was not. He hadn't quite expected that answer, not consciously, but he realized he wasn't shocked.

"You said 'I,'" he commented. "*I* had someone following you."

Bentley nodded. "Mr Pembroke disappeared a couple weeks ago. And he was acting oddly before that. Preoccupied."

Elliot briefly squeezed his eyes shut. He didn't much approve of Pembroke, but he wouldn't wish what he knew must have happened on anyone. Even worse, that made the missing smuggler another possible point of origin for an outbreak of the maddening refrain.

"A couple weeks ago." Not too long after Chester. It almost had to be connected, didn't it?

"When I caught wind of…" Now it was her turn to pause. "Your name I was able to dig up, Mr Raslo. Your friends' eluded me."

"Mr Shiwak and Miss Glick."

"Well. When I learned Mr Shiwak was in Arkham, looking for the *Ujaraanni*, and the rest of you asking around about the boss's newest client, I thought maybe you'd done something to him. That's why I had you all followed. Once you came in here looking for him, though, I guessed I could rule that out."

Newest client. "You mean Chester," Elliot breathed.

The woman paused, her professional – and doubtless habitual – caution flaring, but nodded. "Chester Hennessy. Yes."

Finally. *Finally* it might all be coming together. Elliot struggled to focus on that, and not on the torment shooting through him at each mention of Chester's name.

"That's why you're helping us. To try to find Pembroke."

"So far, I'm only talking to you. We haven't agreed on 'helping' yet. But yes, that's partly why."

"And the other part?"

She didn't answer, instead saying, "You're a close friend of Hennessy's, I understand."

"I… yeah. I am."

Bentley scowled in what appeared to be disapproval. "Your friend isn't good at this sort of thing, Mr Raslo. May be sharp when it comes to his studies, but a real sap. Maybe if he'd been wiser, none of this would have…" She trailed off, gazing at the table, the first time since they'd walked in the door that Elliot had seen her anything but confident.

A few minutes of conversation confirmed what Elliot and the others had already pieced together: that one of Victoria McCutcheon's high society friends had introduced Chester to Pembroke, and the former had then employed the latter to acquire both the *Ujaraanni* and whatever relevant bits of the *Pnakotic Fragments* he might manage to unearth. Due to the infamy of the theft from the University of Virginia, acquiring the stone proved relatively simple. The *Fragments*, however, were far more challenging, and indeed the acquisition had only been made possible by the sheer quantity of money Chester had been willing to throw at the problem.

Every time Elliot thought he'd finally gotten a handle on Chester's obsession, he somehow managed to discover it had been even more consuming than he'd thought.

"That was his mistake," Alice told them. "You just don't toss around sums like that willy-nilly. Mr Pembroke's never outright cheated a client, least not that I know of, but he knew immediately this was something big. A lot bigger than some rich boy's whim, and a *whole* lot more valuable.

"I'm not sure what his end goal was, if he just wanted to squeeze a little more money from Hennessy. Or maybe he figured, if he could learn the whole picture, he could sell information about the kid's discovery. He started looking into everything Hennessy was doing, coaxing more details out of him. He lent the kid one of his rooms – Mr Pembroke owns several properties, flophouses and warehouses – to keep the stone, to do some of his studies."

Another piece clicked into place in Elliot's head. That must be where Chester had stored the *Ujaraanni* – and hidden himself, as well, after his disappearance – before eventually sheltering at his uncle's home.

"He took every opportunity to sneak looks at Hennessy's notes, to study the *Ujaraanni*. He even snuck into the Miskatonic museum to examine some other related piece."

Elliot was starting to have trouble buying this. "Wait a minute. Chester spent months, maybe years, on this, and he was a linguist. I'm sure your boss was a clever guy, but there's no way–"

For his troubles, he earned a return appearance of Alice's hard, cold visage from earlier. "What do you think we do here, Mr Raslo? You figure we just scoop up a bunch of pretties and try to hock them off like some street-corner pawnbroker?"

"Uh…"

"Jebediah Pembroke knows more about the objects he deals in than most of your professors, and he's taught me … maybe not *everything* he knows, but more than enough that I've had no troubles running the business without him. He's an expert in the historical and the occult. So no, he could never have worked out the specifics or the acoustical translations on his own, but he was more than capable of following Hennessy's work."

"I… Of course. My apologies."

"Yeah." Again Alice bowed her head. "Actually, I wish you were right. I wish he hadn't been able. I don't know if he meant to beat Hennessy to the discovery, or sell what he'd learned, or… what. But he vanished not long after Hennessy did.

"So, your turn. What's *happening* out there? And don't tell me I won't believe it."

They told her, or rather Elliot and Billy told her. Ida, perhaps troubled at the notion of revisiting what had happened to her home and her community, once more retreated into her own thoughts. She seemed not to hear a word that was spoken, let alone contribute one.

By the end, Alice gawped at them in horror – but not, much to Elliot's surprise, disbelief.

"Dear Jesus. Jebediah and I, we've come across a few curses in our time, had to rely on protective charms and such, but I've never heard of *anything* like this. Least not quite…"

"Not quite?" Billy repeated.

Alice dithered a moment, then rose and left the room. When she returned, she carried a small stack of old, musty, leather-bound tomes. Had she been present, Daisy Walker would doubtless have been horrified to find them locked away in a private collection, let alone that of a criminal.

Rather than opening any one of them, however, Alice instead drew a scrap of paper, covered in neat handwriting, from between two of the texts. "There's… a language. One that's referenced in more than a few of these books. A specific sentence, if you'd even care to call it that, appears more often than any other."

She cleared her throat, loudly, something Elliot dismissed as a bit of an affectation – until she began to read. Only then did he realize their host had been preparing herself for what could only be a flawed attempt at an impossible utterance.

"*Ph'nglui mglw'nafh Cthulhu R'lyeh wgah'nagl fhtagn.*"

It was ugly, discordant; a snarly, phlegmy thing, grating on the ears, and assuredly on the throat. Elliot flinched, and saw that his friends had reacted similarly.

"What in God's name is that?" he demanded.

Alice frowned. "So that's not how your litany sounded?"

"No! It's…" He struggled for a description, a task made even more difficult by his refusal to think too heavily on the phrases. "The litany is just as alien, but less inhuman. If that's not a contradiction."

"Huh. I don't know if that's a good thing or not." She laid the paper aside and put a hand on the books. "I've read through many of these in my time working with Mr Pembroke, and I've studied several in more detail in the past weeks."

"Felt in the mood for some light reading?" Billy muttered.

"I'm no fool, Mr Shiwak. The boss told me of Hennessy's odd behavior before he vanished, and then he showed the same before *he* disappeared. I knew something unnatural was happening long before you three showed up at my door. I thought I might try to figure out what, but I never came up with much.

"And the language I just read to you is the only one I can't identify that appears regularly in any of these. If it's not the one you're speaking of, I'm afraid none of this…" She thumped the pile lightly, "…is liable to help."

"We should check the *Pnakotic Fragments*," Billy suggested. Then, after several startled glances cast his way, "What? I may not know these writings, but that was the one Chester consulted to transliterate the *Ujaraanni*, was it not?"

"Unfortunately," Alice said, "I don't have access to anything older than an abbreviated English translation of the *Pnakotic Manuscripts*. It took every connection Pembroke had to locate the *Fragments* he sold to Hennessy."

Elliot scratched nervously at his wrist. "We don't need someone willing to part with them, though. Only someone who could help us learn more about what's in them. Does that change anything?"

"You know, it just might." Again Alice rose from her seat. "I have Mr Pembroke's client list. Some of them have private libraries like you would never believe. I'll make some calls." She cast them a mirthless grin. "I hope you're comfortable. This will probably take some time."

"Some time" had stretched itself to four hours, and still counting. Alice Bentley had completed her phone calls in the next room and then rejoined the others after the first hour, and the rest had been spent waiting for assistance she assured them was on the way. The trio briefly discussed the possibility that they might be wasting their time, and any "help" she conjured might prove useless. In the end, however, they had no other real options.

Elliot napped in his chair, head slumped down and – he would have been mortified to know – drooling lightly on his lapel. Ida had attempted to lose herself in one of the modern, non-artifact books the room provided, in this case a treatise on the Massachusett nation, the indigenous people of the region. For a while now, though, she'd simply sat, scarcely blinking, her reading apparently forgotten. She might as well have been as deeply asleep as Elliot.

Which left Billy, his own thoughts awhirl and still seasoned with resentful anger, alone with his host in hostile silence.

A silence he finally elected to break, though he kept his voice low in order not to awaken his friend.

"Do you ever plan to tell us the truth?"

She looked as if she'd forgotten he was present at all. "I'm sorry?"

"The truth. Of why you're assisting us."

"Mr Pembroke–"

Billy snorted. "Mr Pembroke is almost certainly mad, either infected by Hennessy or from his own unwise reading of the *Ujaraanni*. And that assumes he's even alive. If he confronted the madmen, or tracked the boy to his uncle's home, he very well might not be. In either case, there's no guarantee we'll ever learn what happened to him, and if we *do* run into him, we may well be forced to kill him. And I believe you're smart enough to be aware of all that."

"That doesn't mean I don't have hope," she insisted.

"You also said as much, that it wasn't your only motive. Elliot may have forgotten that. I have not."

"Oh, I don't know. Maybe I'd prefer not to see a plague of unnatural lunacy unleashed on Arkham?" She, too, spoke softly, but a growing exasperation rang clear all the same.

"I see. Out of the kindness of your heart, is it?"

Alice sucked in a breath between her teeth. "Just because you think so poorly of me–"

"With good reason!"

"–does not mean it's so. I've no desire to see anyone hurt who doesn't need to be."

"No, you're content to hurt them in ways you *can't* see!"

She stood, fists clenched, and paced to the door, but turned back rather than reach for the latch. "I've seen the aftermath of curses far less severe than the one you've spoken of, and I've no wish to see anything of the sort again. Believe what you like. If it helps, you can assume I'm simply protecting myself and my business."

Billy's expression was less a smile than a baring of teeth. "Yours, is it? Hoping Pembroke's gone for good?"

"Go to hell, Shiwak."

"Wha's goin' on?" Only half awakened by the exchange, Elliot spoke as through a mouthful of cotton.

"A cultural exchange," their host sneered, "with your Eskimo friend."

"Inuit," Elliot and Billy corrected in unison.

Alice snarled and dropped back into her chair.

Perhaps alert enough to sense the tension, Elliot changed the subject. "Would you be so good as to tell us who we're waiting on?"

"One of Mr Pembroke's most important clients," she answered, sullen at first but swiftly regaining her composure. "One of the most discerning collectors I've ever met, and a man of some renown in occult circles. You're fortunate he's even in Arkham just now."

"Oh? He's not from here?"

"No. Louisiana. A small town outside New Orleans, if I'm not mistaken."

Elliot sat upright, now fully awake, and Billy felt his brow furrow.

"Mean something to you?" she asked.

"The client Daisy mentioned?" Elliot wondered aloud.

Billy nodded. "And McCutcheon said her occultist friends were told to stay out of things by someone from out of town…"

"Well, now." It came over the sound of the door opening, in a rich Southern drawl thicker than Arkham's infamous fogs. "I do believe my ears are burnin'."

Everyone stared, though Alice seemed more surprised than anyone. Billy wondered what safeguards she had in place that were supposed to have alerted her when someone entered the outer office, let alone the inner rooms.

The man in the doorway didn't appear to match the voice at all – and Billy realized swiftly that, in fact, he wasn't the source. The first figure wore the formal suit and cap of a professional chauffeur, and kept his gaze turned to the floor, his face partly obscured. After opening the door he stepped aside, allowing another fellow to enter before returning to the outer chamber.

It was this other man, presumably the employer of the first, who had spoken. "Good evenin', my friends. Hyrum Lafayette-Moses, at your service."

Chapter Twenty-Two

Elliot knew he was staring, knew it might come across as rude. He couldn't help himself, and his companions seemed to be waging the same inner struggle. Something about this man *commanded* attention.

Lafayette-Moses was tall, thin without being gaunt; an older man, perhaps a very healthy sixty. The hair on his head was silver, as opposed to the salt-and-pepper mix of his goatee. The charcoal suit he wore cost more than many people's entire wardrobe, and he walked with a cane – probably an affectation, as his steps appeared surefooted enough.

In every way, to Elliot's mind, the very picture of an Old Family southern gentleman.

"Miss Bentley tells me I might be of some small assistance here," he continued, approaching the table. "And I'm quite happy to oblige. Why, I'd feel just awful if somethin' happened to dear Jebediah and I hadn't done everythin' in my power to help."

Elliot found his gaze drawn with an almost magnetic pull to the walking stick. The round head of the cane was made of black glass, perhaps obsidian, but sported an array of white and silver flecks within. It resembled nothing so much as a small piece scooped from the night sky.

And the fingers clasped around it… They were long, thin, swift. The fingers of a pianist, perhaps, or a surgeon.

Or a conjurer.

The nails were perfect, evenly manicured, almost reflective. All save the one on Lafayette-Moses's left ring finger, which was absent entirely. It didn't even appear to have been removed: the finger simply bore a flat and featureless expanse of skin, without even a bed to mark where it should have been.

As the table was a chair short, the newcomer snapped his fingers. His chauffeur appeared almost instantly carrying a chair from the outer office, as though he'd already known what was required. He placed it halfway between the table and the door, then departed once more. Lafayette-Moses seated himself, hands folded atop his cane.

"Tell me, my friends, what it is you require."

And just as before, Elliot, with a bit of assistance from Billy, told their tale. All of it. He hadn't intended to, had meant to gloss over the more personal or uncomfortable details, omit the bits he expected most listeners to discount as sheer nonsense, but somehow it all emerged. It required conscious effort to avoid revealing even the details of his feelings for Chester, something he would never even *consider* sharing under most circumstances.

Only when it was done did Elliot wonder, with a vaguely sick feeling, precisely *why* he'd been so forthcoming.

The peculiar old outsider said nothing at all until the recitation was complete – and when he finally did, it was the last thing Elliot expected to hear.

"You're a student of the mind, Mr Raslo?"

"I... Sorry, what?" Had the man listened to a single word he'd said?

"The human mind. Your field of study?"

Bewildered, Elliot nodded. "I'm a student of psychology, yes."

"Thought so!" Lafayette-Moses rocked back with a smile, almost an aborted cackle. "I could tell that about you. How you speak, how you think. Your thoughts," and here he abruptly grew serious once more, "on the refrain in your head and the dreams you've been having."

His fingers flexed in unison atop his cane, a butterfly slowly fanning its wings.

"You did well to master that protective incantation of the *Livre d'Ivon*. Not an easy thing to do. I'm impressed. Tell me, are you a man of faith as well?"

Elliot was starting to feel dizzy.

And Billy, apparently, impatient. "Mr Lafayette-Moses, time is something of a–"

The old man's head came about faster than a shot, startling even the unflappable hunter, and the jovial charm drained from him equally quickly. "We'll get to you, Mr Shiwak."

Back to Elliot, back to his subtle smile. Somewhat offended on his friend's behalf, the student elected not to answer, not to play along with this any further – except he was already replying before he'd fully made that decision.

"I mean, I was raised a good Christian, and I suppose I believe. It's not much a part of my life, though."

"No, I don't suppose it is. Doesn't mean much to a lot of folks these days. But to others... Oh, to others... Such as your friend here." He waved toward Billy, with no trace of his former hostility. "The Inuit are *fierce* believers, are you not?"

"I wouldn't say we believe," the hunter replied cautiously. "We *know*. We know what shares this world with us, and what dwells in the other, and we fear."

"Oh, but you don't know, my friend. You only think you do. You're right to fear, though."

Lafayette-Moses leaned back in his chair, laying his cane across his lap.

"There are some who still remember gods older than your spirits," he said to Billy, "or your Jehovah in his Heaven," he continued to Elliot, Ida, and Alice.

"You have more than a few here in Massachusetts, in Arkham. You call them 'witch cults,' or think them the primitive superstitions of backwoods yokels. And I suppose that's all some of them are. But only some."

He pointed the obsidian head of his cane across the table at their host. "She knows, if she's paid attention to what Mr Pembroke sells, and to whom. If she's read half as much as she claims. Have you, Miss Bentley?"

She took a deep breath – almost reluctantly, Elliot thought – and once more placed a hand on the stack of tomes she'd produced earlier. "Some of these do speak of cults, yes. Many long gone, but others that, from what I've learned, may survive even today. Not simple religious sects, splintered from Christianity or Islam or whatever pagan faiths you like. They venerate… things. Terrible things that make any conception of Satan and his hosts pale."

Elliot felt a chill, as though the unseasonable weather outside had crept through the closed doors. Alice's words weren't especially frightening of them-selves – he knew humanity had concocted a great many peculiar and even nightmarish beliefs in its time. Today, though, in light of all he'd experienced, and in the presence of the ever-more-disturbing Mr Hyrum Lafayette-Moses, the notion felt far more plausible.

More real.

"What things, Miss Bentley?" the old man pressed, somewhere between a demanding professor and a zealous inquisitor. "Whom do they serve?"

Her posture screamed that she'd no desire to answer, but just as Elliot had felt before, she seemed compelled to respond. "They… appear to have different forms. So many titles. Imprisoned in the far reaches of our world, or our uni-verse, or even 'Outside,' but always lurking at the threshold, ready to cross over at the proper call.

"Some I've only found obliquely described so far. I'm sure their names can be found somewhere in these books, but I've not had access to full translations. The Black Goat of the Woods. The Crawling Chaos. The Dreaming Priest." She swallowed, as though merely speaking of them had parched her tongue. "But I don't know if any of those mean anything to most of you, or if what Hennessy dug up is related to any of these sects…"

"Stop it!" Elliot didn't remember standing, and now that he had, he couldn't say why he'd had so vehement a reaction. It just all felt… dangerous.

The old man raised an eyebrow. "Stop what, Mr Raslo? We're simply havin' a conversation, establishin' some basic facts. You did ask for my help, after all."

Slowly, Elliot sat. Beside him, Alice nervously scraped a fingernail over the spine of one of the books, tracing the title etched into the leather.

"That why you asked about these cults?" Ida asked. Elliot jumped, having once again all but forgotten her presence thanks to her prolonged silence. *She must be having a harder time dealing with her grief than I'd realized.* "You figure the litany's related to one of 'em somehow?"

"It's not impossible. More than a few worshipers of the Ancient Ones are driven mad by the secrets they learn, or the horrors they witness."

All right, Elliot thought, that made some sense. It wasn't identical to the effect they'd seen, but similar enough.

"So," Lafayette-Moses continued, "let us see what answers we can unearth together."

Again he snapped his fingers, and again his servant appeared in the doorway. This time he carried a small wooden box, polished smooth, without adornment or decoration but for a single iron latch. He carefully handed it to his master, then stood at his shoulder rather than retreating.

"The *Pnakotic Fragments*." Lafayette-Moses sounded near rapturous. "Not complete, of course. So many remain undiscovered, perhaps long destroyed, or survive as but a single copy in the hands of others. Still, I think you'll find few collections in the world, if any, as comprehensive as my own."

He leaned his cane against the chair, straightened the box in his lap and flipped the latch with a dramatic flourish.

The scent of old parchment wafted across the room, but what first emerged were several papers of far more modern vintage. These Lafayette-Moses handed to his driver to hold, save for a single sheet, which he kept.

"Now, Mr Raslo, I realize this is likely to make you uncomfortable, and I do apologize, but I'm afraid I'll need to hear a bit of your litany."

"You can't! The infection—"

"Now, son, I was hardly born yesterday. As I said, you did well to make use of even a simple incantation, but let me show you a little of what a true adept can do."

He began to read, then, from the paper he'd retained – or rather, to recite, referencing the writing only occasionally, perhaps to jog a memory. The words were Latin, and carried the cadence of ritual, but this was nothing ever heard within the walls of any proper church. Elliot's education had afforded him only a passing familiarity with the ancient tongue; Chester would doubtless have known what it all meant, but Elliot could interpret only a word here and there.

Yet even without understanding, he sensed its effects. He felt as if he'd been wrapped in something... not constraining but comforting, like a swaddling blanket. The constant infernal echo at the back of his skull grew as quiet as it had ever been since the moment he'd been exposed.

Having reached the end, Lafayette-Moses reverted to English. "Every one of us in this room is protected," he declared. "Not for very long, but most assuredly long enough for you to tell me what I need to hear."

Apprehensive still, Elliot looked to his friends. Ida offered him a shrug, as if she could only just be bothered to care, and Billy a slow nod. Taking a deep, steadying breath, he began.

"*Isslaach thkulkris, isslaach cheoshash* ... Uh ..."

How peculiar. He'd heard the rest of it, numerous times, while under other protections. Now that he tried to bring it to mind, however, he found he could recall only that first phrase, the part that had genuinely infected him. As if the words, unable to take root as they intended, had instead slipped away entirely.

"*Vn… Vnosh?* No, that's not right…"

The old man waved a dismissal. "Not to worry, Mr Raslo. That's enough."

"It is?" Alice dubiously asked the question they were all thinking.

"Oh, yes." His pupils unfocused, delving deep into remembered lore. "That tongue… It's the language of one of the last of the antehuman races."

Alice's jaw dropped, but the others expressed only bewilderment.

"Peoples," Lafayette-Moses explained, "or somethin' like peoples, who walked the Earth before man. This one, in particular… Not reptilian, precisely, but more akin to reptiles than to us. Some few survived long enough to live alongside our first ancestors, and they taught us things. Secrets. Writin's. Magics. Tells me where to start lookin', at least." His fingers darted once more to the box.

Stunned silence wafted through the room like a cold breeze. Elliot looked to each of the others in turn, as if desperately seeking one expression of disbelief, some measure of doubt he could cling to.

He found none. Alice and Billy stared back at him, while Ida gazed at nothing at all. Outlandish as it was, they believed every word. So did he.

He wished he didn't.

"Do you, um, need the table?" their host asked. She sounded hesitant, a reticence Elliot shared. He didn't want the strange visitor any nearer than he already was.

Lafayette-Moses, however, shook his head, then reached out a hand and retrieved the other papers from his chauffeur. Finally, he pointed down at his feet. Without hesitation, the servant dropped to all fours, back held straight. His master placed the box on him as if he were nothing more than a piece of furniture, and began to shuffle through it.

Elliot swallowed a surge of revulsion.

The occultist sorted thick sheets of yellowed parchment almost like a deck of cards, scanning and dismissing. Despite his alacrity, the care he took with the old, crackling material was clear.

"Yes, here we are. Most of the rites and invocations in that tongue are wards and bindin's, shared to protect us and them from forces fearful to both races. They formed some of the very first foundations of humanity's sorceries. Tell me, Mr Raslo, did you see anythin' in these dreams of yours that might help us narrow it down?"

So Elliot once more began revealing to this disturbing stranger intimate details he'd prefer to have held close to his chest. The ice. The screams. The terrible, impossible limbs formed of the mad, and the partial disintegration of his own form.

To each element the other nodded, then asked Billy more of the history and myth behind the *Ujaraanni*, absorbing those answers as well. Until, with a final burst of sorting through the scraps and fragments before him…

"Yes. It's here. A power, a monstrosity, a spirit, a god. An entity formed in part of unearthly matter, but also, in part, a being of *notion*. Of idea. It awoke from within the fears of a people already beset by nature and by angry spirits, and it stretched forth its grasping tendrils from horizon to horizon, through the clouds of storm above and the clouds of nightmare within.

"They called it the Fetid Thought. The Weaver of Flesh. The Thousandfold Dream. But even the *Pnakotic Fragments* don't give its name…"

"Tsocathra." Elliot hadn't meant to speak; it just came out. Yet now that it had, he knew, though he'd never heard it as part of the litany or from any living mouth, though it had come to him only as he emerged from his own terrible dreams. "Its name is Tsocathra."

If anyone wondered how he knew, they chose not to ask. Perhaps they had reached the point, as he had, of taking much of what they learned on faith.

"Well. Tsocathra, then."

"Was this vile toornaq imprisoned in the *Ujaraanni*?" Billy demanded. He leaned sharply forward in his chair, as though straining toward the answers he sought. "Or in the Lindegaard Stele? These ancient, 'antehuman' magics were meant to bind it somehow?"

The occultist glanced again at the parchment, frowning at ragged holes in the material where whole sections were missing.

"To bind it, yes," he answered eventually. "But not in the stone, not precisely. Oh, perhaps that was their intention, but the ancients failed to comprehend Tsocathra's nature. Part physical, remember, and part thought.

"The Old One was not bound in your *Ujaraanni*, Mr Shiwak. He was not bound *by* the spell, but *in* the spell. In the writin's etched into the rock. In the symbols. In the *sounds*."

Elliot choked, which turned into a full-on coughing fit that took minutes of reddened cheeks and streaming eyes to overcome. The words in his head… Shards, seeds, of Tsocathra itself! He felt nauseous, even violated, and had to repress an urge to slam his skull into the wall in a desperate hope to purge the intrusion.

Only after he'd recovered, and Alice had produced a glass of water for him, did he nod weakly for Lafayette-Moses to resume.

"Some of this they learned when those who were meant to guard the great stone fell victim to the madness you've seen for yourselves – to the madness, and worse. The rest, speculation of their greatest wise men and sorcerers.

"Those who read the carved words became obsessed with them, repeatin' them, and that repetition tainted others. Their thoughts, their very dreams, slowly replaced by the essence of somethin' they could never hope to comprehend. If the source lived long enough, infected enough, he'd start to… change, his body growin' as corrupted as his mind. And if ever *enough* minds were tainted, and if even one among them had the *whole* litany in his head…"

"Tsocathra," Elliot whispered helplessly. "Reborn."

"Just so, I'm afraid. Only in a physical body, at first, sculpted and molded of the madmen who'd fallen to the litany, absorbed and remade. But eventually, given the time, and the minds, and the flesh… A *full* awakenin'. A complete transformation. And the Old One would walk the Earth again, in all his unnatural glory."

Elliot found his head between his knees as he struggled not to vomit. Ida, who seemed fully engaged for the first time in a while, leaned over to place a hand on his shoulder.

"How…" Alice struggled with the words. "You said some of the guardians were corrupted. How could they have stopped this? How did they contain…?" She seemed unwilling to utter the name.

"If I'm understandin' this correctly, Miss Bentley, the litany can only spread so far from the source. A can infect B, can infect C… But once you get to, I don't know, E or F or thereabouts, it cannot continue. The words lose their power."

The young student straightened, casting a meaningful glance at Billy and Ida. That, at least, explained why her brother, and some of the others, had proved harmless.

But Lafayette-Moses wasn't finished. "Accordin' to this, anyone infected by the source, by the writin' on the stone, was lost. Anyone else, though, if they could be isolated from anyone else tainted for long enough – months, maybe more – might recover. Without reinforcement, or the chance to spread, it just might fade away on its own."

"Wh- What?" Everything else in the world, everything fell away from Elliot then. Everything but a single thought. *This might end!* He might, one day, be himself once more.

"Says so right here. I won't lie to you, Mr Raslo, the odds are grim indeed. Maybe one out of five, one out of six, ever convalesced. But I do believe that's better than nothin'."

It was, indeed. A slim chance, but it was hope.

A sudden clatter, a chair falling to the floor as its occupant retreated from the table, and then the room filled with a piercing scream, a wail of purest agony and despair.

Ida writhed in the corner, fingers clenched in her hair, yanking several tufts out by bloody roots. Still shrieking, she fell with bruising force to her knees, and finally the throat-rending howl devolved into a series of body-racking sobs.

Oh, merciful God. Elliot was at her side in an instant, trying to hold her, but she shoved him away in a mindless flail. He could do nothing but stand over her, helplessly staring, crying in sympathy.

"Oh, dear," Lafayette-Moses sighed from his seat, shaking his head. "How many of her people did you say she shot? How many of her kin?"

Billy crouched before her. "You couldn't have known, Ida." Elliot wouldn't have believed the implacable hunter could sound so gentle. "And even if you had, you had no choice. We would all of us be dead or insane if you'd not done what you did."

Her weeping didn't stop, but it grew softer, her breathing less ragged, more controlled. This time, when Elliot gingerly reached out, she let herself be held, then guided tenderly back to the table. He placed his own glass of water, only half-emptied, before her. It seemed to be all he could do.

"This must be why the *Ujaraanni* wound up with my people," Billy said after a brief lull. "And no doubt the rest of the stone with others of a similar bent. People who would honor the power within, guard against it – but lacked the knowledge to read it. So the Thousandfold Dream could never come again."

The old man began carefully laying the sheets back in the box. "Indeed so. And it does appear to have been effective. Until now."

"Yes, but 'now' is what we're dealing with," Alice pointed out. "So what do we do? Destroy the stones? Scratch out the writing?"

"I can't say that *that's* a wise idea. It might work, or it might undo the bindin' completely. There's no way to know. Whatever split the *Ujaraanni* and the stele in two, it cracked between the lines, didn't disturb any of them, so we've got nothin' to go on. We've gotta figure there's a reason nobody tried that way back when, and I don't think I'd care to gamble somethin' of this severity on a coin toss."

Elliot actually chuckled. "Yeah, that would've been way too easy." He paused, worrying at his lower lip. "Magic?" he ventured. Even after everything, he sounded silly saying it out loud. "My invocation and Billy's talismans held the litany at bay, for a while, anyway. And you seem to have access to much more powerful, um, spells."

"Oh, son, you flatter me. I can access some potent rituals, sure enough, but the spell that bound Tsocathra was one of the mightiest sorceries ever worked by an entire race. There aren't many in the world today who can rival my mastery of the old secrets, and what you're askin' would be beyond all of us together.

"Which does not mean," he added, "that I can't teach you some invocations of use, Mr Raslo. There are spells, far more complex than anythin' you've yet seen, that might just do you good. The protections you've been usin', and your friend's talismans? They buy you time, but they don't improve your odds. With my instruction, you are far more likely to recover from your unfortunate affliction."

"I…" The temptation almost reduced him once more to tears. "That wouldn't help us with Tsocathra, though."

"No, it would not. You might best be served by simply getting' as far from here as you can before it all goes to hell. What do you think, son? You've got a mind for this."

Elliot was already shaking his head in refusal, though it tore at him. "I can't just abandon my home. My friends." *Nor do I want anything more to do with the occult, or ancient tomes, or spells and magic and "Ancient Ones." And even if I did, creepy and callous as you've seemed tonight, I couldn't even begin to trust you!*

"Well, that's a shame." A flick of the fingers, and Lafayette-Moses held a printed business card. He lifted the box, allowing his chauffeur to rise. With no apparent stiffness from the awkward position, the servant took the card, stepped over to Elliot, and slid it into the student's coat pocket. "In case you should change your mind," the old man said as the chauffeur returned to his side. "Before somethin' else changes it for you, I hope."

"You're all making this more complicated than it is." Billy, who had remained standing since they'd returned Ida to her seat, meaningfully reached under his coat and drew his snow knife. "This creature hasn't risen yet. We still face a collection of violent lunatics, or at worst, if the tales are true, an entity of flesh. And a thing of flesh can die."

"Can it?" Elliot asked. "We initially thought Chester was…" He didn't finish. It still hurt to say.

"We'll have to be more thorough." *As though it were that simple.* "But you heard Mr Lafayette-Moses. The… amalgamation… only happens if at least one of the corrupted knows the entire litany, directly from the stones. Without them, even if we cannot undo the damage already done, we limit how far the litany can spread, and we prevent something far worse from following. Right now, we know that means either Mr Hennessy or Mr Pembroke."

"You're talking about deliberately hunting down a man and killing him." Elliot began to pace, stopped himself, realized that instead he was all but vibrating in place. "Not in self-defense, but deliberate, cold-blooded murder!"

"Yes. I am. It's unpleasant, and if you've a better notion, by all means, now's the time."

He didn't, and a desperate casting about revealed only grim faces, told him no one else had, either.

The notion sickened him outright, let alone the fact that it might be Chester – or what remained of Chester – they were hunting. "What of the others?" he demanded. "The corrupted we'd have to fight through? We know now that some of them could potentially recover, given treatment and time. Are you so cavalier about slaughtering them as well?"

"I am 'cavalier' about none of this, Elliot, and you well know it. But willing? To prevent the alternative? Yes."

Again Elliot saw no disagreement in the remorseful but determined expressions surrounding him, and again, though he desperately racked his mind for some other option, he could provide none.

"How?" he asked, shoulders slumping. "My protective charm and your talismans were barely sufficient before."

"Ah-ha!" Lafayette-Moses stood, leaning on his cane, and now Elliot saw that he had not quite returned all the documents to the box which the silent chauffeur now held. In the old man's other hand were several of the papers he'd first removed before delving into the *Pnakotic Fragments*. "Now here, Mr Raslo, I might be of some further aid. Tell me, do you read Latin? The archaic alphabet, I mean."

"I'm afraid I only know a few words and phrases…"

"I don't believe you follow me, son. It doesn't much matter if you *understand* it, can you *read* it? Aloud?"

"Oh." Elliot pursed his lips, considering. "Most of my reading's been in the modern alphabet, but they're similar enough, and I've seen enough of the archaic that I guess I can puzzle it out."

"Good. 'Puzzle it out' in advance. You can't be hesitatin' or makin' mistakes when it counts." He handed over one of the documents.

Perusing the first few lines told Elliot that this was the ward the old man had used earlier, to protect all present from the recitation.

"You'll have to repeat it," Lafayette-Moses warned, "every few minutes, and keep your companions near when you do. But it should protect you from Tsocathra's refrain better than the incantation you've been usin', and your friends as well."

Elliot felt his stomach churn at the responsibility of warding the others in addition to himself, the realization that the consequences would not fall on him alone should he fail. Nevertheless, he was grateful, and said as much, even if he wondered still why the occultist seemed so eager to help.

For the good of others? That didn't seem like Hyrum Lafayette-Moses; it might be an unfair assessment, but Elliot could not shake his certainty that the man knew little of compassion. Perhaps he simply protected himself, hoping to avoid Tsocathra's rise – or protected Elliot himself, still hoping for an apprentice.

Well, he'd be waiting a long time for *that*, regardless of what the next few days might bring.

It seemed, whatever his motives, that Lafayette-Moses wasn't finished. After a brief hesitation he handed over a second document, also handwritten, but dustier and more yellowed than the first. It, too, was in the archaic Latin alphabet.

"If things grow desperate," he explained in reply to the student's unspoken question. "If you need help and all else has failed. But you heed me, Mr Raslo, I do mean *desperate*. Last resort. There's no tellin' what'll happen mixin' magics like that, openin' yourself to the Beyond in the presence of the litany. Could go poorly.

"But also, it is no friend of yours who'll come to your aid, and these magics are not near so tight a bindin' as you might wish. Once, and once only, you can probably risk it. Once, and you probably remain just another mortal in the tee-min' millions. Any more than that, though, you will be *noticed*. And I do assure you, by whatever god you prefer, you do *not* want to be noticed!"

Unsure what to make of that, but frightened to his core, Elliot took the conjuration with greatest reluctance, holding it between two fingers as if he'd caught a scorpion by the tail.

That swiftly, Lafayette-Moses was all smiles, bobbing his head and taking a firmer grip on his cane. "Might be there are other dangers too, but you haven't time to go over every possible outcome. We'll all just have to… pray. Well, I do believe that's all I can offer. Best of luck with your endeavors, my friends. Mr Raslo, if both you and Arkham are still here when all's said and done, I hope you'll reconsider my offer. I look forward to hearin' from you."

Before any of his startled audience could utter a word, he was gone, his driver following behind with that plain, wooden box.

Nobody moved, it seemed almost that nobody breathed, until the outer office door shut with a solid *thump*. Elliot heard his friends shuffling around the table, but he could not tear his gaze from the papers – the *spells*– that had been left in his care.

And it was only then, too, that all the unasked questions came back to him.

What was Hyrum Lafayette-Moses's connection to the occult circles and witch cults of Arkham's idle rich? Who was he that they had, on his word – and Elliot was certain it had, indeed, been *his* word – elected to remain uninvolved in the search for Chester Hennessy?

Who was he to give that order, and *why* had he given it? How much of what was happening had he already known before Alice called him, before he set foot in Pembroke's office and demanded to hear their story?

What, in the end, was he after?

All questions Elliot had very much meant to ask, and all questions that had totally fled his mind at every opportunity to ask them. A convenient lapse for the mysterious old man – and one, after the compulsion he'd felt to answer Lafayette-Moses's own questions, Elliot wasn't prepared to chalk up to mundane distractions.

Thoughts racing and heart thudding, he turned his attention back to the others. They still had a great many labors ahead of them.

Chapter Twenty—Three

Silence reigned after the occultist's exit until, at long last, it was Ida who broke it.

"How're we even supposed to find Hennessy, or Pembroke, or whoever? The old man ain't said a thing about *that*."

More silence.

"That doesn't seem to be the sort of thing he'd overlook," Elliot said, thinking it through. "So either he couldn't help with that, or he didn't feel we *needed* his help with it."

Alice gave an unladylike snort. "If we don't, that'd be news to me."

Elliot couldn't help but agree. He hadn't the first notion, and all Lafayette-Moses's aid wouldn't count for much if they couldn't piece something together.

Billy stepped to the door, staring it as though he could see through the wood, through the outer walls, to the streets of Arkham. "You've already searched for your employer everywhere you could think of, Miss Bentley?"

She nodded – but then, "Well, almost," she corrected.

He turned back toward her and the others. "Almost?"

"Some of those properties of his I mentioned? A couple warehouses, a flophouse or two, are inside the influenza outbreak. Even if I wanted to risk looking there, it'd be tough to get past the police cordon without being caught – but there's no point in it, anyway. Mr Pembroke wouldn't dare stay there, no matter what he was hiding from. His momma died of the Spanish Flu back in '18..."

She trailed off, and though he'd known her for a matter of mere hours, Elliot swore he could hear the cogs turning in her head.

"Well, I'll be damned," she whispered. Then, more loudly, "Except it's not a flu."

Elliot's jaw nearly brushed the table. "No," he protested. "No, that's not... That doesn't..."

But it did. Hadn't she already told them Pembroke allowed Chester to use one of his flophouses as a place to hide the *Ujaraanni*, to study its secrets? Hadn't they theorized he'd sheltered there, in a period of relative lucidity, before making for his kin in Hockomock?

The authorities hadn't quarantined a sickness, in that handful of blocks in the slums beyond the Merchant Quarter. They'd quarantined an outbreak of contagious psychopathy.

They'd quarantined the litany.

He almost felt foolish for not considering the possibility earlier, except…

"What of the police? Wouldn't they have figured out what they were truly dealing with? Perhaps even become infected themselves?"

"Not if they were warned to keep their distance, maybe even shoot if anyone came too close." It would be an extreme response, certainly, but not one they would disobey, if convinced the epidemic was dangerous enough, though Elliot couldn't begin to guess by whom.

"No," he insisted. "No, they'd still be overrun by even a small crowd. It would only take one to get near enough for them to hear the chant."

In a rough, gravelly whisper, Ida said, "Only if they wanted out." Then, at their expressions, "None of my… None of 'em ever tried to leave. And they always gathered back at the Hennessy place. Maybe this bunch ain't going anywhere, either. Least not yet."

Somehow, Elliot didn't find that notion comforting.

"You suggested the police might have been warned," Billy said to Alice. "By whom? Who would know enough to do so?"

"Do you still not understand? Even after talking to Victoria McCutcheon, and learning the sorts of people she knows just from tiptoeing around the edges of cult circles? There's a good number of the rich and powerful in Arkham who know a *lot* about what's out there under the skin of civilization and science. Some who even dabble in it. And that includes government circles, Mr Raslo, Mr Shiwak.

"If something unnatural's sweeping across whole neighborhoods in this town, people educated enough to notice *will* notice. Even if they don't know near enough what in God's name to *do* about it."

Elliot's head swam; the chamber wobbled until he nearly grew sick.

So a few of Arkham's elite understood – not the true horror, the true danger, of what they faced, but that it was no mundane affliction. "Influenza" was a lie, a pretense for the citizenry, the press. And they'd set the police, albeit in ignorance, between the spreading horror and the rest of the city.

And still, for all that, it was down to *them* – a foreign hunter, an orphaned rustic, a criminal lieutenant they'd only just met, and a half-crazed university student – to stop it. Because while some of the Powers That Be might know something was amiss, none of them knew the *truth*.

It was hideously, grossly unfair. Unjust. Had he not been smack in the center of it, he would have laughed until he cried. But he *was* in the midst of it… and *someone* had to do something. He might wish it was someone else, anyone else, but he wouldn't walk away. Not now.

Billy seemed far less perturbed by their circumstances. "If this is so, it tells us much we needed to know. Not only where the center of the madness might be found, but also that we face only one source of it, not two."

That declaration snapped Elliot from his growing hysterics. "How do you figure?"

"Those afflicted," Billy explained, "cannot help but spread that affliction, and those in turn to spread it further. It is not a subtle thing, else your authorities would not have noticed, and we would not have dealt with… what we dealt with."

Nods, all around. They all followed so far.

"Your police have only cordoned off one area, not two. Your town whispers of one outbreak of sickness, not two. If both Chester and Pembroke were spreading their madness separately…"

Of course. "There would be two outbreaks," Elliot concluded.

"Precisely. As there is only the one, we know that either Chester never returned to Arkham, and the source is Pembroke… Or Chester began the spread before he departed, and may have returned to it since, and Pembroke is either dead or just another of Chester's horde."

"Well, then." Alice pushed back from the table and stood. "I guess that means it's time to figure out how to get you all in there – and how to give you half a shot at surviving once we do."

Alas, though Elliot attempted to convince her otherwise, when Alice had said "you all," she meant it. She would provide supplies, would work to aid them in sneaking past the police, but accompanying them into the lion's den was where she drew the line.

Unhappy as it made him, Elliot couldn't blame her. Although she believed in what was happening, certainly took it seriously, for her it remained theoretical. Tales told by strangers and lore gleaned from old books. She hadn't experienced it, couldn't *feel* the threat posed to Arkham, and God knew how much of the world beyond, as the three of them did.

And she remained, after all, a smuggler and a fence. Not a career path that tended to attract those of an altruistic nature. They had, Elliot knew, good cause to be grateful Alice had proved even as solicitous as she had.

A bit more disturbing, to his mind, was how readily she went along, knowing it might well be her employer they would have to hunt down and kill. When he'd brought it up, however, she'd offered a shrug best described as philosophical.

"If he's become what you say he might, then he's already gone. And we both knew this wasn't the safest business; leaving aside monsters and curses, we deal every week with entitled rich folks who haven't got the slightest compunction about breaking the law. Always figured the day would come when he went out to meet someone and never came back. I can keep this place running. Probably even improve it. I've been handling most of the day-to-day business anyway. And if I've got any mourning to do for my boss and my friend, it's sure not going to happen in front of all of you."

And that was the end of that.

They gave brief consideration to waiting until the following day to act, and just as swiftly dismissed the idea. They had far worse to worry about now than the deadline Daisy had set before she went to the police, and no way to know whether the time remaining until the manifestation of the Thousandfold Dream was measured in weeks or days.

Or even less.

Thus were the following hours occupied by planning and preparation. Elliot found the process surprisingly inspirational. However dangerous and however horrid it was to contemplate, that he was finally *doing* something that might end all this, might spare others a terrible death – or worse – stiffened his resolve as never before.

The Chester he'd known and loved would be proud of him. He smiled at the thought.

He read over the invocations Lafayette-Moses had provided, ensuring he could pronounce them properly when the time came. Ida and Billy loaded weapons – not only the pistols they'd brought with them, but heavier firepower Alice lent them – and then twisted fabric into makeshift earplugs, as nobody wanted to rely entirely on Elliot's constant chanting.

They pored over a map of Arkham, focusing on the restricted blocks and Pembroke's properties. No guarantee the heart of the insanity remained in one of those structures, even if it had begun there, but it was at least a place to start.

They planned how to get past the cordon, what Alice could do to provide a diversion. Once they were inside, she would then use Pembroke's contacts among the rich and powerful to get word to those believers in the municipal government, explaining the greater nature of the threat; what the hazards were; that the afflicted must be fully isolated to have any chance of recovery and to avoid spreading their madness.

They might well not believe her, of course. Even practicing occultists might have trouble swallowing the tale she had to tell. Should they prove at all recalcitrant, it could well be too late by the time they *did* come around to acting.

"And of course," she warned, "if they *do* believe me, they might just send in the police to burn down the entire neighborhood and shoot anything that moves. So I suggest you don't dawdle."

Finally, nothing remained but to gird their loins, say what prayers they felt appropriate, and go.

"Officer. Officer, help!"

Bentley certainly sounded convincing as she dashed toward the police, gathered about their vehicles and the wooden barriers set up along the streets and sidewalks. If Billy Shiwak hadn't known better, he'd have thought she was genuinely frightened.

But then, the woman and her missing employer both had to be convincing liars, did they not?

Crouched in a darkened alleyway nearby, clutching a sawed-off shotgun under his coat and hyper-sensitive to the harsh breathing of his companions – did *none* of these folks know how to be stealthy? – he watched as the blue-clad officers, shaken from their boredom by Bentley's cries, moved to investigate the ruckus.

A research student beset by a curse and a woman choking on grief and guilt. These should have been the last two people he wanted at his side in battle. Yet Billy's nerves, howling over what was to come – though he'd never let it show – were calmed ever so slightly by their presence.

After what they'd shared in the past few days, he was glad to have them beside him – even if they did have all the stealth of a musk ox.

"What seems to be the problem, miss?" the nearest policeman asked from beneath a mustache so thick it mightn't look out of place on the rear end of a small pony.

Gasping for breath, she pointed back the way she'd come, struggling to speak.

Then again, she didn't have to. Taking only a few steps from their blockade, the police found themselves able to see down one particular side street. There, bathed in the light of a street lamp only faintly diffused by a thin fog, a trio of men tussled, two of them shoving the third. A few strained shouts drifted across the way, their words impossible to make out.

Equally unclear, at this distance, were the facial features of the three brawlers. Nevertheless, Billy realized that the "victim" of the other two was in fact the same man who'd been tailing him, on Bentley's behalf, outside the Hennessys' hotel.

Although they gathered a few paces from the wooden barricades to better observe, the police seemed in no rush to abandon their post. It was just a fistfight, after all. If it dragged on much longer, maybe a couple of them would wander over and break it up, but otherwise it was hardly worth–

As if deliberately planned for optimal dramatic effect – which, of course, it had been – only then did the third man, apparently frightened or angry at being outnumbered, pull a revolver from inside his coat and fire.

The round flew well over the heads of the other two, who retreated in sudden fear. The appearance of the gun, however, and the report of the shot, instantly shifted the nature of the cops' response.

Shouting for the suspect to drop his weapon and raise his hands, their own revolvers now drawn, the entire lot charged the intersection. The trio vanished down the side street, where Billy knew they'd already planned their escape routes after putting on their little pantomime. They'd be well and truly gone before the police caught up with them.

The cordon would remain abandoned for mere moments.

Billy hissed something, not really a word, and broke into a sprint of his own. He felt no need to look behind to see if Elliot and Ida kept up; their clumsy steps and, in the student's case, desperate gasps, were evidence enough.

From one alley to another, one side of the wooden barricades to the other. Simple. After all, the police were hardly alert for people trying to sneak *into* a pocket of raging influenza, were they?

And just like that, they found themselves once again within the radius of a madness too terrible to contemplate. Only this time, they had gone knowingly, willingly, with every intention of delving deeper still.

Perhaps, Billy thought to himself, though he would never say such a thing aloud, *we've all truly lost our minds already.* He briefly wished he'd departed Arkham back when he first acquired the *Ujaraanni*, then cast the thought away as unworthy of him.

They crept along, keeping to the shadows between the streetlights, making use of alleys and back ways where they could. Wherever the streets stood open, providing line of sight to other intersections at the edge of the slums, to other police at their cordons, they took greater care still. Often it took them minutes to cross a single roadway, so cautious were their steps.

They had expected, once more than a block or two in, to be able to walk normally, assuming they would appear to be more of the "sick" contained within the neighborhood. They discovered, however, that the streets here were utterly abandoned. Other than a few sporadic lights in windows here or there, they observed no signs of life. If anyone here had managed to avoid being corrupted, they kept themselves locked inside. That much didn't surprise Billy; it was the only sensible choice.

But where were the others? Where were the citizens already corrupted by that foul liturgy? Back at Ida's home, they had wandered the community aimlessly, searching for more ears into which they might spill their poison words, or else gathered about the Hennessy house, the beating heart of their unnatural obsessions.

Here, they found no wanderers. Here, the isolated area was small enough that, if the corrupted were all gathered in one spot, Billy and his companions ought to hear them.

Instead, all he heard was Elliot's constant murmur as he repeated Lafayette-Moses's protective spell, again and again. Billy knew nothing of Latin, of course, but the young man's occasional pauses or stammers as he stumbled over a word here, a pronunciation there, were unmistakable in any language.

"Elliot..." he growled, wincing at a particularly egregious stutter.

"I know. I'm trying!" Even in a hushed whisper, his voice nearly cracked with nerves. He sounded near breaking point, despite all they'd been through already.

Billy had neither the time nor patience to coddle him. "We're relying on you," was all he said, before deliberately turning his focus back to the next intersection.

"We're relying on you."

Yes, I damn well know that. Elliot wanted to scream, rant and rave, to shatter the grating silence until it was nothing but flecks like grains of sand. *That's precisely the problem!*

He couldn't do this. The fear for himself, for his life or his mind; the muttering, ever present, of the infectious litany winding through every thought he had; his awareness that he might be forced to kill innocent souls whose sanity might not be beyond saving; the terrible knowledge he had now of the Weaver of Flesh, of what awaited Arkham, and the world beyond, if they failed... Those were all bad enough, any one of them sufficient to crush the will of men Elliot thought of as far braver than he.

But it was this spell, this Latin chant, that he knew would be his undoing. He'd gone over it a dozen times in Alice's office. He knew how to read it, had readily figured out the differences between the archaic and modern alphabet. It should, by all rights, flow smoothly, close to effortlessly, from his lips.

If it had been like the French charm he'd used before, if he alone had counted on it, it would have.

It was the fact that he protected Billy and Ida too, now – that they were, as Billy said, relying on him – that petrified his tongue until he could scarce form the syllables. The responsibility was too heavy. His fear of failing them would be the reason he failed them.

He couldn't do this, and damn him to hell for not recognizing that until it was too late. They couldn't go back. They had no alternative.

He clenched his teeth, took a deep breath. If it *had* to be him, if he was the one to do this, then he damn well would not let his companions down.

Blinking hard, so unshed tears would not blur his view of the page and impede him further still, Elliot began again at the top.

For some time, he dared not even glance up from the paper. He counted on Billy and Ida to watch for danger, to keep them from discovery, and followed where he was led. He stumbled over the words, far more than once, but at least he made it through *occasional* repetitions without flaw. Without a solid idea of how long each successful recitation would last – he knew only, from what Lafayette-Moses had said, that its effectiveness was brief – he had no way of knowing how well or how consistently they were protected. He felt himself sweating, even in the late-night chill.

When he did look up, look around, his nerves imposed onto this old, ramshackle neighborhood a lowering malevolence. Buildings seemed to sag deliberately toward the narrow streets, as if to slowly engulf, absorb, digest whoever had the misfortune to pass by. The cracks and crevices shaped the stones beneath his feet into unclean teeth, while the sporadically lit windows were the glaring, angry eyes of great beasts only just rousing themselves from a deep yet restless slumber. Although the night's fog was not thick, still each island of illumination cast by the streetlamps was smaller and farther away than the last. Sounds from mere blocks away seemed unable pass through it, leaving them in a pall of unnatural silence.

Or was it his nerves at all? Elliot thought back, despite himself, to the fever-dreamlike trudge through the Hockomock, to the resting place of the *Ujaraanni*, to the swamp's vague corruption and the almost desperate efforts of nature itself to purge the intrusion.

He would never be certain how much of that had been real, but neither would he ever believe it had been entirely in his head. Who was to say, then, that this was?

A frantic study of his companions offered no enlightenment. Billy looked as stoic, as determined, as ever, but even if he were seeing the world as Elliot did, would he have let it show on his face? And Ida… So rarely did she appear more than half present in the moment, who could guess what Ida thought any more?

Then Billy's expression *did* change, but not due to any abnormality in the environment, real or imagined. He raised a hand and hissed at them to halt as the end of the narrow side street came into sight – along with the people beyond it.

Two of them, the first the trio had seen since their arrival, wandered aimlessly about the intersection, a T where this smaller byway intersected with a more major street. They appeared almost stuck; Elliot would have said they looked lost, if their movements weren't confined to so small an area. Over and over, one side of the street to the other and back, from this building to that and then back to this.

He couldn't see their faces, and if they were repeating that dreadful and by now all-too-familiar chant, they did so at a low mutter at best, else he'd have heard it. Nevertheless, the distracted, almost hollow way they moved was enough to convince him they were, indeed, corrupted.

And he wondered: this peculiar, repetitive shambling, constrained to the intersection and a few yards beyond…

Could this be their half-mindless, instinctive version of standing sentry? Were these two men a guard of some sort?

He bent close to Billy to whisper his hypothesis, and the other nodded. "Wait here." Billy didn't utter the words so much as mouth them, then crept ahead, darting through shadows, occasionally crouching behind a hedge or a raised stoop.

Minutes passed. The two corrupted continued their awkward cycle. A streetlight flickered, dimmed, brightened again. Elliot watched Ida's fists clench and unclench, over and over, around the grip of her own weapon, a pump-action Remington she'd gotten from Alice.

He worried about her, in those moments when he wasn't distracted by his own fears. She'd been so withdrawn since they'd reached Arkham, even more so since Lafayette-Moses's revelation… If they survived what was to come, she would need intense psychological treatment. He hoped he could help her find it.

When Billy moved, it was a burst of speed that took even Elliot by surprise. He dashed across the intersection, completely passed the nearer of the two sentries. The second had just drawn near the brick wall of a building across the street and begun to turn around when Billy shot toward him, leaping the last few paces, hand outstretched…

Palm met skull, driving it with brutal force into the bricks. It sounded to Elliot like a baseball bat striking an overripe melon; sickened, he turned away. When he looked back, seconds later, Billy was standing above the body of the second man, his pana bloodied.

The hunter placed a finger to his lips for silence, then motioned his companions forward. Elliot advanced, struggling not to look at either corpse or the smear on the wall. Billy wiped his blade clean on the dead man's sleeve and returned it to its sheath.

"Was that necessary?" Elliot demanded.

"Yes." Billy pointed, first at the structure with the bloodstain, then the building next to it. "Those are both Pembroke's property. Warehouse, flophouse. Not a coincidence these two chose this intersection to guard."

Elliot took a deep, ragged breath, then nodded. "All right. So which do we–?"

It began in the flop joint.

"…*vshuru shelosht escruatha*…"

So many voices, dozens or more. They gradually came into hearing already partway through the chant, a hushed sound becoming audible, so that it seemed they'd moved closer from somewhere distant. Whether their arrival was coincidence or somehow provoked by the death of the sentries, Elliot neither knew nor, in that instant of heart-stuttering terror, much cared.

"*Svist ch'shultva ulveshtha ikravis…*"

The front door flew open and they emerged, one by one, an endless stream. They were, the lot of them, filthy, unkempt, unshaven; some undressed or underdressed, others clad for work, all rumpled and unwashed.

And some… Oh, dear Lord!

Some were no longer entirely human.

Here, Elliot saw a neck that had sagged until the chin melded with the sternum in a permanent, impossible maw. There, a hand and fingers had stretched like putty to dangle and trail against the street. It seemed, impossibly, as though some of these bodies, the flesh and skin, were little more than ill-fitting outfits carelessly donned by something else. Something *other*.

All of them, mangled or not, were a single chorus, orating in perfect unison.

Elliot felt the power of the litany wash over him, but it was muffled, remote – more so even than when he'd been protected only by the French charm and his borrowed Inuit amulet. Even in his mounting fear, he felt a knot of tension uncoil as he realized the incantation over which he'd been struggling was, for the moment, proving effective.

It would do them little good, though, if they were overwhelmed.

"We have to run!" He heard the hysteria in his voice, but couldn't bring himself to be ashamed. "We have to–!"

"*Isslaach ikravis vuloshku dlachvuul loshaa…*"

Not only from the encroaching mob, this time, but also from far nearer. From over his shoulder.

God, no…. Please…

As if dragged against their will, Elliot and Billy turned to look behind them.

"*Ulveshtha schlachtli vrulosht chevkuthaansa…*" chanted Ida Glick.

Chapter Twenty-Four

Stunned, Elliot moved only when he felt something snag him by the collar and haul him backward. He flailed, shouting, until he realized it was Billy, and even then barely got himself under control.

Before him, the throng advanced from one direction, Ida from the other, and cresting like a wave before them, that *Goddamned chant*. Clouded as it was, held at bay by two different incantations and the protective talisman, still it pounded in his head, calling up his own psychic infection in response.

Billy dragged him through a doorway, seeking shelter in the only nearby building from which none of the corrupted were emerging: Pembroke's warehouse. He slammed the door and began piling boxes in front of it; a slapdash barricade, one they both knew wouldn't hold long, but the only readily available option.

"Help me with this!" he shouted, but Elliot couldn't move. The few sane thoughts he retained wouldn't stop racing around his skull, demanded answers.

How had Ida been exposed? It couldn't have happened just now, outside. The ward Lafayette-Moses had given him was working, he *knew* it was working – and even had it not, the transformation should not have been so instantaneous. Elliot knew, from his own experience, from Chester's and from everything he'd seen in Ida's home, that it usually took minutes, hours, even days.

Days...

Elliot sagged, ignoring the increasingly urgent appeals from his friend, the pounding on the door and the muffled refrain from beyond.

So many times since their return, Ida had seemed to fade away, only half present, lost and distracted. He'd attributed it to her grief over all she'd lost, her horror over what she'd had to do. Perhaps some of it had been, but the rest? He should have recognized it. He'd seen it in Chester before his disappearance. He'd heard Alice describe it in Pembroke. He'd felt it himself, that lack of focus, that preoccupation with something only the corrupted could hear.

And he realized only now, when it was far, *far* too late, that in all the chaos, all the terror and exhaustion, and in his own near-maddened state... It had never occurred, either to him or to Billy, to ask Ida the precise details of what happened that night in the swamp, when she'd led her whole community on a lethal chase so the two of them might slip unnoticed into the Hennessy house.

Had she been too scared to tell them, to admit she'd been exposed? Or had her grief and despair been so overwhelming that she'd lost the ability to care about the consequences?

He'd never know, of course. Never know if he could have helped her, as he had himself.

Never fully rid himself of the guilt that now threatened to suffocate him because it had never occurred to him to try.

I'm sorry, Ida.

"Damn it, Elliot!"

It wasn't Billy's admonition that finally dragged his mind back to the present, but the brief thunder that followed. A ragged hole appeared through the door and one of the stacked crates, sending shards and splinters flying. Billy recoiled with a curse, thin streaks of blood welling up on his cheek.

Ida's shotgun. Even in the grip of the litany, she retained the wherewithal to use the tools at hand. A quick nod to his companion to indicate he was with him once again, and then he studied the rude shelter in which they found themselves.

The warehouse was a small manmade cavern, a vast chamber of wooden walls and occasional metal catwalks above. It held little in the way of goods, compared to its capacity; most of it stood open and empty, with only a few sporadic hills of crates, islands in the barren space. A goodly number were covered in a thick frosting of dust, obvious even from a distance. Whatever they contained was clearly not in high demand.

Between the dim lighting and those occasional heaps of boxes, Elliot couldn't see all the way to the warehouse's far side – a realization that finally made him stop and wonder why he was able to see at all. High above, among the rafters, dull electric lights hung in flimsy fixtures. They must have been left on when the warehouse personnel were taken.

Well, he'd accept the tiny lick of good fortune for what it was. "There must be another door somewhere," he said, wincing at the sound of another shot.

"Go!" Billy crouched behind the feeble barricade, his own shotgun in his hands. "Find it."

Elliot ran. Somewhere in the shadows, a window shattered, and he pushed himself faster still.

It didn't take long to find the exit. A small side door, it was conveniently marked with an overhead sign.

It was also, rather less conveniently, blocked by one of those dusty stacks of crates.

Elliot stretched up and gave the top crate a perfunctory shove. As anticipated, it didn't budge. No way he and Billy were clearing the path on their own.

This had to be deliberate. Pembroke's people had blocked the back entrance quite some time ago, probably to ensure nobody snuck in to interfere with any illegal goods they were moving.

A series of shots sounded from across the warehouse. He tried to ignore it, tried to think.

Pembroke was a fence and a smuggler. Which meant…

Elliot dashed back across the massive room, moving in circles, searching frantically. And there it was.

In the back corner, opposite the door he'd tried and failed to reach, a large hatch sat recessed in the floor. Standing over it, he could smell even through the thick wood that it led into the musty, fetid depths of Arkham's sewers.

All right, that made sense. If one could tolerate the filth, the vapors, the rats and the insects and worse, the larger tunnels would make a viable smuggler's route, allowing travel from the Miskatonic River to all sorts of locations within the town.

And if Pembroke's other properties had similar trapdoors, it would explain why the arrival of the corrupted from the flophouse had sounded as though they approached from a distance, already chanting. They'd come from below.

"I've got a way out," Elliot called. "You won't like it, though."

Pounding feet, and Billy was at his side in a flash. "We'll like staying a lot less." As if to punctuate his assessment, a final crash announced the collapse of the partly shredded front door, as well as the broken crates that had blocked it.

Without a word, they reached down and hauled the hatch open.

They fully anticipated the waft of sewer air, and all its varied mélange of scents. It still nearly blew them back from the opening with a physical force. Mixed in with it, though, or somehow beyond it, was another odor, something that reeked of putrescence even more than the sewer's own liquifying waste.

Wincing against the stink, Billy climbed over the edge and began making his way down the rusty ladder beneath.

"Never in all the time we've worked together has anything remotely good come of cellars or underground," Elliot groused. As Billy either didn't hear or elected not to respond, he could do nothing but follow. He'd have preferred they close the trapdoor after them, perhaps hide their trail for a short while, but it had taken them both to open the thing. No way either alone could haul it shut, and the ladder forbade cooperation from this direction.

With a loud click, Billy's flashlight illuminated the passage below. The tunnel writhed in the beam, and Elliot realized with a horrified shiver that he was seeing literal sheets of roaches and other vermin coating the walls, scattering in the alien light. Beyond them was brick, old and worn and glistening with the residue of years, sloping upward in a gentle curve toward the ceiling.

If nothing else, Elliot could at least give thanks that the river of sludge flowing down the center of the corridor was shallow here, in the sewers' uppermost level. The walkways along either side, though filth-encrusted and treacherously slick, remained unsubmerged despite the abnormally rainy season. He and Billy shouldn't need to walk in the offal.

Still, between the scents, the thick, mucous sounds of the flow, and the skittering of a hundred thousand legs, he found himself unable to take that last step off the ladder. Even the driving fear of what followed behind proved momentarily insufficient to overcome his revulsion. His fists tightened despite his commands, threatening to shred skin against the scabrous rust.

"You should probably resume Lafayette-Moses's spell," Billy called softly over his shoulder. "No telling if we're still warded."

The reminder that his friends needed him – well, *friend*, he corrected – was enough to spur him onward. He dropped to the narrow walkway, flailed for balance, then removed both the paper and his own flashlight from his coat. He wondered, idly, if Billy had done that on purpose, had noted his paralysis and said what he must to break it.

Either way, it was a good point. Letting the hunter take the lead, shifting his light from Latin script to corridor floor and back, he once more read through the incantation. Then again. And again. When Billy called a halt, scarcely louder than a whisper, and gestured to a doorway ahead, Elliot felt confident he'd gotten the pronunciation correct more often than not.

"What's in there?" Elliot whispered back – but even as he asked, he heard it. Something, scarcely audible, a peculiar combination of voices and other, more disturbing sounds he could not begin to identify.

Billy looked at him, flashlight in one hand, shotgun in the other. Elliot carefully tucked the paper back into a pocket and drew a pistol: a Remington Model 51 automatic, yet another weapon provided by Alice Bentley. Not a very powerful weapon, but well suited to an inexperienced gunman.

He nodded, reached out and threw the door open. Billy darted past, double barrels raised and ready to fire.

They saw little, even with the flashlights, for the chamber was massive; nearly the size of the warehouse from which they'd come, in length and width if not height, though no such room should exist in the sewers. A few scattered bricks, visible at the edges of their light, suggested that it might have been several separate spaces until recently.

Even nearly blind, however, they knew something was horribly wrong.

The scent hit them again, that decaying, fleshy aroma, but now it was mixed with more familiar, if no less unpleasant, odors: the sweat of unwashed bodies, halitosis, human waste in smaller but far purer quantities than the sewage outside the door.

And dear God, the *sounds*. Elliot heard the shuffling of nervous limbs, a terrible grinding and a wet, slurping noise he could liken only to mud or soft clay being slapped together and squeezed, over and over.

Those, and the litany. Oh, it was different, murky, muddled, as if multiple voices tried to speak through mouths full of old porridge, but he felt the impact in his head all the same. Every nerve screamed at him to back out of the room, to face the horrid sewer or even the mob of corrupted that had doubtless followed them down here, rather than discover what abomination shared this chamber with them.

Then, from out in the corridor, he heard, too, the echoes of far too many footsteps, and a much clearer chorus – fully in sync with the recitation here in the massive hall – and he knew they would come pouring through the doorway any moment. That running was now physically, let alone rationally or ethically, no longer an option.

Billy, as usual, had more quickly assessed the situation and chosen a course of action. A sweep of his flashlight ended on a large handle on a metal bracket beside the door.

A knife switch, Elliot realized, even as Billy lunged for it. Probably for the lights. It made sense. The municipal workers would want it close to the entrance…

A moment of strain, a rain of rusty flecks, and Billy shoved the switch upright, completing the connection. Electricity sizzled, and a series of large, enclosed bulbs lit up along the ceiling, their high-pitched hum all but inaudible in the cacophony.

Together, Elliot and Billy saw what awaited them in that chamber, deep beneath the streets of Arkham, and together they screamed.

Dozens of the corrupted stood around the far edges of the room. In the shadows at the edges of the light, it seemed almost as if they *were* the far edges of the room, their outlines faintly blurred as though they'd begun to conform to the shapes of the corners, the walls, even one another. Elliot couldn't entirely make it out, his eyes somehow refusing to focus where things joined together that should have remained apart.

Lips and eyes fluttered and twitched in unison, still struggling to push the words of their unholy liturgy through malformed orifices. Slow tides flowed through the morass of former humanity, and with each wave and ripple, the wavering bodies moved a fraction of an inch along the wall, along the floor, toward the greater mass at the center of it all.

There, the beating heart of this nightmare in skin, was a column of what had once been a half dozen other bodies, now melded into a single shape. New limbs had formed, whole chains of bones now wrapped in flesh, and had Elliot not already screamed until his lungs ached and he choked on his own bile, he would have shrieked at their *familiarity*.

He had seen those in his dream: the hundred-jointed tendrils of Tsocathra. The Weaver of Flesh sat at his terrible loom, his rebirth already underway.

Only a single recognizable person remained as part of that grotesque amalgamation. Near its top, protruding at a canted angle as though drunk, were the head and a single shoulder of the man around whom all had gathered, the vile sun around which everything else orbited.

Chester Hennessy.

Though some of the wounds they'd inflicted upon him had closed up, his lips were half gone, and his eyes had sunken fully into his head to make way for another, multifaceted, that bulged from his cheek. But his face still retained some of its former shape, and his mustache remained horrifyingly perfect; enough so that Elliot had no doubt who he was.

Behind them, the mob from above filtered into the room, chanting, and Ida was among the first.

Elliot did the only thing he could think of, the only thing that made even an iota of sense. He raised his pistol and opened fire at the thing that had once been his dearest friend.

Beside him, Billy did the same, emptying both barrels of the shotgun and then drawing his pistol, squeezing the trigger again and again.

They accomplished nothing, nothing at all. The bullets and pellets vanished into the hideous mass with barely a ripple, and the creature didn't so much as flinch. Chester's head turned its unblinking insectile eye their way, and the whole thing began to slouch toward them with the most unnatural motion, a combination of worm-ish humps and a sticky slide without obvious means of propulsion.

Face glistening with sweat even in the sickly yellow light, Billy dropped his empty pistol, broke open the shotgun and struggled to reload. Elliot retreated a step, only to hear a metallic *click* from behind.

Ida stood, mouth moving, her own shotgun aimed at Elliot's head. He felt his legs go watery as he realized her inability to keep track of her ammunition, in her tainted state, was the only reason he didn't lie dead on the floor.

Mechanically she turned the weapon around, wielding it by the barrel as a club, and the others began to fill the room around her. The sounds of the litany beat against his wards, and he knew they would not hold for long.

Billy's shotgun fired again, both barrels. And again, he might as well have been hurling invective and profanity at the constantly pulsing, growing mass, for all the good it did.

They had no options. No useful weapons, no room for retreat. So Elliot did what he'd somehow known, though he'd desperately hoped otherwise, he would always have to do.

"Keep them off me!" he shouted, as he drew Lafayette-Moses's other spell from his pocket.

In the corner of his vision, he saw Billy fly past him, calling out in Kalaallisut, pana in hand. He saw fists fly, saw members of the throng hurled to the floor by limbs and joints, saw blood arc as the snow knife struck. But he saw, too, the corrupted gathering, surrounding his friend, and he knew even Billy couldn't stand long against such odds.

Saw it all, and did his best to shut it out, to focus solely on the ancient script before him.

He'd looked over the invocation earlier, tried to master the pronunciation in his head. Unlike the protective ward, however, he'd never attempted reading it aloud; he wouldn't dare, for fear of getting it right at the wrong time. He feared getting it right even now, dreaded to see what it might conjure, yet following that fear came a strange sense of calm. As though he'd somehow known everything would come to this, and it was only a matter now of letting it happen.

He struggled with the text, trying to fit his tongue around the Latin, his brain around the handful of symbols that differed between the archaic and modern alphabets. It wasn't a lengthy text, this spell – in fact, it disturbed him greatly just how brief and simplistic it was – but still he stumbled over it, had to start over more than once.

More of the corrupted swarmed around Billy. Several others, Ida included, advanced on Elliot, and he found himself backpedaling before them, coming disturbingly close to the semi-viscous but still moving bodies plastered against the walls.

They were nearly within arm's reach when he finally shouted the last words of the conjuring, loud enough to be heard clearly over the constant inhuman chorus.

A chilling gust swept through the chamber, bringing everyone, even the corrupted, to a momentary halt. They felt it on the skin, it bit at the lungs, yet it never rustled one hair or scrap of clothing. From far away, Elliot heard… He couldn't quite describe *what* he heard. It was a low, all-but-inaudible roar, the loud silence at the edge of a vast chasm or other unfathomable void. A sound of absence, not of being.

From high above came a hint of motion. It was distant, so distant, unfathomably far beyond the ceiling itself, yet he could see it still, and he grew dizzy at the contradiction. Space itself seemed twisted in that spot, so that the stone he knew was mere feet overhead had instead receded an immeasurable ways.

And from that distance, something approached.

It writhed, twisted, coiled, shadow on shadow. Elliot would have called it serpentine, whatever it was, but it was accompanied by the methodical beat of flapping wings.

He looked away. He had no choice; between the spatial distortion and the winding darkness, it was more than his already battered sanity was worth to do otherwise.

The corrupted began to move again, driven by inhuman will, but the thing above was faster, oh, so much faster. Coils of shadow unwound, wrapping around the nearest figure to Elliot and yanking him into the impossible gulfs above, accompanied by a fearsome hiss, like a hundred vipers at once, and the flash of what might have been the shining of distant stars – or might have been fangs.

The briefest of pauses, as though it were some methodical, horrific hunter, carefully selecting its next prey, and then it lashed down again, a dusk- and scale-wrapped stroke of lightning. Another of the corrupted vanished, hauled away to be consumed or God knew what other fate. And another.

And Ida.

Elliot saw the shadow wrap about her, and he cried as she was lifted upwards. Even at the last, her mouth still moved and he saw no recognition – of him, her coming doom, or anything else – in her eyes.

Over and over, the half-seen thing struck from above, until the horde of dozens was scarce more than a handful. Only then did the distant roar of the gulfs fade, the freezing gusts cease, the ceiling settle once more in its proper place.

Elliot noticed little of it.

With the fourth or fifth stroke, the old occultist's first warning had proved prescient indeed. The combination of magics, the desperate conjuring with Tsocathra's litany, was disastrous.

No way for Elliot to know precisely what had happened, if the presence of the unnatural creature had somehow empowered the growing form of the Thousandfold Dream, if his own brief connection with the thing he summoned left his mind vulnerable, or if it were some other reaction entirely.

He knew only that the wards on which he counted, the discipline he'd built up over weeks of fighting his own burgeoning corruption, were suddenly, woefully insufficient. He had just long enough to observe what was happening to him, to scream inside, before he knew only those terrible words.

"*Isslaach thkulkris, isslaach cheoshash…*"

No, not only those. Elliot knew, too – to the extent he could be said to know anything, to the extent there was an Elliot at all – that Tsocathra called.

His fingers slackened, letting the document drift like an autumn leaf to the floor. Then Elliot strode readily to the pulsating mass of viscous flesh that had dragged itself to the center of the room, let himself fall into it and was gone.

Chapter Twenty-Five

"Elliot!"

A hopeless cry, utterly futile. Billy could do nothing but watch the student slip beneath the undulating surface of the abomination as if its skin were nothing but the muddy waters of the Hockomock. And while he'd never have admitted it to anyone, while he was indeed racked with grief for Elliot, it was a cry mostly of fear.

Alone. Billy stood alone, the recitation pounding as a furious blizzard upon his wards, against this embryonic amalgam that would soon form itself into the Great Old One who had last walked the Earth a thousand centuries gone by.

It scarcely even paid him heed. The face that had once been Hennessy's turned away, the tendrils curled aimlessly rather than reach for him. He was no threat, nor was he fit for consumption.

Yet.

The corrupted fell back, chanting still, letting the profane liturgy do its work. Billy snarled at them, reloading his shotgun again. He would not be a part of this detestation, and he would not fall without a fight. He meant to *make* them kill him. He–

Something *cracked*, a single, sharp sound loud enough to hurt the ear. Billy winced, but what followed was far worse.

From every one of its unnatural mouths, the form that would eventually be Tsocathra howled. Much like those whom it had infected, its voices were many and one simultaneously; some high pitched, some deep, all bubbling and bur-bling with liquid corruption.

Elliot flew from the fleshy mass, purged as though he were some sort of poison, to land in a moist, slick heap upon the stone floor. He skidded sev-eral yards until he fetched up against one of the corpses cut down earlier by Billy's blade. Whether he was sane or whole, Billy couldn't tell, but at least he breathed.

The hunter stepped toward him, jaw agape, wondering why Elliot had been rejected after succumbing so thoroughly as to offer himself up. Wondering…

Until he saw the amulet. The protective talisman, one of the many Billy's angakkoq had provided, that he'd lent to the younger man so long ago. The ward that had, along with his own amateur spellcraft, saved him for so long.

The talisman, carved from ivory and etched with ancient symbols, that was now broken almost perfectly in half.

That's what he'd heard, that ferocious report: the amulet breaking. Breaking, as it exhausted its magics in preventing Elliot from merging with the terrible mass.

Billy didn't stop to think, to ponder whether such a gamble could possibly pay off. He acted, as he'd learned to do in long, treacherous hunts across the icy wilds of Greenland. He grabbed at the leather thongs about his neck, hauling all but one of the dangling charms over his head, and charged.

One of the tendrils struck at him, a fearsome whip that extended near the length of the room, but it was a casual stroke. Billy tumbled under it with ease. The creature that was Tsocathra-to-be still saw him as an irritation at worst, no true danger.

He came back to his feet and leapt with the momentum of his roll. Leapt – and slung the talismans around the protruding head of Chester Hennessy, the heart of the beast and the only man in its entire makeup who had known the *entirety* of the antediluvian litany.

No scream this time. It froze, all of it, then shuddered obscenely, ripples and twitches running through it. The corrupted along the walls, linked to it only by extended limbs that stretched like taffy, moaned and recoiled, their connection severed.

Other bodies fell away from Chester in lumps of meat, masses of tissue that boasted only a stunted arm here, a partial visage there, as a reminder they'd ever been human.

And through it all, the talismans shattered and tore – ivory cracking, leather tearing, wood splintering – in rapid succession.

In the end, Chester stood alone, and now he *did* shriek and burble and howl to the heavens. His face remained mangled, one of his legs split at the knee into multiple smaller limbs like a cephalopod, and his left arm had become one of the great tendrils that had protruded from the larger shape. He was still inhuman, still the core of what would become the Fetid Thought, but he was alone.

With a fearsome shout of his own, Billy fired…

To no more effect than before. Chester absorbed the shot without so much as staggering. A man of less discipline than Billy would have sobbed.

He'd slowed the process, nothing more. He had no weapon that could harm the thing that had been Chester, no means of killing it.

For the moment, Chester merely stood, keening from a handful of separate mouths, the tendril mounted to his shoulder lashing out randomly like a dying eel – not from Billy's feeble attack, surely, but the shock of losing those with whom it had melded. Billy knew, however, that it wouldn't be long before the thing regained control, before it struck out and slaughtered him for daring to hurt it. Then it would simply start anew, with the people still waiting about the edges of the room, the corrupted wandering the buildings above, and whoever else it needed. It would move out from the sewers of Arkham, spreading madness before it, and taking who it needed.

Tsocathra would live.

Billy once more drew his pana and readied himself for one last, purely symbolic, act of defiance.

At the rapid-fire sounds of the amulets shattering, Elliot's eyelids fluttered open.

He watched from where he lay, unmoving, as the outer layers sloughed away, leaving Chester exposed. As Billy tried, and failed, to kill him and braced to go down fighting.

He saw, and he recognized everything that was happening for what it was, but he found it difficult to think. Not because of the litany, oh, no; that had receded once more to its usual persistent itch.

Because of what he'd been forced to *know*.

He had opened himself completely to Tsocathra's call. For endless seconds, what shreds remained of his mind had joined with the others; with the single gestalt built around what had been Chester. They were one.

And Elliot had known that this horror before him was the barest seed, the tiniest kernel around which the Great Old One would form. That Tsocathra would tread over whole civilizations, and never notice, save for the briefest alleviation of its endless hunger, its endless need to absorb the corrupted, to grow ever larger, ever stronger. That it would maim and madden and destroy, not for any cause, not even out of hatred for the lives it would take, but because it couldn't be bothered *not* to.

It was the shock of his ejection that snapped Elliot back to sanity, back to who he was, but it was a brief reprieve. Already he felt the tug of the call, the urge to slip back into the shared oblivion he'd tasted. He had moments, at best – but that was long enough to decide.

If the amalgamation grew beyond these walls, escaped from beneath Arkham, it would be unstoppable. The Weaver of Flesh would never be sated. The Thousandfold Dream would be the nightmare of all humanity.

So he couldn't allow it to escape, no matter the cost to himself. Whatever horrid fate he courted, surely it was better than becoming a permanent part of civilization's destroyer.

Elliot reached out, dragged himself across the floor to the lonely scrap of paper, lying near to where he'd dropped it. Ignoring Lafayette-Moses's sternest warning; forcing himself to be calm, not rush, despite the fear coursing through him… Ignoring the sight of Chester drawing nearer to Billy, step by terrible, limping step, still screaming and lashing out in random fits… He read the conjuration a second time.

Again the freezing wind, the muted drone of the infinite gulfs. Again the first signs of movement far above, so much higher than the ceiling should have allowed.

Yet Elliot sensed, even then, that something was different. Wrong.

The first time – God, was it only moments ago? – he'd had no communication with the nightmare he evoked. He'd given no commands, either aloud or in the silence of his thoughts. He'd simply known, without any idea how, that the entity would prey upon those he needed it to, hunting his foes while leaving him and his companion be.

Now? He felt no such certainty, only a sudden boneshaking shudder that had nothing to do with the cold.

Overhead, the shadows coiled, an expanding darkness that might or might not have been the spread of membranous wings, and the razor-edged glimmer of starlight fangs. They swiftly grew larger, larger…

Closer.

The admonition he'd ignored in his panic had come true. Elliot Raslo had been *noticed*.

It reached down for him in constant winding circles, so that it appeared almost as a sequence of concentric rings descending from above. All the strength drained from his body, and he fell hard to his knees. The painful shock of impact went all but unnoticed, as did the paper once more slipping through his fingers.

His mind began to give way once more, to the call and the litany. He wondered what fate awaited him, within the grasp of the vile predator he'd called, and hoped only that his death would be quick. Let him go with minimal pain, and before his sanity disintegrated once more, and he would call it… not good, but perhaps enough.

Under his breath, he began, brokenly, to pray. The first of the snaking coils surrounded him, started to constrict…

Something else lashed out from across the chamber, wrapping the serpentine body in its own unbreakable grip.

The conjured hunter spun, writhed, spitting its impossible, hissing shriek, and Elliot could only stare as the tendril of endless joints entangled the thing like a chain of flesh and bone, dragging it off him and toward the spindly mass that was the seed of Tsocathra.

It was almost certainly sheer chance that had saved him, Elliot knew. Between the mutated madman's random thrashing, and the sheer size of the other entity, accidental contact had always been possible, perhaps even probable.

But maybe, just maybe, there was more. In the days to come, Elliot would wonder: had his brief melding with the amalgamated creature, the blending of their minds into one, made a connection? There, at the very last, had something of Chester, some final lingering ember, recognized him for who he was?

However unlikely, however much he knew better, he liked to think that his salvation had come, not at the whims of fortune, but from one final act of the man he'd loved and who – in his own way, if not how Elliot might have wished – had loved him in return.

Of course, he would never really know.

He knew only, as the tendril compressed around the shadow serpent, and its own coils wound tight in turn about the shape that had been Chester... As scale and bone and other things shattered with deafening cracks... As the two figures rose, twisting and rotating about one another, until they faded from all mortal sight, accompanied by the methodical beating of unseen wings, leaving only the unmarred and unbroken ceiling behind... As Chester Hennessy vanished one last time...

...That somehow, by some miracle he could scarce believe, they had won.

EPILOGUE

Elliot Raslo and Billy Shiwak emerged, cold and sopping, from the bank of the Miskatonic River.

It had been an easy, if unpleasant decision. Already in the sewers, with the river's muffled rush reverberating through distant halls, they'd chosen to make their exit from the quarantined neighborhood underground, rather than risk being spotted and shot by the police. They'd taken more than a few wrong turns, encountered several dead ends, but eventually the sound of the Miskatonic had guided them true.

Other than the foulness and circuitousness of their route, they had no trouble making their escape. The corrupted had ignored them, standing silent for the first time since they'd succumbed to the litany. Something within them had been shaken, stunned by the loss of their source, their core. It was only a temporary circumstance – they would, before long, resume their wandering, their chanting, their efforts to corrupt others, even if there was no longer any ultimate point to it – but for now, the fleeing pair had been more than happy to take advantage and slip away unhindered.

Elliot knew it was temporary because he still heard the refrain himself, back in its den at the base of his skull, where it had lurked since he'd first heard those cursed words so many weeks ago – and perhaps always would. He was, for the moment, too exhausted to ponder or even truly feel the horror of such a possibility, but he knew that time would come.

Even from the river, they could hear the edges of the commotion, and returned, curious, to the streets beyond the Merchant District. Elliot shivered the entire way, between the unseasonable temperatures and his soaked legs and feet. Billy, of course, gave no indication he even noticed, so accustomed was he to far harsher cold.

Although, once his trousers had begun to dry, Elliot noticed he felt more comfortable than he had earlier that night. Was Arkham growing ever so slightly warmer? Was the lingering winter finally breaking?

He wondered if he were imagining things. He wondered, too, about the timing of the belated spring, assuming he was *not* imagining things, and then firmly drove the question from his mind. Even after all he'd experienced, some questions, some connections, didn't bear scrutiny.

An enormous force of police officers, backed up by a hastily assembled throng of burly citizens – stevedores, brawlers, veterans of the Great War – gathered near the cordons. They wandered and mingled, bragging and questioning; all were armed with firearms or bludgeons, and carried earmuffs and other similar protections. Well-coiffed men in expensive suits worked at separating them into manageable groups, then giving them their instructions. Other Arkhamites watched the proceedings from open windows or nearby side streets, fascinated at the martial gathering. A few were curious or brave enough to call out, but their shouted questions went unanswered.

Alice Bentley had obviously reached someone of power in Arkham's municipal government, someone with a passing knowledge of things beyond the accepted bounds of science, who believed her story. From what Elliot overheard, the police and other volunteers had been told that the "fever" was actually a psychosis caused by a sub-audible frequency whose origins the city was still investigating.

Elliot supposed it sounded a believable enough story to anyone not well versed in the appropriate sciences. In a way, it wasn't even that far from the truth.

He would have to find Alice herself at some point. She deserved to know that Chester had, indeed, been the one and only epicenter of the spreading horror, and thus that Jebediah Pembroke was almost certainly dead or lost among the remaining corrupted. It wasn't much of an answer, but he owed her that.

Later, though. Not tonight.

Just as it began to rain – a warmer, more cleansing shower than any Arkham had seen in months – he witnessed several men and women in hospital whites gathered around a corner, waiting until they were needed. Around them were wheeled stretchers, all equipped with leather straps. They were led by an irritable older man whom Elliot recognized, from having his appendix out over a year ago, as Dr Regensteiner, Chief Physician at Saint Mary's. The doctor was in the midst of arguing with another nattily dressed municipal official.

"… ridiculous expenditure of resources," he was barking. "We'll hold them for testing for a few weeks, but anyone still suffering after that is off to the asylum." He shook his head, oblivious to the other man's efforts to shush him. "I've had it with this, you hear me? This is the last time I'll keep your damn secrets. I'm retiring come summer. Retiring, hell, I'm getting out of this cursed town. Let Dr Mortimore take over, see how *he* enjoys…" Regensteiner trailed off, glaring about him, as he finally realized how loudly he was ranting. Elliot dutifully looked the other way.

"Come on," Billy said, taking Elliot by the shoulder. "There's nothing more for us to do here. Leave them to their cleanup."

A part of him wanted to stay, just to be absolutely sure, to see for himself that it was over. He wondered, furthermore, how the authorities would ensure the silence of anyone who might see the malformed remnants in the underground chamber, assuming they found it. They certainly wouldn't be attributing *that* to any "unheard frequencies". Billy was right, though. It was time, and past time, to go.

They slipped away, just two more curious onlookers who'd decided they'd seen enough.

Elliot sat alone in the dormitory room he had once shared with Chester, and stared at nothing. The silence was broken only by the *flip-flip-flip* of the stiff rectangle of paper he turned over and over in his hands.

They had told the conclusion of their tale to Daisy Walker, or as much of it as they could expect her to believe. She'd shared their regret over Ida, done her best to comfort Elliot for what was now clearly the permanent loss of Chester, congratulated Billy on the completion of his quest. After a bit of discussion, she had also agreed to speak with Mr Combs at the museum, and try to have the Lindegaard Stele locked away where even staff and experts in the field could no longer view it. The odds against anyone else learning how to transliterate the symbols were astronomical, but then, they'd not been any higher when Chester had managed it. And while nobody could master the entire litany without the *Ujaraanni*, another bout of spreading madness would be bad enough even without the threat of a risen Tsocathra behind it.

Daisy made it clear that she was available to talk, should Elliot need anything at all, but thus far he'd not taken her up on that offer. There seemed precious little she could possibly say.

Billy was gone, having left Arkham on a train that was but the first of many stages on his journey home. The *Ujaraanni* went with him, of course, safely locked within several layers of boxes and trunks. Before he left, he had clasped Elliot's hand, called him brother, and then removed the last of his amulets to place it around Elliot's own neck.

"Perhaps it will help until you can finally rid yourself of those damned phrases," he'd said.

Elliot, of course, protested. Hadn't Billy told them that long exposure to the *Ujaraanni*, even by guardians who couldn't read a letter of it, eventually caused a madness of its own?

"Indeed, but that happens only after years. My journey home should take only weeks. Months, at worst, if the weather and the shipping schedules are against me."

"Yes, but you're not a… an angakkoq! What if it works faster for–"

"I don't believe it does. But if so? Then I will manage, and my family will care for me. You need the protection far more than I."

And Elliot hadn't been able to argue any further, because he knew it was true.

Nor was that his only lingering fear. The thing he'd summoned had seen him, turned on him, knew who he was. Did its disappearance make him safe? Was that danger passed? Or did it – or something akin – still lurk in unfathomable spaces, waiting until it was summoned back to the world once more, biding its time until it could hunt him down?

He would never know, until it happened.

So now he sat at home, alone; the talisman about his neck, the words of both French and Latin protection charms fresh off his tongue. Spread out on the bed beside him were copies of both spells, photographs of Chester, and a letter from the Miskatonic administration. The brief, excruciatingly formal missive ordered him to make an appointment with the dean at his earliest convenience.

An appointment to make a case as to why, after missing so many classes and the associated assignments, he should not be expelled from the university. So far, he hadn't thought of a single compelling argument, and he wasn't certain he cared.

Wasn't certain there was a point to caring.

"Maybe one out of five, one out of six," the old occultist had said. A twenty percent chance, at best, that Elliot would ever recover, could free himself of the litany before he lost himself for what, he knew, would be the final time. Lost himself, and began to infect others.

Twenty percent… without help.

Elliot Raslo flipped Lafayette-Moses's business card over and over in his hands, and stared at nothing.

In a very private room, well across Arkham, in a building that nobody knew he owned, Hyrum Lafayette-Moses also sat in thought.

He leaned back in his most comfortable chair, upholstered in rich leather of a sort not readily identified, and held in one hand a snifter of Kentucky bourbon. The drink was entirely illegal, of course – but not nearly as much so, had anyone proved able to identify that leather, as the chair.

To his left, by one of the room's two doors, the silent chauffeur cocked his head in mute query.

"No, Lemuel," Lafayette-Moses said, somehow aware of the gesture without looking. "I won't be needin' anythin' else from you tonight. You go and get yourself some rest, now."

Already rippling and losing its shape, the servant turned and was gone from the room with a terrible liquid sound, leaving only the driver's uniform in a rough trail through the doorway.

His master glanced over at it, and at the coat rack, and shook his head. The creature was so quick to pick up most of the quirks and behaviors of the human form on which Lafayette-Moses insisted, but it seemed utterly unable to grasp the concept of cleaning up after itself.

Well, he'd get it on his way out. For now, the clothes could wait.

Lafayette-Moses took a sip of his drink, swiftly losing himself once more in thought.

They'd done it. He could scarcely believe those fools, those children, had actually *done* it. Oh, he'd hoped, hoped with near desperation that they would, that he wouldn't need to involve himself any further, but he couldn't have dared to expect…

It hadn't gone perfectly, of course. He'd had to reveal himself, to them and to the local faithful, to Carl Sanford and his "Silver Twilight Lodge," who were so much more than the people of Arkham knew. Sanford had almost been a problem, had disliked being told by an outsider to keep his people away from Chester Hennessy or anything to do with unfolding events. Lafayette-Moses had been forced to pull rank, to remind the stubborn bastard that he had come to Arkham on behalf of a power that transcended any mortal cult. He'd worried he might have to prove himself with a show of power, but Sanford had wisely, if sullenly, backed down.

If he'd had to force the issue, or if the rank and file of worshipers – here or across the world – had learned what was happening, it could have sown chaos, and not the proper sort of chaos. Could have cast doubt that the leaders of the many sects and factions knew what they were doing. Could have thrown the entire order of the worshipers of the Ancient Ones into tumult.

And if Lafayette-Moses had been forced to act personally, the old gods alone knew what might have come of it. His own sorceries would probably have been enough to prevent the rise of the Thousandfold Dream, assuming he caught the process early enough – but Lafayette-Moses hadn't lived so long as he had, hadn't obtained his power and his office, by relying on "probably" and "assuming." Even he, for all his learning, had no certain idea how swiftly Tsocathra's power grew, or what the results might have been from mixing human magics with those of the antehuman sorcerers *and* powers far more ancient still. It might have been disastrous indeed!

Still, he'd have done it. Though it would have put him at terrible risk, might even have backfired and hastened the catastrophe he meant to avert, he'd have done it, for that was his duty. The time was not yet, the stars not right, the Others not yet prepared to rise.

If Tsocathra had awakened now, before the proper time, the repercussions would have proved unfathomable, throwing into disarray plans that had been laid down before mortal life had learned to walk upright.

No, it could never have been allowed! But while Lafayette-Moses knew he *wouldn't* have allowed it, the fact that, in the end, he hadn't needed to – that he'd accomplished his goals with a nudge here, a few answers there – was proof enough that something mighty and all-knowing watched over his efforts.

His mouth stretched in an ugly grin, nothing akin to the polite smile he'd offered his pawns. He'd wait here in Arkham a while, see if he might find a way to manipulate the black-market trade in relics through Alice Bentley, or if Elliot Raslo might yet come to him. He'd make a useful apprentice, that boy.

Either way, though, he had to depart before *too* long. He had other duties, in other parts of the world.

He had, too, a man who needed tending, who would require very special care for a very long time.

Because he had to live, this man, perhaps for many years. Had to survive until the stars *did* come right. So that, at the proper time, when the Ancient Ones must rise, the Weaver of Flesh would stand among them.

Hyrum Lafayette-Moses stared at the far wall, at the one-way glass window that allowed him an unobstructed view of the locked room beyond.

And he watched, in silence provided by the thick glass and the padded walls, as Jebediah Pembroke continuously repeated, in its loathsome and apocalyptic entirety, the unholy litany of Tsocathra.

About the Author

ARI MARMELL is the author of the Mick Oberon urban fantasy series, the Widdershins YA fantasy series and many others, alongside novels in *Magic: the Gathering* and the video game, *Darksiders*, as well as writing for several roleplaying games.

mouseferatu.com // twitter.com/mouseferatu

ARKHAM HORROR

IN THE COILS OF THE LABYRINTH

DAVID ANNANDALE

For Margaux, who is the beautiful in my life.

O Rose thou art sick.
The invisible worm,
That flies through the night
In the howling storm:

Has found out thy bed
Of crimson joy:
And his dark secret love
Does thy life destroy.

WILLIAM BLAKE, "THE SICK ROSE"

PROLOGUE

Galloway, Scotland, 1925. The village of Durstal

October ended, and the last of the trucks drove out from the Stroud Estate. They came along the narrow road that ran down the hillside to the village, their cargo shrouded by ropes and canvas. Their loads were as heavy as all the others, Tom Spalding thought. He stood outside his inn and watched the convoy turn onto what passed for Durstal's main road, rumble past the Ash Inn, and head off into the woods, leaving the village behind. He wondered if he should feel relief that they were going. He wanted to. He couldn't remember when he had last felt real, honest, bone-deep relief.

All he felt was the chill in the air, the cold promise of an evening drizzle.

"Do you think things will be better?" Ben Laurie asked. Skeletally thin, his shoulders and back rounded with age, the old man was still half a head taller than Tom.

Tom looked at the old man with some surprise. Direct questions like that weren't the done thing in Durstal. "Hard to say," Tom said, noncommittal and honest at the same time. He stroked his graying goatee thoughtfully. He didn't know. He couldn't guess. But oh, how he wished he could have said *yes* to Ben and meant it.

Ben nodded in understanding. "Fair enough," he said, and shifted the conversation to safer terrain. "Easier to call the weather."

Tom snorted. "I can tell you what tonight's is, right enough. Tonight's is miserable."

Ben nodded again.

The rumble of the trucks faded to silence, and they turned back to the door of the Ash Inn. Before they could go in, Harriet Duncan came hurrying up from the direction of St Andrew's Church. "Is the vicar in there?" she asked, broad face flushed deep crimson with the effort of her run.

Tom shook his head. "He's not at the church?"

"No, and we're coming up to Evensong."

"I think he went up to have a look around the Stroud land," Ben said quietly.

Tom frowned. "Why? I thought no one had been there in weeks except the work crews."

Ben shrugged. "Maybe Donovan came back to close up. Or maybe the vicar just thought he might."

"But why go?" Tom insisted.

The other two said nothing.

Tom grimaced. He could imagine a few answers. Peter Wilson wanting to see if the Strouds were really gone, or heading up for a last chance to satisfy his curiosity while the gates were open. Tom would not have gone, but he understood the impulse. Everyone in the valley lived in the shadow of the Stroud Estate, and the need to do *something* could be hard to resist.

Do what about what?

Always best not to ask that question. Answers might come.

And maybe the most likely thing was that Peter had gone up carrying the same hope that Ben had given voice to, that Tom wished he could feel, only Peter had had the courage to put the hope to the test. Maybe he had gone up to the Stroud Estate to see that, after the weeks and weeks of blasting and the noise of construction, convoy after convoy carrying massive loads, there was now nothing to worry about there. Of course, no one had ever come right out and said they should be worried about the estate. But even so, even so, if whatever might have been there had left, if it was all just ordinary ground up there, that would be something, wouldn't it? Something worth looking into, if you had the nerve.

"What should we do?" Harriet asked. She looked worried. Being even older than Ben, she'd had that much longer to live with all the unspoken fears of Durstal. That made a person fragile, in the long run. And she had taken a maternal interest in Peter since his arrival five years earlier.

If Tom could spare her something, he should.

"We'll look for him," he said.

"Oh, thank you!" said Harriet.

Tom opened the door of the inn. "You come in and have a warm," he said. "I'll fetch my jacket, and Ben and I will be off."

Harriet went in willingly enough. Ben looked grim, but willing too, ready to take on the responsibility Tom had accepted for the two of them.

The two men climbed up the road to the estate. The iron gates were shut and padlocked. The estate would not have them. Tom didn't want to insist. He looked at Ben, who gave him an unhappy shrug.

"I don't think he's in there," Ben said. "But even if he is, we're not going to be able to find him."

"No," Tom agreed. They had come up here because they had to start somewhere, and he had hoped they'd meet Peter coming down the hillside.

No, *hoped* was the wrong word. He'd *wished* that would happen.

"Where now?" Ben asked.

"If he's in the village, he's fine, and he'll turn up," Tom began.

"While we catch our death of colds tromping up and down like fools."

"Maybe." Tom wished again, this time for such an outcome. It would make a story to laugh about afterwards. But if the vicar wasn't in the village… "I think we should try the clifftops," he said.

Ben nodded unhappily.

Midway back to the village, a path branched off from the dirt road and wound back up, making a wide detour around the wall of the Stroud Estate to finally come to the top of the rise, and onto the open moor that ended at the sheer drop down to the sea. A mist began rolling in well before they reached the moor, and by the time they did, visibility had dropped to a few dozen yards and was growing rapidly worse.

"We'll never find him in this," said Ben. "We could be right on top of him and not see him."

"We can at least try. I'll sleep easier knowing I did."

Ben grunted. "There speaks a man expecting the worst."

Tom didn't answer. He started calling for the vicar. Ben joined in. They walked forward carefully, conscious that they were drawing closer to the cliff edge. They called Peter's name, waited for an answer, then called again. The fog gathered around them, turning the landscape into gray, fading dream. The sound of the waves crashing against the base of the cliffs grew louder, a cold and relentless answer, a slow rhythm of mockery.

They heard the vicar just before they spotted him. His cry of "Tom!" sounded mournful. A few steps later, Tom could just make out Peter's shape in the fog, moving back and forth erratically, much too close to the drop.

"Vicar!" Ben shouted. "Stop where you are! We'll come to you."

Peter did not respond. He kept moving, jerkily and too quickly. They hurried forward and caught up to him with less than ten feet between him and the edge.

The call of the waves boomed.

The vicar walked with a harsh, determined gait at odds with his direction. He took ten steps, jerked to the right, went five, jerked back toward the sea for another five, then back, and then another shift. He looked like a puppet being yanked by a capricious showman. Sweat drenched his ashen face. He stared at Tom with pleading, despairing eyes.

"What are you doing?" Tom asked. "Stay still." He took hold of Peter's arm. The vicar kept walking, and he pulled away with a strength that took Tom by surprise. He felt as if he had been trying to restrain a moving vehicle. "Help me," Tom said to Ben, who grabbed the vicar's other arm.

Peter pulled free from them both without seeming to try. "I can't stop," he said. Tears ran down his cheeks.

The fog pressed in closer. If it got much worse, Tom realized, they would have to stay where they were. It would be too dangerous to try to find their way back to the slope leading to the village.

"Go get help," he said to Ben. "Come back with lanterns and torches so we can see you."

Ben nodded and set off as fast as he could. For the moment, they could still tell in which directions safety and danger lay.

Peter had moved off again. Tom caught up and tried once more to hold him. No use. And Peter's twisting path kept bringing him closer by degrees to the drop.

"What is happening?" Tom asked.

Peter tried to speak. His throat seemed to close, and he started choking. The vicar shook his head.

"I'll stay with you," Tom promised. "You'll be all right."

Face agonized, Peter shook his head.

He walked faster. Tom struggled to keep up. The zigs, zags and twists of Peter's path made him dizzy. Cold fingers touched the back of his neck. Then, even as the fear spread through his limbs, Tom felt himself begin to slip into Peter's rhythm. He found it easier to match his pace. He could anticipate when each sudden shift in direction would come. His feet knew the path they had to take. He didn't have to think. He could just let go, and join in the dance with the vicar.

Just let go. Let go. Follow the path.

Let go.

No.

Tom came to himself with a start. They were only a yard away from the cliff's edge. He leapt away from Peter. He threw himself down so he could not take another step. Below, the waves thundered in judgement. The fog came down, devouring the world, and after taking only a few more steps, Peter became a vanishing silhouette.

"Please stop," Tom begged the unseen puppet master.

"Oh, Tom," Peter said, with such terrible grief in two words.

The silhouette vanished.

The waves roared.

"Peter?" said Tom.

Only the waves answered.

Tom stayed down. He clutched at the ground. He would not move, no, he would not, not until the fog lifted and he knew his body would obey him.

He shivered in the whiteness that turned to grey and then to black as the light failed, and he knew all those trucks had not removed the fear from the Stroud Estate.

Instead, they were spreading it.

PART I

CHAPTER ONE

The exhaustion had turned into a python. The image came to Miranda Ventham as she struggled to the end of her morning class. It took all she had to keep upright at the front of the lecture hall. She forced herself not to lean on the lectern, worried she would collapse against it. Heavy as lead, the python wrapped around her and squeezed hard. She couldn't project her voice anymore. She couldn't stop rasping. She managed to hold her cough in check, but only barely. It scrabbled at her chest and throat, demanding to be let out.

She released the students ten minutes early. A few of them had some questions for her, and she supposed that she answered them, but she had no memory of what she said by the time she found herself back in her office on the second floor of Miskatonic University's humanities building. Miranda sat in her wooden swivel chair, head slumped down on her arms.

Somehow, she managed to get through her afternoon class. She remembered even less of it. The students were a sea of blurry faces in the classroom; their questions, when they came, distant signals from a storm-tossed ship.

Miranda ended that class early too, and then returned to her office again to engage in the pretense of marking. She didn't get through a single essay before she put her head down again and fell asleep.

"Miranda?"

She jerked awake and upright, blinking, trying to shrug off the python. It responded by squeezing even harder. Agatha Crane stood in the doorway, frowning with concern.

"Hey," Miranda said. "Sorry."

"You look terrible," said Agatha.

"If I look half as bad as I feel, then I must be a fright."

"You're definitely getting there."

Miranda grimaced. "Thanks."

"Wednesday," said Agatha. "That means you had your freshmen today, didn't you?"

"Two sets of them. Trying to get them interested in Byron."

"That's your field. I hope they were suitably appreciative."

"Ha. Hilarious." Miranda shook her head, trying to clear the worst of the cobwebs. "To be honest, it was a struggle getting through my upper level Romantics class yesterday, too, and at least those students are engaged."

"Byron too?"

"Yeah. Some overlapping prep this week. Small mercies." She chuckled weakly. "We were doing 'On This Day I Complete My Thirty-Sixth Year.'" She recited the last two lines. "'Then look around, and choose thy Ground, / And take thy rest.' I thought I was going to do just that."

"At least you weren't teaching Keats. That would have been a bit close to the bone."

Miranda gave Agatha a hard look, and saw that she wasn't joking. "You're serious."

"I am. Have you seen your doctor?"

"Overwork, he said. Making this cold drag on longer than it should."

"Is that what he said?"

"It was."

Agatha grunted, her expression skeptical. It was a look Miranda was used to seeing on her friend's face. The parapsychologist was in her late sixties, more than twenty years older than Miranda, and she wore her years like an armor of hard-won wisdom. Her wavy white hair framed features that were sharp as a chisel, though not unkind. Agatha was one of those people who seemed to grow stronger with the passing years, as if time were the forge for her tempered steel. Technically, she had retired three years earlier. All that meant was that she no longer taught, and devoted herself entirely to her research. She still came to the university every day.

Miranda had always admired Agatha's strength. Today, she envied it. Miranda was forty-two. She didn't often think of herself as middle-aged, though the signs were there. The crows' feet were starting to gather around her eyes, and the first sprinkling of gray was appearing in her black, upswept hair. But she didn't feel that different from how she had in her thirties, and in her thirties she had felt as she did in her twenties. Hadn't she?

She felt forty-two today, though. Hell, she felt sixty-two.

"Just how long have you had that cough?" Agatha asked.

Miranda tried to think. "This is March?" she said.

"Last I checked, yes."

Miranda counted back, became confused, gave up. "I'm not sure," she admitted.

"You need to see a specialist."

Miranda took a few ragged breaths before answering. She looked around her office, as if something might offer her support, as if the books, overflowing on their shelves and stacked around the edge of her desk in a nearly unbroken wall, should offer her physical comfort. "You think that's what it is, then?" she said to Agatha. She couldn't quite make herself speak the word *tuberculosis*.

"Don't you think that's what it is?"

Miranda closed her eyes for a moment. "I don't know," she said. *Liar.* She heaved herself out of her chair. "I just want to go home."

"Then let's go home," Agatha said, and helped her on with her coat.

Under an overcast March sky, they walked north-east from the university and into Rivertown. The clouds brooded with thoughts of sleet, and it felt much later than five-thirty. They stuck to the main thoroughfares of Rivertown, making their way past warehouses blackened with soot and age.

Never scenic, hardly pleasant, the walk had been a bit more interesting for the past few months. In the northern reaches of Rivertown, where the expanses of the graveyard held sway, renewal bloomed for the first time in Miranda's memory. Decrepit seventeenth century buildings lined the graveyard, and a number of the most decayed had been torn down. Miranda and Agatha had watched the project develop over the course of the winter, going from demolition of the old structures, to the digging of the deep foundations, to the rise of the new walls.

Today, they paused at the iron gates for Miranda to catch her breath.

"It looks like they're finished," said Agatha.

A discrete bronze plaque on the left-hand gate pillar identified the building beyond as the Stroud Institute. Out of the center of the main block, four stories high, a central tower shouldered up, adding one more set of windows. They looked down like vaulted eyes on the grounds. The Institute could almost have been mistaken for a neo-gothic apartment building. Long, gabled wings stretched out from the main block to the east and west. The constructions had not disturbed the thick oaks of the grounds. There had been some landscaping done around the new drive, with trimmed hedges lining the approach and a circular fountain in front of the entrance. The water hadn't been turned on yet, and the stone griffins surrounding the basin looked angrier than Miranda thought. She wondered if the play of water might soften the impression they made. Light, a dull orange, shone from the windows of the tower. Darkness pressed up against the panes everywhere else.

"It opens tomorrow, according to the *Advertiser*," Agatha said. "Our new tuberculosis clinic."

"New." Miranda touched the brickwork of the gate pillar. "Not even open yet," she said, "and it already looks old."

The bricks were dark, pitted, and weathered. They were cold to the touch and felt damp, as if it had just rained. Miranda's fingers ran over a patch of moss.

"It looks like it's always been here, doesn't it?" said Agatha. She sighed. "I had hoped it wouldn't. It would have been nice to see something that actually looked shiny and novel in this town."

"The contractors were from out of town, though, right?" Miranda asked hopefully.

Agatha nodded. "I've been keeping track."

"Really?"

"When something changes in Arkham, I like to know why, and who's behind the change."

"Our guardian," Miranda said, only half joking.

"I try," Agatha said, not joking at all. "Anyway, the contractors and the construction firm are out-of-towners. As far as I know, there's been no local involvement with the project."

So things hadn't altered from what Miranda had first heard. "That's something, at least," she said. New people in Arkham, creating a new thing, even if it did look old, even if the stonework whispered that it predated the town. She shouldn't be surprised by that. Age in Arkham spread through its architecture like a contagion.

Miranda started coughing, and she couldn't stop for a full minute. The fit left her bending over, clutching the pillar for support. She took her handkerchief away from her mouth and saw blood.

She straightened slowly, staring at the plaque. It didn't state the purpose of the Stroud Institute. It didn't have to. The sanatorium's wings, designed to accommodate many for a long time, made its intentions clear.

Miranda glanced at Agatha. She shook her head at her friend's worried stare. "I know," she said. "Wracking cough outside a TB sanatorium. I know. A bit heavy-handed, though, don't you think." She grimaced. "I really don't want this to be a sign." Her voice shook.

"I understand," Agatha said softly. "But if it is, you'd be wrong to ignore it."

Miranda nodded. She started walking again, taking her time. "Yes," she said. "You're right. I'll make an appointment in the morning."

They carried on out of Rivertown and into French Hill. They lived in neighboring buildings, former mansions that had been converted into apartments. Miranda said her goodbyes to Agatha, pulled opened the heavy entrance doors and let herself in to the foyer. The cool breath of the March evening followed her inside and gave her one last shivery touch on the back of her neck as the doors swung closed. Miranda crossed the checkerboard marble pattern on the floor and took the stairs to her suite on the second level. A few minutes later, she had the lights on in her living room, and she was curled up on her couch, blanket around her shoulders, a warming snifter of Armagnac in her hands.

She still felt cold. The cough shook her.

Floor-to-ceiling bookshelves took up most of the wall space in the room. Books squeezed in tightly, defying her to add to their number. She would and she did, and the newer arrivals lay horizontally on top of the rows. One day, she would have to purge and reorganize. Not today, though. Not tonight.

Her windows looked south, down the slope of French Hill, and over a prospect of the graveyard in Rivertown. As night fell, the graveyard became a darker patch surrounded by the lights of Arkham, the silhouettes of the tombstones sinking out of sight into a rising tide of black. In the right mood, she enjoyed the gothic flavor of the view. It didn't appeal to her tonight though, not with her body feeling like a jumble of pain and heavy weights.

From where she sat, she saw only the gables of the buildings across the street, poking up through the bottom of the window panes. Above them, the blank sky shaded darker, the passing minutes turning gray into black.

Miranda's eyes wandered from the window to the walls on either side, the one space in the living room free of bookcases, and where she had mounted some framed prints. To the left of the window, Caspar David Friedrich's *The Abbey in the Oakwood* hung above JMW Turner's *The Fifth Plague of Egypt*. Miranda's favorite painting, Théodore Géricault's *The Raft of the Medusa,* dominated the right-hand section of the wall.

The painting haunted her. It had since she had first seen the colossal original in the Louvre thirty years earlier, when her parents had taken the family to France during her father's research leave. He had taught at Miskatonic too, though she had followed her own path into the English department instead of history.

She stared at the print now, eyes traveling up and down the pyramidal composition of human misery on the raft. The father, grieving over the body of his dead son at the bottom of the frame, had no interest in the frantic activity at the top, where desperate survivors waved rags at the vanishing small sail on the horizon.

Miranda never tired of the ambiguity of the sail. Coming or going? A sign of hope or the mark of despair? No way to know, no way to determine which flavor of human agony Géricault had captured. Most days, Miranda reveled in the perfect undecidability.

Some days, like now, she felt certain the ship would disappear in the next second, even as she needed it to draw closer.

She coughed again. She wiped away another few drops of blood.

Go to bed, she told herself. She would. In a few minutes. When she had the strength to get up.

She sank into a dull stupor. Her attention wandered from the *Medusa* to the window, drifting between pain and dullness. She could have slept, but the cough wouldn't let her. When it came, it shook her entire body with its hoarse, barking strength. Her ribs ached. It hurt to breathe. She felt worse than she had all day, and worse than yesterday.

She would call a specialist tomorrow. She should have sooner. For too long, she had held on to the comforting delusion that this was just a cold, just a bug hanging around longer than normal.

Go to bed.

But if she did, that meant surrendering to the torture of a sleepless night. It meant becoming a thrashing prisoner of the bed and the endless hours before dawn.

She needed rest, though.

Go to bed. Try to sleep, at least.

Her mantel clock chimed eleven before she managed to struggle up from the mire of her stupor and shuffle to the bedroom. The ordeal of changing into her nightgown took the last of her energy. She collapsed into the bed, barely able to pull the covers up to her neck.

She coughed, moaned in pain, and closed her eyes.

So tired. So weak. Maybe sleep would come before the next coughing fit.

It did not.

Hours later, something came for her. It reached out from the night's great dark. She didn't know if she slept or woke, if she felt the touch of a dream or something more frightening. She couldn't move her granite-heavy limbs, but as the vertigo hit, she seemed to be spinning, faster and faster. In a moment, she would fly off the bed.

At the same time, she sank deeper and deeper into the mattress. Stuffing turned into quicksand, pulling her down.

Spinning, sinking, the depths beneath her infinite and hungry.

She tried to scream. She had no voice. She had no breath. Her mouth opened wide in panicked silence.

Spinning, sinking, now drowning.

Down, down, around and around, endlessly, down and down the serpent's coil.

Chapter Two

Miranda sat in the examination room and thought about being in bed. She had to work hard not to topple out of the chair. Exhaustion reached all the way to her bones, and she felt numb with the expectation of bad news. It had taken all of her energy and then some to get from her home to the office of her doctor, Henryk Kravaal. He sat at his desk, going over her test results.

Why she had to come all the way here for the bad news, she had no idea. Miranda already knew what Kravaal was going to tell her. She could read the signs. She had canceled all her classes for the past two weeks because she knew what she had and she wasn't going to spread it to anyone else. Why did she have to put herself through the trip and sit here, teetering? A phone call would have been fine.

Just get it over with and let me go home.

Except home wouldn't be an option for long, would it? And home didn't feel much like home during the night. The dreams kept coming, the variations of the same theme over and over.

"How are you sleeping?" Doctor Kravaal asked, as if reading her mind.

"Not well. Three or four hours a night, tops."

A stern shake of the head. "That isn't enough."

"I know, believe me. What about the tests?"

He turned in his chair to face her. His lined, narrow face, made longer by his gray goatee, arranged into an expression of professional sympathy. "Well," he said, "it's tuberculosis. I guess that's not a surprise."

"Anything else would have been." Exhaustion turned fear into numbness. "What happens now?"

"Now we arrange for your admission into a clinic. You're too sick to be at home, and you're not going to get better without care."

"You mean I would die."

Kravaal opened then clasped his hands. "Nothing is certain. There's so much we don't know about TB. But would things get worse on your own? They definitely would."

"And with care? How are my chances?"

"I'm not in the business of odds and percentages," Kravaal said smoothly. "If I were, I'd be a bookie, not a doctor. You are strong and otherwise healthy, though."

"I sure don't feel it."

"But you are. We've caught this at a stage where I'd think your prognosis, with care, should be a positive one."

That was good news, wasn't it? She supposed so. She felt like she was beyond reacting to anything, good or bad.

"In some ways, your timing is good," Kravaal went on. "If you're going to have TB, better now than a few months ago. You have a couple of options for a sanatorium."

"St Mary's Hospital or the Stroud Institute," said Miranda.

Kravaal arched an eyebrow. "You do your research."

"I walk past the Institute every day after work. It's open now?"

"It is."

"Which would you recommend?"

Kravaal leaned back in his chair and folded his arms. "St Mary's is a known quantity," he said. "Their record for recovery is as good as any other hospital's in the state."

And as bad, Miranda thought.

"It's too early to say anything definite about the Stroud Institute," he said, "but I've heard some promising things about its director."

"But which would you recommend?" Miranda insisted.

Kravaal gave her a knowing look. "For most of my patients, I would lean toward St Mary's," he said.

"Am I most?"

"You aren't. I have an idea that you would not do well under a strict rest cure, and probably make life difficult for other patients and the staff at the same time."

"You make me sound horrible."

"I mean you have a restless mind."

"That's part of my job."

"I know," said Kravaal. "But it isn't a good fit at St Mary's, and I gather they have a different approach at the Stroud Institute."

"Is that a recommendation, then?"

"No. I'm just giving you the information. It's up to you to decide where you want to go. There are some open beds at the moment in both clinics. You make a decision, and I'll get the process started."

A week later, on Friday, under an April sun whose warmth felt thin and brittle, a taxi dropped Miranda and Agatha off at the doors of the Stroud Institute. Agatha helped Miranda out of the cab and held her as she looked up the wide stairs leading to the entrance. Miranda counted the steps. Six. They looked like a hundred. She shoved her hands into the pockets of her trench coat and shivered. The Institute towered over her, as imposing now as it had been at night. No orange eyes glowered in the tower in the day, but now all the windows wore blank, expressionless gazes. The stonework of the building was the color of granite and old sorrows.

"It really doesn't look new, does it?" Miranda said. The building seemed as ancient as she felt.

"Just like the gates," Agatha agreed.

The cabbie put Miranda's suitcase on the ground and drove off. The car passed the fountain, which sent a prismatic spray waving back and forth across the width of the basin. The griffins were as stern as before.

"Can you manage?" Agatha asked.

Miranda still hadn't moved toward the first step. Fatigue hung around her shoulders like a lead blanket. The python squeezed her chest so hard she dreaded every breath. "I think so," she told Agatha. A lie, but she hated how utterly weak she had become.

"There's a ramp," said Agatha. It offered a gradual approach on the left-hand side of the stairs.

Miranda shook her head. The ramp's length frightened her. She couldn't imagine making the journey of a few dozen yards around the porch and up the ramp. "I can do the stairs," she said. She'd managed to get out of her apartment building this morning, after all. But that was down, and it had been two days since she'd last made an ascent.

Agatha picked up the suitcase. Still holding onto her arm, Miranda started forward.

"What do you think you're doing?" a cheerful voice called.

Miranda looked up. She had been staring at the first step as if it were a rattlesnake. A nurse strode out of the entrance, pushing a wheelchair. She came down the ramp at a brisk pace, as if racing to stop Miranda from sprinting up the stairs. As she arrived, the clock tower of Miskatonic University chimed ten.

"You're early," the nurse said, smiling to show she wasn't scolding. Her cap sat on top of tidy curls of red hair. She had a kind face, one that seemed equally disposed to serious purpose and to laughter. "Professor Ventham, isn't it? I *am* sorry. I was going to be waiting for you when you arrived. But all's well, all's well. Sit yourself down like a good girl."

Miranda would normally have bristled at the infantilization. And the nurse couldn't have been more than five years older than her. Yet Miranda suddenly felt ten years old, and embraced by a grandmother's care. She sat down in the wheelchair with a sigh. She had been standing for less than a minute. It felt like an hour.

"I'm Nurse Holden," the woman said, turning the chair around and pushing

Miranda to the ramp. "Let me officially welcome you to the Stroud Institute. Though I'm sorry for the struggle you're having, we're still glad to see you."

"I'm glad to be here," Miranda said. Relief washed over her. She'd reached the end of a hard journey, the end of the ordeal of the last few weeks. She had arranged a leave of disability with the university, feeling guilty about abandoning her students so close to the end of term. Knowing that she had made the right choice for them as well as for her did nothing to ease the irrational, gnawing shame, a shame that seemed to be the only emotion to cut through the numbing fatigue.

Tuberculosis. The word and the reality it signified were hard to face. She had to, though, and being here, at last, made that task easier.

When she had inquired about the Stroud Institute's rates, she had been pleasantly surprised. She could easily afford to stay there, closer to home, and in an environment she hoped would be less depressing than that of St Mary's Hospital.

Less depressing, and most of all, new. That mattered.

They reached the door where Agatha met them, carrying Miranda's suitcase.

"Here we are, Professor Ventham," said Holden.

Miranda's eyes widened at the size of the entrance hall. She had not expected a setting this grand. Two stories high, with a marble floor, it collected the echoes of footsteps and bounced them around for its amusement. Sunlight came in red and blue through stained glass windows, dappling the floor with color. Corridors branched off to the left, right, and straight ahead. Holden went straight, nodding to the nurse stationed at the circular, polished oak reception desk in the center of the lobby.

"Would you mind waiting here?" she asked Agatha. "Professor Ventham and I just have some paperwork to deal with before we can get her settled in."

"Of course." Agatha walked over to the wooden bench that ran along the entire perimeter of the entrance hall and sat down.

Holden took Miranda down a few more corridors, moving at such a clip that Miranda grew disoriented. The halls were more institutional than the lobby, though still more welcoming than a hospital. Above oak wainscoting, the walls were painted a cream color with a slight tinge of green. The effect refreshed, and reminded Miranda of spring as it might be, warm and lush instead of gray and drizzling. Pleased, she didn't mind losing her bearings. When they stopped at a small office and Holden settled herself behind a desk, Miranda no longer had any idea where she was in relation to the lobby.

"Now," said Holden, "we already have most of what we need from you, and we have your case history. You'll be getting a full examination later today. So just a few consent forms for you to sign. We also need to go over some of the basics of your treatment at the Stroud Institute. With me so far?"

Miranda nodded. "In other words, you're going to tell me the rules." She'd done some reading about the rest cure in St Mary's tuberculosis wing and elsewhere. She knew what was coming, and dreaded it. Still, Holden was a lot friendlier than she'd expected. She'd heard the St Mary's crew were dour enough to be gravediggers.

Holden laughed. "I suppose you might call them rules. But I don't think you'll find them all that bad. We're here to take care of you, Professor, not torture you."

That sounded promising. Miranda sat up a bit straighter in the chair.

"Our director, Donovan Stroud, believes that the established approaches to the treatment of TB should be questioned precisely because they *are* established. I know he'll want to meet you, and I'm sure he'll tell you more about his philosophy then, so I won't do him the injustice of getting it wrong now. What you need to know is that though we do practice the rest cure here, we do it with some differences."

"Will I be allowed to read?" Miranda asked. She knew what the answer to that would be at St Mary's. She had spent the days since her diagnosis picturing herself confined to a bed, denied her books, denied any activity of the mind whatsoever, forbidden even from talking. *That's not resting. That's rehearsing death.*

"The Stroud Institute has a very fine library, if I do say so," said Holden. "You're more than welcome to use it. In fact, you'll be encouraged to do so."

Miranda almost wept. "Oh, thank every god above," she said.

"Director Stroud has made reading *The Yellow Wallpaper* a compulsory part of our training."

"I'm impressed," said Miranda.

"So was Director Stroud, by that story. He has ensured that its lessons are not lost on any of us. He believes that a cheerful mind is essential to the success of any kind of rest cure. If the mind is not at ease, neither is the body, and the mind that is not allowed to be active is an uneasy one."

Miranda fought to hold back the sobs of relief. They wouldn't do her cough any good. She felt her body already beginning to relax. She hadn't realized how taut she had been, despite her exhaustion. "You have no idea how much hope you've already given me," she told Holden.

"Oh, I think I might," said Holden. "You are part of our initial intake of patients, but you aren't the first to arrive, or the first to express those sentiments."

Holden spent a few more minutes going over the first stages of Miranda's treatment. "Even though this is the 'bed rest' phase," she concluded, "you'll still have some upright activity, if you feel up to it. We'll monitor your progress and move to total bed rest only if the circumstances dictate it. You're free to converse with your wardmates, but do not raise your voice. No strain is key. We do have a silent ward, but believe me when I tell you that we view it as a last resort."

"I do believe you," said Miranda.

"Splendid. I'll be taking you in a moment to the west wing, the women's wing. Women in the west, men in the east."

"And never the twain shall meet?"

Holden favored her with a wry chuckle. "Only in carefully monitored situations. We do have some rules, Professor Ventham, and they must be respected. They're there for good reasons."

That caution sounded a little more rehearsed than the rest of Holden's delivery. "I wasn't planning on challenging them," Miranda promised. She didn't feel she could ever walk again, never mind cause trouble for the staff.

She signed the last of the forms, and Holden wheeled her into the halls. When they reached the lobby again, Holden waved to Agatha to join them. "We're taking Professor Ventham to her bed," she said.

"Will I be able to visit her?"

"Of course. There are visiting hours on Wednesday, Friday, and Sunday afternoons."

Holden took them to an elevator at the entrance to the west wing, and it brought them to the top floor.

"You don't remember me, do you?" Holden asked Miranda as the elevator doors opened.

"Oh dear," she said.

"Not the first time you've been asked that, I guess."

"It's an all too frequent event. I have the worst memory for faces and names. Did you take a course with me?" Miranda tried to call up the memories of students from years past, but drew a blank.

"I wouldn't expect you to recall," Holden reassured her. "It was more than ten years ago."

"My survey course?" Miranda guessed. "Please tell me I didn't put you off poetry forever?"

"You did not, and you weren't my first-year professor. I took the Romantics with you in my third year. My minor was in English literature."

"Is that right?" Agatha sounded impressed.

"Director Stroud told me it was one of the reasons I was hired," Holden said, not hiding her pride. "He wants his staff to have curious minds too. We aren't resting on our laurels here. The Stroud Institute is committed to continuously finding better ways of treating tuberculosis."

"That would be a feather in Arkham's cap if a vaccine came out of here," said Agatha.

"Don't be surprised if it does."

Miranda let their conversation fade into a comforting background as she took in the surroundings that were going to be her home for the months to come. *Maybe even longer*, she thought, and then chased the idea away before it depressed her. Her nose prickled with the familiar antiseptic smell of hospitals. The halls weren't the stark white she had been expecting, though. They were green-tinged cream instead, and though the lighting was bright, the prevailing atmosphere was warm, as if washed with amber and gold from a source she couldn't quite locate.

She also found the same paradoxical meeting of old and new that had struck her and Agatha about the exterior. Again, she couldn't put her finger on the reason for that impression. The brass railing that ran along the walls gleamed with newness, and so did all the fixtures. The paint on the walls was spotless. The floor was unmarked. She could almost believe no one else had been wheeled down these corridors before her, even though she saw nurses walking briskly from room to room.

At the same time, when she looked up at the slight curve of the ceiling, or let her eyes travel down the full length of the hall, she found herself thinking of catacombs beneath cathedrals, and of cloisters fallen into the silence of ruin. She didn't know why. Nothing here resembled the images that rose in her mind.

Maybe she was feverish. Nothing more than that. Maybe.

She thought about the night the vortex swallowed her, and shuddered.

"Are you cold?" Holden asked.

"No," said Miranda. "No. Just tired."

"We'll have you in your bed very soon."

"That will be nice."

Holden paused outside a room at the intersection of two halls. "Your bed is in here," she said. "We'll leave your things here, get you bathed, and then settled." She looked at Agatha. "Bed B," she said. "To the left, next to the window."

Agatha nodded. "I'll unpack her things."

"Thank you," said Miranda. It felt good to be taken care of, good not to have to decide or do anything for herself for a while. She could let herself go. Embraced by a soul-deep warmth of well-being, she could almost pretend the cough wasn't waiting for her just around the next labored breath.

Half an hour later, Miranda lay in her bed. The formalities were over. She had arrived. A few of her favorite books sat on her nightstand, ready to keep her company – William Blake's collected works, a copy of the 1805 version of Wordsworth's *The Prelude*, Ann Radcliffe's *The Mysteries of Udolpho*. Commanded to rest, she was more than happy to comply. Agatha sat in a chair beside her. They spoke quietly so as not to disturb the other three women in the room, two of whom appeared to be asleep.

"Well," said Agatha, "this seems nice, as far as sanatoriums go."

"I think so too."

They both paused. Their eyes met. Miranda tried to smile. They had both caught the hint of forced cheerfulness in the other's voice.

"It is, though, isn't it?" Miranda asked, needing reassurance as the moment of being left alone in the belly of the Institute drew near. Alone, with three strangers and bare walls for company. The books that gave her friendship and warmth, her prints that gave her eyes joy, she would miss them all terribly. She would miss home. Except she couldn't stay there, and here, she would be looked after. Here was where it was good for her to be. She kept telling herself that, and for the moment, the comfort of the bed made her believe it.

"I'm impressed by the staff," Agatha said, her tone emphatic. "You're going to receive good care here. *Humane* care. So you're absolutely in the right place."

Insofar as anywhere in Arkham was the right place. Miranda couldn't remember when she had first begun to feel the sense of wrongness, like a background electrical hum, covering every corner of the city. Much of the time, she didn't notice it consciously. She had grown used to it, and it wasn't an acute sensation. It had just enough strength to impinge on her thoughts in those moments when silence became a little too thick.

"What do you think of the building?" Miranda asked. She needed reassurance, but she needed her friend's honesty even more.

Agatha cocked her head slightly, thinking. "It's architecturally interesting," she said at last. "More so than you'd expect from a medical facility."

"The old and the new together," said Miranda. "The interior is the same as the exterior."

Agatha nodded. "I'm not sure why that is, but yes."

Miranda turned her head on the pillow to look past the other beds, to the doorway and the long corridor on the other side. She'd noticed something when Holden had been helping her into the bed. She had put the impression down to a fatigue-induced optical illusion.

She had hoped when she looked again, her perception would have changed.

It had not.

"Look down the hall," she said to Agatha. "Do you notice anything?"

Agatha cocked her head. She eyed the walls with a skeptical squint. "Yes," she said after a few moments had passed. "The hall is straight, but ..."

"But it doesn't *feel* straight."

"You're right. It doesn't."

"Like there might actually be a curve in the walls."

"Maybe there is," said Agatha. "Just very subtle."

"Maybe."

"When was the last time you saw a truly straight line in this old town?" Agatha asked. "I can't remember. That could be our problem. We don't know how to look at something that actually is straight and new. We're out of practice."

Miranda turned that idea over. She liked its comforting possibilities. "Do you really believe that?"

"Do we have compelling evidence to the contrary?"

"No."

"No," Agatha repeated, leaning into the word. "So you're going to rest, and you're going to recover, and you're not going to worry."

"Because you'd tell me if I should."

"I would."

Miranda had spoken a fair bit with Agatha about the older woman's research into parapsychology. From the mere fact of living in Arkham and being curious, Miranda knew enough about the history and current events of the town to believe that Agatha's studies were important. She hadn't, as yet, had any direct experience of parapsychological events herself.

As far as she knew. And believed.

And Agatha would tell if she had reason to worry. That reassured her. Even Agatha's preferred word, *parapsychology*, was reassuring, unlike *supernatural*. Miranda liked *parapsychology*. The word had the power of rationality behind it, and stripped mystery away from the supernatural, forcing it to stand up to scientific scrutiny.

So much power in words, and so much treachery. That she knew intimately from her own research. Agatha's hard-headed approach imposed order on the chaotic and kept it at a distance. More than ever, Miranda needed the mere notion of things stirring in darkness kept far away.

But what about that night, the night of the maelstrom?

Delirium caused by fever and weakness. She'd experienced spinning sensations before when she'd been sick.

But not like this. Not with such intensity. Not with the abyssal plunge.

Then again, she'd never had tuberculosis before, either.

She shut the door on such speculation. It wasn't restful. Agatha said she was in good hands. Agatha said she could rest. If Agatha said it, then Miranda believed it.

Miranda sighed. She felt herself sink deeper into the bed, in a good way. "Thanks. I think I really will sleep well here."

"You look like you're going to conk out any minute."

"I just might."

"You really haven't been getting much sleep, have you?"

"I don't know when I last managed longer than four hours."

"Any recurrences?" Miranda had told Agatha about the maelstrom.

"No."

"Good." She stood to go. "Get to work on catching up on those lost hours."

"You'll come by Sunday?"

"Count on it. And I'll keep an eye on your place, so don't worry about home."

Miranda watched her go. She fell asleep before she saw Agatha reach the end of the corridor. On the edge of dreams, she wondered why it took Agatha so long to walk to the elevator.

Chapter Three

Miranda woke shortly before the evening meal. She felt as weak as ever in body, but refreshed in mind, enough to take an interest in the room and in the women who shared it with her.

At first glance, the space struck her as a typical room on a hospital ward, as antiseptically impersonal and predictable as what she would have found at St Mary's. White walls, floor and ceiling, white sheets, iron bedframes. Gradually, she saw that it had a bit more character. The ceiling had a gentle curve, less pronounced than in the hall, but enough to conjure the gentle echo of a dome. The arched windows each had at least one pane of stained red or green or blue glass. Lying down, Miranda could see nothing through them but the sky. She looked forward to seeing the view of the grounds of the hospital when she stood up again.

Not now, though. Not right now.

The windows were shut against the dank, cold spring. That had to be another departure from the norms of tuberculosis treatment elsewhere. Miranda had done her reading and understood that conventional wisdom called for fresh air year-round, regardless of cold or rain, wind or snow. Not so here. The room felt warm, though not overly so. The temperature seemed calibrated to be comfortable when up and about, but just cool enough to give delight in curling up under the covers. *How can they regulate it so precisely?* she wondered. Maybe they couldn't. Maybe she just had the luck to arrive on a perfect day. By purpose or by chance, the air invited her to snuggle down and rest.

I'm going to be okay.

She hadn't been able to tell herself that yesterday.

"Is it always this comfy?" she asked no one in particular.

"It sure is," said Cleo Whitten, the Black woman in the bed opposite hers.

The woman on Miranda's left gave a sniff expressive of disagreement and contempt. Her name was Frieda Fleet, and she wore the whiteness of her skin like a badge of pedigree. When she coughed, which was often, she coughed pointedly. That hacking announced the fact of her illness and demanded that attention be paid. Cleo seemed stronger, her coughing fits ragged, but less frequent. Her eyes were brighter too, and not with fever. Miranda thought Cleo looked like some-one making real progress in her fight against the disease.

You show it what's what. I will too.

Esme Garth, in the bed across from Frieda's, said nothing. She was even paler than Frieda, whiter than her sheets, her face sunken in on itself with weakness and exhaustion. She rarely coughed, but it seemed to Miranda that she rarely breathed, either. Miranda hadn't yet seen her open her eyes. The only evidence she had that Esme still lived was that no one had taken the body away. She only knew the woman's name because Cleo had told her.

After less than five minutes of conversation, Miranda had a sense of the dynamics in the room. She liked Cleo and her expression of knowing amuse-ment. Frieda was going to be much less fun. She had a face chiseled out of ice with harsh, severe strokes. She clearly resented not having a private room, and resented sharing space with Cleo even more. The social leveling of the disease presented itself to her as a personal insult, and no one else in the room had the grace to recognize that fact.

Miranda shrugged inwardly. If Frieda froze the rest of them out, they weren't going to mourn the loss of her sparkling conversation.

Dinner arrived at six, brought in by patients doing well enough to take on light volunteer duties. Cleo greeted one of them, Jennifer Wong, by name, and introduced her to Miranda.

"Jennifer's our good luck charm," Cleo said. "She's been getting stronger by the day."

Jennifer smiled at Miranda. She looked like one of those cheerful people for whom, Miranda thought, smiles had been invented in the first place. "It's true," Jennifer said. "I can't believe how much better I feel. Do you remember what it's like to take a deep breath?"

"I remember the concept," Miranda said.

"I can actually do it again! And you will too. I promise!"

Normally, Miranda found people that bubbly hard to take. Jennifer's enthu-siasm and good wishes were so heartfelt, though, that Miranda found herself grinning too. "If you're the guarantee of that promise, then I'd say it's good as gold."

Jennifer took her by surprise by hugging her, and then finished distributing the meals.

Miranda looked at the plate of breaded veal, mashed potatoes and corn on her plate. It looked much nicer than hospital food should, she thought. It tasted nicer too, she discovered. *And* it was hot.

"I'm starting to think I'll just stay here," she said, then regretted the joke. "I'm sorry. That was in bad taste." No one in the Institute would have been there long, but some of the patients had likely been transferred from St Mary's, and might have been there for months or even years.

"They do make our stay as easy as possible," said Cleo, "and I thank them for it."

"Have you been ill long?"

"Four months trapped in my bed at St Mary's. Don't ask me how long I was sick before that."

"I don't know for sure how long I've had this, either," Miranda admitted.

"It's sneaky." Cleo pointed at Esme. "I knew her at St Mary's. She was there before me. Been like this all along." She didn't have to add that she didn't like the tiny woman's chances.

Frieda sniffed again. "I have no intention of spending the entire summer here," she announced. She gave Miranda a pointed look, as if Miranda had already offered a contrary diagnosis. "There are events, you understand."

"I certainly do," Miranda said with a straight face, careful not to exchange looks with Cleo.

"I won't have them badly run. I won't."

"Nor should you."

Frieda nodded, pleased that Miranda understood. "My husband is Reginald Fleet," she said, and paused.

"I see." *Should I genuflect?* Miranda thought. She knew the name, vaguely. It often headlined the society columns that Miranda flipped past in the newspaper. She knew Fleet owned more than one factory in Northside, and one of the newer, more ostentatious mansions in Uptown.

"I think it's very important that things be done correctly," Frieda said, stating a general principle and implying that this precept was not being followed by the Stroud Institute, at least as far as she was concerned.

"Words to live by," Cleo said, her tone studiously devoid of irony.

Frieda gave her a frosty look.

"I'm going to try to be adaptable," Miranda said. "Whatever I was doing at home wasn't enough to get me well, was it? So I'm going to assume they know better here."

Another unimpressed sniff from Frieda. "I'm sure you hope you're right," she said.

Miranda kept her polite smile in place and turned away from Frieda. She looked across the room to see Cleo's eyebrows raised in amusement. Miranda grinned a little bit wider, turning her smile into satire, and Cleo grinned back.

Miranda dosed fitfully through the evening after supper. When she roused herself with coughing, she and Cleo chatted a bit more. Occasionally, Frieda would hold forth on another of the Institute's shortcomings for their edification. Esme never said a word.

Music began to play from a ceiling-mounted speaker at lights-out. The "Moonlight Sonata" wafted gently through the room.

"Beethoven for bedtime?" Miranda said, pleased.

"The Institute has its own radio station," said Cleo. "Sometimes we get music. Sometimes a reading."

"A story?"

"More like a homily," said Frieda.

"Things for us to think about," said Cleo. "Nice things."

The music wasn't loud, but neither was it so quiet that Miranda had to strain to hear it. The piano soothed her. She turned onto her side and stared sleepily at the open door and the dim lighting of the hall.

She closed her eyes.

She still saw the corridor, in every detail.

Am I asleep? She didn't know.

The corridor twisted. Floor and walls and ceiling turned over and over, a ribbon of madness. The vertigo seized her, and she spun counter to the rotation of the hall.

She had to be asleep. She had to be dreaming. *Wake up! Wake up! Wake up!*

An old reflex kicked in, a desperate childhood defense against nightmares. If she hyperventilated, she might escape. She tried to take deep breaths.

Immediately, a flood of black water roared down the hall. Her breath, caught in her chest, turned into a scream, and the water swept over her and silenced her.

Down again, dropping and spinning as she had that night in her home. She flailed at the dark. Drowning. She was drowning. She couldn't breathe. Her chest burst with pain.

She surfaced, gasping and coughing.

Darkness around her. Motionless shapes in the other beds, shapes she sensed without seeing. The hall lay before her, an expanse of gray and dim amber.

Miranda didn't know the hall, didn't know the room, didn't know where she was.

She felt the rub of the cotton sheet against her arms, and the pain in her chest from another day of coughing.

She was awake. Had to be. But why didn't she know this place? Her mind fumbled in total disorientation.

A dull roar, and then the black water foamed down the hall again.

She couldn't make a sound. The scream stayed inside her skull. The water carried her away into the depths of the nightmare once more.

She surfaced again, praying that this time she was awake, that she had broken through the strata of dreams.

She faced the room, the hall, the disorientation. And then, to her despair, the black water.

Over and over, spinning and drowning, a false waking that felt completely real, and then the night flood churning and foaming as it came to swallow her.

The cycle did not end until dawn found her. Limbs tangled in twisted, sweat-soaked sheets, every breath a punishment; she didn't trust the reality of wakefulness until she heard Esme cough, and the Stroud Institute settled itself around her for the day.

Chapter Four

Agatha kept her promise. She arrived in Miranda's room on Sunday, just after lunch.

"Would it be all right if she took me to the library?" Miranda asked Nurse Revere. "I feel up to it." She did, in spite of the bad nights. She knew better than to believe she was on the mend after barely forty-eight hours, but she was sleeping well during the days, and the lack of teaching and marking and not worrying about working was making a difference. The nights were the nights, and she needed to talk to Agatha about them. Other sources of stress had been lifted from her, though, and that mattered.

Nurse Revere didn't answer right away. She scrutinized Miranda's chart as if there were already months of data on it. Miranda did her best to look meek. Revere was older than Nurse Holden, and carved from much sterner rock. She had eyes of flint, and the face of a granite axe. To Miranda's relief, Agatha picked up on her strategic approach and adopted an expression as close to innocence as she could manage.

Whether Revere believed in Agatha's act or not didn't matter. After making them wait a full minute, she gave a curt nod. "You've been resting," she said. "That's good. You're going to behave yourself, Professor Ventham, aren't you?" The question sounded like a command. "You're not going to be a patient who doesn't want to get well."

"I *do* want to get well," Miranda reassured her. "I'll do anything to kick this. Show me the hoops, and I'll jump through them. I want to feel normal again."

"Then you'll behave."

"I will."

Another curt nod. "No exertions," she said. "Not too long." Then she turned to Cleo's chart, dismissing Miranda and Agatha.

Miranda made sure to take her time getting out of her bed and into the chair, accepting help from Agatha. Nurse Revere glanced back once, and seemed satisfied that there was no misbehavior.

"Which way to the library?" Agatha asked.

"This floor," said Revere. "Follow the signs."

Agatha pushed Miranda out into the corridor. "Do you see any signs?"

"Not here. Don't ask again." That would be asking for permission to be revoked. "Let's just go."

At the end of the hall, they found the first sign. Agatha turned right, down another long corridor. At the next intersection, they were sent left.

"These halls…" said Agatha.

"I know," said Miranda. "Just pretending to be straight, all of them. I think I'm getting used to them, though. Almost. I try not to focus just on what's immediately in front of me. That helps, anyway. And it's not like I'm out of the room much."

"How have things been?"

"I feel taken care of. Had more tests and my X-ray done yesterday. Now all I have to do is keep resting."

"And they're helping you do that?" Agatha asked.

"They are. The food is good. There are enough little things happening in the day to keep things interesting."

"Such as?"

A coughing fit seized Miranda, and it was a long, painful moment before she could speak again. "Puzzle sheets that come with lunch," she said, her eyes watering. She rubbed them clear. "I hear there are counseling sessions for those well enough to attend, so that's something to look forward to."

"That doesn't sound like a lot happening," said Agatha.

"Weirdly, it's enough. There hardly seems to be enough time for all the napping I want to do between meals."

"You really are resting then. That's good."

"Plus, we get piped-in music in the evening."

"This place has its own radio station?" Agatha sounded surprised.

"Seems it does."

"Have you been doing any reading?"

"Not really," Miranda said. She thought about her little pile of books with a pang of guilt. "I haven't felt up to it yet. This will be my first visit to the library. But we get things to read with the meals along with the puzzles. Quotations for the day."

Agatha laughed. "No doubt very inspirational. Lifted from *Reader's Digest*?"

"Want to know what today's was?"

"Tell me."

"'I saw from afar and from before what I was to see from behind,'" Miranda recited.

Agatha was quiet for a moment. They reached another junction and turned right again. The complexity of the route struck Miranda as excessive.

"Can't say I've heard that passage before," said Agatha. "Doesn't sound very *Reader's Digest*."

"It's from Thomas de Quincey's *Suspiria de Profundis.*"

"I see," Agatha said slowly. "And what are you supposed to do with that line?"

"Think about it, I supposed. Puzzle it out. It does give us something meatier than a platitude to ponder."

"Granted. What did your roommates make of it?"

"We didn't talk about it. It made Cleo frown, I think. Frieda barely looked at it."

"And the other one?"

"Esme? I'm trying to think. I haven't spoken to her at all yet. She sleeps almost all the time. She *did* surface for the meals, briefly. I didn't notice if she read it."

They turned another corner, and at the end of a short hall the library entrance waited for them, wooden doors open, the high, wide space beyond inviting.

Miranda read the inscription on the lintel. "'The unexamined is the unquestioned'. Magnus Stroud."

"Stroud," Agatha repeated. "Is the director immortalizing his thoughts?"

"His first name is Donovan, I think. I'm going to guess these are the words of an illustrious ancestor."

The library had a high ceiling, much higher than anywhere else Miranda had been in the Institute, with the exception of the lobby. A row of arched, floor-to-ceiling windows poured daylight into the center of the space, where leather armchairs clustered. Bookshelves took up the other walls, resting in cool shadows and the gentle, warm light of lamps mounted along the ceiling's periphery.

Agatha brought Miranda to the window. There were other armchairs here, with plenty of space between them for a wheelchair. Agatha sat down next to Miranda. They looked down into the grounds together.

"Huh," Agatha grunted.

"Yeah," said Miranda. "Did you keep track of all the turns we made?"

"I thought I had. I must have miscounted."

The library was in the central tower of the Institute, and faced in the same direction as Miranda's room. From this vantage point, she would have guessed that a single corridor would have taken her straight back to her bed. "I wonder what the architectural reasons were for that route," she said.

"Someone thought they were very sound," replied Agatha. She took Miranda's hand. "You said the days helped you feel rested." She gave her friend a searching look. "How are the nights?"

Miranda sighed. "Not good." She told Agatha about the dream of her first night. In the daylight, it was easier to think of it as a dream. She also distrusted that ease. She wanted the truth to be that she was just having nightmares. She could deal with that reality. But their insistence and repeated imagery were new, and that disturbed her.

Agatha listened carefully. She prodded Miranda for a few more details, then asked, "What about last night? Any better?"

"Different," said Miranda. "Again, I couldn't tell if I was asleep or awake, but I wasn't drowning or spinning this time. I was just staring down the hall the whole night."

"The hall that you try not to look at during the day?" Agatha asked, eyebrows raised.

"I know what that sounds like, but yes. I couldn't help myself. So I'm lying on my side, eyes open, looking down its length. Then I'd wake up and realize I'd been dreaming of looking at the same thing I could see with my eyes really open. Or so I thought. Then I'd wake up again. And so on and on until morning."

Agatha had taken a pen and a reporter's notebook out of her handbag. She wrote in it, then frowned.

"You know more about this kind of thing than I do," Miranda said. "Are these more than bad dreams?"

"Do you think they are?" Agatha's tone was carefully neutral.

Miranda's instinct was to say yes, unequivocally. But a gut response was not what Agatha was interested in hearing. So Miranda thought through her answer. It was still a yes. "I've never experienced anything like them before," she said. "And though there are differences, there is also a consistency to them that I don't associate with dreams. I do think they're something more."

Agatha jotted down a few notes. "All right," she said. "You might be right. Then again, you might not be."

"I understand."

"This isn't me saying that I doubt your word."

"I know that's not the issue, Agatha."

"Good. We have to approach the problem with rigor. If we don't, we're being fantasists, not scientists."

Miranda almost pointed out that she *wasn't* a scientist. She decided that a plaintive cry of "But I'm in the Humanities!" wouldn't be helpful.

"Agreed," she said instead.

"Before we can seriously consider the possibility that you're experiencing a parapsychological phenomenon, we have to eliminate all other explanations," Agatha went on, almost as if Miranda were one of her pupils.

Miranda didn't object. Agatha had often expounded on her frustrations with the emerging discipline of parapsychology. There were too many self-styled researchers who didn't know the first thing about the scientific method. Too many proponents who believed in everything they encountered because they wanted to, without even consulting stage magicians to see if they didn't have ways of duplicating the reported wonders. Agatha feared the disrepute that hovered around parapsychology, not because of what might happen to her own academic reputation, but because of how that ridicule could bring down the entire field and destroy the good that it could do.

"We don't dismiss the parapsychological possibility," Agatha insisted. "But we don't make it our first assumption."

"Things happen in Arkham, though," Miranda said quietly.

"Yes." Agatha was somber now. "Yes, they do." She took a breath, straightened up in the armchair, and put pen to paper once more. "Tell me everything again," she said. "Let's start at the beginning. Go through it slowly. We want every detail."

Miranda relived the nights again, breaking them down, under Agatha's prompting, into phases, and the phases into beats.

"What is it?" Agatha asked after Miranda paused for an extended period.

"I was thinking about the corridor," said Miranda. "It feels like a fixation."

"Why do you think it might be one?"

Miranda shrugged. "Maybe because there's something about the hall that's significant."

"The one you see in… let's call them dreams for now, or the real one in this building?"

The question made Miranda feel queasy. She made herself examine it. She was going to beat TB, so she was going to beat whatever these dreams were too. "Maybe both," she said. "They both feel weird."

"Maybe they are," said Agatha, and Miranda did not find that answer reassuring at all. "And maybe that's the answer. Maybe a quirk of architecture is affecting your dreams."

That was more like it. That was reassuring. Except… "But my first hall dream was before I came here."

"And that's something we can't ignore. All right. Think about how you experience the hall. Tell me its defining features in the dreams."

Defining features? "Length," said Miranda. "It's too long, or longer than it seems." She remembered watching Agatha's departure on the first day. "I think I might have had one of the dreams right after arriving," she said, and told Agatha about the endless journey she had appeared to make. "And it twists," Miranda said, details becoming clearer as she thought about them. "Even when it isn't spinning around, somehow there's still some kind of twisting." She shook her head. "No, that's not quite right. *Coiling.* Yes, that's more like it. And it's old. Too old."

"How do you mean?"

"I can't say. That's just the impression I have." Miranda looked around the library. She eased herself up out of her wheelchair.

"Easy," Agatha warned. "Where are you going?"

"Nowhere." Miranda took a step forward and touched the wall between the windows. "Feel this," she said. She sat back down and wiped her palm against the dressing gown. The wall had been dry, but her hand suddenly felt clammy, as if she'd run it down a slimy surface. "Feel it," she insisted.

Agatha followed her example, and then she too was rubbing her hand against her coat sleeve.

"It's wrong, isn't it?" Miranda said. "I don't know why, but it is. Like the contradiction of the new and the old. In the dreams, the corridor seems ancient."

"I see," said Agatha.

They sat in silence for a few minutes. "Do I need to worry?" Miranda asked.

"I always worry," said Agatha. She gave a brittle laugh, then sighed. "I'm sorry. That's not what you were asking. Do you need to worry about this place specifically? I don't know. I would like to think that our initial impressions were correct, and that you don't. I want to think that the new that we see here matters more than the old. There's so much of the old in Arkham, and not just here. And you're clearly receiving good care."

"So I don't need to worry."

"I didn't say that."

"No. I was sort of hoping that you had."

"I wish I could too."

"Right," said Miranda. She drummed her fingers on the arms of her wheelchair. "So what's the plan?"

"For now, we monitor your dreams closely. And we learn what we can about the Stroud Institute."

"Just to be on the safe side."

"Exactly."

"Shall we start in here?"

"Why not?"

No one else had come into the library while they talked. They had the place to themselves. Agatha wheeled Miranda around the shelves, and they scanned the spines. Miranda expected to see a lot of popular titles, and she did. Mary Roberts Rhinehart, Edna Ferber, Zane Grey and Rafael Sabatini jostled for space. Their competition surprised Miranda. "I wouldn't have thought *The Waste Land* to be comfort reading," she said.

"Plenty here from your field," said Agatha. "Lots, even."

She was right. At first blush, Miranda had the impression their shelves held more Blake, Byron, Keats, Wordsworth and the other Romantics than any type of literature.

Then there was the philosophy.

"Boethius," said Miranda. "Hume. Kant. Light, bedtime reading." She took the Hume down to bring back with her.

"I don't know whether to be impressed or confused," said Agatha.

"I'm starting to think the quotation over the lintel is a real statement of intent for this library."

"Agreed." Agatha turned them back toward the doorway to start the return journey to Miranda's room. "I'll say this. I have a few questions I'd like to put to Donovan Stroud."

"You'll have the chance."

"Oh?"

"I meant to tell you. Friday evening. The director has invited me and a guest, and that's going to be you, to his quarters for a personal welcome. The invitation is on fancy stationery and everything."

"Now that is an evening I don't want to miss."

Miranda felt lighter for the first part of the way back. She felt as if she had taken concrete steps to deal with the bad nights.

Her mood faltered as they retraced their steps through the halls. It seemed to take even longer to return to the room than it had to reach the library.

Chapter Five

Miranda had two nights of something that could almost have passed for respite. No spinning, no drowning, no visions of twisting halls. No dreams of any kind, as far as she could remember. But not much rest, either, at least none that she could feel in the mornings. The threat of the nightmare's return simmered just below the surface of reality, waiting to stab through and set the world to howling.

Miranda actively dreaded the nights now. The possibility of nightmares was enough to trigger her anxiety. The days were good. They *were* restful, and she thought she was feeling a bit better. She had longer periods between coughing fits. A little energy had returned, and she could read for more than five minutes at a stretch now. She kept up her journal again. She was so used to the sounds of women coughing in her room and others that she barely noticed it any longer. And she could keep thoughts of the coming night at bay for most of the daylight hours. She could make it until after supper before she really became anxious.

But the worry was growing stronger. Soon it might become terror.

Miranda controlled the fear by taking notes. If Agatha wanted documentation, then she would have it. If, through meticulous observation, Miranda could help Agatha prove that her visions meant nothing more than that she was tired, sick and worried, then she would anatomize each day down to its component seconds. And if she was experiencing something worse than bad dreams, then they would need every detail she could glean if they were to learn how to fight it.

Fight it, she thought. *Fight what?*

She had no idea. The very thought of there being something that had to be fought bothered her. She had always found Agatha's research fascinating, but something to be examined at a remove. Just like the low-grade awareness she had that there were things that were not right in Arkham. That was knowledge she had taken seriously, while also filing it away as something that did not apply directly to her. In that, she believed, she followed the everyday practice, conscious or unconscious, of most of the population of the town.

Tuesday night, she was on her side, facing the hall at the moment of lights out. The hall's illumination dimmed, and the room went dark. The light seemed to rush out of the room, pulled down the length of the hall as if it were a physical thing being sucked into the depths of a throat.

Miranda jerked up. She swung her legs over the side of the bed, got up, and shuffled to the doorway as if to follow the fleeing light.

Nurse Revere would be angry to see her up. She didn't care. She would even welcome a scolding. The pain in her chest and the strain of her lungs kept her grounded in the real. She knew she wasn't dreaming.

Miranda held on to the doorway. She looked down the hall into dim stillness. No nurses walked by. The entrances to the other rooms yawned blackly. She heard coughing and moans. She saw no further plays of light.

Beneath the stillness, the dreams waited, even closer to the surface.

She did not want to go to sleep. She also knew she had to. Her body demanded it. Her legs threatened to buckle and drop her to the floor.

Miranda turned around to start the long voyage back to her bed. And Esme spoke.

"You shouldn't look."

Miranda jerked her head to the left. She could barely see Esme. The woman was a bundle of shadows, her face turned away from the hall.

"What do you mean?" Miranda asked.

Esme said nothing. She didn't move. Her breath deep and slow, sounding like sleep.

Miranda left her. Passing a snoring Frieda, she made her way to her own bed and struggled back under the covers.

"Did Esme speak to you just now?" Cleo asked.

"Yes," said Miranda, grateful not to be the only one awake. "At least, I think so."

"It's spooky when she does that, isn't it?"

Miranda rubbed at the gooseflesh on her arms. "Yes," she said. "I'd say so. Has she spoken to you?"

"She used to all the time at St Mary's. In the early days. She hardly does at all now, and when she does, it's upsetting."

"Because of what she says?"

"Because it's so rare," said Cleo. "She goes so long without saying anything at all, I just give up. And then, once in a while, she whispers." Cleo sighed. "We were friends at St Mary's. Now she just reminds me of death. She makes me think of what might be coming for all of us. Is that awful? Am I terrible for thinking that?"

"No," said Miranda. "I'd feel the same. I'm pretty close to that after just a few days, and you've seen her change."

"Thanks," said Cleo. "Still feel guilty though."

"Can I ask you something?" Miranda said after a few moments.

"If it changes the subject, I hope you will."

"How are your dreams?"

"My dreams," Cleo repeated. She paused, then said, "Not sure that I've had any, recently. Huh." She sounded surprised. "I used to. Haven't in a bit. Kind of a relief not to, you know? I need the rest."

So do I, Miranda thought. Cautiously, she said, "So you're getting that rest here? You feel good here?"

"I do," said Cleo, emphatic. "I feel something here that I never did at St Mary's."

"Which is what?"

"That I'll get to leave. Because I'll be cured."

Tuesday night, Wednesday night, Thursday night. The hours of darkness passing without relief. Always, the sense of the nightmares poised to strike, their claws inches from Miranda's throat, the jab and tear held back out of a dark sense of amusement.

By contrast, Wednesday and Thursday mornings and afternoons were measured out by blessed naps and the soul-deep joy of being looked after, and of feeling safe. Wednesday meant another visit from Agatha, and this time they stayed in the room, talking about ordinary, comforting things. Miranda's apartment was fine. Agatha brought a get-well card from the members of the English Department. The weather was still miserable.

Thursday brought the visit of a dignitary. With breakfast came the word that Councilman Payton Wallace would be touring the wards.

Frieda looked ready to clap her hands with glee. Miranda had never seen her in a state of unbridled joy before. The effect was jarring.

"Payton is a close family friend," Frieda confided to the room after Holden had left.

The way she said *Payton*, with too much emphasis on the first syllable and a bit too much of a stretch of the first vowel sound, turned the name into something unctuous. Miranda was sure she had had Paytons as students in the past. She had never had anything against the name. Until now. With one sentence, and one utterance of the name, Frieda had turned her against the very concept of men called Payton.

"He and Reginald went to college together," Frieda continued.

"Let me guess," Cleo deadpanned. "They were fraternity brothers."

"Why yes they were, as a matter of fact," said Frieda, missing the veiled sarcasm completely and delighted the question had been asked. "Reginald says you learn a lot about a person in a fraternity. Really get the measure of a man."

"Which is what going to college is all about," Cleo said. She turned to Miranda. "Isn't it?" she asked, raising disingenuous eyebrows.

"So I'm told," said Miranda. If Cleo was going to try to make her laugh, she would fire right back.

"Yes," said Frieda. She nodded sagely. "That's right. Payton gets things done," she said, her tone implying that Getting Things Done was humanity's highest calling. "He has great things ahead of him. He'll be mayor before long. Mark my words."

"That's nice," Miranda said. "What Things has he Got Done?"

"Well!" Frieda puffed up, as if Payton's accomplishments were her own. "This sanatorium, for one thing."

Miranda mused of that statement for a bit, fascinated by a world where a civic politician somehow deserved credit for the vision governing a medical facility, and where Frieda could bask in some sort of reflected glory as if she, too, had had a hand in the Stroud Institute's foundation.

"That's pretty impressive," said Cleo, who was not buying anything Frieda was selling.

"How did he manage that?" Miranda asked, and this time she was genuinely curious.

"Payton was a big supporter of the Institute from the start," said Frieda. "He pushed hard when the rest of the Council was slow to see the benefits. He kept pushing, and he brought them around."

"I guess he must have," said Cleo, looking around the room as if surprised to find that it existed.

"Why was he so keen on the Institute?" Miranda asked.

"It should be obvious, my dear," said Frieda. Her smile was patiently understanding and condescending. "Think what it's done for the economy."

Miranda had no idea what that meant, and she suspected that Frieda didn't, either. If that was what Payton had used to make his case for the Institute, and if that was what he really believed, then that said nothing good about him. This was taking the concept of doing the right thing for the wrong reasons to the point of absurdity.

The great man arrived shortly after the lunch trays had been cleared away. Nurse Revere acted as his escort. He stepped into the room with a broad, very pleased smile.

That was the look, Miranda decided, of a man who believed congratulations were due for the accomplishment of being himself. Napoleon arriving in Egypt could not have been more certain that he was the conquering hero.

Payton Wallace was a man who, she guessed, had been very thin in his youth, had come to think of that condition as eternal, and still thought of himself as a thin man even as middle age proved him wrong. His blue suit was expensive but too tight, his pants squeezing his midriff because he refused to admit he needed a larger size. The orange of his ascot, brighter than it needed to be, declared his love for the flourish. His face was handsome in a self-conscious way that made Miranda's skin crawl. He struck her as a man who believed in his own beauty as an article of everyone's faith. His thick black hair, slicked back with Brilliantine, and his small, perfectly trimmed and waxed moustache, were more than carefully thought out grooming. They were the official presentation of Councilman Payton Wallace to the world, delivered with an expectation of applause.

"Ladies," he said, with a knowing smile and nod after Revere had introduced him. There was more oil in the word than in his hair.

Miranda wished she had the energy to get up and belt him.

Cleo stared back at him, stone faced. Frieda, though, blushed and simpered. Even Revere seemed, by her standards, disarmed. She didn't exactly smile, but she looked out across the room with an air of smug pride.

Esme, as ever, did not react at all. Miranda thought her eyes opened briefly, but the moment passed too quickly for her to be sure.

"It's a real pleasure for me to see the Stroud Institute in action," said Payton. "It's so good to know that our faith in Director Stroud has been well-placed. And what an honor to have so informed a guide as Nurse Revere to show me around."

The corners of Revere's mouth twitched, as much of a smile as she could allow herself. Her cheeks took on a hint of color.

"And it is *so* good of you to come and see us," said Frieda. "I can't tell you how much it means to see a friendly face."

Payton looked at Frieda. "I'm so glad," he said, smooth as plastic. "And how are you doing?" he asked, the inquiry about as genuine as a three-dollar bill.

Miranda watched the exchange carefully. *He doesn't recognize her.*

"Reginald will want me to give you his best," said Frieda, and Miranda heard the desperation in her voice, the need to prevent, above all other things, the moment where Payton asked her name.

Miranda *almost* felt a twinge of sympathy for the councilman. She had wrestled with remembering faces and names most of her life, and though, by the end of each term, she was usually pretty close to knowing which student was which, all it took was to see one out of context, at the movies instead of in class, for instance, for her to stare blankly at the young person chatting happily about running into each other.

But then Payton said, "Dear Reggie," and turned around to announce to the room, "Now there's a man with a wicked backhand!" He spoke with such easy practice, such perfectly tailored but false enthusiasm, that Miranda's sympathy shriveled into contempt.

He didn't know who you were, Frieda. That's how much your friendship means to him.

"Do tell Reggie I'm ready for a rematch whenever he is," Payton said, addressing Frieda again, leaning forward slightly over her bed in a show of intimacy.

"I will!" Frieda promised. "Oh, it really is so nice to see you, and to have the chance to thank you for everything you've done."

Payton shook his head. "Now aren't you just the kindest?" Modest as a peacock. "But I really can't take any credit for the wonderful work being done here, and the vision it represents," he said, taking all the credit. "I have to congratulate Director Stroud on his accomplishment."

Miranda noted that Payton used the word *vision* in a way that separated it from Stroud, who merely had an accomplishment.

"But most of all," Payton said grandly, "the praise should go to Nurse Revere and her sisters. They are the beating heart of the Stroud Institute."

"Merely our duty," Revere said, unable to keep every trace of pleasure from her voice.

Payton smiled at her, and then toured the beds. He hesitated at Esme's, his mouth open to spout something meaningless, but her immobility stopped him. Marginally off his stride, he swerved to Cleo. "Taking good care of you, are they?" he said. "Good, good," he added before Cleo could answer.

Then he was at Miranda's bedside. He patted her stack of books. "My my," he said. "Lots of reading to get through there, I see. Taking the opportunity to improve our mind, are we?"

"Absolutely," Miranda said, her voice high and sweet. "We little women have to keep busy or who knows what trouble we might get into."

Payton blinked. His smile wavered, then steadied. "Good, good," he said, grasping for the first words he could find. Then a spin on his heel took him out of danger and back into the comfort of Frieda's worship. He took her hands and gave them a visibly hearty squeeze. Miranda choked at the display and started to cough, but Frieda glowed.

"You will tell me if there's anything I can do," Payton said.

"Oh I will," Frieda reassured him. "I will. You're too kind."

Payton waved off the praise.

"Reginald will never forgive me if I don't invite you over for dinner," Frieda rushed on, gushing. "Once I'm out of here, of course." She reddened.

"I'll be there with bells on," said Payton. "How could I refuse, after what you served last time?"

And just what did she serve last time? Miranda wanted to ask.

Frieda giggled at the empty praise.

His poise reestablished, Payton left as he had arrived. "Ladies," he said, bowed, and swept out after Revere.

Frieda glared at Miranda. "How could you be so rude?" she demanded.

"He was your husband's frat brother, he's eaten at your house, and he can't remember who you are," Miranda said. "What does that say about him?"

"That's just nonsense," Frieda said. She turned on her side, away from Miranda, ending the conversation.

Cleo shook her head. "That man," she said. "He could take credit for a sunset."

"And make the sunset dirty," said Miranda.

• • •

And then Friday came. In the afternoon, Holden helped Miranda to the shower room, ran the water until the chamber filled with steam, and left her to it. For several minutes, Miranda reveled in the privacy and the luxury. The water beat against her skin, hard and soothing with warmth. She was in no hurry to leave.

When she turned off the water, the steam coiled in patterns a little too distinct for her liking. Now she was in a hurry. She toweled off as quickly as her weak arms allowed, wrapped herself in her robe, and wheeled out of the room. The coughing that hit her as soon as she breathed the cooler air of the corridor undid all the therapy of the shower.

Agatha arrived just after supper for the evening visit to Donovan Stroud.

"So they're letting you stay up past your bedtime," she said.

"I'm sure Nurse Revere has opinions about this," said Miranda.

"Not her place to have them in this case though, is it?"

Miranda grinned. "Not when my invitation is from on high."

Agatha had stopped by Miranda's apartment and brought the simple black dress Miranda had requested. She didn't want to feel like a patient for a couple of hours. It took her a long time to get into it, and triggered another coughing fit. Her weakness alarmed her. But she triumphed over her body, and then sank into the wheelchair.

Agatha took her through the tangle of corridors that led them to the central block of the Institute.

"Does the layout bother you?" Miranda asked.

"You've been thinking more about it."

"I have, and you didn't answer my question."

"It seems more convoluted than it needs to be," said Agatha. "But I also don't want to assign malign intent to something that may just be bad planning, or an architect's whim. What about you?"

"I am fascinated," said Miranda. "All these straight lines, but so few straight paths. Are you ready for me to sound pretentious?"

"Always."

"Have you read any EE Cummings?"

"Can't say that I have."

"He's one of a number of poets who have been making quite a splash recently. He does fascinating stuff with typography and grammar. He uses the typewriter, this machine designed to regularize print, to defamiliarize words, and even letters and punctuation. And he'll use language to make us acutely aware of the rules we take for granted, because he uses those rules to produce combinations of words that are beautiful, but whose meaning we have to come at sideways. Do you follow?"

They had reached the tower, and they waited for the elevator that would bring them to Donovan Stroud's quarters.

"I think so," said Agatha. "But I don't see where you're going with this."

"Goethe said that architecture is frozen music," said Miranda.

The elevator arrived with a clanking hum. Agatha pulled the gate aside and Miranda wheeled herself in.

"I think it can also be embodied poetry," she went on. "The floor plan of the Institute makes me think of a Cummings poem. It has straight lines like the rules of grammar or the regularity of a typewriter's print, but the lines are breaking the rules."

The elevator jerked into motion.

"All right," said Agatha. "I see what you mean. The question is, do we conclude anything from that?"

"I don't know," Miranda admitted. "It just feels important."

Donovan Stroud greeted them as they emerged from the elevator on the top floor. Dressed in a dark brown suit and sporting a brown, polka-dotted bowtie, Donovan was old enough to come down on the right side of the boundary between dignity and foppishness. Miranda placed him in his early seventies. Yet with his gray hair neatly trimmed, and his sharp eyes looking out fiercely from his thin face, he looked like a man still just getting started with the projects of his life. Within seconds of meeting him, Miranda had the impression of a young man with much to prove. Nothing in him suggested a man looking back on the accomplishments of a lifetime.

"Welcome," he said, smiling broadly. "I'm so glad to meet you finally, Professor Ventham."

"Thank you," said Miranda, and she introduced Agatha.

Donovan shook her hand and ushered them down the short hallway to his apartment. "I hope you don't think I'm trying to be flattering when I tell you that I've been really looking forward to this evening." He spoke with an animation that made his sincerity palpable.

"You may not be trying to flatter, but you're doing a nice job all the same," Miranda smiled. "Don't let me stop you."

Donovan laughed. He brought them through the open door of a vestibule and into a lounge whose windows looked out over the front grounds of the Institute. Donovan had apparently jumped with both feet into Art Deco. The room was richly furnished, and bathed in warm reds and blues from light filtered through stained glass lampshades. Logs crackled in a fireplace, and Miranda felt cozier without having realized she'd been cold.

An oil painting, set off by a gold-leaf frame, hung over the mantle. It was the portrait of a young, early-nineteenth-century nobleman. He stood with his left hand behind his back, and his right appearing to gesture to the landscape behind him. Moody cliffs brooded beneath dark clouds. At the top of a cliff, the ruins of an abbey jutted up, tumbled and vacant. The man had a look of quiet satisfaction. At the same time, it seemed to Miranda that his eyes held a sparkle of wonder. The family resemblance to Donovan was unmistakable.

"An ancestor, I take it," Miranda said, pointing to the painting as Donovan invited Agatha to sit on a red velvet sofa with its back to the window.

Donovan helped Miranda out of the chair and onto the sofa next to Agatha. "That's right," he said. "Professors, I'd like you to meet Lord Magnus Stroud, my great-I-forget-how-many-times-grandfather. You see him with a backdrop of his estate in Galloway, Scotland." Donovan spoke with pride.

"Lord Magnus of honored memory, I gather," said Miranda.

"Indeed. He set an example that all of us since have tried to follow. Can I offer you a drink?"

"Is that allowed?" Agatha asked.

"If I say it is," Donovan said, and he smiled. "Don't worry. I'm not being cavalier. I've checked Professor Ventham's charts, and a little cognac won't do her any harm."

"In that case, yes please," said Miranda, and Agatha joined her.

Donovan served them, then took an armchair facing them on the other side of the fireplace.

"You said you try to follow Lord Magnus' example," Miranda prompted.

"Yes, I did." Donovan glanced up at the portrait. "I think you might appreciate this, Professor Ventham, given your field." He nodded at Miranda's raised eyebrow. "Oh yes," he said. "I've read some of your essays on Blake."

"Really?" Miranda asked, surprised. No one outside the walls of Miskatonic University had ever told her that.

Donovan nodded. He pointed to the middle shelf of the bookcase that took up the wall opposite the windows, and she recognized the spines of *The Review of English Studies*.

"I'm flattered," she said.

"I'm genuinely interested in your work," Donovan went on. "My family history makes that rather inevitable. You teach and study the Romantics, but Magnus knew them personally."

Miranda's jaw dropped, and Donovan laughed, delighted by her response. "Lord he may have been, but he was a radical. Cut from the same political cloth as Byron, if you will. He believed in the promise of the French Revolution. A poet in his own right, too, though, as he would be the first to admit, in a very minor way. He was friends with Wordsworth for a time. In fact, unless I'm mistaken, Wordsworth visited him in Galloway around the same time this portrait was done."

"Friends for a time?" Agatha asked.

"Yes. Magnus stayed true to his radicalism throughout his life. He and Wordsworth inevitably drifted apart. I do often wonder what they might have accomplished together, if Wordsworth hadn't tacked into more conservative waters."

"Together?" said Miranda. She sipped her cognac, enjoying the warmth in her chest. It eased the pain that lingered after the coughs.

"Magnus invited Wordsworth to collaborate with him in the creation of a community of writers. A physical one, founded on the Stroud Estate. Wordsworth declined, in the end."

"Did Magnus succeed anyway?"

"He tried." Donovan gazed into the fire with a regretful, melancholy air. "In the end, he failed. But I think the fact that he tried at all is important, don't you?"

"I think it matters," Miranda said.

"It does matter. It does very deeply, at least for those of us who count ourselves as descendants of Magnus. I like to think that we're following his example here at the Institute."

"How so?" Agatha asked.

"By not being afraid to challenge conventional wisdom. By thinking radically. Always for the good of our patients, of course."

"Of course," said Agatha. Her tone, Miranda noted, was carefully neutral, scrubbed clear of any possible trace of sarcasm.

Donovan smiled at them both, then raised his glass in a silent toast to the portrait, and took another sip.

"I hope you don't take this the wrong way," he said to Miranda. "I don't mean it to sound like I am celebrating your illness. Having said that, though, I am glad you're here." He smiled.

"What do you mean?"

"I mean it's a privilege to have a mind like yours within these walls. I feel you might be able to help the Institute almost as much as, I hope, it will help you."

"I don't see how I could," said Miranda. "You're saving my life, after all."

"I'll tell you what I mean," Donovan said. "We can talk about details much later, when you're in the next stage of your convalescence. When you're up and about, and more active again. Part of our treatment, you see, involves discussion groups for the patients. Those who are up to it. The active mind."

"The active mind is important," Agatha agreed, still innocently neutral.

Stop it. Miranda didn't want to start laughing. It wasn't that she even disagreed with Donovan. He just sounded a little too evangelistic, and a little too much as if he had invented the concept of thinking.

"The active mind," Donovan repeated once more, nodding sagely. "Keeping busy even when the body cannot. Good for morale, and for mental energy. You'll be invited to take part in due course, and I can't help but hope that perhaps, down the road, you might think about leading some. Again, once you're at the more active stage of your cure, naturally."

"I will think about it," said Miranda, and she meant it. Donovan's delivery aside, what he said made sense.

"I can't ask for more, and I won't," said Donovan.

Fatigue caught up with Miranda a few minutes later. First, she left Agatha and Donovan to carry the conversation. Then she began to have trouble following it. When the painting began to writhe at the edge of her vision, she knew it was time to go and face what the night would bring to her.

"You look tired, Professor Ventham," Donovan said, pre-empting her.

"Yes," she said. Speech came with effort. Breathing felt like a boulder rested on her chest.

She barely took in the goodbyes. The next thing she knew, Agatha was wheeling her out of the apartment. She looked back to wave at Donovan. Leaning against the mantle, he waved back.

Above him, in the background of the portrait, the ruins of the abbey squirmed.

Chapter Six

Miranda spent Saturday quietly. Her bed held her in an embrace of heavy comfort. She felt herself sinking into it as if the Earth's gravity had suddenly tripled. Her exhaustion worried her. Was she really this weak? Was this what even a short evening of conversation would do to her? Had she set herself back? Recovery became hard to imagine. The illness had become her life. It defined her existence. She could not see beyond its horizon.

And she was too tired to care.

The bed was soft. It took care of her, as did the staff of the Institute. She didn't have to worry. She didn't have to think. She could drift through the leaden sea of the illness, floating on numbing tides.

So unlike the woman she had been. The old Miranda would be bored stiff, desperate to find something to occupy her mind. Traces of the old Miranda had been present as recently as last night.

She didn't mind. She was safe. All was well.

Distantly, the old Miranda called to her. Rest, she said, but don't forget you have to fight, too.

Even when the evening came, she didn't have the energy to become anxious about the night. She barely stayed awake long enough to be aware of lights out. When she woke on Sunday, she realized, gratefully, that she had slept through the night. There had been dreams. She had a vague impression of long, twisting movements, but nothing specific. The night retreated with nothing worse than a faint, residual shudder.

Miranda felt refreshed, too, more like herself, and actually restless. Energy, that had seemed an impossible mirage the day before, a delusion that had vanished and would never return, was back. The fear that tuberculosis was forever receded. She could imagine getting well.

Up and down, she told herself. She should get used to this. Up and down, weak and strong, resigned and hopeful. There were no forevers. *Keep hold of that.*

"You look bright this morning," Nurse Holden said when she came by on her rounds after breakfast. "I think that's some actual color in your cheeks, and not the feverish kind."

Miranda touched her face as if her fingers could feel the color. "I had a good night," she said.

"You have a question," said Holden, reading Miranda's face.

"I was wondering if I could be up for a bit today."

Holden picked up her chart, gave it a scrutiny, and took out a pen to update Miranda's readings for the morning. "All right," she said.

"Thank you."

Holden held up a finger. "With conditions."

"Of course."

"No more than half an hour," Holden said, and now she enumerated the restrictions with her fingers. "You stay on this floor. And you stay in your chair. No walking. Are we clear?" She sounded almost as stern as Revere.

"I understand."

"Good." Holden smiled, and the angel of the ward returned, reassuring Miranda that she was still a good patient, and that the strictures were for her benefit, and not a punishment.

After Holden had left, Miranda put on her dressing gown and settled herself in her wheelchair. She ignored Frieda's stare and disapproving frown. When it was clear that her silence wasn't going to have the desired effect, Frieda cleared her throat. Even that sound was sculpted by breeding.

"Do you think you're accomplishing something?"

Across from Miranda, Cleo snorted. Esme had her eyes open, or as open as they ever got, their lids half down, shielding her from the world.

"I hadn't actually set out to accomplish anything at all," Miranda said. If she'd been speaking louder than a murmur, she would have used a bright and artificial tone. Instead, she gave Frieda a wide, false smile.

"You should be resting," Frieda said. "We don't want this room to have a reputation."

Miranda's eyebrows rose. "And what reputation would that be?"

"That we can't keep still. That we're difficult patients. Troublesome."

Miranda stared at her until she was sure she could speak without laughing. "I wouldn't worry," she said. "Your reputation is secure. I'd wager my lungs on it."

Frieda sniffed. "I should hope so."

Cleo made a choking noise. Miranda wheeled herself out of the room before she lost her composure.

She had lied to Frieda, though. She did intend to accomplish something. She had had enough of disorientation. Her sense of her room was of an island in the middle of a tangle of corridors. She had no real conception of where the library was in relation to her room, and that was just one instance of her frustration. She had always had a good sense of direction. When she visited a new city, it usually only took her a few minutes to get its cardinal points fixed in her mind, especially if she was getting around on her own, and on foot. Like the first time she had been to New York City. She had been six, on an outing with her parents. Manhattan's grid between rivers had clicked into her mind so completely that, when a woman had approached her mother and asked for directions, it had been Miranda who had answered.

It offended her vanity not to know her way around the Institute. She told herself that her confusion was due to having been wheeled from place to place by other people. It always took her longer to get her bearings in an unfamiliar place if she was a passenger. So today she would start to sort out the vague tangle of the Institute's geography, beginning with the route to the library.

She started off by looking for a map of the floor, hoping to find one posted at a hallway intersection. No luck. Plenty of signs pointed the way to the library, X-ray lab, surgery, elevators, and every other destination she could imagine, but no map. When Miranda started following the signs to the library, she stopped after the first few turns. She felt like she was being taken around again, invisible hands pushing her chair and giving her no say in where she went.

She worked her way back to the hall leading to her room and started again. She took note of signs, but instead of following them, she concentrated on choosing the corridors in a systematic fashion. She took her time, not heading down another until she felt confident about the relation of the current one to the previous hall. If the Stroud Institute refused to post its floor plans, she would create her mental one.

She went past the doorways of rooms of coughing women. She smiled to the staff she encountered, and most of the time received smiles back. The overall atmosphere of the Institute was as cheerful as she imagined it was possible for a tuberculosis sanatorium to be.

I'm lucky to be here. I am.

She took her time. Mindful of Holden's admonitions, she took care not to tire herself. She would be the good patient. She would do what she must to get well.

Most of all, she didn't want to have future wanderings forbidden.

She took her time, too, to make sure she learned the floor plan. But when she finally made it to the library again, her mental construct of the layout collapsed. She had made some progress, but she was still confused. There were gaps in her understanding of the corridors. She felt as if she had arrived sooner than she should have. And she had a growing conviction that the walls of the Stroud Institute were too thick, the halls too spaced out from one another.

She checked her watch. Her half-hour was almost up. Time to be good and head back. No point fighting the maze any longer today. She followed the signs to return to her room, Ariadne's thread leading her back to rest. Every intersection seemed to be a false choice, as if no matter which direction she chose, her path would always be between the library and bed.

She returned to the room a minute before her half-hour. She passed Holden in the last hall, who gave her an approving nod. *Good girl. Good patient.*

She spent the rest of the day retracing the halls in her mind, fighting to turn the web into a map. The web fought back.

And the halls followed her into her dreams that night.

On Monday, Agatha Crane marched up the steps of the Miskatonic University's Orne Library, determined to become acquainted with Count Magnus Stroud. Gray gargoyles lined the roof of the gray building, ancient guardians of still-older knowledge. Rain dripped from their jaws like venom. The damp came in through the door with Agatha, clinging to her bones as she made her way into the stacks.

She was worried about Miranda, worried about more than her health. The quality of care at the Stroud Institute struck her as excellent and progressive. Miranda was strong. She would beat the TB. But her dreams and visions concerned Agatha; they were not to be ignored.

Agatha considered herself a rationalist. That position was core to her identity. She hadn't set foot in a synagogue for more years than she could recall, but she treasured the tradition of asking hard questions that was the gift of her ancestors. Investigation, interrogation, the demand for evidence as extraordinary as the theories it meant to support – these were the tenets she lived by. Parapsychology had to hold itself to the most rigid of standards if it wanted to take its place among the established scientific disciplines. And it *needed* to reach that status. It *had* to be taken seriously. The matters it dealt with were too important, and too dangerous, to dismiss. The more Agatha encountered in the realms of the paranormal, the harder she found it to credit traditional conceptions of the divine, and the more she worried about what these forces, unopposed, might do.

She hadn't come to any conclusions yet about Miranda's night visions. They might be more than nightmares; they might not. She had to find out, and not just for Miranda's sake. She had to be sure.

Agatha began her search on the ground floor of the Orne, in the reference section. She gathered armfuls of biographical encyclopedias. Sitting at a wooden table scuffed and scratched by generations of researchers, surrounded by her stacks of thick volumes that smelled of dust and dry, crackling years, she started off on the trail of Magnus.

The initial volumes did no more than confirm that there had been such a person, that he had been born in 1770, and died in 1858. Older editions, though, referred briefly to the fact that he had been a writer as well as a friend to writers.

Agatha found nothing by him in the card catalogues. She consulted with the one of the librarians, Abigail Foreman. Severe in posture and dress, her hair in a bun so tight it seemed to be pulling her straight, Abigail got back to Agatha after an hour of searching and informed her that the archives had no record of any works by Magnus Stroud.

Agatha kept looking. She followed some pathways that Miranda had suggested, looking for references to Magnus in books about people connected to him. She had her first real luck in Besselman's biography of Wordsworth from 1896. It touched on Wordsworth's friendship with Magnus. Agatha learned the count's nickname among his friends was "Merrick", because of his habit of climbing the Merrick in the Range of the Awful Hand alone to look out towards the land in Galloway that would, eventually, be his.

Agatha went back to the card catalogs, and then to the librarian, this time looking for works by Merrick.

Her prize emerged from the archives. She took it back to her table. The reading lamp cast an amber glow over the book, and the gloom of the hall pressed in closer. Agatha turned the pages of the *Miscellany of Merrick*, which had received limited publication in 1806. The black covers contained a smattering of poems, some satirical jabs at politicians, philosophical musings, and journal entries.

Agatha started to read.

The afternoon darkened. The light coming in the Orne's stained-glass windows turned sullen. Through the words on the page, the past shifted uneasily.

Chapter Seven
Scotland, 1805

They were about a mile south and east from the summit of the Merrick, and the wind had turned ferocious. It no longer felt like August. The light rain turned into a horizontal attack. William Wordsworth squinted into the stinging wet and pulled the collar of his coat tighter. The footing was becoming treacherous, so he walked steadily and with caution, putting more weight on his walking stick.

"William! Keep up!"

Count Magnus Stroud had put a good fifty yards between them. No caution in his stride, he hurried up the slope, at times almost running. He laughed, giddy, and waved, urging speed.

William shook his head, grinning. "I'm not as young as you are!" he called back.

"We're the same age!"

"You're still younger!" Magnus raced on with the remembered energy of a child. He kept laughing, growing younger by the moment in William's sight. He didn't set a foot wrong. William wasn't surprised, though he was envious. Magnus knew the Range of the Awful Hand in Galloway like he knew his own hand. The Merrick, in particular, had been the count's home of exile, the land that gave him succor while he was denied the freedom of his true home.

Today, the exile was coming to an end, and William was glad Magnus had asked him to share the moment. He loved these hills too. If only the rain wasn't driving quite so hard and trickling cold inside his collar. He tried to find the enthusiasm of the child who ran through the hills and didn't care about the rain. It usually came to him a bit more easily. Maybe it was seeing that exultant freedom of movement in Magnus that made him feel a bit older and a bit more distant from his former self.

Or maybe it was just the years and the experiences. Maybe it was what he had seen in France. Magnus had been there too, more than once, in the last fifteen years. He must have seen the curdling of the Revolution's dream into the Terror and the Empire. Didn't that weigh on him?

Today, apparently nothing did.

Look around, William thought. *Look at these hills.* They elevated his soul, even with the wider view shrouded by the rain and clouds. He moved faster to catch up with Magnus.

"Are we not heading for the summit?" William asked. They were not taking their usual route.

"Not today," said Magnus.

"I thought you'd want to look out towards the estate." Stroud Hall and its grounds had been the possession of Hugo, an elderly cousin. Complex lineages had granted Magnus the title of count and possession of another house in Yorkshire. But that mansion had been a place of cold comfort for Magnus since childhood. His heart belonged in Galloway. With Hugo's death, he was coming home.

"We wouldn't be able to see the grounds today," Magnus said.

"True," William admitted. The horizon had drawn close. Even the nearest hills were pale gray shapes, becoming insubstantial in the squalls. The estate, on the coast, would be invisible.

"We'll be walking the grounds soon enough," said Magnus. "We're here because I have to pay respects to their guardian."

"Their guardian?"

Magnus winked.

They came around a bend and over a rise, and William understood.

They approached the Grey Man of Merrick from its east side, the perspective from which the illusion was most convincing. On this side, the rock formation of a cliff face became a man's profile. Aged, contemplative, serene, the Grey Man gazed downslope into the distance and rain, unmoved by the turbulence of the world.

William slowed, savoring the sight. Magnus ran forward. He reached up, reverently, to touch the Grey Man's pointed chin. He bowed his head, and William held back, giving him the space for his moment of communion with stone.

Magnus lowered his arms. He looked up at the Grey Man, grinned, then called to William. "What say you? Is there a family resemblance?" He turned to look down the hillside, and William had to concede some parallels in the profile. The heavy brow, the pronounced bridge of the nose, the pointed chin; yes, the two could have been hewn by the same artist.

"There is no doubt," he said as he joined Magnus. "You are brothers."

The count took a deep, happy breath of air. He took off his hat and lifted his face to the rain. The wind gusted. He didn't flinch any more than did the Grey Man.

"You called the Grey Man a guardian," William said.

"He is." He pointed into the limbo of the rain. "He looks directly toward Stroud Hall. He has watched over the estate for me all this time. He watches over it even now when we can't see it."

William nodded. "You were right to give him your thanks. He has been a good friend to you."

"He has," Magnus said with feeling.

Two hours later, they were back in Magnus' carriage, rattling along the uneven road toward the estate. The rain had let up, giving way to rolling patches of mist.

"This day has been a long time in coming for you," William said.

Magnus shrugged. "I knew it would. I didn't mind the wait."

"Even though you and Hugo didn't get along."

"Hugo didn't get along with anyone. I did not take his animosity as a personal attack."

"But what about what he might have done to the Hall?"

"What of it?" Magnus' serenity was unbreakable.

"Aren't you worried? You told me that he had spent himself into bankruptcy."

"He did, yes. And yes, his taste was abominable. But I have my own fortune, so Hugo's sins on that front die with him. And I'll tell you this, William. As for the crimes he might have committed against the Hall, he could have burned it to the ground and it would not trouble my happiness one jot. What is the Hall? A building, and so by its very nature, ephemeral. The land, though. The land persists. Hugo could not make that vanish."

"He might have sold it."

"Not without my consent, and I made sure the funds to prevent that, at least, were present. The grounds are intact. They are as they were in my childhood."

William leaned forward to shake Magnus' hand. "Then you have my congratulations."

"And your approval, I hope, old friend."

"That goes without saying."

The day was failing when the carriage came to the wrought-iron gates of the estate. An attendant had been waiting for them, ensuring the gates were open before the carriage had time to stop. Magnus shouted his thanks to the man, and the horses carried on up the oak-lined drive, and to the graveled forecourt of the Hall.

The ancestral seat of the Strouds thrust its square battlements up into the gathering gloom of the late afternoon. Descending from the carriage, William looked up at the Hall, and it glared back at him, sullen, glowering. It was more a keep than a mansion, its walls built for defense, not comfort. A few of the windows glimmered with the light of fireplaces in their rooms, but many others were glazed with darkness. The hulk of a building felt cold, unwelcoming.

The servants waiting at the entrance seemed pleasant enough, though. Three came forward, accompanied by the butler, to take down the luggage chests from the carriage.

"My lord," the butler said, "welcome to Stroud Hall."

Behind him, the other servants were lined up, waiting for inspection.

"Thank you, Phillips," Magnus said. "It's good to see you again."

"It has been a long time, my lord."

It would have been, William thought. Magnus hadn't been here since his early adolescence. White-haired but rigid of posture, Phillips seemed as old as the oaks on the drive, and as unlikely ever to fall.

"You can all carry one," Magnus said. "Mr Wordsworth and I will stretch our legs a bit before coming in. I'd like to see the grounds while we still have some light."

The wind blew hard from the nearby coast. When William turned into it as he and Magnus left the carriage behind, it roared at him with greater ferocity than it had on the Merrick. He embraced its challenge, more eager to test his mettle against it than venture into the cold arms of the hall.

Past the small woods that circled the hall, the land became open and barren, and the wind howled in unbridled freedom. Midway between the trees and the cliffs overlooking the Irish Sea, huge shapes grouped together, behemoths whispering secrets to each other.

"Are those standing stones?" he asked.

Magnus just grinned.

"No," William said, answering himself. "They're too large."

Magnus' grin became even wider.

"But there's something about their arrangement…" William trailed off.

Magnus clapped his shoulder. "They're one of two things I wanted you to see here before the day is done. Come and see!" He broke into a run, darting like a deer over the moor. William followed.

He slowed as he drew near the boulders. They were immense, the smallest at least thirty feet high, the largest twice that. Some were rounded, almost spherical, while others, narrow and tall, loomed over them like sentinels. They were clearly natural formations, yet William was sure he saw a pattern in their positions.

"What is this?" he breathed.

Magnus urged him on, and they passed beyond the nearest stone and into the embrace of the cluster.

"I call it the Stroud Spiral," Magnus said. "That's what it's always been for me, and no one has told me otherwise. Maybe it doesn't have a name, though that would be strange."

"Strange indeed," said Wordsworth. His voice had dropped to a whisper. He felt as if he had crossed the threshold of a cathedral. He stared up at the boulders. They leaned toward him, wise and secretive. On instinct, he reached out and ran his hand on the moss-covered flank of the nearest. A profound sense of touching the ancient struck him. He didn't want to let go. He walked around the curve of the rock and removed his hand only when he could transfer it immediately to the next behemoth. He moved from boulder to boulder, losing himself in a waltz with stone.

This was a spiral, and it had caught him in its coil. He followed it willingly, breath held in anticipation of revelation.

And then, as he felt the possibility of a center to the spiral approach, he pulled back. He wasn't ready. He shouldn't look. He didn't want to see.

The effort of pulling his hand away from the rock sent him stumbling, and for a moment he didn't know where he was.

Had he been released, or had the coil flung him away?

Magnus took his arm to support him. "It is an experience, isn't it? Do you think Coleridge would like it?"

William rubbed his eyes. "I don't think it would be healthy for him." He looked about. The new surroundings had come upon him by stealth. The ground was barren rock, with no trace of heather or moss. The land rose to the cliffs. It ended suddenly, and the booming of waves came from far below. On the highest point, ruins cut a jagged silhouette against the darkening sky.

"The abbey," said Magnus.

"Does it have a name?"

"No more than the stones, and don't you think that's fitting?"

"I do," William murmured, uneasy. The abbey seemed to flow up out of the rock on which it stood, as if it too were a natural formation. It declared its kinship with the boulders of the Spiral. They were one.

William looked back and forth between the abbey and the Spiral. He shuddered with awe. His throat went dry.

"Such a wonder," said Magnus, his face ecstatic.

A wonder? Yes, it was. And it upset William that he could not share his friend's joy. He did not want to be here.

He believed in the inherent goodness of nature. Every landscape could be a balm to the soul. But he also believed in the presence of the land, in a sense of being so huge that it called out terror that was the necessary element of awe. He thought about the strongest, most frightening sense of that presence he had ever felt. As a child, he had taken a boat out one night on Ullswater. Partway across, the mass of Glenridding Dodd had appeared to rise up before him from behind other peaks. The peak came for him. It was not a question of changing perspective. The mountain advanced. It rose higher and higher, and it *saw* him.

He had rowed back across Ullswater with fear driving his strokes, the mountain's silent pursuit bearing down upon him.

That had been the fantasy of a child. In the years since Glenridding Dodd had hunted him, he had looked back on the incident with fondness, the terror softened by memory to a delicious shiver. The experience came back to him now, primal and real, and there was nothing delicious about it.

The fear was there again. The cliffs with their ruins and the spiral of boulders knew he was there. They had him between them. If he stayed where he was, the trap would close.

"I would like to go back," he said.

Magnus didn't hear him. The count stared at the abbey, his face frozen in rapture.

"Magnus," said William. He spoke louder, and could not keep the tremor from his voice. He shook Magnus by the shoulder.

Magnus jumped. He blinked, coming back to himself.

"I'm sorry, William. What did you say?"

"I would like to go back." Urgency squeezed his chest. In another few moments, it might be too late. A coil he could not name would have them.

"Of course," said Magnus. "It is getting late. We won't have the light much longer."

They started back. William did not breathe easily until they were on the other side of the Spiral. The sense of danger receded. The fear that he had been seen did not.

Even when caught by the most violent storms in the Alps, he had never wavered in his belief in the benevolence of nature. He held firm to that tenet even now. He had to.

But this place was wrong. It was evil. Nature had been distorted into something else.

"I've long had dreams of what I might be able to do here," said Magnus.

William glanced at him uneasily, then concentrated on the land ahead. He strained to see some hint of light from the Hall shining through the woods that waited for them.

"Now you can realize them," he said. The response came automatically. He hated the idea as soon as he spoke.

"I will tell you my plans tonight," said Magnus.

William nodded.

He didn't want to know.

He wanted to run.

Chapter Eight

Agatha's studiously neutral expression made Miranda brace herself. She waited until Agatha had sat down at her bedside and they could speak quietly before saying anything.

"You've either made no progress, or the progress you've made is worrying," Miranda said.

Agatha grimaced. "Are you up to a visit to the library?" she asked.

"Not today. I overdid it the other day. I'm to stay put and rest until the weekend." The prospect didn't bother Miranda as much as she would have expected. The effort to map out the floor had taken so much out of her, physically and mentally, that she had accepted the strictures from Nurse Revere without complaint. Even getting up for visits to the washroom was an ordeal.

"I see," said Agatha. After a moment's thought, she shrugged. "Maybe it doesn't matter."

Miranda followed Agatha's gaze around the room. Esme was asleep, as usual. So was Frieda, her snoring coming out in sharp gasps and snorts. Cleo was reading a magazine. Agatha looked at her a few moments longer, then back at Miranda, her eyebrows lifted in a silent question.

"She's okay," Miranda mouthed. The subterfuge felt surreal. What reason did she have to worry about what Cleo or the others overheard? Did she think they were spying on her? For whom? For Stroud? Why? Was he responsible for her dreams?

Of course not. Ridiculous questions, all of them.

But at night, when they waited for sleep and the possibility of dreams lurked, murmuring in the dark, the questions would come back to make her heart pound. Better to face them now, in the daylight, and try to strip them of their power.

Did she believe Cleo meant her harm? No, she did not. Impossible to conceive of the other woman as dangerous.

Agatha seemed to be wrestling with the same debate. Then she nodded, ready to speak.

"You've found something?" Miranda whispered. No need to wake Frieda or Esme. No need to bother Cleo.

There. Good, sensible, *thoughtful* reasons to be quiet.

"Some material by and about Magnus Stroud," Agatha said. She took a notebook out of her leather briefcase and went through her findings. Miranda listened, struck by the fact that she had somehow never heard of this figure from her field of study. A friend of Wordsworth, another Romantic idealist, another *writer*, it seemed, no matter how minor, and, somehow, he had been completely forgotten.

"The lands that form the background to the painting reverted back to Magnus in 1805. He describes visiting them with Wordsworth," said Agatha.

"It's a shame Wordsworth never wrote about that visit," Miranda said. "At least, I'm pretty sure he didn't."

"You would know."

"I've never encountered any reference to Magnus in either Wordsworth's poetry or his correspondence. Which is strange, given their friendship. You'd think there would be some letters somewhere."

"Destroyed?" Agatha asked.

"That's what I'm thinking. The absence feels telling."

"But absence isn't evidence," Agatha pointed out. "And evidence matters."

"Granted. *Did* you find anything?" She still didn't know what she expected to uncover. Something sinister about Donovan Stroud's ancestor? Or maybe proof of his benevolence? What would that prove or mean in the present? And would any of it stop her worrying about her nightmares?

"I don't know if I'd call it evidence," Agatha said. "Have a look at this. Tell me what you think." She took an old compass from her briefcase, flipped open the cover, and passed it over.

Miranda frowned. She turned back and forth in her chair, holding the compass in different directions. "That's not north," she said. The needle, defiant, pointed south-west.

"Keep watching," said Agatha.

After a few seconds, the needle began to jerk wildly, then settled to the east. After another few moments, it sprang to life again.

"That looks unusual," Miranda said.

"Doesn't it?" said Agatha. "And listen to this. That behavior only starts once the compass is inside the Institute itself."

"It's normal otherwise?"

"It is, until I'm close to the Institute. At that point, the needle swings from the north to point at this building, and doesn't budge until I'm inside."

"What does it all mean?"

"I don't know," said Agatha. "It's suggestive, at least. Something real is affecting magnetic fields in the Institute. That doesn't necessarily imply parapsychological phenomena. The explanation could be something completely mundane. But it's a start. I'm going to perform some other tests. If you are having more than dreams, and the reason for has to do with the Institute, then there must be a way of physically registering its influence."

"That's fine," said Miranda. "But what does all this have to do with Magnus?"

"That remains to be seen. Maybe nothing. As for him, though…" Agatha produced a sheaf of papers from her briefcase. "Have a look at these. I transcribed some of his journal entries."

Miranda read them. Her stomach clenched with unease. "He's obsessed with that abbey," she said. The ruins came up over and over in the entries. Magnus visited them day after day, and each time he felt that they were suggesting new mysteries to him. They teased revelation but never delivered, offering instead always another secret, a different configuration of shadow. When Magnus wasn't writing about his explorations of the abbey, he was musing about it, speculating about its origins, regretting that Wordsworth hadn't wanted to share the experience with him, and anticipating his next visit.

"The full manuscript is more varied," Agatha said. "Theories of art, plans for his community, but it was the way he hammered on about the abbey that really struck me. And as best as I can tell, Wordsworth's friendship with him ends after their visit to the estate. At least, Magnus doesn't mention any further visits."

"So these regrets that Wordsworth won't be part of things is the end of it?"

"As far as I can tell."

Miranda let the papers drop on her blanket. "Suggestive," she said.

"But not conclusive."

No. Nothing to tell her to worry, or to stop worrying. She might be looking at the traces of a friendship that sadly fell apart, and Magnus was not the only Romantic to wax enthusiastic about a Gothic ruin. He would have been a rare one not to have done so.

Suggestive. Sure. Only if read while also thinking about the Institute's unmappable geography.

She told Agatha what had happened to her. "Maybe I'm just too weak to be exploring right now."

"Maybe."

"Too many maybes," said Miranda.

"And nothing that says the mundane answers are the wrong ones."

"We need to know more."

Agatha gave a short, emphatic nod. "I'll keep digging."

"You said he writes a lot about that community of artists he wanted to establish. It would be good to know what happened with that, if anything."

"It would," Agatha agreed. "And you should try exploring again when you're able. And you'll tell me if anything else happens."

"You know I will."

They chatted a little longer, letting their voices rise a hair above a whisper now as they stuck to banal topics. When Agatha got up to leave, Miranda made herself get up too.

"I thought you were supposed to stay lying down," said Agatha.

Miranda eased herself down into her chair. "Just going as far as the doorway to see you off," she said. "To see if I can."

She managed it, but when she had said her goodbyes to Agatha and turned around again, the distance back to her bed looked like miles.

She was about to begin the trek when she saw that Esme's eyes were open and staring at her. Miranda smiled. Esme did not. Her cracked lips parted, and she formed words. Miranda wheeled herself next to the head of the bed and leaned forward.

"I'm sorry," she said. "I didn't catch that."

"What were you doing?" Esme's whisper was softer than air, thin as tissue, weak as a sigh.

"Just visiting."

The tiniest movement of Esme's head. A little bit more than a tremor, just recognizable as a shake, *no*. "Don't," Esme whispered, her eyes wider now, urgency flickering in their exhausted depths.

"Don't what?"

"Questions," said Esme. "Stop." Each word came out with the effort of hauling a boulder up from a well.

Miranda leaned in closer. "Why are you afraid?" she asked. She spoke as quietly as Esme.

Another shake of the head. "Don't… Quiet… Just be quiet…"

Esme closed her eyes. Her shallow, rasping breath slowed. She had willed herself back to sleep.

Chilled, Miranda left her. Esme might have been rambling, delirious. If they had been in a clinic in Manhattan, Miranda would have dismissed the warning. In Arkham, she could not. She crossed the room and put herself back to bed as silently as possible.

By then, Frieda was awake. She and Cleo were both looking at her.

"So," said Frieda. She glared at Esme and then back at Miranda. "You're worthy of conversation, then."

"We barely exchanged two words."

"Two words more than she has ever said to *me*. What did she say?"

Miranda could say that it was none of Frieda's business. She could tell her off, and wouldn't that feel good? It also would do nothing to douse Frieda's curiosity, and the next thing that might happen was her going over to Esme and confronting her with indignant shouts.

No one needs that. Least of all Esme.

"She asked what Agatha and I were talking about," Miranda said, deflecting Frieda's interest away from Esme.

"Which was what?" Frieda demanded.

"Wow!" said Cleo. "How have you never had that nose of yours broken, Frieda? Shove it into my business like that and it's pulling out bloody."

"We have a right to know," said Frieda, tilting her head up, the wounded party, the picture of aggrieved dignity, "if she was talking about us."

"We weren't," said Miranda.

"Then there's no need to be coy, is there? That will only make us think the worst."

"*Us*," Cleo repeated, disgusted.

Miranda wondered if she should come clean. If she should ask if they had dreams that frightened them, dreams that might not be dreams. She could ask if anything at the Institute didn't feel right.

But she already knew the answer. Frieda would be shrieking in terror or anger if she saw so much as a spider. Cleo had already said how good she felt being at the Institute, and Miranda believed her.

Nothing to be gained in frightening them. She might set their recovery back, and she didn't even know if there was a reason to frighten them. Warn them of what? Of the misfiring fancies of her subconscious?

And Esme said to be quiet. Esme urged silence, and lived by that principle.

Be small, be unnoticed, draw no attention.

No attention from whom?

Could she trust the others?

The question startled Miranda. *Why am I even thinking things like that? What's wrong with me?*

What if there was nothing wrong?

But no. Cleo was definitely not the problem. Frieda was *a* problem, but not one that worried Miranda.

"We're planning a trip to Scotland," she said. She lied so they wouldn't worry. She lied because Esme feared questions.

"Scotland?" said Frieda. "Why Scotland? Now, Monte Carlo, there's a place. Reginald took me there the summer before last." Frieda took off on an extended list of recommendations, their details endless, the personal anecdotes epic in their self-regard. Miranda watched her take pleasure from the belief that no one else in the room would ever be able to replicate the experiences she had had thanks to dear Reginald.

Good. That was Frieda deflected. Cleo wouldn't pry. Miranda could relax a little. Because the sun had not yet begun to set, all was still well. Miranda didn't have to think about the night and dreams – not just yet.

Miranda knew she was dreaming. Floating through the corridors of the Institute, she saw them from a perspective wrong for her memories. She was too high, too tall, only a few feet down from the ceiling. She had left her body and the chair behind. A being of pure awareness, she flew with effortless freedom toward Donovan Stroud's apartment.

She knew she was dreaming. But the details were so precise. The geography of the Institute did not distort. She heard the coughing from the other rooms. The antiseptic tang stabbed at her absent nose and throat. And the dream did not let her transport herself without transition to the apartments. She came to the elevator. Though she had no fingers, she felt the touch of the button. Her spirit had to wait for the Institute's automatic elevator to arrive, and, clanking and whirring, take her up the tower.

The apartment doors opened to her on their own. She flew more quickly now, hurrying to her destination. She tried to hold back, realizing the goal of her journey and frightened of it.

An ethereal rip tide had her, and it yanked her toward the painting. The canvas filled her vision, and she passed into it. Brush strokes resolved into reality, and now she flew over the grounds of the Stroud Estate.

The abbey ruins loomed ahead. A sense of being watched made her look back. She saw no one, only a cluster of huge boulders. The eyeless shapes gazed steadily at her.

Twenty feet above the ground, she sailed toward the ruins, ensnared by their command.

Before the orphaned archway, the entrance to roofless emptiness, Magnus Stroud capered, spinning around and around in a spiral dance. He saw her, and he stopped. The end of his dance froze her flight. She hovered, suspended, directly above him, the threshold of the ruins hungry and waiting.

Magnus smiled. He put a finger to his lips. *Hush.*

The ruins heaved, the earth buckling with the promise of a monstrous birth. The walls, tall and majestic despite their gaps and wounds, swayed. Stone rippled, then began to flow like candlewax.

The abbey melted, becoming a river of rushing, foaming stone. It flowed back toward the ring of boulders, and it took her with it. She flew back, even faster than she had arrived, and Magnus laughed to see her flight.

She hurtled at the boulders. The moment that she understood this was where she had emerged from the painting, she plunged into the center of the spiral and shot out across Donovan's apartment again.

The river of stone came with her. It thundered out of the painting in a torrent, and it caught her, submerging her in mossy gray as it spread over the Institute. Crushed, suffocating and drowning all at once, Miranda caught one last sense impression before the darkness. A serpentine vastness shifted, tightening coils.

Miranda jerked awake, gasping. She sat up, clawing at her chest. Her lungs fought to draw air thick as molasses.

In her panic, and in the dimness of the Institute's night lighting, it took her almost a minute to notice that Esme's bed lay empty.

PART II

Chapter Nine

"Esme passed away sometime after midnight," Nurse Holden said. She stood near the foot of Esme's bed. From that position, she could address the entire room. She turned her head slightly with each breath, looking directly at Frieda, Cleo and Miranda in turn. She spoke calmly, matter-of-factly, but also with genuine sorrow.

Holden, Miranda thought yet again, was *very* good at her job. She had come to tell them the truth, to give them leave to grieve, and to reassure them.

"The night nurse discovered her during one of her rounds," said Holden. "Director Stroud thought it best to take her away without waking the three of you. It would not have done you or anyone else on the ward any good to be woken in the middle of the night to that news."

All very true, all very correct, but the reference to a night nurse made Miranda flinch. Of course every ward had a night nurse. It would be strange, and worrying, if they did not. It was just that Miranda had not thought about there being one before now. She had always felt alone during the nights, the halls empty except for the visions that haunted them. The sudden reminder that she was not alone, that someone walked the corridors while she slept, disturbed her. Instead of being a comforting presence, a guardian of the sick, in her imagination the night nurse became a faceless, roaming presence.

Esme had died and vanished, and Miranda hadn't known. This was how things were supposed to work. Nothing odd or abnormal here.

Still, she flinched. She wished Holden had given the night nurse a name.

"What happened last night is hard for you," Holden went on. "It is for all of us. The goal of the Stroud Institute is to cure everybody who comes through the door. The fact that this is impossible doesn't make the reality any easier to accept. Now, I don't say this to make light of what happened, but this is not just a day of mourning. We have something to celebrate too."

Holden turned to the doorway. "We're ready, Jennifer," she said.

Jennifer Wong stepped into the room. She was dressed in her own clothes and wore an overcoat. She clutched a suitcase in one hand and gave them a little wave with the other. "I'm going home," she said. "My lungs are clear."

Miranda and Cleo applauded. "Well done!" Miranda cheered, as loudly as she dared without straining her voice.

"Good for you," Frieda muttered, glaring at Jennifer as if her recovery were a personal insult.

"You'll all be going home too," Jennifer said. "I know you will. You should have seen me when I first arrived."

"We'll miss you," Holden said, "just as much as we're happy to see you go."

When Jennifer left, Holden became solemn again, though she spoke with a determination meant to be contagious. She was there to stiffen their spines, Miranda thought.

"TB is a serious illness," said Holden. "I don't need to tell you that. Not everyone recovers. Deaths happen. But because Esme succumbed, that doesn't mean that any of you will. All your conditions are different, and none of you are as ill as Esme was. When she arrived at the Institute, her case was already extremely advanced."

"I always thought so," said Frieda. "Yes, clearly very advanced. And she was weak." Frieda spoke with too much vehemence. Her relief sounded forced.

Cleo said nothing, but her shoulders dropped, her body relaxing. She *was* relieved.

Everything Holden said was true. Miranda had no reason to doubt a word.

But having seen the empty bed in the aftermath of her vision, she could not shake the idea of a causal link.

On Wednesday, when Agatha arrived at the start of visiting hours, Miranda felt stronger again, and Agatha took her to the library. They had the room to themselves once more.

"Does anyone else use this place at all?" Agatha wondered.

"Maybe it only exists for us," said Miranda, only half-joking.

They sat by the window, and Miranda told Agatha about the vision. "Does Magnus write about boulders at all?" she asked. "Arranged like standing stones, but too big?"

"He does," said Agatha, looking grim. "The Stroud Spiral, he calls it. I found an entry about it after I'd left you." She held a finger up. "And that, Miranda, is our first real evidence of the parapsychological. You saw something you had no prior knowledge of. Can you describe it in more detail?"

Miranda did, and Agatha's expression became more certain and more grim.

"So it wasn't a dream," said Miranda.

"No. I think we can be definite about that. And you didn't need me to tell you it was more than a dream, did you?"

"It helps to hear it from you." Miranda took a long, slow breath that rattled. "I feel less alone. When the visions come, I really am alone. It's hard, Agatha."

Agatha took her hand. "I'm sorry. I wish I could do more."

Miranda nodded, grateful that Agatha was there and believing her. "So what now? Have you made any more progress?"

"On a couple of fronts, maybe, but the progress isn't reassuring."

"I haven't been expecting any reassurance from your research."

"That's good. First, then, I thought it would be worth looking into this particular site, see if there's a reason why Donovan decided to build his sanatorium here."

"And is there?"

"I haven't found a direct connection between Arkham and Galloway, though I didn't expect to. Arkham itself is enough of a reason to draw the attention of people like the Strouds."

"What do you mean?"

"You grew up here. You went away, though, for your doctorate. Did you notice anything when you returned? Did Arkham *feel* different after having lived somewhere else?"

Miranda thought about it. She remembered her first day back, after several years in New York City, when she had come to be interviewed for the post at Miskatonic. Arkham *had* felt different, yes. The ground did not feel the same as in New York. Even the air had seemed foreign. At the time, she had put the impressions down to the effect of having become used to the sights, sounds, and pace of a big city. She had stopped noticing the taste of the air, or thinking that the ground was somehow less stable. But the more she thought about it, the more Miranda had to concede that a faint, barely noticeable background sense of *wrongness* had never gone away. "Yes," she said, "it did feel different. It does now too."

"Good," said Agatha. "Not everyone can feel that, I don't think. Many who do, try to argue themselves out of their own perceptions. That's a mistake, and I'm glad you're not making it. There is something about this town that... I'm not sure how to put this... causes or invites certain kinds of events, and certain kinds of people."

"What something?" Miranda asked.

"I wish I knew. I've made it my life's work to find out. In the meantime, what matters is that Arkham is Arkham, and whatever that means, it's enough to justify Donovan's eye falling on our town. As to this location, though, I did find out something more specific. There was a pest house here at the end of the eighteenth century. Built in 1794. It was gone by 1840, as best as I can tell."

"A pest house," Miranda repeated.

"I wish I could say it was a proto-sanatorium," said Agatha. "It wasn't, not the Arkham one."

"Let me guess. More like a storage facility for the sick."

"Yes," said Agatha. "Tuberculosis, cholera, smallpox – the whole nine contagious yards. If you had it, and you could spread it, then you were quarantined here."

"Would I be wrong in thinking you just used *quarantined* as a euphemism?"

"You would not be. Not many of those who crossed its threshold ever came out again."

"What happened to the dead?"

"Buried on the grounds," said Agatha. "Unmarked graves. No graveyard for them."

"And now a sanatorium erected over their bones," said Miranda. "Were they exhumed before construction began?"

"I wondered about that too. I went through everything I could in city archives. No sign of any such order."

Miranda grimaced. "We saw how deep the foundations were dug during construction. If the bodies weren't removed…"

"Right. Then they were disturbed violently by the process. They'll have been scattered around. Some of them, or parts of them, hauled away with the dirt and disposed of who knows where. Others might still be in the grounds."

"Or ground to dust."

"That too. Now keep all this in mind while I tell you about the test I performed. I have an Atwater-Kent battery radio. I drove down here with it last night."

"Why did you do that?"

"It's an experiment I've preformed at or near other sights with reported phenomena. It's another way of trying to register their existence. I tune the radio to static, and see if I hear anything unusual."

"And did you?"

"Not exactly. I didn't hear anything *at all*."

"I don't understand."

"I set the radio to static before I left home. I had it on as I drove. I heard nothing but static all the way down. But when I came close to the gates, the static cut out. Dead silence."

"Dead silence," Miranda repeated.

"Sorry. Not the best choice of words, given what I told you about the grounds."

"Maybe exactly the right words," said Miranda. "Does that silence tell you anything?"

"Not yet, but it is a clear symptom. This is how we gather the evidence. Individually, the pieces might not look like anything. But I do believe, I *have* to believe, that eventually a picture will emerge."

Miranda thought again about the dead beneath the Institute's foundations. "Do you think building here, on this particular site, was deliberate?" she asked.

"On Donovan's part?" Agatha shrugged. "Did he even know about the bodies? Maybe. Could he have arranged for nothing to be exhumed? Not impossible, I suppose, but this could easily be explained as bureaucratic negligence."

"The innocent explanation we can't dismiss," said Miranda.

"*Innocent* might be a bit of a stretch, but yes."

"Only you don't buy that any more than I do."

"It's definitely not the first on my list of likely scenarios," Agatha said. "And there's something else interesting I found. The land originally belonged to the family of Payton Wallace."

Miranda felt her lips twitch in disgust. "The good councilman who worked so hard to get the city's approval for the Institute's construction."

"He certainly did. You should see the transcripts of the debates. He was most eloquent."

"Did he still own the land?" Miranda asked.

"I wondered about that. The archives weren't much help on that front. Too many gaps. So I don't know."

"He could be involved with Donovan in some way, then." Miranda examined the idea, and wasn't satisfied. "Payton strikes me as too callow to be deliberately engaged in something sinister."

"It may be a case of simple bribery, then," said Agatha. "Or maybe not even that. I'll see what he has to say for himself."

"You're going to see him?"

"I managed to get a late-day appointment. I'm not expecting much from our meeting, but I don't want to leave any possible lead unexplored. And he has tied himself to the sanatorium, one way or another."

For a brief moment, Miranda allowed herself to entertain the idea that they were about to uncover mundane corruption. It was pure pretense, one she just needed for a few seconds, a reprieve from the more terrifying prospects. Fiddled deals at city hall didn't explain anything, and she knew it. But it was nice to pretend.

The moment passed, and she let the dream of a normal world flutter away. It had been sweet while it lasted.

Her mind went back to the pest house.

"It would be nice to take comfort in the fact that the Stroud Institute's track record is better than its predecessor's," she said.

"It would be," Agatha agreed. "You might as well hang on to the comfort you can for now. At least the track record is real."

"You checked on the people who've been released?"

"I have. They're doing well."

Miranda sighed. "Well, that's something, anyway. And I guess we know why the Institute is here."

"Not exactly," said Agatha. "We have established a connection, a reason for Donovan to be interested, but we don't know his purpose."

"That brings us back to the Strouds, then. Any more luck with Magnus?"

"That's where the research hasn't been as productive," said Agatha. "I've gone through the *Miscellany* backwards and forwards. I've squeezed everything I could out of it. I haven't found any other promising sources. It ends with him going on and on about his dream of a community of artists. There's no indication if he actually did something about it."

"So that's a dead end."

"Yes. I don't think we've learned all there is to learn about Magnus."

"As far as what Arkham offers, you mean."

"That's right."

They sat without speaking for a full minute, both of them conscious of what had to happen next. Miranda didn't want to give voice to the words. If she did, she would hurry the moment of being truly alone. Agatha seemed just as reluctant to broach the subject.

Miranda forced herself to break the silence. "Galloway," she said. Speaking the word felt like putting wheels in motion. She looked at the months ahead with a sharp spike of dread. The library seemed to grow dim, motes of darkness gathering in the air around her.

"Yes," said Agatha. "If we're going to learn more, that's where I have to go. And given your vision, I'd say my being on-site is imperative. The sooner the better." She grimaced. "I don't like saying this, but it seems to me that whatever is happening is getting worse."

"My visions sure are."

"And though we don't know that Esme's death is connected in any way…"

"We don't know that it isn't, either."

"And that's the problem."

"Yes," said Miranda. "We need to know."

Agatha squeezed her hand. "I don't like the idea of leaving you alone."

"I'm not wild about it myself."

"Maybe there's an alternative."

Miranda shook her head. *Come on now. Be strong.* "No. You have to go. We can't pretend nothing is going on."

Agatha gave her a tight, approving smile. "No, we can't."

"And I'm not alone, not really. Or at least, I won't be worse off with you gone. It isn't like you can be here during the nights, and even if you were, what could you do? I have friends here."

"We could see about having you transferred to the hospital," Agatha offered.

"No," Miranda said hesitantly, and then more emphatically. "No. The care here *is* good. And I'm feeling a bit better. Better than I was before being admitted."

"That's some good news, then."

"This is the thing," said Miranda. "We know something is happening in Arkham, and it looks like it's linked somehow to Magnus Stroud, but we don't know that it's centered on the Institute. My first vision was in my apartment, after all."

"The night before you came here," Agatha pointed out.

"I know," Miranda conceded.

"Tell me the real reason why you don't want to leave," Agatha said. "This is important. If you're making this choice, it has to be a clear one." She held up that finger again. "No rationalizations."

"Right." Miranda gave herself a moment. She needed to be sure. Putting the thought into words had consequences. "If there is something happening here, then someone has to fight it. There's only so much you can do from the outside. I'm here. If I don't fight, who will?"

There. She had said it. There could be no more pretending, ever, that nothing was wrong, and that she had just been imagining things. She couldn't hide behind that delusion any longer. No going back. Only forward now, into the gathering darkness.

Agatha squeezed her hand. "I'm proud of you," she said.

Miranda forced herself to smile. "Thanks." She knew she had made the right choice. She just wished she felt more proud than frightened. "How long will you be gone?" She had already begun the countdown to Agatha's return.

"Hard to say. Depending on the bookings I can make, let's allow for a week each way for the Atlantic crossing. Another few days of travel to and from Galloway, and that's assuming I can find an inn close to the Stroud Estate. As for how long the research will take me there, and what other travel might be involved, I don't know. Any guesses?"

"You might have to chase down records and look through archives in Edinburgh or Glasgow," Miranda said bleakly. "Or elsewhere." Agatha could be gone a month or more. An eternity, Miranda thought. She would be alone, and would have no idea when Agatha might be back.

"I'm not gone yet," said Agatha. She put her hand on Miranda's.

"No, but you must," Miranda told her. "If you don't, we won't be doing any good." She tried to shake her apprehension. "I'll be fine. It's not like the corpses are stacking up outside the Institute. Esme died, but Jennifer went home. This is still a place that's making people well."

"All right," said Agatha. "This is what we're doing, then. I'll head off as soon as I have tickets. I'll be back as soon as I can."

"Please do," Miranda said. "Please hurry."

A draft touched the back of her neck, the library breathing down on her, its teeth about to brush against her skin.

The councilman kept Agatha cooling her heels in the waiting room until the very end of the working day. The reception area had a carpet in rich red, and some gilt-framed paintings that were very passable pre-Raphaelite imitations. Agatha sat on a wooden chair, an antique clearly valuable, and strategically uncomfortable, and refused to give in to impatience. The struggle was hard. She should be home, preparing for the trip. Time wasted here was time she could not get back, and she had really hoped to be on a train by the evening. Yes, that might not be realistic, but she didn't want to dismiss the hope. If she lost a day, that could mean a day longer for Miranda to be left on her own. Not necessarily, but maybe.

So many maybes, and so much time slipping away pointlessly.

Still, Agatha held her temper. Losing it would be a defeat. It helped that the receptionist was a young woman with, Agatha suspected, definite views about the utility of anyone over the age of fifty. She glanced at Agatha from time to time as if gauging whether the peasant had been taught her place yet. That gave Agatha someone to fight, so she kept her face placid. She barely moved, didn't even glance at the three-day-old newspaper insultingly set out on the low table before her.

Finally, more than an hour after Agatha's appointment time, the receptionist's phone rang. She picked it up, listened, acknowledged, and then begrudgingly informed Agatha that Councilman Wallace would see her now.

"Thank you," Agatha said without rancor, and also without the gratitude that was clearly due for being permitted to see the great and busy man.

Agatha had been surprised by the visual luxury of the waiting room. It turned out to be as nothing compared to Payton's actual office. Its polished dark wood, spacious dimensions and treed view were there for the clear purpose of creating envy and awe. So were the plentiful paintings and objets d'art. The councilman was not a man, it seemed, who had to rely on his salary as the sole source of income.

Then there was the larger-than-life portrait of Payton. Its scale and the heroic pose of the model made Agatha feel better. Instead of holding back her anger, she now struggled to suppress her laughter.

Payton stood up behind his huge desk. "Do please forgive me for the delay," he said. "Pressing business. I'm sure you understand."

"I do," she said, with enough edge to let him know he wasn't fooling anyone.

Payton smiled. "Please sit down." He gestured to the chair in front of the desk.

No, she thought, she would not sit in that. It was so low, she would barely be able to see over the top of the desk. Payton could have his little games with someone else.

"Thank you," she said. "I'll stand."

Payton missed a beat, thrown by her refusal to follow the script. "As you wish," he said. Another beat, as he debated whether to sit or stand himself. He sat, and from the look on his face, regretted his choice immediately. He was stuck now, though. He couldn't stand back up without looking ridiculous.

He folded his hands and leaned forward, making a concerted show of being comfortable in her presence. "Now, Mrs Crane–"

"Professor Crane," Agatha corrected him.

Payton coughed. "Excuse me," he said, the purpose of the apology ambiguous. "What can I do for you?"

"I was hoping you could fill in some research gaps for me," said Agatha.

"About what?"

"The Stroud Institute."

Payton's right eye twitched.

"Specifically," said Agatha, "why you fought so hard for it."

"Why would I not fight for what is so clearly a good thing for Arkham?"

"Your passion for this cause seems to me to have been of a different order than you usually display in council, I have to say. I've read the transcripts."

Payton smiled patiently. "I fight for what I believe in," he said.

"And your belief had nothing to do with your family's ownership of that land."

"That's outrageous!" Indignation reddened Payton's cheeks. He pointed a warning finger at Agatha. "You're fortunate there is no one else present to hear you say that, or I would be starting legal proceedings against you. I resent your implications about my character. And that land has not been a Wallace possession for a long time."

"That doesn't explain why there was no exhumation of the human remains."

Payton's jaw dropped. He recovered quickly and didn't even stammer, but Agatha knew she had struck home.

"The land is not a graveyard," he said. "It has never been zoned as such. There was no need for an exhumation. If there were any remains found, they were treated with due respect."

If there were any remains found. In other words, Payton had made sure not to know, one way or the other. Maybe his involvement with Donovan was one of basic bribery after all. How Payton expected Agatha to see the flaunted art in his office and presume him to be honest was beyond her. She gave the councilman a long look, and what she saw in him, she decided, was a mixture of ignorance and cunning. A dangerous combination, because it was also the right sort of politician's recipe for success.

Agatha found that she believed Payton's anger. He didn't know anything bad about the Institute, and therefore didn't know anything useful to her. That didn't mean he couldn't be of some use himself, though. She wondered if the right words might turn another set of suspicious eyes on the place.

"I apologize," she said, and he leaned back in his chair, somewhat mollified. "Your conscience may well be clear when it comes to the construction of the Stroud Institute. Do you think the same will be true of your political record if something is wrong there?"

That got his attention. She finally saw genuine concern on his face. "What do you mean? What's wrong?"

"Possibly nothing, but then again, possibly much. This is what I am investigating."

"Surely the police…"

Agatha shook her head. "I'm not talking about criminal activity. What may be wrong there is outside the authority of the police." She braced herself. What she said next might have her thrown out of the office on her ear. "My particular study consists of the careful, scientific investigation of parapsychological phenomena." Better to multiply the syllables, hit him with words he might not understand but have to pretend that he did, and so couldn't easily dismiss. "I have evidence of such phenomena occurring at the Institute. The evidence is tentative at this point, but it is of concern." She didn't say to whom. Let him wonder if other people, perhaps ones he had to take seriously, were also taking a look at the Institute.

Payton said nothing for a long moment, his brow furrowed as he tried to parse what she had said, and what it might mean for him. "Has something happened to the patients?"

"Nothing that can't, *as yet*, be presented as natural causes." Everything she said was true. The presentation, though, she shaped to worry Payton.

I should have gone into politics.

Her tactic worked. He looked very worried now, and he hadn't even asked her what *parapsychological* meant. "I appreciate your bringing this to my attention," he said.

"My investigations are taking me away from Arkham for a while," said Agatha. "So I won't be able to provide you with any updates." She spoke confidentially now, as if he were a long-term ally and part of the small group that was in the know.

"I will be taking a closer look at the Stroud Institute myself," said Payton, his voice stronger again, closing in on being condescending again as he reassured her that he was now on the case.

"That's very good to hear," Agatha said. She gave him her best grateful smile. And she *was* grateful. She didn't think for a moment that he could do anything except make his scrutiny visible, and that might impede Donovan in some way.

Maybe.

If something was happening at all.

"If I may make a suggestion," she said, all deference. She even sat down.

"Please do."

"If there is, in fact, something going on, it will be well disguised. Be wary of what is normal and the easy explanation. Be especially wary of the explanations for things that bother you, even if you aren't sure why."

For a moment, Payton looked like a little boy who had been told a very scary bedtime story.

Good. The visit had not been a waste of time, after all.

"Did you get through?" Agatha asked Wilbur. Her husband had been on the phone in the apartment's entrance hall, calling the ticket offices of the shipping lines, looking for a last-minute third-class tourist booking that wouldn't bankrupt them. They had no children, and inheritances on both sides had left them comfortable in their retirement. Agatha's research called for travel, and they'd been able to afford her voyages up to now. She had never gone with such short notice before, though.

"Had some luck with White Star," Wilbur said. "You're on tomorrow's sailing of the *Leviathan*."

Agatha turned away from the suitcases opened on the bed and kissed Wilbur. He smiled, and lost some of the *this, again?* look in his eyes. He was a small, thin man, his bald head just a bit large for his slight frame. He was built for a quiet retirement, and Agatha loved him all the more for how well he had accepted that would not be their lot.

"So," he said. "Off again."

"Only because I have to." She went back to her packing. She stuffed another notebook into one of the cases. Better to have too many than not enough.

"An Atlantic crossing," Wilbur said. "In early spring, no less. Sure to be smooth sailing all the way."

"Lucky I don't get seasick, then."

"I was thinking about my own poor stomach."

Agatha paused, a sweater half folded. She looked at Wilbur.

He grinned. "Got us two tickets," he said. "Seemed like sense."

"Oh, you sweet old fool!" She threw her arms around him and hugged him tight before releasing him to become all business again. "You're sure you're up for this?"

"Well, I'm sure that I'm not going to be without you for this long again."

"On your head be it, then." She kept her tone light, but she wasn't joking. She went to her dresser and unlocked the small, dark chest that sat on top. She looked at the amulets and rings inside, thinking about protection for two.

"Are you doing something dangerous?" Wilbur asked.

"I don't know. I really don't." Just like she didn't know which object would help or why. Belief? Actual properties that obeyed a scientific principle she hadn't yet discovered?

"And if you don't go, will something bad happen?"

"I'm worried it might. Though I also don't know if my going will make a difference."

She chose two silver medallions. She had had them made two years earlier, commissioning a design that replicated one on a medallion in the special archaeological collection at Miskatonic. No one had yet been able to date the object. It appeared to be much older than the detail of the design permitted.

Agatha held the silver disks in her hand and felt comforted. She gave one to Wilbur.

"Keep this with you once we get to Galloway," she said. "*Always.*"

"If you say so."

"I do." When he put it in his pocket with the care he might have given to explosives, she kissed his cheek. "You do put up with a lot from me, don't you?"

He shrugged. "I don't understand any of it. Probably best that I don't. But who is going to stop you? Not me. And I don't think I should."

He shuffled off to get his suitcases out of the storage closet.

Agatha moved to the bedroom window. She looked down toward the Institute. "Sleep well and be strong," she murmured. "I'll be back soon."

She hoped she would be soon enough.

Chapter Ten

The first two weeks after Agatha left were quiet. Miranda's dread receded to the point that she felt the temptation to consider everything she had experienced as a dream after all. She hadn't had any further visions. She slept through most nights, and the few times she had woken up, anxiety crawling over her skin, there had been nothing to alarm her. She had calmed down and gone back to sleep.

She also felt better. Her sense of increasing well-being was real. She was sure of it. Her chest still ached, her energy was a fraction of what it had been before she fell sick, and fever gave her alternating chills and sweats during the night. But none of the symptoms were as bad as when she'd arrived. She sometimes went for half an hour or more without coughing. Breathing had become less of a strain. She had enough energy to be bored during the day, and even enough to do something about that boredom, crack a book, and read for entire minutes before falling asleep again.

Rested, feeling stronger, she found it easy to believe all was well. Easy to tell herself she had been imagining things.

Except she had seen the Stroud Spiral before knowing it existed. And Agatha had gone to Scotland. Agatha believed Miranda had experienced something real, and that worried the parapsychologist.

Even so, Miranda accepted the reprieve gratefully. She wanted to believe she was improving even more strongly than she wanted to believe nothing had happened.

Miranda took advantage of the calm to think about *why* she had the respite. The absence of evidence made it hard to theorize. All she had to go on was her experience, and she wondered if there was a pattern to the ebb and flow of night terrors. At first, she pictured the movements of a tide. During the one night that she did lie awake in the pre-dawn hours, she found herself imagining the whirl of a slow vortex with her at the center, terror spiraling to and away from her, tethered to her and following an arc she could not quite see.

Turning and turning in the widening gyre…

Yes, but in this instance the falconer was at the mercy of the falcon. It flew at her and away, responding to whims of horror. The center could not hold, and neither could she flee. The falcon would whirl and whirl, near and far, and always the talons would come again.

She did not like the image, or the way it resonated with her heart as truth. It kept her awake for much of that night, the fourth after Agatha's departure. In the morning, though, the conceit lost some of its power. It seemed too convoluted, too much the product of a fatigued imagination. She did not abandon it. She kept it in the back of her mind. But she did not feel its claws during the night.

Two days after Esme's death, Lupita Guerrero became the new resident of the fourth bed. Lupita was in her mid-70s, her hair white and streaked with black, as if testifying to her strength. Intensely pious, she knelt by her bed to pray every night. She did so in silence, holding hard to her crucifix, and with an unshowy dignity that met with Cleo's approval, and annoyed Frieda, who somehow took it as a rebuke.

Ten days after the night of the vision, Nurse Revere informed Miranda that her tests were looking good, and that she now had permission to take short walks. Revere delivered the news with the severity of a judge pronouncing sentence, and Miranda took the message that she should not take her new privilege for granted.

"Thank you," Miranda said, with all due solemnity. Keeping a straight face was hard. She felt giddy. She really was getting better. She wanted to leap up and drag Revere into a dance. Instead, she said, "And thank you for your guidance."

Revere's stony gaze stayed on Miranda a few moments longer, as if scanning for sarcasm. Then she gave a curt nod and left.

Miranda's first journeys without the chair, just to one end of the corridor and back, went well. Her energy levels fluctuated, but her breathing remained steady. And so, two weeks after Agatha left, Nurse Holden told Miranda that she was well enough to start attending the counseling sessions.

"Is it mandatory?" Miranda asked. She had no objection to going; she was simply curious.

"No," said Holden. "It's up to you. I do recommend the sessions, though. They keep your mind more active than the mental exercises you've been doing here, and the active mind helps lead to a healthy body."

"I'll look forward to them," Miranda said.

Cleo and Frieda had just started going the week before. The privilege of doing something that Miranda was not yet part of turned the sessions into Frieda's new obsessive focus of conversation, even though she struggled to be specific about what was actually said. Cleo didn't help her out.

"They're interesting," she said to Miranda without elaboration. "You'll see. I know you'll be going soon too."

Lupita, much stronger than Esme, and – Miranda enviously suspected – stronger than she was herself, was also invited to start the sessions. On Friday, the four women wheeled themselves to what Holden had called the seminar room. As they made their way there, Miranda said, "I don't think I'll ever get the hang of the layout of this place." She kept her tone light. Just a casual remark, a random cast, nothing more.

She watched the others carefully.

Frieda clucked her tongue. "If you can't follow signs, then you deserve to get lost."

Cleo rolled her eyes at Frieda's remark and gave Miranda a sympathetic grimace. "Hospitals," she said. "I kept getting lost at St Mary's too."

Lupita bit her lip. She said nothing. Her reaction made Miranda feel a little less alone, and more than a little guilty for poking at a sore.

Miranda's first sight of the Stroud Institute's library had surprised her. The seminar room surprised her again. It had smaller windows than the library but seemed much airier and brighter. Cream and light green washes defined the wallpaper, with energetic lines and splashes of bright color conjuring irises, lilies, and entwining vines, a garden spare and lively, calming while bursting with life. Tall, potted ferns in the corners extended the soothing energy of the wallpaper into the room. A dozen leather chaise lounge formed a circle, with enough space between each to make it easy for the patients to park their wheelchairs and transfer onto the furniture. The circle surrounded a table, a pole raising its narrow surface to the height of a podium. It held a few books, some pens, and a sheaf of papers.

Once all the patients were settled, the door opened again and a woman walked into the room.

No, Miranda thought. That was wrong. She did not walk. She *flowed*. She moved with a dancer's grace, a dancer who never left the stage, and whose every gesture was part of a lifelong motion of grace. She had her black hair in a flapper's cut. Miranda put her in her late twenties, and her skin had the eerie perfection of a porcelain doll. She smiled at the group as she made her way to the center of the circle, and her teeth were perfect too, dazzling white between shining lipstick of a red so deep it was almost black. When she spoke, her voice seemed to be an extension of her body's endless grace, soft and low, the caress of a summer's breeze. She wore a black top and skirt; at odds with her haircut, the skirt was long and swayed with her movements, a partner in her dance.

"Welcome, welcome!" she said, making a graceful turn that extended her greeting to every woman in the room. Miranda felt seen. She felt cared for. The woman had only spoken four syllables, and Miranda couldn't wait to hear more.

"I'm so glad to see all of you back, and to see some new faces as well. To those just joining us, don't worry about catching up. We only just started this group of sessions last week. My name is Daria Miracle." She rolled her eyes. "I know. That last name is a bit much. But it's the one I have, so please be gentle with me."

Daria grinned, and Miranda grinned back. If Miracle was her name, then let her be one. Miranda was already halfway to believing Daria would embody her family's name.

She noticed the other women were grinning and laughing with Daria too.

Daria clapped her hands together in delight. "Splendid! We're all having a good time together, and we haven't even got going, yet. I think we'll have a fine afternoon. Don't you?"

More smiles. Everyone nodded.

"Good, good. So, for our new friends, let me tell you what we're up to during these hours." She paused and grew serious, her voice even more gentle, a balm for the soul. "TB is scary. Of course it is. It's a serious illness, and, well, all of you know what can happen. TB can make you feel like you've lost control. Or that you are lost, plain and simple. What I want to do is to help you feel stronger. Just because something *can* happen, that doesn't mean it *will* happen. After all, you're here to get well. Aren't you?"

"Yes," Frieda breathed. It was the closest to pleading Miranda had ever heard from her.

"You're not lost," said Daria. "You do have agency."

"We also have faith," Lupita said.

"That too."

Daria's agreement sounded genuine. Yet Lupita's lower lip trembled. Very slightly, very briefly. As if she had felt stricken, and then the moment had passed, virtually forgotten, but leaving a faint residue of confusion behind.

Why? Miranda wondered.

Lupita seemed to be wondering too.

Daria carved an arc in the air with her arm as she began to recite. "*In middle of the journey of our days / I found that I was in a darksome wood– / The right road lost and vanished in the maze.*" She lowered her arm. "Dante felt lost on his journey in mid-life. Some of you haven't reached that point yet. Oops, I mean *none* of you have."

More general laughter. Frieda looked schoolgirl-pleased.

"My point is," said Daria, "that we can feel lost on any stage of our journey. How did we get to this point? To every point? Is it fate or choice that decides?"

"God's will," Lupita murmured under her breath.

Daria heard, all the same. "Or God's will?" she added, and winked at Lupita. "These are big questions. I'm not the one with the answers."

The confidence in that last sentence suggested to Miranda that Daria didn't have the answers, but she knew who did.

"None of you chose to contract TB," said Daria. "Or am I wrong?" A chorus of "No!" answered her. "So it's understandable if you feel confused." Daria began to walk slowly around the circle. She came close to every chaise lounge, creating greater intimacy between herself and the patients. "If you didn't choose to get TB, why do you have it? Is fate cruel? Is God punishing you? Are you just the victim of meaningless chance? Does any of that sound right?"

More denials. Daria walked a full circuit in sympathetic silence. Then she returned to the center of the circle. She picked up two pieces of paper from the table. "Does anyone know the difference between a maze and a labyrinth?" she asked.

Miranda knew. She said nothing, growing more and more conscious of the performance nature of Daria's presentation. The initial seduction had worn off, and now Miranda was feeling played rather than seen. So she watched the session from a distance, curious instead of involved.

"Aren't they the same thing?" Frieda asked.

"They aren't," said Daria. "Many people think they are, and it's easy to see why." She held the two pages up and turned around slowly, showing them to the entire group. The illustrations on the sheets were similar. At first glance, the only difference between them was that one was a square, the other a circle. Both contained a density of lines.

Daria lifted the square higher. "This is a maze," she said. "The difference is not in the outer shape. That can be anything. It's what's inside the walls that matters. When you enter a maze, you must constantly decide what branching path to take. There are so many choices, but only one correct route. The maze is designed to be frustrating. The labyrinth, though, is soothing. The labyrinth has only one path. No matter how many times it turns and twists, there are no forks in the road, no wrong decisions to make. When you enter the labyrinth, you know you will reach the center. In a maze, you are lost. You might never find the way. In a labyrinth, you are never lost."

Riveted, Lupita said, "The labyrinth is God's plan."

"If you like," said Daria, "in whatever way you choose to understand that idea."

Again, Miranda thought Lupita looked a little betrayed, as if her revelation had met with dismissal.

Daria put the papers down. "You are at a point in your lives where you seem to have no choice. You feel powerless."

Miranda had to admit Daria's bolt struck home there.

"I want to invite you to walk the soothing labyrinth with us. Think of your treatment as a labyrinth. There will be many turns. You can't see far ahead. You can only see to the next bend. But you know you'll make it to the center. That's what you came here to do."

Daria paused, her smile fixed and caring while she waited for her audience to take in her words. Then she went on.

"Maybe the image of the labyrinth is useful just for your time with us. If that's the case for you, then I'm glad it's useful here and now. But I encourage you to think about the labyrinth as the symbol for your entire path through life. You'll never know for certain if your outcomes are determined by choice or by destiny. But maybe that doesn't matter. Maybe you don't need to worry about that debate at all. What if you simply accept the twists and turns in your life as being the path of the larger labyrinth that you walk? After all, whatever choices you have made, and whatever chance events you have encountered, they have all been paving stones in the one route that is your life."

Daria paused again. She touched one of the books with a pensive finger.

Nice theatrics, Miranda thought. Was she not going to talk about the books at all? Were they just for show? They were good props, then, leather with old, cracked spines, ancient soldiers recruited for this mission from the library.

"If you see your life as a labyrinth," Daria said, speaking more slowly, delivering the lesson, "then you know that whatever happens, this is *your* route, and you can never be lost." Yet one more pause, and a solemn nod before she blazed with fervor again. "We're going to explore the labyrinth together. So you won't be lost, and you also won't be alone."

Applause all around, even from Miranda.

That was really good. Very entertaining. First rate show.

Daria never did do anything with the books. She did distribute pens and paper, though. The patients went back to their rooms with a maze and a labyrinth, and the challenge to find a path to trace.

The puzzles impressed Miranda. They reinforced Daria's points, and they made Miranda *feel* the argument. She solved the maze, but not without cursing under her breath as she crossed out one wrong route after another. When she reached the center, her paper looked a mess. *And this is why Daria gave us pens, and not pencils.* No erasing of mistakes. She had to live with the growing, unsightly mess of the dead ends.

Miranda could tell when the other women in the room were working on the maze. They frowned, bit their lips, glared at the paper, and did lots of angry scribbling.

The labyrinth, by contrast, soothed her, just as Daria had promised. The convoluted path seemed to take hold of the pen and gently pull her through to the end. As she traced the line back and forth, up and down, left and right in zigs and zags to its single end, she felt herself easing into a meditative state, less conscious of her tired, laboring body.

She finished by blinking, as if waking up from an unexpected nap.

Miranda looked around at the others. It was strange to see Frieda thoughtful; Cleo and Lupita were deep in their own musings too. The room felt strangely quiet.

Miranda broke the silence. "What did all of you think about today?"

"Daria Miracle is a wise woman," Frieda pronounced. "Everyone would do well to heed her lessons." She nodded in agreement with herself, and in anticipation of a consensus. "I wonder if she speaks elsewhere. Reginald and his friends should hear her."

Cleo grunted. "She knows how to speak, that woman. She surely does."

"Does that mean you buy what she's selling?" Miranda asked.

Cleo made a face. "Don't like not having a choice." She folded up the two puzzles, creasing them with decisive energy. "I make my own choices and my own mistakes, thanks all the same."

Was she protesting too much? She spoke more loudly than necessary.

Lupita said nothing. She kept looking at her crucifix as if she didn't recognize it.

Miranda had another night without dreams. Lupita did, though, and her dreams woke Miranda. An hour before dawn, Miranda opened her eyes, startled awake by pleading and the sounds of loss.

Chapter Eleven
Scotland, 1806

Magnus walked through his grounds, trying not to look a fool by grinning too broadly. He had to work hard, and he almost didn't care. He felt giddy. He had turned the Republic of the Arts into a reality.

It had only been a couple of weeks since the first poets and artists had begun to arrive, and only today could he say that all of the cottages he had had built were occupied. The Republic had only just been born. But it lived. It no longer existed only in his dreams. People of revolutionary creativity lived together and worked here. He had created the conditions for his estate to become the artistic pole star for the young century.

The cottages were scattered by design. Some nestled in the trees closer to the Hall. Others braved the elements on the open moor. Magnus had directed that enough space be left between the thatched cottages that the inhabitants of one would barely be aware of those of another. The privacy and isolation necessary for artistic endeavor had to be preserved.

At the same time, the Republic should also be a community. So he had created what he called a village square in the shadow of the Stroud Spiral. It was a simple affair: a fire pit large enough for a proper bonfire, stone benches forming a semicircle around it. Anyone present would be facing the boulders and see them lit up by the flames and dancing with shadow. Magnus had ordered that a bonfire be lit every night. It initiated the gatherings, drawing the artists and writers to the heat and light.

They had need of both. Fall had come early, and the first days of September felt like mid-October. A chilly, rainy start to the Republic of the Arts, but Magnus didn't care. The weather created the need for more community in the evenings, and the days were warm enough for the work of creation to carry on uninterrupted.

Magnus stopped beside the fire pit for a moment, watching his servants prepare the wood for the evening. One of the poets, a slight, limping young woman named Christina Blackstone, sat on a bench, scribbling in her notebook.

Magnus sighed with delight and satisfaction. He had done it. He had told William of his hopes, and he had made them concrete in just over a year.

He wished that William had wanted to be part of it. He had been an eager collaborator in shaping the early forms of the dream when they were at St John's College in Cambridge together. But he had shown none of that interest when Magnus had brought him to the estate. William's mood had chilled; he had been uninterested in any of the schemes Magnus had tried to lay out for him, and he had left the estate the next day, in a sudden hurry to get away when the original intent had been for him to spend the week in Galloway.

William had not returned since. He wrote, but only when Magnus did first. His letters were civil but distant. Magnus grieved to think he had lost a friend without knowing why.

William, I wish you could see what I've done. Why did he draw away? Why wouldn't he rejoice in the realization of the project? The closer Magnus came to welcoming the first citizens of the Republic of the Arts, the slower and more curt William became in answering letters.

Maybe it was disillusionment. Magnus had noticed William turning more and more away from the promises of revolution. The souring of the dream in France had also soured William on its principles too, it seemed.

Magnus shook away his gloom. William's apostasy, if that's what it was, didn't matter. The Republic mattered. Its reality mattered. Magnus had created it himself. His dream, his accomplishment.

Arranging for the construction of the cottages had been the easy part. He had the means to hire whoever he needed to make small, simple, but comfortable homes. What had been more difficult had been finding a population for the Republic. That had taken time, research and patience. The Republic had nothing of interest for the more established or dissolute creators of revolutionary poetry, and that seemed, unfortunately, to account for a great many of the people Magnus thought of as the sort of poet or painter he wanted to support.

He tried courting William Blake. Magnus admired his work and knew he was part of a very select number to do so. Blake was poor; Magnus could do a lot for him. Six months after William Wordsworth had departed the Stroud Estate, William Blake had come for a visit.

Things did not go well. Blake arrived late evening. During the night, he woke the entire Hall with his screams. The nightmare left him pale, shaking and weak, but he refused to talk about it. Refused, also, to set foot outside the Hall. For hours, Blake stared out at the grounds from the front windows as if demons lurked beyond the trees. He left for London without breakfasting.

Then, as if fate decided it had to make amends for the disaster with Blake, Magnus' luck turned. He combed through issues of *The Edinburgh Review* and *The Gentleman's Quarterly*, searching for hints of other poets, other artists, less well-known but still of the right sort. Disapproval from some quarters became signs of hope for Magnus. He would be the patron of the reviled and the abandoned. They would come to him because they would see that he shared their vision.

And they came. First one, then a few more. Soon, the Republic of the Arts counted twenty-three citizens.

I've done it.

The thought made him feel giddy again. Regrets about what had happened with the two Williams evaporated.

Magnus wandered over to where Christina Blackstone sat. She looked up at his approach and rose to curtsey.

"Please sit," he said. "I hope I'm not interrupting the flow of your composition."

"Not at all, my lord. I don't think that's even possible here." She sounded as giddy as he felt.

"So the grounds here aren't too sylvan for you?" Christina was a poet of the Graveyard School. Her work that Magnus had seen was icy meditations on gloom and loss. "I'm sorry I don't have a graveyard to offer you." No Strouds had been buried on the grounds since the dissolution of the monasteries, and the earlier markers that must have been present had been removed when the abbey fell.

Christina smiled. She ran a hand over the page of her notebook. "I have been visiting the ruins of your abbey, my lord. There is fuel enough for a lifetime of inspiration there."

"I'm very glad to hear it."

"I was wondering if the abbey's crypt is safe to visit."

Magnus frowned. "The crypt?" In all his childhood explorations of the ruins, he'd never seen the entrance to a crypt.

"It's in what I judge was once the chapel," said Christina. "Near where the altar might have been."

Magnus knew where she meant. "You saw a way down?" There had been nothing there the last time he had been, just before the first citizens of the Republic had arrived.

"I did, but I did not know if it was safe, or permitted."

"Your caution does you credit," said Magnus. "I will have to see for myself, and I will let you know." He thought for a minute. "If there is something there, I find it remarkable that it has been hidden for so long, and even more remarkable that it suddenly became visible at this juncture."

"Like an omen," Christina breathed, her eyes shining with excitement.

"Quite so."

"I have been feeling, my lord, as if my entire life were a path leading to this place. It is a sense of destiny."

Magnus' blood thrummed with euphoria. Destiny. He wasn't alone in feeling it. The Republic was going to be more than a center of creation. It was something that was *meant* to be.

To what end?

He didn't know yet. He might never know. Its purpose might not be revealed until long after his death. But he had a new certainty now: the certainty of legacy.

He had to see what Christina had found in the abbey.

"I believe all of us are here in answer to a calling," he said. "You have just confirmed that belief. We will speak of this again soon."

She blushed and smiled with shy pride.

He left her, making his way toward the abbey. Midway between the Spiral and the ruins, he saw that Alfred Claymot had set his easel up on the moor, a short distance away from his cottage. He lived in one of the loneliest and most wind-battered homes on the estate. He had two canvases with him, one on the easel, the other leaning against its legs. Hands on his hips, Alfred looked from the canvases to the abbey and the Spiral, and then back again.

As Magnus drew close, he saw that the two paintings were unfinished landscapes. They looked like dreams of the moor, their details yet to emerge from a fog of colors. There was little indication of what the completed work would look like, and that, Magnus knew, would be impressive. Alfred's landscapes had a special weight to them, as though when he looked at the land, he saw more than its appearance. He saw its *meaning*. That insight was why Magnus had commissioned Alfred to paint his portrait.

The artist ran a hand through his long, disheveled hair. He had a soft, nondescript face pinched into a permanent scowl of dissatisfaction, as if his features were outraged by their own banality.

"My lord," Alfred said, bowing distractedly, his attention held by the problem he saw on the canvasses.

"What ails you, Alfred?" Magnus asked.

"I have been trying to settle on a backdrop for your portrait, my lord."

"I do like the idea of the moor," said Magnus.

"The problem is the perspective. I have been trying to experiment with either the abbey or the Stroud Spiral as a backdrop."

Magnus looked more closely at the two paintings. He couldn't make much of the blur of color. He wanted to squint, as if facing a thick fog. "I don't really see either here," he admitted. He had trouble making out a clear distinction between the two.

"Neither is there," said Alfred. "And both are. When I try to paint the abbey, I keep seeing the Spiral in my mind, and the reverse is true when I try my hand at the Spiral. Each refuses to be portrayed without the other, and so all that I produce is confusion."

"How very curious. Do you have a solution?"

"Not yet. I will find it, my lord. You will have a worthy backdrop."

"I am confident you will, Alfred." Magnus placed a hand on his shoulder. "Have faith in your skill. I do."

He carried on, marching up the slope that led to the ruins.

Though the abbey had lost its roof and none of the walls were completely intact, its ruins were extensive, as if instead of being destroyed, it had transformed into a new kind of structure. It cut an imposing silhouette against the sky, its facade and shattered columns both massive and jagged. Magnus thought of it as the skeleton of a behemoth, the beast so huge it could not truly die, and instead slept, its new body as vital and even more imbued with meaning than its old one.

Magnus passed through the isolated entrance arch and into a space where stone, tumbled and standing, created the ghosts of chambers. The gaps in the walls formed junctions that had never been, and the concrete memory of the abbey's interior was a more complex web than it had been before the dissolution.

More arches stood on their own, inviting Magnus to go under them, though there was no need. It felt right to accept their invitation. Doing so made a ritual out of his path through the ruins, and the path felt like the true one, the only one he could trace despite the gaps and openings everywhere around him.

Magnus wended his way through the center of the ruins and to the biggest open area of the abbey, at the very edge of the cliffs. A jumble of fallen stonework took up the western end of the chapel's space. Magnus went up to the heap and examined it.

He found what Christina had seen almost immediately. Three large chunks of masonry leaned at angles against each other, leaving a dark gap between them, just large enough for Magnus to squeeze through, if he felt brave.

It had not been there before. He would have noticed. The abbey had been his special domain as a child. Every day of his stays on the estate, he had explored the fallen walls and archways. He had lived with every stone preserved in memory during the long years of his exile, and he had walked through and around it several times daily since his return. The abbey had always called to him. The ruins were a special kind of perfection, granting the site far more meaning than if the building had been intact. Destruction had profundity. In being broken, the abbey had changed character. For Magnus, it was no longer a site of something as mundane as Christian worship, but speaking somehow to mysteries more ancient.

More ancient than stone.

The mysteries were his to plumb, his to learn, *his*. He would have known if this secret had been visible before. It was for *him* to be the first to cross this new threshold.

The rubble must have shifted very recently, maybe even today. Christina was not the only artist to frequent the ruins. Someone else would have mentioned this before her, and maybe been foolish enough to venture down.

Which was it, brave or foolish?

What made the stones move, and why now?

What was he going to do?

Magnus supported himself against the stones and poked his head into the gap. Darkness breathed cold against his skin. It smelled of the sea.

He thought he heard something, the hint of a whisper, a trace of syllables.

He held his breath and strained to listen. Silence waited for him.

Magnus examined the stones. They seemed to be solid in their new configuration.

That meant nothing. The rubble had appeared unchanging all his life. And now it had moved.

But the darkness called.

He stepped away from the gap and looked around. The poets especially liked coming to the ruins at night for the atmosphere. He found some stubs of candles, and someone had left flint, steel, char cloth and some tapers in a bowl for the use of the night visitors. Magnus got a taper burning and lit three of the stubs. He crouched at the entrance and reached inside with a candle. The space beyond widened quickly, and there were worn steps just past the threshold.

He dropped the candle. It rolled down a few steps, gave him a hint of a long descent, and then the dark breeze snuffed it.

Magnus sucked in his breath. His heart beat fast with excitement. He would come back with a lantern. He had to go down.

He would go, and no one else.

This is mine.

He walked slowly from the chapel to the abbey's entrance. He looked down the slope toward the Stroud Spiral and, beyond it, the woods with their cottages. The bonfire had been lit, its orange glow growing brighter in the waning day.

This was his republic, spread out for his inspection. This was his dream made real. This was his destiny, he only now understood, coming into being. He was more than a patron for these poets and painters. The unheard whisper from beneath the abbey embraced him and showed him the truth. He was the conjurer of change. He had gathered the artists of true revolution. They would achieve, thanks to him, the promise that had been squandered in Europe.

The breath of the dark reached out from the crypt and touched his neck.

Look. See. You are the guide and the light.

You are inevitable.

But how? *How?* He didn't know what the revolution should look like.

The crypt called to him. His descent would reveal all.

Come and see.

Come and see.

Chapter Twelve

Another week passed, another week where the night terrors lurked as a potential, but did not strike.

Grudging as ever, Nurse Revere gave Miranda permission to extend the length of her walks. Miranda practiced for her exhibition by repeating her now-familiar stroll up and down the corridor outside her room. She knew this hall. In the day, it held no surprises. It was a straight line. It was not a labyrinth.

Was it part of one?

What if she ventured down other halls and couldn't find her way back? Miranda pictured herself without her chair, collapsing in an unknown region of the Institute, calling for help and water while staff ignored her because she was not one of their charges.

A silly image, one she should laugh at.

One more length of the hall, she decided. Do one more length of her hall before she ventured further.

She thought about the confusing layout of the Institute. Was it a maze or a labyrinth?

The question refused to be set aside. Miranda couldn't stop thinking about labyrinths and their natures. Whenever she gave free rein to her thoughts, they ran down the paths Daria Miracle had opened. She saw labyrinths everywhere, the metaphor multiplying like twists in the road.

And there, now she was using the labyrinth as a metaphor for the metaphors.

In another context, she would have been amused or annoyed. She had been amused after the first session. She hadn't thought Daria's lectures had any real significance for her. She was too skeptical to take them seriously. But then the ideas wouldn't leave her alone, and she saw them at work on her roommates. There was nothing she could find objectionable in what Daria said. But the way her words lingered in the mind began to feel like a symptom.

Miranda wished she could speak with Agatha.

She reached the far end of the corridor again, hesitated, then forced herself to go further. Hiding in her room until Agatha returned was not an option. She had the responsibility to search for answers herself.

What answers? Where? Search how?

She didn't know. But she did know that she would find nothing if she did not look.

An experiment occurred to her: find the library without reading any of the signs. She had gone there and back enough times in her wheelchair that, if this were any other building, she would know the way without thinking. But no matter how much she had tried, she still had no mental image of the floor's geography. Maybe, though, maybe she had a better instinctive sense of where to go than she thought.

She headed off, keeping her eyes on the floor, carefully avoiding sight of the signs. At the first intersection, she was already at sea. Left or right? She had no idea. She went left before she gave in to the temptation to look up.

She kept up her momentum after that, taking each turn at random. If she didn't know which choice was the right one, then it was pointless to debate. Every hall was both unfamiliar and identical to all the others. She had no idea where she was.

Irrational worry nagged. What if she couldn't find her way back? That was stupid. All she had to do was stop being stubborn and follow the signs. Nothing to it.

What if the signs were gone?

Ridiculous. That was a thought for three in the morning, not the hour before lunch. But the fear that all the signs would have vanished when she looked for them kept growing.

That was the irrational trying to break her resolution. She refused to give in.

But she really did not know where she was.

And then she was standing in front of the library door.

Miranda felt no sense of victory. She couldn't pretend that instinct had brought her here, not when she had felt so completely disoriented.

She had set out for the library, and the halls had brought her here. As if all her choices were an illusion, and there was only one path.

It is a labyrinth.

One path. Leading where? To being well, Daria would offer. But that wasn't true for everyone.

Too many questions, and no answers. Not yet. Miranda promised herself she would find them. And she promised herself that she would not submit to the mercy of the halls. She would find her own way. She would learn to navigate the Institute. She would defy its will.

Determination renewed, she opened the doors and entered the library. In one of the chairs by the window, Lupita huddled miserably, her hands clutched in fists before her lips.

Miranda sat in the other chair. She leaned forward, offering comfort but not touching Lupita unless invited. "Are you all right?" she asked.

Lupita turned a tear-streaked face to her. "There's no chapel here," she said.

Miranda had never thought about looking for one. "You've asked, I gather," she said.

Lupita nodded. "I did. Why isn't there one? What kind of place is this?" She spoke as if she had woken to find herself in a burning speakeasy. "The hospital has one."

"It does," Miranda agreed. "But this is a private institution. It is not under any obligation to provide a chapel." Though that was true, she didn't want to push too hard to be convincing. She heard Agatha's voice at her shoulder, warning her not to leap to conclusions. Of either kind, she thought. She mustn't read malice into the banal. She also mustn't dismiss the threatening as banal.

"Private or not, shouldn't they be doing everything possible to help their patients? Don't they understand how not having a place of worship makes things for some of us?"

"I guess they don't," Miranda said.

Lupita wiped the tears from her cheeks. "I thought, if I came here to pray, I might feel better. I thought, this is a quiet place. I thought it would be better than nothing."

"Did it help?" Miranda asked.

"No!" Lupita choked back a sob. "It's been getting harder for me to pray in the room. But it's worse here."

"Do you know why?"

"The thoughts here are too loud."

Miranda's breath caught. Her skin began to crawl. "What do you mean?" she asked. She realized she was whispering, as if the walls might overhear.

Lupita looked stricken. She squirmed in her seat, trying to get away from her own words. "I don't know." She shuddered. "That didn't make any sense, did it?" She squeezed her hands together. "You shouldn't pay attention to what's coming out of my mouth. I'm babbling."

"I don't think you are," said Miranda. She held out a hand, and Lupita clutched it gratefully.

"I'm so upset with myself," Lupita said. "I keep trying to find things to blame. Why can't I pray the way I used to? Why is it so hard? Is it my fault?"

"I'm sure it isn't." Miranda found it hard to look at the pain in those eyes. "You should try to be kinder to yourself. Maybe you should stop attending the counseling sessions." Miranda had always doubted. She treated all orthodoxies with suspicion. Yet she was finding the sessions sinking hooks into her mind. For people who did not like doubt, the hooks had to be more painful, and sinking in more deeply. All her roommates had been looking more and more thoughtful, and, it seemed to her, more worried.

"I have to go," said Lupita.

"Why? They aren't compulsory."

"What if what Daria says is true?"

"What if it is?" said Miranda. "Why should that affect your faith?"

"I don't know!" Lupita wailed, her voice high and thin. She held Miranda's hand harder, then let go, embarrassed. "I'm sorry."

"Don't be."

"I have to go," Lupita insisted. "I have to follow her thread."

They were both quiet for a moment, conscious of the labyrinth that had crept into Lupita's words.

Miranda almost asked if Lupita was afraid of where the thread might lead. But she didn't, because Lupita's face made the answer clear.

Durstal's small cluster of houses huddled in the shadow of the slope that led up to the Stroud Estate. The nearest railway station was two miles away. A narrow road, badly in need of repair, twisted through until it reached Durstal's hollow and came to an end in the village.

"We should have waited for a cab," Wilbur said again.

"I didn't see any at the station, did you? If we had waited, we'd still be waiting. Spending the night on a railway platform wouldn't be comfortable." Agatha spoke gently. Wilbur was exhausted after the trek. He was entitled to a few grumbles. They were the first he'd made since leaving Arkham, and the trip had been a long one.

The ocean crossing had been pleasant, with no storms to trouble Wilbur's stomach. Once they had arrived in England, though, Agatha had pushed them hard. She didn't want to be away longer than she had to. Once she learned how awkward a route the journey to Durstal would be, she had realized that it would make more sense to stop at Glasgow and Edinburgh first. Wilbur only had a couple of days in each city to recover before Agatha bundled them on to another train.

She was tired too, but the call of the hunt kept her energized.

Agatha had hit dead ends in the cities. She found almost nothing about Magnus Stroud. The university holdings there had even less by or about him than Miskatonic. Frustrated, she wondered if the absence was significant, history erasing Magnus' presence, or Magnus erasing his tracks.

But absence was not evidence. And so she and Wilbur had come, at last, to Durstal.

Night was falling when the road took them out from the trees and down toward the village. They had been using flashlights to see their way for the last few minutes. Wilbur heaved a sigh of relief at the sight of lights glimmering in windows.

"It's very small, isn't it?" he said, clearly hoping for reassurance that it wasn't *too* small.

"There will be an inn," Agatha said. *There had better be.* "Come on." She gave her suitcase a bit of a heave. "Almost there!"

To her relief, there was a *there* at which to arrive. They found the Ash Inn at the edge of the village. The tree that gave the inn its name towered over the small buildings, its limbs thick and twisted with age. It stood out in the village, a moody sentinel waiting for the ephemeral humans to pass away and leave it in peace.

Inside, they found a pub on the ground floor. All but two of the tables were occupied. The volume of the conversation had not been loud, and it dropped further as they walked inside, but did not cease. The locals eyed them curiously, and with something that surprised Agatha. She had been prepared for hostility; she had not expected hope.

Agatha strode over to the bar, Wilbur shuffling behind her. The landlord, a small man with bulging, perpetually surprised eyes, regarded her with a wary, but not unfriendly, expression.

"We're hoping you have a room available," she said.

The landlord laughed. "Oh," he said. "I was worried you were going to tell me you were lost!" He reached over the bar to shake hands with them. "Tom Spalding," he said. "Let me get you your room."

A quarter of an hour later, Agatha left Wilbur gratefully collapsed on the bed. It was late for what she had in mind, and dark, but she was too restless to wait until the morning. She needed her first glimpse of her goal.

Tom had given her directions to the Stroud Estate readily enough when she asked, though he had not hidden his concern. "You'll hardly be able to see to find your way," he said. "You wouldn't prefer a seat by the fire and a brandy instead?"

"I would prefer such things," Agatha agreed, "and I'll look forward to them when I get back."

The landlord nodded solemnly. "Don't be long, then." He had to be fifteen years her junior. His worry made him sound like her father.

The bar's patrons watched her with open curiosity. When she had asked Tom how to get to the estate, this time the conversations *had* stopped. She smiled on her way out, and a few people shifted, as if about to say something to her. One old man gripped his pint with both hands. He looked at Agatha with pleading eyes.

What do they want?

Tomorrow. Find out tomorrow.

With her flashlight, she had no difficulty following the landlord's directions. There weren't many ways to choose from. Agatha felt a sick, vertiginous inevitability about the way her steps had brought her to the threshold of the Stroud Estate.

A dirt road wound from the center of Durstal and up the slope. With no trees to flank the road, Agatha had to walk slowly, careful not to step off the track and into the thick gorse on the hillside. Partway up, the moon came out from behind clouds, and the cold, bleaching wash of its light showed her the path ahead.

At the gates, she moved her flashlight beam back and forth, examining the obstacle. A chain and padlock held the gates shut. It would take heavy bolt cutters to break the lock, and she had no intention of leaving signs of her passage, if she could avoid it. The dry-stone wall, though, was not much more than six feet high. If she could borrow a ladder…

Easier said than done. How did she plan on acquiring one? Walking up to a random villager and explaining that she needed to break into the Stroud's property?

The villagers' desperate looks came back to her. The old man clutching his beer, on the verge of calling out to her. Maybe just asking would be the right approach after all.

Worry about that in the morning. Get some sleep, be less tired, and think more clearly. She had made it this far. She'd find a way in.

And then what? What did she hope to find?

She had no specific hopes. She had run out of leads, except the goal to stand on the ground depicted in the portrait of Magnus, and see what there was to see. Miranda's vision had meaning. Agatha had to find why it linked Galloway to Arkham, and the abbey to the Institute.

She went right up the gates and aimed her flashlight through them. The trees on the other side of the wall held on to the darkness, nurtured it, and thickened it. Silence coiled with the night.

Agatha took her compass from her jacket pocket. The needle pointed quite a bit west of north. It held steady, just as it did outside the walls of the Stroud Institute.

The air, still as a held breath, chilled her. The space beyond the gates felt hollow, abandoned.

It also waited, anticipating her arrival. If the chain slipped open and fell from the gates, she would not be surprised.

She turned back and hurried away before that could happen.

The moon painted swirls of shadow on the gorse. The secret paths grinned at her as she hurried down the hill.

Chapter Thirteen

Lupita calmed down, and, after a little while, she left the library, declaring she needed to lie down. Miranda believed her. She had the face-sagging look of someone feeling the numb exhaustion that comes after grief. Lupita paused at the exit, as uncertain of direction as Miranda. She looked up for the signs, then headed right, walking slowly. The door swung closed behind her with a soft sigh.

The walk here had tired Miranda, but not overly so. She didn't feel the need to head back just yet. She sat and listened to her breathing. It strained and rattled. The iron band around her chest seemed looser than it had been. Any better than yesterday? Hard to tell. Better than before coming to the Stroud Institute? Definitely. Again, a fact to remember. She was being well cared for, and she wasn't a prisoner.

Really? What if she tried to leave?

She hadn't reached that point. Especially not with her health improving.

And what if the night visions followed her home? What if they had no connection to the Institute?

The vision of the painting said otherwise.

When she became too conscious of her breathing, Miranda pushed herself up from the chair. Enough of chasing her own tail. Time to be useful. Don't leave all the research to Agatha. She moved slowly around the room, scanning the titles on the shelves, looking for the name that stood out, or the pattern that was less innocuous than a first look had suggested.

She found nothing.

Miranda started pulling books off the shelves at random, flipping them open to see if they were, in fact, what their spines purported. She found none in disguise. Someone had left a bookmark in a copy of *The Magic Mountain*, and it fell when Miranda riffled the pages. She knelt to pick it up, and noticed the carpet for the first time. It had barely registered on her awareness before, a deep burgundy with a pattern of black stripes. Up close, she saw that though the stripes gave the impression of being arranged in tight, angular, parallel formations, they actually connected. The positions of the links varied, never too close to each other, so they were easy to miss.

Miranda put the book back and focused her attention on the carpet. She picked the nearest connection and followed the stripes on the right to the next link. She frowned, crouching down to look more closely.

She'd been wrong again. What she had thought were links were a line making two ninety degree turns. The gap between the stripe that turned and the one above was so thin, so close to being indiscernible, that it looked as if two stripes were one longer one.

Miranda straightened. She swayed, fighting vertigo as her understanding of the rug's pattern shifted, tilting reality. There were no links. A single stripe covered the entire carpet.

A labyrinth.

Now that she saw it, she had to work to pull her eyes away. The labyrinth called her gaze, inviting her to lose herself in its contemplation. She walked to the door on unsteady legs. The zig-zag path tried to capture her steps. She swayed, off-balance as if on a ship in a storm. The distance to the door stretched, endless, across a carpet as wide and treacherous as the sea.

Miranda closed her eyes to escape the labyrinth's grip. It held on. She felt the stripes beneath her feet. The soles of her slippers squirmed, trying to shift so they faced in the direction of the stripes. They wanted her to walk the labyrinth.

She dragged herself forward, pulling against glue. She opened her eyes and kept them focused on the door. She stared at it fiercely, making it her beacon, her lighthouse that would save her from the undertow of the pattern. It taunted her, unreachable, miles and miles away. She would never get there.

She put one dragging foot in front of the other, to no point, to no end. The labyrinth would take her. It would not let her escape.

One step, one step, one step, her breath scraping, exhaustion hauling at her. She would fall. She would sink through the carpet into the true labyrinth beyond its simulacrum.

One step, one step, one step. She couldn't go on.

She touched the door. The pull of the labyrinth ceased so suddenly that she stumbled. She breathed in, out, steadying herself. She risked a look at the carpet. The pattern was there, and that was all it was. No danger to her. Just a carpet.

"Nice try," she whispered.

She stepped into the hall and closed the door behind her. She would not be returning to the library.

She was more than ready to be in her bed now. And she would follow the signs. She wanted only a clear, rational reason for getting back.

First, though, she looked closely at the wall. She didn't believe the labyrinth only existed in the library.

There were no patterns in the paint. No stripes, no shifts in tone of the greenish white.

Miranda ran her palm along the wall. She felt a slight unevenness. She traced it with her fingertips. It was so slight, she almost lost it. It took her three tries to follow the bump, and learn that it became a ridge.

She pressed the side of her face on the wall. Deep age reached through institutional paint to chill her cheek. She looked down its length, focused on the line she had under her fingers, and there…

There. The ridge extending, then turning back, and turning again, and again. The endless switchback and relentless, single-minded advance of the labyrinth.

In the morning, Agatha left Wilbur to linger over his coffee at the inn and strolled through the streets of Durstal. Under the brittle sunlight of spring, she smiled at the people she passed, said hello when someone smiled back, and started conversations wherever she sensed an opening. She kept her initial comments banal while giving the villagers the chance to take things further.

"Durstal is very pretty," she said to an older, broad-faced woman who smiled at her as she came out of a newsagent's.

The woman's smile became strained. "You'd think so." She seemed to be looking at something a long way off, an unpleasant memory ducking behind the mountains.

"You don't?" Agatha asked.

"Pretty to see and pretty to live in are two different things. You stay here for any length of time, and you'll see what I mean."

"Have you lived here long?"

"We all have. Our whole lives."

"I can't help but notice there aren't a lot of young people about."

"If they have the chance, they leave. More power to them. Best they're gone."

When she returned to the inn late in the afternoon, Agatha had put together a mental mosaic of Durstal. A cloud hung over the spirits of its people. She couldn't make out what lurked in the cloud and gave it shape and power. She didn't think any of the villagers could either. Again and again, they surprised her with the way they opened up to her, as if by being an outsider, by being someone who came from a place without a cloud, she had the means of lifting its oppression.

They had clearly never been to Arkham.

By four, the ground floor of the inn had filled again. Agatha ordered a round for everyone and did so again a couple of hours later, when she and Wilbur sat down to their dinner. The locals greeted her as one of their own.

"Are you planning something for tonight?" Wilbur asked, digging in to his fish and chips.

"Nothing frightening," Agatha told him. "I won't be heading out."

"Good."

"I'm going to spend some time here, talk to people."

"You've been doing that all day."

"Yes, I have. I've been making myself known. And now that the beer has been flowing, I hope I'll hear more. I think these people are frightened. I'd like to know why."

"That's very reassuring." Wilbur contemplated his fish as if it had suddenly spoken. "If you find out, does that mean we head home tomorrow?"

"No. I still have to get into the Stroud Estate."

Wilbur grimaced. "I keep hoping you'll change your mind about that. What if you get caught?"

"Then that will be a problem."

"What's the charge for trespassing here?" Wilbur asked. "Does bail work like it does back home?"

"I don't know," said Agatha. "With a bit of luck, you won't have to find out." She didn't say that being caught by the police was the least of her worries. "I'll be careful," she promised.

Wilbur didn't try to argue. He went back up to the room when he'd finished eating, and Agatha sent still another round for the company. She looked around the room, and met the gaze of an old man sitting in the far corner. She took her own beer over and sat down at his table. "Agatha Crane," she said, and held out her hand.

"Ben Laurie," he said, shaking her hand. "So, what brings you to these parts?"

"Events at home."

"Oh?" he looked surprised.

"I think there might be a connection between home and Durstal."

"Oh." He sounded guarded.

"I'm here to find out what that might be, if I can."

Ben took a thoughtful sip of his ale. He kept his eyes on the table. "You want to be careful, doing things like that," he said.

"I always am," said Agatha. "And I get the feeling that you would like to tell me more."

"Mmm," said Ben, very neutral.

"I'm curious as to why that is."

Another sip, another pause. Then Ben looked at her. "An outsider is a rare thing in these parts. When we see one, we like to hope they've come to help."

"Help with what?" Agatha asked.

Ben shrugged. "Not sure that we know."

"Then I'll tell you what I'd like to know. I'm curious about the Strouds."

"Ah." Ben made a sour face, his weathered skin wrinkling like a walnut.

"Do you like them?"

"We should." He looked ready to spit.

"But you don't."

"Well, they've spent enough money in Durstal over the years. Enough to make most kinds popular."

"But…?" Agatha prompted.

Ben lowered his voice. "They're a wrong bunch. Have been for a long time. You know how some folk'll give you money but are laughing at you?"

"The Strouds are like that?"

"No, they're worse." He paused, then corrected himself. "*He's* worse, I should say. Only ever one Stroud at a time up at the Hall. Just the master. Don't quite know how they manage it. Must be wives and children, but all we ever see is the master and the servants. I've seen three different ones in my years, one at a time. Always one at a time."

"You said he was worse," Agatha said, bringing Ben back to his point when he looked like he was going to nod to himself and consider his piece spoken.

"Worse, aye," said Ben. "He's not laughing at you. But it doesn't half feel like he's bought something from you that you shouldn't have sold. D'you see?"

"I think I do."

Ben opened his mouth, then shut it again as Tom Spalding walked by. His attention shifted again to his ale. Agatha felt dismissed. Ben had said all he would.

She got up and went to the bar. Tom, cleaning some glasses, smiled apologetically. "Sorry if I made old Ben shut up," he said. "Didn't mean to."

"Why would he feel comfortable talking to me, but not to be overheard by you?"

"Not me specifically," Tom said. "Anybody but you."

"I don't understand."

"You're not from here. By your accent, you're *really* not from here. That makes people feel safe. They want to talk, and they can talk to you."

"But not to each other," said Agatha.

"Now you're grasping it. Any of us might be getting Stroud money to keep an ear and an eye open. No way of telling."

"I might be too."

"Maybe. Seems unlikely. And if you need to let something out, you're a safer bet than our neighbors."

Lucky for me. "So if I'm a safer bet, can I ask if you see Donovan Stroud much?"

"Hardly ever," said Tom. "And not at all for some months now. Not since all those lorries."

"Oh? What were they up to?"

"Who knows? I couldn't tell you if they were bringing things in or taking them or both, but there were a lot of them."

"That sounds like something was done on the grounds," said Agatha.

Tom wrapped his dish towel around a hand absently. "We've all been too scared to try to have a look," he admitted. After a pause, he added quietly, "All but one of us."

"Oh?"

"Our vicar, Peter Wilson."

"I'd like to speak to him."

Tom looked grave. "You can't. He went up to the estate, and then he went over the cliffs. I was with him at the end."

"I'm sorry."

"We've all been careful not to go near the grounds since."

"I don't blame you," said Agatha. "And I appreciate the warning. It does, however, make it even more important that I get over that wall."

Tom nodded. He gave the towel a nervous tug, then nodded again, this time to himself. "I'll help," he said.

"Thank you."

Tom held up a hand. "Don't thank me. I owe the vicar that much. And if you can do anything to help us, it'll be me thanking you."

"I won't make promises I don't know that I can keep, but I'll do what I can."

"Can't ask fairer than that."

"I don't suppose," said Agatha, "that you have a battery radio? It would be useful to bring along."

Tom blinked in surprise. "I do, at that. We don't like to use it much." He sounded uneasy again.

"Why is that?"

"Hard to get anything at all in these parts, and…" He hesitated. "To tell you the truth, the static gives us the shudders."

"Because you hear things in it."

Tom twisted the dish towel and said nothing.

CHAPTER FOURTEEN

The days passed, and the night visions still held off. Their absence ceased being a relief. It became a false recovery. Miranda felt her tension growing worse every day. She wasn't sleeping well again, lying awake waiting for the blow that threatened but never fell.

The arc of its path must be huge, she thought. Its momentum ferocious. The impact, when it comes, will be awful.

The Thursday after her encounter with Lupita in the library, Miranda revised her understanding of her vision of the abbey and the river of stone. The connection between the Institute and the Stroud Estate was profound. Somehow, she thought, the Institute and the abbey and the stones were one and the same.

She wished she could speak to Agatha.

She wished she could warn her.

This is much worse than we thought. Age and the labyrinth defined the halls of the clinic.

In the days before Thursday, she became more and more aware of the malaise running through the Institute like a new infection. As she walked the halls, she would sometimes poke her head in another room and get to know other patients. Two more deaths occurred during this period, two more faces disappeared just as she was getting to know them. The change in the mood of her roommates, though, seemed independent of the bad news. It began before they heard about Ingrid Shelley and then Angel Hayden. Lupita's crisis of faith continued. Cleo was subdued, the closest to withdrawn Miranda had ever seen her. And Frieda had started crying too during the night. The sainted Reginald came to visit her, and she barely spoke to him.

Miranda took comfort in one thing: Cleo's health was improving, and quickly. She had already reached the stage where she would normally have been moved to another ward. No beds were ready for her yet, so she stayed in the room and spent most of her days taking part in the volunteer work, delivering food trays, collecting puzzle sheets, arranging ornaments on bedside tables. They all expected her to be going home soon. An iron determination to make that expectation a reality seemed to animate her. When Miranda looked at her, she saw a woman willing herself well.

Then Thursday came, and with it another of Daria Miracle's sessions, as hopeful and as metaphysically troubling as ever. Miranda now thought of herself as an enemy agent when she attended the lectures. She held herself as far as she could from the sweep of Daria's oratory and the hypnotic dance of her body. She had to know what Daria said. She told herself she rejected everything the woman said.

Daria's words flowed like her gestures, comforting and seductive, and there was nothing wrong in what she said, nothing to take exception to. Her labyrinth of hope beckoned, and Miranda fought its pull as she had the pattern in the library.

If only she could identify the foe hiding in the loving platitudes. She couldn't fight what she couldn't see.

And on Thursday, after the session, she walked the halls at random, walking for exercise and the chance to think without interruption. She turned into a long corridor and saw, at the far end, Nurse Holden silhouetted by a window.

Holden stood perfectly still. She could have been a mannequin. Unnerved, Miranda slowed down as she approached. Holden did not move. Her arms hung down at her sides. She faced the window. Miranda had the sudden conviction that she did not want to see Holden's eyes.

She stopped half a step from Holden. She looked around. Some orderlies crossed from one room to another at the other end of the hall. Coughs and the occasional moan rasped out of the doorways. Signs of life and signs of illness, and Miranda felt profoundly alone.

"Excuse me," she said.

Holden did not react.

Miranda reached out. She didn't want to touch Holden. The nurse would feel like stone, like death. She made herself tap Holden's shoulder.

Holden jumped with shock and gasped. She spun around, her eyes wide and stricken, and for a moment they didn't see Miranda. The inward vista held them fast. Then they focused and Holden tried to recover herself. "I'm sorry," she said. "I was miles away. You startled me."

"I didn't mean to," said Miranda. "I apologize."

"No, no, I'm the one woolgathering on the job." Her lips stretched into a sick imitation of a self-deprecating smile. "Can I help you?"

"Can *I* help *you*?" Miranda asked.

Holden's professional mask fractured, then reassembled itself.

She wanted to say yes, Miranda thought. She wanted someone to help. She wanted to lean on a shoulder.

She could not.

"That's very kind of you, Professor Ventham. I'm quite all right. A long day. You know what those are like, I'm sure."

"I do." *And I know the difference between being tired and something worse.* She listened to a hunch and asked, "Does the staff have sessions with Daria Miracle too?"

"Are you enjoying them?" Holden deflected. She didn't wait for an answer but instead made a show of looking at her watch. "Is that the time? Duty calls, and I'm remiss!" She laughed with forced humor. "Must run!"

Miranda watched her go.

Later, after supper, when Nurse Revere came to take their temperatures, Miranda studied her. Revere's stony face gave little away. Her eyes, though, barely took in the patients and the thermometers.

"You're looking lovely today," Miranda said, probing for a reaction.

"Hm," said Revere.

"I saw fairies dancing in the grounds today."

Revere grunted, and moved on to Frieda.

Cleo stared at Miranda. "What are you doing?" she mouthed.

Miranda shrugged and grinned, hoping she looked more impish than she felt.

A preoccupied Revere disturbed her almost as much as a motionless Holden.

That night, in the dark, the thought came that she had been wrong about her vision. She had feared it was a prophecy. What would be worse was if it were history. An event that could not be prevented, because it had already occurred.

She thought of the river of stone flowing from the abbey to the Institute.

What if that was what really happened? What if, in some way, the abbey and stones had come here?

Miranda turned her head to face the doorway. Gazing at the wall outside the room, and the paint above the wainscoting, she could not see the labyrinth of barely raised texture. She knew it was there, though. She could feel it.

Feel it snaking across the entire Institute, capturing them all.

Daria's voice came to her, inviting them to walk its path.

Why resist? You're already here.

Tom carried the ladder to the wall of the estate. Agatha and Wilbur shared the awkward load of the radio. It was a rectangular console, not unlike her Atwater-Kent, and weighted a good thirty pounds. The men seemed eager to carry as much weight as possible, as if to compensate for a different weight, the weight of shame for staying on the other side of the wall. The burden was unnecessary, but she knew it would be pointless to tell them.

They reached the wall and Tom placed the ladder against it, about twenty feet down from the gate.

"Should we come with you?" Wilbur asked.

"No," she said, and they both looked guiltily relieved. "I need to do this alone."

She had no idea what she might find on the other side of the wall. She had her medallion, as did Wilbur. Unlike Wilbur, she had some ideas of how she might use it, if she had to. Tom had no protection at all. "What you can do for me is monitor the radio." She turned it on.

"That's odd," said Tom.

The radio had been full of static when Agatha had tried it at the inn. Now it was silent.

"This isn't entirely surprising," Agatha said. She spoke as if studying a lab report, but her mouth had gone dry. "Let's leave it on. If you hear anything, anything at all, please make a note of it."

"We can do that," said Tom.

"I wish you wouldn't do this," said Wilbur.

"I wish I didn't have to," she said. "But it's why we're here." To Tom she said, "Thank you for lending us a hand. Again, I can't promise I'm going to find anything that will help you."

Tom shrugged. "I don't expect you to. We don't even know what it is we need help with."

Agatha gave Wilbur a hug, then climbed the ladder. Perched on the top of the wall, she pulled the ladder up with Tom's help, lowered to the other side, and descended into the estate.

The weather favored her again. With the full moon out, she didn't need her flashlight, except to check her compass, once she worked her way through the brush and onto the drive leading from the gate. She turned it off, hoping she could manage without it at least until she was well past the Hall.

Her sense of the estate's geography was two centuries old. She expected changes, and she crossed her fingers that they wouldn't be so extensive that she would get lost.

In fact, there were no changes at all until she reached the Hall. Moonlight reflected like cataracts on the windows. The house was dark, silent, and the east side looked as if a bomb had hit it. Only bits of walls still stood, broken and unwanted. The interior was gone. Agatha wondered if the entire house had become a shell.

No one would be living there. She relaxed and used her flashlight again.

She looked at the compass, wondering if the needle would indicate the Hall. It did not. It pointed in the direction she planned to go, as steady as it had been at the gate.

Beyond the Hall, a new gravel road cut through the woods in the direction of the Spiral and the abbey. If this was his doing, Donovan Stroud had made life easier for her. She would have to thank him.

What were you doing with all those trucks?

She found the answer a few minutes later. The road brought her to a quarry where the Stroud Spiral had been. The boulders had vanished, the ground excavated to the point where all trace of the stones had been erased. They had been extracted like teeth.

Based on the descriptions in the *Miscellany of Merrick*, the stones would have been much too huge to load onto trucks. Donovan would have had them broken down; he had done so cleanly. Agatha swept the beam across the shallow crater next to the road. She didn't see a single stray fragment.

The road carried on up the slope to the abbey. The ruins were gone too, the top of the cliff unbroken by the silhouette of fragmented stonework. Agatha followed the road to its end, urged on by the compass whose north, she now realized, was the site of the abbey. She had to see everything, even if all she saw was absence.

Not every trace of the abbey had disappeared. The last remains of its corpse lay before Agatha, broken stones strewn like barren seeds. The abbey had become a carcass picked over by scavengers.

What did Donovan want with the Spiral and the abbey?

She knew, of course. She should have guessed sooner. She should have pieced it together when Miranda had told her about the vision of the abbey flowing through the Spiral and into the Institute. She should have realized because she had wondered about the sense of age the new building radiated.

The abbey and the Spiral had become the Stroud Institute.

A deep, circular shadow swallowed the moonlight. Agatha walked over to it, and shone her flashlight beam into a shaft. It looked like the mouth of a wide well, with a rough staircase carved into its sides, circling down and down into the night of the earth. Agatha peered into the depths. They kept their secrets, inviting her down.

She picked up a fragment of masonry and put it in her jacket pocket. Something to test back in Arkham.

She looked at the compass again. The tip of the needle was stuck flat against the housing, pointing down. It vibrated hard, as if trying to escape.

Agatha took a breath, then started down the stairs.

She walked carefully, one hand on the wall to keep her balance on the narrow, uneven, treacherously smooth steps. She paused after a minute and looked up. The pale, moonlit circle above her had shrunk, as if her way back to the surface would close behind her.

"Don't be stupid," she whispered. Echoes slithered down the shaft ahead of her.

Which was stupid? To be afraid or to keep going?

She started forward again, more slowly now, making sure of her footing before each step. She could smell the sea. The salty tang grew stronger as she went down, and soon she thought she could hear the surf too, the rough, grating rhythm crawling up the stairs toward her, as if in answer to her whisper.

Instinct made her stop again. She listened carefully, eyes starting to water from the smell.

That was not the surf. The sound scraped too hard, too heavily, scales against stone. The indrawn rasp of the surf became a breath, a murmur, the expectation of words.

Agatha turned around. She headed back up, forced herself not to run. If she did, she would slip. She climbed, steadily, her movements calm but her heart pounding, the blood in her ears roaring as it tried to drown out the rhythmic scrape and hiss below.

The circle above expanded grudgingly. It taunted with the hope of light and air, so far out of reach as the sounds below grew louder, and Agatha did not look back. She must not see what might be closer.

She climbed, and the wall turned slick and clammy under her palm.

Below, the presence shifted. The hiss, the hiss that sounded like wave on rock but was infinitely older, began to shape itself.

Hurry, Agatha's panic urged. Hurry, or you'll hear your name.

If she hurried, she'd fall.

Maybe if she screamed, she would not hear the call.

No. She would not scream. She would not betray who she was, even now, even now with the hiss ready to form a first syllable.

The circle widened at last. She breathed clean air. She gave in to the panic and ran up the last few steps. She burst out of the shaft and now she really ran, leaping over the broken stones, rushing headlong for the road that would take her back through the grounds, back to the wall.

The road was true and straight. But when, behind her, the hiss became a snarl, and the snarl uncoiled into the laughter that lingers over dying stars, the road groaned. The gravel vibrated. The road strained against its path, trying to wrench itself into sharp angles and turns, trying to become a new journey that would spiral down into the depths and bring her back to the danger she had fled.

The flashlight beam bounced over the quivering road. Agatha clutched the silver medallion that hung around her neck. She felt squeezed, as if she would imprint its configuration of lines into her flesh. She used precious breath to chant a few words. They came from the Last Prayer of Evashallon, preserved on a few tatters of parchment, a fragment of a much longer work, as lost now as the language in which they were written. She did not know the meaning of the words, only their effect. They anchored reality, and they fought with the road, holding it back from the thing it wished to become.

Cracks opened in the surface, racing along the track, chasing after Agatha. The gravel rolled and squalled like an infant.

Agatha's shoulders tensed. The hair on the back of her neck bristled. The false sound of the surf thundered, close, so close, the entire sea rising above the cliff and waiting for her to look back, look back, and see the wave gazing down at her.

Don't look, don't look, don't look, don't look.

She ran past the gaping wound where the Stroud Spiral had been, and things slithered in the crater. She ran past the broken Hall, and though the moon still shone, the windows reflected nothing, darkness pressing close against them to witness her flight. As she left the Hall behind, the dark shrieked, harsh and high, like a fox, like hunger, like rage.

Then she had the ladder in her hands, and she went up and over the wall in a single breath.

"Did you hear it?" she asked the two men, shoving the ladder at Tom and hurrying down the road.

"Hear what?" Wilbur asked, jogging beside her. "The storm coming?"

"Storm," Agatha repeated, and held back a frightened moan.

"That wasn't wind?" Tom asked.

And then a snarl broke the silence of the radio, deep and long, grating low in a thing of many throats. Tom recoiled, then smashed the radio with the ladder.

Agatha grabbed him and Wilbur and pulled them after her down the slope. The sound behind the wall grew louder, a precursor to a more terrible snarl. Tom began to turn his head.

"Don't look back," Agatha said, and he snapped his head forward. "Don't ever go into the estate. Leave Durstal, so you will never be tempted. All of you, leave Durstal behind. The land here is blighted." She had none of her precious physical evidence. Only a stone to investigate later. And she had never been more sure of anything. "Run, Tom. Run."

Chapter Fifteen

Scotland, 1806

Partway down the shaft beneath the altar, terror almost sent Magnus rushing back up. He fought the urge. He leaned against the wall, the lantern swinging softly in his grip as he breathed in and out. He sought the excitement that had accompanied him on the first part of his journey. Why did the exhilaration abandon him? Every step of his descent made the discovery even more wondrous.

His discovery. It didn't matter that Christina had told him about it. No one else had gone in before him. His were the first feet to walk these stairs.

First for more centuries than he could guess. There was no record of what lay beneath the abbey in any chronicle he knew of, and he had read them all, many as a youth when he visited the estate, and many more in the years afterward, when they gave him leave to dream of the land that would one day return to him.

His land. His abbey. His discovery.

The fear receded enough to let him resume his way down. New waves of it washed over him with every crash of the surf below.

"You behold the sublime," he said to himself, speaking aloud. "Terror is meet and right."

Sublime, said the echoes. *Sublime, sublime, sssssssublime.* The word spun down ahead of him into the shaft, distorting, becoming one with the next crash of the surf.

The stairs carried on before him into the dark, and into the endless turns.

Magnus examined the wall as he walked. It changed as he dropped down, becoming a greater source of wonder in its own right. At the top of the shaft, the walls had been stonework, in the same style as the abbey, and for the first twists of the staircase, Magnus had thought Christina right to think this was the crypt. Now, though, carved stones became rare objects, fading into the naked stone of the mountain. The shaft seemed neither artificial nor natural. It blended both states, an impossible construct. Magnus no longer believed it had been built with the abbey.

This is older.

Who created it? He asked himself the question with growing urgency and wonder. The Romans? The answer seemed absurd as soon as he thought it. He looked at the play of the lantern's light over the wall, at the way it was a cavern one moment, a well shaft the next.

"Human hands did not build this," he announced.

This, this, this, thisssssssss, said the echoes, merging with the hiss-roar of the surf.

No, not the surf. He admitted that to himself. It was that knowledge, instinctive at first, that had frightened him. That knowledge now kept him going, dropping down and down to greater revelation.

He began to breathe in time with the hiss and crash. Then he imagined the sound changed, became precise, became a voice directed at him.

Mag… nusssssssssss

Withdraw and crash, withdraw and crash.

Mag… nusssssssssss

Destiny and revelation were one, and the one called him by name.

"I hear you," he said. "I am coming."

No echoes of his own words now, just the call.

Mag… nusssssssssss

Around and down, darkness above and darkness below. Soon the sound surrounded him, and he lost all sense of progress. The stairs could go on forever. He had been here always, answering a call that would never cease. He became frightened again, but the wonder kept him going. How far had he descended? Hundreds of feet, miles and miles, a drop beyond measure without beginning or end.

He took the stairs faster. He knew he would not fall. He didn't have to look. His vision blurred. The walls rotated around him, their glistening black shadows at play in the lantern's light. Nothing changed and everything was change. He no longer had a body. He had become his soul, plunging through the forever toward the summons.

The voice in the depths roared his name once more, and then, louder and more demanding and more sinuous than before, it spoke new syllables, a new name.

Crothoaka

The name uttered, the light went out. Magnus stepped onto level ground. The jolt returned his body to him. He staggered in a half circle, then stopped, breathing hard. He could see nothing. Fully terrified again, conscious of the mass of earth above him, he tried to find the stairs. The roaring, hissing voice had fallen silent.

Alone, abandoned in the dark, he fell to his knees. He curled up and closed his eyes.

He tried to pray. He had admired the courage of the atheists of the French Revolution, and he had voiced that admiration sometimes, much to the consternation of William Wordsworth. He hadn't really believed in his ostentatious radicalisms, though. Not those ones.

But now…

The prayers fell into emptiness. No one heard. No one answered. The darkness took apart his certainties and left him with nothing but doubt.

No one heard his prayer. Some*thing* did, though, and when the dark had done its work, the voice returned, the voice of a god that *would* answer.

Mag… nusssssssssss

Crothoaka

Magnus opened his eyes. Light, green and slithering, leaked over the floor to him. He stood and followed the trail.

The light bloomed. Magnus saw walls now, rising up to the hint of a vault. He could not say that the walls were stone, or that they ran straight or curved. They had been carved from doubt itself.

The floor sloped and then dropped steeply. The light intensified, and Magnus looked down into vastness and a serpentine nightmare. Below him waited the architecture that was the truth of the abbey. The ruins he had loved since childhood were, he now saw, the extrusion of the immensity below. Perhaps there had never been a true abbey. Perhaps there had only ever been the ruins, the pretense of ruins, waiting for the chosen Stroud to see more deeply, and to take the lure.

The twists of the structure below reflected the shape of the ruins on a grand scale. That was Magnus' first thought. Then he understood that the reverse was true. The abbey, the mere extrusion, was the poor, shallow reflection of what lay beneath, the monstrous and the sublime reduced to a scale that could be encompassed by human understanding.

The serpentine structures captured his eye, his mind, and his soul. Magnus sank to his knees again, in weakness and in awe, and because his body had become irrelevant. His consciousness fell down into the twists of the path below. He traced the convolutions of the halls, more dense than the surface of a brain. He traveled up the corkscrewing towers that reached toward him. He listened to the ocean surge darkly through the veins of the inhuman temple, and heard its commands. He heard, too, the shifting of the inhabitant of the labyrinth, the coiling of the thing that used the ocean for its voice.

He heard the summons of Crothoaka.

The dweller in doubt devoured all his beliefs but the ones that it had whispered to him before. It had planted in him the seeds of a cancerous truth, one that had strangled every other conviction with its roots. Now the truth had ripened, and Magnus understood that all his choices had been delusions, and all the paths of existence were a single, inevitable march to this point, and to this god.

Kneeling, he submitted.

Kneeling, he began to worship.

Later, when he rose, he rose to obey.

Chapter Sixteen

Cleo's suitcase sat packed on her sheetless mattress. She looked awkward in her street clothes, uncertain where and how to stand, as if the act of wearing anything other than the hospital gown were unforgivably rude.

If so, Miranda thought, Frieda shared Cleo's opinion. She sat up in bed with arms folded, lips pressed in a thin, sour line. She watched Cleo with sovereign resentment and judgment.

"I'm going to miss you," Cleo said, her smile unusually shy. She looked at Miranda and at Lupita when she spoke. Then, with a return of her spark, she cocked her head at Frieda. "You too!"

"It would be a shame if it turns out that you're being hasty," Frieda said, snipping each word. "You don't want to find yourself worse than before."

"Cleo isn't the one making this decision," Nurse Holden put in. She had arrived with supper, which included chocolate cake and ice cream for dessert for the farewell celebration. "Cleo has been given a clean bill of health. Her lungs are clear."

"Thank you so much for everything," Cleo said to Holden. "You've taken such good care of me."

Holden took both of Cleo's hands in hers. "It's been my pleasure," she said, and then, after a slight pause, "I know you'll walk the path in strength."

Sitting on the end of her bed, legs dangling, her plate of cake in hand, Miranda watched the two women carefully. Cleo's smile became strained. So did Holden's, as if her own words had thrown her off her stride. Her delivery had been mechanical, but at the same time emphatic. Her gaze becoming distant again, Holden said another goodbye to Cleo and left.

Cleo gave Lupita a hug, then looked around the room, awkward again, waiting for the right cue. "Well," she said. "I guess ..." She picked up her suitcase and turned to go.

"Wait for me," said Miranda. She got up, linked arms with Cleo, and walked her to the door.

"Going to see me out?" Cleo asked.

"That might be a bit too long of a walk for me," said Miranda. "But let me take you to the elevator, at least."

Cleo squeezed her arm. "I really am going to miss you."

"I'm sure going to miss you," Miranda said with feeling. "You're walking away with all the fun in the room." Conscious of the invisible pattern on the walls, she lowered her voice as if the lines could hear her. "I am glad you're going, though."

"Me too," Cleo whispered back, and Miranda wondered if some part of her sensed the need not to be overheard. "I feel guilty saying that. I've been treated so well. I just… I just don't feel right here anymore." She shook her head. "You must think I'm silly."

"I don't," said Miranda. "I think you're absolutely correct. Things feel wrong to me too."

"Do you think you could leave?"

"No," said Miranda. "I'm too ill. I can't be on my own and I have no family. And I think I'm where I need to be. Do you think *I* sound silly?"

"You don't. I get you. I don't know why, but I think it's good for the others that you're here."

"That helps. Thank you."

They arrived at the elevator.

"I'll come and visit," Cleo offered.

"No!" Miranda hung on to her whisper. "When you're out of here, you're gone. Please?"

"Okay," said Cleo.

"Promise me," she said as the elevator doors opened.

"I promise."

They hugged. Cleo stepped into the elevator. They held on to each other's gazes until the doors closed.

Miranda listened to the hum of machinery taking Cleo away. She felt very, very lonely.

Miranda woke up around three. She climbed out of bed and padded quietly to the bathroom next to the exit from the room. She closed the door before turning on the light, and held her breath during the brief second of total darkness. The harshness of the overhead light always came as a relief.

While washing her hands, Miranda realized she was squinting. The light had dimmed from sharp yellow to a dirty orange. Miranda's face in the mirror became grainy. She dried her hands, and they became distant and grainy too. Motes of darkness danced in the light.

Miranda looked up at the light. She reached up to tighten the bulb. It dimmed to red as her hand drew near.

The motes swarmed, multiplied, thickened. They came together. They became worms, twisting angrily in the air.

A nightmare. She wasn't awake, just dreaming. Had to be.

Please, she begged to anything that would listen.

The worms grew longer. They coiled around the bulb and draped their bodies over the mirror. Some, grown plump and heavy, dropped into the sink and squirmed around in bunches at the drain.

The childhood reflex came again with the terror, and Miranda started hyperventilating.

Wake up, wake up, wake up.

But in the nightmares of her early years, she could breathe freely, even when drowning. Now her gasps hurt, and she lapsed into a coughing fit. It bent her over the sink. He lungs heaved, and a worm, coming up from inside, caught in her throat. She gagged. It wriggled on her tongue, slimy and furry at the same time. She tried to spit but choked. She couldn't breathe at all. She put her fingers in her mouth, tried to grab the worm. It was like trying to pull out her tongue. She gagged again, and this time the worm came out in a ball of phlegm, landing with a wet smack in the sink.

She moaned, eyes watering, and the dim red light flickered.

Wake up, wake up, wake–

No. She couldn't wake because she *was* awake.

A vision, a terrible vision, but just a vision, let it pass, know that it will end.

The worms gathered, fused, became longer coils, became serpents.

Miranda closed her eyes to shut the vision away. She could not. The growing serpents still writhed in the air before her.

Impossible. So this had to be a vision. The inescapability of the sights gave her hope, until a coil tightened around her wrist.

She opened her eyes again, and now that she wanted to see, she could see almost nothing in the dimming light, just the snakes, no, the single snake, and yet again no, it was not a snake, but something else and darker, not worm but wyrm, scales and muscle and a head she could not see and hoped she would not.

The wyrm pulled at her arm, and she pulled back, fighting a physical force. Nightmare or vision, it had flowed out of her mind and into reality, as the abbey had flowed into the Institute.

With a yank, Miranda hurled herself against the door. She grabbed the handle, but more coils wrapped around it, thinner than the greater mass and yet part of its single length. Her hands slipped on the slimy cluster. Long, glistening strength looped around her midriff and pulled her back. It had a path for her, and it would drag her down its dark road.

Whispers crawled up her spine. They squeezed into her skull. They searched for her certainties, bringing the venom of doubt.

But doubt was already hers. She valued doubt, and its shield against doctrine and dogma and pride. She doubted even the truth of the serpent and the pain of its grip. She clutched *her* doubt like a sword, and lurched forward to grab the door handle again. Both hands now, squelching through slime and gelid flesh, and she would not let go, not ever, and before the wyrm could constrict and devour, before the light failed and the snarling dark came, she pushed down with all her force on the handle.

It turned.

The door opened.

She fell out of the bathroom and hit the floor with a bruising impact.

The bathroom light blazed yellow into the room. In her bed, Lupita stirred and whimpered a complaint, shut eyes squeezing tighter.

Miranda got up, turned off the light and closed the door on the empty bathroom. She tiptoed back to her bed and nestled under the covers, breathing as deeply as she could without pain. She rubbed her hands, her blessedly dry hands, together, and interlaced her fingers.

She had survived the blow. She wondered, terrified, how much worse the next one would be.

She vowed, determined, to ward it off too.

Chapter Seventeen

The storm hit on the third day of the *Leviathan*'s return crossing. The wind came up and the clouds gathered. The rain came down in angled torrents, chasing passengers off the decks. Then the swells grew. The rocking of the ship became noticeable by lunch. The people most prone to seasickness took to their cabins. Many people, especially children, had fun with the movement of the hallways, laughing as they teetered back and forth, banging into doorways and grabbing onto rails. By dinner, the waves were twenty feet high, and the novelty had worn off.

The Tourist Third dining room was half empty. Agatha had to keep catching her plate to stop it from sliding back and forth on their table. The folds of the white tablecloth brushed against her knees, drew back, and touched again, an insistent linen ghost. Wilbur stared at his food, his complexion a pale shade of green. Finally, he closed his eyes and shook his head.

"I can't," he said.

"Can you manage a bit of water?"

Another shake. "No." He breathed through his mouth. "I need to go back to the cabin."

Agatha stood up. "Then let's go."

She held his arm, and they walked slowly. Wilbur winced every time he swallowed, waging a last-ditch battle against nausea. He spoke with pauses for shaky inhalations. "Didn't I say… a spring crossing would be fun."

"You did, and I am sorry, my dear. This has been a rough trip all around."

"Was it … worth it?"

"I think so. I learned something important."

"Will it help?"

"I want to believe that it will." She didn't know.

The storm grew worse in the time it took them to reach their cabin. The ship climbed and plunged down such mountainous waves, Agatha and Wilbur had to clutch the rails with both hands to keep from falling. The struggle actually seemed to help Wilbur. He had to work so hard to stay on his feet that he forgot how sick he felt.

Once in the cabin, he tumbled, sick and relieved, into the lower berth. Agatha tucked him in, pulling the covers up to his chin. He looked so frail, and she cursed herself for having given in to the selfish impulse to have his company on the trip.

"Are you going to be all right?" she asked.

"I will be when we get home."

She stroked his forehead. "I'm sorry this is so hard."

Wilbur took her hand. "We will be all right, won't we?"

"Of course we will. This is a good ship, and the storm isn't *that* bad."

"That's not what I meant. I know the ship will make it to port. Will *we* be all right?"

"Yes," Agatha said, firmly, because that was what he needed to hear, and she needed to believe. "Why?"

"Is something following us?"

Her throat dried. "Have you seen something?"

"No," said Wilbur. "It's just… Sometimes I think you have."

Agatha bit her lip. She had felt tense the entire trip back from Durstal. She had kept checking behind them whenever she thought Wilbur wouldn't notice. She should have known he would pick up on her anxiety. From the moment she had come down the outside of the wall around the estate, her overriding drive had been to put as much distance between them and the blighted ground as possible. The trains had not been fast enough. They did not accumulate enough miles. No distance felt safe. Rationally, she knew she couldn't hope for that safety, not when the abbey and the Stroud Spiral had become the Institute, not when a link of that kind existed between Galloway and Arkham.

Irrationally, she felt the need for flight. And she did not have a reassuring answer to Wilbur's question. Was something following them? She couldn't lie and say no. She couldn't terrify him and say yes. She couldn't even give herself a definite answer. Several times on the train journey that took them to Southampton, she thought she saw something in the corner of her eye. A flicker of grey, the vibration of a thread, a cracked and fluttering angle. When she turned and looked directly, she never saw anything.

But her shoulders ached from the tension and the watching.

She hadn't seen anything since they'd boarded the *Leviathan*. The last few days had been the first restful ones she'd had since the night on the estate. She didn't even mind the storm, though she wished it wasn't so hard on Wilbur.

"We're fine," she said. "I encountered something frightening and dangerous on the Stroud Estate, but it isn't here. We're safe."

Wilbur sighed and gave her hand a grateful squeeze.

"Thank you," he said. "I think I'll sleep now."

"I thought I'd read in the lounge for a while." It was barely past seven. She wouldn't be ready for bed for another few hours.

"Good idea," said Wilbur. "I'll be fine here. Go and relax."

There were even fewer people in the Tourist Third cabin lounge than there had been in the dining saloon. Agatha had most of the lounge to herself. She settled in an armchair next to one of the wooden pillars. A potted fern nearby swayed gently with the motion of the ship, as if remembering the feeling of wind.

She hadn't been there more than a minute when two of the small handful of passengers present hurried out, hands over their mouths. The rise and fall of the ship leaned Agatha back and forth in her chair. She found the side-to-side motion almost soothing in its rhythm, and she sank into her book.

She had chosen to be in Leo Selig's company tonight. She had read *The Ascended Treatise* more than once, but the massive volume warranted return visits for new arguments. Agatha found Selig as interesting as he was frustrating. Selig, who eccentrically followed both Aleister Crowley and Helena Blavatsky, managed to avoid the worst features of his inspirations. That didn't prevent his book from being a mess of conjecture and foundationless theories. In spite of that, over the course of a thousand pages of dense, recondite prose, he kept giving Agatha interesting things to argue with, and insights that she had never considered.

Lost in the thickets of Selig's thesis, she didn't look up for a couple of hours.

The sound of gnawing broke her concentration. The noise seemed to be coming from inside the pillar. She tried to tune it out. Rats, she thought. Every ship had them. She went back to her book.

The teeth chewed through something that snapped like bone. A body rustled. Then it slithered.

Agatha put the book down. She looked around. There was no one else in the lounge.

Slither. Scrape.

She stood up, then backed a few steps away from the table, her eyes on the pillar.

A long scrape, the sound of a claw dragging down against the interior.

The wood rippled.

Agatha fled the lounge, moving as quickly as the heaving deck permitted. The sounds followed her, snaking out of the pillar, into the floor, and then up into the walls of the corridor.

Her first impulse, a primal instinct, was to find other people, as if nightmares could not exist in the presence of a crowd. She saw no one. The hall from the lounge stretched out before her, a deserted perspective to the vanishing point.

She hesitated. Go where? Run where?

A tongueless voice moaned like a dog. The slithering sounded familiar, and claws scrabbled at metal.

The walls began to ripple.

Agatha held her medallion. She whispered another portion of the Evashallon prayer, almost as afraid to speak those words as she was of the thing that had come for her. She did not know what cost might attach itself to the prayer, or what alliance she might invite.

The uttering of a few syllables seemed to push at the enemy. The rippling ceased. The clawing became frenzied, and it moved away from her.

Then it paused, and a liquid snarl came from the ceiling. At the same time, on her right, the slithering rushed ahead, leaving her behind.

Leaving part of itself behind.

Unless more than one being had come.

Agatha heard the sound of a long, sinuous body shooting down the corridor in the direction of her cabin.

Wilbur.

She hurried forward again, struggling up sudden inclines and then running down them as the ship climbed and plunged. She had to reach the cabin first, had to save Wilbur.

How?

Fight how?

Why had the thing chosen them as prey?

No, she thought. She had it wrong. They had not drawn the horror to them. Not directly. It was the stone she had taken from the abbey. She had created the same link between herself and the abbey as the one between it and the Institute.

You fool. You damned, damned fool. Why not summon it deliberately and get it all over with right away?

She chased the sounds now, racing to get to the cabin first. And the heaving of the ship mocked her. It took her balance away, changed the direction of her momentum up and down, back and forth. The corridor stayed empty of people and hope, but no, it was not truly empty, because there were things here, things inside the walls, and the walls were rippling, ready to tear like bad skin.

The hallway reached to infinity, taking the cabin away, so far away she would never get there.

Except she did, with the walls bulging now, the metal thin as a film of surface tension, turning translucent, and Agatha saw the squirming within, the strong twitch of a coil, and the flex of claws.

She burst into the cabin, accompanied by a scraping cacophony of the long, slithering thing changing course to follow her from the inside of the wall.

"Agatha!" Wilbur cried. "What is it? What's happening?" Eyes wide, he had his covers pulled up past his chin. He stared at Agatha so he would not look at the walls. "What is happening?"

"It will stop," she promised. She flew across the cabin to her suitcase. She rooted through it as, above her head, the metal of the wall began to tear.

Her hand closed around the stone.

"Stay here," she ordered Wilbur and ran for the door.

"But…" he began.

A claw as long as her hand poked out of the wall between the berths. Wilbur yelped and tried to shrink down into his mattress.

"It will come with me," Agatha promised, hoping that was true.

She ran from the cabin and pounded down the corridor again, making for the door to Tourist Third promenade deck. A hiss, outraged and hungry, pursued her.

She did not know if one creature or many were in the walls. The snarling and the rasping of movement surrounded her. Clawed rents opened up in the ceiling and on either side of her, horror keeping pace, horror toying with the moment to strike.

Agatha threw the door to the deck open. The wind screamed at her, seized her, and almost lifted her off her feet. Spray lashed her like a whip. Skidding and stumbling, she hurtled across the deck to the railing.

Though the ship's bow aimed into the wind, the chaotic swells of waves slammed against the sides in fury. Their white anger blinded Agatha and left the deck soaking in water deep enough to pull at her feet as it withdrew. She weaved back and forth, and the railing hit her so hard it knocked the breath from her lungs.

She hurled the abbey stone overboard, then clutched the railing. The wind and waves surrounded her with their rage. They wanted to take her with the stone.

Behind her, horror tore itself out of the walls of the ship. It surged past her, a being not yet fully born into the material world. It howled through the air. She had a sensation of monstrous length whipping by in the spray and vanishing into the roiling depths.

Gasping, choking, her ribs a mass of pain, Agatha fought her way back across the deck and inside the ship. She slammed the door shut and leaned against it. She slid to the floor, soaked, drained with relief.

She did not want to think. Her mind betrayed her and leapt forward to the next terrible thought.

If this was what a single stone had called, what would the transported totality of the abbey and the Spiral summon?

Chapter Eighteen

The Stroud Institute shifted. It changed. Its anticipation blew through the wards, an intangible yet insistent breeze that chilled Miranda. She could not feel the touch of the breeze, but she felt its effects. She could not get warm. The breeze followed her down the halls. It insinuated itself under her blanket. Darker than a promise, its smile wider than a threat. *Soon*, it whispered.

Soon.

Soon.

And sometimes, she thought, it laughed and said, *Now*.

She couldn't treat all change as sinister, yet with each change the breeze seemed to creep closer to being a wind, a storm to end all things.

She had expected the first change, inevitable with the departure of Cleo. Barbara Paul was her replacement, and she was not going to be nearly as much fun as Cleo had been. Not that Miranda felt humorous these days, but Barbara sucked the energy from the room. She lived and breathed her terror of her illness. She regarded every cough as a sign of terminal decline and imminent demise. "Am I going to die?" she asked endlessly.

"I hope so," Frieda muttered a few hours after Barbara's arrival, her words just audible enough to make Miranda wince, though Barbara gave no sign that she had heard. She was too consumed by her attempts to feel her pulse, to see if it was beating too strongly, or perhaps not at all.

"You are not going to die," Miranda told her. Tall, broad-shouldered, Barbara looked like she could take on a quarterback and come out the victor. "I guarantee it." With an inner sigh, she accepted that she had just committed herself to making that same guarantee on a daily basis, at the very least.

The other change came the day after Barbara's arrival. Exercise was not just permitted now. It was encouraged. At least, *encouraged* was the word Nurse Revere used. Coming from her, it sounded more forceful than a suggestion.

"How long can my walks be?" Miranda asked her. Revere had just announced the new regime to the room before doing the usual check of vital signs at each bedside.

"As long as you can manage," Revere said, whipping off the blood pressure cuff, her movements as brusque as ever, as if the cuff had offended her and needed punishment.

"Every day?"

Revere looked down her nose at Miranda. "Why?" she asked, suspicious. "You aren't thinking of shirking, are you?"

"No, no," said Miranda.

"You wouldn't want to be thought of as *difficult*."

"Of course not."

"This is how you get well."

"I know."

"You aren't going to pretend you know better than the doctors."

"I never meant that."

"Walk the path," Revere commanded.

Miranda said nothing. She just nodded. Did Revere mean what she had just said? Was she even aware of it, and of how out of character it sounded? The order had come out as a mechanical compulsion.

Revere looked at her, motionless, waiting for a satisfactory response.

"I'll walk the path," Miranda said softly.

Revere jerked back into motion. She gave Miranda a curt nod and turned to Frieda.

For the first time, Miranda doubted the wisdom of the care. That was a change that truly belonged to the cold, impossible draft.

She obeyed, though. She would not be difficult. She would not call more attention to herself than necessary. Not until she knew what she had to do. Not until she knew how to fight back.

Fight back against what?

Find out. Somehow, find out.

Miranda went out on longer walks. Everyone did. The corridors became crowded with patients shuffling along or wheeling themselves on journeys without destinations. Miranda changed her approach to the halls of the Stroud Institute. She accepted that she could not map the floor in her head. She shifted her attention to her fellow patients and watched them instead, searching for patterns.

Miranda wished for larger groups at Daria Miracle's counseling sessions. She didn't like being part of a single circle of participants. Mentally, she had moved to the back of the room, where students could pretend the teachers did not see them. She wished she could really be there, lurking in the background of the session, observing without being observed.

Miranda maintained her camouflage instead. She knew what bored students looked like, and made sure to appear otherwise. With a bit of effort, she kept her face bright and interested.

Daria began the session by asking the circle how everyone was doing.

"I don't know," Frieda said, sounding genuinely upset instead of chagrined.

"What don't you know?" Daria said, moving to Frieda's chair with feline grace.

The question seemed to throw Frieda, as if it struck home in a way she was frightened to understand. It pulled the pain out of her in words. "What am I supposed to believe?" she cried.

Other patients nodded. Some leaned forward, hanging on Daria's answer. Lupita squeezed her hands together in distress.

Daria knelt beside Frieda. "Why ask me?" she said, soft and kind. She touched Frieda's hand. "This is for you to know. Your journey is yours. As it has always been."

"Where are you taking us?" a woman called Perla Todd asked.

Daria rose from Frieda's side. Pure dance, she turned and moved to smile down at the teenager. "I'm not taking you anywhere," she said. "You're taking yourself."

"But we're asking questions we shouldn't," Lupita said, on the edge of a quaver.

Daria flowed in her direction. "Why forbidden?" Always gentle, always soft, always welcoming, never stern.

"Because…" Lupita said. She searched for words. "Because they're wrong."

"Wrong? But why? Is it because they don't have answers?"

"I don't know." Miserable, Lupita stared at her hands.

Daria leaned and touched Lupita's chin, soft as a breeze, a breeze from the ether.

Are you cold, Lupita? Miranda wondered.

Lupita jerked her head up to meet Daria's warm, piercing gaze.

"Is faith fragile?" said Daria. "Is yours?"

Lupita's breath hitched.

"You don't have to answer," said Daria. "I'm here to help, not upset you. And I don't think faith is fragile at all."

She did not say *your* faith, Miranda noted.

Daria moved to the center of the ring, carrying all attention with her. "We don't like doubt," she said. "No one does. It hurts."

"It does," Lupita whispered. She hugged herself against the cold.

"I'm sure you're not alone, my dear," said Daria. "How about a show of hands? How many people here are wrestling with doubt?" She raised her hand high.

After a moment's hesitation, so did everyone else. Miranda did too. Did it count if, instead of wrestling with doubt, she embraced it? That didn't matter. The point was not to stand out. Not yet.

Appear to be one of the flock.

"There," said Daria. She turned her smile on Lupita. "See? You're not alone at all." She went back to addressing everyone, walking slowly around the circle again.

Miranda watched her spiraling, spiraling.

"What should you do with doubt?" Daria asked. "You should ask yourself why you are encountering it. Let the questions come. Find the true source of the doubt. Get to its core. Can I let you in on a secret?" A conspiratorial smile. "Doubt is the path to certainty. Follow the doubt all the way, and you'll come out the other side. Walk the path of doubt to its center, and there you will find knowledge. There you will find truth."

The pattern of Daria's movements changed. Instead of circling inside the ring of chairs, she went back and forth across the circle, gracefully bouncing from one patient to the next. The directions seemed random at first. Then Miranda caught the way the tight turns created nestling lines. Daria was walking a labyrinth.

"Don't stagnate in dogma," said Daria. "You won't find certainty there. The harder you clutch on to dogma, the worse the doubt will become. Find your way to a living belief. It will change you."

Daria kept speaking, urging the audience on their journeys. Her voice pulled, and her words pushed. She created a powerful current. Miranda felt it, and even braced as she was, she had to fight hard to keep from being swept off her feet. She distracted herself and tuned Daria out by focusing on the others. The current had them. Their faces were rapt. They were happy to drown for Daria. The wind from the ether blew stronger, stronger, becoming a gale, and the waves it conjured could not be swum.

But doubt was her element. Miranda lived for the questions that troubled. That was why she could fight. She had always lived in this sea. She would battle the currents, and not fear the gale.

After the counseling session, after an afternoon rest, Nurse Revere called on them to go walking again. Miranda watched as she strolled slowly, noting the changes caused by the Institute's wind in the faces of her fellow patients. In some, she saw the look of gnawing obsession that haunted Lupita and Frieda's features. In others, she saw a kind of blank determination. Barbara had it, when she wasn't swamped by her health terror of the hour.

Beyond the shared expressions, Miranda finally began to see a pattern in the walks. Daria's ballet had taught her what to look for. No one moved with Daria's elegance, but the pattern was there. It defied easy definition. It lacked location or clear direction. Miranda found it concentrating on the turns she saw the other patients make. She kept herself a dozen steps behind Barbara and counted her left and right turns. When Barbara returned to the room to lie down, Miranda kept going, following another, and then another patient.

She counted, and she found the pattern. She found the labyrinth path they were walking.

Her legs ached with fatigue. She wanted to lie down. She made herself keep going. She had to see how far the pattern went.

She took the elevator to the next ward down. There, as with her floor, every mobile patient was walking. She didn't stay long. She didn't want to be noticeable. She strolled casually, looked pleasant, and counted turns just long enough to be sure that everyone walked the same path here too. Then she took the elevator again.

The ward above hers was the one where Cleo would have gone, had she not recovered so quickly. Here were the patients closest to being given a clean bill of health. These were the volunteers, the active residents of the Stroud Institute, the ones learning how to adjust to active life once more.

They walked quickly, and there were many of them. Miranda shrank back next to the wall, fearing the traffic would carry her off at a pace that would overwhelm her. She could not keep up with anyone she chose to follow. She didn't have to. The sheer number of walkers, and the purpose of their stride, made the shape of the pattern so much easier to see. Miranda didn't have to count the turns. She knew what to expect from the floors below, and so now she could predict which way any of the patients would turn.

The intersections were lies, she thought. There were no choices here at all. Not a maze, but a labyrinth, a single path leading to the center.

What center, though? Where was it?

She walked for as long as she could, taking in the full force of the walk's flow, and the chill of the blank, straining faces.

She wondered how close to the center these people had come.

Perhaps because of the greater freedom of movement of these patients, with the chains of illness fallen from them, she caught the flaws in the walking more easily. They stood out more. Every now and then, a stuttering twitch interrupted their gait, a splice in the film of their movement. Miranda slowed down to a mere shuffle, watching closely. The twitches, she saw, happened when the patients passed particular spots of the walls. No features stood out about the locations. That meant nothing. Miranda knew about the lines of the labyrinth beneath the paint. They didn't stand out, either.

Miranda became conscious again of the wrongness of the intersections, of the Institute's skewed architecture. The rooms were not big enough. The corridors extended too far beyond the end walls of the last rooms before they turned.

Miranda ran her fingers gently on the wall starting a few yards away from one of the twitch points. She felt the lines, and walked as slowly as she had to so she would not lose them. Remaining wary of falling into its rhythm, she let the pattern draw her on.

She came level with the point where the patient ahead of her had jerked. Her fingers found a slight, circular depression. The lines coiled around it. She took her hand down and moved away from the wall before she attracted attention.

That night, Miranda waited until her roommates slept, and the night nurse had come by on her first round. She wouldn't be by again for at least fifteen minutes.

Miranda rose and, barefoot, padded silently into the corridor. She went down to the end of the hall, close to the intersection. Battling the misleading geography of the Institute, she searched for the point equivalent to the one she had found on the floor above. It took her a minute or two of going back and forth for her fingers to follow the pattern to another depression.

Miranda took a breath. She checked the hall. She was alone.

She pushed.

The circle of wall went deeper in, then stopped with a faint click. A vertical line appeared and the wall parted before it, the two halves of the stone portal pulling back with unnatural smoothness of motion and a silence that sent goose-flesh up her arms.

A passage led into the dark. No paint on its walls; the stone was rough, damp, reveling in the glory of its age. The smell of the sea crept out and wrapped around her.

Miranda pushed the depression next to the opening again. It clicked back out, and the walls closed once more. She could see no sign that the portal had ever been there.

Still alone, she hurried back to the room.

The others were awake, sitting up, and staring at her.

"Sorry if I woke you," she said, slipping back into bed. *Please don't ask what I was doing.*

Lupita asked something worse. "Are we in danger?"

"No," Frieda snapped, and the danger was in her voice.

"But…" Lupita began. Frieda's glare stopped her.

"Is there something wrong with this place?" Barbara asked.

What could she say? Miranda wondered. How could she help them? If she took them into her confidence, what would that do? Could they fight, when she didn't know how? Would she just be putting them in danger?

"If you can leave," Miranda said, feeling a gamble in each word, "I think you should."

"Nonsense," said Frieda, brittle and angry. "Whatever is wrong with you?"

Lupita shivered and pulled her blankets up to her chin.

"Oh dear," Barbara whispered shakily. "Oh dear, oh dear, oh dear. My brother is a police officer. Maybe he can help. I'll speak to him in the morning."

He wouldn't be able to help, Miranda thought. But if the idea gave Barbara some comfort, or he could find a way of taking her out of the Institute, then well and good.

Miranda managed to fall asleep an hour later. She did not dream.

In the morning, Barbara was gone. A different woman slept in her bed.

CHAPTER NINETEEN

Breakfast came, and no one said anything about Barbara. Miranda recognized the new woman from the counseling sessions. Her name came back to her after a minute – Norma Reese. She had been in a room four doors down.

Frieda chatted with Norma as if she saw nothing unusual in the other woman's presence. Lupita joined in too, a bit shyly, but also with a dogged commitment to normality. Miranda couldn't manage more than some grunted agreements and noncommittal mumbles when one of the others spoke to her. How could they be talking about the orange juice, and whether it tasted more chilled than usual this morning, and how nice it was that the eggs were a proper over-easy with lots of runny yolk? How could they not ask Norma what she was doing here? How could they not raise the alarm and demand to know where Barbara had gone?

The questions shrieked in Miranda's mind. She did not voice them. She didn't do any of the things she wished the others were doing. Instead, she watched them closely, looking for signs of things that were wrong, or she hoped, that were still right.

Was there any hint that they knew something strange had happened?

In Lupita, yes, Miranda thought. Her contributions to the conversation were tentative and brittle. She reminded Miranda of a dog licking the hand of an unpredictably violent master.

What master? She didn't know.

Frieda, on the other hand, seemed resolute. She would impose normality on the situation through sheer, bulldozing belief. That was Miranda's more optimistic reading. She didn't want to think that Frieda really did believe all was fine. But if she had to face that reality, she would.

"Eat up," Norma said, eyeing Miranda's barely touched breakfast. "Got to keep your strength up for all the walking later." She laughed, and Miranda did her best not to cringe too visibly. Norma was one of those people who laughed at the end of every sentence. "We need to get lots walking today," Norma added, nodding at her own wisdom.

The other two nodded as well. Walking must be done. Consensus reigned.

Were they all mad? Miranda wondered. Could they hear themselves?

Maybe something had happened during the night. Maybe the effects of all the walking of the day before had sunk in, only these three had not woken with sore muscles because the walking had nothing to do with exercise, not really. Just like a communion wafer wasn't about food. The walking was a ritual, Miranda knew that. What kind, and to what purpose, she didn't know yet.

They were changing, she thought. Through the ritual came transformation, one deeper and darker than transubstantiation.

Nurse Holden came by on her rounds after breakfast. Her movements seemed stiff, as if her body had become unfamiliar to her. When she smiled, the smile came from a distance. It looked like plastic.

"Where's Barbara?" Miranda asked.

"Who?" said Holden.

"Barbara," Miranda repeated, her pulse skipping beats. "She was here yesterday. Very frightened about every single symptom. Big, strong woman." She kept piling on the details as if that would force Holden to acknowledge Barbara's existence.

Holden frowned. She shook her head. That was when Miranda noticed the twitch. It had no rhythm between occurrences. She picked up on it this time because it happened twice in a few seconds. After Holden shook her head *no*, she shook again, so quickly her face blurred. And then, as she started to speak, the sudden, rapid shake happened once more. "I'm sorry, Professor Ventham," she said. "I don't know who you mean. Norma has been in this room since Cleo left."

Miranda stared at her. *Liar*, she thought. And then: *What if she isn't?* It might be worse if Holden believed she was telling the truth.

Worse yet if she was right.

Or perhaps Miranda should be hoping that was the case. If the problem lay with her, and her grip on reality, then there was nothing for the others to fear at the Stroud Institute.

No. She could not take refuge in that lie. That would be cowardice. She had made a promise to fight.

Frieda and Lupita were staring at her. Propped up against their pillows, they were very, very still. They didn't want to be frightened. Norma was looking at her in confused expectation. She needed her cue to laugh again.

"Oh," Miranda said. "I see." *No, I don't, but I'll play along for now.* "Sorry. Rough night. My dreams must have confused me." A weak explanation, but it seemed to satisfy Holden and the others. She had given them something they could choose to believe.

After Holden left, Norma decided she had her permission to laugh. "That must have been quite the night!" she said to Miranda.

Miranda gave her a weak smile. "Seems so." She braced herself for awkwardness.

None came. Norma chatted happily, bubbling on about how much she was looking forward to the day. "It's so exciting, isn't it?"

"What is?"

"Our journey! That is something I really didn't expect when I came here. I'm not just getting well in body! I'm walking the path! Isn't that wonderful?"

She laughed and laughed, and Miranda didn't have to answer.

When Norma went to the bathroom to get washed up and ready for her exciting journey, Miranda confronted Frieda and Lupita.

"Well?" she asked. "Did I really just imagine Barbara?"

Lupita squirmed and didn't answer. Frieda rounded on her with a ferocious, frightened glare. "Why are you being like this?" she demanded.

"You didn't answer my question," said Miranda. "What about Barbara?"

Lupita kept her eyes down. She pulled a rosary back and forth between her fingers, her lips moving in an unconvincing, heartbreaking mimicry of prayer.

"Just stop it!" Frieda hissed. "You aren't helping. You're being scary."

Miranda didn't reply. She saw that she would not get the answer she wanted from either of them. She couldn't even tell if they believed in Barbara's existence or not.

"Let's just do our walk," Lupita whispered. "We'll all feel better."

"Will you?" said Miranda. "Did Daria help you yesterday, or make you feel worse about your doubts?"

"We have to reach our center," Frieda said, pronouncing judgment from on high. "Once we get there, we'll be better."

"No more doubts?"

"Stop it!" Lupita pleaded.

Miranda took a breath, then nodded. She was doing no good. Lupita and Frieda were clinging to the labyrinth and the promise of certainty. If she insisted on asking about Barbara, she would only make their doubts more painful, and they would clutch Daria's promises with even greater desperation.

They had nowhere to go. They had to feel safe here. They weren't, but she couldn't save them through terror – if she could save them at all.

If she could save anyone.

After breakfast, the walking began. Frieda, Lupita and Norma threw themselves into the exercise with a fervor that gradually became a blank effort. Miranda stayed close enough to watch them. She saw their features loosen, their eyes become dull. The ritual had them, its grip stronger than yesterday. She could feel its power now, and it wanted her to take part. It would be so easy. She could walk the path to certainty too. She could stop worrying about Barbara. She could stop worrying about everything, if she walked the path all the way.

New doubts crept into her mind, squirming in like spiders, doubts inserted by a force outside her, but so perfectly shaped for her that, if she had not been on her guard, she would have thought they came from within. They were doubts about her doubts, insinuations that she had misread everything, that she and Agatha were sabotaging her recovery, to the point where she could no longer tell the difference between fever dreams and reality. How could she really believe she had found a secret passage in the Institute? Gothic nonsense, so obviously born of her research field that it was amazing she could credit the thought in the light of day.

It would be easy to walk the path. It would be restful, in the end, to let the doubts take her, and follow Daria's prescription to certainty.

Miranda shook herself. *No*, she thought. She pushed back at the doubts. The inside of her head itched from their scrabbling legs. *No*. She knew what she had seen. She knew what was real. She would not accept these doubts. She had plenty of her own to turn against the enemy and the blandishments of certainty. That, above all things, she distrusted. The Great War and the physical, emotional, cultural and spiritual devastations it had left behind had proven the wisdom of that perspective.

She resisted the currents of the ritual. She eyed the location of the hidden door every time she passed it. She wondered how many other entrances there were. At least one on every floor, she guessed. She pictured secret halls, thick with age and the smell of the sea, spreading out through the Stroud Institute, an inner rot. The scale of what might be present made her feel very small. She walked closer and closer to the edge of despair. How was she going to fight this all alone?

Where was Agatha? When would she be back?

The awful possibility: *What if she's dead?*

The rooms Miranda passed were largely empty. Almost all the patients in the ward were walking. Miranda thought the numbers were wrong. If there was no one in the rooms, she should be seeing more people in the halls. She wondered how many other Barbaras had disappeared.

She felt the crisis padding down the halls with her, gathering its forces, growing ready to complete its great work.

A desperate thought came. She could burn the Institute down. She pictured the flames rising high in the night, engulfing the roof, billowing out of the windows, roaring down the corridors.

She shuddered. Even if she could find a way to do this, how many patients would she kill?

Nauseated, she banished the idea.

She turned a corner and saw Donovan Stroud coming down the hall, against the tide of walkers. He smiled at everyone, stopping every few steps to exchange a word. His approach was casual.

It was also purposeful. Miranda knew he had come to see her.

He stopped in front of her. "Professor Ventham," he said. "How nice to see you looking so much better than the last time we met."

"That's kind of you to say."

"I was wondering, do you think Nurse Revere would object if I stole you away from your exercise for a little while?"

"I owe you and myself an apology," Donovan said when they were settled in his lounge.

They sat as they had before, with Miranda on the couch and her back to the window. She tried to not stare too fixedly at the painting over the mantle. Had it changed? Had the abbey vanished? No, the ruins still loomed on the horizon behind Magnus Stroud, as if mocking her for believing in her vision.

She felt something had changed in the room, though. Something more concrete than her trust in the place.

"An apology?" Miranda asked, scanning the room.

"Yes, for neglecting my opportunities to talk with you." Donovan pulled a wry face. "And after all my fancy talk of being delighted to have a scholar in residence, as it were."

"Flatterer."

"Not at all. Not at all. But it is good to see that color in your cheeks. How *are* you? I'm told you're improving."

"So I am," Miranda said.

On the wall behind Donovan, that wood-engraving, its lines dense as a Doré. She didn't remember it from before. She hadn't noticed it, at least. In a storm of wind and waves and fire, a serpent and a dragon entwined in combat. The twisting of limbs and scales leapt out at her, rich with meaning. She saw in the print the symbol of the Stroud Institute's architecture. She saw two sets of corridors entwined, one hidden by the other, a double labyrinth, the true center concealed from the walking patients. For the moment.

"Does Agatha Crane still pay you regular visits? It would be lovely to speak with her again too."

Miranda tore her eyes from the print. She focused on Donovan. "Agatha's away," she said. "She'll be back soon, I would think."

"I'm sure you will be glad to see her." Donovan smiled.

How many layers should she read below the innocuous surface of his comments? How deep a threat?

The skittering, spider-legged doubts scratched to be let in, to tell her that in her paranoia, she turned pleasantries into murder.

"It will be nice when she's back," Miranda agreed.

"Tea?" Donovan asked. "I think it has steeped enough." He picked up the Wedgwood teapot from the table between them.

"No, thank you."

Donovan poured himself a cup. "I've been meaning to ask you," he said, "what you thought of our counseling sessions." He added a teaspoon of sugar, hesitated, then another. He looked up as he stirred, all attention.

"I didn't know what to expect," said Miranda, ready for a trap to spring, not knowing which word, look or hesitation could trigger it. "Daria Miracle is an extraordinary speaker."

Donovan chuckled. He wagged a finger at Miranda. "I detect diplomacy behind your words. You have your doubts about her teachings. I can tell."

"I always have doubts." So there would be fencing today. Very well. She would not retreat, in spite of the traps.

Donovan looked pleased. "That's what I thought," he said. "They're a necessary part of your pedagogical practice, aren't they? They're needed for critical thinking."

"That's right."

"You teach your students to have doubts."

"I do."

A wide grin. "I imagine that makes for some lively dinner conversations at Thanksgiving for them, when they trot out what they've learned from you."

"You're flattering me again," said Miranda. "You overrate the impact I have on my students."

"And I think you're being too humble."

"You wouldn't if you were nodding off at one of my lectures."

"I'm sure I wouldn't. I can't imagine anyone could."

"Then you would be surprised."

Donovan sipped his tea. "I suppose anything is possible," he said. "The fact remains that I know I would be riveted. We have very similar philosophies, you and I."

"Oh?"

"Yes. We simply apply them in different fields. I, too, firmly believe in the need to foster healthy doubt."

"Healthy," Miranda repeated.

"Naturally."

"So you think being wracked by doubt helps the body combat TB?"

Donovan raised his eyebrows in mock surprise. "Wracked?" he said. "*Wracked*? That doesn't sound like the language of someone who believes in the value of doubt." He raised a hand before she could answer. "But I see what you're doing. You're making me apply the principals of critical thinking to my own system. Give it a shake, eh? Make sure it isn't brittle dogma? Yes, in answer to your question. Because doubts and curiosity are intimately related. A curious mind is an engaged mind, as I have always maintained, and that is the way forward."

He wanted her on-side, Miranda thought. Why?

Donovan put his cup down. He brought his hands together and leaned forward, delivering a confidence. "If I could cure this century's ills," he said, "I would. And one of the greatest of those ills is misplaced certainty." He lowered his voice and carved his words out of solemnity itself. "Look what certainty has done to the world."

Miranda held her face still. *Don't let him see you're startled.* Donovan hit too close to her thoughts of earlier. The doubts from outside plunged through her defenses. Her lungs felt thick and cold. She struggled to breathe.

"Magnus saw the same thing," Donovan continued. "He saw what the cancer of certainty did to the French Revolution. He witnessed the Terror, and Napoleon's betrayal that became the Empire. He saw that he had to fight, to carve the path through the reeds of false certainty, wielding the blade of doubt." He leaned back with a theatrical grimace. "I am very sorry about that metaphor. That was a bit much."

"How did Magnus fare in his struggle?" Miranda asked.

"He made a start. It was always a project that would span generations."

"So the torch has fallen to you now."

"Yes, it has." Donovan's eyes burned as he spoke the boast, the promise, and the warning.

He knew she was fighting him. He was telling her that he knew. They weren't even pretending to be talking about the treatment of tuberculosis anymore. She still wondered why they were speaking at all. Barbara had mentioned a brother in the police, and she had vanished. Miranda's visions, when they came, were worse than ever. But she was still here, physically unharmed.

Donovan wanted her for something.

And the currents in the Institute kept trying to pull her down the labyrinth's path.

Donovan had all the advantages. He knew what was happening. She didn't.

I'll fight you anyway.

"And are you the one to bring Magnus' work to completion?" she asked.

"I am. And I will."

The impossible wind blew hard through the halls. It blew through the lounge. The windows rattled. Though it was spring, Miranda shivered with the coming of winter.

Chapter Twenty

Agatha and Wilbur arrived at their apartment well after ten at night. The last task of the journey looked like it was going to break Wilbur. He tottered as he got out of the taxi outside their apartment building, and he carried his suitcase as if it were slowly pulling his arm out of its socket.

"Almost done," Agatha encouraged him. She hooked her arm in his, and they made their way up the porch and into the building.

When they unlocked their apartment, Wilbur went straight to the bedroom. Agatha heard his suitcase thump on the floor, and the squeak of mattress springs as he threw himself on the bed.

"Get into pajamas before you fall asleep," she called out.

"What are you doing?" he answered.

"I'll be there in a minute." She had an inspection to make.

Agatha moved through the rooms, turning on all the lights. The apartment exuded that chilly stillness that settled over rooms left empty for longer than a few days. The familiar had taken on a sheen of the uncanny. Furniture and possessions looked back at her, inviting her to wonder if any had changed positions while she had been gone. None had, but it took the tour, and several minutes of reacquainting her with her space, to make the home hers again.

She banished shadows and stood in each room, turning around slowly, until she satisfied herself that nothing had come here ahead of them, and nothing waited in the dark corners.

She ran her hand over the books, crammed and bursting from shelves, and stacked in precarious piles on every flat surface. She walked down the hall, with its lithographs of Paris, London and Prague, and asked herself if the lighting was not a bit dimmer than it should be.

No, it wasn't. She could see down the corridor's length as well as she ever had.

She had left a small, protective circle, drawn in salt, in every room. Nothing had broken the boundaries of the circles. She did not really know what, if anything, could shield her against what she feared was coming to Arkham, and that might still have its sights on her. But her home felt right, and she sighed, grateful.

She went to her office, opened the large wardrobe next to her battered, cluttered desk, and opened the tool box inside. She took out a geologist's hammer, then went back to her suitcase in the living room to dig out her flashlight.

"Agatha?" Wilbur called, suspicion shaving the sleep from his voice.

She poked her head in the doorway. "You get some sleep," she said. "You need it."

"So do you. What are you doing? Why do you still have your coat on? You're not going out again?"

"Yes. Sorry, but I have to."

"But you must be exhausted too. Can't it wait?"

"I'm fine," she lied. She was ready to drop. "It can't wait." That was true. She had been racing against time since her flight from the estate. What worried her was the growing conviction that the race had started much earlier.

Tuesday night in Arkham, after eleven. The streets of French Hill and River-town were quiet. Nothing unusual in that. But the quiet felt deeper than normal to Agatha. She saw no one else. No cars passed her. The streetlamps created pools of stagnant light. It had rained earlier in the evening, and the water from the eves broke the silence only to have it return with greater force after every echoing drop.

The night was taut with anticipation. It watched her, muscles coiled, coiling tighter the closer she came to the Stroud Institute. A current ran through the dark too, picking up strength and speed, trying to rush her to the Institute. She had to pay attention to each step, had to work to ensure her approach was on her own terms, her action, not a passive acceptance.

She would not be swept through the gates by the unseen river. She was heading to the Institute, but she would leave it again.

It would not devour her.

The gates were shut when she arrived. She hadn't expected them to be open, not at this time of night. Still, irrationally, the barrier felt like an angry response to her resistance. The current flowed hard, and the night was ready to pounce, and now she would have to work to get in.

"If I want to," she whispered to the Institute. "If I choose to."

The gate's pillars were made of the same stone as the Institute itself. She might not have to go any further.

So she told herself. It was the right kind of comforting lie for this moment. She didn't know if she had the energy to try to enter forbidden grounds again. The symmetry of the effort made her uneasy.

And yet. And yet. She knew she shouldn't make do with "good enough", not with so much at stake. She eyed the wall. It was higher than the one around the estate in Galloway. She didn't have a ladder. She could not climb it, and she could not squeeze through the pickets.

No way in. Not tonight, at least.

With a tired sigh of relief, she moved into the shadows of the left-hand pillar and pulled out her hammer. She looked up and down the street. She was alone.

Water plinked. The night watched.

Agatha struck the pillar. The hard *crack* of the hammer sounded like an explosion in the deserted street. She hit the pillar three more times before she could lose her nerve. The fourth hit dislodged a small piece of stone. She snatched it up, put it in her coat's pocket, then listened for the sounds of running footsteps and outraged shouts.

Nothing.

She let herself breathe normally. Time to go home, even with an imperfect sample. The way the atmosphere of anticipation built as she closed in on the Institute suggested that a sample taken from the building would be worth getting.

Before she could start moving, she heard a vehicle heading her way. She froze, convinced it was coming for her, that someone had heard her and triggered an alarm. She stared at the headlights, unable to run.

The electric gates swung open, eerily quiet.

And the vehicle turned, its headlights swinging away from Agatha, and she saw that it was an ambulance, bringing another patient to the Stroud Institute.

The ambulance headed down the drive. After a slight pause, the gates began to close again. Before she had a chance to think her actions through and talk herself out of them, Agatha ducked out from behind the pillar and hurried between the gates.

They shut behind her with a metal click.

Now I have you, said the Institute, its words self-evident to her imagination.

No, she told it. You don't. I'm the one who's hunting you.

She half-convinced herself with her bravado.

The Institute loomed over her, glowering with the dim light that shone, colder than the moon, through a few windows. At the peak, the windows of Stroud's apartments blazed red, a cyclops's eye.

Agatha turned off the drive and into the trees, away from the eye's gaze. The lampposts along the drive gave her just enough illumination in the shadows to see her way. She went left, to the side of the building, and rushed in a crouch across the grass to the black stone mass.

No windows near here, and no door. She was hidden. She raised the hammer, winced in anticipation of the noise, and hit as quickly as she could.

Four taps, their echoes high and clear, and she knocked a piece of stone from the body of the building. The heavy darkness over her seemed to quiver with a snarl. On instinct, she raised a hand to protect her face from the teeth or the jet of blood about to hit her.

Nothing touched her.

Silence clamped back down hard. Agatha felt the reach of the Institute across the grounds. The grass flexed under her steps like muscle tissue. The earth, hating her, paused on the edge of violent, carnivorous movement. She grabbed her sample and hurried back to the wall.

No way through the locked gates, and no way to climb the wall.

I have you, the Institute said again.

Not yet. You forgot the trees.

The oaks, thick and gnarled and ancient, lined the wall, and some of their branches went over it. It took Agatha a few increasingly frightened moments to find a tree she could climb, but there was one. She took hold of the lowest branch. The wood felt wrong, a heartbeat away from squirming. She fought through her disgust and held on. She climbed up, away from the tainted ground, knowing the tree could crush her with its limbs if she gave it a chance.

She climbed as if she were a child again, old moves coming back, fueled by adrenaline. A frightened squirrel, she hauled herself up to the branch that stretched over the wall, inched along it, and then dangled over the sidewalk. She let go, dropping a good five feet. She landed awkwardly. It hurt. She bit down on her yell, and it came out as a long, painful hiss.

She straightened, found her balance. Nothing broken, and she didn't have time for the pain of sprains.

She walked away from the Institute, its silent fury boring into her back.

She was shaking with cold and fatigue when she let herself back into the apartment. She couldn't sleep, though. The need to know kept her going a bit longer.

Agatha hurried to her office. She put her samples down on the laboratory table that sat against one wall and readied her microscope.

When she looked at them, her first thought was that she had pushed herself too far, and that exhaustion had wrecked her vision. She would have to try again tomorrow. The samples refused to come into focus. When she looked up, though, she could see clearly. There was nothing wrong with her vision. She peered through the microscope again and realized that the blur came from the sample. The stone was vibrating. Not enough to be detectible with the naked eye, or enough to be felt consciously by touch. It registered at the subconscious level, though. The stone felt unpleasant. Under high magnification, Agatha could see the thrum, and its irregular, complex rhythm.

The sample from the building seemed to be vibrating with a slightly greater intensity than the one from the gate.

A stronger link, she thought.

Link to what?

To the thing in Galloway. To the thing that would be coming.

She sighed, frustrated. She knew she was right, but her conclusions weren't based on science. She had evidence of something, but the specifics were still her intuition.

The specifics, but not the fact of the danger itself. She had felt it in Galloway. She had witnessed it on the *Leviathan*.

She knew it was coming. But she didn't know how she and Miranda, or anyone else, was meant to fight it.

We need to know more.

The terror, the time, and the expense of the trip, and had she gained anything?

Maybe. Confirmation of the threat, and that Donovan Stroud was involved.

That meant a clear direction of investigation. Except it was a direction closed to her. Only Miranda could follow it.

Could Agatha ask that of her? In all good conscience?

In all good conscience, could she not?

Fatigue finally caught up with her. She fell into bed, the unresolved question swirling in her mind. She fell asleep, and dreamed of serpents and the smell of the sea.

In the morning, while Wilbur, looking more rested than she felt, puttered about in the kitchen getting breakfast ready, she had another look at her samples.

She had no way to establish a quantitative measure of the vibrations in the stone. Even so, she could tell that the intensity of the blur had increased.

It's getting closer.

She went out again before breakfast, walked past the gates to the Stroud Institute, and tossed the samples inside. She didn't think she would learn any more from them, and she would not draw the horror to her home.

She listened to the warning of her dreams.

Chapter Twenty-One

Miranda flew out of bed, across the room, and into Agatha's arms. She hugged the older woman fiercely, reassuring herself that she was real. Agatha hugged her back, just as hard. They stepped away and grinned at each other, giddy with mutual relief.

"I am so, so glad to see you," Miranda said. "I can't tell you how good it feels."

"You don't have to. That's how I'm feeling too."

Conscious that they were standing in the middle of the room, and that the other three were staring at them, Miranda led Agatha back to her end. They sat down on the edge of her bed and spoke in quieter tones, the ones people used when visiting, as if this would make them inaudible to the other occupants. It would, Miranda hoped, make listening in a bit more difficult and less interesting. Either way, torn between suspicion and the need to help, she had to be guarded in what she said.

"How was your trip?" she asked.

Agatha nodded to herself and gave an expressive sigh. "Exciting," she said.

"Good research for your book?" Miranda settled on their cover story for the moment.

"I think so. I feel like the book has some direction now, at least."

Nurse Revere appeared in the doorway, and Miranda fell quiet. Revere scanned the room, lips pursed in disapproval.

Agatha looked at her watch. "I'm sorry," she said. "Did I get the visiting hours wrong? Am I interrupting rest time?"

"Exercise," Revere said. "They should be exercising." Frieda, Lupita and Norma got out of bed. They shuffled past Revere and into the hall.

"Even during visiting hours?" Agatha asked, looking at Miranda instead of Revere.

"It's strongly encouraged," said Miranda. She stood up.

"You can talk and walk at the same time, can't you?" said Revere. She ignored Agatha and gave Miranda a scolding look.

"You're absolutely right," Miranda said. She put on her most obedient face, doing what she could to avoid being on Revere's list of problem cases. The instinct was a futile one, she knew. Donovan had her in his sights, so what difference did Revere's opinion of her make? Eyes were on her, whether they were Revere's or not. "Would it be all right if we went outside?" she asked. She hadn't ventured out of the Institute's doors since her arrival. The thought appealed to her now, especially since it would be easier to speak freely with Agatha on the grounds than in the halls. Other patients did walk outside. She saw them from her window.

"In the rain?" Revere asked sharply.

"Oh." Miranda looked back at the window and the drops running down the pane. "Never mind, then."

"That's all right," said Agatha, taking her arm. "Why don't we go to the library again?"

Revere pointed at Miranda. "Just be sure you don't go there to sit for ages. If I don't see you, I'll come looking."

"I'll be good," Miranda promised.

Revere sniffed, then swept out of the room.

Miranda and Agatha headed out into the corridor. Agatha looked dismayed when she saw the parade of shambling patients.

"What…" she began, then trailed off.

"Exactly," said Miranda. "There have been developments in your absence."

"They aren't encouraging ones."

"Why? You don't believe in exercise."

"This isn't exercise," said Agatha, her voice barely above a whisper.

"No," said Miranda. "It isn't."

Agatha took the first turn, following the signs to the library. Miranda slowed down. Agatha looked at her.

"You don't want to go to the library?"

Miranda waited until they overtook an old woman shuffling along with a cane. A few more steps, and they were in a bit of a gap between patients. "I had a bad experience there last time," Miranda said.

"Should we avoid it?"

She wasn't sure. Did it matter anymore? Was anywhere in the Institute safer than anywhere else? The library, at least, would give them a chance at some privacy. She wouldn't be there alone, and she knew to be guarded about what she looked at.

"Let's go," she said. "Be careful, though." She glanced around before speaking again. "The floor pattern is a labyrinth. Don't let it catch you up."

They arrived outside the library door a few minutes later. Miranda could feel the undertow of the pattern. It wasn't strong, no worse than the withdrawing of a wave at her ankles.

"Are you all right?" said Agatha.

"Can you feel it?"

"Yes. I can fight it too, though."

"Then so can I."

She opened the door. Going in was like stepping into a hard smile. *Been a while*, said the empty room. *Remember me?*

Miranda kept her gaze level. She walked over to the window and stood facing out.

The rain made patterns on the glass. Miranda looked past it, to the grounds below.

"I see what you mean," Agatha said at her side.

"You saw?"

"I did. Funny that we missed that before."

"We weren't looking before."

"Do you think we can speak freely here?"

Miranda shrugged. "Do we have a choice? No people here, at least. I don't know what else might be listening."

"Or if it can listen in other places, beyond these walls. I think it might."

"Then it's not going to like what I have to say," said Miranda. She told Agatha what had happened during her absence. Speaking quietly made it a little easier to stay calm. When she finished, the relief of having opened up to someone left her weak. She sat down, daring Revere to come in and object.

Agatha sat too. "Has there been any sign of Payton Wallace on the premises?" she asked.

"No," Miranda said, surprised. "Should he have been?"

Agatha sighed. "I'm pretty sure he's been Donovan's useful idiot. I had hoped I'd made him mine. I guess not." Then she talked about her trip.

Miranda's relief bled away.

Afterwards, they didn't speak for a few minutes. They held hands, processing the horror.

"So," Agatha finally said, "secret passages. How very gothic."

"Very," Miranda agreed.

Their forced levity rang cold in the hostile space of the library.

"You aren't planning on exploring them, are you?" Agatha asked.

"No! Not before we have a plan."

They looked at each other. They both knew she would have to go into that darkness sooner or later.

Miranda ran a hand down her face. "What *is* this place?"

"The abbey rebuilt," said Agatha, "and fused with the Stroud Spiral." She grimaced. "I shouldn't say *abbey*. I don't think the ruins were ever an abbey at all. Not a human one." She paused. "That's one answer. That's what this building is made of. But that isn't really what it *is*."

"Architecture is frozen music," Miranda quoted, thinking back to an earlier conversation, when it had still seemed possible that the Stroud Institute was a place of healing. "Architecture is embodied poetry."

"Architecture is ritual," Agatha finished.

"Not just the architecture," said Miranda. "The people in it. The walking."

"Yes," said Agatha. "The right kind of movement in the right kind of structure."

"A ritual to what end, then?"

"A summoning, I think." Agatha held up a hand and Miranda held back the question she had been about to ask. "To summon what?" Agatha went on. "We don't know. What will the being do? We don't know. Though we know it will be bad."

"Things are bad enough now. I don't want to imagine what they'll be like when whatever it is gets here."

"I think," Agatha said, "that it may already be present. Partially. We're looking at a gradual manifestation."

"Why do you say that?"

"The vibrations in the stone of the building. They're already happening, but growing stronger."

Miranda thought about her most recent vision, and how horribly tangible it had been. She still had the taste of the worms in her mouth. "All right," she said. "I can buy that. So what do we do about it?"

"You could see about leaving," Agatha said.

"To go where? Be safe how? Anyway, you know I can't leave. I can't run away. I won't."

"I know." Agatha squeezed her shoulder. "I had to suggest you get away. I couldn't live with myself if I didn't, even though I knew you'd stay to fight. You understand?"

"I do," said Miranda. "I do. Thank you. But since I'm not leaving, what do we do?"

"We have to learn more," said Agatha. "What I found out in Scotland has helped, but it isn't enough."

"Right, then." Miranda braced herself. "What's our path for finding out more? Is there another archive to comb through?"

"If there is, Donovan Stroud has it."

"I see." Miranda's mouth went dry. "We have to break into his quarters."

"You say *we* ..." Agatha began.

"When I should be saying *I*."

"I can't ask this of you," said Agatha. "No one can or should."

"I know." Miranda's stomach fell away from her when she thought about what she would have to do. It dropped into darkness, leaving her hollow. "I said I would stay and fight, and this is how I can."

"I'm not even sure what you should be looking for." Agatha sounded both sorrowful and frustrated. "Papers or journals relating to Magnus Stroud would be a start, but there may be more, items I can't imagine."

"I've done research before where I didn't know what I was looking for until I saw it," Miranda said.

"This will be more dangerous than the British Museum's reading room."

"Don't I know it."

"So you're sure?" Agatha asked.

"Positive." Terrified, but positive.

"Then I have something for you." Agatha opened her bag and pulled out a thick volume. She handed it to Miranda.

"A Wordsworth collection," Miranda said. "This is thoughtful, but–"

"Open it."

She did. The center of the pages had been cut out. A set of lockpicks sat in the rectangular hole.

Miranda smiled. "You knew I'd say yes."

"I felt guilty bringing them, but I knew I had to. There's no way I could gain access to his apartment. It will be hard enough for you, but at least you're already on the inside."

"It might not be as difficult as you think."

"Oh?"

"Next Friday, there's a special session being conducted by Daria Miracle, one for the entire Institute. It's going to be held in the theater. A true occasion. Donovan is going to be in attendance." She gave a crooked smile. "It has been Announced."

"That sounds perfect," said Agatha. "Very convenient."

"Isn't it just. That worries me."

"You think he knows you'll try something?"

"What if he *wants* me to?"

Agatha didn't answer. Miranda kept her eyes on the world beyond the window, but what she saw was the labyrinth.

She had no choice, and a single path to walk.

All the way to what waited at the center.

Chapter Twenty-Two

The dreams and the visions pulled back again. Miranda's nights calmed. She slept well, and the instinctive anticipation of a blow melted away.

As her body relaxed, her dread grew. She had been right before to see a pattern, and that the waters of nightmare were just withdrawing ahead of a tsunami. She feared how terrible the next blow would be. It might deliver a nightmare from which she could not wake. Or one that would swallow all of Arkham.

Or worse.

She did nothing in the days before the grand event on Friday. She ate her meals, slept, and she walked, like all the other patients. She continued to feel better, too. No more fever, much less weakness. The cough left her alone sometimes for an hour or more, as long as she didn't take a deep breath. Her energy seemed almost normal.

She distrusted her recovery. She didn't believe in it because she could find no reason for it. Rest and then exercise were not cause enough. She found that she could believe in some force that gave her the strength to walk and walk and walk, because it needed her, and everyone else, to enact its ritual.

She walked, and she did as the nurses said. She read, and she took on her first volunteer work. The duties were light, limited to delivering a few trays on this floor. That gave her the chance to get to know other patients a little more, but she restricted her conversation to mundane subjects. That wasn't difficult. Her roommates had become less and less talkative, withdrawing into the inner vistas of their own dark paths and doubts. She accepted the reality that she could not count on any of them to be allies in the fight, because they could not fight. How could they, when she didn't know how to yet herself?

Maybe the summoning could not be fought. Maybe she would only make her suffering worse by trying to hold back the tsunami. Maybe she should just let the wave wash over her.

Maybe, maybe, maybe. At least the doubts were still her own. She did not have to face the collapse of faiths and certainties that she had never had.

Could any of them be saved? If the coming horror were defeated, what would happen to all patients who had followed the path so deep into the labyrinth?

She didn't know, and the question tormented her. She didn't want to believe that anything she did would be too late for them. She had to hope that they could be helped.

But the days went by, and they went further down the path. And more patients disappeared. The corridors were full of the walking obsessed, but not as full as they should have been.

Payton Wallace put off visiting the Stroud Institute for as long as he could. The things Agatha Crane had said bothered him. They nagged at him during the day, gnawing at the strength of his smile, and at the pleasure he took in public appearances. At night, they niggled at his sleep, fraying the edges of his dreams. He kept touch on anything that hit the news about the sanatorium, and he spoke to Donovan Stroud a few times on the phone. Nothing turned up that seemed alarming. Of course, that was precisely what Agatha had told him not to trust.

He heard about the deaths, and they made him think he should worry. There were also reports of the people released, cured, and those made him feel better. Never enough, though, to relax completely.

Payton knew he should go to the sanatorium and see things for himself. Look around with new eyes. Put his acumen to work. The problem was, being seen there would connect him to the Institute, and he didn't want that, not if things went wrong.

On the other hand, what if things went wrong, and he hadn't made a show of investigating? Wouldn't that be worse?

He went back and forth on the question and finally decided to go. On a gray Wednesday, with the wind blowing hard, he called Donovan to say he was coming over, and drove to the Institute.

The wind sprayed water from the fountain over him as he got out of the car. He wiped his face and looked at the grounds of the Institute. All of this used to be his family's. But it wasn't any more, just as he had said to Agatha. Whatever happened on this land, it was not his responsibility.

Then why, when he looked at the lawns and the trees, did he feel a connection? It was almost as if the land owned him.

Nonsense. Where did that idiocy come from? It wasn't worthy of him. Payton was a practical man. He dealt in the realities of the political world. The reality he had to face here was the political fallout if he had helped push through some kind of disaster. If he got out in front of the problem, though, and warned of the disaster, then he might save his career.

He trotted up the stairs and reached for the doors, and they startled him by opening before his touch.

Donovan stepped outside. "Payton!" he said. "Always wonderful to have you here. I was in my office and saw you pull up, and I thought we might give ourselves the gift of fresh air for a bit. What do you say?"

"Sure," said Payton, wrong-footed.

"Excellent!" Donovan took his arm and guided him back down the stairs. "A stroll through the gardens will do us both a power of good." He turned right at the bottom of the stairs and started down a narrow path, marked out by gray flagstones, that meandered away from the drive.

They wandered around to the back of the Institute and then away from the building and into the trees, always following the stones. The path's direction looked random to Payton, a pointless meander in and out of the trees, yet as he walked, he felt himself drawn from one stone to the next as if a clear purpose guided his steps.

The ground kept drawing his eyes. He thought about the dead that had lain here, and perhaps still did. He thought about Donovan's reassurances on that front, and about the money that had made even the possibility of a problem go away. The old pest house was a forgotten piece of Arkham's past. Payton had been surprised Agatha had known about it.

"So," said Donovan. "To what do I owe the pleasure?"

"I thought I'd drop in, find out how things are going. It's been a while."

"Far too long! You know you're always welcome here, councilman. And things are going very well, very well indeed."

"I've been told there are some issues."

Donovan laughed. He clapped Payton on the back. "Show me the institution, of any kind, without issues, and I'll show you a miracle. Or a lie. There are always issues, and each one is an opportunity, leading to greater perfection."

"So there's nothing to worry about."

"I can't begin to imagine why you'd think there could be."

"You'd tell me if there was," Payton insisted.

"What possible business could this be of yours?"

Donovan's smile was so wide, his tone so cheerful, that Payton thought he had misheard. He had to remind himself that he was Councilman Payton Wallace, and that people didn't speak to him like that. "I staked my reputation on this place," he snapped. "And if I have to call in an inspection to preserve that reputation, I will."

"You should feel free to do so at any time," said Donovan. "But why would you? Tell me, are you in some way threatening me with something? I ask only for the purpose of clarification, you understand."

"No, I'm not trying to threaten you."

"Because you were very well compensated," Donovan continued. "So a threat would be very ill-mannered. Not to mention foolish. I doubt any sort of public outcry would do you any good."

"I wasn't–"

Donovan didn't let him speak. He carried on, relentless, smiling the whole time. "And you shouldn't ever imagine you can distance yourself from the Institute, councilman. Not with your connection to the land."

"It isn't mine."

"Isn't it? Perhaps the ownership runs the other way, then. You may have no legal ownership, but there is the fact of history, and you still saw to it that the land was untouched, as I asked. You exercised control. You are linked to the ground we walk on. Don't you feel it?"

Payton did. He felt heavier, as if each step reverberated to the center of the Earth.

"I would even say that you couldn't leave this path even if you wanted to."

The thought that Donovan was right terrified Payton. "That's nonsense," he said, his mouth dry, his voice weak. He didn't try to break from the direction of the stones.

Donovan laughed again. "Of course it is! All your worries are! Let me prove how well things are going. We're having a performance for all the patients on Friday. Why don't you come? It will put your mind at ease. You'll see that we are moving in exactly the right direction."

Friday evening arrived as both a threat and a relief. The thought of what she had to do frightened Miranda so much, she could barely swallow. But at least she would act.

After supper, the nurses swept through the wards, shepherding the flock for Daria Miracle's performance. Miranda had hoped she could duck aside without being noticed, but no such luck. Revere marched behind her and her roommates, guiding them through the halls to the theater.

She wondered if Donovan had told Revere to make certain that Miranda attended. She found that possibility preferable to the one where Donovan wanted her to do what she was about to attempt.

The theater was in the central block of the Institute. It took up most of the floor one up from the lobby. Miranda and her roommates were in the last crush of arrivals, and she managed to take a seat in the back row, close to the door and away from the people who knew her.

The theater could hold hundreds. There was room for every patient, and all the staff, and there were still many empty seats. Miranda wondered what Donovan had in mind for this space. What events did he imagine it could host? What call would there be for twice the current number to be present?

Unpleasant possibilities hovered, half-formed, at the edge of her mind.

The ceiling, a shallow dome like the one of the entrance hall, called Miranda's eyes with such insistence that after a first, stunned glance, she knew she should not look at it and tore her eyes away. A massive fresco of a storm dominated the entire dome. The swirl and clash of dark clouds had such detail and a sense of depth that it seemed to move. It lured the eye and the mind to its center, where the darkness became deep and secretive.

Miranda looked around at her fellow patients. Many of them had their heads back, mouths open and slack, as they stared at the clouds, following the convolutions of the storm. Though seated, they were still traveling the labyrinth, their minds tracing the paths marked out for them by the clouds. The ritual had not paused.

The stage below was bare except for a single chair made from dark wood, polished with age and upholstered with material the faded red of old tapestry. A relic, Miranda guessed, brought over from Stroud Hall.

A movie screen dominated the wall behind the stage. Beneath the stage, a full orchestra tuned up.

At eight, the lights dimmed, and a spotlight shone on the chair and the center stage area. Donovan Stroud walked out from the left wing and into the spotlight.

He waved at the audience. "I'm Donovan Stroud," he said. "Some of you know me, and I know some of you. But we don't all know each other nearly as well as I would like. And though some of you have just arrived, and some of you have been here since we opened, I want to take this opportunity to welcome all of you. I mean that. I really do. This isn't just me spouting off the usual pat phrases. I'm speaking from the heart. Don't believe me? Then look!" He stretched out his arms, hands wide. "See! No notes! No cue cards!"

Applause. Laughter, followed by a lot of coughing.

Donovan grinned. He shook his head and shrugged in self-deprecation. "You're too kind," he said. "Too kind, my friends. And you *are* my friends. Even if we haven't met in person yet – and we will – you are my friends just by being here, and entrusting yourself to my care. The Stroud Institute is a dream, a potential, and you are going to turn that dream, that potential, into a reality. Have no doubts about that."

More clapping, and he applauded the audience. "Give yourselves credit. Please. You aren't my patients. You're my partners. We are going to achieve extraordinary things together. We already have, and just you wait!"

Rapturous applause. In the thunder, Miranda heard the energy of the desperate. The man before them spoke with energy, confidence, and an absence of doubt. They needed him. They needed the rescue he promised.

"I'm here to introduce a woman who doesn't need an introduction. All of you know her. All of you have been working with her. What I'm going to introduce, then, is what she will present to you tonight. Daria Miracle has spoken to all of you about the path, about walking through your troubles and your anxieties until you come out the other side. She has taken you by the hand and helped you find the way. Tonight, she is going to *show* you the way. Tonight, you will see the other side of Daria. You know her as counselor and philosopher. Now you will know the artist. Art is the voice of what cannot be said or conveyed through explanation. Art is transcendent. Let yourselves be transported. Let us *all* be transported. My friends, my partners, I give you Daria Miracle."

To more applause, the loudest and most desperate yet, Donovan bowed and sat down in the chair. The orchestra struck up. It played a sinuous, insidiously infectious melody. It coiled through Miranda's blood, urging her to rise, to follow, to descend. Daria came in from the right. She wore a black bodysuit wrapped in yards of flowing, diaphanous veils and scarves. She was the night and its clouds, come to dance with the wind.

She twirled once, then leapt into the spotlight. She landed in a crouch, arms wrapped around herself. Her head jerked up, her eyes wide. She stared into the spotlight. As if it were the sun, and she a dark flowering, she rose from the crouch, face ecstatic, arms stretching out to embrace the light. She arched her back, stood on pointe, and at the moment of her greatest extension, the spotlight went out.

The screen came to life. An experimental film unspooled. No, Miranda thought, correcting herself, this wasn't experimental. She would have called the film that in the innocent times before the Stroud Institute. There was nothing *experimental* about this. Donovan knew exactly what he had created. The ritual of the Stroud Institute continued, now in a different, more intense form.

Images cascaded across the screen, none visible for more than a few seconds, most barely a bright flicker before they vanished. Some frames were blank emptiness. Others appeared to melt and burn away, backdrops for Daria's gyrating, convulsing silhouette. Narrow paths and labyrinths appeared, vanished and returned. Patterns in stone, in hedges, in sand and in snow, hypnotic, insistent, calling, commanding.

Donovan wasn't even trying to hide the existence of the ritual any longer. He had dropped the mask.

Miranda felt time slipping away.

She wrenched her eyes from the screen. She stared at her feet, steadying her mind and trying to tune out the music. When she felt ready, she got to her feet. She edged past the few patients seated between her and the door. At the closed door, she hesitated. When she opened it, light from the hall would flood in. She would be seen.

She had no choice.

Her path, determined for her.

The screen flashed white, and she took the moment. She pushed out through the door and closed it again as quickly as she could. Then she hurried to the elevator, her rasping breath sounding deafening in the empty halls.

She could hope no one noticed her leave. The audience dazzled by the bright screen, Donovan facing the projector beam and seeing only a black mass of the audience.

That was reasonable, right? That wasn't just wishful thinking, right?

She wasn't doing exactly what Donovan had laid out for her, right?

It didn't matter. No choice, no choice. The only way forward. The only way she might be able to fight.

She took the elevator up to Donovan's apartment. She tried the door and was relieved to find it locked. Maybe he didn't want her in there after all. She fished the picks out of the pocket of her robe, knelt in front of the lock, and got to work.

She wished there had been a way to practice. Agatha had explained, in detail, how to use the tools, but the instructions, full as they were, had also sounded second-hand. Someone else had explained to Agatha how to pick locks, and she had passed the knowledge on to Miranda.

She was going to look very silly if this didn't work.

She felt in the lock, probing and trying to visualize the mechanism she was supposed to be moving. When the clicks came and she had the door open, she grunted with surprise. She looked at her watch. It had taken her less than five minutes.

"You have a future in this," she muttered.

Donovan had left a table light on – most likely to light his way when he returned, not for her benefit, she told herself. She took a quick look in the living room, but saw nothing she hadn't seen before.

She found his office at the end of the hall. She had to turn the light on here. She rushed to the window and closed the Venetian blinds, adding the hope that no one could see the light from outside to her lengthening list of wishes.

The room's roll top desk was open to her inspection. A quick look at the papers on its surface showed her administrative memos and receipts. She pulled open the drawers and found dozens of file folders. She would never have the time to go through them all. She took a step back from the desk, despair forming in the pit of her stomach.

She looked around, then moved to the display case in the opposite corner of the office. Its glass shelves held jewels on violet cushions and small sculptures that made Miranda hiss in distaste. They seemed to be mythological serpents of some kind. She had never seen anything like them before. They made her want to scratch inside her head. Their stone looked old. And wet.

A book sat on the bottom shelf, hard to see unless she crouched down. The dark leather cover was battered and cracked with age.

Too much to hope for that this was what she needed to find?

Another lock to struggle with. More to go wrong and more time to eat up, so the book had better be worth it.

The lock on the display case, smaller than the one on the apartment door, gave her more trouble. She swore at it. Stubborn, it taunted her. Finally, it relented, and she opened the case.

She picked up the book. It felt cold and damp. She opened the cover, and found the journal of Magnus Stroud.

Too easy. Too easy. It couldn't possibly be this simple, could it?

Yes, because it wasn't that simple. What was she going to do with the journal? She couldn't steal it. Not if she wanted to have some chance of pretending to herself that Donovan didn't know how much of a threat, if any, she and Agatha might be.

No. She had to read it here.

She had no idea how long Daria's performance would last, no idea when Donovan might come marching through the door.

No idea, and no choice. The realization made her hate Donovan all the more. She felt as if all the choices in her life had been illusions, every step a predetermined one down a single, twisting path, bringing her to this moment, when she finally saw that there had never been any branches off her destiny at all. The place had always been her destination. She had always been fated to move to the desk and sit, perched and tense, on the edge of Donovan's swivel chair. Always been fated to read this journal with her heart in her mouth, terrified of what she might hear in the apartment.

Terrified of what she might learn.

"Damn you," Miranda whispered, cursing all the souls and entities and currents of events that had brought her here.

She could not fight her destiny. So she didn't. Under the familiar but alien glow of a banker's desk lamp, with shadows lapping at the edge of her awareness, she began to read.

Chapter Twenty-Three
Scotland, 1807

When the nanny was installed in the carriage, Magnus handed her his infant son, swaddled in blankets in spite of the August heat. Millicent Hardwick took Braden Stroud into her arms and held him protectively.

"I'll watch over him well, my lord," she promised.

"I know you will," said Magnus. His eyes never left the child. He could almost see down Braden's road of service to Crothoaka. *Your destiny is already written, my son.*

"Such a terrible shame," said Millicent. "Such a shame." She shook her head. "To have fallen so ill, so quickly, and for so long."

Magnus nodded, patient. He had all the time in the world. Millicent had served at the Yorkshire estate for years, looking after Magnus' young cousins. She had only just arrived, and he was sending her back immediately. She would not set foot in Stroud Hall, or see Braden's mother.

"If you don't mind my saying so, my lord, though I know it isn't my place, you're doing right by the wee thing. He'll be better off elsewhere until his mother isn't so poorly."

"I appreciate your saying so, Millicent. Those are my thoughts exactly. We will join you when we can."

He shut the carriage door and watched it drive off through the gates, dust rising in its wake.

Magnus started back to the Hall. The heat was suffocating. It had been a broiling August to date, excessively so, and there hadn't been a drop of rain in over a month. Magnus felt the heat go deep into his lungs when he breathed, as if the air were burning.

A perfect day for the culmination of his efforts.

Back at the Hall, he climbed the grand staircase to the second floor, and went down the west wing to the locked door at the far end. He leaned his forehead against the door. "It is done," he said to the being inside.

A faint stirring answered him. Magnus' hand brushed against the door. He almost knocked, but restrained himself. What lived in the room had forbidden him to enter, and he would not disobey.

He didn't know what to call the being on the other side of the door. He could not think of it as *Christina*, not since Braden was born and the transformation had begun.

Perhaps it had not really been Christina who had come back from her journey beneath the abbey. The real Christina, the poet whose work he admired, had pleaded with him to show her what lay below. He had found that he had had no choice but to let her go. He did not own the secret of the ruins. Crothoaka owned him, and Crothoaka wanted Christina to see, and know, and for her to do that alone.

Magnus stood sentinel in the ruins until she returned, and when she did, she was transformed. She spoke to him with a tone of command, and with eyes would brook no contradiction. "We must have a child," she said. "A child of destiny."

He had obeyed.

And so Braden had come into the world, to be raised in the knowledge of Crothoaka from the very beginning, to be taught the way of the labyrinth from his first day to last, and so be the first of the new line of Strouds.

Braden had only been a day old when Christina locked the door and forbade anyone from entering. The servants exchanged looks, but Magnus told them to do as she said, and they could hardly challenge him. Phillips asked just once whether the count wished him to send for the doctor. Magnus told him no, and Phillips let the matter drop.

"Farewell," Christina said as she closed the door on Magnus. "Do not look to see me again."

Magnus had obeyed, just as he had in everything else concerning Braden and, today, the Republic of the Arts.

The climax of his labors was at hand.

"I go to finish things," Magnus said. "I will return tonight."

More stirrings in the room. Eager ones.

Magnus left the Hall and walked through the heat to the Stroud Spiral. The sun speared his eyes. He held his hands up to his face. It seemed astonishing that they did not blister in the heat.

All perfect, all as it should be.

At the Spiral, he walked into the gap between the two most massive boulders, and he began.

Crothoaka guided his steps. He gave himself over to the impulse that came from outside his own being and told him when to turn left, when right, when to double back, when to circle which boulder. He never hesitated. He never had a choice to make. His feet walked the true path through the Spiral as surely as if it had been marked out in crimson light before him.

The afternoon fell away. Magnus had no sense of time. Nothing mattered, and nothing existed, except the need to trace the labyrinth, to perform the slow, utterly precise dance that was itself yet one more step of the larger slow, yet utterly precise dance he had been engaged in since the night below the ruins, and even before. Without knowing it, he had been dancing all his life for Croth-oaka.

When he finished, he found himself outside the Spiral, leaning against the stone that, in defiance of the heat of the day, was cold.

The sun had set, leaving the land to an evening as oppressive as high noon.

Magnus jerked into motion again. He made his way out from the trees, onto the moor, and to Alfred's cottage. The painter opened at his knock. Alfred looked drained, starved. His skin hung in folds on his emaciated frame. He had lost much of his hair.

"My lord," said Alfred, his voice weak and hoarse. He stepped aside to let Magnus in.

The interior of the cottage had become a frozen vortex of art. Canvasses covered every square inch of every wall, every flat surface, and slid over each other in chaotic piles on the floor. There were still landscapes here, recognizably in the style of the Alfred Claymot who had arrived at the Republic of the Arts. Many more paintings, though, showed his new more obsessive and more sinuous brushwork. Perhaps they were landscapes. They were certainly nightmares.

"I wanted to tell you once more," Magnus said, "how pleased I am with the portrait you did for me." Alfred had completed it just before Braden's birth. It was, Magnus thought, a masterpiece. It looked, from anything more than a few feet away, like the work of the old Alfred. The new one, though, seethed beneath the surface appearance, visible only up close, and at the right angle. Or by touch. The portrait squirmed when touched.

"You honor me, my lord," said Alfred. "It does my soul good to know that I have done something that feels important." He coughed, and his entire frame shook.

"Your work is not done yet," Magnus said. "You may take my word for it."

"Thank you, my lord, thank you." Alfred struggled with a bow. He had to use the edge of a table to push himself upright again. "May I ask how you… ah… how… Christina is faring?"

Magnus smiled at Alfred's hesitation. He and Christina had not wed. The great work of the summoning had no room or time for such pointless customs. "She is deep into her journey," he said, finding it odd to refer to Christina in the present tense. "As are we all."

Alfred nodded. He coughed again, and clutched the table for support, knocking a canvas to the floor. "I am finding the way so hard, my lord. So very hard. And I cannot see the center of the labyrinth."

Magnus put his arm around Alfred's shoulders. "But you have reached it," he said.

"I have?"

Eyes shining, Alfred looked up at him, so he didn't see Magnus pull the dagger from his belt. Magnus rammed it up through Alfred's throat. Alfred jerked. His feet danced with the shock of death. Blood rushed warm down Magnus' hand. He withdrew the dagger and let Alfred's body fall. The artist's head bounced sharply off the corner of the table on the way down.

Magnus broke the leg of an easel, wrapped the top in paint-soaked rags, and lit them from one of the candles Alfred had been burning for light. It took no effort at all to set the cottage on fire. So dry, so hot, so filled with fumes, the room burst into flame at the merest suggestion from Magnus' torch.

He left the cottage at a run, dagger and torch in hand, and the fire followed in his wake. It spread out behind him, over the moor, and roared with crackling eagerness as it reached the trees.

Fueled by ritual and commanded by it, the fire traced the path of its own labyrinth. When it was done, it would consume the forest, but it had to follow the lines of the dance, and Magnus led it. He ran from cottage to cottage, tireless, ecstatic. He slashed throats and thrust the torch into faces. He killed every one of the artists whose patron he had been for a year. He destroyed the Republic of the Arts, and he rejoiced in the sacrifice. The Republic, he now understood, had only ever been created for this purpose, to be the offering to a greater dream.

The fire surrounded the Hall when he walked back up the drive to the front entrance. The earth moaned, its voice deep and pained. Magnus had seen the boulders of the Spiral burst into flame, one more wonder on a night thick with them.

The servants had gathered on the porch, terrified by the conflagration. Huddling together, they reminded Magnus of his arrival at Stroud Hall. They had been outside then too, to greet him.

He killed them. They were so stunned by his attack, so baffled by the sudden end of their world, that only the last few even tried to defend themselves. They went down easily.

Magnus entered the Hall and ran up to the room with the locked door. He reached for the key, but the door opened on its own. A young, dark-haired woman emerged. She was beautiful, her every movement a serpent's dance. Magnus stared at the being forged out of the flesh of Christina Blackstone. He bowed his head in worship.

"Truly," he said, "you are a miracle."

"Then Miracle shall be my name," said the woman.

"The ritual is complete," Magnus told her.

"Is it?" she asked, and though she smiled, her voice was stern.

"… no," Magnus admitted. If all had been accomplished, Crothoaka would be in the world. The god was not. "I don't understand."

"Come," said the Miracle. She hooked her arm through Magnus' and led him slowly back down to the ground floor, and to his study.

Waving, orange light bathed the room. The windows looked out onto an unbroken wall of flame.

The Miracle guided Magnus to his desk. She sat him down, put his journal before him, dipped his quill pen in ink, and put it in his hand.

"The work of all your life before tonight has been but a prologue to the great ritual," she said. "Tonight is not the end, but the real beginning. The writing of the first chapter. And even that is not yet complete."

She opened his journal to the first blank page. "Write it down," she said. "Write everything down. This will be the work of generations of Strouds, and I will be there to guide them."

Magnus had begun writing as soon as the Miracle told him. He paused now, the nib hovering over the page, not quite touching. "Will it not fall to me to guide my son?"

"It will not."

He looked up at her. "Why not?"

She smiled again. "Because the sacrifice of this night must be complete."

"I understand."

And he did. Nothing more needed to be said. He saw what he had to do. He saw it in such precise detail that he wrote his coming actions down too as if they had already been done.

"There," he said, satisfied, and presented the journal for the Miracle's inspection.

"Good," she said. "The work is good."

"Thank you," said Magnus.

He left her in the study without looking back. He walked out of the Hall, out onto the drive. The barrier of flame rose higher than the trees, blinding, impassible, devouring, and yet advancing no closer to the Hall itself. The fire obeyed as he did.

He didn't hesitate. He walked off the drive and into the fire. He knew he would scream when the pain hit.

He did. For much longer than he had expected.

The journal smelled of smoke, Miranda thought. It smelled of horror.

She knew more now, but still not enough, and still not how to fight. Maybe this would make sense to Agatha, though. She might draw some conclusions from what Magnus had done that might help them.

The journal didn't end with Magnus' atrocities. New hands took over, the lineage of the count chronicling the growth of the ritual year after year, decade after decade. Always more sacrifice, more murder, more cruelty, and more philosophical ravings.

Miranda started. Was that someone in the hall? In the living room? She listened, breath held.

The apartment clicked, the sound of a pipe in the walls, not the tread of footsteps.

She read again, and she came, at last, to the final hand. She read Donovan's entries. She read about how he moved the ruins and the Spiral to Arkham, and rebuilt them as the Institute. His words and his penmanship became frenzied as he drew near the completion of the ritual.

Hail Crothoaka, the Worm of the Labyrinth! Hail the conjurer of dark exegesis! Hail the sower of doubt! You have been with us always in the interstices of belief, and in the fractures of contradictions of faith. Come now and teach us the unity that comes through final collapse! Come, Great Labyrinth, and takes us all to the heart of your devouring!

That was all.

Miranda looked at her watch. She gasped. She had been here for well over an hour. She slipped the book back into the display cabinet and locked it again, Donovan's encomium ringing through her mind. She had memorized it without trying.

She tiptoed out of the office, down the hall, and to the apartment door. The emptiness of the rooms felt like the camouflage of a predator. She put her hand on the door handle and held one of the lockpicks like a dagger, ready to stab Donovan in the eye if she found him in the corridor.

She yanked the door open, and more emptiness confronted her.

Shut the door, lock it, and now hurry, hurry, take the stairs and not the elevator, and why do you have to breathe so hard, and why are your legs so weak, can't you go faster, go faster, go faster?

She made it to her floor, and to still more emptiness. No one was back from the performance.

That had to be it. She told herself she was not suddenly alone in the hospital. She told herself the hidden passages were not filled with things that had been patients and nurses, all watching her and hungering.

She hurried again, feeling so weak now, so tired, ready to drop, and the trip back to the theater was much too long. She would never get there in time, and she would have to explain to the people she would suddenly run into why she had left and where she had been.

But she saw no one, and as she approached the theatre, she heard the booming of music rising to a crescendo.

Instead of trying to slip back inside, she waited just to one side of the doors.

When, a few minutes later, the performance did end, she let the first dozen or more audience members walk by, and then she joined the stream. No one seemed to notice. They were all too dazed.

Or too far down the labyrinth.

Back in her room, in her bed, the blanket drawn up to her chin, Miranda thought about how smoothly, really, everything had gone, and she wondered why Donovan wanted it so.

PART III

Chapter Twenty-Four

Miranda slept.

Lupita lay awake, staring up. In the dim light from the hall, the ceiling was a doubtful mist of gray. Deeper and less solid than it should have been, it promised and threatened visions. Its murk might produce the shape of her fears. Would it not offer her hopes too?

But she would need hopes for her imagination to shape them, wouldn't she? They couldn't come from nowhere.

The ceiling's blur deepened with her tears. She wiped her eyes. Stop being like this. You weren't like this before getting sick. And definitely not before coming here.

She thought not, anyway. The memory of who she was like before became elusive. Hadn't there been a Lupita strong in conviction, and strong in faith? Had that been a real person, or just the construct of what she wished she were like?

She wanted answers. The ceiling offered nothing. In the night, the only answers were ones that hurt.

Daria offered things that seemed like answers. *Seemed.*

Lupita turned on her side. She looked toward Miranda's bed. She wanted to speak with Miranda very badly. Miranda was like the Lupita of memory or imagination. She had made it clear to Lupita that she was willing to talk and listen, but the new Lupita had been scared to accept the offer. Now, though, after the evening's performance, she needed to talk. Not to Frieda. The old Lupita would have laughed at the idea of confiding in that woman. Even the new Lupita saw the humor in that. And she didn't want to talk to Norma, either. She didn't trust Norma.

She trusted Miranda, because Miranda didn't appear to trust anything.

Lupita wanted to know what Miranda thought about Daria Miracle's performance. Lupita had been mesmerized every second of its duration. She had been unable to look away, even though a part of her had known she should. The ecstasy, and the sense of revelation, that she always experienced during the counseling sessions had been a hundred times more powerful. But when the performance ended, and she had shuffled with the other dazed spectators back into the halls, and the magic began to slide away, she began to feel unclean.

She felt even worse now. Everything was wrong. She didn't know where to turn. She kept trying to pray for guidance and failed. The words would not come, or if they did, they seemed alien to her, as if she were pretending to be a woman of faith, as if she did not deserve to call for help. She held tight to her crucifix, clinging to it as she would a life raft, but she knew it would not save her from drowning.

Doubt surrounded her. It mocked her.

Miranda seemed troubled too. Perhaps they could help each other. Perhaps together, they could keep their heads above water.

She had to speak to Miranda.

Lupita got up. She padded over to the other woman's bed. "Miranda," she whispered. "Are you awake?"

Of course she wasn't. She looked profoundly asleep, so far down into unconsciousness she might have been in a coma.

"Miranda," Lupita said again, a little louder. She shook her shoulder, and it was like trying to move a boulder. Could people grow heavier in sleep?

Miranda's stillness frightened Lupita, and she checked to make sure Miranda was still breathing.

"Miranda," she said again, despairing now. There would be no help for her tonight.

Frieda's sudden hiss almost startled Lupita into a scream. "*What are you doing?*"

Lupita turned around, shaking. "I'm sorry. I–"

"You'll wake everyone."

Lupita glanced at Norma. She slept on, her breathing slow and even, a placid smile on her face. Was she really asleep? Lupita didn't fully trust her appearance. Miranda, though, didn't stir.

"I'm sorry," Lupita said again to Frieda. "I just wanted to talk to Miranda."

"Why?" The question was sharp as a dart.

Lupita hesitated. Then, desperate to find a companion for her fears in anyone, anyone at all, even Frieda, she plunged in. "Don't you feel it?" she asked. "You know there's something wrong here."

"I don't know what you're talking about. Go back to bed."

"Please, Frieda. I've seen you looking worried."

"No, you haven't."

"*Please!* Please listen to me. Do you really believe all the things Daria has been telling us? Do you believe in the labyrinth?"

"I want to sleep. Stop being a ninny."

"But do you? Aren't you worried that–"

"I don't want to hear it."

"But–"

"Shut up, shut up, *shut up!*"

Lupita drew back from the venom in Frieda's voice and eyes. Norma slept on in bliss. Miranda remained submerged, as if being held down forcefully in sleep.

Lupita went back to bed. "I'm sorry," she began.

"*Quiet!*"

Lupita froze, motionless. She didn't dare move in case the rustle of a sheet enraged Frieda even more. After a few minutes, Lupita heard long, steady breaths coming from Frieda's bed. They sounded like a point being made.

Lupita closed her eyes, trying to silence her racing mind, trying to sleep.

She failed. She couldn't even keep her eyes shut, or find a comfortable position. Lupita turned onto her side, then her back, and then her side again, twisting and wrinkling the covers, making everything worse and more uncomfortable, her body an enemy, the bed an enemy, and the two at war with her and with each other.

With a sigh, she turned on her back yet again. The sheet tangled around her legs, tying them together. A lump of covers pressed hard against her right flank. She tried to smooth it out.

It moved. The ripple of a hundred tiny legs tickled her through her nightdress.

Her breath hissed out of her lungs in sudden terror. She beat against the sheets, fought to free her legs, kicked and struggled and finally fell out the bed, whining in horror.

She jumped up. The bump under the sheets still moved. She snatched the sheet away. The thing on the bed was almost a foot long. It had the segmented body and legs of a centipede, but was thick as a slug. Its black carapace glistened with slime.

Lupita backed away from the bed, hand at her mouth, scream caught in her throat. She couldn't get the shriek out. She breathed faster and faster, and the scream kept growing, becoming too great. It would break her jaws if it escaped.

Trapped voiceless by nightmare, she fled the room for the corridor. There was light here, at least, but weak. It made everything gray when she needed the blaze of sunlight.

Something skittered behind her.

She ran, desperate for help. The hall was empty, and everyone slept in the rooms she passed. No one saw her and asked what was wrong. If they had, perhaps that would have freed her to speak, and she could have said, and she could have begged anyone, everyone, to do something, anything.

Instead, she saw only nothing, and behind her, the skittering grew louder.

There was more than one, she realized. God in heaven, there was more than one, and they were hunting her.

She couldn't be alone. There had to be staff. If she found no one, then she had to be dreaming, and none of this was real, and she could survive the terror of a nightmare, because it would end, and she would wake.

But she felt the jarring of the floor against her feet, and it hurt for her to breathe, and she had never felt anything, not really, in a nightmare before.

She turned a corner, the skittering closer, and saw the night nurse halfway down the hall. Lupita hurried to catch up with her. She would welcome being scolded. She would welcome embarrassment. She would welcome any unpleasantness as long as it banished the skittering.

"Please!" She had her voice again, but it came out as a wheeze, no louder than a whisper. The night nurse didn't hear her, and marched on.

"Wait!" Lupita begged. No response, but she had almost caught up. She grabbed the nurse's shoulder.

The nurse turned around. She had no face. A mass of worms, each as thick as a thumb, squirmed where there should have been a face.

Lupita found her scream. She stumbled back, arms flailing, as the night nurse reached for her. Wailing, she turned around and ran again. Daggers of broken glass scraped through her lungs, but she ran. She had no direction, no refuge, no thought, but she ran. Screaming, despairing, she ran.

She had no sense of her flight, only the need to escape the nurse, and the skittering that still followed. Lupita only realized where she was when a wooden barrier stopped her. Jerked to full awareness again, she found herself in the entrance hall of the Institute, and stood before the main doors.

She grabbed the handles and pushed, pulled. Locked, the doors did not even rattle. She sobbed and pounded on them, hitting so hard the skin on her knuckles broke open. She looked over her shoulder, dreading the sight of her pursuers.

There was no one.

A cathedral's silence filled the hall.

Lupita's fists paused against the doors. She listened.

No more skittering. No footsteps of the approaching nurse.

Reflexively, she pushed the doors again, and they opened. She stepped out onto the porch. She took a deep breath of the night air. She was free. She could go.

And because nothing stopped her, she hesitated.

It had rained again. The ground was wet, the night cold. She didn't even have a dressing gown.

What was she doing? Only a fool would head out into the night like this. Did she want to make herself even more sick?

But the worms…

Not real. They couldn't be. She had had a nightmare. She must have fallen asleep after all. She had had a nightmare, a very bad one, yes, and she had leapt out of bed, maybe still half-asleep, and tried to escape the dream.

Wasn't that so?

Yes?

No?

She rocked from side to side. She couldn't decide. The reality of the nurse faded with the immediacy of the terror.

But what if she hadn't dreamed? She couldn't go back inside.

She hugged herself. It was too cold. Where did she think she would go? She had no money with her. Home was miles away. Any taxi that would even stop to pick her up would take her right back to the Institute.

Or to the hospital. She could say she had wandered away from there, and got lost. She could.

Every scheme seemed more senseless, more pointless. But going back was still too frightening to contemplate.

She had nothing but doubts.

Descending the steps, she started down the drive. With no goal, she moved because she couldn't stay still. She walked down the wet pavement, hoping for purpose, praying for salvation.

She only found more doubts. They wrapped around her chest, making it hard to breathe, and coiled around her legs, weighing her down. Lupita's feet dragged, as though struggling through ankle-deep mud.

And then she was. She looked down. The pavement of the drive flowed around her, viscous, sucking. The worms of doubt were real, thick as pythons, and they had her. They pulled her legs deeper into the asphalt mire. Lupita screamed, her voice lost and tiny in the vastness of the night. She tried to pull free. The coils squeezed tighter and hauled her down, past her knees, and then up to her thighs. She had no purchase for her feet. The impossible quicksand went down forever, and the depths, hungry, awaited her. She screamed again, and then a length of worm wrapped around her chest. Its embrace tightened. It forced the air from her lungs.

There would be no more screams now.

She flailed, sinking to her waist, and then her ribs. She pushed against the ground and her arms went down to her elbows. The sucking grasp refused to let them go.

Mouth open, tears streaming, hope fleeing, she struggled on, but she could barely move now. The worms had her. The doubts had her. As they pulled her into the ground, and the muck pushed into her mouth and nose, they cursed her with understanding. They had won when she lost the last of her purpose and the last of her certainty. When she lingered on the porch, all direction and faith and belief gone, she had already begun to sink.

She went down into the darkness. Certainty had at last come for her, and it dragged her to the center of the labyrinth.

•••

Frieda stopped pretending to be asleep when Lupita fled the room. She sat up, furious with Lupita for waking her, and even more furious with her for being gone and out of the range of her anger.

She hung on to the rage. As long as she felt it, she could keep the anxiety at bay.

She waited for Lupita to come back, rehearsing the scolding. The minutes went by, and then a half-hour, and Lupita did not return. Frieda wondered where she had gone, and when she did that, she lost hold of her anger. It slipped away, and the gnawing in her chest came back. She frowned hard. *Go away. Go away.* She didn't want the worries. They weren't her. She had felt them too much of late, and she didn't know what had happened to her old confidence that the world was meant to behave as she wished.

This was Lupita's fault. And Miranda's too. And while she was at it, where did Norma get the right to look so serene all the time?

She stirred the ashes of the anger with resentful thoughts. It refused to catch fire again.

She stared absently at Lupita's empty bed, stewing. She chewed her bottom lip.

Something moved under Lupita's sheet.

No. She was not having this. Frieda looked away. She got out of bed. She kept her eyes averted from Lupita's corner of the room as she pulled on her dressing gown and stepped into her slippers. She needed certainty to get rid of the rat in her chest, and to banish the terror that would come if she looked at the sheets and saw them move again.

The labyrinth was the way. So Daria promised. Walk the labyrinth. Reach the center.

The way to feel better. The way to *get* better. The way to be good. Frieda was anxious to be good in the eyes of the Stroud Institute. She needed to be one of the gifted, the special, the chosen. Whatever one of those was the right word, Frieda needed to be that perfect thing.

She started walking the halls, taking the familiar turns, as she had done so many times. She would walk the labyrinth, and that would make her feel better, and then she would sleep, and not think about things that worried her, or imagine things that frightened her, and Lupita could go to hell for starting all this nonsense in the middle of the night.

Frieda was alone for the first few minutes of her walk. She had fallen into the rhythm and was feeling she might walk all the way to dawn when she saw Nurse Holden walking toward her. Holden's rapid head twitch had grown worse, and Frieda couldn't look at the nurse's blurring face without feeling pain behind her eyes. Holden walked with steady, graceful, direct purpose, though. Frieda wondered briefly if she should be surprised Holden was here. Frieda hadn't thought she ever worked the night shift. The questions passed.

They didn't matter. What mattered was showing Holden that Frieda was behaving, and doing her duty by walking, even when everyone else slept.

Holden held up a hand, and Frieda stopped before her.

"What are you walking?" Holden asked. Her voice had a new rasp.

"The labyrinth," said Frieda.

"Do you embrace the labyrinth?"

"I do," said Frieda, and she meant it. She realized that she had never been more certain of anything.

"Are you ready to greet the center?"

"I am."

Holden touched the wall. It parted. Frieda looked into the dark passage that had opened before her. It did not frighten her. She felt excited. She had come to where the path of her life had always been heading.

"Then come with me," said Holden.

They walked into the dark. Frieda knew the dark would soon move, and she welcomed it. She had moved beyond choice, and new worship bloomed in her heart.

In the morning, Miranda woke from a sleep so profound, for a moment she didn't know where she was. Then she took in the room.

And the empty beds.

And Norma's empty smile.

Chapter Twenty-Five

"Good morning, sleepy head," Norma said.

How did she talk without losing that sickening wide smile? Shouldn't she be moving her lips?

"Morning," Miranda muttered.

Norma cocked her head. She blinked with a concern as plastic as her smile. "How are you feeling? You look done in."

Miranda felt worse than that. She felt as if a boulder rested on her chest, while her limbs had turned to lead. She couldn't imagine getting up. She didn't know what was happening to her. She also refused to confide in Norma.

Instead of answering, she said, "Where are the others?"

Norma ignored her question in turn. "Are you looking forward to walking? It's a lovely day."

As opposed to any other day inside the Institute? Miranda grunted.

"I'm sure you're as eager as I am to get going," Norma went on. "It's so invigorating."

"Is it?" Miranda couldn't help herself. She couldn't subject herself to Norma's artificial good cheer and not fight back.

"It really is," said Norma, the smile impervious and eternal. "If you're in the right spirit."

She knows, Miranda thought. She knows where the others are. Or she knows what happened to them. That's what's behind that smile.

She should have pitied Norma, who had been seduced by the power that whispered down the halls of the Institute. She did not believe for a moment that Norma had served Crothoaka before coming here. Norma had been changed, twisted into something other than her true self.

Not made to reveal her true self? Are you sure?

No. She wanted to think no one but Donovan and Daria had been corrupt from the start. She wanted to think that. And if she held true to that belief, she should pity Norma. She really, really, should. But right now, she hated and feared her.

"I'm not one for being in the spirit," Miranda said, encasing her words in ice.

Norma didn't answer. She just kept smiling.

Breakfast came, and there were no trays for Lupita and Frieda. Miranda didn't ask again where the other two were. She would only get lies or confusion in response. And she was so tired. She didn't have the strength for a pointless fight. She had to preserve her energy.

Get through today. Tomorrow, Agatha will be here. Tell her what you learned. She'll know what to do after that, right? Right.

Just because Miranda couldn't see how her knowledge of what had happened and the name of what was coming would help, that didn't mean Agatha would be stymied.

Agatha *had* to know what the next step would be. She had to.

Miranda conserved her strength. Eat, rest, walk, and do as you're told. Get through to tomorrow.

She found that she couldn't imagine the future beyond Sunday.

After breakfast, Nurse Revere appeared. "Time to walk," she said.

Norma leapt out of bed as if it were Christmas morning. Miranda could barely sit up. She had to use her hands to get her legs into position. She pushed off against the mattress to get herself on her feet. She wobbled back and forth, then fell back, knees buckling.

Revere rushed into the room. "What's the matter?" she asked.

On her hands and knees, Miranda said, "So tired… Can't stand." Her breath came in painful gasps. The boulder on her chest was flattening her lungs.

Revere lifted her, the nurse's wiry strength disturbing in its power. *How will I fight you when the time comes?* She settled Miranda back in the bed.

Miranda sighed, and the breath happened all wrong. It hurt her chest and made her cough. Revere stood motionless, looking down at her. Miranda couldn't focus on her.

She just wanted to sleep.

Revere was speaking. "… a doctor…"

Yes, yes, get a doctor. That was a fine idea. Someone ought to do that someday.

Miranda closed her eyes. She floated for a moment on top of the pain, and then she coughed and started to drown. She bobbed in and out of consciousness.

What's happening to me?

When the fever let her think, she understood. She had regressed. All the progress she had made towards recovery had vanished. She felt far sicker than when she had arrived at the Institute.

Down into the delirium of exhaustion and pain. Surfacing for moments. A doctor came. She didn't know who it was. Another of Donovan's useful tools. She had a vague awareness of being spoken to. She didn't answer. A stethoscope touched her chest. Someone gave her commands. Her body obeyed, though her brain barely registered the presence of others in the room. Voices spoke to each other, but not to her. At some point, the doctor left. She was alone again. The day slipped away. Everything slipped away.

She was slipping away.

I can't fight.

You *must.*

She forced herself to break through to the surface again, and to stay there. She would not let Donovan win like this. She wouldn't be a good little victim and fade into nothing, leaving the field clear for him and his nightmare ambitions.

She kept her breath as shallow as she could. Her head cleared. She looked around. From the light, she judged it was mid-afternoon.

Donovan sat in a chair beside her. There was no one else in the room.

"Hello there," he said.

Adrenaline spiked.

I *will* fight you.

"Hello," Miranda croaked.

"What a setback you've had," he said, still wearing the mask of the concerned administrator. "You shouldn't scare us like that."

Miranda said nothing.

Donovan discarded the mask. His eyes glittered, hard. His face seemed to age, furrows deepening like knife slashes as he leaned forward, his expression determined. "Very well," he said. "Shall we speak of doubt?"

"I doubt there's anything to say."

His lips twitched briefly in a sour facsimile of amusement. "Wit," he said. "You must be feeling better."

"Doubtful."

The twitch again. "What is this? Mockery? That's beneath you, professor. You're disappointing me. I would have thought you might be curious about where absolute critical thinking can go."

Miranda shook her head slightly. Her skull felt heavy as a cannonball. "It goes against absolutes," she said.

Donovan's thin smile seemed genuine this time. "There you go," he said. "Proper engagement."

Miranda mustered the energy for an attack. "Yes," she said. "I engaged, and you diverted. Or didn't you understand what I said. There are no absolutes, and you should know that."

A shadow of uncertainty flickered over his face. It passed. He had shrugged off whatever she had said to disturb him. "You're wrong," he said. "I have the advantage over you in knowing that utterly and completely. But I would have thought you'd know better than to say that. After what you read."

There. So he had wanted her to find the journal. And she saw why now. He wanted her conversion.

Why, though? A point of pride? Why not just dispose of her otherwise, if she refused to march down the path laid out for her?

Well, he hadn't. Maybe she would find out why not. She *would* make him regret playing this game.

"I do know better," she said. "I know better than to bend the knee to your god, and to your foul philosophy."

Donovan stood up. "My my," he said. "I have to agree with the doctors. You do seem to have overdone things rather badly. I hate to see such a decline, and after all the way forward you had come." He made a show of sighing. "This goes against everything I want the treatment to be for our clients in this Institute, but your condition leaves me no choice. Following medical advice, I'm afraid you're going to have to cease all exercise. Nothing but bed rest for you."

Fine by me. She wanted no part in the walking ritual. She would rest, store up her strength, and then, when Agatha came by on Sunday…

"Bed rest," Donovan repeated, "and no more visitors. You're just not up to the excitement."

His grin was nothing like Norma's doll-like rictus. It dripped venom.

Gathering reality, Crothoaka flexed its coils. And Arkham shuddered.

Payton Wallace loved his office. It was, he sincerely believed, a statement about who occupied it. Payton had, since his first election, added to the prestige of the office with the careful choice of decor and accessories. "Clothes might not make the man," he liked to say, "but the office does." He was only half-joking.

The silver inkwell, more than a hundred years old, purchased at an estate sale three summers ago. The ornate mantle clock, its baroque bronze housing culminating in a figure of Venus seated on the top. The equally ornate frame he had found to complement his portrait on the wall. These things and more came together as one to announce the quality of the man who sat in this office. The people – the ones who crossed the threshold into his space, at any rate – deserved to know that they had elected someone of substance, someone who *mattered*.

Payton liked to take the lunch hour to spend some time alone and bask in the space of his accomplishment. He would sit at the desk and look at one object, and then another, and feel warm, and know that what he enjoyed and what Arkham needed were one and the same.

The comfort and warmth were what he needed now. He couldn't get Daria Miracle's performance out of his mind. It had dominated his thoughts since he had seen it, and he didn't know why. He kept trying to believe that the spectacle, so sublime, so captivating for the patients, showed him that all was well at the Institute. He tried very hard, but all he could think about was her movement, and how it seemed to push his soul down a coiling path he did not understand, but could not refuse.

Being in the office helped. Looking at the familiar and the beautiful helped.

Payton leaned forward to touch the clock. It sat across from him on the desk, at the edge, in the precise, measured-to-the-quarter-inch center, lengthwise. He ran his finger down the sinuous convolutions of the bronze.

It hurt. Pain, stabbing, sharp as a razor, sliced deep. He jerked his hand away and scattered drops of blood over the surface of the desk. He stared at the cut. It ran the entire length of his index finger. He made a fist, dripping more blood, and clutched his hand to his chest. He looked back at the clock.

Had someone broken something on it? One of the cleaning staff? If they had…

A shimmer passed over the clock, stopping his outrage cold. Thick, oily streamers dangled off Venus' upraised arm.

Payton jumped up and backed away from the desk. In the center of the office, he turned around slowly, his eyes caught by the sudden hostility of the room. It radiated from every object, and from the walls and ceiling and floor. He suddenly could not be sure that he had bought any of the things he saw. He would never have purchased that clock, not when it was so vile a thing. Then how did it get there?

How did anything get here?

The room did not want him. Its contents were foreign to him. A sheen of the strange covered them.

"What…" he said, but only in a whisper. He did not know whom he should call. He did not know if he should call anyone. What if they meant him harm? What if they had brought the clock?

What if they were responsible for that portrait? It looked like it was meant to be of him, but he distrusted it now. He did not know its intent.

He did not know anything. He was surrounded by strangeness and uncertainty. Mewling, he curled in a ball on the carpet. He rocked back and forth, eyes darting around the office.

On the clock, Venus turned her head to look at him. She hissed. The ornamentation writhed, and then it began to crawl off the clock, across the desk, and down its sides, making for him. On the ceiling, shadows of serpents moved with heavy grace.

Councilman Payton Wallace began to scream. He was still screaming when the ambulance came, and the men with the stretcher bore him away. Though his voice eventually gave out, the screams in his head never stopped again.

Cleo Whitten opened the door of her Southside house. She planned to walk down to the drugstore a few blocks away and pick up some odds and ends. The novelty of being able to go for a stroll whenever she felt like it, and not feel out of breath, had not worn off. Since leaving the Stroud Institute, she had taken new pleasure in the mundane, taken-for-granted events of a day that became out of reach when she had fallen into the depths of her illness. She was well again. There had been times when she feared she never would be. Those memories were still sharp. She treasured the gift of living normally.

She also welcomed each day that came and put the Institute further into her past. She couldn't complain about her treatment there. And her stay had cured her. For most of her time there, she had felt safe, comfortable, and lucky to be receiving care of that level. She had felt less comfortable during the last part of her stay. The sessions with Daria had been the turning point. She had welcomed them, at first, but the more she thought about them, the more they troubled her. Daria's words, her grace and her lessons, had followed Cleo home from the Institute. They were beginning to fade, she thought, and with them the discomfort they created.

As the everyday returned, and the old habits returned, the old certainties did too.

But now, as she closed the door behind her and took one step down the wooden porch, she froze. She suddenly did not want to put her foot down on the sidewalk. The instinct stopped her so abruptly that she almost lost her balance and fell. She windmilled her arms, barely holding on to her purse, then steadied.

The ripple of a wave passed over her small yard. The grass rounded itself over the mound, and so did the concrete slabs of the sidewalk. Another ripple followed the first, then more in quick succession. Her yard undulated. The movement surrounded the house, and it extended out into the street. Cleo looked left and right, and saw the ripples move up the walls of her neighbors' houses.

With the ripples came a call. The image of the Institute filled Cleo's mind. The center of all things summoned her. She had to go back.

"No," she told herself, and wrapped her arms around one of the porch's posts. She shut her eyes so she would not see the hypnotic movement, but then the Institute became even sharper in her head, insistent, commanding.

"No," Cleo said again. "*No!*" She clung to the post, fighting against the psychic undertow that pulled her. If she let go, she would run to the Institute, and to the labyrinth.

Don't let go, don't let go, don't let go.

She would not walk that path. She would not go back.

She was trying to keep her footing in the torrent of a flood. But she held on.

At last, the current released her. She opened her eyes. The ripples had ceased. Her yard was still, the grass unbroken, the sidewalk no more cracked than it had been yesterday.

Cleo let go of the post with one arm, then the other. The urge to return to the Institute had passed. She had fought it off.

But she didn't know what she had fought.

And if it came again, stronger, she didn't think she would win.

She went back inside the house and locked the door.

In the streets and in the stores, in bedrooms and in cars, in Southside and in Rivertown, in Easttown and in Uptown, in all the corners of Arkham, the tightening of the coils made itself felt. The citizens felt the touch of the gathering god. Some barely noticed. It marked others forever.

An overture to the coming reign.

CHAPTER TWENTY-SIX

In French Hill, Wilbur called out to Agatha in a voice trying hard to be brave.

"Dear," he said, "is it possible that we have snakes in the building?"

Agatha looked up. She had been scouring her desk with cleaner. Some faint traces of the samples she had taken from the Institute must have remained. She had found what looked like slug trails on the surface in the morning. She had thrown herself into a full purge, while at the same time gathering all the protective amulets, of confirmed value or otherwise, that she could find. She grabbed two now. She had convinced Wilbur to continue wearing the medallion she had given him for the trip. Hearing the fear in his voice, she acted on instinct, taking the flat iron discs engraved with the elder sign.

She hurried to the living room. Outside, the afternoon had become overcast, and the light seemed much dimmer than it should be, the clouds drawing a lead lining between Arkham and the sun. Wilbur stood in the center of the room, eyeing the walls nervously.

"Snakes?" Agatha asked, following his gaze.

"I keep hearing sounds in the walls."

He held up a hand for silence, and they both listened. "There," he said after a minute, his face turning white.

Agatha heard it. She heard the awful, familiar scrape and slide from the *Leviathan*. She tried to follow the sound with her eyes. In the corner of the walls and ceiling, where the shadows had thickened, she caught the afterthought of movement.

It's here, she thought. Her chest tightened with despair.

Then she shook herself. Surrender would not help. And the sounds were not as loud as on the *Leviathan*. Here but not here, not fully, not yet, still some time. Not much, but some.

"Those aren't snakes," she said to Wilbur.

"Oh," he said, and visibly relaxed.

"It's something much worse," she said, hating that she had to scare him. But he should be frightened. Being scared could mean staying alive.

"Do I want to know…" Wilbur began.

"No, you don't," she told him. "Even if I could explain, and I'm not sure that I could."

Wilbur swallowed. "I suppose ignoring the sounds isn't an option?"

"It isn't."

"That's too bad."

He was doing his best to put on a brave show, and she loved him for it, but his voice cracked at the end, and his hands trembled.

Agatha knelt and grabbed one end of the Turkish carpet that covered most of the living room floor. "Help me with this," she said.

They rolled the carpet, and she moved the coffee table out of the way. She had Wilbur stand in the middle of the bare floor, then raced back to her office to fetch chalk. She stopped in the kitchen on the way back for a pitcher of water and a glass. She gave them to Wilbur.

"What are these for?" he asked.

"For you if you get thirsty."

"If I get…?"

"You're going to stay where you are for some time," she explained. She left him for a minute, then came back with a bucket. "You might need this, too. You can't leave the circle. For *any* reason."

"Oh," Wilbur said in a very small voice.

She brought over one of the dining room chairs and a throw cushion from the couch. "For sitting, and for if you want to lie down," she said.

Wilbur sat. He didn't ask any more questions as she drew a protective circle around him. She marked it with elder signs and all the other symbols of protection she knew.

So much fumbling in the dark, she thought as she worked. So much she, and the other people who fought to hold back the dark in the world, did not know. Agatha believed that there had to be a way of understanding the threats, and the science behind the words and the incantations and the sounds and the symbols that seemed to help. There had to be rules that governed the universe. They just needed to be found.

She didn't know what the rules were today, with the light bleeding away from the day, and sounds in the walls. Did the ones she had half-glimpsed in the past even apply? She just had to hope they did. And so, she drew the circle around Wilbur and hoped it would keep him safe. She needed him safe.

"Do not step outside the circle," Agatha said again.

"Okay."

"Don't do anything to break it."

"You already told me that."

"Promise me you won't."

Wilbur nodded. "I won't."

"Stay right where you are until I get back."

He paled again. "Where are you going?"

"To the Stroud Institute. That's the heart of what's happening. I have to do what I can to stop it."

"But what is *it*?"

"The thing I have to stop."

"You're not being funny."

"I'm not trying to be. I wish I had better answers. I just know that I have to try."

She hugged and kissed him, stepped out of the circle, and drew its final segments. Then she left the apartment.

The journey to the Institute showed her how much worse things had become. The air tasted wrong. It tasted of anxiety. She kept looking over her shoulder along the sidewalk, and the people she passed had a hunted look, their eyes darting about. She flagged a cab down after a block, and the cabbie seemed distracted. When she told him where she wanted to go, he looked puzzled for a moment, as if he didn't know the way, and when he did get going, she could see his uncertainty unnerved him. She didn't blame him. The closer she came to the Institute, the more uncertain she felt. Doubts crawled over every thought.

The cabbie drove hesitantly. He kept starting to brake, then muttering to himself. "Nothing there. Stupid."

He slowed down as they approached the gates of the Institute. "In there?" he asked.

Agatha knew how he felt. The building loomed. It governed the day with malice. At the same time, it pulled the eyes and the mind its way. The closer one came, the harder it would be to get away.

"Drop me off at the gates," she said. She could spare him the approach.

The cabbie nodded gratefully. He pulled away as soon as she got out, not giving her a chance to pay him.

It took an effort to pass through the gates. The grounds felt much more dangerous, much more infected, than on her last visit. She thought about how relieved she had been to get away.

And now I'm back.

She had no choice. She had to do what she could for Miranda, and with her. She had to warn her how badly things were going outside the walls of the Institute, how imminent the disaster must be. And she had to know what Miranda had found, if anything, in Donovan's apartment. Waiting to learn that, waiting to know that Miranda was all right, that all had gone well, had made the night and day an agony. At least she wasn't going to wait for Sunday's visiting hours. No point in keeping up appearances anymore. The crisis had come, and it was time to fight back, even in total ignorance. It was that or surrender. She would never do that.

Agatha jogged down the drive and up the stairs to the Institute's entrance. She tried the doors; they were locked. She pounded on them, and no one came.

She backed down the stairs and looked around. No sign of life on the grounds. No ambulances arriving, no groundskeeper working on the lawn. Only stillness, and the silence before the storm.

She looked up at the building. Could she work out which window was the one for Miranda's room? It looked out on this side. Yes, she thought so. She counted, picturing how many rooms she went by before she reached Miranda's room. The confusing geography of the interior didn't help, but from the outside, she could tell where she had to be to get the view from Miranda's bed.

There. That was the one. Two in from the end of the wing.

Agatha picked up a handful of stones from the edge of the drive. She threw them one after the other at the window. They bounced off with sharp ticks. After the fourth, the window opened. Miranda leaned out.

Agatha hissed. Even from this distance, she could see how haggard Miranda looked. She leaned on the windowsill as if it was all she could do to keep from falling. She lifted a hand for a moment and waved feebly.

"I can't get in," Agatha called. "The doors are locked."

Miranda nodded, as if this news did not surprise her.

"It's happening," Agatha said. "We're out of time. The ritual is almost complete."

Miranda straightened with visible effort, steeling herself. "Crothoaka," she said.

Agatha winced at the cost Miranda's lungs must have paid for her to make herself heard. The word she spoke had no meaning, and it had too much. Agatha recognized it as a name, and understood that Miranda must have learned it from what she found last night. Agatha clenched her fists in frustration. Miranda knew more now, but there was no way for her to pass the information to Agatha, no way for them to fight together.

Miranda managed some more words. "What do I do?" she asked.

I wish I knew. "Fight," Agatha said, hating the burden she was placing on Miranda's shoulders, raging against her helplessness. "Fight in any way you can." She pulled a medallion out of her jacket pocket. It was an iron disc, etched in silver with an elder sign. "Keep this with you. It will protect you." *I hope.* She threw the medallion at the window. Her aim was true. Miranda reached out to catch it, missed, and it sailed past her into the room.

Miranda nodded. She closed the window.

Agatha stayed put. "I'll wait," she promised.

The medallion clattered to the floor behind Miranda. She shut the window, the cooling air raking her lungs, and turned around to retrieve it.

Norma had it. She held it up, examining it as if it were a dead toad. "What is this?" she said.

Miranda hadn't heard her return. She hadn't come back since the morning exercises had begun. Miranda had drifted in and out of wakefulness all day. When Agatha's stones had brought her back to full consciousness, she had noticed how still the hallway was outside her door. There were no walkers. No one around at all. But now here was Norma.

The other woman made a face at the medallion. "This is garbage," she said.

"Maybe," Miranda said. It hurt so much to talk. "But it's mine. Please." She held out a hand.

Norma closed a fist around the disk. "I don't think this is healthy for you," she said.

"Not … your business."

"I'm going to show this to Nurse Revere."

Miranda took a step forward. "Give it."

Norma turned to go.

Miranda lunged. It felt like she was trying to jump underwater. The weakness of illness and the sluggishness of nightmare fought her. She grabbed the back of Norma's robe as she fell, and they both went down. Norma snarled, teeth bared, and she clawed at Miranda's face. Miranda jerked her head back. Norma punched her, hard.

Miranda saw stars. She tried to hold on to Norma, her vision graying. Norma kneed her in the stomach, and Miranda slumped down, pain exploding in her head and wounded lungs. She was only vaguely aware of Norma pulling away.

Lying on the floor, her body a single bruised mass, she went down into unconsciousness again. The last image before the darkness was the medallion. She had only had one good look at it, when Norma gave it her hateful stare. The design leapt out at her, carved itself into her imagination, and kept her company when the lights went out.

She didn't know how much time had passed when she opened her eyes again and managed to use a bedframe to haul herself up from the floor. Hours, she guessed. The afternoon had been turning black, but now night had fallen. She dragged herself to her bed. How could she do anything? She didn't have the strength for anything except to collapse in bed.

You promised.

And there was no one else. Agatha couldn't get in. If Miranda didn't fight Donovan, then he would complete the summoning of Crothoaka.

He probably will anyway.

How did she think she would fight him? Norma had stolen the closest thing she had to a weapon.

The image of the elder sign burned in her mind's eye, as sharp as ever. She sat on the side of the bed and took up a pad and pen from her nightstand. She drew the elder sign, the blazing memory guiding her hand. She examined her work when she was done. Hardly silver on iron, but the symbol looked right. She traced its lines with her finger.

The worst of the exhaustion dropped away. She could move again. She stood up without having to lean on anything. She no longer felt the overpowering urge to sleep. Her lungs were still congested, her breathing ragged. Whatever force had alleviated her TB had given it all back. Her empirical physical health was not good. But the force, perhaps the same one that had been oppressing her all day, had lifted.

She got dressed. The process felt like donning armor. She would not confront Donovan clad as a patient. She shrugged into her coat and belted it tightly. Then she tore the sheet with the symbol off the pad, folded it, and put it in her pocket.

"Be thou my shield," she whispered to the elder sign.

Here we go.

She left the room. In the silent hall, she took a quick look in the nearby doorways. The rooms were not all empty. The beds were far from being full, but she saw at least two or three patients in each room. Wherever the others had gone, whoever had become like Norma, full converts, Miranda saw enough to allow her the hope that many of the people under the roof of the Stroud Institute were not her enemies.

She didn't know how she could help them, though. And they certainly couldn't help her. Without exception, they slept deeply. She tried calling out, and then clapped her hands, the sharp sound echoing weirdly in the silence. No one stirred. The power that had tried to pull her down had them in its coils.

"Stay safe," she said to them. "I'll do what I can."

She turned to the wall and felt carefully along it. She found the tactile pattern of the labyrinth, and then she found the circular depression that marked the trigger for the hidden passage. She steeled herself and opened the wall.

She had no flashlight or candle. Nothing to light the way. It looked like she wouldn't need one. The passageway was dark, but not black. A faint, green-tinged luminescence came from the walls. The path before her was clear.

The way of pilgrims, she thought. The labyrinth had welcomed all to its center. It wanted them there.

It wanted her there.

She accepted the invitation, and started down the path.

Chapter Twenty-Seven

The passageway turned sharply, and then again, backtracking on itself before turning again and descending. After another short stretch, it curved, sloping upward. The curve went on so long that Miranda realized she had entered a spiral, one that somehow switched from going up to going down, and then up again.

The inner labyrinth made the rest of the Institute seem rational in its layout. Miranda had no idea where she was in the building. Within minutes, she gave up trying to locate herself. Soon, she found it hard to believe the world existed outside the labyrinth. She had always been in this passage. She always would be.

The walls changed the deeper she went. From the start, the air was damp, and the stones glistened with trickles of slime. Carved into rough, rectangular slabs, pitted and scarred, the stones brooded with their age and seemed to press closer to her, alert to the movement of prey. Gradually, the lines between the slabs became vague, as if the walls and ceiling and floor of the passage were made of a single mass.

The transformation pointed to revelation ahead. Miranda dreaded it. But she did not turn back. She doubted she would be allowed to, and she would not back down. She would see the path through to the end.

You say that like you have a choice.

The thought chilled. She resented it, all the more furiously because she couldn't deny it. She had a single path before her, with no branches, no junctions, no choices.

You are here, the labyrinth whispered, because that is your fate.

Her victory over fatigue was no victory at all. It was a capitulation to the inevitable.

Inevitable. Her life had turned into mere inevitability. She looked back at the moments that had brought her here, to walking endlessly through the damp, green twilight, and saw how all her options had been stripped away from the start. In Donovan's apartment, reading the journal, she had felt the same sense of iron destiny. The steps through the winding labyrinth from her home to this darkness were so obvious.

All the steps, all the little moments, some trivial and unremarked when they happened, others massive, but whose interconnections she had not seen at the time.

All the steps. Walking by the Institute every day, observing it gradually come into being. The thought of the place as her first choice for help when she fell sick. The days of care and nights of fear, the visions and the suspicions teaching her to be wary, to look for the danger.

She had resisted Daria's lessons. She did not want to walk the path Donovan had laid out for her. But then she read the journal he wanted her to read, and now she walked the labyrinth: could she say that she was here against his wishes?

No, she could not.

She thought about the mission she had given herself. She came to stop the project that Magnus Stroud had begun. She, a Romanticist, had come to destroy the work of a zealot of Romanticism. The symmetry of the conflict defied chance. If she tried to put down all the events that had produced this result to coincidence, her reason turned away, revolted.

Coincidence had not brought her here. Fate had. She accepted that.

Back and forth. Down straight halls, then curved ones. Up and down, twisting around angles so sharp, the passage should have crossed its own path.

The stones continued to change. The divisions between them had shed their disguise. They were wrinkles. As if the walls were flesh.

The passage twisting and twisting, like a thing alive.

The turns and the rises and the falls felt like the pattern of her life, seemingly random but destined.

She grew dizzy with the turns. She coughed, and she stumbled. She put out a hand to stop her fall. Her palm touched the wall; the stone was warm and wet, and it gave beneath her touch.

Like flesh.

Flesh that clung.

And she was in a lecture hall at Miskatonic, her lungs clear, her voice strong.

"My question for you," she said to the class, "is this: do Byron's heroes have free will? Think about it. Wouldn't that affect our judgment of them and their actions?"

"They do have free will," said one student. Miranda should know her name by now, this late into the term. She had trouble making out her features. Was the lighting dim? "Their tragedies are their fault."

"I see," said Miranda. She drummed her fingers against the lectern and nodded. "Their circumstances are the results of their actions, then."

"Yes," said another student, and Miranda couldn't quite place his name, either. She should be doing much better than this.

"And their actions are chosen, not preordained," said Miranda.

A half-dozen heads nodded. Most of the class regarded her neutrally. She couldn't tell if they were engaged by the debate or not. They sat very still.

"But is it possible," Miranda said, "that the choices themselves were determined by the formation of character? Were the Byronic heroes always going to sin because of all the life experiences that brought them to the moment of sin?"

She saw some frowns.

"You don't agree?" she said to the first student who had spoken. *What is her name?*

"I think that's a cop-out."

"How so?"

"Because that way, you could excuse anything."

"That's true," Miranda agreed. "Anything except the god who caused the circumstances to occur. And so the Byronic heroes rail against the gods and fates, but in the end do what has always been destined."

"*Exactly.*" The students spoke as one, the class pleased that she had learned her lesson.

Miranda frowned. The class had been going well, the students not just accepting what she said uncritically, but now she felt as if she had completely misread her own circumstances. Wasn't she the one lecturing?

Undulating movement passed over the class. The students' arms and limbs lengthened, turning into tentacles, their leathered skin a blotchy patchwork of red and white and dark green. The lecture hall trembled. The walls cracked, raining wood and plaster down. The ceiling broke open. It peeled away like burning paper, and Miranda looked up into a sky that had become a bulging, translucent gray membrane, ready to tear and unleash the writhing shapes and eyes behind it.

Miranda raised her hands to her own eyes, and she could see right through her flesh and bone, see and see and see, and…

She tripped and almost fell as the passageway sloped downward again, the gradient steeper than before.

She stopped, waiting for her breathing to calm and her head to stop spinning. She couldn't remember pulling her hand away from the wall. She didn't know how far she had come since she had touched it. There had been no slope, then, and she had been in a straight portion of the hall. The path here curved ahead and behind her. She had walked without seeing where she was going, while she had been caught in that…

…memory? Maybe. She couldn't be sure, except about the last part. What about the rest? She had given more lectures about Byron than she could count. She didn't remember the events of every class from term to term. There could have been such a debate. The memory now felt so clear, or at least what had been said. The faces of the students remained frustratingly vague.

Had the labyrinth plucked a forgotten moment from one of her classes and, in using it for its own ends, given the memory back to her? Or had everything been an invention? Her fists clenched in frustration, nails digging into her palms to remind her that real was real. She felt as she did when she woke from one of those dreams that claimed to be a recurring one, without any way of telling if she had really dreamed this before, or if the memory were itself a creation of the dream.

She mistrusted the reality of the lecture. It was too convenient. But when she denied it the stature of fact, all its elements receded from certainty too. She couldn't see the students' faces, so they weren't real – but when she tried to picture her students from this term, the ones she had taught not that long ago, their faces were misty too. How could she know if any memories were truly hers?

If she had always been in the labyrinth, then she had never taught. Her students, her office, her books, the essays she had to mark and the exams she had to invigilate, all of them delusions.

"No," she said aloud. She started walking again. "It is the…" She couldn't remember the date. She tried again. "I came to the Institute in March. I had a life before. I have not always been here."

But the memory of the sky, of the disintegration of the lecture hall, so real, so vivid, more precise than the ordinary, familiar recollection of the lecture.

"No," Miranda said again. "No, no, no." She put her hand in her pocket and clutched the paper with the elder sign. Such flimsy material, so weak, yet the comfort it gave her was real. A folded corner poked her palm. She felt the texture of the paper against her fingers. The strength of the symbol reached to her soul.

It didn't matter if the lecture had ever happened or not. The horror at its end had not happened. Not yet.

"Not ever," Miranda promised herself.

Air, warm and clammy, pushed against her. In the unknown, unseen center of the labyrinth, something hissed. The flesh of the walls moved. They shifted, a muscle stretching, coming to know itself.

She clutched the elder sign harder as she understood what Donovan had written.

Hail Crothoaka, the Worm of the Labyrinth!

Donovan's words, and words were important. Precision mattered. *Of* the labyrinth, not *in* it. The worm and the labyrinth were one. The twisting passages inside the Institute were becoming the summoned god. She was within the manifesting Crothoaka, swallowed already, and when the summoning ended, the Worm would burst out of its stone cocoon.

Miranda fought back a wave of panic and the need to turn around, to run and run and run, to be out in the clean air and not be in the monster, go now now *now*, before it's too late.

She forced herself to keep going, and even held back the grunt of terror that tried to force its way out from her chest.

"I will fight. I will fight. I will fight." The sound of her voice helped, another reminder of existence beyond the confines of her head.

The path kept going down, and kept turning. The way became narrower, then wider, and then narrower once more. As the expansion began yet again, Miranda realized that the walls were moving. They were contracting and expanding with a slow, measured rhythm, and the sluggish breeze blew and stopped, blew and stopped, and she should recognize breathing when she encountered it. She had grown so conscious of her own lately.

She kept to the middle of the path, trying to draw her shoulders in. The walls came in close, and she didn't want to touch them again.

She refused them. They insisted. The walls curved inward, stretching, an echo of the membrane of the sky; before she could deny that memory again, they squeezed her from both sides.

And she was ten years old, in her parents' house, bored of her books one Sunday afternoon and looking for something else to read, something *grown-up*; she had been told that she could try anything that interested her from the *grown-up* bookshelves.

That Sunday, a warm fall day, she found *Frankenstein*. She started reading it. She didn't understand it all. She persisted, though, getting through more each day. When she ran into passages that she felt sure were crucial but couldn't puzzle out, she spoke to her mother.

A few days into her project, in the evening, a wet one now, with the leaves turning into brown mulch in the gutters outside, she asked her mother why Victor Frankenstein, when a child, seemed angry with his father about some alchemy books he had found.

They were sitting beside each other on the couch. Anne Ventham put a bookmark in the volume she had been reading and looked at the page Miranda was showing her.

"He's trying to blame his father for what happens later," Anne explained. "He says that if his father had explained things a different way, then Frankenstein would have agreed with him that the books were nonsense. Then, he would not have become obsessed with them and their ideas, and he would not have made all the other choices that finally lead to creating a monster. Do you understand?"

"His whole life is his father's fault?" said Miranda.

"That's more or less what Frankenstein is saying. That doesn't mean he's right." After a thoughtful pause, her mother continued. "I think he's just making excuses and trying to shift the blame. But I think it *is* true that reading those books did influence who he grew up to be in a very, very important way."

"Can that happen? Can just reading a book change you?"

"Or maybe decide who you are. Yes, honey."

Miranda didn't know if she found the idea exciting or frightening. Either possibility seemed like a good reason to hug her mother, so she did, and her mother hugged her back, and hugged her, and hugged her, arms reaching around and around and around, slithering and squeezing, rough with scales, crushing now, and Miranda couldn't breathe, and her mother hissed, and her long, twitching tongue tangled in Miranda's hair.

Miranda gasped, her chest filled with broken glass, and she rushed forward, down the sinuous path, away from the memory and its horror. The memory had to be false, another construct of the labyrinth, except that it was all so vivid, and she remembered everything else about that fall and her first encounter with *Frankenstein*. It was true, true, true, that the right book at the right time could shape you, could set out the path of your life. Because she had read *Frankenstein*, she had become a Romanticist, and so she was here, in the labyrinth, the right book dooming her to this horror, the right book appearing not by chance but by fate, her path decided from childhood, and earlier, from birth, and earlier, always already decided, her descent into the labyrinth always already mapped out.

And if she said no, if she denied this truth, then what – were all her memories wrong? Were they all illusions, thin dreams of free will and mirages of life? All wrong, all lies, all fed to her by the labyrinth at its pleasure, in its perversity, because she had always been here, only been here, the labyrinth the only reality, the only truth?

"No," she said again, then louder, to prove that she could. "No!"

The floor of the corridor had leveled off, and the walls had become sinuous, curving left and right and left and right, as it breathed in and out and in and out.

"No," Miranda said again, not as loud, but with determination. She twisted sideways to avoid the touch of the walls. She would refuse the binary choice of horror the labyrinth offered her. She would not accept its truth. She would disprove it through victory, by freeing the patients of the Institute from the labyrinth's grasp.

She heard human voices chanting. She listened with care, and rubbed the paper of the elder sign for some reassurance of reality before she could be sure that the voices weren't in her head. They grew louder. Each curve of the corridor brought her closer to them.

She couldn't make out the words. Meaning crouched just out of reach. She strained to hear better, to make out the call, because it was a call, yes, she made out that much, and the satisfaction pushed her to move faster, to get closer, and learn the rest. Only then did she realize that she was answering the call.

Miranda forced herself to slow down, and put her fingers to her lips. They were moving, trying to shape the syllables, as if she were five again, and sounding out the words on a page. She pressed her lips together, held her mouth closed. Crothoaka would get no summons from her.

She slowed down some more, making her steps deliberate, advancing with caution, keeping clear of the walls.

Here we go. Almost there. This is when you fight, really fight. The journey here had been a prologue.

Another bend, and the corridor ended. Beyond an archway lay the center of the labyrinth. It was a huge chamber, much larger than the Institute's entrance lobby, much too big a space to be contained within the walls of the building. Perhaps Miranda had descended far below the foundations of the Institute. The chamber could be a cave. It had rows of twenty-foot stalactites and stalagmites running down its left and right sides, except they weren't mineral formations, because they were too smooth, too perfectly shaped like fangs, and they weren't sculptures either, gleaming with venom and the imminence of motion.

The mound in the middle of the room, around which all the people had gathered, was an altar, with a rounded top, and a front that sloped, undulating, nearly to the archway. Yes, an altar.

But also a tongue.

Green, pulsating mist oozed around the chamber, jerking and turning to the rhythms of the chant. Donovan stood directly opposite Miranda, on the other side of the altar, arms outstretched, fingers crooked into claws, his head tilted back in ecstasy as he led the song. Maybe fifty patients and staff were gathered in a semi-circle around the altar. The light and their worship had transformed their dressing gowns and uniforms. To Miranda's eyes, they looked like ceremonial robes to her now.

Daria danced. She moved among the worshippers, around Donovan and the altar, and back to the patients, weaving a path, and marking it too, because her arms stretched long, serpentine and boneless. Her hand on one shoulder and the limb weaving around the shoulders of a dozen other celebrants before the caressing hand followed, leaving a gleaming, viscous trail behind on faces and necks.

Miranda stayed just inside the archway. They hadn't seen her yet. She had this moment to act. She didn't know what to do.

Then Nurse Holden shot around the side of the arch from where she had been hidden against the near wall. Her head twitched up and down and side to side, the movement so harsh and rapid it should have broken her neck, but her smile was wide, so wide, and as she struck rattlesnake-fast and grabbed Miranda's arms, her gargling voice repeated the first words she had said to her when Miranda had arrived at the Institute, a thousand centuries ago.

"What do you think you're doing?"

Chapter Twenty-Eight

Holden dragged Miranda into the chamber. Her hands were rough, covered in minute insect legs that scrabbled against Miranda's skin. Her grip was unbreakable. Miranda tried to pull away, but Holden didn't seem to notice. The ring of worshippers parted, and Holden pulled Miranda toward the altar.

The chanting changed. The people turned from the altar to face Miranda, and they shouted what sounded like hails, but using a word that Miranda had never heard, that she could never pronounce without her tongue being transformed. The word slithered into her ears. It wrapped around her mind and tried to burrow in deep. In that repeated syllable she felt the taint of triumph, of welcome, of delight and of hunger.

She saw many faces that she recognized in the congregation, all changed as the culmination of the great ritual approached. Norma's smile had grown until her lips reached all the way around to her ears. Her teeth had grown too, longer and wider and brighter. She chanted, and she laughed at Miranda, her teeth clacking together with castanet mockery.

Frieda's eyes had crept out of their sockets and clung to the lower cheeks, just above her chin. They stared at Miranda with cold fury. Pale, grub-like things filled Frieda's eye sockets, twitching with tension.

Nurse Revere's face flowed with movement. She looked like herself for a moment, and then her head became a writhing explosion of great worms. They flailed out from her skull, reaching for Miranda as she passed, then curled back in on themselves, the markings on their bodies reforming the illusion of a human face for a moment, and then repeating the cycle.

A choir of horrors, a congregation of monsters. Any thought of appealing for help, of trying to break through the Institute's conversion, died. Miranda would find no help here.

Holden presented Miranda to Daria. The Miracle's arms twisted like rope around Miranda's, brought her to the altar, and forced her to lie down on its rounded surface. It moved under Miranda's back, a muscle tasting her presence.

"You are loved," Daria said. Her voice changed, sliding across registers to one painfully familiar.

No no no, Miranda thought. *I will not allow it.* Her mother had died three years before. She would not let this creature taint her memories.

But Daria kept speaking in the voice Miranda knew, and the taint spread. "You have always been loved, because of who you are, and who you would become, and of this moment, when you would do what you were born to do. How proud I was, when you asked me about Frankenstein." The serpent arms tightened in a parody of reassurance. "How I loved to hold you close."

No no no no. Miranda fought against the insinuations. But the re-experienced memory, turned monstrous, held on to her with a grip as unbreakable as Daria's. She could not split the real from the false. The joyful and the evil were alike in vividness and detail. They were one.

Daria held her down, and Donovan smiled at her. He wore a gray, hooded robe. Symbols sewn in black thread adorned it. Miranda recognized none of them, but she saw the labyrinth's pattern in them. They were all formed from a single, unbroken line, and a thin trace connected them all. Donovan was the only one of the faithful who had not been transformed. His face was as it always was, and he looked at Miranda with the same open friendliness as ever.

"This is the greatest moment of your life," he said. "You don't believe me right now, but you will."

This was the fight, Miranda thought. Somehow, this was when she had to strike back. She had no strength against Daria. She had no hope against the congregation. But Donovan needed something from her. If she could deny it to him... If she could use it against him...

But what did he want? Her conversion? What did one more or less believer matter?

"You're very sure of yourself," she said, stabbing in the dark. "So sure that all the physical changes are for other people."

No crack in Donovan's joy. If anything, he seemed pleased by her defiance. "It isn't for me to decide the fate of my body. That will come soon, I'm sure." He produced a dagger from somewhere in the folds of his robe. "Everything will be soon. The waiting is done."

He ran a finger down the length of the blade. The knife had been forged of a metal blacker than obsidian. It had a rough texture like iron, yet shone in the green light like glass. The twists in the blade gave it the impression of being in motion.

"How many people have you murdered with that?" Miranda asked, revolted.

"Sacrificed, you mean," said Donovan. "And the answer is none. Nor will I today. You will complete the summons by sacrificing yourself to the Worm of the Labyrinth."

"If you want me dead, I am not going to do your work for you."

"But you will!" Donovan assured her, eyes shining with zealotry.

"How can you be so certain?" Miranda saw the hint of a way to fight back against Donovan. Doubt and certainty lay at the core of Crothoaka's spell. Donovan was, truly, Magnus' heir. Both men were idealists, driven to take their tenets to the ultimate conclusion. Men who rejected the orthodoxies of their times, but then kneeled before another dogma.

"I am certain because of who you are," Donovan said. "You are here for one purpose alone, and not the one you think. You were chosen long ago, you know. You were chosen long before you came to the Institute."

Miranda struggled against Daria's grip. She didn't want to hear. She began to lose hold of the embryonic tactic against Donovan.

"You must have known this," said the priest of Crothoaka.

She thought of the vision the night before she came to the Institute. She thought about the intimations of destiny that had assaulted her mind during her journey through the labyrinth.

Lies. All lies. She mustn't grant them the status of truth.

The thoughts would not shake loose. Insect legs in her brain, scratching, scratching.

"You can't think your tuberculosis was the result of a chance infection," Donovan scolded. "There is nothing random in the steps that brought you to the Institute. It took no effort at all to put you in the presence of contagion. We had time, after all. Months of construction before we would be ready to receive you."

"Why?" she asked before she could stop herself. She knew she shouldn't ask, but she had to know.

"Because you are the perfect final sacrifice. You complete the art of the ritual."

"Because I'm a Romanticist?" Even in her terror, she almost laughed at the absurdity of the idea. Then she remembered how she had seen the dark perfection in the nature of the conflict, and absurdity melted away before destiny.

"Not just that," said Donovan. "Not even principally that. Your scholarship is not the totality of your identity. It isn't your primary marker. You are the great doubter, Professor Ventham. You distrust all orthodoxies – social, political, and religious. You doubt all authority. You question everything. That is why you are here. Yours is the perfect conversion."

"Then you'll be disappointed."

"I won't." Always that confident smile. "Confronted by the god of doubt, and the certainty of its existence, you *will* convert."

"No," said Miranda.

Donovan didn't answer. He didn't seem to hear her. She tried to shout louder and found that she couldn't speak. The refusal stayed in her head, weak and alone. The chanting had changed again, become much louder, become an incantation and a call, directed at her and her alone. Rhythmic, hypnotic, it swamped her hearing, and then all of her perception. Her vision tunneled. Donovan receded from view as she fell down the well of consciousness.

Her awareness floated in deep nothing. Something in the void stirred. She mustn't look. But she had no body here, no eyes to avert, only her soul caught by its awareness of the serpent divine.

She witnessed the uncoiling of Crothoaka. Sublime, vast beyond her conception, the god appeared to her first as a storm of tentacles, a grasping, flailing maelstrom. Then, as the god filled her perception to the shattering point, she saw that the tentacles were the folds of a single, linear being, the labyrinth incarnate.

The vision changed, then. With the insect legs scrabbling deeper into her mind, her awareness multiplied. She became legion, seeing everywhere in Arkham first, and then more and more and more. She witnessed the reign of Crothoaka begin. She saw the spread of the plague of doubt. It vectored through the population on the wings of thought, in the disintegration of all assurances, and it came for the people in physical form, in devouring coils of insect and worm, in the disintegration of physical identity, in the end of every kind of self. And behind the doubt came the wave of the new certainty, the only one, the certainty of cataclysm that was Crothoaka, and all was devoured by the labyrinth.

Miranda saw it all. She saw the inevitability of it all, and she was the tiniest, most miserable of creatures doomed to be consumed, and what was there to do but submit before the truth? As the crawling things in her head dug deeper and deeper, she asked herself: would she dare to stand before a god? How could her feeble doubts compare before the Lord of Doubt? Crothoaka lived and waited in the fissures and contradictions and lacunae of every structure of belief, ready to bring them all crashing down.

In the end, Crothoaka was beyond all doubt. In the end, she had to surrender.

The pummeling cascade of visions of nightmare ended. Miranda returned to her body. It weighed her down with weakness. There was barely any need for Daria to hold her. The Miracle made a sound between a hiss and purr. Her limbs shifted around Miranda's arms, a spiral hug in preparation of release, because the time had come for her to take the knife and do what fate demanded.

Submit.

No.

Her defiance, so small, just a spark, but silver and precise. She could speak again, and she muttered. Donovan looked startled. He had expected to hear something else from her lips, and its absence threw him.

"What did you say?" he demanded.

"Paradox," Miranda said, a little louder, the spark gathering strength, lengthening, a silver thread now, a thesis in formation. She called on the image of the elder sign. She traced its shape. She made it into an argument. "Why do you accept it?"

Donovan didn't answer.

Miranda pressed her advantage. "Crothoaka is ultimate doubt, and therefore absolute certainty. You don't believe in critical thought. You don't suspend belief. You just sought a new dogma."

Donovan stared at her. His face twisted in confusion and anger. "You reject your fate, then," he said.

"Not my fate."

"You would have experienced the new perfection of sacrifice."

"I will not give you the perfection you need."

He shook his head, even more angry. "Not that I need. That I want. Your death is still the full accomplishment of the summoning."

"Is it?"

"*Yes!*" His voice broke with the shriek.

She wilted and went limp.

"Crothoaka!" Donovan shouted. "Your reign has come!" Instead of ecstasy, desperation filled his voice.

Desperation born of doubt.

He raised the knife with both hands. He brought it back over his head. Miranda saw the arc, and the pause before its descent as if she had all the time in the world, as if she had always known this moment, as if she had seen it so many times in forgotten dreams that her role in the event had become instinctive.

With a surge of energy her body must have been saving since she arrived at the Institute, Miranda snapped out of her possum act. She slipped out of the grip of the startled Daria. She grabbed Donovan's wrists as he brought the dagger down, used his momentum against him and turned the angle of the blow. She pushed with all her strength, and plunged the dagger into the stomach of the doubting priest.

Donovan gasped. His eyes widened in shock. His face went gray.

The chanting stopped. A second of perfect silence fell over the chamber.

Then Donovan fell. And Daria began to scream. And a hiss built up, a hiss greater and older than the voice of mountains, and the hiss became a roar of anger, a roar to shatter thunder.

The chamber began to shake.

Chapter Twenty-Nine

Agatha felt the roar as much as she heard it. Tremors rolled through the grounds of the Stroud Institute, knocking her off her feet. She struggled to her knees, looked up at the building, and braced herself for the monstrous emergence.

It did not come. Cracks appeared in the foundation; they raced up the walls. Windows frosted, then shattered. Glass and fragments of stone rained down. Agatha shielded her face, managed to get to her feet, and staggered over the bucking earth, out of the range of the glass.

With a deafening crash, the entrance doors blew inside, as if a giant's mace had smashed them in. The stained glass of Donovan's apartment flew into bits, but most of it went in, not out. The roof over his quarters buckled.

The facade began to distort around the cracks, forming concavities.

There would be no emergences, Agatha realized. The Stroud Institute was in the earthly throes of an implosion.

She's done it.

Screams came from the rooms with broken windows.

Agatha raced to the entrance, the momentary exultation at Miranda's victory gone in an instant. The building had turned back into a hospital full of patients, and it was about to come down around their ears.

And Miranda was in there, somewhere.

The floor of the lobby trembled, its surface breaking up like an eggshell, tiny pieces of marble bouncing up and down, like pellets on a drum. Agatha ran to the fire alarm on the wall behind the reception desk. The shrill clang of bells erupted in the halls, cutting through the deeper sound of the agonized roar, and the ever increasing groan of the Institute's walls.

The shaking was worse than outside, but Agatha found her balance. She started up the stairs, coughing in the clouds of dust that wafted down. She crossed paths with the first of the patients before she reached the first floor.

"What's happening?" one woman asked, her eyes wide with terror.

"A collapse," said Agatha. She kept climbing, and called back, "Get out as fast as you can. Stay on the grounds and wait for help, but keep well back from the building."

She went up, and the traffic of fleeing patients increased. She urged them on, but they didn't need her encouragement. The rattling and shaking of the stairwell gave them all the incentive they needed.

Agatha hit the top ward of the west wing, breathing hard, and got out of the way of the patients lining up for the stairwell. No one, she saw, seemed willing to risk the elevator. Most of the patients were able to walk, and they carried the ones who couldn't.

All the windows on this floor had disintegrated, their shards littering the floor. As Agatha ran past a deserted room, she heard, drawing closer, the *clang clang clang* of the fire engine bells.

She made for Miranda's room, and the position in the halls where she had described finding the passage.

Be open, Agatha thought. Please be open.

The gap in the walls was there, its sides ragged, cracks spreading out along the walls, the labyrinth pattern clearly visible now as it began to disintegrate. Beyond the threshold, the passage sloped down sharply.

Agatha hesitated. Miranda had said it started off straight and level. Her first impression had been that it was specific to this floor. Agatha wondered if she had found the wrong entrance.

No, it had to be this one. The location was right.

Everything collapsing, she thought. Everything changing – just like the odds of finding Miranda, and of either of them getting out alive.

No choice. She didn't care about the odds. She cared about the right thing to do.

She rushed down between the writhing walls.

Miranda felt the inversion of the summoning as clearly as the tolling of a cathedral bell. She saw the logic of the catastrophe as if she had commanded it herself. Magnus had walked into the flames of his estate strong in the full certainty of his cause. Donovan died in the agony of doubt.

The ritual died too in the moment of its completion, riven by its own contradictions. The serpent of doubt turned on itself and devoured its own tail.

Miranda felt a certain pride to perceive the nature of her victory even as she accepted that she was about to die.

The fangs of the cavern crumbled and withdrew into the stone. The chamber itself began to contract. The walls pressed in toward each other, and did not withdraw. The ceiling bulged down, splitting open and dripping pink ichor.

Miranda slid off the altar. She stood, stunned and off-balance, expecting to fall, surprised when she managed to take a step, and then another.

Daria wailed, her voice rising and falling through multiple octaves of ululation and base snarl. Her limbs whipped around, slashing the air, and then her body lost coherence. Her final, grotesque dance began, her flesh ballooning and contracting, stretching and flowing, becoming a perpetual inhuman transformation.

The congregation joined her in the dance. No chanting from the throats now, only screams, and the screams came from mouths that opened in arms and chests and foreheads. Then they were simply indiscernible shapes as the skeletons broke down. Caught in the logic implosion of their god, the things that had been people flowed together, and toward the flesh vortex of the Miracle.

Miranda weaved between them. The last face she saw before there were no faces was Holden's, and she thought she saw sorrow mixed in with the agony.

At the archway, Miranda looked back; all the flesh was still screaming.

She turned away. A vicious tremor shook the chamber, smashing her against the side of the archway. She sagged in pain.

She could give up. She had done what she had come to do. Why pretend she could work her way back through infinite length of the labyrinth?

Because she had won. She had fought with nothing, and she had won. She wouldn't stop fighting now.

She headed into the tunnel. Spasms shook the walls. Their breathing came in tubercular gasps. The tremors rocked Miranda back and forth, and she had to work hard to keep her balance and not touch the flesh of the dissolving god.

The tunnel began to climb. A massive tremor hit, and with it a violent, hissing shriek and a blaze of silver, the lightning strike of pain. When Miranda's dazzled eyes cleared, she faced a junction for the first time. The walls were splintering open, the path turning into a web of fragments. The labyrinth had become a maze.

Miranda hesitated over the choices. Then she forged ahead. This passage was narrower than the others, but it went straight, and it went up. Space had become meaningless on her journey to the center of the labyrinth, but she clung to the intuition that the great chamber was beneath the Institute. So she had to climb up, up out of the darkness, up towards the light – if there still was light to find, light that did not squirm with green agony.

The flesh of the walls tore into flaps. They whipped across the passage, snapping like torn sails. Miranda tried to run past the rags. They touched her but just for fractions of a second. They had lost the power to hold her. During the brief contact, she encountered shards of memories and possibilities, but they did not swallow her consciousness. She still saw the hall and its billowing curtains of skin. The memories burned all the same, bright and jagged as trauma. None were true, or all of them, or some. Miranda cried out against them, against the violence being done to her history. Would she ever know what was real in her past again?

She forced herself to move faster, to turn the pain in her lungs and the pain in her mind to anger, and the anger to energy, the energy she needed if she hoped to have a future.

The slope steepened, becoming a mountain path for her to climb, and she didn't have the strength for speed now. All she had was the will to force herself to take one more step, and then one more, and no, I can't, it's too steep, too far, no, I can't, I'm too weak, but yes, a step, now another, now another, keep going, don't fall, don't fall, don't…

Finally, the pain and the exhaustion and the disease won. She tried for that one extra step, that last one that could be turned into maybe one more, but she couldn't move, and she was blacking out. She tried to shout – for help, for defiance – but she had nothing left. She fell.

Arms caught her.

Agatha caught her.

Miranda blinked. Her breath stopped for a moment in the fear that this was a delusion, a final wish instead of a memory. But Agatha held her, and joy gave Miranda the power to stand again.

"How…?" she began, in a voice like a crow's.

"You're just a couple of floors down from the entrance," Agatha said, shouting to be heard over the roars and screams of the labyrinth. She put Miranda's arm over her shoulders and started them both up the slope. She laughed with relief. "Not far at all. And not far to go."

Not far, but far enough. Hope of escape turned the final minute of the climb into an eternity. Ichor flowed in torrents from the ruptured walls, making footing treacherous.

I'm getting out, Miranda thought. Damn you, I'm getting out.

Another huge tremor slashed through the passageway as she and Agatha lurched out of the ruins of the labyrinth. The passages screamed and devoured themselves. The walls crashed together in a futile attempt to take Miranda down with them.

She was back in the ward she had come to know so well. It was dying too. The ceiling pressed down, and the floor had split into slabs that leaned in every direction. Dust choked the hall. The building shook as if a titan were pounding it flat.

Alarm bells rang and rang, and they were the sound of the real world, a mechanical cry, and Miranda embraced the din of normal. She focused on it, instead of the rumble of the building that sounded too much like the rage of the thing within it.

Agatha hauled them to the staircase.

"The other patients?" Miranda asked.

"Outside," said Agatha. "The fire department is here, too."

Good, good. Miranda took comfort in the emptiness of the halls.

Let us be the last ones here.

The stairwell swayed. Heavy chunks of masonry smashed down after the women. Agatha pushed Miranda against the wall and the railing to avoid being hit. And when they finally reached the lobby, fires had broken out. Dragged by Agatha, Miranda stumbled across the floor through the final convulsions of the building. Flames exploded out of a gap in a wall, licking the air just over Miranda's head. She heard a deep, crackling groan, and looked up to see a slab of stone ten feet wide break free of the ceiling and fall their way. Her determination not to die inside the monster gifted her with one more burst of adrenaline, and she sprinted, actually *sprinted*, side by side with Agatha.

Through the doorway and down the buckling stairs of the porch, and she took her first breath of outside air in a century, and she learned how sublime a single breath could be.

And now her weariness would not be denied. The debt of strength her body owed came due, and she couldn't go any further on her own. She leaned on Agatha, and they moved down the drive to where the patients clustered around the fire engines and the ambulances.

They turned around to watch the end.

The great thunder of the implosion came from the depths, and it seized the Institute. The roof went first. It fell in, and then the walls rushed at each other. The building went down like a closing fist, and Miranda heard the firemen shouting in as much surprise and shock as the patients. They had never seen a structure devour itself. The tremor of the final collapse split the grounds open. A wall of dust swept out from the grounds, choking and blinding.

Miranda coughed and kept coughing, sure she would finally expel her lungs from her body. When the dust cleared, and she could finally draw breath again, murmurs of wonder ran through the crowd.

The Stroud Institute had vanished. It had compacted itself down into a crater.

"I don't get it," one of the firemen kept repeating. "There should be more. Shouldn't there be more? I don't get it."

The wreckage was too small, too concentrated.

"Where's the stone?" Miranda whispered to Agatha. Twisted metal protruded from the heap. Smashed beds and doors and medical equipment lay entangled with one another. Glass lay everywhere. There was stone, but it was marble, and there were pieces of concrete. She saw almost no trace of the rock that had come from Scotland.

"Gone," said Agatha. She hugged Miranda. "Killed and gone."

EPILOGUE

The snow fell in thick flakes, as it should in mid-December, when Miranda came out of the main entrance of St Mary's Hospital. Agatha and Wilbur were waiting for her. Wilbur had the passenger door of his Model T open, and he rushed forward to take Miranda's bag. Agatha embraced her and asked, "Ready to go home?"

Home, where Miranda had not been for the best part of a year. Oh yes, she was more than ready. But she was also not in a hurry. She wanted to savor the day.

Wilbur stashed the bag and then hovered. "We should get you out of the cold," he said.

Miranda laughed. "I'm all right," she said. "I'm better, really. The cold won't hurt me. In fact, if I could just have a minute…" She tilted her head back and let the flakes fall on her face. She stuck out her tongue and laughed again at the gentle fairy-touch of the snow. She breathed deeply, enjoying the sharp, clean cold, the cold that would no longer make her cough.

"I'm so tempted to walk back," Miranda said.

"It's miles back to French Hill," Wilbur objected.

"What if we split the difference?" said Agatha. "You said yesterday that you wanted to pick up a few things at your office. Wilbur can drop us off at Miskatonic, and we'll walk the rest of the way."

Miranda nodded. "That would be nice." It had been too long since she had really, properly stretched her legs. The exercises she'd been allowed to do in the hospital grounds for the past several weeks had felt too limited. They were the promise of a walk, not the real thing.

They piled into the car and Wilbur drove off.

"You're restless," Agatha commented.

"Can you blame me?"

"No."

At St Mary's the rest cure for tuberculosis had been strictly enforced. During the first part of her stay, she hadn't even been allowed to read for more than a few minutes a day. Days and weeks and months of nothing in the days, of boredom such as she had never imagined possible. Having her lung collapsed through a pneumothorax procedure had been welcome as an event that broke up the monotony at least as much as the help it might or might not bring to her condition. There had been times when she found herself thinking fondly of the early days at the Stroud Institute, when she had still thought of it as a place of healing.

Cleo had come to visit her, too. Miranda treasured the friendship as one of the truly good things to have come out of the darkness of the Institute. Miranda had to reassure Cleo that she shouldn't feel guilty about being one of the Institute's success stories. Cleo didn't know what had happened in the end, but she had told Miranda about the movement in her yard.

"Do you think the place left a mark on me?" she asked.

"No," said Miranda. "You're better. You're well, and that's all that matters. The Institute is gone. It can never hurt anyone, and you're not the only one it actually helped."

Miranda did think about that, another of the paradoxes that circled Donovan Stroud. He and his ancestors were idealists in every sense. The Institute might have been a facade and a means to provide the bodies necessary to complete the ritual, but Donovan couldn't do anything in half measures. He made the facade so convincing, it was real.

Wilbur left Miranda and Agatha at Miskatonic University and took the bag home. Miranda kept the empty briefcase she had asked Agatha to grab for her at her apartment. She and Agatha strolled across the campus to the Humanities building. The Quad was deserted, classes and exams over for the term. The snow fell, shrouding the roofs and ground with calm.

Miranda had wondered what setting foot in her office for the first time in so long would feel like. She was prepared for the space to feel strange, someone else's place of work. Instead, she stepped into the warm embrace of the familiar. The stacks of books had waited patiently for her, and were glad to see her. The desk invited her to sit, and she looked out at her view of the Quad with a real sense of homecoming.

"Do you know," she said to Agatha as she put the books she needed in the briefcase, "I'm actually looking forward to the start of the winter term."

"Would you like me to check if you still feel the same way once you're marking papers again?"

"You can, but I know I will. It's going to feel good to be back."

They headed home in the gathering white of the afternoon. By unspoken agreement, they did not alter their route from the usual. Agatha did touch her shoulder as they drew near the gates of the Stroud Institute.

"Are you going to be all right with this?" she asked.

"Yes. I want to see it."

They stopped at the gates. The pillars had fallen with the rest of the Institute, and concrete ones had been raised in their place. The gates never opened now. They sealed off the gangrenous limb from the rest of Arkham.

Snow covered the ruins, softening their shape. Miranda looked through the bars at a vista of drab emptiness.

"It was looking pretty overgrown before the snow came," said Agatha. "City council is just letting it go. Use the wall and gate to keep the kids from hurting themselves in the ruins, but that's about it."

"Is anything going to be built here?"

"Not that I've heard."

"Just as well," said Miranda. "I wouldn't trust that ground."

"Nor would I. Better to just let it be another Arkham eyesore."

They walked on.

"That wasn't too hard?" said Agatha.

"No. I'm glad my first look at it was in the snow. Makes it look so changed, different. It's just a place now."

"That's good."

Miranda felt a slight clench in her chest when she unlocked her apartment. She was more nervous about what her home would feel like than her office. She hadn't had the night visions in the office. She was glad to have Agatha's company.

Once inside, she relaxed. This *was* home. The space belonged to her, and she to it. She walked through the living room, running her hands on the back of the sofa. She smiled at the prints on her wall. She'd missed them.

"Good to be back?" said Agatha.

Miranda smiled. She gave a happy sigh, and all the tension flowed out of her limbs and shoulders. "So good," she said. "Glass of wine?"

"Please."

When they were both on the couch, glasses of pinot in hand, Miranda said, "I worried home might feel tainted. Things started here. But it just feels right. No more visions."

Agatha said nothing.

Miranda looked at her. "What?" she asked.

"Not necessarily anything."

"But not necessarily nothing, then. Come on, out with it."

"I can't promise that you won't ever have visions again."

Miranda took a healthy sip of her wine. "I am so grateful you waited until I was out of the hospital to say something like that."

"You were supposed to rest. I wanted you to."

"Thank you." She steeled herself. "All right. Tell me what you mean about the visions."

"Just what I said. No promises. They might never recur. But Donovan targeted you for a reason, and you also saw things that helped us understand what was going on. You might have some powers of sight, and that's something you'll have to accept."

"Okay," Miranda said slowly. "But it's over, right? Everything we fought. It's over."

"Yes…"

Miranda began to wish she'd poured herself a much bigger glass. "That sounds like a qualification."

"Donovan is dead," said Agatha. "What he tried to do is finished. You destroyed the ritual, and sent Crothoaka back across the veil. Yes, all of that is over."

Miranda rolled her eyes. "All of *that*, she says. Are you trying to worry me?"

"No. Not at all. I guess you could say I'm trying to issue an invitation."

"Oh?" Miranda felt curiosity now. It took the edge off the dread.

"I don't think it's an accident that Donovan came to Arkham to complete the ritual," Agatha said. "And just maybe it isn't an accident that you were here. The right person in the right place at the right time."

"Didn't feel right to me," said Miranda.

"It was, though. You stopped him, and the horror he tried to unleash." Agatha gave her a solemn look. "Other things have happened in Arkham," she said. "Other bad things."

"I can well believe it."

"And there will be more. I don't know why they happen here, but they do."

Miranda nodded, realizing that she didn't feel surprised. The atmosphere of the town, one she had only half-noticed but had also been unable to completely ignore, began to make sense as Agatha spoke.

"I try to understand what's happening, and I try to help stop the bad stuff. I'm also not the only one. You've been through a lot, and you'll get absolutely no grief from me if you just want to put it all behind you."

"No," said Miranda. "I can't do that. I won't pretend it didn't happen, and that nothing has changed."

"Then would you help us with our work? There is so much to be done."

"It's going to be scary, isn't it?"

"Yes." Agatha grinned. "But not boring."

Miranda grinned back. "You should have led with that."

Tom Spalding walked along the cliffs beyond Durstal. He stopped about a mile from the edge of the Stroud Estate. He watched the angry December waves slam into the base of the cliffs. A freezing drizzle had started. The wind blew needles of water against him, which ran down his hair. He wiped the water from his face. It would be getting dark soon. He should head back to the inn, where light and warmth waited.

He should. He had come here hoping for some clarity. He would turn around in a minute.

The land here is blighted. Agatha Crane's words. *Run, Tom. Run.*

He hadn't run. Durstal was home. Run to where? Anywhere, he supposed. But he had roots here, deep ones. And if he left, what about all his friends? What about the rest of Durstal? Did Agatha expect him to organize an exodus?

That wasn't fair. She hadn't asked him to do anything. She had warned him. Anything else was his responsibility.

He had done nothing after Agatha and Wilbur left. He had gone on as he always had, as everyone in Durstal did. Chin up, make the best of things, and be wary if things look wrong. Don't disbelieve the stories you hear, and don't go looking for trouble.

Durstal was home.

The storm that had come in the spring, not much more than a week after Agatha had left, had frightened him badly. It had torn roofs off and felled trees, and there had been sounds in the wind that no one talked about afterwards. He had spent the night with his hands over his ears. He knew he had not been the only one.

Since then, he hadn't slept well. Months of broken nights, and worse now that the winter storms had come and kept coming. He was so tired. And he couldn't stop thinking about the estate.

He watched the waves. He listened to their crash and boom. Gradually, he realized just how deep the boom seemed to go. Or perhaps, from how deep it came. Rhythmic, huge.

Furious. Like a voice.

He found his clarity.

Run, Tom. Run.

Acknowledgments

I do so love writing horror fiction, and so my first thank you is to you, the reader, for having accompanied me on this journey.

When it comes to the research for this novel, I owe a particular debt to Betty MacDonald's *The Plague and I*, her sparkling, witty memoir of her experience in a tuberculosis sanatorium. I have taken all kinds of liberties with the details of treatment, the better to serve the dark purpose of the Stroud Institute, but to put it most succinctly, any accuracies are entirely thanks to this book, and the errors are all mine. My debt to the book goes beyond its value as research, too. It was hearing about *The Plague and I* on the wonderful podcast Backlisted that provided the initial inspiration for *In the Coils of the Labyrinth*. For more specific inspiration as to the Stroud Institute itself, I must credit Dario Argento's films *Suspiria* and *Inferno* (especially the latter).

Huge thanks to Marc Gascoigne, Lottie Llewelyn-Wells, Nick Tyler, Anjuli Smith, Paul Simpson and everyone at Aconyte Books for all the support. Special thanks to Charlotte Bond for her superb editing, which I know will serve me well in many books to come.

Thank you to John Coulthart for his amazing cover, which provided me with further inspiration as I wrote.

Thank you to Katrina Ostrander, Claire Rushbrook, and everyone at Fantasy Flight Games for their guidance, and for entrusting me with this little corner of the *Arkham Horror* universe.

Thank you also to my fellow writers Michael Kaan, Stephen D Sullivan and Derek M Koch. Our online sprints and mutual support were wonderful motivators.

And, as always, my heartfelt, loving thanks to my wife, Margaux Watt, and to my stepchildren, Kelan and Veronica, for everything and more.

About the Author

DAVID ANNANDALE is a lecturer at a Canadian university on subjects ranging from English literature to horror films and video games. He is the author of the *Marvel Untold* Doctor Doom trilogy, and many titles in the *New York Times*-bestselling *Horus Heresy* and *Warhammer 40,000* universe, and a co-host of the Hugo Award-nominated podcast Skiffy and Fanty.

davidannandale.com // twitter.com/david_annandale

THE DEFINITIVE GUIDE TO THE WORLD OF ARKHAM HORROR

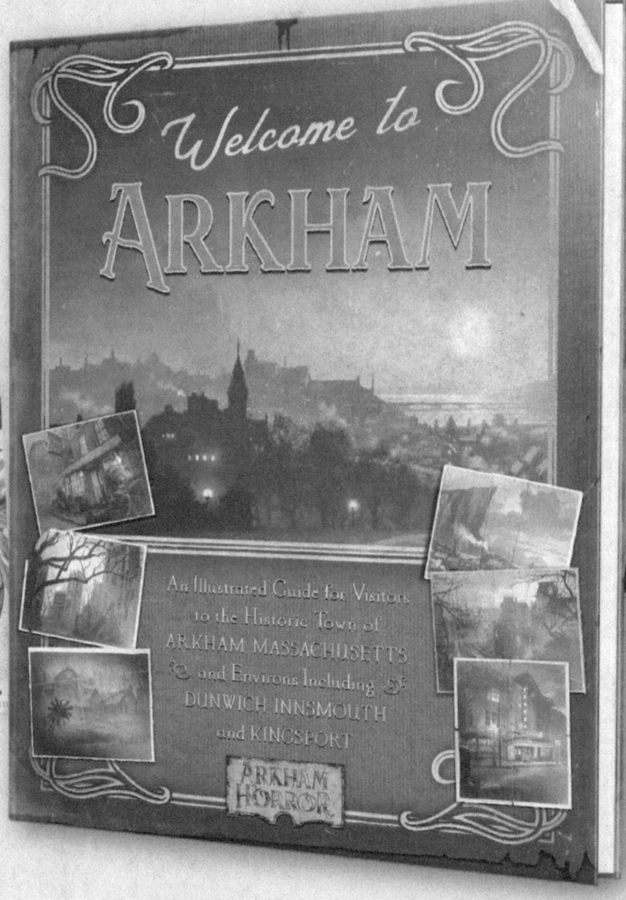

Venture deeper than ever before into the legend-haunted city of Arkham and its neighboring towns of Dunwich, Innsmouth and Kingsport. Explore 115 fabled locations with more than 500 illustrations in this gorgeous, full-color hardcover guidebook.

24 POSTER-SIZED PRINTS OF ICONIC ART FROM ARKHAM HORROR

Bring a touch of madness and Lovecraftian horror to your coffee table or pull out your favorites to use as posters or frame as prints, with the Arkham Horror Poster Book.

ARKHAM HORROR

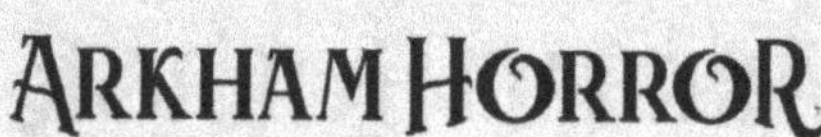

A darkness has fallen over Arkham. Who will stand against the dread might of the Ancient Ones?

Explore riveting pulp adventure at

ACONYTEBOOKS.COM